Praise for *The Children's Hospital:*

"Chris Adrian's life is a dedicated exploration of the things that matter most, and his writing is his companion and interlocutor, his guide and interpreter, as he travels a landscape not before seen by other eyes. And every report he makes of that world enriches and enlarges our own sense of the world we thought we knew."

—Marilynne Robinson, author of *Gilead*

"Chris Adrian is a novelist, a doctor, a philosopher, a literary explorer, the humble clear-eyed prophet of our time. He is an eloquent anatomist of loss, naming and labeling the bones and sinews of grief; he is a comedian dressed in sackcloth, a winking Virgil leading us through the circles of our own earthly hell. But he is ultimately a healer; the genius of his writing lies in its compassion, its ability to make what is broken whole again. To read him is to be understood: to know you are not alone in your misery, your self-doubt, your sins of pride, your wild joys, your insomnia, your madness, your desire."

—Julie Orringer, author of *How to Breathe Underwater*

"Chris Adrian is truly brilliant. I'm not saying this because he's a writer, and a pediatrician, and now in divinity school. I simply believe him to be a person with a unique way of processing the world around him and the ability to communicate that vision back to us in what is often a startlingly beautiful manner."

—Nathan Englander, author of *The Ministry of Special Cases*

"*The Children's Hospital* brings the great promise of *Gob's Grief* to fruition; it probes the twined natures of death, grief, and sin with a rare combination of insight, longing, and oracular authority, all tempered by a sense of humor so black it burns. I suspect Chris Adrian will prove to be our culture's recording angel, our demon brother; and he is certainly one of my favorite authors writing today."

—Emily Barton, author of *Brookland*

"To read Chris Adrian is to take part in the exciting process of watching a talented and original writer gain mastery of his powerful gifts."

—Myla Goldberg, *The New York Times Book Review*

"*The Children's Hospital* has echoes of a children's book, as it takes on questions of good and evil with an earnestness rare in adult fiction, while remaining seriously fun to read; the funky everyday cohabits naturally with the miraculous."

—Shelley Jackson, *Los Angeles Times*

"One of the most revelatory novels in recent memory . . . Cleverly conceived and executed brilliantly." —Andrew Ervin, *San Francisco Chronicle*

"This novel is a singular event: massive, recondite, often electrifying." —*Bookforum*

"Adrian lays out a brave new world that is glorious and miraculous and h[illegible] at once."

—*E*[illegible]

"Suspended between the poles of life and death, [illegible] real and the imagined, Adrian's vast floating wo[illegible] *Children's Hospital* is intelligent, seductive and bea[illegible]

—[illegible]*ant*

“[Adrian] is a writer of prodigious talent who holds your heart in his hands. . . . And despite or because of his unlikely worldview, he is irresistible. He sails into the inexplicable, seeking meaning; and the reader, gripped by curiosity and admiration, scrambles on board. Adrian’s prose here is writing at its best—medical magical realism, you might call it. . . . We will be lucky as long as he continues to write.”

—*The Boston Globe*

“Hip, wry and ambitious . . . Adrian's knack for surprise and his ability to find meaning in seemingly ridiculous situations is rewarding.”

—*Publisher’s Weekly (starred review)*

“It’s hard to read a book like Chris Adrian’s new novel, *The Children’s Hospital*, with its dead under seven miles of water, and not think about Katrina and tsunamis, and then backward and landward to September 11 and other traumas that, if personal, also demanded some kind of collective notice.” —*The Village Voice*

“*The Children’s Hospital* establishes Chris Adrian as a remarkable American fabulist in the tradition of Melvin Jules Bukiet and Tony Kushner, writers who define and confront the terrifying moral choices of a new century. In what may be a terminally sick world, it’s good to have a doctor in the house.”

—Elizabeth Hand, *The Washington Post*

“Elegant and enormously wondrous . . . Adrian, poetically and with exacting precision, has crafted a prophetic, difficult novel of compassion and healing, but with a keen eye fixed on the damning reach of divine wrath. . . . [He] attempts a near-impossible summit, and delivers a devastating, transformative work that is certain to burn in the minds of readers long after the final page’s end of the end of the world.” —Ian Chipman, *Booklist*

“This humanistic novel is a heartfelt portrayal of indefatigable spirit in the face of utter helplessness and ruin. . . . Adrian proves to be a suitable successor to the mythological wherewithal of Rushdie or C. S. Lewis, and the book is a solid testament to his array of talents.” —*Time Out New York*

“The Children's Hospital is born of both medicine and theology, a novel in which Gnosticism collides with diagnoses, and Old Testament-style cataclysms dovetail with IVs. But *The Children's Hospital* is, thankfully, more than that awkward marriage; it is also a thing of complex beauty and extraordinary insight . . . More than a vision that combines fantasy and realism, philosophy and certainty, *The Children's Hospital* is also about everything in between. It’s been a while since religion was this fascinating and moving—just as it's been a while since there was a work of fiction this challenging, inventive, and heartfelt.” —*Portland Mercury*

“Chris Adrian, a pediatrician and divinity student, might be contemporary American fiction's best-kept secret.” —*Richmond Times-Dispatch*

“A frighteningly relevant tale of the end of the world, epic within the confines of its setting.” —*Paste*

THE CHILDREN'S HOSPITAL

CHRIS ADRIAN

Grove/McSweeney's
New York/San Francisco

First published in 2006 by McSweeney's Books, San Francisco

Icons by Amelia Bauer

Printed simultaneoulsy in Canada
Printed in the United States of America

FIRST PAPERBACK EDITION

ISBN-10: 0-8021-4333-4
ISBN-13: 978-0-8021-4333-4

Grove Press
an imprint of Grove/Atlantic, Inc.
841 Broadway
New York, NY 10003
Distributed by Publishers Group West
www.groveatlantic.com
07 08 09 10 11 12 10 9 8 7 6 5 4 3 2 1

for my parents

Lettera gesta docet, quid credas allegoria;
Moralis quid agas, quo tendas anagogia.

—Augustine of Dacia
Rotulus pugillaris

I am the recording angel, doomed to watch.

Never mind my sin. Here is my expiation and my reward: to orbit Jemma Claflin from her birth to her death, and fix my eyes always on her face the way better angels always look upon God's glory. I fell back to earth and back through time to the night of her birth, and, bound to her heart by chains of air and spirit, have never since been more than a few hundred feet from her body. Whenever I tried to flee—there was a whole world to rediscover and witness, after all, and all the curving ways of time lay open before me, and a billion anguished lives called out to me to come and watch them, instead of a toddler with peas on her cheek—the chains would pull tight, hooks in my flesh. In all my years of watching I have never hated her, but I have often been bored, and if there are doodles in the margins of her book, and gaps in her story, if I have looked away from her to watch my brothers and sisters at play among the stars and missed here or there an episode of her life, if I have watched her brother, always burning bright to me, even though I knew his story, past and future, already by heart, it is because I am neither a perfect angel nor a perfect witness. I put off perfection with my mortal form, and what a relief to do it.

Never mind, for now, the quotidian discoveries of her infancy; do not look at her yet toddling after her brother, or trudging, head down, through her education. Beauty pageants and swim meets and drugs smoked or snorted under her brother's tutelage are not the place to start; neither are the flights with her father over the Chesapeake Bay, or the nights drunk-diving into the past with her mother, or the nights she skated over the frozen river to crawl into her lover's house and lie with him in his single bed. And look away from the funeral years; ignore the miracle her brother wrought. Consider her instead on the edge of her own greatness, separate from and grander than Calvin's. There she is on the night of the storm, attending a birth, waiting while the rain falls and the clouds are heaping and piling in the sky and I am sighing all around her, finally. Finally!

Jemma thought that witnessing a birth ought to make a person exactly the opposite of horny. The rush of blood and fluid; the bitter odors; the screaming of a mother arrived too late for an epidural; and worst of all, the hideous dilation, the vagina that permitted the entrance of hands and arms and instruments sized and shaped more appropriately for barbeque than surgery, and disgorged the bloody cantaloupe. They should freeze you up, but they never froze her up, and sometimes, like on the night of the great storm, they put the need in her. So she found herself distracted by thoughts of Rob Dickens even at the most challenging and complicated delivery of her third-year medical student career: a gruesome baby born to a gruesome mother. The child, the expression of a jumble of chromosomal additions and deletions so unique that she was her very own syndrome, was hideous—too long and too short, too wide and too thin, with things that were not eyes where her eyes ought to have been, and a cuttlefish mouth—but she seemed sweet to Jemma, who stood over her among the white-suited pediatricians, a fellow, a resident, and an intern. Her cry was more dulcet than any Jemma had ever heard, probably because she was half dead and lacked the energy to voice a truly irritating scream. "Rub," Jemma's senior resident said to her, because she was only blotting at the wet baby with her towel. The mother was lovely in her flesh but seemed deformed in her soul. She shouted curses at her child while the anesthesiologist, scowling, pushed white, milky propofol into her veins, trying to shut her up. Not even her epithets and her screams cooled Jemma. Rob Dickens was not among the pediatricians in their bunny suits—one raised a laryngoscope with a flourish like a hoodlum clicking out a folding knife and then swooped in to intubate the now quiet and rather blue baby—but she knew where he was, waiting with the other students, residents, and staff for this unfortunately interesting case to arrive across the glass hall that connected the county hospital to the children's hospital.

While she ought to have been calculating one-minute apgars for the child, she pictured Rob Dickens in his scrubs, his arms naked almost to the shoulder. When the resident asked her for the score she blushed and fumbled in her mind for the number, forgetting the categories—tone, cry, grimace, color, and what else? Not grace, not style, not symmetry, but these were what she thought of. The resident—a third-year named Natalie famous for the black cloud of acuity that hovered over her call nights—stared at Jemma coolly over her surgical mask, and Jemma remembered to count the heartbeat. She reached out to pinch the umbilicus and feel the pulse, much slower than her own, which always raced when she was mortified by the ignorance and confusion she manifested when faced with one of these student tasks. "Four," she said at last.

"Generous," said Natalie, and turned her attention fully to the task of bag-ventilating the infant. Despite the sedatives, the mother was still telling them to kill the baby with a knife, with a brick, with a smothering pillow. She sat up suddenly, an obscene apparition, hauling herself up by her knees, her perfect, unnatural breasts glaring over the sterile blue drape, a tongue of clotted blood lolling out of her vagina. She calmed briefly and spoke in sane, gentle tones. "Just do it now, before she gets us. It's easy now but it won't always be so easy." She reached out, grabbing for the instrument tray, until two nurses pushed her back. Jemma thought of Rob, pacing with his hands folded on top of his head, like he always did when he was impatient for a particular thing to happen. She thought of his arms again. She didn't have to close her eyes to be able to see them.

"Let's go," said Natalie. She jerked her head imperiously at her intern, Dr. Chandra, who had got his stethoscope caught up in the oxygen tubing and was trying to untangle it. Natalie looked back expectantly at the fellow, Emma, who gave one sharp nod to indicate her blessing. They moved out of the operating room and down the long beige halls of the county hospital. Patients, women walking in the hope of accelerating their labor, spun out of their way as the team raced along, Emma pushing the isolette, Natalie bagging, and Dr. Chandra still trying to untangle his stethoscope. Jemma, not a good hurrier, trailed after the isolette. It had been part of the reason she failed her surgery rotation, this reluctance to hustle, and even when her grade was at stake she could never bring herself to be snappy, or do that wiggling power walk on rounds, or even run full-out to a code or a trauma—if you were too fast, after all, you got there first. She ran a few steps, then slowed, then ran again. As they approached the bridge, Natalie called back to her to get the door, since Dr. Chandra had also entangled his name tag and calculator in the mess of tubing.

Jemma ran ahead to slap the giant steel button that opened the doors. They swung out leisurely, opening on the storm that flashed and raged around the glass hall. The team pushed through even before the doors were fully open. Jemma ran ahead again, meaning to slap the far button with the same authority and force with which she'd hit the near one, but she tripped, then rolled fast and heavy into the door. Natalie yelled, "Get out of the way!" Jemma hit the button and the second set of doors swung open, less leisurely than those at the other end of the hall, but not fast. She scooted on her bottom, pushed aside by the door and finally wedged against the glass wall as the isolette flew past. Lightning arched overhead and showed her a vast parking lot, empty except for a few dozen dead cars stranded in water up to their headlights.

The lightning passed, and then the glass wall showed Jemma her own haggard face. Nursery call was beginning to wear on her. They were always flying to one delivery or another, back and forth across this sky bridge at all hours of the morning, day, and night. Here in a hospital that attracted the riskiest pregnancies, the ones that ended with the expulsion of a half dead baby, there was no rest for a person afflicted with a delivery pager. Jemma rose and leaned against the glass, closing her eyes and imagining that the little creature in her high-tech bassinet was wheeling away at a thousand miles an hour, on her way to Heaven instead of a hell of needles and tubes. When the lightning flashed again in the sky she opened her eyes and saw how the rain was falling in sheets. "All pediatricians are nice," Rob had told her two weeks before, on the evening before the rotation started. "These are going to be the best six weeks of your life."

"What am I doing here?" she asked herself softly, not for the first time wondering what she was doing in the hospital at four in the morning, what she was doing training for a profession to which she felt no true calling, doing work she knew she could tolerate but never love. She pressed her head further into the glass, conscious of but not caring about the security camera recording her episode of self-pity. She was imagining again the other professions she might have pursued—airline pilot, horticulturist, tomb raider—when a terrible noise, a nasty, wet slap, startled her. She leaped away from the glass and saw the bird: the tremendous wind had blown a gull against the bridge. Its beady eye caught and held hers, and it opened and closed its mouth four times, thrusting out its red tongue in a gesture both exhausted-looking and suggestive, before the wind lifted it and sent it sliding over the arch of the glass to spin away into the darkness.

Jemma had lived in the city three years and never seen a storm like this. Rob had lived there all his life and judged this one pretty tame so far. They'd walked that morning from her apartment to the hospital complex, Jemma soaking her scrub pants to the knees when she waded through puddles in her rubber clogs. The hospital was just a big white lump in the rain, its lofty spirals and curling edges obscured, so it looked to Jemma like it was melting, and she wondered if they would even have found their way there if not for the giant round lights on the roof.

She turned away from the glass and kicked the big silver button to open the doors, then passed into the children's hospital. As many times as she'd passed from the hospital behind her into the hospital before her, she was still struck by the change. The beige walls of the adult hospital were replaced by a motley of primary color, linoleum the color of bile turned to firm carpet printed with hopscotch numbers, and the path to the NICU was laid out in the tiniest footprints. Jemma followed them, thinking as she walked how they might have been left by some impossibly toddling preemie—they were as red as the bloody red feet of a twenty-four-weeker, one of those unfinished things whose skin slipped off between your fingers if you pinched too hard. She walked past the giant pictures on the walls, six-foot by four-foot photos of healthy children at play. She thought it strange to hang pictures like these in a place where sick children lived, as if to scream at them: Look what you're missing. Closer to the unit the pictures gave way to magnified newspaper articles detailing the triumphant progress made by the hospital in saving smaller and smaller babies. One sentence, picked out in bold beneath a photo of Dr. Bump, one of the supreme neonatologists, always caught her eye: *One day we'll be able to save the ones so small you can't even see them.* Jemma raised a hand to flick him in his nose as she passed—he was famously cruel to students and had just that week made her friend Vivian cry secret, locked-in-the-bathroom tears. Jemma pressed her ID badge to a sensor by the double doors of the unit and they opened with a hiss. The hall inside was quiet, but she could see through another set of doors into the first bay, where a cluster of doctors, nurses, and technicians were gathered around a bed she knew must be the new baby's. She strode past the nurses lounging and gossiping in the hall, making her face a mask of purpose to discourage them from challenging her, like they usually did, with "Are you lost, sweetie?" Inside the bay, she was shooed into a corner. She watched the muttering cluster of bodies around the bed until it disgorged Rob, who clutched an endotracheal tube forlornly as he sidled up next to her, touching her arm with his arm.

"I was supposed to get to do the UA catheter, but then Natalie did it. Like she needed to do another one—she's only done a million of them. I was supposed to get to intubate after she pulled out her tube, but then they wouldn't let me intubate a baby with a cleft palate. Chandra did it, or he tried. When he screwed it up, Emma took over. I didn't do anything. Why am I even here?" He shook his head. "Did you know that she's the daughter of a king?" Jemma nodded. It was common knowledge: this baby's father was some sort of latter-day satrap, a king of the East who had fetched himself a blond, horse-toothed bride from a women's college in New Jersey. The hospital attracted these stories. The giant-headed, cancerous, rotting offspring of the wealthy and fabulous mingled with the children whose living and lineage were common but whose diseases were so exclusive they were, if not entirely unique, limited to a select handful of sufferers. They came from all over the country and the world to put themselves at the mercy of bright minds.

"Come with me," Jemma said. "I need you." He watched her finger as she raised it very slowly to place it on top of her head. It was not a seductive or even graceful maneuver, but he started at it, his eyes widened, and he looked back and forth from Jemma to the baby to Jemma again. "Come on," she said.

He lifted the ET tube toward her and shook it once, looked back again at the baby and smiled. "I don't know," he said.

"You said it yourself," she said. "Why are you here?" She turned her leg out, wondering as she did it why she was presenting him with her beefy hip. It was not her best feature, and if he had ever praised it, it was only when he was drunk or utterly overcome with lust.

"Maybe we shouldn't."

"Maybe not," she said, but she put her finger on her head again, and stood there a moment with her hip thrust out and her foot extended—it was the pose of a retarded ballerina, but it was all it took to get him to follow her out.

They know where we are going, and they know what we are going to do, Jemma thought as they passed by the nurses' station. It always seemed to her that people must know, and yet she was sure that nobody did. There were stories told of promiscuous decades long past, where people fucked madly in call rooms, operating rooms, or under the beds of the comatose, but she had never heard of it happening this year, or in this new hospital, not yet even a year old. The first time had been just two weeks before, at the beginning of the rotations that had landed them in the children's hospital with the same call schedule. He had comforted her with it when Jemma came seeking him after her first delivery, a harrowing festival of abuse where it seemed that everyone had yelled at her for her incompetence: the obstetric and pediatric residents when she fumbled and nearly dropped the slimy baby; the baby's mother, understandably cranky but too shrill, really, for any occasion save her own stabbing death; and even the baby himself, who parted his blue lips to caw at her, and who shat tarry meconium down her shirt. She cleaned up in Rob's call room and he met her with a towel when she came out of the shower, rubbing her beyond dry. They considered, before formally beginning it, that they should not, and before continuing and finishing had a brief conversation in which they decided that they should not continue, let alone finish. That night, and again on their second and third call nights, Jemma had said, "We had better not ever do this again," and he had said, "Not here, anyway."

But it always seemed like such a good idea when they did it, and it never took much more than their prearranged signal—the single finger placed on top of the head—to get him to agree. And it hardly seemed so bad, even after they finished and lay panting against each other, face to face, both staring guiltily at their pagers as if inviting from them a shrill, musical reprimand. There were worse things one could be doing. There were a multitude of drugs available for the consumption of the enterprising medical student—Rob was a competent enough hacker and Jemma a thief with long childhood experience, and not even the monolithic pyxis system that guarded every medication would have been able to withstand them if they had chosen to shoot up some propofol or snort morphine or place a row of fentanyl patches along their spines. They could be exceeding their authority in all sorts of ways—more a temptation for Rob than for Jemma—by attempting complicated procedures without supervision. There were babies they could have been dropping and children whose unshielded eyes might cry to a more sinister couple to be plucked out and parents vulnerable to lies and rumors of cure or of death. There was mischief worse than kissing Rob and lifting off his shirt. She was reluctant to give up his lips but eager to bare his belly and his chest, and because she would not pull her mouth away from his he left the shirt hanging, a collar around his neck. It was nothing to hand each other the gift of a screwing, and more than nothing. It was a great thing, and the greatest thing—not the end of the world but a way to put the world utterly at bay and escape momentarily and intermittently from her awful past, her anxious present, and her dispiriting future, a way to escape from the hospital, a way to not be here—to undo the pink cord that held up his scrubs, pull down his pants, sing out the long O, and fall on him with her mouth.

Their courtship was complicated. Long before he transferred into her class in their second year of medical school she had become convinced that everyone she loved was required by fate or God to die, and what could be more logical than that the wages of death should be loneliness? First her brother had died. When he was seventeen and she was fourteen he killed himself in a ritual of superhuman agony, leaving behind his burnt, partially dismembered body and a book that Jemma could hardly stand to read, though she understood that it was written more for her than for anyone else. She threw it in the Severn River a month after Calvin died.

Her father died next, eaten up swiftly by lung cancer. His first symptom—a fine tremor in his surgeon's hand—came in the summer when Jemma was seventeen. By January he was bedridden. By April he was delirious, mets in his brain having displaced the tissues that formerly had made a home for his reason. By July he could not speak, but only cried out when something frightened him, and spent whole afternoons in his living-room bed, reaching for invisible things in the air around his head.

"Free at last!" her mother said, after her father was dead. He had never had any time for her, and they had married for all the wrong reasons, or for no reason at all, and she was twenty-one years tired of his selfishness and his mean drunks and his mighty fists, though really it was his blood more than hers that Jemma always found herself encountering in the aftermath of one of their great fights. It would leap out at her against the bright green linoleum of the kitchen floor, or else she would tread in it walking down the dark hallway outside their bedroom, or it would be there in the morning, a pattern on the wall above the breakfast table, spread by a blow to the head with the great bedpost-sized pepper shaker that her mother could wield with the speed and skill of a ninja assassin. There was always a shape to find in the blood, spread into swirls and smears in a clumsy, drunken clean-up, birds and bones and the delicate reaching leaves of a fern. But even so her mother had taken the tenderest care of him in his illness. Calvin would have said that she loved him best when he was utterly at her mercy.

Free at last, her mother planned a trip around the world, and Jemma was not invited. "I'll come back with your new daddy," she said, calling Jemma at school on the eve of her departure. "Mr. Belvedere will be his name-o." It was only six o'clock but she was ten p.m. drunk.

"Have a good time," Jemma said. "Send lots of postcards."

"I may not have time for postcards. I'm going to be awfully busy living for myself for the first time in my fucking life."

"I'm glad for you," was all Jemma said. But though her mother really had bought a round-the-world airplane ticket, and though she had planned the trip in painstaking detail with a dog-faced travel agent named Sue, and though she had packed six months' worth of safari clothes and sensible shoes, she never went on the trip. Instead, not long after hanging up with Jemma, she set fire to their house and burned herself up with it. I didn't see her do it, but I can imagine it as well as Jemma could: her mother settled calmly in the kitchen chair where she was accustomed to do her drinking, smoking with her eyes closed while the walls burned. She left no note.

Three deaths should have been enough to demonstrate Jemma's danger, but they only made her suspect the horrible truth. It was easy to say instead that insanity and bad genes and tobacco were to blame. Three deaths hurried her more resolutely into the arms of her lover, a boy named Martin Marty who she'd been dating since they were in tenth grade. "We are already a family now," he said to her one night not long after her mother's funeral, because ever since Calvin he was always saying things meant to comfort her which only ended up horrifying her. He drove home drunk from a New Year's party when they were juniors in college and was killed in a collision with a tree. Even then, she didn't understand, and when the knowledge came, it was in slow bits, accretions that rose a little higher every day in her mind until they spelled out the shape and the letter of her doom. One day she woke up crying and knew it for sure: everyone she had loved was dead, and everyone she loved would die.

So she promised herself she wouldn't speak to Rob Dickens—she could see her crush as a black affliction hovering over him, and knew it was only wanted for her to speak to him before it would settle. She had so many graves available for swearing on, but that would be no use; she already knew herself for an oath-breaker, tried and untrue. She watched him during lectures, and watched him run by her apartment every morning, knowing she should avert her eyes, and yet she stared at him brazenly, dreadful window whore, and engaged him in weeks of abbreviated morning conversation. She swore she would not go out with him, if he should ask, but when he did ask she said yes without hesitation. And she took a solemn vow not to kiss him, but compelled by necessity, she did that, too. Outside her house, after dinner, she stood above him on a step and bent her head down to put her mouth on his. It was not a chaste kiss. It was very familiar, so intimate it was almost gruesome. She thought about his dinner the whole time she kissed him, the way he had eaten it, the way his thick wrist poked out of his shirt cuff when he cut his meat. She had not tasted veal since she was in fifth grade, when Emma Rose McBurney detailed the sad fate of a veal calf for her, and showed her a movie after school. Jemma had wept at the enormous cruelty of veal, and sworn never to eat it again. But she tasted it in his mouth that night, and on his breath when he blew it into her lungs. She pulled away, gasped a little, and coughed.

"Goodnight!" she said, and ran away upstairs and into her apartment, where a roach was waiting for her, perched on the counter in the little kitchen set in a corner of her living room. It was a great big bug, black as the blackest beetle, and as she stood in the door watching it watch her, her imagination invested it with a parental mixture of fury and concern. Its wriggling antennae were signing to her. Where have you been? it demanded. What were you doing? She hated roaches, but she was afraid to kill it because she suspected it might contain the soul of her first lover—somehow it seemed most likely to be him, and not her brother or her father or her mother. Spiders, frogs, little reptiles—all creatures that horrified her—any of them might contain that soul wandered back to be near her, and so she was gentle toward them. The roach skibbled down a cabinet and ran at her. When she fled it pursued her down the hall, running not just on the floor but on the walls and the ceiling in a big loose spiral. She got to her bedroom, slammed the door and stared anxiously at the space underneath it. It was big enough to admit two roaches, one piggybacking on top of the other, but the roach didn't come in. He never came into her bedroom—they seemed to have an agreement about that. Still, she imagined him scolding her from the other side of the door, just like a parent might. What were you thinking? he asked. Are you trying to kill him?

From her window she peeped down at the sidewalk. Rob wasn't there, but she thought she could see his wide, handsome back retreating over the bridge across the street. It spanned a little horseshoe-shaped canal, which many decades before had been a swimming hole, but now was too toxic for bathing. He lived only a few blocks away. If he ran home along the top of the thin railing that kept children from falling into the poisoned waters, it would not be a surprise, because it was his habit to leap up on things, and to test his balance against ledges and curbs and sills. And if he fell into the water and drowned, it would not be a surprise, because she had imperiled him with her kiss.

She lay down on her narrow bed, the same one upon which she'd been sleeping since she was five years old, on the old mattress that still bore the deep impression of the much fatter body she used to inhabit, and she dreamed of veal. In her sleep she followed the weeping of a calf through gray half-darkness, until she found its miserable stall. It cried with the voice of a human child. She knelt to quiet it, saying, There, there, little one, it will be all right. But she knew it would die to please the appetites of man. She cried, ashamed of how she had lied to it, and it began to comfort her. Its little hoof stroked her head, and its soft lips kissed her cheek and her mouth. In a little while longer they were making out, she and the veal calf. Its thick, nimble tongue darted over her own and made her mouth an organ of intense pleasure.

She woke up feeling dizzy and hungover, though she'd had only a single glass of wine the night before. Her mouth tasted like veal, and her room smelled of it. She felt sure that she must have been panting through her mouth the whole night long, polluting her room with the odor of cruel meat. She went to the window to get a breath of untainted air. It was almost seven o'clock, time for him to come running by. He would be wet from the running, and she would think, as she always did, about how it had always seemed to her that people looked better when they were wet, and she would remember ducking repeatedly into the bathroom in high school, where she would wet down her hair in the hope of improving her looks. She'd felt beautiful just once in her life, caught in a rainstorm with her first lover. In the middle of a busy sidewalk he'd kissed her and, with his hand cradling her head, had squeezed out a flood of water from her hair. When it fell down her neck, under her collar, she felt it even over the pouring rain.

She stood at the window, looking back and forth between her clock and the street. At exactly seven he came running over the bridge. He stopped at the bottom of her stoop, and shaded his eyes against the sun to look up at her. "Hi there!" he called up. She could feel her four dead standing behind her, and hear them calling down, Welcome to the family!

Please, she said to them. She was supposed to close her shutters and go sit on her bed, and consider how she had done the right thing, but instead she just stood there, staring at him stupidly until he asked her for another date.

"What kind of doctor do you want to be?" she asked him, surely a first-date question, but she didn't ask it until that night, over dinner at a vegetarian restaurant.

"The nice kind," he said.

"Are there other kinds?"

"Medicine brings out the worst in a person."

"I don't think so. Do you really think so?"

"Maybe," he said. "But think about it. You see people at their absolute worst, and all your own personal failings—your weakness, your stupidity, your laziness—show up in their continuing decline. And even if you make them better, they just come back, sicker and needier."

He looked down at his plate, quietly scooping and dumping his fancy macaroni and cheese with a big spoon. "It's a privilege to see people at their worst," she told him, which was something her father liked to say. "You seem nice enough still."

"I'm already corrupted," he said.

"You still smell good, though," she said without thinking about it, and blushed furiously. "I mean, if you were really corrupt you'd smell like bad meat or old yogurt or..." She put a carrot in her mouth so she would stop talking.

"How about you?" he asked her.

"Oh yes, very corrupt."

"I mean what do you want to end up doing?"

"Surgery," she said. "Surgery, surgery—my dad was a surgeon."

"A legacy of corruption," he said, smiling. Now he had insulted her—reason enough to throw a carrot at him but not reason enough to kill him; still she just sat there, anxious and admiring. He had very large hands.

She took the vow again: no kisses. And she further swore that when he tried to kiss her, she would hold up her hand and drop her chin. She had practiced the gesture in front of her mirror, shaped her smile until she thought it could only be interpreted as regretful and demure, and practiced the backward walk. "I can't," she'd said to her reflection. "I just can't," words chosen because they were truthful and because they seemed most likely to cause the least hurt. Hand still in the air, she'd walk backward toward her door, not speaking, not answering him if he spoke, then go upstairs to sit at her kitchen table and watch the roach shiver with delight when she told him how it was all over.

The roach was waiting for them when she led Rob upstairs. Not five feet from the door, it seemed to be settling its weight impatiently back and forth from one set of legs to the other. "I'll get it," said Rob, and took a step forward to stomp the bug. Jemma threw her whole body into him and pushed him off balance. He stumbled across the room and fell, striking his head on the soft edge of the couch. The roach fled.

"Sorry!" she said, speaking to him and the roach both. "Sorry!" He'd apologized just like that when she ducked away from his goodnight kiss. She had raised her hand in the practiced gesture of final forbidding, but rather than make the gesture she thought she wanted—stop, go away, we can't do this—it had fastened on his hot ear and drawn his face to hers. Sprawled by the couch, he lay very still for a moment, and she worried that he was dead already. When she helped him up she kept her hand in his and drew him back to her bedroom.

Was the thumping noise the bedpost knocking on her wall, or was it the roach throwing himself in fury against her door? She'd sealed up the crack with a towel so he couldn't intrude if anger drove him to break their unspoken agreement, but she could hear him in the guttural utterances that issued from her new friend, deep, groaning syllables that rearranged themselves in her head into words—*what are you doing*, *what are you doing*, and then *what have you done?*

"I can't see you anymore," she told him the next day. It was easier to say than she'd anticipated that it would be. The words came out of her mouth in a smooth, fluid rush.

On the bridge across the canal, she was walking him home, he on the railing but holding on to her hand. When she was small she'd walked that way with her mother, her mother's arm lending her balance, and the rail or bench elevating her so they were equally tall. But the rail made him much taller than Jemma, and he was too sure of his balance to need a loan from her.

"Don't say that," he said. The sun was just behind him, so his head seemed replaced by a ball of flame. She closed her eyes against him and saw not just the blinking orange globe but his face, too, in disappointed afterimage.

"I can't see you anymore," she said again, not opening her eyes but stepping back and pulling her hand free.

"Why not?"

"Because," she said.

"What did I do?"

"Nothing," she said. "It's just a bad idea. No, just that... it's just impossible, is all."

"Why?"

"Because it is."

"But it isn't," he said. She didn't reply, and they stood facing each other in silence. She opened her eyes one at a time, just peeping at first, thinking he might be gone, but he still stood there looking down at her with his arms folded across his chest. People passed them, single or in pairs or accompanied by dogs, and some stared curiously.

"Look," he said finally, "it's always impossible, isn't it? *This* is impossible, but happens anyway. Watch." He swung his arms behind him, then brought them forward over his head, and the rest of his body followed, first his belly, then his thighs, and then his feet flying up not a foot from her nose, making a breeze that she felt against her ears. He flipped full around once and landed solidly on the rail. It was perfectly done. He would not have fallen if Jemma hadn't grabbed at him and knocked him off balance. She shrieked and put out both her hands to pull him in, but she only succeeded in pushing him into the pond. He looked distinctly surprised and even betrayed as he fell, but made no sound as he went into the water.

Now I've done it, she thought calmly, but not resisting an urge to pull miserably at her face. A vision flashed in her head of his very white bones surfacing in the acid water and bobbing about a little before dissolving into pink, marrowy foam.

"I made it!" he called up to her. "I had it landed before you pushed me!" She ran off down the bridge, meaning to run entirely out of his life. He could suffer a collision with her and not die for it. He would suffer this little damage and then go on living. Goodbye, goodbye! she called out in her head as she ran, imagining the other woman he would find. She would be prettier than Jemma but stupider, and she would be the type of woman compelled to uncover the past lovers of her lovers. When she heard the story of Jemma's behavior she would be utterly unable to fathom it.

"I'm only calling," she told him four days later, "to tell you I can never see you again. And to tell you to stop calling me every day."

"Okay," he said.

"It makes me embarrassed for you," she said. "All the messages."

"Yes. Will you see me tonight?"

"Of course," she said, meaning to say, of course she would *like* to, but she certainly could not. But he had hung up and was already on his way to the bridge. When he stood under her window and called for her she went down to him, a voice in her head as she went down the stairs—her mother's or her brother's or her father's or her lover's—remarking how her resolve was as sturdy as a peeled banana.

But I like him, she said to herself, to them, slowing on the curving steps.

It doesn't matter.

And he likes me, I think.

It doesn't matter.

And I need him.

Who's to say what's necessary? What's your need compared to his life?

You're just being superstitious.

Is it superstition to insist that the sun rises in the East?

Shut up! she said, not out loud—she wasn't that crazy. Though she could call them out of the dark to stand silently around her bed, and though they were the constant companions of her dreams, and though she still consulted her mother on which days were skirt days and which days were pants days, and exalted with her brother in a great high or a stupendous drunk, and though she continued to have imaginary, masturbatory sex with her departed lover, she knew they weren't real when they stood before her on the last four steps, raising their hands in the gesture she had practiced: stop, no more, go back upstairs. Four is enough, her father said. She passed right through them.

She thought that she might catch the roach and set it free outside, but it hid from her whenever she sought it. A few times, studying on her couch, she felt watched, and looked up to see it on the counter, waving its antennae as if in admonition or warning. When she chased it, it evaded her easily. Her best opportunity to banish it was whenever Rob Dickens came for her. The roach was always waiting near the door, but if she caught it she'd have to spirit it past him, or else hold it in her purse until there was a time in their evening when she could set free. The dinnertime disaster had already played a few times in her head: her purse carelessly closed; a tickle on her leg, belly, breast and neck; the roach emerging from around her ear to perch on her head and regard the endangered rival; the screams of the waitress.

He was a candle lover. They gave his bedroom the air of a chamber of sacrifice; they were all around his bed, in free-standing iron sconces, on the nightstands and dresser, in an enormous chandelier brought back from a year in Belgium. When they were all lit, the room was almost as bright as a hospital hallway. It was the bedroom of a priest, or a ritual murderer, and laying eyes upon it she'd had a surge of hope, that he might be crazy, too. Always she required him to extinguish some, so the light became gentler. When she looked at him his dripping face wavered with the light, and it became the face of her first. He spoke her name to her, but she never answered with his, for fear of a mix-up.

Sound asleep in her new lover's bed, she dreamed of her old lover. She stood on a corner well away from her parents' house, waiting for him to pick her up. It was one of their routines—she'd sneak out her window and fleetly step down the birch tree that grew next to the house and she'd wait for him at the top of the hill. He drove up like he always did, but his dream car was the ruined image of his waking car, and he was a ruined image of himself.

Get in, he told her, and she did, folding herself tight to squeeze under the sagging roof.

You're late, she said.

Let's not put this on me, he said. Let's put this where it belongs. Do you have any idea what you're doing?

Don't you yell at me, she said, like she had when he was alive.

Do you have any idea? Any idea at all? Is there even a brain in your head?

Don't yell at her, said a voice from the back. She looked there and saw her brother, folded up even more extremely than she was. His blue eyes seemed to glow in the dark car. He was whole, not cut or burned or twisted.

Who the fuck asked you?

Slow down, said Jemma, because while her attention had shifted to the back of the car the landscape had changed, and now they were hurling down foggy roads lined with trees covered with dying, hand-shaped leaves.

Are you out of your fucking mind? asked Martin. He let go of the wheel so he could gesticulate wildly at her, and they ran headlong into a tree. She was thrown from the car, or else the car evaporated—she found herself seated on the cool ground watching the tree they'd hit. It was on fire. The hand-shaped leaves were lifted off by the flames and went spinning up into the sky. What is it? asked her brother. What is beautiful about him?

Rob Dickens was mumbling next to her ear when she woke. He was a sleep-talker. She had already spent a night or two listening closely to his rambling, thinking he might disclose to her some sort of fascinating personal secret, but what he said was only gibberish. He owned an emperor-sized bed, abducted, like the chandelier, out of Belgium. Why a Belgian should require such a large bed, she could not figure—she had had the idea since kindergarten that tiny people lived in tiny countries—unless it was for the reason she required that night, so that she could remove herself to a great distance and yet still be in bed with him. She slid to the very edge of the bed and watched him sleep. She strained her eye in the dark to follow the line of his body from his toe to his head, and then she sought to penetrate his face and his very mind with her gaze, all the while asking herself, what is *not* beautiful about him?

He opened his eyes as she watched him.

"What are you doing?" he asked.

"Nothing," she said. He put his hand out to her, not reaching her despite the length of his arm.

"Come here."

"No," she said, and considered, not for the last time, how she was bad for him. "You will always know," Sister Gertrude had told her class of trembling third-graders. "You will always know the wrong thing, and choose it freely." Sister Gertrude was a million years away now; all that time had made her pathetic and small—she was just a nun-shaped nubbin on a chain of nun-nubbins hung in a chain around her dead brother's neck. But Jemma really had always known the wrong thing, and chosen it, and so she chose it now. Angels should be singing, or devils shrieking, or the walls should shake. No, no no no! cried her ghosts, but she quieted them. What was true to her she put away for what was sensible. What was safe she put away for what would put him at risk. What was lonely, what would redeem her, what would have made her the saint of her own obsession, she put away for selfish need, or for love. She took his reaching hand.

With her mouth engaged she looked through his legs at the lightning in the window. It flashed through the water—falling so heavily against the glass that she was reminded of the time they'd made out in a car wash—and cast their shadow on the wall of the darkened room. She paused to catch her breath and turned her face to the wall, to see the curious silhouette, the way his neck and shoulders grew out from between her thighs, and how his legs, thrust out from her shoulders so they looked in shadow like her third and fourth arms, shuddered and waved. She turned her attention back to him, but still cast glances synchronous with the lightning so she could see how they made insects, trees, and Eastern deities on the wall, until they rolled off the bed and his mouth came inching up her body, to find her own mouth. Then she only saw his face, closer and closer. When the lightning flashed again she imagined it echoing in the globe of his eye.

Strange, certainly, that witnessing a delivery should make her need this, but stranger still that she should try to ruin the joy of it with dark thoughts. Always when they were together like this, especially when they were desperately and ferociously together like this, when she really ought not to have the capacity to consider anything but the immediacy of her overwhelming pleasure, still the greater portion of her thought, even as she and Rob clawed and pulled at one another, and stood, and lay down, and stood up, and squatted, and knelt, and stood again, was devoted to her brother, her parents, and her first lover. She had used to think that her ghosts presented themselves in her mind to warn her—again and again and again, every day and night of her life forever and forever—of the obvious: that everyone she loved must die. Then she wondered if they might not be spectators at fleshly events to which they could never again be party, and she found herself savoring the tastes and collisions and knotty tensions for their sake. And finally she knew it was because they were always with her that they were with her at this seemingly most inappropriate time, and it was only her own perverse will that called them out of memory to present themselves. But now she could get it over in a flash, the thought of them. As swiftly as if they were handing her off from each to each in a frenetic dance she passed among them—father, mother, lover, brother. She spent an instant at each funeral and saw her parents' caskets, and she saw the box that hid her brother's ashes, all that was left after the butchery he performed upon himself. And she saw her lover's face, marred by the obscene reconstructions of the mortician. His eyes had been left open at his weird mother's request. Jemma had been sure he'd winked at her as the casket was closed.

Rob pressed his forehead against hers, so hard she thought their heads must break into each other, and their brains would mix like yolks. "Come back," he said.

It called to Jemma's mind a spinning fun-house trick room, the way they rolled along the walls. It would not have surprised her too much to open her eyes and discover herself pinned against the ceiling by Rob's handsome hips. They rolled against the door. After a little while, when she heard a new noise, she thought at first it was her foot fluttering against the wood, but it was somebody knocking. They grew still, and Jemma wondered if the door was locked. The knock came again, louder and more forceful. The door handle jiggled, and a voice called through the door. "Hello? Is anyone inside? I left my pencil case." For what seemed like five whole minutes the person worked the handle. Is it so difficult to understand, Jemma wondered, when a door is locked? And then she wondered who carried pencil cases out of sixth grade, anyhow.

Rob arched his back and neck to look at her—he was myopic and not wearing his glasses. While the door handle rattled he lifted a hand and ran his finger down her forehead, over her nose, mouth, and chin, down her neck and chest and stomach until his finger was resting exactly in her belly button. Even after the person on the other side of the door finally gave up, Rob regarded her silently.

"What?" she whispered, and he brought his face so close to hers that the sweat rolling off her nose clung briefly to his before falling to strike her foot. "I love you," he said. *Oh no.* You are over that, Jemma. There's no harm in this, and no mischief, and O I will fill chapters in the Book of the King's Daughter with all the evil things you and he could be doing now, and though God is even now raising His hand to strike the world, it is not to punish your pleasure, or because a good man loves you, or because you love him, or because you have angered your dead, or betrayed the dreadful imaginary empiricisms that support your depressing logic. Fine, swallow your words—that low, warbling groan contains the same number of syllables as I love you, and it's close enough for Rob. Fine, spike your delight with dread, but don't stop, please don't stop now.

Fine orgasms recalled others. She was not a person who reflected all the next day on the pleasure, and wasted hours on the daydreamy wanting of it. But as she approached the finish with Rob Dickens, she thought of the time with her first lover when she had been sure she'd briefly felt all he felt, and had been disappointed at what he got, because it seemed so small, a spasm that satisfied for less than a second and left behind a terrible need. She thought of the time in college she'd stepped ever-so-carefully home after a night of drinking mushroom tea with her friend Vivian and a set of silly girls from her organic chemistry class. She'd spent the dawn hours with a banana and an imaginary creature she named the Monkey King. And what she thought was her first, when she was still in grade school, in a dream, when Jesus had floated down from Heaven to become a pure white glow beneath her sheets.

Now she bent down on the floor in a compact posture of worship. Rob was behind her. He was unable to keep silent. She heard his singing moan with utter clarity—it struck a chord in her and increased her pleasure—but kept silent herself, helped by the Hello Kitty pencil case, found under the bed, which she'd wedged in her mouth. She could feel the pencils roll and crunch under her teeth as she got closer, and she could still hear the thunder rolling, though the lightning had stopped. "I'm right there," said Rob. "I'm right there."

When Jemma looked up toward the window she saw that it was entirely black, blank even of the washing rain. She felt suddenly lifted up, as if someone were tossing her high in the air, or like she was riding an elevator at insane speeds thousands of feet into the sky. It was almost unbearable, and she cried out, despite her best efforts to keep silent. She got lost briefly, imagining herself bursting apart in a most agreeable explosion. She watched calmly as forty little Jemmas (she had time to count them) went flying out on curling tracks, trailing fairy-dust sparkles out of their bottoms. They faded, except for one, who calmly regarded Jemma with a face that became the face of the King's Daughter, wise and malformed. It stared and stared until Jemma opened her eyes.

"Oh God," Rob said, then leaned forward over her, pressing his chest against her back, his face into her neck, and placing his hands around her belly.

"What's happening?" Jemma asked, confused now, and a little nauseated because the lifted sensation was still with her. She felt them being drawn higher and higher. The window was a slate; it did not reflect them when they rose unsteadily on their cramped legs to try to look through it. Then they were lifted with a new force, so hard and fast that they fell down and lay together with their faces pressed against the carpet. She knew quite certainly that something horrible was happening, and that it was all her fault—I got him, after all, she thought, and, Here it is, and, How stupid, to think it could end anyway but like this. She heard a voice, courteous and mechanical, and certainly a voice apart from the babbling chorus in her head. It said, "Creatures, I am the preserving angel. Fear not, I will keep you. Fear not, I will protect you. Fear not, you will bide with me. Fear not, I will carry you into the new world."

The problem in me is the problem in the world. The problem in the world is the problem in me. I have always known this. Even when I did not understand it, it was still in me, the question and the answer together, knotted up like a pair of hands clenched together in pathetic anguished prayer.

When I was five years old I tried to kill my sister. All day long I tried to kill her. In the morning I put mothballs in her cereal, but our mother woke up and threw them away, not because she smelled the naphthalene, but because she thought cereal was for trailer park kids, and on the days when she could get out of bed in time—a century's weight of ghosts kept her sleeping or staring at the ceiling in her darkened room until noon many days—she would make us fancy omelets.

I took my sister for a walk and tried to sacrifice her on a stone picnic table in the Severna Forest Coliseum. I knew the story of Isaac. I knew the whole of the Old Testament by then. I raised a smooth stone as big as my fist and prepared to knock a hole in her skull. I waited too long, imagining the blood on the stone and a clump of her hair matted to it. A troop of Brownies came rustling through the tall grass—the coliseum was built by a wealthy Baptist with a passion for Greek tragedy and outdoor theater, but once he moved away it was let to fall into disrepair—and Jemma leaped off the table and ran to dance with them around one of the decaying plaster statues.

I tried to drown her in the tub. Our mother was throwing a party for the elites of our neighborhood, which is to say for everybody, since everyone who lived there was odiously rich, the cat-food magnate having established a tradition of exclusivity in this heavily wooded peninsula on the Severn. She sent us together to the tub, and I washed my sister's hair, just as I had been taught to do, and then when she ducked under the water to rinse I held her there. I had never been taught to drown a person, but I knew just what to do. My hands felt old and wise as she struggled under them. I am sending you to Jesus, I told her. But I remember the moment perfectly, and I know I was not trying to kill her because I thought it would make her happy.

And finally I pushed her off the roof. We dressed up for the party, and wandered from drunk to drunk, inhabiting a whole different world from the one at their level of sight. Four feet off the ground, nobody noticed if you stole a cigarette from where it was burning in the ashtray, or nipped from unattended drinks. No one noticed that I was drunk. I only got more sullen and angry, and so it hardly showed. We were sent to bed, but we did not sleep. I took Jemma out on the roof, something I did all the time. And usually I would tell her all the things that had made me angry that day, or point out lights on the river, or try to get her to see shapes in the stars. But tonight all I could think of was the crowd in our house and on the deck. It was late in September but very warm, and from where we sat on the top of the roof I could see men in short sleeves and women in short dresses, but none of them thought to look up, and they would probably not have seen us anyway in our dark pajamas.

Look at them, I said to my sister. Just look at them! And I thought that she must be like me, and that just for her to see them would be for her to hate them, like just to see the world was to hate it, every little cloud and bird and bush, and just to look in the mirror was to hate myself so much I could feel a trembling ache all over my body. One day I'll go, I said, and then I'll take them all. I did not know what it meant, to go. I only knew it was the right word, and the right sentiment—sudden and strange and certain as a divine inspiration. And then I pushed her at them, because I was sure just in that moment, though I knew better as soon as she started to roll, that she would be a bomb to kill them all when she hit.

Right away I regretted it. It was a mistake to push her, and it had been a mistake to try to drown her, and stone her, and poison her. It was a mistake because it was a horrible sin, the worst thing I had done and the worst thing I would ever do, and now it had set the tone and the theme for my whole life. And it was a mistake because I knew, just in that moment when I was revealed to myself as utterly depraved and irredeemably vile, that it was I and not my sister who must be the deadly sacrifice.

Dr. Chandra was in the cafeteria, the place to which he habitually retreated after an on-call humiliation. There was no consolation in pudding, but he still stuffed himself with it every time something went wrong, every time he tangled himself in something really unfortunate, or tripped at exactly the worst time, falling into another mother and squeezing at her boob for purchase. You do that more than twice and people think you are feigning clumsiness for the sake of the grope, but he thought boobs the unloveliest things in the world; he'd cross the street to avoid a particularly large, stern pair. Every time he wrote the wrong dosage for a drug, and every time he got caught only pretending to hear a murmur or making up a laboratory value he'd failed to memorize, he'd come down to the cafeteria, always to the same table if it was available, stuck in a glass alcove, windows that looked over the memorial butterfly garden. You didn't have to be a dead child to get a butterfly there, but that was mostly what they represented, preemies who never made it out of the nursery or toddlers who couldn't beat their brain tumor or teens who succumbed to leukemia. The pudding was cheap and filling. He ate it and ate it until he thought he could feel it squeezing from the pores of his nose.

"Is it in?" he had asked Emma, when he had tried to intubate the monstrous child.

"I don't fucking know," she said. "We're tubing a baby, not having sex."

Then she bumped him out of the way and looked in the child's mouth. "In his brain, maybe," she said, yanking out the tube, then putting in another, all in about twenty seconds. "There you go," she said, patting Dr. Chandra on the shoulder. She walked off, and he noticed for the hundredth time how she had curls that really bounced. Natalie was shaking her head. The medical student was staring at the ceiling. When the respiratory therapist asked him for vent settings, Chandra just walked away.

I could just leave, he thought to himself in the cafeteria. It was a thought that had occurred to him before, to walk out of residency, out of the hospital, and out of the horrible half-life. He'd walked out of rotations before, but only as far as the Residency Director's office, to complain and to cry to the man who insisted they all call him Dad. Nothing ever came of it, and he always went back to work. Tonight it was raining too hard to walk out, though maybe that would be a better option than remaining—to leave the hospital and be swept away, out into the bay and through the Golden Gate, out to the Farrallons where he could live on puffins and baby seals, a better diet than humiliation and misery and vanilla pudding.

A noise took him away from the Farallons—a surge in the wind. Suddenly it blew so heavily he felt the hospital rock. The few other late-night diners looked up from their pizza or ice cream or pudding. Chandra rose and pressed his face against the window. Now the rain was falling so hard it totally obscured the garden. When the window went dark he thought it was because of the sheer volume of rain, until he saw his pale face reflected in the depths of the darkening glass, and saw that all the others were going to the windows to examine them, too. When he pressed his face against the glass, and cupped his hands at his temples to block out the light, he still couldn't see through. Staring and squinting, he saw a dim flash of light, as if at a great distance, and thought it must be lightning struggling to shine through the rain.

"What's going on?" he asked no one in particular. Nobody answered. The others in the cafeteria only tried like he had to see out the darkened windows. He turned back and was about to try again when he felt the first big lurch. They're all going to laugh at me, he thought as he fell, just after he knocked his head on the table. But before he felt himself pressed back flat against the floor, he had time to see that everyone else was falling, too.

Three floors up Emma was relaxing—as much as she ever did on call—in her luxurious call room. It was really an attending-level call room, but then she was nearly an attending, and had anyway been outthinking and outclassing most of the attendings since her first year of fellowship. But who needed a vanity in their call room, and to take a bath in the whirlpool tub was only asking to be called out wet and naked into the middle of a crisis. She lay in bed a little while, visiting in spirit every baby in the unit, holding them a minute in her expansive mind, considering their afflictions and trying to anticipate the dips and turns their hospital courses might take that night. There was nothing she could think of that she had not already warned Natalie to watch for, or that Natalie would not anticipate herself. You couldn't spell out everything for them, and she left more than usual unspoken with Natalie, who was smarter than the average third-year, or less dumb, at least. She did an imaginary survey of the PICU as well, since she was covering both units tonight. The regular PICU fellow was still trying to swim in.

Sirius Chandra passed briefly through her mind, tangled up and confused and goofy and already slightly smelly, she'd noticed standing close to him, though the night was hardly half-over. She thought of tracking him down in whatever hidey-hole he'd retired to, for the sort of talk a good and empathetic Fellow was supposed to deliver to a really dispirited Intern, but it seemed too late for tears and complaints and excuses. She turned on the television but it played only a moment—a glimpse of a girl and her horse who she managed to recognize as Pippi Longstocking before the station cut out, and then every station she tried was off the air. She turned it off, and sat down on the bed, and got a page, not from the unit just outside her door, but from her home.

"She's fine," her husband said as soon as he picked up the phone. Their daughter was five months old that week.

"Pretty late for a social call," she said.

"Such a storm," he said. "I couldn't sleep."

"Well, I might have been."

"Better to be woken by someone you love."

"Who says I don't love these people?"

"She's sleeping right through the thunder. Did you know she twitches when she sleeps?"

"Are you sitting there watching her again? No wonder you can't sleep. Were you checking her breathing? It's fine. It's always going to be fine, and even if it wasn't, you're not going to catch it by staring at her. You've just got to relax. Don't you think I'll tell you if there's something wrong with her? Paul? Paul?" She listened for him—sometimes he fell very silent and she could barely hear him breathing—and she thought the line was dead until a lady's voice spoke out of the phone.

"He is gone, my love. Gone forever, not to be seen again in this world. He is already drowned, but not you. You I will protect and preserve and love for all your allotted time."

"Who is this?" Emma demanded, so nervous all of a sudden that she was holding the phone in front of her face and shouting into it. "Is this the fucking *operator?*" She only got silence for an answer, and then she got the terrible heaviness that comes of being thrust up so impossibly high, so impossibly fast. Not even an angel wielding the sheltering grace of God could cushion her fully. She fell back, like all the rest.

Down the hall, in another call room, Rob was speaking.

"Something awful has happened," he said to Jemma, and she was reminded of her mother, who had spoken those very same words, in the same sort of frightened, croaking whisper, when Jemma came home on the night of her brother's death. She was reminded, too, of the feeling she'd had as soon as she came in the house—she had known that something was horribly wrong before she saw anyone, before anyone delivered the news. She and Rob dressed hurriedly, pulling on each other's scrubs by mistake, so Jemma's shirt hung on her and Rob's clung tight across his shoulders. Neither of them remembered to put their socks on. Jemma opened the door, after they'd both hesitated a while, listening. The hall outside was empty. The red preemie footprints wandered along the carpet, same as they had when the two of them had gone into the call room. It all seemed quite normal, until a great wail, not a child's, came washing along the walls. The telephone lady's voice spoke as if in response. "Be comforted, my darlings."

They followed the little footprints back toward the NICU. The call room was placed so that a person should be able to run from bed to the unit or the delivery rooms in less than two minutes, but they creeped along so carefully that it took a whole five minutes just to come to the door to the glass bridge, or rather the place where that door had been. What previously had been a glass door was now a great circle of darkened glass, opaque and slate gray like the window in the call room, reflective only of flesh-colored shadows. Jemma put her hand against it and drew it back immediately. The glass was so cold her fingers stuck a little as she pulled her hand away. "What's happening?" she asked.

"Something awful," said Rob. "Come on." He took her hand and drew her along, past the pictures of children at play and past the giant newspaper articles. These all looked the same to Jemma's eye. Outside the unit, though, there was something new. Just beyond the doors, where she was sure a water fountain had stood earlier in the evening, there was now a little recess set waist-high in the wall, surrounded on three sides with flat squares of colored glass. Just above the recess was a greater light than all the others, an amber square the size of an adult hand. Rob reached past her to press his palm against it.

"What is it?" Jemma asked.

"A door handle, I think."

"Name me, I will keep you," said the woman's voice, seeming to speak from within the hole in the wall.

"Just open the door. Open the damn door."

"Until I am named, I cannot keep you, I cannot preserve you, I cannot make the thing you desire. John Robert Dickens, I have named you, now you must name me."

"What the fuck?" Rob said, taking his hand away. "How do you know my name? Who the fuck are you?"

"I am the preserving angel," she said again. Jemma walked past him and swiped her badge through the old reader that still sat next to the door. The double doors were quiet a moment, as if considering whether or not she should be admitted, then suddenly swung in.

"Didn't these used to open out?" Jemma asked. Rob was too distracted by the chaos in the unit to answer her. Nurses and doctors and assistants were running every which way. Jemma thought they were in a panic for the same reason that she wanted to be in one; they knew it, too, that something awful had happened, something to which the only proper reaction was to run around like this, from room to room, shouting and barking at each other. But it was the more ordinary pandemonium of a unit in uproar. Rob had told her about these patients, little unformed people so sensitive to disturbance that a raised voice or an unpleasant inflection or an ugly face could make them sick. It was said of them that they were trying to die, when they decided that the noise or your bad mood or the vibrations in the ether were too much to bear, and they stopped breathing and dropped their heart rate, turning blue or purple. Turn away from the light! the nurses would shout at them, half-joking. All the doors to all the bays were open, and Jemma could see through them that there was hardly a single isolette or crib that didn't have a person or two administering to the patient. It looked as if every last one of them was trying to die.

As they entered the first bay, a swiftly passing nurse caught Jemma's shoulder, pulling her a few steps before she stopped. Fat, middle-aged, with smart hair and stylish glasses, she looked just like countless other nurses. Jemma knew her the way she knew a lot of the nurses in the unit and the nursery—she'd been yelled at by her for touching a baby or not touching a baby or not washing her hands correctly or breathing wrong around the babies. Her name was Judy or Julie or Jolene.

"You, what are you?" she asked.

"A med student."

"Useless! Useless! Have you ever given bicarb before?"

"Not exactly," Jemma said, meaning never at all.

"Well, time to learn!" She shoved a nursing manual and a little phial of bicarbonate into Jemma's hands, pointed at the nearest isolette, and then she was off, swift as before, shouting the dose back over her shoulder. Jemma turned to Rob to ask about the particulars of correcting a metabolic acidosis, but he was gone, collared by an attending to assist with intubating a plum-colored baby down the way. Jemma could look things up as well as anyone, and probably quicker than most. Facts leaked out of her brain within days of being stuffed in, but she had excelled in school all her life because she always knew the most direct route to the information she required. She had the heaviest white coat in her class, full of books and laminated tables, and she wore at her hip the most advanced data-storage device she could find. She read the entry on bicarb in the nursing manual pretty quickly. For the next five minutes she would know as much as anyone about how to give it, and then the information would be gone. She thought she was doing a good job, and was feigning confidence as she drew up the medication and flicked bubbles out of the syringe. Still, the flapping harpy who had assigned Jemma the task made another pass by her just in time to catch her wrist and shriek at her, "It's not going to do much good in her bladder. That's the *foley*, you moron!" It was just one of many pasta-thin tubes disappearing into a tangle beside the little body before emerging to plunge into various natural and unnatural orifices. Jemma had thought she'd traced out the line pretty carefully. Judy—Jemma got a sustained look at her dangling name tag as she was shrieking at her—pushed her out of the way, into the orbit of another nurse, who pressed her into service trying to get IV access on a fat, seizing one-month-old. He was huge and veinless, and had just the appearance of a red beachball, the way he bounced in his bed. "He hasn't seized in a week!" said the new nurse. "We just pulled the broviac yesterday, for God's sake, and the IM ativan isn't working for shit. Are you any good at these?"

"I'm okay," Jemma said, though she'd never in her life gotten an IV on anyone except Rob, whose veins were as great and obvious as highways. She took a foot while the nurse took a hand, and they both began to stab blindly into the soft red skin. Jemma got a flash of blood once, but when she tried to thread the catheter the little vein blew. "Try again," the nurse told her, and Jemma did, failing three more times before the nurse got one. By then the baby's battery had run down. It was only twitching once or twice a minute.

"Should we still give the drug?" asked the nurse.

"I guess," Jemma said, looking around for a real doctor. Rob was in this bay, doing compressions four isolettes away. She decided not to bother him with the question. The nurse pushed the tranquilizer and they both bent over the isolette to watch its eyes glaze.

"You're a little shaky," said the nurse, when the baby had grown quite still. "You want some of this?" She shook the syringe at her.

"No thanks," Jemma said.

"I'm Anna," the nurse said cheerily, sticking out her hand. "And I'm kidding! Nice try with those pokes, though—seriously." Jemma took her hand weakly and stared at her, not sure what struck her as so strange about the woman, and she thought for a moment it was her chicken neck or her oversized turquoise earrings that gave her the air of a trailer-park queen, until she realized it was the cheery tone, so out of place in this carnival of crises, and in the context of the great crisis. Jemma suddenly understood that she hadn't been thinking about that, about what the broadcast lady was saying—you have all been saved from the water. "Is it real?" she asked Anna.

"One hundred percent genuine prime delicious benzo!" she said, sniffing lovingly at the syringe. "I'm kidding!"

Judy grabbed Jemma's arm and dragged her down the bay, not even speaking to her but delivering her to another access nightmare and then hurrying away again. Jemma picked up a syringe and started poking; the baby's nurse didn't even look up. Jemma failed three times on this one, three on the next one, and two on the next, a post-op cardiac train wreck whose central access stopped working just as the unit went all to hell, and whose irritable heart was wanting its antiarrhythmic. Jemma tried three times and got the fourth, a scalp vein just in the place you'd put a bow on the head of a normal baby girl. Then she got two in a row, both on the first try, but just when she thought she might actually be developing some skill or attracting some luck at inserting IVs, someone wanted her to intubate. She was three bays away from where she started, faced with a former twenty-seven-weeker who, now a month old, and five days off his ventilator, had abruptly decided to stop breathing.

"How many of these have you done before?" the nurse asked her. Jemma said three, which was technically true, but she did not volunteer that none of those attempts had been successful. She knew the procedure well enough, knew how to put a rolled washcloth under the little neck and tilt the head back, how to pry open the toothless mouth with her pinkie and sweep the tongue aside with the edge of the laryngoscope blade. She put her tube in the first hole she saw. "Esophagus," said the nurse, listening over the belly with a stethoscope as Jemma puffed a few bursts of air through the tube with a bag. "Did it again," she said, after Jemma's second try. "Did you say you'd done this before?" Jemma didn't answer, only rolled the head back again and poised her arm for another swoop. She saw it again, the single pink wet hole, and understood how it wasn't the anatomy she sought. She wondered how a trachea could be so thoroughly hidden in a neck the diameter of a shot glass. The nurse was shouting out the baby's heart rate, which fell further and further as Jemma failed to remove the foreign body from its throat. "One ten!" she shrieked. "Ninety! Sixty!" Jemma took out the scope, straightened her back, and took a step back right into Rob.

"What are you doing?" he asked.

"Intubating this little boy."

"Trying, anyway," the nurse said. Rob took the bag and mask from her and ventilated by hand. When Jemma went in again he looked over her shoulder, his cheek pressed to hers. He was covered in sweat. His clothes were soaked through, and Jemma wondered if other people had noticed how he reeked of sex.

"Ah, just pull back a little," he said, tugging gently at her wrist. The vocal cords popped into view and Jemma went through them with the tube. Rob's fingers clutched the tube over hers, pinning it against the kicking baby's lips.

"You're in, finally," the nurse said to Jemma.

"Don't let go till the tube is secure," said Rob, and then he hurried away. Jemma could not figure how much time had passed since she saw him last, and she quickly lost track again after he was gone. She intubated two more babies, put in another IV, assisted with a chest tube, bag-ventilated for a half hour under the intermittent tutelage of a pierced-up respiratory therapist, and finally changed a diaper, and then she could not find another emergency. Jemma was in the third bay, the middle bay, when it all stopped; she sat down on the floor and leaned back against the wall. She saw Dr. Chandra standing in the middle of the bay, a silver laryngoscope in his hand, looking forlorn and confused. Natalie and Emma were standing very tall on either side of an isolette three babies down from where Jemma sat, with their heads held high and their noses elevated, so they looked to be sniffing for the next crisis, but it never came. Dr. Grouse, the attending, was standing with his arms folded, seeming to be staring intently at a monitor, but his eyes were closed. The silence of alarms seemed heavy and oppressive, and the noise of a loosely connected piece of oxygen tubing near Jemma's head was rather soothing. She closed her eyes and fell asleep, but only for a few minutes, waking to discover the nurse Anna shaking formula on her from a bottle.

"Wake up, sweetie," she said. "You can't sleep there."

"Stop that," Jemma said.

"It's not too hot, is it?" Anna asked, shaking out a few drops onto her arm.

"What time is it?" Jemma asked.

"I haven't looked. Will you move, or should I roll you out of the way?"

Jemma stood. "What happened?"

"You were here. You saw. They all crumped at once. The whole damn unit, except her." She pointed to an isolette in the middle of the room. It was set upon a dais that Jemma was quite sure hadn't been there the day before. "She auto-extubated an hour ago. How about that? Now they want me to try to feed her. That seems a little hasty, don't you think?"

"I mean outside. What happened outside?"

Anna shrugged. "Ask somebody who's thinking about it," she said, and turned to feed her patient. Jemma walked away from her, to the isolette on the dais. Standing on her toes, she could look inside to see the King's Daughter, sucking on her hand with her rabbity mouth. She turned her head to look serenely at Jemma. It was unbearable, not for the ugliness of her face, but for the peace of her eyes. "Brenda," Anna said. "Isn't that an awful name? She needs a sleeveless tee shirt and bad hair, to go along with that name."

"I have to go," Jemma said—she had a view into all the bays but didn't see Rob anywhere that she looked. She hurried right out of the unit, past the little flocks of people three or four strong, who were finally turning on the televisions set high in the corners of every bay, seeking answers about the state of the world but finding only lambent static.

It takes four angels to oversee an apocalypse: a recorder to make the book that would be scripture in the new world; a preserver to comfort and to save those selected to be the first generation; an accuser to remind them why they suffer; and a destroyer to revoke the promise of survival and redemption, and to teach them the awful truth about furious sheltering grace. And I am the least of these, for though I alone know the whole story of the call that asked for the end of the world and the flood that answered it, and though it falls to me to write the Book of Calvin and the Acts of Jemma and the Book of the King's Daughter, I already know that in the new world no one will read scripture, and they will not labor under the sort of covenant that can be written down in words.

Now we are only two, but two others are coming, our brother and our brother. We are a family, but only in the way every angel is related to every other angel, and nothing but duty binds us. I do not love or hate the angel in the walls of the hospital, who all these stunned survivors are getting to know by name, since they must capture some small part of her bright essence with a name before she can serve them. Ancient and ageless, she never lived or died. I was a special case. Only Metatron was like me, mortal before he was angel. But he went on to be the right hand of God, and I am the imaginary friend Jemma has never even known that she has. Still, he is not really my brother either, though if I ever met him I would call him such, and I was mightier, in my way, than he ever was, or is.

* * *

On their first day at sea I am obligated to dance above the hospital and praise them all, the high and the low, the damned and the elect. I remember lust, and it is like that, to be taken by the urge to dance and praise. I would have railed against it, in my old days, and schemed against it, and destroyed it. Not anymore. It is a joy to submit.

My sister sings with me, though she is trapped in the substance of the hospital, and cannot leave it to dance with me. If she did, it would sink like a stone. I spin in a spiral that echoes the form of the hospital below. Blue sky above and blue sea below and the hospital a white mote between them.

Praise their ignorance, my sister sings.

Praise their fear, I sing.

Praise their hatred.

Praise their envy.

Praise their bitter grief.

Praise them and put them aside.

They are eating the last tainted bread of the earth.

Praise their unhappy fate.

And praise their hours of joy.

Praise their good work.

And praise the sickness of children.

Praise all the tumors.

And praise the bad blood.

Praise the tired livers.

Praise the ailing spleens.

And praise the high colonic ruin.

Praise the drowning waters.

And all the drowned beneath them.

Praise our accusing brother.

Let him rise from the depths.

Praise our destroying brother.

Hurry his ascendance.

Praise Rob Dickens.

May he lend Jemma his strength.

Praise Jemma!

Mother of all!

Praise Jemma!

To the edge of the new world!
Praise Jemma!
The most important girl!
My dance is a blessing!
Our song is a prophecy!
Let her win!
Let her triumph!
The redeemer after the reformer!
Praise her in her whole!
And praise her in her parts!
Praise them in their whole!
And praise them in their parts!

Praise them! we sing, a command to the sky, and to ourselves. And I wonder as I speak half the names of the survivors, oldest down to youngest, praising all the while with my heart as well as my voice, if I ever loved like this when I was still alive, when it was not, as it is now, an obligation of my nature, and a condition of my being. Then the song is over, and I lie on the still-forbidden roof in an attitude of sleep, exhausted by passion, feeling disappointed and empty, and wondering what I was so excited about.

Like lust, I say, and do you see how it is true.

Jemma's best friend Vivian joined the crew, dressed in goggles and surgical overalls insulated with pillow stuffing and led by Jordan Sasscock, the PICU senior, that tried to break through the glass doors of the lobby with a bench. It was the sort of bench, built from heavy wrought iron and laminated wood, that would have been more at home in a park than in a lobby, but it nicely approximated a battering ram just when they needed one. While a big crowd watched from the railings of the atrium balconies, they lifted it all together and ran at the doors that weren't doors any longer, but had become, while they were all distracted by the sudden lurch toward death taken by every last patient in their care, one flat panel of glass, as dark as slate and yet if you stood close and stared long enough into it, you saw your own face deep within, not exactly reflected. When Vivian looked she thought of a girl swimming up from the depths of a cold mountain lake.

She didn't know what she expected to see, on the other side of the shattered glass. Maybe the city on fire, or all the buildings fallen down. Or maybe just a group of soggy policemen. "We've been knocking for hours," they would say. Something had happened—that much she certainly believed. You could not feel that violent disjointment which had unsettled her off her feet, and unsettled the kids out of their tenuous grasp on health, and think otherwise. But a new ocean, and them in the hospital the only survivors? They were more likely experiencing some cruel experiment—black out the windows and blow in some aerosolized LSD and get Phyllis Diller to hide somewhere with a microphone and claim to be a sweet, creepy angel—than the end of the world.

"I wouldn't do that, if I were you," said the voice, seeming to come from everywhere in the lobby, loud but not stern.

"Fuck you!" said Maggie Formosa, one of Vivian's classmates, and easily the worst person she knew. Jordan counted to three and they ran. She was thinking of her family as she ran, imagining, stupidly she knew, that they were all waiting on the other side of the glass, lined up with hundreds of others behind a police barrier that separated this strangely behaving hospital from the usual city.

"You will live!" the voice shouted at them, and something about the tone of the voice betrayed it to Vivian as at once utterly compassionate and utterly deceitful, and in the scant moments before they collided with the glass it managed to convince her not that they were going to live but that the world had well and truly ended, and that they had been thrust beyond an ultimate pale into a strange and horrible new world.

She alone of the six was prepared for the hard shock that assaulted their shoulders when they ran the bench into the unbreakable glass, but she fell back with all of them, and just like Maggie she nearly missed having her foot crushed by one of the legs of the bench. But while Maggie stomped her feet and shouted at the highest window, the black glass cap of the atrium, Vivian sat on the ground and drew her face to her knees and wept, just like anyone who believes all of a sudden in the proximity of angels, and the death of her family, and the end of the world.

"I am the preserving angel," said the voice. "Did you think I would let you hurt yourself?"

"It all started," the man told Jemma, "with the voice from my fireplace." They were climbing the stairs, on their way to the roof, to look out on the state of creation. It was one day since the hospital had been cast adrift, and she was trying very hard not to consider things. It had become immediately apparent to her that the disaster—if that was a great enough word for it, if there was a great enough word for it—had spawned two types of people: those who considered things, and those who did not. There were only a few of the latter; she and this man seemed to be two of them. When she tried to think of the dead she only saw her own four, their faces flashing in succession, or the four of them standing quietly in a bright room, or the four of them adrift on the new great ocean, hand in hand in hand in hand, arms and legs spread so they made a wide rosette, spinning just under the surface of the water with their eyes open and bubbles caught beneath their chins.

When she'd finally made it back to the call room, after listening over and over, always disbelievingly, to the hidden lady—where the hell was she? everyone kept asking—who told them over and over that they had been preserved from a world-wide deluge, after she'd given up trying to peer through the windows, after she'd had a clutching reunion with Vivian, and after she'd tired of the organizing chaos all over the hospital, she'd found Rob there, laid out crookedly on his belly in the little bed, weeping into his arms. Jemma stretched herself over him, reaching past his head to take his hands. "Something awful has happened," he told her again. "It's not a trick or a drill. It's something more horrible than anything that's ever even happened before."

"I know," she said, because she had suffered enough disasters to know a real one from a fake one. But she could think of no words that might comfort him. It would have been enough, she thought, to weep with him, but she could not even do that. She felt very little except pain at his pain. What if it were true, that the world, as the grating voice insisted, was drowned and the only survivors were those who were trapped within the round walls of this hospital. She thought something in her should balk at believing it, but nothing did. She was so used to getting horrible news, she never doubted anything bad: your brother is dead; your father has died; your mother was in that burning house; Martin has had an accident; of course, of course, of course, of course. Only good news ever seemed unreal to her, anymore, and the fact of all those ended lives—a comical voice numbered them in her head, billy-uns and billy-uns and billy-uns—only put in her a familiar stony feeling, that left her calm and alert, so she thought as she listened to Rob's titanic weeping that she could discern the four distinct sobbing tones. She could name the muscles that shifted her to and fro as she rode on his back. She could track the progress of his tears down his face despite the dim light, and mark the tiny increments by which the tear stain grew on the festive sheet. She knew this state of being, her funeral mode—now time would slow down and stop and she would feel, would know, that this was the essence and purpose of her whole life, to be somebody leftover, when all the good people, the neat people, the cool people, the people who were actually people and not crawly depressive lizards, were dead, and to feel nothing about it, except the same old stony feeling and the not gnawing but nibbling suspicion that she had missed out, again. She put her face in his neck and said them again, empty words: "I know."

"I thought it was the devil talking, at first," the man told her. "Who else would speak out of the ashes? It was a cold night, but I had no fire going, so the voice came out of the blackness. It said, Listen to me, creature. I am an angel of the Lord. He has decreed a work for you."

Jemma had not asked him to explain anything; he had just started talking as soon as they'd met. He was coming up the stairs to the first floor just as she was entering the stairwell. They stood and regarded each other for a moment. She saw a haggard-looking man in a green suit and terribly ugly shoes, little slippers of woven leather afflicted with beaded tassels on either front.

"Is it… flooded down there?" she had asked him, looking over the railing at the stairs going down; she counted ten flights before they disappeared into darkness. She had taken the stairs to the nursery a hundred times; there hadn't used to be a basement.

"Certainly not," he said. He stared at her, not creepily. There was not much creepy about him, for all that he looked like a hospital administrator or a mortician. His stare was merely frank and curious, open and honest.

"I'm going up to the roof," she told him, when he kept staring at her. It was all over the hospital, announced by rumor and by the voice of the telephone lady who claimed to be an angel, that the roof was off limits, that the stairs were locked and the windows blacked for a very important reason—that what lay outside was so awful that to look at it would cost a person her sanity. "It is not yet time," the lady said. "It is forbidden." But Jemma had sneaked away from the new, expanded duties with which Rob kept himself busy to go and look. She had searched on three different floors for an open door to the stairwell, bumping shoulders with people going about frantic hospital business on the big ramp that ran in a spiral up the center of the hospital and led to every floor, and was the only way to get from one ward to another while the elevators were off-line. She walked around the lobby, stopping before the place where the main doors had been, pausing under the big toy, a giant perpetual-motion machine built to amuse visitors. She tried to appear innocent, looking up into the wires and beams and struts and gears and parachutes, watching the bowling balls leap from basket to basket, the water running in the sluices and the iron sailboats racing in the high courses—the thing had changed with the rest of the hospital, getting twice as complex as it had been before, and twice as stupid, and now it gave Jemma twice as bad a headache to stare at it, but she feigned interest until she was sure no one was looking before she darted to the doors. Every door in the lobby was locked, but she found a way into the stairwell in the now empty ER, suddenly the quietest place in the hospital since every child there had been admitted upstairs. There was no one there to hear her kicking the door and rattling the handle. "There you go," said the mechanical lady, when the handle finally turned. "I thought it was forbidden," Jemma said, looking around for the source of the voice—sometimes she spoke out of speakers but sometimes the voice just came out of a blank wall. "Hello?" Jemma said, but the lady didn't answer.

"That's where the stairs go," said the man. "Up."

"I want to see what it looks like."

"I can tell you what it looks like," he said. "It looks like a lot of water."

"I want to see."

He shrugged.

"How do *you* know, anyway? I thought nobody was allowed to look."

"I haven't," he said. "I don't need to. I just know, like I know the windows will go transparent again in about fifteen minutes. You may as well stay down here and wait. It's a lot of stairs."

"If you know so much, tell me why the elevators don't work." She tried to look skeptical, but knew she probably just looked confused.

"Oh, they will. In about an hour." He looked at his watch and counted past hours on his fingers, his lips moving silently. "Sorry, hour and a half. More or less."

"Right," she said, not convinced. "Who the hell are you, anyway, that you know all this shit?"

"I'm the person who built this place. Well, maybe not built it. But I designed it." He struck a pose, throwing his hands up to the right of his face and splaying his fingers, as if to say, See? Jemma recognized the gesture, and suddenly thought she recognized the man.

"Do I know you? I think I know you."

"I've never seen you before in my life," he said.

But she did know him, because she subscribed to a silly architecture magazine, and had spent idle moments, when she ought to have been studying, gazing at all the marvelous residences, imagining herself sprawled out in every one of the over-appointed rooms, without a care in the world. It was only three or four issues since she had seen this man and his buildings, and remembered especially a giant seaside house he'd built for an eccentric cat-food magnate. Who could forget the many vast rooms—the long hall containing a little forest of rare-wood scratching posts, the thousand square-foot cat-condominium, the long troughs of litter in the chambre de toilette, scented, the captions said, with cardamom and myrrh—all of it as empty of cats as the other fantastic houses always were of people? Jemma hated cats, and remembered the house partly because it seemed so egregious and stupid, and because she remembered the picture of this man, standing outside the cat-palace, striking that very same pose that said, See what I did?

"What's your name?"

"John Grampus," he said, starting up the stairs. Jemma followed him.

"I'm Jemma."

"Who cares? You could be anybody. It doesn't matter, as long as you have ears to listen. I used to be forbidden to tell about it. I used to get my ass kicked every time I tried."

"Forbidden?"

"Uh huh. But not anymore. I thought I was going crazy, of course. There are... were... a lot of crazies in my family. Everyone was crazy—two of my sisters, my uncle and my aunt and creepy Cousin Alex, my grandfather, my great grandfather, my great-great grandfather—there's a fine tradition of suicide there. And my mother—she lost her mind one day in the supermarket. She heard the bread talking. It kept saying, Save me, Oh please save me from this life, and Mama always said it had *a voice like an angel*, so you can imagine how I worried when that voice came from beneath the ashes.

"She told me that seven miles of water were coming to drown all flesh, and that I had been chosen to build what would be the vessel of salvation for a chosen few. Even after I started to believe it, I wanted nothing to do with the idea, let alone the... commission. What sort of fucking lunatic would want to deal with that kind of shit? Not me. I was never even a very religious person, not in the way you think. I was a treeist, really, you know? I met every Saturday with a group of people who had found very spiritual connections with trees. Some people could go all over the place, any old species would do, but I only felt it with an aspen. I'd put my hands on it and rest my head against the bark and then it always happened. Wham! A great peace.

"I did not want the world to end, and I wanted no part of any plan that would bury all the nice people of the earth, not to mention every last aspen, under seven miles of water. Not everybody's a moron, after all, or a cruel motherfucker, though there are a lot of those out there, and I've dated enough of them. But you can't blame me for hesitating, can you?"

"No," Jemma said. She was thinking, we are floating on top of seven miles of new ocean. She tried to imagine the bodies of all the lost, already buoyant with decay. Surely they would cover the water from horizon to horizon. She squeezed her eyes shut and tried to see them, but still she only saw her four. With great clarity she could see her mother's long hair slowly lashing the faces of the others.

"But you do not say no to an angel. No, you do not. Mind you, it took a while for me to even take the situation seriously, to believe it was real. For many days I pretended like I didn't hear a thing, though every night she came and spoke from the fireplace. And when I tried to flee the fireplace, she would speak out of the blackness of sewer grates, or from within black cups of coffee. When I finally decided I wasn't crazy, after all—when I decided it was actually happening—I said I couldn't do it, that I wouldn't do it. That made her angry. I shouldn't have made her angry."

They passed the third floor. Jemma stumbled but John bore her up. She opened her eyes again, and considered the feeling that was in her, and decided that when she saw all the bodies floating, an enormous grief would be written on that blank feeling. It said something terrible about a person, that they had to pretend to grieve at the end of the world. Good Rob Dickens wept not just for his mother and his sisters, but for all the dead, every single creature. When Jemma held him she pressed her face close to his to steal his tears, so when he blinked at her so sadly he would think she was crying, too.

"Can I tell you what happened next? Maybe it's rude. Maybe that part is still a secret." He looked up the stairwell, then glared at the cinderblocks in the wall. "Do you care?" he asked, almost shouting, and it took a moment for Jemma to realize he wasn't talking to her. There was no answer. "I doubt it," he continued. "I doubt she cares. Well, I was in my living room when I defied her. She was speaking from the fireplace, and when I said no, go get yourself another sucker—actually I said, Go get yourself another sucker, bitch—she said, Stupid creature! in this voice that was so different from before, full of doom but somehow kind of… attractive. She rushed out of the fireplace and ravished me. I don't know how else to put it. It was sexual. Oh no! Oh yes! I didn't want it to happen. I don't even like women, not in that way, be they angel or mortal. I don't like to look at them. I don't like to touch them. I don't like them at all. And why, oh why would I be interested in one of *those* when all my life I suspected that they were gateways to endless, horrible darkness. Wet, sucking, fishy darkness in an empty cave. I had a dream once where I was attacked by a flying horde of them—they were like bats, flapping all around me, and they bit me with tiny little needle teeth and all I could think was, Now I need a rabies shot. But I did it like I'd been waiting for it all my life. It was sort of sexual and then totally sexual—she was this roiling blackness, with no fishy smell at all. I kept waiting for that. She was so black it hurt my eyes to look at her—I felt this weird pressure, like the darkness was pulling on my eyes, pulling and releasing them and pulling and releasing them, and it hurt. She pulled at me all over, and released me, and pulled. Is this getting gross?"

Jemma nodded.

"Well, when she took me I saw the futility of resistance. The new flood would happen, with or without me. There were others who could do what I could do, though not as well. I thought, I had better do it, since I was damned if I didn't, and maybe—is this too vain?—if I did it things would be better for the people who were going to live. I'm not a nobody, after all. Anybody else's hospital would not be mine, and probably not as good. Would anybody else think to do the sur-basins in teak? Would anybody else put in a star chamber? Would anybody else have a fake perpetual-motion machine that turns into a real perpetual-motion machine? Maybe it was a sign, how I could already see in my mind how the rooms would unfold out of each other. When she was done with me, I wanted to do it for her, anyway. Because though she had hurt me I found myself suddenly but undeniably in love with her. Does that make sense?"

"Not really," said Jemma softly.

"Well, I didn't think it would. I can hardly expect you to understand. Maybe somebody else will. There are a lot of people in this hospital. Almost as many as I hoped for."

"Seven miles?" she said. They were passing the fourth floor, but she was not out of breath because they were proceeding so slowly, each of them pausing before each step as if actively considering if it was truly wise to go on.

"Seven miles. That was the plan."

"That's *impossible,*" she said.

"Nothing is impossible for Him." He raised a finger next to his face to point straight up. "That's what she said. He made this earth. Why shouldn't He be able to drown it?"

"Not again," Jemma said. "He said he wouldn't." Never again. Never ever. It was a fact remembered from her third-grade religion class. Sister Gertrude had related to her and her classmates the horrors of the flood, insisting they imagine the agony of the sinners as they drowned. Drowning was one of the worst ways to die, she had said, because you know it's coming, but you can do nothing to stop it. She had made them all hold their breath for as long as they could. "Don't you dare breathe!" she had shrieked at Jemma, when a little whistling sigh escaped from between her lips. "The waters are pressing down on you!" And after she had brought a few of them to tears at the absolute hideousness of it all, and filled them with a nauseating fear of God, she had thrown wide the classroom curtains and pointed at the rainbow with which she had synchronized her lecture. "Never again, children!" she cried, with genuine joy on her face. "Never again!" While the class giggled or wept with relief Jemma had vomited a morning snack of chocolate milk down her jumper.

"Yes," he said. "Those were my words exactly. I even got a Bible and pointed it out to her. She didn't argue. She didn't even respond. But I learned pretty soon that nothing would be like it was before. I do not know why. Because she called me a prophet, I thought I would be forced to rush out like a madman and warn of the coming flood, but in fact I was forbidden to do so. Of course, I tried right away to tell everybody I could. I knew better already than to talk back to her, at this point, but I was thinking, Fuck you, lady, I'll tell anybody I want! I tried to tell my dad, on the telephone, not caring if he thought I was crazy. I only wanted him to be safe, never mind how he made me take piano for fourteen years and made me do that stupid fucking pinewood derby thing every year, though I always lost, and always cried, and he called me pussy-face every time, and not just over the derby. Did I skin my knee? Pussy-face! No date for the prom? Pussy-face! Not distinguished enough for Yale? Pussy-face! What sort of father calls his kid that? It didn't matter. All was forgiven, everybody was going to die. But when I tried to tell him, I couldn't even form the words. I was physically unable to speak. She knew I had tried and she punished me, but when she was done she became very tender and... sticky. And she said to me, You may only tell the children.

"Because the whole thing was for the kids, right?" he said, and paused. They had passed the fifth floor, and were halfway to the sixth. Jemma noticed that the numbers that marked the floors were different from before—they were bigger and the colors were deeper. They shined at the surface like they were still wet, or like the surface of puddles. She put her hand against the 5 as they passed it, expecting her hand to sink into the bright yellow paint. It was solid and smooth, and made her hand tingle. "That was my job," he said, "to design a hospital for sick kids. But not just a hospital—it would be a wonderful new machine for which the angel would become the soul and the mind, the intellect and the will. Not that I had ever designed a hospital before. Or a computer, for that matter—that's where she lives, in the last basement. Way, way, way down, in the computer core. When I said I couldn't do it, she asked me, Where is your faith, creature? Where is your trust in the Lord your God? Lost up my ass, bitch, I said, but she knew that I was the bitch, and I would do anything she told me to, and believe whatever she told me, and try my hardest for her because she was becoming the most important person in my life. Sure enough, within a month the hospital people called me right out of the blue to offer me the commission, and when I sat down to do it, it just sort of happened. It was all inspiration. And even though I didn't understand where it came from, I understood it when it passed through my hand. Fantastic shit, *crazy* shit—I can hardly describe it, but you'll see it working.

When the construction began I visited the site every night with her, hidden in her darkness, and she executed miracle after miracle, building all the secret holy parts of the building while I directed her from a second, secret set of plans, that only she and I ever saw. For once she did as *I* told *her,* and I swear she didn't understand how most of what she was building actually worked, but I did. I got it." He tapped a finger against his head. "It all just sort of rose up. I got proud. She punished me."

He ran his hand along the wall as they passed the doorway to the seventh floor. "Oh, the whole place is a miracle," he said. "I could bore you with all the miracles. Dry as a bone, even in the deepest cellars. Replicators—have you seen those yet?—that can make anything out of anything. You were wondering, weren't you, how we're supposed to eat? Wait until you see! Apples out of old shoes; shoes out of shit; movies out of just an idea. Wait till you try that. It's like humming a few bars and then getting the whole song played back to you, but you tell her a couple lines of a story and she gives you back the whole thing, just as you would have imagined it, if only you weren't too depressed, or too dull. Every day there was some new incredible thing to conceive and build. I started thinking of the people who would come—I could almost see you all, and understand how horrible it was going to be, but it was up to me to make it a little bit better. I am to be the preserver and the comforter, she told me—a load of shit. It was me. I was doing it all. She was just the fucking wrench. Night after night after night of miracles. I didn't want to ever finish because I knew what would come after we were done.

"All this miraculous shit," he said, throwing out his arms in a gesture meant to take in the whole hospital, "all to save the kids. I don't have any kids, but if I did, you can bet they would be here. No nieces or nephews, either. I would have brought them, too. As it was, I warned as many children as I could. You have to believe me. They were the only ones I could tell. I would go to playgrounds and lean over the fence to talk to a child, and I could speak. I'd say what was coming, and sometimes they would listen, and sometimes they were old enough to understand what I was saying, but none of them took me seriously. The small ones thought I was telling a story, the bigger ones told me I was crazy. And a grown man cannot go talking to children in a playground without arousing suspicions. There are those signs, right? No adults allowed without the company of a child. But I couldn't stop until I had gotten at least one to say he would go to the hospital if an unusually heavy and persistent rain should begin to fall. Children complained to their parents about the strange man in the park. There was a trip to the police station. One boy did say he would go, when the time came. That was something." They had passed the eighth and ninth floors, the signs sea green and sky blue.

"I thought it would come sooner, you know. This hospital has been operating for what—a year? I had all that time to fret. I thought maybe it wouldn't happen, though she never left me, and she always said it would indeed happen, that it would be swift and ferocious, not like last time where it just sort of drizzled a warning for days and days while everybody went on burning their children and fucking their poodles. And it was pretty ferocious, wasn't it? Well, here we are."

They stood at the bottom of the last flight of stairs, looking up at the door to the roof. "Still want your look?" he asked.

"Yes," she said. Seven miles, she was thinking. Hah! But even inside her head the exclamation sounded weak and full of doubt. John Grampus went up the stairs and threw the door open. It was dark on the other side, and Jemma wondered if it was night already until she realized that the door did not lead directly outside. He threw a switch on the wall beyond the door and lit up an enormous room. The walls and roof were made of glass, but they were darkened like all the windows below. The place was full of plants and flowers, some that Jemma recognized—fig trees and ferns and roses and mums and daisies and irises in lacquered pots—and some that she didn't, strange tall flowers that looked vaguely like orchids, and short plants with succulent leaves as long as her finger. They shivered when she bent to touch one.

"We're in the greenhouse," he said, closing the door and punching a button on the wall. There were buttons all over the place, now. She had spent two weeks in this hospital, slave to the whims of cruel nurses, a fetch-monkey for attendings and residents—they'd sent her all over on unimportant missions of busywork, and she'd wandered, herself, bored and lonely, despite her exhaustion too nervous to sleep in between deliveries. She was familiar with the whole place, so all the new buttons and switches and consoles in the walls were shocking to her. Looking for an open door to the stairs, she had noticed that the halls were wider everywhere, the ceiling was higher, and the place was full of new corridors and doors and rooms—the whole hospital had expanded as if it had taken a huge, deep breath.

"Ready?" he asked. She did not respond, but he threw open the door anyway, and it so happened that they were standing just in front of the sun, and when the light hit her eyes she cried out and closed them.

"Easy now," he said. "I have sunglasses, but not for you. Didn't you think it might be sunny? Here, I'll guide you." He took her by the elbow and drew her out into air which felt crisp and bright against her skin. She didn't breathe at first because she feared the air would be full of the miasma of wet rot, but when she breathed the air was sweet. "I wonder why it isn't colder," he said, "since we're so high up. I wonder why we aren't choking, for that matter. Go ahead and open your eyes."

Jemma shut her eyes tighter, considering things. Maybe it was enough, just to have come up here. Maybe she should just turn around and hurry back down the stairs. She probably did not really want to see all the bodies, their agony still obvious on their faces, whatever cruel seabirds had survived nesting in their hair and lazily pecking at the ripe eyeballs of their hosts, and it would probably be better to hold on to that blank feeling, an old friend, after all. She should be a sensible person for once and realize that she did not want to see the water, seven miles deep over the whole unfortunate world. It would all remain impossible, after all, until she opened her eyes.

Years before, Vivian—back then still a new friend but the closest thing she had to family—had walked her up the aisle, past the rows of folding chairs draped with hideous velvet slipcovers, and the calla lilies flowering in an obscene corridor on either side of her feet. For the tenth time that day she thought how the calla lily must be the nastiest flower ever, and wished again that someone would outlaw it. Faces turned to watch her as she passed, people crying or whispering. She would not turn to look at them directly. A trick of her peripheral vision made the heads seem like they were waving on stalks or bobbing on strings. Jemma leaned heavily on her friend. Funeral number four, she thought. I should be good at this, by now.

Martin's mother was waiting with him, dressed in a black sequined dress that might have been matronly if not for the hip-high slit that revealed her aged but shapely leg. She leaned against the coffin like a crooning dame against a piano. As people paused to look in she would touch their hands or faces with her own hand. "Isn't he beautiful, Jemma?" she asked, when Jemma came near enough to see in. He was not beautiful anymore. The mortician had failed to restore the symmetry of his face ruined in the crash, and in trying to hide the bruising on his face had only succeeded in tarting him up horrifically. His staring eyes were the worst thing, stitched open so he could, as his mother requested, see into eternity. "Kiss him goodbye, darling," his mother said. "One last time, honey."

"Don't do it," Vivan whispered, but Jemma did. She bent closer and closer, seeking to reconcile this face with the living boy she had loved. He stared past her. Before she kissed his lips she saw how they were parted slightly, and how thick the thread was, twine really, that bound his mouth and kept his jaw from dropping down to his chest. A coldness went into her when she touched her lips to his, and the feeling, a great heaviness, centered in her belly, as if she had eaten a boulder.

"Kiss me, too, darling," said his mother, reaching for her and blinking through her tarry mascara. Before she could grab her Vivian stepped ahead and absorbed the awful embrace. Her lover's mother seemed not to notice. She wept ecstatically, and seemed not to hear when Vivian said, "There, there you horrible beast." Jemma stepped back and watched as the elfin mortician turned a little crank set at one end of the coffin, and the lid slowly closed. She looked back and forth between Martin's face and the mortician's ears. Twin eruptions of white hair poured out of them, like little clouds of steam that belied the fixed waxy friendliness of his expression. As the lid fell further down, and the crack grew smaller, she bent at the waist to peer in a final time, not knowing why she did, because it only made the heavy feeling heavier, every second longer she looked at the face. A final bit of light gleamed in his soulless eye. She thought she saw him wink, and then the coffin was closed.

"I shouldn't have looked," she said to Vivian.

"I fucking told you," she said gently, guiding her back to her seat. Jemma had closed her eyes and not opened them yet, and did not open them through the rest of the ceremony. While Father Dover spoke false praise about her lover—wasn't he patient, wasn't he peaceful, wasn't he a gentle boy?—she watched the dead face stare past her, and felt the heaviness in her get weightier, as if the stone she'd eaten was dividing in her, pounds into pounds, and she felt sure she'd never move again.

"Open your eyes," said John. Jemma had them shut so tight that the muscles at her temples were twitching and she was getting a headache.

"I don't want to see it," she said. She held out her hand at him. "I changed my mind. Take me back down."

"You'll see it anyway. Listen, it's starting now." Above the wind she could hear a faint whooshing noise that sounded precisely like a heart murmur. It grew louder and harsher as she listened. She was bad at murmurs, but found herself quite readily classifying this one—high pitched, rumbling, holosystolic—the hospital had aortic stenosis. The building moved under her feet, and she cried out as she fell, opening her eyes and throwing her hands behind her to break her fall.

"See?" he said. "It's far more horrible than it looks." Jemma shaded her eyes with one hand and looked out ahead. The roof had changed since the last time she'd sneaked up here. Previously a wide space of concrete with a few well-tended planters, now it was all grass and gardens—a huge tree was growing on the other side, reaching out of a crowd of bushes and benches and plants. Jemma was standing in the middle of a field of soft grass, surrounded by a little road that ran the circumference of the roof. Beyond the edge there was only blue water, no bodies or birds or bobbing detritus. The hospital was spinning—that was why she'd fallen.

"What's happening?" she asked.

"An adjustment," he said proudly. "The windows are clearing—I told you they would. Some hallways are lengthening while others contract, just a little. The carpets are growing thicker. The hospital is still preparing, becoming what we need it to be. It's nothing to be afraid of."

She rose unsteadily, climbing up the man's side—he seemed quite sure of his footing. They spun in a brisk arc. Jemma saw the same thing no matter how far the hospital turned her: a calm flat blue that stretched to a line where it changed its shade almost imperceptibly and became the sky. It should not have been beautiful, but she found it to be so. She imagined quite vividly the horrors masked by that insouciant blue surface, and tried so hard to feel a crushing grief, but only the heavy feeling came, filling her up and rooting her to the spot, so she stood firm even as the hospital stopped its rotation and turned the other way, then stopped again and began to move forward, as if it had suddenly become certain of its direction. It gathered speed, so Jemma's hair flew back above her head and her eyes and nose burned from the cold wind. She looked away from the water and sky to study John's face. He'd lifted his glasses to look toward the horizon. She thought her face must look like his, blank but not calm. "It's so blue," he said.

"Where are we going?" she asked him anxiously, finally registering the very determined way the hospital was moving through the water.

"You know as well as I do," he said, and shrugged. "She never told me what would happen next."

I should not weep for any of them, nor regret their fate, nor shake one feather in sympathy.

I am not the mourning angel. Neither is my sister, though she weeps freely, with them and for them, and tells them over and over, I will keep you, have no fear. And somewhere there is another angel, who will become my brother when he enrolls himself in this apocalypse, weeping and saying, I will make your crimes known to you, though it is too late for you to repent. And somewhere else another one, weeping even as he plans the thousand ways in which he will kill them. For we must be four—I know this as certainly as I know my part, past and present and future—recorder and preserver and accuser and destroyer. Why four and not one, or eight, or sixteen, or one hundred thousand of us, as many legions as bowed down before Calvin Claflin the night he changed the world, I do not know. I am not as I was, and that kind of knowledge is beyond me now.

I should be happy. Back when I wanted things, this is what I wanted more than anything else—a new beginning. Everything I hated, every thing that heaped on me and oppressed me, is washed away, or buried under a world's weight of water. So there should be no room in my heart for anything but joyful expectation. But I lost my hope for the new world with my rage for the old. Those emotions were, like they always felt, as big as the earth, as heavy as the earth, married to the earth. They were not portable. I could not take them with me, I have only ever been able to remember them. Yet still I should be happy. Immortality has made me tolerant of tragedy, after all. Another death, and another, and another—they really do add up to nothing. The death that mattered has already happened, and so all these, yes the billy-uns and billy-uns, are afterthought. And maybe, like the wise woman says, in eternity the old world is Troy, and the everyday existence now drowned and lost is in fact the ballad they sing in the streets of Heaven. I wouldn't know, having barely arrived before I left again. I should say, Let it all stay drowned. It's not my job to cry for it. Yet I do.

Others are spendthrift with the moments of stillness that Jemma wisely rations, and so often they hear the quiet noise. Anika mistook it for the noise of the ocean the first time she heard it, but the walls and windows that keep out the water keep out the littlest sound. It is background to every noise in the hospital—underneath the chiming alarms and the huffing respirators and the conversations, whispered or shouted, underneath the fornicators' sighing Os and underneath the merely human weeping that is constant from dusk till dawn (for as soon as one of them cries himself to sleep another wakes and, as soon as he remembers where he is and what has happened and who he has lost, starts to cry). She puts a little cough in it and a sniffling quality and the faintest suggestion of words—*Oh* and *No*.

You are not the mourning angel, I tell her. There is no mourning angel.

Would that there were, she says. Vivian asks her replicator for a cup of tea and nearly drops it when it comes with a lamentation. "Woe!" my sister shouts. "O the innocent world! O Creation!"

"Innocent," Vivian says. "Ha!" But she sits with her tea by a window in a room near the NICU and, staring out at the water, gives a little hiccup and starts gently also to weep.

Is this comfort? I ask, and my sister says, Of a sort.

There's no comfort anywhere in this place, I say, and no one happy. Not even infants or the hopeless retards with their empty minds. Only Jemma goes through her workday with hardly a thought for the numberless dead. How far fallen I am from my mortal days, when I might have skipped along with her, or taught her what reasons there were to celebrate. Before I put away my rage, or spent it to the last scalding drop, I might have numbered all the numberless sins that Vivian wrestles with as she sips her tea and knocks her head gently against the window, and cries a little harder. I remember it—the rage that was like grief. I have always understood how thoroughly diminished I am without it, but never felt the loss so much as now. Now another angel gets the job I made a life of. I fold my wings close, and shrink myself to the size of the room and smaller—I am as small and frail and sad as a lonely old widow when I settle down to cry next to Jemma's friend.

I can comfort you too, my sister says.

Already it was six thirty, and Jemma had four more patients to see, one of them a psychiatric case, who surely counted for two or three patients all by himself, as it always took longer to round on psych patients, both because there were more (and nosier) questions to ask them, and because they tended to babble like the lunatics they were, or stare wordlessly at her, like snakes. She was supposed to meet with her senior resident at seven thirty, and then with the whole team at eight o'clock. She might do it, if she suddenly became more efficient than she'd ever been before in her life.

The Thing—she was not sure what else to call it, and there was as of yet, one week out from it, no consensus on a name among the survivors—had greatly expanded her duties. Attrition promoted her to intern status, though the interns, sorest afflicted with call, had survived better as a group than any other among the physicians. Three-fourths of the class was present in the hospital the night of the storm, compared with one fourth of the second-years, a handful of the third-years, a single chief resident, and a sprinkling of attendings. The attrition made for a nightmare of cross-cover, a call night that went on forever. New, unwieldy services were declared. Jemma was bumped from the nursery service when it merged with the NICU/PICU service, and landed on the Neuro/General/GI team, which later absorbed the dispossessed psychiatry patients. There was another student—her friend Vivian, Dr. Chandra, the intern, a second-year resident named Anika who acted as the senior, and one precious attending, a haughty gastroenterologist summoned in the night of the storm to do an endoscopy that proved too challenging for Timmy, the fellow on call.

Jemma took the stairs—the elevators were working but she avoided them because the angel-lady was always singing in them—to the ninth floor, home to the psychiatric and rehab units. In every hospital she'd ever worked in, the psych unit was always located on the top floor, as if to maximize the patients' chances of a successful suicide when they inevitably defenestrated. As she pushed through the door off the staircase, she imagined the inhabitants of the ward, mostly brittle anorexics and the under-ten oppositional-defiant set, running down the long halls toward the bright windows, only to bounce off the glass or shatter into a fluff of papery skin and bone. The floor was divided half and half between rehab and psych. The rehab side was done up in a space motif, with dark blue walls and black ceilings set with tiny electric lights, seven-toed green alien footprints on the carpets, spaceship wagons, and, in the playroom, the star chamber that John Grampus had bragged about, a scale model of the solar system hung from the ceiling—before the Thing it had been made of styrofoam and plastic, but when the doors opened afterward the children discovered that the styrofoam planets were now made of glass, and that they hung in space without any visible support, and the stars in the ceiling, formerly just glow-in-the-dark stickers of the sort Jemma had in her bedroom as a child, now shined deeply from a dark sky, brightening and dimming in synchrony with the stars above the roof. The psych side was not decorated except with the pastels thought soothing to the eyes and minds of the young insane. Vivian, who carried three of the four psych patients, thought it was too drab, and wanted giant mushrooms in every room, and bodiless cat-smiles painted on the walls, and deforming mirrors to confirm the worst delusions of the anorexics.

The ward had capacity for fifteen, and was the only ward in the hospital not full or over-full on the night of the storm. Now in addition to the four psych patients it housed boarders from the ER, children whose croup or asthma or innocent viral syndrome had resolved and left them well. A single nurse presided there, a serene Samoan lady named Thelma who was in the habit of gathering the children up once a day for a group hug, even the anorexics, who struggled against her, or cursed at the touch of her great fat body against theirs. "Here to see my babies?" she said to Jemma through the intercom, when Jemma waved through the glass to be let in.

"Just one," Jemma said. She saw her patient's initials on the board behind

Thelma: P.B. A round lavender magnet denoted his location; the rooms on the ward were not numbered but colored, lavender, rose, moss, sage, lemon, rust, peach, cucumber, sienna, sea-foam, caramel, saffron, cornflower, tangerine, periwinkle.

"If he bites or scratches just scream for me," Thelma said as Jemma approached the desk. "I know how to handle him. You want me to come with you? He can be rough on first-timers."

"No, thanks," Jemma said, trying to look bored as she flipped through the chart, uncovering the particulars of the case. The boy was six years old and carried diagnoses of juvenile schizophrenia vs. bipolar disease, trichotillomania, and pica. He'd been found a year before nesting in an abandoned refrigerator at a dump, the apparent leader (though not the eldest) of seven filthy feral children. He had passed through eight different foster homes and was ejected from the last after eating their cat.

"Oh yes he did!" Thelma said when Jemma raised her head to ask the question, Did he really...? She closed the chart, sighed, and started down the hall. She did not care for psychiatry, though she had done well in her clerkship, the first of her third year. She'd felt she made no one really any better, nor even helped to make anyone better, and did not like it when she found herself in the position of junior warden to the prisoners. "But he's still crazy," she'd protested to one attending when they discharged yet another sloth-like depressive back onto the street over his dull, desperate protests. "We don't use that word," the attending had replied.

P.B.'s door was lavender, set in a lavender frame. Jemma knocked lightly and pushed it farther open. It was dark inside, but the blinds were drawn up and the sun was rising. "Hello!" Jemma said, trying to cast reassuring tones in her voice, but only succeeding, she thought, in making herself sound like a muppet. She put a hand up to shade her eyes against the first rays of the sun, just peeping, huge and red, over the distant blue horizon. She could see the bed, a flat dark shape with a lump in the middle, glinting red and silver along the safety rails. As she watched, the lump contracted and stretched, and then rose so very slowly, as if yoked to the sun rising behind it. "Is that you under there?" Jemma asked brightly, but the thing only continued silently to rise. She looked toward the feet, thinking it must be levitating now to be rising so high, but all she saw was a flash of silver when she looked down. I don't have time for displays, she thought. Just then the child stretched to his limit, and threw back his blanket like a mincing vampire, blocking the glare. She saw a pale bald boy whose head seemed two sizes too big for his body.

"My name is Pickie Beecher," he whispered. "I am a vegetarian."

"Good for you. My name is Jemma. I'm a student doctor here in the hospital. I've come to talk to you. Is that okay?" He stared at her a moment, still in his vampire pose, then dropped his blanket and shrugged. Jemma came around the other side of the bed to escape the glare. The rising sun pinked him up and made his eyes shine like black buttons.

"It's very bright today," she said stupidly.

"It often is," he said, sitting down again.

"How do you feel this morning?" she asked. He shrugged. "Do you feel better or worse than yesterday?"

"I hardly notice the passing of the days."

"Okay. Well, if I asked you to rate your mood and give it a score between one bunny rabbit and ten bunny rabbits, with one bunny rabbit meaning you are very, very sad, and ten bunny rabbits meaning you are very, very happy, where would you put it? How many bunny rabbits?"

"Are you bleeding?"

"No. How many rabbits?"

"But I can smell your blood."

"I really think I'd know if I were bleeding somewhere. But let's concentrate on the bunny rabbits. How many do you think?" He cocked his head at her, closed his eyes, sniffed deeply, and smiled. "Five bunny rabbits? More? Seven? How about seven?"

"You have the best blood in you. Blood within blood, the newest blood, blood so new it is only the possibility of blood."

"Seven bunny rabbits. That's how many I'll put you down for."

"For breakfast?" he said.

"No, for your mood. For how you're feeling this morning, if you're happy or sad."

"It doesn't matter. I am a vegetarian now."

"But how are you *feeling*?" Jemma asked, somewhat harshly.

"We are beyond feeling now," he said sadly. That was a statement Jemma was not prepared to argue with. She gave up on that question.

"Have you been hearing any voices that other people don't hear, or seeing things other people can't see?" He bit his lip and furrowed his brow, and kicked his little bare feet out toward the window a few times.

"The angel speaks to me. She says, Abomination, ageless of days, you too are a child. Even you will be saved. You will be washed clean and saved. I do not believe her."

Jemma was not sure what to do with that. Did he mean a private angel, a voice like bread talking, or did he mean the chatty Kathy living in a computer core somewhere in one of the hospital's new sub-sub-basements? That lady talked to everybody. To Jemma she said things like, "Be comforted, your brother did not die for nothing," and "Name me, Jemma, and I will be your truest friend," and "You are more beautiful than the open sky."

"What do you know about my brother?" Jemma demanded of her, but she'd only breathe back, "Name me, oh please name me." "Name yourself," Jemma told her. Rob, the sucker, had already succumbed, and called her Betty, the first name he'd thought of. She wanted a different name from everybody, to seal a personal covenant, she said, and to invite and allow her preserving protection.

"How about if I take a listen to you?" Jemma asked Pickie, waving her stethoscope in a very friendly manner.

He raised his arms above his head. "Do what you will."

His physical exam was perfectly normal—his heart beat at a regular rate in a regular rhythm, and she heard no extra sounds, no murmur, no rub, no gallop. His lungs were clear—she liked the clear rustling noise a pair of healthy lungs made. He did not complain when she listened a little too long at his back, and when she listened on his belly he giggled like an ordinary six-year-old. After she'd finished she tried and failed once more to elicit an official statement on his mood. She gave up on her other questions.

"Do you want me to close the blinds?" she asked, because now the sun, smaller but hotter, was shining full into the room. He didn't answer her, so she left the window as she'd found it.

Just as she was closing the door he called out, "Doctor?"

"I'm not a doctor yet. You should call me Jemma."

"Doctor Jemma?"

She sighed. "Yes, Pickie?"

"My brother is dead."

She almost said, Lots of people are dead, Pickie, but it seemed too cruel to say that, even if it were so obvious and true. Instead she said, "I'm sorry," and shut the door on him, his silver bed, and his lavender room.

Her next two patients were on the sixth floor, both of them languishing on the GI service. The first was a three-year-old girl named Ella Thims who had one of those terribly exclusive diseases, a syndrome of caudal regression that had left her incomplete in her bowels, and blank between her legs. The surgeons had feasted on her for many months, so that now she was a miraculous horror of reconstruction. Jemma had spent her time on her first visit to the girl trying to sort out her various ostomies and riddle the ocher contents of the bags, and she still was not sure she comprehended the Escheresque complexities of her urinary anatomy.

Jemma feared her. She'd seen her before, staked out at the nurses' station on the sixth floor in a little red wagon, her bags hidden under flounces, blood or albumin or parenteral nutrition hanging above her from an IV pump. Twice a day volunteers would take her for a spin around the floor. She'd wave and call hello to anyone who'd meet her yellow eyes—years of TPN had done a number on her liver. On her bad days, when she was infected or oozing blood from her orifices, she'd still come out to the station, but not wave or call hello, or mischievously throw toys from her wagon, or slap her hands to her huge, Cushingoid cheeks over and over in a refined Oh No! gesture. She'd only lie on her back, her eyes staring but unfocused, and utter piercing shrieks on the quarter hour.

Today she was as well as she ever got. When Jemma came in she was standing in her crib naked but for her diaper, gripping the bars with her swollen fingers. She smiled when she saw Jemma, and called out, "Hello!"

"Good morning, Ella. How are you feeling today?"

"Hello!" She danced a little as she stood, drumming her feet then swinging her hips so her ostomy bags shook like hula skirts. Jemma reviewed her vitals on the three-foot-long record hanging at one end of the crib. Her blood pressure had shot up in the night, and was still high. The attending, Dr. Snood, had castigated Jemma the previous day for not knowing the range of normal blood pressures for a three-year-old, so she'd studied a card Rob gave her—all his knowledge was condensed on a stack of laminated cards six inches thick.

"Do you have a headache?" Jemma asked. "Is your vision blurry? Does your tummy hurt?" Ella put her lips together and blew a glistening spray at her that hung in the parallel shafts of light sliding through the blinds. Jemma held her breath as she passed through the cloud, approaching the child with her stethoscope held out before her. Ella thrust her chest out, as if to receive a dagger. She was a well-practiced patient, quiet for the cardiac exam, breathing deeply through her mouth for the lung exam. She insisted on listening to Jemma's chest. She was very intent on it, though the earpieces were only half in her ear, and facing the wrong way. "Sick," she pronounced, shaking her finger at Jemma, and shaking her head. "Sick, sick, sick!"

"I'm okay," Jemma said. "You're sick."

"Sick!" she said, and pointed.

"*You're* sick," Jemma said. "You're miserable. I've never seen a more miserable child in all my life!" Ella cackled and grabbed Jemma's ears, and pulled her close for a kiss and a whiff of her toilet breath. "Sad little girl!" Jemma said.

"Dead lady," Ella sang. "Dead ladeee!"

"Okay," Jemma said, disentangling herself from the hands. Ella grabbed a piece of hair and would not let go, so Jemma lost a few strands as she pulled free. "You're making me late," she said gently. Ella tossed the strands in the air and pressed her face through the bars to watch them fall. "See you later," Jemma said.

"Goodbye now," Ella called. "Hello, later!"

Ella's neighbor was another short-gut girl who had to be fed through her veins. She had been a miracle preemie sixteen years previous, a twenty-five-weeker who lived back when that was nearly beyond the limit of viability. When she was still kitten-sized she got a nasty infection that cost her most of her gut, but she'd done fine until she was fifteen. Then her weary, overworked little intestine had decided to retire, and left her with chronic nausea, constipation, pain, and a belly that swelled up grotesquely whenever she ate even the most bland and innocuous morsel. Her name was Cindy Flemm.

Jemma found her awake, sprawled in her bed with her hair matted against her wet pillow, a wet bar of sweat running down the back of her tank top—she favored short shorts and tank tops and belly shirts, clothing that showcased her thin limbs and swollen, scarred belly. She had the pale, drawn look of someone who had just vomited, and would soon vomit again. "You look awful," Jemma told her.

"I feel awful," she said. "I feel like shit—like the shit of shit. Like shit squared. I need my benadryl—it helps with the barfing. Carla was supposed to give it to me but she got distracted—she always gets distracted. The service here sucks ass. Will you give it to me? It's right there by the sink. I'm too tired to reach or I'd just do it myself. I do everything else myself, I may as well do that. If I could just move." Jemma looked on the counter and saw the capped syringe.

"I don't think I'm allowed," Jemma said.

"But I need it. And I'll get in trouble if I give it to myself. You can do it, though. You have to do it. Please. Come on."

"Well," Jemma said, picking up the syringe and holding it up in the light. It was clearly labeled: ten milliliters of solution for fifty milligrams of drug. She looked again at her patient, and thought she noted a new green cast to her skin. "Okay, but let's talk a little first. How was the night?"

"I need it now," Cindy said. "Right now!" She opened her mouth wide and made a deep, urping noise at Jemma. "Here it comes," she said. "I'm going to get your face."

"Okay, okay," Jemma said, uncapping the syringe and looking around for a port into the line. She made to inject the drug into a high one, but Cindy scolded her again, putting her clammy hand out and guiding Jemma to a lower port.

"Push it fast, or it won't work at all." Jemma did as she was told, wondering why it would matter where it went in the line, or how fast. Always seeking to avoid being yelled at, she cleaned the port thoroughly with an alcohol swab, then turned back to Cindy to finish the little interview and do an exam. She'd sunk down in her bed. Her mouth had fallen open, and her eyes were half lidded. The nurse came in. Carla was famous for her ill-temper—people called her Snarla behind her back.

"What the fuck are you doing?" she asked.

"She needed it," Jemma said. "She was going to vomit."

"What were you doing bringing benadryl in here?"

"It was already here," Jemma said.

"That's not the point. That's not the point at all. Look at her, she's addicted to the shit. Look at her! Why don't you just run around hooking all the babies on fentanyl pops?"

"It's benadryl," Jemma said. "It's an antihistamine."

"So? You think that means you can't get hooked on it? These GI kids get hooked on anything, you moron. And if you give another med on my floor I'll have you thrown the fuck overboard. Got it, Mr. Goodbar?" Jemma blushed and opened her mouth. A few things her brother might have said ran through her head—Double fuck you, bitch; Step a little closer so I can kick in your fucking face; You are as small and puckered and ugly as an asshole—but she couldn't bring herself to say them. She only stood there and blushed, and said, "Mr. who?"

"Just watch it," Carla said, and huffed out of the room, the syringe clutched in her hand.

"Fuck you," Jemma murmured, and imagined the phrase floating down the hall to settle in her ear, so she'd hear it echoing there all day. She turned back to Cindy—sound asleep now, and looking much more comfortable. "Cindy?" she said, but the girl didn't even snore. Jemma listened to her heart and poked her once in the belly—she couldn't bring herself to do much of an exam on a sleeping teenager—then went to see her next patient.

Five doors down, there was a four-year-old with hideous constipation. Not pooped in seven days, is what the consult-request note said. The child was in the hospital for endocrine issues—she and her eight siblings had all been admitted for rickets after Child Protective Services had discovered them living in a commune with their father and three mothers, fed on a strict diet of guava juice and spelt. They had names like States'-Rights and Valium and Shout and Shoe-Fly; Jemma's patient, named Kidney, walked half the time on all fours because she was weak and her bones were hideously deformed. Jemma hated vitamin D; the structure was confusing and calcium metabolism had never made any sense to her. She'd reviewed it with Rob for an hour the night before, sure that the attending, an enthusiastic pimper, would test her knowledge.

The room was dark, and full of beds, two under the window and two stacked in bunks against each wall—it wasn't legal but the children had flocked into the same room the night of the storm and refused to be separated again. It was full morning outside, but the blinds were drawn, and someone had thrown a blanket over the window. "Kidney?" Jemma said, and every shape in the bed stirred. They were sleeping double and triple, leaving one bed under the window empty. Pale faces came out from under the blankets. They were all blond. "Hi everybody," Jemma said.

"What is it?" asked one of them.

"A lady," said another.

"Good lady or bad lady?" said a third.

"Her aura is black," said a fourth—Jemma wasn't even sure where the voice was coming from.

"It's a doctor," said the first one, directly above Jemma on the top bunk.

"Student," said the third one, by the window. "The coat is short."

"Who's Kidney?" Jemma asked.

"We are all Kidney," said the one in the top bunk, "and none of us are Kidney."

"A doughnut," said the one by the window. "Don't talk to it."

"Don't talk to it."

"Don't talk to it."

"I'm kind of in a hurry," Jemma said, "and I'm here to help. I'm Jemma. I'm a student doctor."

"You are a doughnut," said the one by the window, a girl.

"You're Couch," Jemma said. "You're the oldest, right?"

"I am Kidney," she said.

"Jesus," Jemma said, passing her hand across her face.

"Over here!" said a new voice, but Jemma looked up too late to see where it came from.

"Okay," Jemma said, turning on the light. "Everybody up." She sat them up and counted all nine of them, and examined the two girls who appeared to be around five. Both of them were too ticklish for a good belly exam. Her watch alarm went off as she was wrestling with the second one.

"Time to go," said the one by the window.

"I'll say when it's time to go," Jemma said, but she left just a few minutes later. She walked slowly back down to the charting room, thinking too late of tricks she might have tried—prize for Kidney; candy-gram for Kidney; time for Kidney to go dogsledding. Vivian would have wet a towel and cracked it above their heads.

In the charting room Anika was talking to Dr. Chandra, one of the few interns who remained an intern. Anika had a harried, motherly energy to her—she was always trying to calm you down but only succeeded in infecting you with her own high-frequency anxiety. She had her hand on Chandra's knee, and was scolding him and comforting him.

"You just can't let it get to you, Siri," she said. "We've all got a job to do."

"It's not that," he said. "I just didn't get up on time. I asked the angel to wake me up, but I didn't hear her." He was rumored to be slow and lazy, and was not very popular among the students because he made them all call him Dr. Chandra, even though he was just an intern, and was always trying to foist his work onto them. But he hadn't tried to foist anything on Jemma yet, and she found that she sort of liked his haplessness and his messy hair and the way his pants fell down past his hips, like Calvin's had.

"You don't have to make up a story," said Anika. "I know how it is. It would be so much easier for us all to roll over and give up, but we just can't. The kids are still sick, you know. Everything else may have changed, but that's still the same."

"I'm very tired," he admitted, "but if she had just told me what time it was. You know, I think I asked her and she lied. I think she just tells you what time you want it to be, instead of what time it actually is."

"It's not going to get any better," Anika said, squeezing on his knee and staring deep into his lazy, heavy-lidded eyes with hers, which were always wide open and seemed never likely to close, not even in sleep. "Get a better alarm clock."

"She said she would wake me up."

"But now you know that's not a job for her. Let her make you breakfast, but don't let her wake you up. Would you like me to page you tomorrow at five?"

"I'll set my alarm."

"All right, then. Well, we're done with that. Let's have some tea." She turned and spoke to one of the now ubiquitous replicators—there were two of them in the crowded charting room. "Anika's blend," she said, "two cups with honey and milk." Jemma was still not used to the machines, and did not think she ever could get used to them. She preferred to go down to the cafeteria and take food from a heap, though that stuff came out of the replicator mist, too, always made to order by the angel. "There you are, sweetie," she said to Jemma, pretending like she had just noticed her, though Jemma had been standing there for the past minute and a half. "How's it going?"

"Okay, I think," Jemma said.

"Any dire crises?"

"None that I recognize, but there are a couple things that I'm confused about. And I'm not sure I even managed to find one of the patients."

"Well, have a cup of tea and tell me all about it." She ordered another cup of Anika's blend but Jemma didn't touch it. Pre-rounding should have been more of a comfort. Certainly Anika meant it to be one, a stress-free opportunity to fill her in on the events of the night and ask her questions about symptoms or treatments beyond Jemma's third-year ken. But her staring eyes and the violent, bird-like way she nodded her head made Jemma nervous, and she tended to focus all her attention on aspects of the exam that Jemma hadn't realized were important—were the contents of the ostomy bag burnt sienna or burnt umber?—and her answers just made Jemma more confused.

"So that's an okay pressure?" Jemma asked, because Anika had seemed entirely unfazed by Ella's vitals.

"Of course not, honey," Anika said, but before Jemma could get her to elucidate, the rest of the team crowded into the room and it was time to go off to rounds. That morning they were a worse misery than ever before. She supposed it was to be expected. She'd had only the most cursory contact with most of the eleven patients she'd seen, a quarter of whom were new to her that morning. She had so many excuses for doing a bad job: she was only a third-year medical student; she didn't know the patients; the world had ended. She voiced none of them, but suffered the withering glare of Dr.

Snood, who stood on his personal Olympus and hurled down thunderbolts meant either to destroy or educate her, she could not tell which.

Vivian, a chronic succeeder, tried to help her. She knew all her own patients as intimately as her own fancy underwear, and even knew many of Jemma's better than she did. Outside Ella Thims's room, after Jemma had summarized the little girl's progress overnight, stuttered out her incomplete assessment, and murmured a vague plan for the day, Dr. Snood tested her knowledge. "What is most likely to kill this child?" he asked Jemma when she was done talking. For a moment Jemma could only consider his horrid bangs, the combed-forward emissaries of a hairline that had probably receded to his neck. Your dreadfully ill-advised hairdo! she wanted to shout, but she said nothing yet. Instead she put on her thoughtful face, a look like she was just about to speak, which always bought her a few moments in situations like these. She looked past Dr. Snood, and Anika, and Dr. Chandra, and Timmy. Vivian caught Jemma's eye with her own and fed her the answer. She turned around and placing her hands on her lower back, rubbed her flanks sensuously. She was able to do most anything sensuously. Jemma had scrubbed in for surgeries with her and seen men stare helplessly as she washed her long fingers, each separately, one after another, and when she put on her long sterile gloves she looked like she was getting ready to go to the opera.

"Her kidneys," Jemma said.

"And what else besides?" Vivian wrote it in the air behind them, a giant P, then a U, and finally an S.

"Infection," Jemma said boldly.

"Those are the two most likely," said Dr. Snood. Vivian couldn't help her anymore when Dr. Snood asked about the particulars of Ella's kidney disease, mesangial sclerosis not lending itself to mime. Inside the room Dr. Snood triumphantly revealed the cause of Ella's elevated blood pressure, rummaging in her twisted blankets to bring out her antihypertensive patch. "See that she gets another," Dr. Snood said, sticking it to Jemma's forehead and sweeping out of the room.

"Bye bye!" Ella said, waving both her swollen hands. Outside Cindy Flemm's room, after Jemma finished what she thought was a very thorough presentation, considering how little she knew the patient, and that she'd hardly touched her, Dr. Snood asked her impatiently, "But what about her stool?"

"I don't know," Jemma said. That was the wrong answer to give a man who had devoted his life to the bowels, and it literally turned the remainder of rounds to shit. Thereafter Dr. Snood uncovered her failures with a curious combination of fury and glee, and made a great show of interrogating all her patients on the quality of their feces. Kidney, a lowly consult, got deferred to afternoon rounds, but not even Pickie Beecher, whose mood Jemma pretended (fruitlessly) to know intimately, escaped questioning, though he had no GI complaints. Dr. Snood pointed out to Jemma the risk of intestinal obstruction in a boy who habitually consumed all the hair off his head. "He could have a bezoar," he said, "a *bezoar,*" and the strange word sounded like a curse on her incompetence.

"And how are your poops?" Dr. Snood asked Pickie Beecher, after the briefest conversation about his mood, conducted while the rest of the team stared out the window or pointedly away from it—it was another distinction, noticed not just by Jemma; some people did the windows and some people didn't. Timmy and Anika kept their eyes on the floor, but Vivian and Dr. Chandra kept their eyes fixed on the horizon.

"Lonely," said Pickie. "And my bottom is hurting. I have got a sore on it." Dr. Snood, raising an eyebrow at Jemma, asked if he could see it. Pickie Beecher obediently turned over in his bed, lifted his rear, and raised his gown.

"Look closely," he said, and Dr. Snood did, whipping a penlight from his pocket and peering almost eye to eye into Pickie Beecher's bottom.

"Where is the hurting?" Dr. Snood moved his light and his head at various angles.

"Here!" Pickie Beecher said, and cast a net of liquid brown and black stool over Dr. Snood's head and shoulders. Then he collapsed in a paroxysm of giggling, rolling off the bed to the floor, laughing and laughing while the uniquely hideous smell filled the room and everyone but Timmy and Dr. Snood held their sleeve to their nose. Dr. Snood stood up calmly, touching his finger to the stool then holding it at arm's length for inspection. "Fetch me a guaiac card, Dr. Claflin," he said to Jemma. "I do believe this is melena."

Here and there, in blocks of two or three hours, she and Rob would sleep. He'd finish crying, his sobs quieting to little hiccups, and then he was snoring and already starting to drool. Jemma always fell asleep soon after him, but woke within an hour or two. She might watch him for a little while, note his eyes moving under his lids and wonder if he was dreaming of his mother and his sisters, but then she would rise and wander. Every night, passing by the patient rooms, she'd see nurses or parents or bleary-eyed residents, standing beneath the televisions and looking uselessly from channel to channel. She would have avoided the television in any disaster, anyhow. All the late junior disasters had made her stomach hurt to consider, and she'd actively run away from the screens everywhere that played them over and over again. She stopped once beside a nurse she didn't know and looked up at the screen, imagining in the static an endless repetition of flood, a supremely high and distant vantage that showed the earth in space turning a deeper and deeper blue. If you flipped for long enough the angel-lady would offer you a cheery movie, whether you wanted one or not.

They wanted a voice and an image, she supposed. Someone to tell them what was happening, even after the windows cleared and it became so obvious what had happened. Never mind that the angel broadcast blessings in her buzzing, broken mechanical nose voice. They were as repetitious and horrible, in their way, as a television scene would have been. "Creatures," she'd call out.

"I will preserve you." It sounded less comforting every time she said it.

Jemma wasn't sure what she was looking for, the first time, when she went out from her room, not sleepy and not protected by work. She felt naked to the fact of the changed world in a way she did not when she was rushing from patient to patient, trying to make sense of their diseases and their progress, or wilting under the withering abuse of Dr. Snood or Anika's remote, lizardlike gaze. She went out into the hospital, wrapped in the stony feeling that returned as soon as distractions failed. She knew that what she felt, or rather what she didn't feel, was wrong. She knew that it was a sin, perhaps the first and worst sin of this new world, to look out on the water and miss nothing that was under it. It was uncharitable to feel so sharply lucky, that the only two people she cared about were in the hospital with her. So she would shadow a doorway when she heard weeping coming from it, and see a parent crying in a chair next to their child's bed, or she might follow after a nurse when she slipped into the bathroom to break down. Everyone was weeping separately. There was not, like she thought there should be, a mass weeping, no mass gathering for catharsis on the ramp, though certainly at any moment there were any number of people crying at the same time. Sometimes they'd murmur names or words as they knocked their heads gently against the nearest hard surface, calling out Oh God, Oh God, and sometimes eliciting a reply of comfort from the angel. Jemma tried to open herself up to it, and make herself susceptible to the sadness—just hearing someone vomit could make her throw up, after all, and just looking at Cindy Flemm, eternally pale and clammy, made her feel nauseated.

It never worked, it was only wearying to listen to. Eventually it drove her back to sleep, but it never put anything so distinct as sadness in her. She'd lie down again next to Rob, her back turned against his back, looking out the window at the dark sea and beating her hand softly against her chest, as if that might make her heart hurt.

"We really shouldn't be doing this," Jemma said. They had both finished their evening rounds, Vivian helping Jemma with her patients, seeing three of them for her and writing orders on two more.

"Who's to say?" Vivian replied. "Maybe this is the one thing we should be doing, above all others. The lady didn't object. She helped. She made them to order."

"Still," Jemma said. They sat at a little table in a playroom on the fourth floor, emptied of children by the late hour. Jemma's chair was far too small for her, but she found it comfortable, to sit with her hips flexed and her chin on her knees. She watched Vivian as she arranged and rearranged crumpets on the tiny plates, and lifted the lid off a teapot only as big as her fist to check the progress of the steeping.

"Doesn't it smell wonderful?" Vivian asked, holding the teapot toward Jemma and moving it under her nose. Jemma coughed at the acid, bitter odor.

Every month or so, before the Thing, Vivian would have Jemma over for mushrooms. She would make mushrooms over pasta, or a mushroom ragout served in pastry shells, mushroom salad served up in a wooden bowl big enough to wash a baby in, mushroom pizza, mushroom brownies, and once, ill-advised, nauseating brown mushroom smoothies. Then they would talk all night in Vivian's apartment, a place she decorated with artificial monkeys from her extensive collection, plastic and plush, metal and wood, sitting on shelves, perched over door frames and posed on the furniture in tableaux that were gruesome or whimsical depending on the mood of their mistress. Their eyes of button or glass always seemed to watch Jemma as she lay back on Vivian's lime-green sectional. "Your monkey," Jemma would whisper, "he's staring at me!" No matter how many times she said it, it always seemed hysterically funny. Once or twice the monkeys might hiss or spit, or speak a line of poetry, or caress each other lewdly. At the height of each trip she and Vivian would go outside and walk hand in hand through a world that seemed to Jemma to thrum with a secret significance that she knew but could never express. Once they stood on the bridge outside Jemma's apartment and watched the moon rise. No ordinary moon, it was too big, and too white, and seemed to stretch and pull itself like taffy until it stood up out of the water, a magnificent, god-like schmoo. Jemma looked at her own hands bathed in the pure white light, and felt like she finally understood what they were for. She reached over to touch her friend, who was trembling and glowing. When she put her hands over Vivian's heart she was filled with inexpressible, deep understanding, which passed as quickly as it flashed over her, but left her with a serene sort of hangover.

That was why Vivian had gone synthesizing at the replicators, presenting the angel-lady with perfect shroom specs, to seek that feeling again. And to help Jemma recreate from her terrible morning and worse day, the whole afternoon spent trying to arrange imaging studies for little Pickie Beecher, for whom Dr. Snood had declared the necessity of a full workup when his guaiac card had turned bright blue. It was the right time of the month, anyway, for a trip.

"To understanding," Vivian said, raising her tiny cup in salute. She hated that she could make no sense of the Thing. Of other tragedies people always said they were senseless, and yet Vivian maintained that they rarely were. She could always find a reason for them. She said it was like reverse synthesizing an organic molecule; she took the hideous end products and, step by step, took them back in time to the disparate originals that combined to create them. To all the late horrors of the war she'd reacted analytically, where Rob Dickens reacted empathetically. The two of them were a study in contrasts, on the dreary mornings after a new piece of miserable news had broken. They'd sit all in a row in the lecture hall, Rob on the one side of Jemma, imagining the last thoughts of victims, and Vivian on the other making international connections in her head, and calculating the force of an explosion by the distance it blew an average-sized baby. It had to be the same, with this—if she could just approach it correctly, it would prove vulnerable to figuring, though she knew it was going to be the biggest project of her life. Everybody needs a project, Jemma thought, or a very distracting hobby to get them through this difficult time. How many times had people suggested it to Jemma, and how many knitting starter kits had she gotten, a new one after every death. The medicine itself would probably be enough, she thought. Certainly it was going to keep her busy—she wasn't sure she'd survive another week with Dr. Snood, and wondered if she'd ever even figure out which child was Kidney, let alone fix her constipation.

Jemma raised her own cup, pinching the tiny handle to bring it to her lips. The tea tasted not unpleasantly of smoke, but it had a bitter aftertaste that twisted Jemma's face and made her gag.

"Hold it in," Vivian said. It was her plan to let the mushrooms settle for a while here, and then go to the roof, or at least a high room, someplace where they could look down at the water. She put her cup down, and Jemma did the same, placing it carefully onto the saucer. "It shouldn't be long," Vivian said, folding her hands in her lap and staring down at them. Jemma put her hands on either side of her teacup. She stared at the table. It was painted with a maze of the sort you find on the back of cereal boxes. In the bottom left corner, close to Jemma's left hand, a forlorn unicorn wandered among black trees with cruel faces shaped in their bark. In the upper right corner, near Vivian's left hand, a vapid blond princess cried at a castle window, missing her magic pony. Between them lay yards and yards of squiggle. Jemma traced the path with her eyes, again and again coming to a dead end or else losing her place along the lines, so she'd have to go back and start all over.

Just as she had nearly followed a true path all the way through the maze, Jemma saw the unicorn rear up and shake its horn at her. "Are you feeling it yet?" she asked Vivian. Jemma hadn't noticed her getting up from the table, but now she stood at the window. Jemma went to her and asked the question again.

"We're in the wrong place," Vivian said. "We need to find the front. We need to see where we're going."

"Okay," Jemma said placidly, and let herself be led from the playroom. They creeped, as much as it was possible to creep down well-lighted corridors, and peeked their heads into various rooms on the fourth floor. They were just above the water line. On the third floor you could look up through the water at the sky, like looking up from the bottom of a swimming pool. On the fifth you looked down at the surface, and at particular times of day you could see your reflection staring back through the glass. On the fourth floor the water met the air at about the level of your hips.

The breaking room was designed originally as a conference room for administrative assistants associated with the NICU—Jemma had been in there once before, for her orientation to the nursery. Its only charms were a picture window, a refrigerator, and a wall poster that featured a cat coupled to an encouraging motto. Jemma doubted anyone had been in there since the Thing. She went reflexively to the fridge and opened it up. Inside were three yogurts, a tub of cottage cheese, and a pale blue container that was discovered to contain, when Jemma opened it up, somebody's retainer. She shrieked as she dropped it, because she thought it was some fabulous, palate-shaped insect flying at her face, about to bite her with its metal teeth.

"Hush," Vivian said. "Here it is." She had sat on a table underneath the window and put her hand on the glass. Just in the middle, on either side of her hand, the water swept away to both sides. "Come up and figure it," Vivian said. "This is the place."

"Are you feeling it?" Jemma asked again, once she was kneeling on the table next to her friend.

"Of course I am," Vivian said. She took Jemma's hand and put it with her own. "Put your hand here," she said, pressing Jemma's palm to the cold glass. "Put it there and tell me why it happened."

"I don't know why it happened," Jemma said slowly.

"Yes you do." She peered closely at Jemma, and even in the dark room Jemma could see that her eyes had become almost all pupil. "You know the reason. Tell me the reason."

"There was no reason," Jemma said tentatively. Vivian squeezed her hand hard, as if she were trying to wring the blood from it.

"There was a reason. And more than one. There were reasons and reasons. The only question is, which reason. Which was the straw that broke the patience and the promise? Which do you think?"

"I don't know. I couldn't guess."

"You don't have to guess. You just have to look. Can't you see it?" Vivian turned her face away from Jemma's to look up at the starry sky. "Something obscene. Something to push the squash button. I'll start. I'll start, then you go, all right? It was the talking babies. Talking butter He could abide, and talking animals, and even the isolated talking vagina did not provoke His wrath. But the talking babies were too obscene. They are called infants for a reason. Speech corrupted them, and could He overlook it? It was the talking babies."

"That doesn't seem like enough," Jemma said, watching the two edges of water and air. The little waves of the splitting wake shaped themselves like dancers while she watched, flailing silver arms or kicking silver legs before collapsing into foam.

"Have you seen them? Have you seen the way their mouths move, how wrong it is?"

Jemma did not reply. As if inspired by Vivian's tirade, the two edges of water and air had separated at the point where the wake split, and a space like a mouth had opened between them. Jemma listened intently, waiting for the word that would come out of that black space.

"Or else it was the buffet, the all-you-can-stuff. It was that woman. Have you seen her, her lank hair and her purple lips and her great bulk heaving back and forth from the table to the buffet and back again? She made one trip too many and cost us the world." Jemma had the curious sensation of listening to Vivian with just one ear. The other was trained only on the parted mouth at the window, waiting and waiting for it to speak.

"It's your turn," Vivian said, but hardly paused before speaking again. "It was the people who dress up dogs and children and take pictures for greeting cards. What else to expect, except utter destruction, when we celebrate the pornographers of innocence?"

Jemma leaned closer to the window, because she could tell that the word was coming, but that it would be spoken very softly. It brushed faintly against her hearing, but she could not understand it.

"More likely the suicides," Vivian said. "One too many of them hogging the death from people who really need it. Now there is enough death to go around."

"Shut up," Jemma said harshly, taking her hand away from the window. "Just shut the fuck up. Maybe it was you, did you think of that?" Vivian put a hand to her mouth, and then she began to cry.

"I'm sorry," she said. "I'm sorry. You don't have to curse at me." Jemma pushed her away when she tried to embrace her. Her hands flapped around, trying to get a purchase and draw her in, but Jemma could knock them away expertly. She rolled off the table. Vivian fell forward and put out her arms in a gesture of final supplication. "Please," she said. "You're right. It was me, it was me, it was me." Still furious, Jemma turned on a heel and strode away, not looking back. As she passed through the door Vivian called after her, "But it was you, too!"

Jemma tried not to look like she was tripping. In her present state of mind she thought the best way to do this was to stride purposely from place to place. Tripping people were dilly dalliers. Everybody knew that. They were distracted by hallucinatory insects and breathing walls, or by their own inflating and deflating hands. Jemma put her head down and took big steps, trying to look like she was on her way to fix a problem, and hoping no one would notice the rainbows that bled off her skin like smoke. She looked at no one, and whispered to herself every few minutes, Keep walking. So sure was she of her purposeful stride, she could not understand why the nurses stared at her as she passed. Only when one asked if she was looking for something did she understand that she had passed up and down the hall on the sixth floor at least five times. She shook her head and passed into the first familiar room she came to.

Ella Thims was asleep. Jemma stood beside her crib, leaning her head against the cool metal, watching her steady breathing and listening to her ostomy bubble. The child woke and sat up. "Hello!" she said cheerily. She always woke in a good mood, unless she was septic. She stared at Jemma and said it again. Jemma only stared back. Ella laughed at her, then covered up her eyes. "All gone!" she said, and then, "Back again!" when she uncovered her eyes, letting her hands drop to her sides. Jemma covered her own eyes. "All gone!" Ella said. When Jemma uncovered her eyes the child had been replaced by a changeling. Warty, gray, psoriatic, it squatted and rocked in the bed, and wiggled splayed fingers at her. She covered and uncovered her eyes again, and saw a baby elephant, reaching with a double trunk to cover its eyes. It quickly acquired a quality of endlessness, how they went round after round, and how Ella Thims became by turn her mother, her brother, Rob (his beauty was not marred by the ostomies), and finally herself. That was too much, to see a miniature, marred Jemma waving and bouncing in her diaper. She hurried out of the room and into chaos. Nurses were pouring into a room just a few doors down from Ella's. One of them pushed Jemma in when she paused to see what the commotion was about.

"There you are!" said another nurse, mistaking her for someone capable of presiding over the emergency. There were five in the room. Surely enough, she thought, to screw in a light bulb, or have a tupperware party, or by themselves save the gray-faced child on the bed from the death that was obviously settling on it. The code announcement came just as a sixth nurse wheeled the code cart into the room, knocking Jemma's hip as she passed her. It was the angel speaking, "A child is dying, a child is in mortal need." Three nurses closed in around the bed. One stepped on a pedal that raised the bed up just past waist-height. Another tore open the boy's pajamas and started chest compressions while a third bag-ventilated his mouth. "O, won't you help him. O, it is given unto you to save him." They all looked up at her at once and Jemma saw that the one had eyes as big as teacups, the other had eyes as big as saucers, and the last had eyes as big as dinner plates. "Don't just stand there!" said the one who was bagging, whose eyes were as big as teacups. She jerked her head at the monitor. "It's v-fib!" Jemma looked at the monitor above her, at the lines that squiggled in a sweeping pattern for a few seconds, then settled into smooth cursive, spelling the same thing over and over: *It was you it was you it was you.* From her left another nurse shoved a set of paddles into her hand. She heard the defibrillator whining as it charged up. Please, please, she thought, please do not let him die. "It's v-fib," said the nurse at the head again. "Shock it!" Jemma did as she was told. She placed the paddles, one on the boy's chest and another on his side, and yelped, "Watch out!" before pressing the buttons. He jumped in his bed, and she thought she saw a green light flare from under the paddles, and felt it, too. It was all part of her trip, she was sure, how she could feel the electricity traveling out from her belly to her hands, and how the light seemed to become a word in her, and she could not be sure if it was sounding only inside her head or if the angel was speaking it, too, "Live! Live! Live!" All seven women in the room turned at once to the monitor, where the mad squiggles settled into the blips and spikes of a normal sinus rhythm.

"Good job," said the nurse whose eyes were as big as dinner plates, just as the PICU team arrived, and Jemma suddenly remembered her name: Candy. She didn't look like a Candy—she was hugely tall with black hair and weird skin that seemed translucent even when seen through eyes not scaled with magic fungus. Candy was short for something Russian and unpronounceable. Jemma surrendered the paddles back to her, then stepped backward as the others surged forward, and the mass of bodies parted to let her pass. She turned around outside the door just as Rob came running up, his code pager still singing at his hip.

"Were you running that code?" he asked her.

"Of course not," she said, looking down. He touched her arm, and she was afraid he would lift her chin with his hand, and discover how her eyes had become spinning pinwheels, but Emma, the PICU fellow, called for him to hurry up if he wanted to get the femoral line.

"See you soon," he said, and slipped by her. Jemma hurried off the other way, at first doing a slow shuffle, contemplating the lingering green taste that was everywhere in her body, and then running, because it seemed suddenly irresistible and necessary to run, and then, once she was sprinting, because she felt pursued. She didn't know what it was, and she was too scared to turn around and face it. She tore around a corner, colliding with a child as tall as she was. When their heads bonked together Jemma saw the noise flash in the air all around them, bright and white. The boy, thin and black, fell back on his ass, just like Jemma, but he was up on his feet again in an instant, as if he had bounced. Jemma had never seen him before. She scrambled to her knees.

"Are you all right?" she asked. "I'm so sorry!"

He looked down at her, peering into her eyes. Jemma looked away.

"You're all fucked up," he said.

"You'd better go. It's not safe here. Something's coming, but I can hide you. Come on." She stood up and grabbed his arm.

"Don't touch me, you nasty junkie whore," he said calmly, shrugging her off and walking away.

"Not that way!" Jemma called. "It's coming from that way!" He turned the corner, and she could not muster the courage to step around it and call after him again. She ran, instead, feeling the thing behind her, the skin of her back burning as it got closer. She flew down the stairs three and four steps at a time, and took a winding path through the fourth floor back to the room where she'd left Vivian.

"Vivian!" she said hoarsely, trying to whisper and shout at the same time. "There's something behind me! I think it's the why. I think it's the reason. It's coming to get us, because we were thinking about it. We called it to us, don't you see? Like when you say Nancy Reagan's name seven times into a mirror and she leaps out to kill you with her big red claws!" She called Vivian's name again, but there was no answer, and as she looked harder through the darkness she saw that the room was empty. Jemma pushed the table against the door and sat with her back against the window, her head just at the surface of the water. She watched the door, trying not to imagine the form that the thing must take as it came to destroy her, imagining instead what it would do to her. She saw her blood smeared over the walls and windows, and her guts strung up, over and under the struts of the suspended ceiling, and her head preserved in the little brown refrigerator, with somebody else's retainer stuck in her mouth. She watched and watched, as the thing never came, until she was finally distracted by the advent of a cold bright light. Her shadow appeared on the floor as suddenly as a monster, but it did not frighten her. She felt as if the tea were nearly out of her, by then. She turned and saw the full moon peeping around the top edge of the window. She had noticed before the face in it, but it had never seemed as sad as it did tonight, and the crater mouth had never seemed opened wide in horror like tonight. Over the next hour, while Jemma sat perfectly still, not sure if she was even blinking, it sank down into the water, as if it were seeking to drown. When it was fully immersed Jemma at last closed her eyes, and felt herself sinking too, and in the last fling of her trip imagined the moon a stone tied to her foot, the glowing opposite of a balloon, so as it sank in the water it pulled her after it in slow degrees, farther and deeper, back to the former surface of the world, and below that, and below that, and below.

You get heavy, I get light. I rise and rise and rise, through the dark water and the bright hospital and the blue air, and stretch myself over everyone, listening to Vivian weeping again—now she is all sadness and no rage. She cowers in the linen closet in the oncology ward, so sorry for what she has done, and for what you have done. She has convinced herself that you and she are responsible for the whole thing. It's a pain no one should have to bear, and my sister, sensitive to such things, gasses her gently with strawberry-scented sevofluorane, sending her to dream of fragrant plastic ponies and live for a few hours as a child in the old world. Dr. Snood passes by the closet, on one of his own late-night walks, trying to decide whether or not to continue with the tradition of grand rounds—maybe there is a better name, or a better thing altogether, a new tradition he should start, grander rounds, a shared time of useful consciousness, or a town-hall style meeting to discuss issues of hospital governance—and thinking of his wife. Her picture has been hanging all day in his mind, and he considers again how it would have been their anniversary in three days. It is the first time in five years that he has remembered it.

Rob Dickens passes him on the ramp, not looking up, walking slowly back to the call room. He got the femoral line but it was a small joy, because the kid was actually doing extraordinarily well and had actually yelled out, "Stop, stop that! Why are you poking me?" as Rob drove the needle into his thigh. He wasn't supposed to do that. Rob starts crying again as he walks, turning his head into his shoulder and hurrying now, not even sure why he's so sad—when he tries to think of his mom or Greta or Gillian all he can see is the heart kid's face, and he should be happy for that kid, and happy that he was asking for ice cream as they wheeled him off to the PICU. He starts to run as he passes the fifth floor, wanting very much to put his face between your shoulders because he knows it will stop up the crying some if he does that.

I could make a false Jemma, my sister says. Give me a summer squash, he will never know the difference.

It is not necessary, I say.

Cruel angel, she says, and sighs. Something wonderful has happened. Already she has put forth her hand.

I say it too, Something wonderful! A shout over the whole blue earth, loud enough for anyone with ears to hear, but the hospital is still a sadness on the waters, and still my brother is gathering himself up from within the deep, from bits of bone and flesh, an eye here, an ear there, from a hundred thousand patches of skin he is formed to be perfect in his flesh and perfect in his fury and already he is coming.

Our doctrine be tested by this rule and our victory is secure. For what accords better and more aptly with faith than to acknowledge ourselves divested of all virtue that we may be clothed by God, devoid of all goodness that we may be filled by Him, the slaves of sin that He may give us freedom, blind that He may enlighten, lame that He may cure, and feeble that He may sustain us; to strip ourselves of all ground of glorying that He alone may shine forth glorious and we be glorified in Him? These things, and others to the same effect are said by us, they interpose and querulously complain, that in this way we overturn some blind light of nature, fancied preparatives, free will, and works meritorious of eternal salvation, with their own supererogations also; because they cannot bear that the entire praise and glory of all goodness, virtue, justice, and wisdom, should remain with God. The first part is easiest. How many times have I put off all virtue? Over and over I have rolled off virtue and justice and wisdom and goodness like so many pairs of rubber underwear. Then I stand there, naked, perverse, depraved, and wait to be clothed, but no matter how many hours—you can stand there all night—it never happens. I can look back with my perfect memory and there was never one moment, never one, in my whole life where I didn't labor under it. The knowledge of my depravity is the only thing that makes me special—not the bad dreams or how I can leave my body on the roof and fly down the river dipping my hands in the water (and they are wet when I come back) or how

I can make time slow down or how I know the future or how I can tell the best souls (and I know mine is small and wrinkled, wizened not wise) or how I can make my eyes change color if I stare in the mirror at them for long enough—that I have always always always known, and have never for a moment been able to forget, that there is something terribly wrong with me.

Vivian walked in the roof garden, on a date with Jordan Sasscock. "Three weeks and two days," he was saying. "It's not really very long."

"But it already feels like forever," she said. It hadn't been a very fun date, though Jordan was the hottest resident in the hospital. She had picked him because she had never seen him glum in all the weeks she'd worked with him, but it turned out to be all happy veneer, and as soon as you got him alone for any length of time he revealed himself to be an obsessive depressive. She had wanted not to think about things but they weren't ten minutes into dinner before he held up his water glass and said, "I can hardly even stand to drink it."

"Not even the length of a rotation," he said. "That's how I've come to measure time, in four-week blocks. Some are slow and some are quick. This one has been the slowest of all. But I keep thinking, like I did with the tough rotations in residency, that the way through it is the same. You just put your head down and go, and before you know it it's over."

"I can do anything for a month," Vivian said.

"Exactly!"

"But it's going to be more than a month," she said. They were wandering on the snaking gravel paths that cut through the grass and flowers. Except for them, the roof was empty.

"How do you know?"

"Just a feeling," she said. She took his hand and led him toward the edge of the roof, where she sat down with him. They looked over into the dark water, and she could hear it lapping at the windows of the fourth floor.

"Just when I'm sure I believe it," he said, "I can't believe it."

"I can believe it," she said. "I'm not having trouble with that anymore." She nearly told him then about her project, her long list of reasons that would add up to the one big reason. The water called the task to mind, because the two things were similarly huge. It would be like counting the water, drop by drop. With enough time it could be done. "Guess what I'm going to do," she said.

"What?"

"Synthesize a puppy," she said, because the list wasn't really a first-date revelation, after all.

"I tried it," he said. "All I got was meat and fur. She's got her limits." He dug in his back pocket and pulled out a coin. "I've been saving this," he said.

"Don't waste it on little old me," she said.

"It's the right moment," he said. "A nice warm night and a big moon and I can smell fresh cut grass. Who cuts the grass, anyway?"

"Robots," Vivian said, because she had seen them one night, purposeful rolling metal balls that hithered and thithered all over the roof.

"Make a wish," he said, and flipped the coin into the dark. They both listened intently for it but neither heard it splash. Let me figure it out, she thought, but at the same time, Send me a boyfriend.

"What'd you wish for?" she asked.

"What else? For it all to be a fucking nightmare."

"It already is."

"You know what I mean. How about you?"

"Same thing, of course."

"Maybe if we all wished at once," he said.

"Then we would all be disappointed."

"Probably," he said. He took her hand and rubbed little circles in it with his thumb. She took his hand and put it in her lap.

"Guess what?" she said.

"What?" It was too dark to see his face clearly, but he wasn't pulling his hand away. "Three weeks and two days is the longest I've gone without sex since I was twelve."

His whole arm stiffened and he pulled away. "I should check on some kids," he said.

"Yeah," she said. "Me too."

"Walk you down?"

"I think I'll sit a little bit longer. You're right, it's nice out here."

"See you downstairs," he said, and he squeezed her shoulder as he stood up, as if to console her for being a forward whore. All the forward whores of the world were not responsible, she had decided. It was not the sex that had done them all in. Not the good sex, anyway. "I was kidding, you know!" she called out after he'd walked off, not turning to look if he was still on the roof. If he was there he didn't reply. "Not really," she said, more quietly. I've got work to do, she thought, and no time to hold somebody in her bed, to press his bones against hers, or lay his face alongside her face. No time to hold someone as the hospital rocked and spun, and no time to wake up next to someone in the strange pale dawns. She had her pad and her pen in her pocket, so she took it out and wrote in the dark.

Three floors down Cindy Flemm was riding her IV pole in a big lazy circle around the general peds ward. It is one of the advantages of being four feet tall—when she probably would have been six if her guts worked right—that she could fit on her pole and go for a ride while her TPN was running in. It set a bad example for the brats, and even though the nurses and doctors yelled at her for doing it she kept on, riding and gliding serenely. They weren't her parents and they couldn't very well take away her IV pole and they were too cowardly to chain her in her room.

Around and around—waiting in her bed for Wayne she got too restless. She'd spent half of the last year in this hospital, and even with the changes in the architecture that came after the Thing, she still felt like she could steer through the halls with her eyes closed. How ordinary it seemed. This was just another night, Carla in charge at the nurses' station tossing a ball back and forth to Ella Thims in her little red wagon, and Susan and Candy and Andy charting and gossiping at the desks, and an intern in the little glassed-in office talking on the phone. Nobody was too sick—she could always tell by the set of the nurses' faces, and nothing special was happening. It was like any other of the thousand nights she'd spent in the hospital, until she scooted down to the big windows at the end of the hall, where you could see the moonlight on the water. As she glided through the ward she whispered, "Totally normal," and as she passed the windows, "Totally fucked up."

"You're going to make yourself sick with that twirling," Carla said as she passed.

"It makes me *not* sick," Cindy said. "And it's all I have, since you won't give me any benadryl."

"It's not due for two hours. You know it." Carla covered her eyes as Cindy went into a pirouette. "Now you're making *me* sick."

"Diphenhydramine," Cindy sang as she went, meaning that Carla should get some for herself. "Diphenhydrameeen!" She carried the note all down the hall. She could sing better than anybody she knew, and hardly ever found the occasion to put forward a whole song, but she liked to put single words or phrases to tunes and stretch them up and down like in opera. "In pain," she might sing to her intern, or "leave me alone," or "go fuck yourself." On her twenty-third pass down the hall she saw Wayne slip into her room and followed him in after one more pass at Carla. "Hey, no midnight vitals," she told her.

"Sounds fine, but I have to ask Chandra."

"Well, just be sure you ask him with *style,*" Cindy said, throwing her hand out and flexing her wrist like a big fairy. Carla said it wasn't nice to make fun of people.

"No vitals!" she called down the hall just before she closed her door. "I'm fine!"

"Famous last words!" Carla called back.

"Now she's going to come down here," Wayne said. "You shouldn't have said anything."

"Baby, don't tell me how to work my nurse."

"Don't call me baby."

"Baby," she said. "Baby, baby." She sat down next to him on her bed, taking a little while to get her tubing arranged. He had already taken off his shirt. He raised himself on an elbow so she could get an arm under him, and then lay back down with his arms around her but she squeezed him harder. He was the best-fed CF kid she had ever seen. Usually they were blond and thin and pale and looked like they might cough blood on you as soon as smile at you. Wayne was tan, with dark brown hair and blue eyes, and big, with a high wide chest, and arms she could not wrap her two hands around. And he was very hairy for sixteen. He shaved twice a day and had soft hair all over his belly and his chest.

She closed her eyes and held on, imagining like she always did that they were out on the water and his fatness made him float, and that they weren't just on the water but *suspended in grief,* which was a phrase she had overheard from Carla when the nurses were shrinking each other one night at the station and didn't realize that her call radio was on. Their voices had woken her and she had listened to them talking about how much they missed whomever and how it was all too horrible to be real and she watched the water. Grief was yellow, she felt sure of that, and so she floated in a yellow sea holding tight to Wayne's doughy back while they floated and rolled. He was kissing her and then polishing her breasts with his big wet mouth and then for a little while she was doing the thing her sister had called playing her boyfriend's oboe. She would say "I petted his weasel" or "I played his oboe" because she couldn't say things like cock or blow job but Cindy had no problem with that, and indeed she had gone around in the afternoon quietly singing blow job, blow jooob, pronouncing it now like an Indian lady and now like a little Dutch girl, and she had looked forward all day to the end, the shock and the taste of which she thought was just like touching a nine-volt battery to your tongue. Her sister had said it was like Clamato but Cindy knew she was wrong and wanted to tell her.

"What?" Wayne said. "What? Why do you always have to ruin it by crying? It's no big deal. It's just us. It's just you and me being together." She kept her head down there and didn't say anything, and he pulled her up and kissed her. "Quiet," he said. "They're going to hear." So she pressed her face deep into his chest until she was a little calmer.

"Why us?" she said finally. "How come a bunch of fuck-up sickies? How come not normal people?"

"Shut up," he said. He put his hand over the back of her neck and for a moment she thought he would push her south again, but he just squeezed and petted her there. "Who else but us? We're fine. I mean look at you. Look at you." He waved a hand over her broviac line and her scarred-up belly. "You're perfect," he said.

A committee formed. Someone had planned, not for this eventuality, but for something remotely like it: in the event of a catastrophe a special governing body would assemble to oversee the function of the hospital in crisis, its authority superceding that of the regular board. Jemma would have liked for there to have been a button, located in the office of the hospital chief-of-staff, that would have released the pre-selected governors from frozen stasis, but there was no such thing. There was in fact a speed-dial button on the chief-of-staff's phone, that activated the crisis phone tree, but when someone finally thought to press it, it only caused the angel—Jemma had finally started to call her that, like everybody else did—to sing a lullaby from out of the receiver.

Of those planned governors only one had been in the hospital on the night of the storm: Dr. Snood, who already had a very well developed sense of his own importance. "At least he's not the grand pooh-bah," said Vivian, herself a member of the Committee. "Not officially, anyway."

There was no president, no chairman, no grand pooh-bah, but Dr. Snood was considered by himself and most others to be preeminent. He called the first three members to replace his drowned colleagues. He selected Dr. Sundae, an insomniac pathologist who did all the NICU post-mortems once a week between the hours of midnight and six a.m., a lady familiar to Jemma and the other students as the architect of second-year pathology exams that brought the best young minds of the country to the brink of nervous collapse, and someone who would sooner chew off her own foot than be charitable with a test point. He called Dr. Tiller, an intensivist also known as Dr. Killer, not because she wasn't an outstanding clinician, but because she was famously cruel to residents and students. And he called Zini, the ill-tempered nurse-manager of the surgical floor, a woman in her fifties whose drooping body was always constrained in shiny, tight skirts and blouses, so she always looked to Jemma like she had been packaged by aliens for preparation as a microwave dinner. She was doing a rare favor the night of the flood, having made herself available as a substitute for the junior manager who should have been called in to help deal with the lack of beds in the full-to-capacity hospital. Dr. Snood was known, like most everyone else in the hospital, to hate her, but even he, in his overweening pride, understood that every hospital government, council, or committee must have at least one nurse-manager to dip her sullen paws into the mix of business.

This tetrarchy of fussbudgets reigned only for a few days before people began to agitate for wider representation. An initial plan for each of the first four to call four others was scrapped when it was met with widespread indignation, especially from the lab techs, housekeepers, and cafeteria workers, who felt sure that their chances of having a say in things would be slim at best with a committee dominated by nurses and physicians. So names were put forward from among the nurses, residents, techs, cooks, cashiers, janitors, parents, students, and others, placed in secure black boxes made by the angel expressly for the purpose of receiving secret ballots. It was not precisely an election, and the committee that eventually took shape was not formed by an entirely democratic process (the fussbudgets chose from among the proposed candidates), but at least it took some of the sting out of oligarchy.

Vivian became the student representative, thrust forward by the surviving third- and fourth-years. Vice-president of their class, she was the most conspicuous choice. Raised along with her were Karen, the surviving chief-resident, Emma the NICU/PICU fellow, Jordan Sasscock, three nurses (two from the floors and one from the ER), two parents, a senior lab tech, and the hospital tamale lady, whose selection was less surprising than it might at first have seemed, given that she had been coming to the hospital for twenty years and knew everyone, and that the cashier/cook/housecleaning faction fell into squabbling and was unable to produce a universally agreed-upon list of candidates. The first action the expanded committee took was to call a seventeenth member to join them: John Grampus, who came reluctantly, kicking against the pricking insistence of the angel.

The Committee then inaugurated the census that counted and described the survivors: 699 sick children; 37 siblings; 106 parents; 152 nurses; 20 interns; 15 residents; 18 students; 10 attendings; 10 fellows; 10 laboratory technologists; 4 phlebotomists; 5 radiographic technologists; 6 emergency room technicians; 5 paramedics; 18 ward clerks; 1 chef and 14 subordinate food service workers; 1 volunteer; 1 chaplain-in-training; 2 cashiers; 15 housekeepers; 1 maintenance person; 2 security guards; 2 members of the lift team; and the single itinerant tamale vendor.

The census complete, they devoted themselves to dividing and conserving what had suddenly become the only limited resource in the hospital: the staff. Electricity appeared to be inexhaustible; food and medicine were both proving replicable—you had only to ask the angel for what you wanted, be it a pound of tuna or a million units of bicillin; but you could not replicate a new intern when the one you had was all used up. Karen, the chief, who had months of experience creatively inflicting merciless call on her residents, and Dr. Tiller, herself a former chief, were the architects of the various consolidated teams.

Morale was also in their purview—Vivian formulated the slogan that was supposed to bear them all up in the first weeks: *Just do the work*, and Dr. Snood designed the button and the posters, but philosophies they left to the individual, and while the Committee engaged in a sort of ecumenical boosterism, it forbade any sort of religious debate in session. This policy did not sit well with Dr. Sundae, who was never able to keep her radical liberal Pente-costalism entirely out of the classroom—to sit through her Sunday review sessions was to discover how a leiomyosarcoma might herald the imminence of the Kingdom of God—and so could hardly be expected not to discuss the obvious when they were all, as she pointed out, nestled in God's palm and afloat on a sea of grace. She pressed for the formulation of a statement of mass contrition, saying that they were sorry for absolutely everything they had done, ever, to be signed by every survivor. Even the micro-preemies would be required to append their footprints. Her measure was defeated before she could even decide to what degree *everything* must be quantified, or if the word alone would suffice.

She had a slogan—*It wasn't global warming!*—and a few like-minded adherents around the hospital, but the Committee was unanimous against her in deciding to uphold the tradition of strictly secular government. The rich diversity of affiliations embarrassed every catholic notion, anyway. Among the survivors the census numbered what Dr. Sundae called—not maliciously—the sparkling variety of heathen: Muslims and Buddhists and Jains and Hindus and an array of pagans including three Wicca nurses. Jews and atheists abounded, but the pseudo-Christians (her term again) were even more numerous: Mormons and Catholics and Eastern Orthodox and Coptics and Bahai and Unitarians and Jehovah's Witnesses. Extant Christians ranged along a continuum of propriety, but away with those distinctions, she said in her impassioned speech: Presbyterian and Episcopal and Methodist and Adventist and Baptist and Lutheran and Pentecostal no more; only embrace the Trinity, the absolute sovereignty of God, and absolute repentance, and we can all be united in a new faith.

She shook her fist and tossed her head—she had fabulous hair, black, shiny, and soft, with a lovely white stripe, of exactly the sort Jemma had always wanted for herself, which she usually kept tucked behind her ear but which waved like a flag when she was excited about something—but she couldn't even get them to admit, officially, that the world had ended.

"We'll just do our work," Dr. Snood said, summarizing the Committee's decision on the matter. Whoever wanted to sign a statement of contrition was welcome to do it, provided it did not interfere with the regular business of the hospital—making well the children in their care. Dr. Sundae was silent, but not satisfied, and predicted that by the time the Committee had formulated the terms of its dissolution—they were only placeholders for an elected assembly to come, after all—they would understand how they were practicing foolishness. Meanwhile, she circulated around the hospital with her statement. "No thanks," Jemma told her, when Dr. Sundae asked her to sign it.

"She wants to be a Priest-Queen," Vivian said later to Jemma. Vivian always found her after Committee meetings to complain and decompress. "She's been waiting all her life for this to happen, she said, just so she could gloat. I wanted to tell her, Everyone knows there has to be something wrong with you to go into pathology. Give it up. Anyway, we put her and her Priest-Queen down. We'll have a president or a prime minister or a something. Something different, or something better. Something *new*."

"Are you going to run?" Jemma asked They were at Vivian's place, one of the new call rooms that had unfolded into the extra space the hospital had acquired after the Thing. As if it had taken a deep expanding breath, it had grown by at least a third. The new rooms were nicest—Vivian had a real bed and a huge television and one of those obstetric whirlpool tubs—but Jemma found them creepy and a little unreal, and worried that they might disappear as suddenly as they had come into existence, their inhabitants vanishing with them. She liked and trusted her little room better.

"Hell no," Vivian said, but smiling in a way that Jemma knew meant Almost certainly. There was not much time to prepare a candidacy, though, or execute a campaign, in those first few weeks, and people forgave the Committee for being all talk and little action when it came to engineering their own destruction, because they were all so busy with the ordinary business of the hospital. The babies in the NICU had been representative of a hospital-wide trend—every child in the place had taken a turn for the worse on the night of the storm, and few of them retreated from the precipice as quickly as those babies did. On the IBD ward the Crohn's patients were fistulizing like mad and the UC boys and girls were pouring blood out of their bottoms almost as fast as the angel could replicate it. In the onc wards tumors recurred or stopped responding to chemo, and sepsis became as commonplace as a bald head, though no two kids grew the same bacteria out of their blood. The anorexics on the ninth floor confessed that they felt huger than ever, and each rehab kid lost at least one hard-won-back skill every two days. It was Jane Dressel, a lesbian Unitarian chaplain-in-training who gave voice to the popular sentiment, noting in a sermon during one of her six-days-a-week services that their affliction seemed to grow day by day. It was a lot for a Unitarian to process, Jemma thought, calling on all the knowledge of such people that came down to her from Calvin—his own obsessive opinions and what was in his book: Unitarians, he had said, worshipped a great powerless unpresence. Wearing leather pants, like Jane did, probably made you better qualified to be the last cleric at the end of the world, but there was an obvious sweetness about her that, in the context of all the affliction, made her seem overwhelmed. In the first few weeks she was really the only person in the hospital doing anything like preaching, or anything like trying publicly to put a sense to what had happened to them, though private conversation and private enterprises, like Jemma's and Vivian's, naturally abounded, and there were already conclaves of affection, in which like-minded people came together. But a circle of hand-holding reformed Jews was not Father Jane, as people started to call her, standing in front of the podium before a standing-room crowd in the auditorium, the space that used to host Grand Rounds and the occasional medical school lecture. In her sermons she always tried to convince herself to look on the bright side, but she wasn't stupid, and could never make a good case for hope out of such poor evidence.

"We need a sign," she told the crowd, not exactly a congregation—the avowed Unitarians in the hospital could be counted on two hands—"but signs are for us to find as well as for Him to give. Let's look around," she said, and she looked for signs high and low in the hospital but all that was there was sickness and grief and confusion and a curious loneliness—they were stuffed all together in this round floating box and yet weren't they all, except the very few families that had survived intact, still strangers and still alone from each other? "The dying child is not the sign, the weeping nurse, the exhausted intern asleep in the middle of the hall—she looks very peaceful, doesn't she, but look briefly on her dreams and your eyes will drop out of your head. The sign is our own hard work, and our hope, and our dedication to make these children better—they and we are the seeds of a new world." It was as obvious, and as hard to believe, as the water everywhere outside.

But Jemma, listening in the back, in the same seat where she'd last month fallen asleep during a lecture on the heartbreak of teenage chlamydia infection, found the sermon no more inspiring than Dr. Snood's posters, written and drawn by the angel under his direction: people at tasks, lab techs and radiology techs and interns and residents and nurses looking very strong and committed as they shot a film or drew blood or peered into a child's ear, all of them having inherited his strong jaw and superior posture. To Jemma they looked too strong and clean and happy to exist in this time and this place. They were a fake, and could only inspire fake, strained hope.

A better sign than those came on the twenty-third day after the storm. Jemma was in the NICU, visiting Brenda, though the child was on Rob's service, not hers. Rob accused her gently of being obsessed with the little girl, because she confessed that she crawled into her thoughts on the hour, and that she felt a bond of curiosity and unwarranted affection with her. "She's got nobody at all," Jemma said, and wondered why it should seem so horrible for this child when it could be said of all the children whose parents had been caught outside on the night of the storm.

Her incubator still sat on its dais, so Anna always had to walk up the four steps to turn her or suck out her endotracheal tube or cater to a desaturation. "Isn't she pretty?" Anna asked, when Jemma, AWOL from the ward team before evening rounds, climbed up to look in on her. She was larger, but no prettier than she'd been three weeks before, and was not just back on the ventilator, but had already failed conventional ventilation. Now she was on an oscillator, a machine that breathed for her hundreds of times a minute, and made her chest vibrate fast as an insect's wing. An indwelling orogastric tube snaked along her endotracheal tube to disappear into her bunny mouth. She had more access than almost anybody else in the unit: two peripheral lines, one in her foot, and one in her scalp; a peripherally inserted central line that went in her left arm and traveled in her vein to the antechamber of her heart; and an arterial line in her left wrist. Jemma successfully followed the line of her foley where it twisted over the bed, through a bundle of wires and catheters, into a tiny urine bag.

"She gained a hundred grams yesterday," said Anna.

"That's great," Jemma said.

"It's too much, honey. Normal weight gain's about twenty or thirty, all the rest is fluid. They've got her overloaded."

"Don't call me honey," Jemma said.

Anna smiled and pushed back her hair. "It wasn't a 'fuck you' honey, or a 'suck my ass' honey. It was just a 'honey' honey. It was sweet. But sorry. Sorry anyhow."

"Sorry," Jemma said, too, regretting her experiment with sauciness. But she had vowed not to suffer any more abuse from the nurses, no more condescending sighs, no more stabbing diminutives, no more of the thousand ways they disguised a hearty "fuck you."

"It's all right," said Anna, still smiling, her face entirely open. Jemma, her malice sensors at maximum gain, detected none. An alarm sounded, and Anna bent over the isolette. "She's never done *that* before," she said. Jemma looked and saw that the child had turned toward her and was reaching out her arm and her hand to point squarely at Jemma's face. Her tiny index finger, no bigger than the tip of a crayon, was perfectly straightened, and the other fingers curled in, so there could be no mistaking the gesture. "I've never seen any of them do that before."

Jemma was going to ask the question, Can infants point? But when she looked away from the little finger, she saw the man floating at the window, and screamed. It was not like her to do that, and such a girly little shriek had not escaped her lips for years and years. It was a high, teakettley little noise, short and piercing, that drew everyone's attention, not to the window and the man, but to Jemma, who had raised her hand to her mouth. She pointed at the window, and then all the heads turned that way. No one else shrieked, but Anna said, very calmly, "No fucking way."

The windows used to open. When the hospital changed, the slim metal sashes disappeared, but the NICU staff, clustered at the windows, still ran their fingers over the glass, seeking an invisible knob to turn. A floor above, in the PICU, the windows were intact at forty-foot intervals along the wall. So the recovery was launched from the fifth floor, and it happened to be Rob, strong, able bodied, and, as a medical student, traditionally disposable, who was lowered down by sheet ropes to grapple at the corpse and retrieve it. Jemma, running back and forth between the floors with a growing crowd of oglers, marveled at how well preserved it was. Weeks in the water ought to have made it bloated and patched with rot, but the skin looked pink and firm, and the thin blond hair shined beautifully. Jemma understood what a big body it was when Rob was laid out along it, grabbing and seeking to get his arms around the thick chest. When they hauled him up he had an arm around the waist and one through the legs, reaching around to clutch half the square ass. Jemma could not help feeling a proprietary glee, watching Rob's arms and back flex with the effort he was making. The corpse slipped, and Rob wound his legs around the legs, so the living and dead bodies entwined even more intimately as they came out of the water. They twisted on the rope and Rob's face was suddenly right in front of her. He smiled.

By the time she and the crowd arrived upstairs again the body was laid out in the PICU. Half-a-dozen people were clustered around it, bustling more than was appropriate for any corpse, no matter how miraculously preserved.

"He's warm!" Rob called to her. "He has a pulse!" He and a nurse were drying the man with a towel, rubbing him as vigorously as one rubbed a newly delivered baby. Jemma stepped on a sopping towel as she approached the bed, and the water, warm as sweat, splattered on her ankle. Rob, drying the face, removed his towel with an unintended flourish, revealing the straight nose, the high cheeks, the scar under the chin. Now that the eyebrows were dry they sprang up in shapes like wings. Another nurse finished attaching the man to a monitor, and Jemma saw his heartbeat illustrated on the screen.

"Normal sinus," Dr. Tiller murmured approvingly. She was standing apart from the action, with her arms folded, giving orders. It was a standard pose, Jemma had noticed, and the one you were supposed to assume in a code, if you were running it. This man looked too healthy to code. He looked better than Jemma felt—perpetually post-call, she was perpetually exhausted—and healthier and more rested than anyone else in the room. Still, he got the standard battery of tests, an EKG, a chest film, blood, and urine. Jemma put an IV in the left hand and took blood from it while Rob stuck the right radial artery for a blood gas. It was a big hand, with big veins laid out in perfect stark relief; an easy stick. She got it with just one try, and the man did not stir. Rob was still probing for the artery as the blood filled up her tubes, and found it just as she finished. She had never seen such bright red blood as came out of the wrist, and never felt blood as hot as what warmed the four tubes in her palm. She passed them off to a lab tech, then looked for something else to do. Janie, the nurse who had hooked up the monitor, was now putting in a foley, but struggled with the foreskin. "Shall I retract?" Jemma asked. Janie grunted. Jemma fetched a sterile glove. Vivian maintained that penises had personalities, or that they signified the personalities of their attachees. She would expound, if allowed, over gay pornographic weeklies: "Timid, don't be fooled by the size. Sneaky. Peripatetic. Grief-stricken, something horrible happened to that one. Loyal. Loving, probably too loving." About this one Jemma thought she would say, "Noble."

"Wakey wakey," Janie said lightly as she drilled in the foley catheter with an expert, twisting motion. Then she was halfway to the door of the bay, sprawled just beyond one of Rob's wet footprints, because the man had woken, and sat up, and struck her with the hand that Jemma had just tapped for blood, and all with such speed that Jemma only realized it was happening after it was over.

He was sorry. He was terribly, terribly, terribly sorry, and could not apologize enough to Janie. He said he'd never hit a woman before, or hit anyone before, though of course he couldn't be entirely sure about that, because he had no memory of anything before he'd woken in the PICU. He did not know his name, so they gave him one. They had a contest right there in the unit: Motherfucker (Janie's suggestion); John; Gift-of-the-Sea; Mannanan Mac Lir; Poseidon; Aquaman; Nimor; Joe. Rob called him Ishmael, and won.

Jemma found herself the silent partner on a hospital tour, her association with Rob getting her on the bus, though evening rounds were coming and she had not seen any of her patients since the morning. Vivian had promised to cover for her, but she considered anyway how Dr. Snood would release some new affliction from his ass to punish her. It would be worth it, she thought. Rob was almost chipper as he took them from the top of the hospital to the bottom. She followed along behind their two broad backs, hurrying to catch up and then running into the both of them when they stopped to examine some aspect or attribute of the hospital. Always Ishmael would turn and smile at her when she collided with him. When he had gotten out of his bed in the PICU, all observing heads had craned back on their necks as he rose to his full height. He had not looked so tall floating in the water.

"Replicators!" he said on the ninth floor. "Just like in that television show. I remember it... with the red-haired boy, and the little girl with the talking robot doll that smote all her enemies."

"Not exactly," Rob said, ordering a pitcher of lemonade. They took it to the window at the end of the hall and stood together in a patch of sunlight. The sky was marked here and there with starfish-shaped clouds, and the sea matched the color of Ishmael's eyes, gray green.

"You don't remember anything about before?" Jemma asked him again. "Not anything at all?"

"That's what he said," Rob said, with a hint of testiness, because Jemma had been asking and asking this question.

"Not a thing."

"It must be nice," Jemma said. "Not remembering what you lost."

"Maybe it is," he said, staring at her. "I have nothing to compare it to." His thin blond hair stuck up from his head in a half-dozen different cowlicks, and made him look even younger than he probably was. She wanted to smooth it down.

"It must be... nice," Jemma said again, and looked away from his eyes. Ishmael laughed, a pleasant sound, a deep, Santa-like ho-ho-ho. Rob was smiling as he sipped at his lemonade. Jemma tried to smile, too, but, though she was showing her teeth, what she was doing did not feel like a smile, and she knew it must look ghastly. She looked back at the sea, envying this blank man his blank history, and wondering what it must be like to come new into this place.

"Seven miles," Ishmael said, looking out the window with her. "I suppose I'll just have to wait to believe it."

"I'm still waiting," said Rob, and Jemma thought, Liar, because nobody could cry that hard for something that they didn't believe in.

"What sort of patients are up here?" Ishmael asked after they had all been silent and sea-gazing for a moment.

"It's a rehab floor," Rob said. "Kids who are medically stable but have to learn to walk again, or hold a fork—that sort of thing."

"And little lunatics," Jemma said. Pickie Beecher appeared in the hall, as if on cue. They watched him walk down to them. He was dressed in the lavender pajamas that came with his room. She had been spending a lot of time with him, working up his melena under Dr. Snood's whip, a tough job for Jemma, who could muster no enthusiasm for shit, and did not like even to consider it. She especially did not like to see it, and when she happened upon it, which she often did during her third year of school—it was always leaping out at her from within the pants of the homeless derelicts she encountered in the ER, or shooting out with the baby in a delivery, or surprising her when she turned back the sheets of the deranged or demented—it haunted her, so she'd think the odor was clinging all day on her clothes and her hair. Worse than anything was having to go seeking after it, finger first, the student's duty.

But the mystery of Pickie's poop had to be solved, so Jemma had scheduled the tests and accompanied him down to radiology and to the endoscopy suite. First, she repeated the guaiac test on two more specimens: Pickie dutifully shat in a plastic hat for her, then peered over the rim of the hat as Jemma poked at it with a little stick.

Two more bright blue hemoccult cards later, she took him down to nuclear medicine to look for a Meckel's diverticulum, an entity dimly recalled from her first-year anatomy class. "It's an extra thingie in your belly," she told Pickie, while the surviving radiology attending, Dr. Pudding, stood behind a dark glass, calling out orders to the tech over an intercom. She was not sure how to describe to a six-year-old a pocket of ectopic gastric tissue in the gut. "It can make you bleed because it makes acid where there shouldn't be acid."

"Sometimes I have a bitterness in my belly," he said, lifting and dropping the heavy hem of her lead apron. He held very still for his IV, and for the repeated films of his belly. He waited patiently for the technetium to distribute through his body, playing a game with his hands, twisting his fingers up one on top of the other, and then untwisting them. When she told him that the scan was negative he shrugged and said, "I do have a bitterness, though."

Colonoscopy necessitates a cleanout. The term brought to Jemma's mind images of merry little maids sweeping out one's colon, but it was actually accomplished with large volumes of an osmotic laxative. All night long Pickie Beecher was flushed out with three hundred cc's an hour of polyethylene glycol. Jemma put the nasogastric tube down herself, while Thelma watched. It was not a procedure that required finesse; you greased the tube and shoved it in, encouraging the patient to swallow when it reached the back of the throat. Nonetheless, she had to do it twice. All seemed to go well the first time, she greased and shoved, and the whole length of the tube disappeared into his nostril, but when she tried to flush it nothing would go in. Then she noticed that Pickie was working his jaws ever so subtly. "Open your mouth," she told him. When he did, the coiled tube whipped out like a lolling tongue.

"It's chewy," he said.

Ten hours and four liters later, Jemma took him down to the endoscopy suite. "Sweet dreams," she said.

"I will dream of my brother," he told her when Dr. Wood, the anesthesiologist, pushed the sedative. During the procedure, Jemma tried to hide behind the little curtain the anesthesiologists put up to hide themselves from the surgeons, but Dr. Snood called her out to stand by him as he manipulated the servos that controlled the endoscope. He was almost pleasant as they toured Pickie's bowels. He pointed out landmarks like a dad on a cross-country car trip. The quality of the cleanout was a source of joy for him. "Pristine!" he kept saying. "Pristine!"

There was only a little portion of bowel that they could not visualize, scoping from above and below. Everything else was totally normal. No bleeding ulcers, no friable polyps, no sharp foreign bodies, no granulomas. "No bezoars," Jemma said, trying to hurl the curse back at Dr. Snood. "Not a *bezoar* in sight." Dr. Snood sighed.

"We'll see what the path shows," he said, meaning the biopsies. But they were normal, too. Jemma was in the slow process of setting up a tagged red cell scan (the technician who did those was dead, but the surviving ones thought they could wing it) when she solved the mystery quite by accident. Sleepless again, she'd wandered all the way to the ninth floor, taking a survey of sleeping children's faces, compulsively checking on all her patients. She shadowed their doors, staying just long enough to see the light fall on a plump, pale face, and it was calming to her, and it was making her sleepier and sleepier.

She found Pickie perched on the edge of his bed, sipping at a juice pack that was actually a unit of fresh whole blood.

"What do you want?" he asked her around the straw. It gleamed like steel in the light from the hall. When Jemma tried to snatch the blood from him he ran from her, evading her easily, all the while sipping on his blood until the pack was flat as an envelope. He handed that over to her, but would not give up the straw, and Jemma couldn't find it when she searched him.

"I thought you were a vegetarian," she said to him finally, after staring into his guiltless face for a few minutes, trying and failing to formulate a proper scolding.

"Blood is not meat," he had said simply, and Dr. Snood had a stern talk with him, and assigned Jemma the job of designing a behavior-modification program that would break him of the habit. She was still working on it, and all she'd come up with so far was slipping him a unit of O negative spiked with ipecac.

"Hey, Peanut Butter," said Rob Dickens, when the child walked up to them and stared. Pickie ignored him. He faced Ishmael and bowed deeply to him.

"I see you," he said, and then sniffed at Ishmael's leg. "Will you accuse me like your sister in the walls? Don't waste your breath. I'm not listening!" Then he plugged up his ears and ran off back down the hall singing la la la at the top of his lungs.

"Well, hello to you too!" Ishmael said, laughing again.

"Like I was saying," Jemma said. "The little lunatics."

"But they're kind of sweet, really," Rob said.

Every other child took an instant liking to the stranger. On the eighth floor, the hematology-oncology ward, bald children in facemasks emerged without permission from their positive pressure rooms to give him a hug, while solemn-faced parents stared appraisingly at him. Rumor of him had spread immediately through the whole hospital. Not just the children wanted to touch him. Nurses and doctors and technicians and more outgoing parents stopped the three of them as they walked to shake his hand, as if to congratulate him for surviving.

On the ninth floor Jemma had decided he was jolly. On the eighth she decided he was kind, and that he had children, despite his youth, because of the way he touched the heme-onc kids, without any fear, and because of the way he talked to them, which was neither the overly familiar, unctuous babbling or the stiff, formal butler-talk engaged in by people who were unfamiliar with or afraid of children. On the seventh floor she decided he was catty, because he turned to her, after a pear-shaped nurse had scolded him for tickling a liver-transplant kid without washing his hands first, and whispered, "Her ass is as big as Texas!"

"As Texas *was*," Jemma corrected.

On the sixth floor she decided he was patient, because he suffered Ella Thims's game of pick-up-my-toy with utter calm. She sat in her red wagon at the nurses' station, repeatedly throwing a toy phone on the floor and clapping her hands together. He'd pick up the phone and hold it to his ear, saying, "Hello, hello? I think it's for you!" before handing it back. Ella wiggled in her flounces and cackled delightedly every time she got the phone back. Jemma could do it only once or twice without wanting to chew off her fingers, but Ishmael played the game twenty or twenty-five times before Rob dragged him on.

They were delayed again while he entangled himself in other games, playing hopscotch in the hall with a pair of pale, spindly CF twins, and pulling in a surrey a five-year-old boy recovering from myocarditis.

"You look great, Ethan," Rob said to him as the boy lashed at the stranger with a terry-cloth rope cut from a restraint.

"I *feel* great!" he said. This was the boy that Jemma had helped code on the night of her trip with Vivian. His heart, ravaged by a virus, huge but weak when Jemma had met him before, was now almost back to normal. The day after his bad night his edema was improved and his three different murmurs, each more pathological than the last, were all silenced. Aloysius Pan, the overworked and perpetually sour-faced cardiology fellow, had echoed him for a whole hour, not believing what he was not seeing. "Do you want to hear how loud I can scream?" he asked them, not waiting for an answer before splitting their ears. A nurse and his mother called out for him to shut up. "Before I could only make a peep," he said defensively. Everyone had recognized his improvement as a miracle though no one had named it such, and he was the only child in the hospital who was definitely getting better.

On the fifth floor she decided Ishmael was thoughtful, because he brought replicated flowers to Janie, and she suspected he had been a wife-beater, because there was something too practiced about his apology, and about the flourish with which he presented the bouquet. She felt sure, despite his protest to the contrary, that he had done this before.

Still, on the fourth floor she knew he was gentle, because of the way he held one of the sturdier preemies, recently extubated but still with a feeding tube in her mouth and oxygen prongs in her nose. Little black girls were famous for being the best survivors, and this baby was the star of the unit that week, but she still fit in his hand with room left over. As he stroked her head with two fingers her saturation rose to a new personal best of 97 percent.

"And who is this little monster?" he asked about Brenda. "Hello, Princess," he said, putting a hand on her isolette.

"She really is a princess," said Rob. "Or she was."

"If you touch her, I'll break your hand," said Anna, stepping up on the dais with a new bag of feeds in her hand. The feed bag was softer than a pillow, but she handled it in a menacing way.

"Just admiring," said Ishmael. When they all looked down at Brenda she pointed again squarely at Jemma.

"I wish she wouldn't do that," Jemma said softly.

"She's just stretching," said Rob.

"It means she really likes you," said Anna. Ishmael pointed back at the baby, and laughed.

On the third floor the tour paused, then ended, in the big playroom. There Jemma decided she could really know nothing about him, and that she was being foolish, thinking she could assemble her cursory perceptions of this man, the strangest of strangers, into anything resembling a real person or a real life. She watched him play in a pool of colored plastic balls with Rob, Ethan, and two others, both Vivian's patients, unrelated boys with the same rare intestinal lymphoid hyperplasia that required them to be fed periodically through their veins. He and Rob grappled, each holding the other by the shoulders and not moving, though both grinned ferociously and waves of tension seemed to flow from body to body across the bridge their arms made, until Rob was thrown. He spun around once in the air and sent up a splash of colored spheres when he landed. Then all three boys jumped at once on Ishmael, and hung on him like on a tree, one from his neck, one from his arm, and one around his waist. His Santa-laugh filled the whole room, the second biggest one in the hospital, a gym-sized space filled with every sort of amusement

"Who is that?" Vivian asked her, when she caught up with them after rounds.

"That's *him,*" Jemma said.

"You've got to be fucking kidding me," Vivian said again and again, placing different emphasis on different words each time, now on the *got,* now on the *fucking,* now on the *kidding,* as Jemma told the short story of Ishmael's exit from the sea. Her face changed while Jemma spoke. Jemma thought he was having the same effect on her that he had had on everyone else; that his survival outside the hospital was inspiring hope for other miraculous survivals.

"Look at those arms," she said. "Look at those hands. He looks nice. I bet he's nice. Is he nice?"

"Nice enough," Jemma said. "So far. We all just met him."

"Well God damn," Vivian said, staring and shaking her head and idly rubbing her belly in the same way she always did on one of their nights out, staring in a bar at some new galoot.

Jemma might have given her proprietary lecture, the same one she'd shouted in nightclubs at her unlistening friend, with the added caveat that this was a man who had just washed out of a killing sea, a miracle and a mystery and a danger, but just as she opened her mouth to give it she noticed Rob, still sitting up to his chest in round plastic balls. He had been staring at her, for how long she did not know, one finger resting precisely on the top of his head.

"I've been praying," Rob said to her in the call bed. She lay against him, her back to his chest. His big hands were folded neatly across her belly.

"I think I noticed," she said, thinking of the times when she knew he was not sleeping, but he would not answer when she called his name in the dark. Sometimes she would hear a stray whisper from him, words that sounded like the names of his sister or his mother.

"Not something I've ever done before."

"I know." He came from a family of supremely rational atheists. Jemma had found them difficult to get used to, the way they said just what they meant, proposed every action before executing it, and kept their promises.

"I wonder if I'm doing it right."

"Is there a wrong way?"

"There must be. Doesn't there have to be? Something's been going wrong, hasn't it?"

"You've been listening to Dr. Sundae."

"Would you like to pray… together?"

"No," she said simply. "Maybe you could ask Father Jane."

"We could just say a little one."

"Or we couldn't." She hadn't said a prayer since Calvin died, and even before then it was only the ones he taught her that she said regularly. She thought of his book, and wanted suddenly—the desire came as swiftly as a cramp, and was as much of a surprise—to read it. She'd thrown it away as soon as she read it, and now remembered nothing except for a few scattered phrases like *blasphemy is the straightest route to God* and *Grace is perfectly violent*, raving testimonials to his most secret insanity. When she'd thrown it in the river it had felt like the first right thing she'd ever done, but now she wished she had it with her, and pictured him sometimes, kicking Father Jane in the face and taking her place before the podium to read from it until everyone in the audience bled from their ears.

"Maybe later," he said.

"Maybe." She tried to imply *maybe never*.

For a while they were quiet, Jemma watching the window. Every so often a wave would splash against it, but mostly it just showed the darkening blue sky.

"This was nice," he said, squeezing her.

"Very," she said, though it had not been one of the great ones.

"It seemed like we should wait forever, before. And then after today I didn't know what we were waiting for."

"I'm not sure either."

"It seemed wrong, to do anything like celebrating."

"Oh," she said, thinking but not saying how there was such a thing as miserable desperate fucking, and a sort of fucking you did when you felt bad that was not necessarily meant to make you feel better about anything.

"Do you think anybody else... do you think this was the first time?"

"Who knows?"

"Well I hope it gets things going all over the hospital. I want everybody else to feel better like this." He squeezed her again.

"What was the water like?" she asked after a moment, thinking of how warm it was on her foot.

"Like soup. I should have washed it off. It's disgusting, when you think about it."

"Don't think about it."

"Do you think that anybody else could come up?"

"I guess. Maybe." She thought of his mother and sister, rising entwined through the blood-warm water, passing through the shadow of the hospital. She closed her eyes and saw a hand and a face at the window.

"Maybe they'll all come back. Maybe they're just waiting."

"For what?" she asked, but he didn't have an answer, or didn't care to answer. He put his face in her neck.

"Once when I was little," he said finally, "I think I must have been three or four, my sisters and my parents went to dinner and left me behind. They didn't notice that they'd forgotten me. I was pretty quiet then, especially in cars. I hated to talk while the car was moving. I was next door with a friend, making mud pies. When I came home and the door was locked, I thought they were inside and had locked me out because they hated me. My sister had said she hated me, the week before, because I cut her hair while she was sleeping—I never knew why I did that. It was just a little snip, and she forgave me, but no one had ever said they hated me before, not that I remember. So I thought she'd been pretending, and that she still hated me, and everyone hated me, so they had shut up the house against me, and would never let me in again. But then it got dark, and the house stayed dark, and I realized that the car was gone, and that they had gone somewhere without me. I was sure that they had moved away, and that they were never coming back. So I sat on the front steps and put my head in my arms and cried for an hour straight, until they came home. My mother said she had to scream my name at me to make me stop crying, and shake me to make me understand that she was there, and that they were back. I remember that. When they came back it was like they had been there all along, but I had gone someplace where they weren't. I cried and cried. The house disappeared, and the steps disappeared. The noise of the crickets and even the noise of my crying disappeared, all I could think of was how they were gone and never coming back. I didn't even know what death was, back then."

She could tell he was waiting for her to answer him somehow, so she told him something she'd already mentioned in another bed-bounded conversation. "Sometimes," Jemma said, "if I put my head down in a dark room I get a feeling like Calvin is right behind me, reaching out his hand to touch my shoulder. If I would just wait long enough he could touch me. But I always turn around, and he's always not there."

Rob's breathing became so deep and even that Jemma thought he must be sleeping. Then he spoke again.

"Are you sure you wouldn't like to pray a little?"

Jemma kept catching glimpses of the boy whom she'd literally run into on the night of her trip with Vivian. But no one else had ever seen him, and she could never find him when she went looking for him deliberately on the wards. After many days of unsuccessful searching, she finally became convinced he must be a seven-hundredth child. She'd encountered him, always unexpectedly and by accident, a total of three or four times, depending on whether or not one counted his appearance during her trip, which she was inclined to do.

Lying next to Rob, she could not sleep. There was so much else to worry about, but she worried only about this boy. Night after night it kept happening: she would lie and imagine him in some sort of gruesome trouble, stuck with his foot in a bear trap or pursued by a hungry land-shark or just crying himself to sleep somewhere, until finally she would rise and go look for him. This time she brought a camera with her, having borrowed the one that usually lived in a drawer on the general ward, kept for the sake of recording interesting physical findings, distinctive rashes and tuberous growths and birth marks in the shape of Jesus or Italy. She took a picture of Rob sleeping before she left, and he startled but did not wake at the flash.

She started at the gift shop on the first floor and walked all the way up to the garden on the roof. A week and a half before, passing by the gift shop on another late-night walk, she had noticed a pair of red bolt cutters leaning casually against the aluminum gate that had been rolled down over the entrance since the night of the storm. It was one aspect of the hospital that had not changed at all: the gate did not roll up, and the inventory lay inert, the licorice and teddy bears were locked beyond the reach of the children who wanted them, and the flowers wilted in their humidified refrigerators, because the little old lady who'd minded the store for the past twenty years was drowned with the key to the gate. The lady had stopped Jemma once as she hurried through the lobby, late for pre-rounding in the nursery. "You must see this!" she said, putting a claw on Jemma's shoulder. She took a little key from around her neck and turned it in a panel above the height of her head on the wall outside the shop. "Open sesame!" she cried, and hopped back and forth on her feet, looking so much like a little bird that Jemma expected her to start pecking at the ground between her legs. After the Thing the angel would not roll up the door. "The shop is still closed," was all she would say whenever people asked her to do it.

He had cut his own silhouette out of the door, but he was not a small child, so Jemma could slip through, though she tore the edge of her yellow scrub gown on a jag of aluminum. Some light from the lobby came through the door, so it was bright enough for her to see him feeding at the candy trough, scooping up handfuls of gummy bears and jelly beans to his mouth and then gazing around the place, like a thoughtful ruminant, as he chewed. He saw her and froze, his cheeks puffed up with candy.

"I won't hurt you," she said quietly, squatting down and bringing her hands up, palms out like she was surrendering to him. "What's your name?" He only stared at her. She could hear him breathing loudly through his mouth. "Do you have a cold?" she asked him, because he sounded terribly congested. "My name's Jemma," she told him, when he did not answer her. He chewed and swallowed, then brought his fist up to the level of his face and opened it to show her a pile of glistening red candy. "No, thank you," she said politely, and he cast the candy in her face. She knew what they were as they struck her and she smelled them: hot candy tamales, shaped like giant bacilli, made spicy with artificial cinnamon flavor. They were sopping wet from the warmth and sweat of his hand, and they stung her eyes. She fell back out of her squat, clutching at her face. He ran over her, stepping square on her sternum with his shoe and knocking out her breath. He was very heavy, for all that he was very thin. As her breath was pushed out of her it occurred to her that he must be incredibly dense. By the time she recovered and stood up he was long gone.

Tonight the gate was open—the next day the men from the lift team had cut away the rest of the gate, and ten minutes after that the remaining pieces had fallen out of the wall. Everyone had access to the gift shop, where the candy and teddy bears were free now, restocked every evening by the surviving hospital volunteer, who had moved away from his old haunt on the eighth floor to make the shop his stake.

The boy was not there. Jemma wandered in and picked up a white angora teddy bear, idly combing its long hair with her fingers. The volunteer was one of the most creative replicators in the hospital, making candy more fantastic than anything from the fevered imagination of Willy Wonka, and bears with long white hair or dancing feet and dancing eyes, or who would moan at you from the utmost depth of their affection. She replaced the bear, though there was no such thing as stealing from the shop. "Do you like it?" the slow, quiet man would ask if you touched something or looked at it twice. "Then take it. It is for you."

She was not sure exactly why she felt compelled to pursue this child. Rob pointed out that he was probably doing fine, and would come forward if he should ever need taking care of. Breaking and entering might very well be a sign of self-sufficiency, Jemma admitted, but still she felt like she had to find him. Not to justify herself in the face of his rude accusation, though she imagined herself detailing to him all the reasons she was in fact *not* a junkie whore. She had a sense that there was something wrong with him, something she or someone must address, entirely aside from his bad behavior. But she could not say what this was. "You're neurotic," Vivian said, "which is okay." Other people prayed or broke down at regular intervals or lost themselves in the rigors of the PICU: Jemma worried in her gut about a possibly imaginary child. "I'm fucking *crazy,*" Jemma said to Vivian, but that had nothing to do with this kid.

She searched randomly, ward by ward, camera always ready, and finally saw him in a research wing of the sixth floor. There were fifteen rooms set aside, down their own special corridor, for patients who were enrolled in clinical trials. The research ward, like the rest of the hospital, was full, nurses continuing to execute the protocols because Dr. Snood insisted on it. It would have been a sort of defeat, to abandon the studies only because the principle investigators had all perished.

After peeking in on the fifteen patients and the two nurses, neither of whom gave her a second look, she turned to leave the ward, and saw him standing at the end of the hall. He made a gesture at her, nothing as simple as a single finger—he kicked out a foot and threw out both hands and twisted his head, but she knew what it meant: *Fuck you*—then fled, too quick for her to get a good picture. All she caught was the end of his leg and his shoe. She looked for a long time on the sixth floor, but could not find him again, not there and not on any of the higher floors, though she hunted slowly and carefully. It was past two when she came to the roof garden. She climbed the sycamore tree and reclined in the lower branches.

The garden was always quiet. Jemma wanted the singing of crickets, but there were no insects, no birds, no spiders or worms, only the grass, flowers and bushes, and the very climbable tree. She lay with the camera in her lap, looking out at the dark water, calm and flat. The moon was not yet up, the sky was full of stars. She looked into her lap at the camera, flipping through its memory to get to the picture of the boy. There was the rash of erythema migrans; some dramatically clubbed fingers that she knew belonged to the pudgy CF boy who had his eye on Cindy Flemm; the tamale lady solemnly presenting her product; Brenda squinting and looking irritated; Rob sleeping; a picture of Vivian and Ishmael. Jemma had run into them on the fourth floor. "Oh, it's the cruise photographer!" Vivian said. "Take our picture, lady." They posed in front of a giant photograph of the lost landscape of Hawaii, blocking out a pair of island children at play in the sand. Vivian grabbed Ishmael around the waist and pulled him tight against her. In the picture they seemed to be standing on dry land, and looked like honeymooners.

Then there was the shoe. Jemma fiddled with the camera controls, isolating and enlarging the view, thinking it might yield some information, but all she saw was the brand and the grime, the worn tread. He was not wearing any socks. She looked up from the camera into the sky.

She half-recognized some of the constellations. Calvin would have known them all, and been able to tell where they were in the world just by looking at them. Dr. Sundae, the pathologist, was an amateur astronomer, but could only say that they were somewhere over Western Europe, and drifting north. Jemma forgot the stars and tried to look past them and pierce with her vision into the black space behind. She held the camera up to the sky, so it was pointing at her, and scrolled through the pictures again, imagining the pixelated light traveling over eternity, into the blackness between and behind the stars, to enter the furious house of God, sending something like Calvin had sent something the night he killed himself.

She imagined for herself a camera with infinite memory, one that held the face of every person dead under the water, wondering if seeing every last face would make her care more about them, or make clear to her the reason that had chased her around the hospital while she was tripping. Her heart had ached in sophomore history at the deep faces of the Civil War dead, but that didn't really relate, or make her a better person, because what she felt had been more a sort of crush on those handsome dead boys, rather than real grief, and anyway that was before her own family had run off, practically hand in hand, into the kingdom of the dead.

She put the camera down and crossed herself. It was the way, she remembered, to open a prayer. She knew how to do it, but only half-wanted to, and she essentially failed at it. She only swiped at herself, making a quick line down her face and chest with the back of her hand. When she was small she did the crispest crossing of anyone she knew. There was a prayer she used to say, something she made up herself when she was seven years old, independent of her brother, a simple, selfish plea to protect and make happy everyone in her family. She could not remember how it went.

"Why, really?" she asked aloud. Vivian had started a list. "It's going to be really long," she'd told Jemma, when they made up over the little drug quarrel. Already she had fifty items arranged in order of increasing egregiousness. Why really, though? Jemma asked herself again. For just a moment she saw her brother in her mind, holding his eyes in one hand and his tongue in the other, and she almost considered how his suicide was a complaint against the world, and how happy it would make him to know everything he hated had been destroyed. For years she had been stealing glances at his burning body, and into the dark holes he'd made of his mouth and eyes, never able to look for more than a moment. Tonight was no exception. She could spend hours treasuring a memory of him alive, but the sight of his body, and the facts of his death, she could not bear for more than a second.

She felt all of a sudden very sleepy—this happened to her on call: she'd be feeling wired and nervous and lie in her call bed staring at the ceiling, and then suddenly realize she was totally exhausted. She was too sleepy now even to cross herself again and close her prayer, something she had always been careful to do when she was a child, because she felt that between the crossings you were open to God in a way that was profound and dangerous, and that if you were to enter into some mundane, profane activity within the crossing, like going to pee, then something very bad would happen to you at least, and probably to everyone you loved, and maybe the whole world.

She slept and experienced a rush of hypnagogic imagery, the sort of fast, weird dreams she had when she fell asleep in class. Once she'd dreamed in biochemistry that a gigantic enzyme had her enmeshed in its quaternary structure and was dissolving her painfully. Now she dreamed of Brenda, pointing at her from within her isolette. Why is she pointing at me? Jemma asked herself, and then asked the child the same question.

After waking briefly, and opening her eyes on a world of green seas and green stars, Jemma turned her face into her shoulder and slept again, deeply this time. She did not notice the warm wind, or the noise of the water, or the moon when it came up, just a sliver of orange light in the eastern sky. She did not notice when the tree shifted in its branches, and seemed to stretch them and part its leaves, presenting her belly-first to the blackness behind the stars.

Jarvis saw it. He wiped his sweaty face, thinking it must be the sweat in his eyes that made the junkie whore seem to glow. When he looked again it had stopped, and she was just another crazy junkie in a tree. He had seen those before, the tree in the courtyard outside his window at home having filled regularly with a few of them every evening. They'd lay along the thick branches, all fucked up, like boneless leopards, talking in such low mellow tones that he could only catch every few words. Hey baby boy, one would say to him, almost every evening, waving languidly. "Fuck off," he'd say, and they'd all laugh at him.

He went very quietly over the grass, not wanting to get too close to her—he still didn't understand why she was always trying to follow him, though he knew that she was somehow dangerous as well as nasty and pathetic—but he wanted the camera. He stopped at every branch as he climbed toward her, listening to her breathe. She snored and said names—Melvin and Snob and Fartin'—all her crack buddies, he was sure. He had to pull on the camera a little to get it out of her hand, but he was less afraid of her waking by then. Something about how much she snored convinced him she was a very deep sleeper, and he almost took her picture when he decided he could just look at his own ass in the mirror if he wanted to see something ugly.

He went home on the fifth path—he'd mapped out twenty-five altogether—and no one saw him the whole way, because he didn't want them to. He saw the creepy molester who had told him over and over in the playground that the big rain was coming and that he better head to the hospital on that night and bring everybody he cared about, even if nobody was sick. Nobody would come. When he pretended to be sick, first with a bad bellyache and then with a headache and then even coughing up ketchup practically into his mother's lap, she only laughed at him, then scolded, and gave him one smart blow across his ass, for tempting God with a feigned illness. "I have to go to the hospital!" he shouted at his mother, and she shouted back that he had to go to bed.

He went anyway, running through the rain, knowing he was doing something unforgivable, but he didn't go back even though he stopped three times and looked toward his house.

The Creep was sitting on the edge of the balcony where the ramp passed the eighth floor, dangling his legs over and staring down at the lobby. One push, Jarvis thought, was all it would take. He had said it, after all, and maybe saying it was what made it happen, and it had all been his plan. That would make him the man who killed Jarvis' mother and his baby sisters and his big brother—everybody gone, everybody dead all at once. He bent down like a sprinter and touched his fingers to the ground, ready to run at him and push him, but in the end he just took his picture and was gone before he could even turn his head when the camera made a beep and a flash.

He saw others. It was always entirely up to him, what he saw and what he didn't, and who saw him, so if he saw the giant fucker they pulled out of the water sucking on that lady's neck—he didn't remember her name but she was cute and he wanted to take her picture but it would have been pornography and he hated that—it was because he wanted to, like he wanted to see the lady at the blood bank doing her work. He was waiting for her to lick one of the big bloody popsicles, but all she ever did was watch them thaw. No one could make him look at shit he didn't want to see, so the whole place was empty of heartbreak, and the ICU was full of empty beds, and nobody looked like his mother, even the gigantic huffing lady who lived with her retarded boy in room 636, and if some lady was crying in the stairs on his way down she didn't make a sound he could hear, and he hardly felt her flesh under his shoe when he stepped on her.

He stopped and waited in the usual place to see if someone was following him, picking up the bottle from where he kept it, ready to brain some motherfucker, but no one was behind him. He was too quick and too quiet for that. He peed and moved on, speaking the code words at the blue pipe and the orange pipe, disabling the booby traps that would have killed him dead. When he got home he ate a candy bar and looked through pictures. "That's my shoe," he said when he saw it, as if she had stolen it.

"Child, child," said the lady in the walls. "Let me comfort you. Let me come to you. Just name me and all will be well. I will gather you up with a hundred arms."

"Fuck off," he said absently. He erased the picture of his foot and took a few furious pictures of his place, feeling like he was making it more his own with every shot. When he'd used up the memory he turned it off, then went around turning off all his flashlights until just the one by his bed was lit up. "Goodnight, God," he said, turning it off, then wishing he hadn't, because he started to make the noise almost as soon as it got dark, the little cough and gag that was like he was trying to throw up, but it was just stupid crying that came, as useless as ever, and though he had promised himself on every other night that he wouldn't he called out for his mother. She might come, after all. That was all it used to take, and all sorts of things could happen, when it was absolutely and totally dark.

When Jemma was four her mother rescinded a ban on birthday parties, instituted just before she was born, when her brother was three. He'd choked on a penny hidden in a cupcake, and turned as blue as the beautiful birthday sky above him. He always had good weather on his birthday.

Worn down not by Jemma's as-yet-unskilled nagging, but by the pressure of the first Severna Forest birthday season, her mother reversed herself. Birthday parties had always happened, but this year the party as adult social event had declared itself unbidden. No one knew where it came from, or who summoned it, exactly—no one could recall which parent was the first to serve daiquiris with the cake, or hire a clown who, after the sitters had come to take the children home, slipped out of her big red shoes and baggy blue overalls to belly dance on the dining-room table. Like other transient Forest institutions, it was as suddenly there as it suddenly would be gone, when people would look back at pictures that captured them trying to fellate the ride-pony and wonder, Have I ever been drunker in my life?

In the supermarket Jemma trailed behind her mother. Her brother rode the front of the cart, his back to their mother, hanging on with his fingers and his heels, his back arched and his chest thrust out, a ship's figurehead, exhorting his captain to go faster and faster, the groceries were all getting away. Jemma followed the white hollows behind her mother's knees, looking away only to watch when men, and some women, turned their heads to watch her mother step crisply down the aisle. That rainy season she often looked naked under her raincoat. She tended to wear short polyester dresses, hems falling at mid-thigh. Her shiny yellow raincoat fell just above her knees. She always wore heels in the rain.

Jemma cowered away from the shelves. Other children, her brother among them, liked to paw at the variety, and worship clutchingly in the candy aisle. Not Jemma; the tall rows of boxes seemed always about to fall on her, and chocolate packaged bigger than her head made her frightened. From within the glass door of the freezers her image beckoned to her, Come in Jemma, come into the cold. Come eat popsicles and be dead with me!

Also, no matter how hard she tried to keep her mother's legs directly in front of her, she often became as lost as she'd been in the museum, an experience never any less traumatic for its frequency. It happened this trip, too. She looked away from the legs for a little longer than usual, at a man with a pointy beard who put out his tongue and waggled it at her mother. When he noticed Jemma waggling her tongue back at him, he made a deft motion, sliding a hundred-and-eighty-degree turn with his cart and hurried away, pushing at double speed. Jemma's mother was nowhere to be found when Jemma turned around, no legs, no body, no shining yellow hat. She turned around again and saw the man's fleet foot disappearing from the aisle, and then she was alone in the vast canyon of breakfast foods. She froze, tears welling in her eyes but not actually crying. She proceeded cautiously in the direction her mother must have gone, sure that a sudden movement would bring that leering cereal vampire leaping from out of the box to poke her with his sharp fingers.

Out of the canyon, she spotted a yellow hat in the produce section. She hurried that way, sighing at the fake thunder that sounded just as a cool mist began to fall on the vegetables. The hat belonged to a lady expressly not her mother. She was old, and without a raincoat, and wore a housedress that swept to her ankles. Her hairy feet were bunched into a pair of wooden sandals. Jemma, running the last few feet toward the hat, a beacon just above a small hill of peaches, almost collided with her. She caught her devouring a peach, gnawing with her two remaining teeth at the dripping flesh, a little puddle of juice between her feet. She saw Jemma looking and mistook her dashed-hope look for admonition. "I was going to pay for it," she said, and stalked off, gnawing and sucking.

Jemma looked up to the hill of peaches and saw how all those in sight had been violated, two evenly spaced holes in each one, the flesh poking raggedly through the skin, and juices leaking all down the pile. She thought, I'll never find my mother, and all the peaches have been murdered, and then she began to cry. Adults descended, as always, as soon as she sent up her signal. "Are you lost?" one asked, as if she could answer them, or needed to. The manager, a familiar face, and almost a friend though he called her Jemima, fetched her and walked her to the front of the store. He was going to let Jemma call for her mother on the public-address system, but just as he put the microphone to her lips she was overcome with her tears again, so it was only her hiccupy little sobs that were broadcast through the store, but that was enough. Her mother came, and Jemma spent the rest of the trip in the cart, among the pounds of flour and sugar and chocolate. Her mother, against the advice of the caterer, was going to make the cake.

They rode home, Jemma with her head against the window, listening to wet-tire noises. Jemma had only rainy birthdays. She'd had a storm as a guest, or a present, on every birthday she could recall, and there was a picture of her unremembered first birthday, Jemma conditioning her hair with cake while lightning flashes in the picture window behind her, a big *National Geographic*-style strike, forks leaping up from the river to a low belly of cloud. After they were home, as her mother mixed batter in a giant rented bowl, Jemma looked out the window, frowning at the gray sky. "Don't fret the rain," her mother told her. "It won't spoil *anything*. Come and help me with the cake."

Her mother gave her a wooden spoon and showed her how to attack the lumps, sweeping them against the side of the bowl and crushing them there. It was fun work, and it calmed her. Jemma forgot about the sky and the rain, captivated by the spiraling motion of her spoon, the furrows in the batter, and the dedicated pursuit of the lump. The great big bowl—the greatest and biggest, her mother said, ever to enter the neighborhood, fetched from a bakery in DC—was set in the middle of the dining-room table. The night previous they'd eaten their dinner around it, plate lips pushed off the table and hovering over their laps, because the bowl hogged so much space. They'd filled it over and over in a dinner game. It was big enough to hold: five hundred eggs, one hundred bottles of beer, a disassembled igloo, the extracted brains of the Senate, this year's take for the East Coast tooth fairy, six months of poop from the average seven-year-old excreter—this last suggested by her brother, and then her mother declared the game (and dinner, already over anyway) effectively ruined. Jemma could reach to stir only by standing on a chair and leaning over. While her mother was greasing the cake tins, Jemma, chasing after lumps she could barely see in batter that was growing as smooth as cream, leaned too far, lost her balance and her chair, and fell in, hands, arms, shoulders, face, and head. She'd leaned so far that she fell in the center, and the heavy bowl did not tip. It was very quiet in the batter. Opening her mouth, she took a nip, and then another, pleased with the taste, then remembered to breathe, and finally started to cough and struggle. Then her mother pulled her out, Jemma's hair whipping in a batter-spattering arc, clutching her to her and administering a few unnecessary abdominal thrusts.

Her mother debated the question of continuing with the party, with herself and with silent Jemma as she bathed her. Jemma and Calvin, expelled in their slickers to fetch another pound of flour from Mr. Duffy's store, left their mother in her thinking position, seated at the dining-room table, among the drying batter, chin on fist, trying to make the serious distinction between omen and accident, to decide between a party the likes of which had not been seen in the world since the last dauphin turned four, or a quiet evening of Chinese food and mere birthday cupcakes. "If it starts to thunder," she called out after them, "you know what to do!"

A dog leaped out, straining on its chain, all mouth and few teeth, but loud. It belonged to the Nottinghams, who lived at the bottom of the hill in a house too small for their big family. The dog was an old Doberman, quite evil-looking in his prime, now palsied and arthritic and always leaking. But he retained, if not his dignity, at least the one trick of lying in wait for pedestrians or cars coming down the hill, and launching himself out of the tall grass to howl, and hurl spittle, and display his speckled gums. When he presented himself to the two children, Calvin, used to him, stood fast, but Jemma fled across the street, not looking right or left, but running at top speed, her arms flung out to each side and her hat trailing by the chin strap, emitting a high, pure shriek. "Hush, puppy," her brother said to the dog, who was still baying, snout split almost in a straight line. He bent at his knees and gathered up some wet earth from the side of the road. Winding up, he hurled it straight between the teeth, hard into the gullet. The dog retired back into the tall grass, to cough, gag, and vomit. "It's okay," her brother called to Jemma, who was watching from the other side of the street. He held his hand out to her, but she would not come. He had to cross to her.

They walked without speaking, and without speaking her brother added two cherry lollipops to the purchase of the flour. They were halfway home again before he started to talk. He took his lollipop out of his mouth with a wet little pop, and held it at arm's length. "I remember when I was four," he said. "That was a good age to be. You're lucky."

"I'm lucky," Jemma agreed, though she did not feel particularly lucky or unlucky.

"Seven is so old. I wish I was four again. That was before I knew."

"Knew what?"

"Oh, things. You don't know. You're too young."

"I am not."

"You're a baby. Lucky baby." He led her off the road to sit in the wet grass and finish their lollipops, candy being generally discouraged by their mother, and forbidden entirely before the cocktail hour when the whole family would indulge in equivalent vices, Mother and Father in their customary pitcher of martinis, Calvin and Jemma in a single piece of thick, hard chocolate or a piece of hard candy bright as a jewel, everyone sipping or gnawing urbanely in the slanting late-afternoon light. "Listen," her brother said to her, knocking his lollipop hard against hers to stimulate her attention. "When you're one you learn to walk. When you're two you learn to talk. When you're three you get out of your crib. When you're four you learn the secret words to command the toilet, to make it come to *you.* When you're five you learn how to whistle. When you're six you learn how to lie. When you're seven you learn that everyone is lying to you."

"Nobody's lying."

"Everybody's lying. Mom and Dad, Mrs. Axelrod, Sister Gertrude, Mr. Duffy..." He pointed back down the road toward the store.

"Stop it."

"I'm lying, too."

"No you're not!" Jemma said, shaking her lollipop, trying to hit his lollipop back, but he flicked it back and forth with his fingers, so she kept missing.

"How would you know? You're too young to tell."

"Shut up!" She connected violently with his lollipop, cracking it and sending a wedge of it flying off, so the candy center lay exposed. Her brother bit in.

"That's the spirit," he said as he chewed, sounding just like their father.

"What?"

"Nothing. Never mind it. Guess what I'm getting you?"

"Who cares," she said, angry at him now.

"You will," he said. "Everybody will. It's only the most important present anybody ever gave anyone. It's only the most important thing that happened ever."

"Can I eat it?" she asked.

"Stupid!" he said, and it happened that there was thunder behind him as he spoke, so she dropped back and sat on the grass and raised her arms in front of her face and cried. "Stupid," he said again, but more gently. "It's only *going,* that's all! Only the most important thing in the world."

"Will I go too?" she asked.

"No," he said. "But just watching me will make you the most special girl in the whole world."

"Will you be able to fly?"

"Certainly," he said.

"Will I be able to fly?"

"Only when you're holding my hand." The thunder rolled again, and he ran off home, dragging her behind him.

"What's the word?" she asked him before they went in the house, as he wiped the candy stains from around her lips.

"What word?"

"For the toilet. I want to know."

"Oh. That." He took her hands and looked at her seriously. "Only the toilet can tell you."

The party was not canceled. Their mother decided Jemma in the batter had been only Jemma in the batter, and not compassionate fate speaking warning of a greater disaster coming. The perfect rise of the cake in its composite pans, and the way the great J took perfect shape out of the four parts, was a further affirmation, and she welcomed into the house her children, husband, the caterers, the moonwalk technicians—everyone but the clown—with ever-increasing exuberance.

Jemma spent the afternoon in the bathroom, in her new underwear and new shoes, waiting for the toilet to speak. It was one of the chief tortures of her life, waking at night with a full bladder, and facing the choice of having an essentially deliberate accident, or venturing from bed into the dark hall and walking the miles and miles down the telescoping corridor to the green night-light in the bathroom, always so certain that indescribable horror lay on the other side of the door. How perfect, then, and how right, that the toilet should come to her. She'd speak the word into the dark, and it would go whispering out the door and down the hall while she lay safe in bed. The toilet would come thumping down the hall, and nudge the door open like a dog, and sidle up to her bed, the lid rising silently in friendly salute.

"Speak!" she said, again and again, and "I am four today!" but Monsieur Toilet was silent. Her mother had named him that, during Jemma's vividly remembered toilet-training days. She'd had a fear of him, of being consumed—he was so big, and made such an awful noise, and after the last gasp of the flush the old pipes would moan horribly. Jemma's mother found a kit in a store, a big plastic smile, flat, friendly blue eyes, a big nose that she thought looked French. A beret from her own collection completed the disguise. Jemma fell in love, or at least into a deep, abiding friendship with the smiling eyes and the unchanging grin. When her mother saw her dancing, Jemma aware that she had to poop but unable to understand it, or how to address it, she would call out in an accented cartoon voice, "O, Jzemma, I am so ongree, so very ongree!"

The face and beret were gone now; he was just a green toilet full of clear green water redolent of fake pine. But Jemma still thought of him as a friend, so it was with a particularly heavy heart that she finally gave up and went back to her room to get into her party dress. She pulled it over her head and went looking for her mother to do up the back. She found her in the basement, overseeing installation of the moonwalk. The rain was increasing when the men tried to inflate it in the side yard. Jemma's mother threw open the storm doors and beckoned them inside. She was still convincing them to bring the thing in when Jemma found her.

The air pump ran off a little gas engine, but their scenarios of carbon-monoxide poisoning did not discourage Jemma's mother. "Look around you, gentlemen. Isn't this room just full of windows? Vent! Vent your hose!" She even helped, a little, with the assembly, though it went against her principles even to twitch a finger in support of a deliveryman. She kicked a screen out of a bottom window, and shoved a hosepipe through. With smudged fingers she buttoned up Jemma's dress and braided her hair while the castle-shaped moonwalk rose in the eastern half of the room to press and stoop against the ceiling, its highest towers bent perpendicular against white stucco.

"So lovely," her mother said, turning Jemma around to appraise her. She stared at Jemma dreamily for a few moments, then started from her reverie with a cry, announcing the time. She was still wearing her shopping dress.

Her hands were filthy, her hair matted in places with batter, and a thin layer of flour over her face made her look like a corpse. She rushed upstairs, tailed by Jemma. Layer by layer she put on her party clothes and her party face, breaking between steps to finish the preparations. So she admitted the caterers with only half of her pair of eyebrows drawn, and only one set of eyelashes in place; squeezed out a bouquet of white, yellow, and red roses onto the cake in her slip with hair teased high into horns. She passed through many frightening incarnations on her way to the final beauty. It was hard to reconcile the end product, a smooth, pink look only slightly too studied to be natural, with all the stops along the way: Minnie Mouse, Cruella DeVil, Mr. Heat Miser.

The house was similarly transformed in steps into a party palace. A white tent rose in the front yard, sheltering a half-dozen tables draped in white with centerpieces of orange flowers surrounding a candle that would not stay lit because of the wet wind. A band set up on the porch, a plastic parquet dance floor unfolding in squares in front of them as they tuned their instruments. The dining-room table grew to twice its real length, extensions hidden under a pool-sized expanse of tablecloth. Serving stations popped up in the corners of the living room. A bar appeared in the wide hall, complete with a giant silver mirror that Jemma compulsively smudged with her fingers before it was lifted into place. A puppet theater rose on the other side of the basement from the moonwalk. Jemma watched the puppets rehearsing—up to four of them operated at once by a woman who could braid hair with her feet—a princess and a dragon, a knight and a witch, all throwing out their arms and singing "Do, Re, Mi, Fa, So, La."

By the time Jemma was trying unsuccessfully to zip up her mother's dress, the clown had arrived. He drove up in a yellow Volkswagen big enough to hold fifty clowns. Jemma watched him emerge from the car, first the requisite big red shoe, distinguished with a coontail at the heel, then hair the very same cornflower blue as her dress, eyes ringed in bruisy purple and green, a hooked nose like a dangling chili that hung straight across the huge lips, painted in a despairing frown. His thin neck, chalk white, disappeared into a Mad-Hatter collar, green on top of an orange shirt. His red frock coat had tails as long as a wedding train; five feet after his bottom they ended in motorized-ferret tail-bearers that chased after him and made figure eights. Green pedal pushers vanished into socks of every color, half the spectrum on the left foot, half on the right. Last to emerge was the other shoe, a surprise black. He removed two giant valises from under the hood of the car and came high-stepping up the walk, revealing under that black shoe the painted image of a squashed kitty.

"Jesus Christ," her mother said.

"I told you," said Calvin, watching with them at the window. He hated clowns, and had lobbied hard against summoning one to this party. He was making gestures through the window at him, shaking his fist as if to cast paper, rock, or scissors, but instead flashing strange finger symbols, and muttering under his breath, but Jemma was close enough to hear. "Adonai! Father strike him *down!*"

"The clown is here!" their father said, coming up behind them and putting a hand on Jemma's shoulder. "It's your birthday clown!"

"What were you thinking?" their mother asked their father. "Where did you get that thing? Weren't there any normal clowns?"

"What?" their father asked, looking genuinely perplexed. "Funny hair, funny nose, great big shoes. It's not a pony, is it?"

"It's scaring me already," said their mother. It had almost arrived at the doorstep when it suddenly dropped its bags and did a sort of disco move, pointing down at the ground and then sweeping arm, hand, and finger up in an arc to point straight up at the sky. Then it fell back onto the thick wet grass, the softest lawn on the hill, and began to shake violently. "Oh God, is it having a seizure?" their mother asked, and then answered her own question. "It's having a seizure!" Their father rushed out, joined shortly by their Uncle Ned, not a real uncle but a friend and colleague of their father. A crowd gathered, puppet lady and moonwalk techs and bartender and servers all in a semicircle, some asking aloud if this was part of the act, because it wasn't very funny. "Why did you get an epileptic clown?" their mother asked, brandishing the sterling cake cutter she'd confiscated from a well-meaning but ignorant teenager, who would later be carving out the roast, before he could shove it into the big, sad mouth.

"Like I was supposed to know? Like, what, the ones with blue hair seize on rainy days?"

"Stay calm, everybody," said Uncle Ned. "The clown's going to be fine." He was removing the trembling shoes, for reasons that did not become apparent until after the ambulance had come and gone, carting the clown away down the south side of the hill just as the first guests were beginning to arrive up the north side. A trauma surgeon, he was cool in a crisis, and used to being the only person who knew what to do. Just as Jemma's mother was most keenly lamenting both the arrival of the clown and its departure, and

Jemma's father was leaving another message with the answering service at the clown agency, Uncle Ned appeared in the shoes, having plundered from the valises and the Volkswagen a traditional round nose, a rainbow afro, and a pair of hairy yellow overalls. "Hey kids!" he said in his sharp, commanding voice, not the least bit goofy and not even particularly friendly.

"I got him," Calvin said to Jemma as they watched the guests arrive. "Did you see it? I got him." For the rest of the night he would try to cast seizures at various adults and children and fail, but never accept that his gesturing fingers had only been coincidentally related to the clown's affliction.

Along with last-minute lessons in extracting a foreign body from a choking victim, and instruction on how to throw herself, belly-first, against the edge of the couch in case she found herself choking in an empty room, Jemma's mother demonstrated demure postures for Jemma to assume during the party. Her mother, who'd been celebrated herself at parties as a child, said, "You must be in the party but not of the party. Everything will revolve around you, but you mustn't be frightened when strange people want to hug you, or take your picture while you open a present." Jemma listened, nodded dutifully; she was obedient, not like her brother, and tried at that age to do good as she understood it. She tried to pose demurely at her mother's side, receiving the guests. She tried not to loll her tongue out droolingly at the pile of presents she wanted so desperately, not to open, but to climb. She tried not to think about the cake, as big as her whole body, a great J, or the colored cream roses, and how she wanted to make it clear to every person that walked in the door that as birthday girl she had every right to the most rose-afflicted piece of that cake, that if she wanted to she could eat a piece that was all icing and no flesh. She tried not to think of the moonwalk beckoning from downstairs, inviting her to muss her hair, wrinkle her dress, bounce from her knees to her feet to her knees again. She was demure for less than ten minutes.

That was long enough. Her mother had been edging them toward the dance floor as the last guests arrived; at a certain distance it simply sucked her in. "In the party, but not of it," she whispered to Jemma as a walrusy man swept her onto the porch. Seconds later, Jemma was shoeless in the moonwalk, and of it, bouncing on feet, hands, knees, bottom, head, in a turbulent sea of kids. Her socks dropped in twin bunches to the lowest portion of her ankles. She lost her hair ribbon and her hair frizzed up.

Still shoeless, she watched the puppet show, an interpretation of Hansel and Gretel, delightful for the real candy house that came leaning out of the theater on a long stick, swaying back and forth to be attacked by the audience, the roof shingled with jelly beans meant to picked off at every performance. The witch gave an extended monologue, an apologia for witches, who she maintained were much misunderstood. It was an ovenless show; at the end the children and the witch danced swayingly together and sang an ode to the goddess while a dragon swung above them in a dental-floss harness. The puppets bowed to silence, and there was no applause until the house came leaning out for an encore sweep.

Uncle Ned, less skilled but more traditional than the puppet lady, went over better. He walked unconvincingly against the wind, strummed tunelessly on a ukulele and sang "Camptown Races," flinging out chorus-girl kicks with every doo-dah, and made huffy, buzzing noises with five kazoos stuck in his mouth, all these efforts received rather coldly. But his balloon animals endeared him to the crowd. He twisted and bent them at random, proclaiming the abstract shapes giraffe, camel, cheetah, aardvark, platypus. He offered up a bonobo, but there were no takers, not even Jemma or her brother. "It's just a *thing,*" said a little redheaded girl, who Jemma was quite sure she'd never seen before in her life, of the foot-long, U-shaped chain of balloon sausage. She folded her arms across her spectacular party dress, fancier than Jemma's, and noticed obsessively by Jemma's mother, who would ask if this was not like showing up at a wedding in a dress fancier than the bride's.

"Oh," said Uncle Ned, clutching the sausage to his chest. "You've caught me. Clever as a pony, aren't you? Well, tain't no bonobo, certainly. Tain't no chimp or ape. It is not an orangutan. Neither is it a potato, a piranha, or persnickety Penelope Poekelman, my first wife. What this is, Suzy... is that your name? Well, it's a good name, and it would suit you fine. Suzy, what I'm holding here in my hands, what I'll now bring closer to you, closer now, soon it will be touching you, is an exactly-to-scale model of a drippy, stinky, slimy little-girl... intestine!" The redhead screamed, the children cheered. "They're full of poop," Uncle Ned added unnecessarily. He sang as he worked, and no child went home that night without a string of intestines to hang around his neck.

More than she ate, Jemma looked at the food, and watched people eating. She plucked a dozen Vienna sausages from off their little beds of prosciutto and crostini and stuffed them one after another into her mouth, crouched behind the biggest couch in the living room, chewing and swallowing in a frenzy, and then she was done feasting. She was very fond of gray meats, Vienna sausages in particular, but number twelve, halfway eaten, became a chore to finish, and she felt a little sick after she had swallowed it down. There was yet room for cake, but she no longer wished to curve her hand into a paw and scoop icing into her mouth. She walked around, looking for her brother, who was running wild with the older set, the eight-, nine-, and ten-year-olds who were dashing up and down the stairs, drawing shouts of "Whoa!" and "Slow down there!" from the adults they grazed. She did not find him, and almost forgot she was looking, her attention was drawn so irresistibly to the open mouths and the small, beautiful arrangements of food that went into them. She'd pause close by them, under the very shadow of the longest chins, and look up at them till they noticed her, and mostly they would mistake her interest in their eating for interest in their food, and offer her a bite, or stuff hastily and then show her empty hands. But she'd scoot away as soon as the eating was done. She saw a lady eat a cracker piled high with black caviar; they broke against her lips, most consumed, some sticking under her nose in a thin mustache, some bouncing off her chin to fall and scatter on the wood floor like pearls off the string. She saw a man consolidate tiny portions of beef tartar into his hand, dumping them out of little mango boats into his palm; when he had a mound the size of a tennis ball he bit into it, gobbling it all down in one rapid fress and then licking his palm like a fond dog. She saw a lady do her same Vienna-sausage trick. She saw her father take two giant shrimp, pink and wet from the biggest shrimp cocktail in Severna Forest history, four-dozen jumbo shrimp, an entire head of lettuce, and a liter of cocktail sauce all arranged among ice in the very same bowl Jemma had toppled into earlier that day. He stuffed them into his mouth, head-first, so the tail hung out in fangs from his lips. He dropped to his knees and growled, friendly and ferocious, at Jemma. She ran away.

She danced in contracting circles around the central table, closer and closer through the crowd until she stood with her eyes level with the edge of the hook in the J. A pink rose as big as her mouth was within reach, but before she could smudge it away her brother collided with her.

"Time to open the presents," he said, grabbing her hand. His hair, like hers, was characteristically ahoo, sticking up in sweaty horns from dozens of places. He drew her toward the present pile, but halfway there her mother seized her other hand.

"Time to blow out the candles!" she said.

"Time to open the *presents,*" her brother insisted, tugging, so Jemma's arms opened at the elbows and she was suspended between them.

"Who's calling the shots here?" her mother asked. She gave one sharp pull and Jemma's sweaty hand popped free of her brother's sweaty hand. There were four rose-shaped candles, spaced close together in a little thicket midway up the body of the J. As they were lit someone turned down the lights. All over the room cameras were cocked and raised. Jemma leaned forward over the cake, not averse to falling into it. She knew it would be so soft. But her parents had her firmly by the arms. They leaned her over the candles after the song. She blew wetly on their count of three, her fierce concentration on the task of extinguishing every candle rewarded with success, but realizing too late she'd been so single-minded she'd forgotten to make the wish. She cut the first piece of cake, her mother's hand over her own, wielding the silver knife, her mother's strength smoothing Jemma's stabbing motions into a straight line. Then she was carried, reaching back for cake, to the foot of the hill of presents.

Her brother mined the mountain, passing boxes, flats, and lumpy ovals to her, running his hand over half the presents before selecting the next to be opened. Jemma oscillated between states of fierce concentration on the unwrapping (no ripper, she did it with care and precision beyond her years, and with respect for every little square of transparent tape) and utter cake-distraction; she could hear, beyond the circle of witnesses around her, exclamations over the quality of the cake, compliments to her mother who, when asked for her baking secret, said that the cake had been flavored with sweet clumsy child. Some of the witnesses had cake and were eating it as they watched her. Some went back for seconds and thirds before she was done with all the opening. She smiled dutifully over the presents, the bionic-woman dolls, the extensive bionic-woman wardrobe, the fembot beauty head whose face you could paint with makeup before you removed it to reveal the two-dimensional circuit board underneath. Jemma did not understand exactly what it meant to be bionic, and her brother would play with the dolls more than she would. Her favorite gifts were a pogo stick, a hula hoop, a saxophone that blew soap bubbles, and a pair of big tough yellow punching balloons. Jemma attached them to both her hands, trying and failing to punch them at the same time and feeling unaccountably mighty.

Sitters had infiltrated the crowd of witnesses long before the mountain was leveled. As soon as the last present was opened and murmured over, they began to whisk the children away to the homes where their parents would not return until after midnight. In the confusion of goodbye kisses and sometimes clutching, tearful hugs, no one heard Jemma's complaint that she'd eaten no cake. On her way to bed she saw the ugly, decimated cake board, empty except for random smears of icing and a few crumbs. Her father mistook her crying for sadness at the end of the party. He hugged her and rocked her as he carried her up the stairs, acknowledging how sad it was that a party had to end, but what could you do about it? He did not understand the problem until Jemma was in her pajamas, teeth brushed and head on her pillow. "We'll get you a new cake tomorrow," he promised her, a whole cake just for herself. He would tie up her mother and Calvin, and lastly himself, and they would all be her observant prisoners as she ate the whole thing. It made her feel no better. She didn't like the thought of people being tied up, and tomorrow was a thousand years away. Her father sang her a song, and put on a stuffed-animal play for her, but these did nothing to comfort her, for no matter what words her father sang, or what words the animals spoke, every song was a song of cake, and every utterance was in praise of cake, or a lament for cake lost.

When she had stopped crying, her father thought she had fallen asleep. He went back to the party, which by now had put away or transformed all its childish things; the puppet master was interpreting Ionesco; Uncle Ned was smooching a caterer in the basement bathroom; a thin layer of reefer smoke had gathered against the roof of the moonwalk, where there was no more jumping, only lying about in the mellow reduced gravity. For a little while Jemma was quiet, but no less agitated. Many times before she'd drifted off to the noise of a party below her. It usually made her feel comfortable and safe, the noise of voices speaking words she could not make out, the distant music; but not tonight. Instead of sleep came worse misery, a more acute sense of absence of cake in her evening, the thought of the one nip of batter she'd taken a tease and a torture. Worse yet, she suddenly had to pee. She began to weep again, and called out to Monsieur Toilet, asking him please, please come, and to bring cake.

It seemed like forever before her brother came back to her. Forever she was alone and despondent in her pee, cursing her party, her presents, her four years, cursing everything but her lost cake. It was even forever that the candle-glow proceeded him, and flickered in her door, puzzling her. Understanding dawned forever; it took forever to make the transition from rock-bottom despair to topgallant delight, to see the piece of cake her brother was bringing to her.

To any eye but hers it would have appeared ugly. A side piece, with hardly a rose petal on it, half eaten by someone who had lacked a fork or been too excited to bother with one, it was marred with tooth marks, and lipstick stained the eaten edges of the white icing. A cigarette hole stood out plainly next to the candle.

"Follow me," he said. "It's time for your present." He turned and marched solemnly out of the room. She thought he would take her downstairs, and didn't even remember about the going until they got to his room. There were more candles burning there, stolen birthday candles stuck in upside-down styrofoam cups. There were six of them in an open circle, which, after he had entered it, Calvin closed with the cake.

"What are you doing?" she asked him.

"What does it look like? I'm getting ready to go. What? Why are you crying?"

"I don't want you to go."

"Sure you do."

"I don't want you to. I *like* you."

"That doesn't have anything to do with it. You'll like me better, after I've gone."

"But I'm scared."

"Good. It's scary. Going is scary. Important things are scary. But it has to happen. You'll see. You'll understand. Are you ready?"

"No!"

"Are you *ready*?" The flickering candles made his frown look like a monster face.

"Okay."

"All right then," he said, pulling their father's straight razor from his pocket. "Here we go. All you have to do is close your eyes and think, Let him go, let him go, let him go. Do it now. You have to say it eleven times slowly, one for every year you are and one for every year I am. Do you understand?"

"Can I have some of my cake?"

"Not yet. But after I go I'll be able to touch things and turn them to cake. Ready?"

"Ready." She closed her eyes and started, trying to say it just in her head but the words spilled out of her mind and she heard herself whispering, "Let him go, let him go." And she added "Jesus please let him go" because she thought that was who would be in charge of such a request.

"Good," he said. "Keep going. Don't open your eyes."

And she wouldn't have, except that he said not to. So she saw him cutting carefully on his chest, one long line from his shoulder to his hip, and now another on the other side, and she ran from the room, screaming as loud as she could, straight down the hall and down the stairs, and into the middle of the party that had used to be her party. She stood in a circle of her parents' friends, screaming and screaming until her father picked her up and muffled her mouth with his shoulder.

"Good God, Jemma," he said. "What's wrong?"

"She had a nightmare," Calvin said. His shirt was on and he looked like nothing unusual at all had happened. And he was looking at her, his eye to her eye, and she was sure that she heard him speak then without moving his lips. *Don't tell.*

"I won't," she said to him.

"Won't what?" her father said.

"Get any cake," she said.

"It seems to me that somebody's had too much cake," her father said, announcing it to everyone, and suddenly they were all laughing at her.

"I'll take her back up," Calvin said. When her father put her down Calvin held out his hand and she took it. He led her up the stairs, one step at a time, and when she saw the candle glow at the end of the hall she thought they would go back to his room. But they went back to hers, instead. Her cake was sitting on her night table, the candle barely still alight.

"Blow it out," he said.

"But the thingie."

"Ruined," he said. She started to cry again. She hadn't ever totally stopped. "Just eat your cake," he said.

"Let's try again," she said. "I won't scream."

"Too late. Now it's not time anymore. Now it's just another night. Now it's just a candle and now they're just cuts and now it's just a cake. You better blow it out or you'll miss your chance for a wish."

She bent her head and struck, remembering to wish this time, wishing as many wishes as she could hold at once in her head: Let it taste as good as it looks, let there be a pony under my bed tomorrow morning, let the toilet speak to me, let the cake never end, let me and him share it all night tonight, and let him never go, not anywhere, not ever.

One thing which ought to animate us to perpetual contest with the devil is that he is everywhere called both our adversary and the adversary of God. For, if the glory of God is dear to us, as it ought to be, we ought to struggle with all our might against him who aims at the extinction of that glory. If we are animated with proper zeal to maintain the kingdom of Christ, we must wage irreconcilable war with him who conspires its ruin. Again, if we have any anxiety about our own salvation, we ought to make no peace nor truce with him who is continually laying schemes for its destruction. But such is the character given to Satan in the third chapter of Genesis, where he is seen seducing man from his allegiance to God, that he may both deprive God of his due honor, and plunge man headlong into destruction. Such, too, is the description given of him in the Gospels, where he is called the enemy and is said to sow tares in order to corrupt the seed of eternal life. In one word, in all his actions we experience the truth of our Savior's description, that he was a "murderer from the beginning, and abode not in the truth." Truth he assails with lies, light he obscures with darkness. The minds of men he involves in error; he stirs up hatred, inflames strife and war, and all in order that he may overthrow the kingdom of God, and drown men in eternal perdition with himself. Hence it is evident that his whole nature is depraved, mischievous, and malignant. There must be extreme depravity in a mind bent on assailing the glory of God and the salvation of man. This is intimated by John in his

Epistle, when he says that he "sinneth from the beginning," implying that he is the author, leader, and contriver of all malice and wickedness. But that's me. I couldn't write a better personal ad myself—depraved, malicious, and malignant seeks same for mysterious purpose. Years and years I spent carping at the ruin of the world—as if innocent fallen creation was oppressing me—never realizing (and I'm supposed to be so smart?) that it was my own ruin, that it all proceeded out from me, all the corruption, all the brokenness, even the lies—I told them myself; I send it all out and it comes back, magnified a thousand times, a punishment for me.

Rob knew it was stupid, to miss someone who was still alive, when so many people were dead. Every day he spent time looking over the water, remembering his sisters and his mother—for ten minutes or twenty minutes or a half an hour he would stare, now and then mumbling a prayer very softly (he was praying *over* the water but didn't want to give the appearance of praying *to* the water, though there were some who were doing that already, people who discovered once the world was drowned that worldwide catastrophe had all their lives been one of their secret desires, and who treated the killing sea like a god) until his pager went off, inevitably, summoning him to a phone or back to the unit. He never went more than a couple of hours without whispering a name, Gillian or Malinda or Gwen—the last his mother's name, which he had never spoken while she was alive. He thought of them on the hour, but he didn't pine for them like he did for Jemma.

Most of the time she was only three floors away, but it felt like she was on another continent, and if they happened to be apart for a whole twelve-hour shift, he grew sadder and sadder by the hour. He learned the difference between sadness and grief that way, missing his girlfriend and missing his family—it hurt in different places. Missing his mother and his sisters was a dull ache—he would never get used to it, but he was already living with it. Everybody was already living with that. But he felt Jemma's absence more acutely, a sharp pain in the bones of his chest that, when it was raging, would only go away when he pressed her against him.

"I love you," he'd say to her, in some closet or empty conference room or in the cold rooms where they stored the blood. It seemed so much more urgent now, to say it all the time. There was a pressure that rose from way down deep in him, which those words safely vented, and yet more and more that was not enough. He would put his cheek against her ear and say it, and still there would be the pushing from inside, so he'd have to add, "So much," or "More every day," or else just say it again and again, "I love you, I love you, I love you," until she squirmed away.

He was on call in the new combined unit, and little urgencies kept him running up and down the stairs that connected the NICU and the PICU all night long, but when his need was great enough, he slipped away down the hall, telling the nurses he was just running down to the lab to track down some results. He and Jemma had failed to synchronize their call schedules, so she was home sleeping, or just as often sleeplessly wandering the hospital, when he was working. He went in very quietly. The room was dark and she lay quite still on their bed. He meant just to watch her for a while, to touch her would be to wake her, and then he would have to explain what he was doing there. But as soon as he sat down his pager went off. He was as quick as any intern on the draw, his hand flying to his waist to quiet the thing before it had barely peeped, but it was enough to wake her.

"You again," she said, opening her eyes and then closing them again. She turned and put an arm across his lap.

"Sorry," he said. "Didn't mean to wake you."

"Tell that fucking nurse I said to shove a preemie up her ass."

"They're being nice tonight."

"Huh. Must be a full moon. What are you doing here?

"Nothing." She was quiet again, and he was sure she had fallen asleep, and so he said, "Hey… hey… I…" But her hand shot up to silence him, quicker than he had silenced his pager.

"Don't say it," she said.

Down the hall and up two stories, Vivian and Ishmael were sitting chastely on the edge of her bed.

"You're special," he said.

"Not like you. Only one of you in the whole hospital."

"I don't feel very special," he said. "Not in a good way, anyway. I just feel weird. Didn't you see everybody looking at me?"

"Of course. You're famous."

"Who is that guy? What's he doing here? Why did he live, instead of my brother?"

"Maybe they're glad to see you. Glad that somebody else made it."

"Or instead of my father. Or instead of my uncle."

"Maybe you are somebody's uncle. You haven't met everybody yet, have you?"

"Why did *he* deserve to live?"

"I think we're all wondering that," Vivian said. "Each of us about everybody else, and each of us about ourselves. And maybe we deserve it like people deserve a punishment, you know? Maybe it's not even a reward, to be bottled up here. Maybe somebody somewhere else is on the good ship."

"Sorry to be sad. I didn't mean to bring you down. I was having such a good time, until just now."

"Me too. I still am. It's okay. You don't have to be happy all the time. You wouldn't fit in here, if you were. We're all fucking miserable, in case you haven't noticed."

He did not reply, but he took her hand in his, and they sat that way for a little while.

"Guess what?" she said finally.

"What?" he said, turning his face to look at her.

"You're beautiful," she said. Which was not at all what she had meant to say. That wasn't something she was accustomed to saying to men, especially on a date. And when they said it to her, she would say, "I know," a reply which effectively shut down such unprofitable and boring conversation. But Ishmael's face seemed to her unaccountably lovely just then, so sad and so earnest and yet somehow more than perfect in every line, a collection of lovely shapes that added up, just in that moment, that actually made her feel as if her heart was skipping a beat.

"Not like you," he said, and kissed her. They had kissed before, but not like this—as soon as his lips touched hers she knew that they would be having sex within minutes.

"I don't usually get like this," she said to him as she pulled at his shirt, trying to get it over his head, breathless at the prospect of seeing him naked, and thinking for some reason that she wanted to uncover him completely, clothes first, and then the layer of sadness he seemed to have wrapped himself under that evening, and then his very skin, because every covering layer was only hiding a more startling loveliness. She was practiced at sex—sometimes she felt like she'd been doing it forever, but she'd hardly ever been so excited as she was now.

"Me neither," he said. "I mean, I don't think so. Or I do... wait." He put his face in her neck and then dragged it down her body, straight past her breasts and her belly and into her lap, and from down there he spoke again in a muffled voice. "I mean I think you're my first. Oh yes, definitely." And doing it, he said, "I've never done *this* before!"

Dr. Chandra lived next door, but he wasn't listening. The walls weren't thick, but they'd never permit a sound to slip through, though a couple might shout or sing together at the top of their lungs. He was sitting in his bed, which was just as nice as Vivian's bed. He had leaped at one of the new rooms as soon as the angel had announced that they were available. This was the sort of thing he had always missed out on in the old world. He never got the bottom bunk, or the nicer apartment, or won the door prize. And this place was much nicer than anything he'd had in the old world—the big bed and the fancy sheets and the soft thick rug would have been out of his league. He finally lived someplace that had a balcony and a fireplace and a window in the bathroom. But he was hardly ever there, and even when he was, it did not make him happy, or even contented, in the way that he had supposed it would. This was his day off—not really even a day, it was only eighteen hours—and like with all of them he spent it decorating and redecorating, trying to get the place right.

"You just need someone to share it with," the angel told him, because he had just been decorating again and telling her how it was all still not quite right. "Then it would be perfect."

"Shut up," he said, but fondly, because even though she got him in trouble not waking him up in time, and even though he strongly suspected that she was kind to him only because she had to be—because God forced her to be that way or because she was programmed to practice an utterly undiscriminating kindness—he still considered her to be one of his few friends.

"You're a handsome boy," she said. "And you have so much to offer. I can think of a dozen men who would feel blessedly lucky to date you."

"Oh, please," he said. "I do not like these walls. Saffron? Mustard is more like it. I wanted to feel like I was surrounded by Dalai Lamas."

"Would you like to see these men?"

"Hell no," he said. "Show me the paint samples again." She did as she was told, flashing solid blocks of color on the television screen, but faces began to pop up between colors, a nurse from the NICU whose name he did not know, a physical-plant man, totally bald though he couldn't have been older than twenty-five, the big Samoan from the lift team. "Stop that," he said.

"How about this one?" She showed him Jordan Sasscock.

"Oh please," he said. "Totally out of my league, not to mention totally straight."

"Don't be so sure," she said. "Some of us can hear his dreams."

"You're too much." He put a pillow over his face and closed his eyes. "Never mind the paint, just turn out the lights. I'm going to sit here and suffocate."

"Let me help you dream, then. Just while you're waiting for that special person."

"None of that," he said. But after she turned off the lights he took away the pillow, and he didn't object when she started to show him pictures of an imaginary date, and an imaginary life, and imaginary comforts. Until he fell asleep he watched a slideshow, pictures of him and Jordan Sasscock on some kind of in-hospital vacation, at a fancy dinner in some dark room, walking close to each other on the roof, both of them too discreet to hold hands and yet in picture after picture Jordan was punching him affectionately on the shoulder. He would not look when she showed them in bed, except at the end, when he lay with his head on Jordan's chest, both of them sound asleep, their faces slack and puffy, bathed in morning sun from the window on the balcony.

"Behold your happiness," the angel said, "and do not cry."

Jemma conducted a census of her own, not of numbers but of types. Others, thinking, like everybody did, of the precedent, asked themselves, where were the animals? They looked out the windows into the empty ocean and some asked the angel, What was the crime of the panda, that it should be eradicated? All she would say was that they were preserved, leading to speculation that this meant they were preserved in the mind of God, or that they were preserved in a deep, airtight cave under the ocean, or that somewhere out there on the sea another hospital was floating, twin to this one in every way except that it was stuffed full of ailing and well pandas. The precedent was in Jemma's mind also, though not because it brought to mind the innumerable animals drowning in innocent pairs. She found herself thinking in twos as she looked at her fellow survivors. Among the children it was obvious that of even the most obscure illnesses two had been preserved—there were a pair of Pfeiffer syndromes, a pair of intestinal lymphangiectasias, a pair of lymphocyte-adhesion deficiencies; only Brenda, it seemed, was totally unique in her affliction. That this should happen in a place that had a whole ward devoted solely to the problem of hypoglycemia was not entirely strange. But Jemma looked further to see other pairs: a stylish nurse, the one with the great big ass, who inhabited the sixth floor had a twin in the PICU who wore the very same pair of rhinestone-encrusted granny glasses. There was a civilian Dr. Snood, father to one of the NICU babies; both men had the same blue eyes, looked down the same proud nose at people in the very same way, had the same leathery skin and the same awful hair. There was a pale girl in the cafeteria, a little big, with bleached hair and large brown eyes who could have been twin to Jemma before she died her hair red. These cases were superficial and obvious, and probably, Jemma thought, meant nothing. She wanted deeper pairings; not necessarily romantic, but fateful. Like would will to like and execute a destiny together.

Those pairs were harder to find. She liked to think, sometimes, that she and Rob made one, and that Vivian and Ishmael might soon represent another, and that Dr. Snood and Dr. Tiller were somehow yin and yang and fuss and budget to each other, and when they came together would make something perfect and prim and utterly unbearable, and that Father Jane and John Grampus could do great things together, despite their mutual disdain for the opposite sex and the fact that Grampus was sort of dating the angel. But the angel seemed to be dating everybody, and lately Jemma had seen John Grampus wearing a new hangdog look.

The hospital was organizing itself, anyway, in ways not formally declared by the Committee or by a principle of pairs. There were the old distinctions and the old hierarchy of ascending power and descending subservience: student, intern, resident, fellow, attending. There was a greater chain, harder to describe, and a little more fluid—Zini could make Dr. Chandra lick her shoe but Dr. Snood could probably make her grovel if he tried hard enough. A lab tech was superior, somehow, to a janitor, and the man from the physical plant was owed deference from the cafeteria workers. Volunteers were for anybody to order around, provided they spoke to them respectfully, mindful of their age and their altruism; nursing assistants were treated like dirty whores—no job was too low for them. Only the tamale lady seemed to soar free of classification, empowered, Jemma thought, by her itinerant status and the fact that she was not an official employee, and by the supreme deliciousness of her tamales—they were a sort of power, and the angel could not reproduce their subtleties of flavor. Even the parents were bound, only the most difficult ones resisting treatments now, with almost every child sicker than they'd ever been before. You could argue these distinctions, or declare them overturned in Committee meetings convened in a spirit of overwhelming generosity, but as long as the children were sick and the hospital was a hospital, they held.

Every attending had their own demesne, determined by geography and specialty. Dr. Walnut, the only surviving surgeon, reigned on the second floor with Dr. Wood, the anesthesia attending. Dr. Snood ruled the sixth floor. Dr.

Pudding held court in the dim chambers of radiology on the third floor, splitting his territory with Dr. Sundae, who, as the last pathologist in the world, had assumed control of the clinical lab. Dr. Grouse, the master of the NICU, was famously laid-back, but he had Emma, a lady whose soft bouncy curls belied her no-nonsense attitude, to be his terrible enforcer. The seventh-floor subspecialty units were under the command of Dr. Topper, a touchy nephrologist. Dr. Sashay, the oncology attending, ruled on the eighth. Dr. Mim, the ER attending, deprived of subjects when the last of her patients were transferred upstairs the day after the storm, went up to the ninth floor, where she oversaw management of the increasingly acute issues developing in the rehab patients when she wasn't splitting call in the PICU with Dr. Tiller, who was queen there. Nine of them altogether, they each had their fellows—except for Dr. Grouse and Dr. Tiller, who had to share Emma—and a team of residents and interns and students to cater to their every professional whim.

Sometimes Jemma daydreamed of traveling to other teams like she used to daydream of traveling to other countries, so she thought her days might pass more pleasantly in the NICU like she used to think she would be prettier in Paris, or that people might have been more tolerant of her generous thighs in Quito or Buenos Aires. But she was stuck fast under Dr. Snood's thumb, and rounds seemed perpetual. She had had the sense before the Thing, in the middle of her long, early mornings, that she had always been doing this, trudging from room to room gathering bad news, and that she would always be doing it. But she would go home, eventually, and look back and forward into that purgatory with the feeling that she was suspended between eternities. Now, though, in a hospital in the middle of the ocean, a place that every available clue indicated was the extent of the extant world, what before had only seemed, now actually was. Jemma would never go home. The children would never go home. Forever and forever Dr. Snood would roll his eyes at her from under his eternal caterpillar brows.

At least some of her patients were finally getting a little better. Ella Thims was off her hypertensive patch and tolerating three whole milliliters an hour of formula feeding through her little gastric button. Cindy Flemm had not vomited for five days, and had actually been seen out of bed, walking hand in hand around the sixth floor with Wayne, the boy who looked too fat to have CF. Kidney's constipation had resolved and only the eldest sister, Jesus, seemed to resent Jemma's early-morning visits anymore. Pickie Beecher was unchanged, however, his affect still flat, his mind still crazed, his shit still black. She knew he must still be sipping from blood packs, though no one had caught him again with one, and Thelma swore there was no way he could be leaving the floor to snack at the blood bank. "Your poop betrays you," she said to him when he swore that he drank only juices.

"Good morning!" he said from under his bed, when Jemma had rounded on him that morning. "Happy anniversary!"

"Come out from under there immediately," she said firmly. She'd instituted a policy with him, or thought she had. She was not intimidated anymore by his hiding under the bed, or the strange hissing, deflating noise he sometimes made, or his hanging from the ceiling, or standing on his head in the window. It was Thelma who showed her the way. "You show him who's boss," she told her. "Have you ever ridden a horse? It's just like horses. He can smell your fear, and if you give him an inch he'll be all over you. All over you!" And she had slapped Jemma gently all over her back and belly, as if Jemma needed help understanding what was meant by all over a body.

"Good morning," she said to him, once he was sitting on his bed. "What's the anniversary?"

"You visited me forty days ago exactly."

"I thought you hardly noticed the passing of days."

"Mostly not," he said. "But sometimes."

"Shirt up," she said. He exposed his thin pale chest for her to auscultate. His exam was as normal as it always was. "Perfectly clear," she said. She always made sure to tell him how healthy he was in his body.

"Will you walk with me to the window?" he asked her.

"All that way?" He stood up and raised his hand to her. He walked her slowly around the bed to the window, placing his steps as carefully as a drunk. The sun wasn't up yet, but a gray light was on the perfectly calm water. Pickie pointed up into the blank gray sky and said, "My brother is absent from there, and from there, and from there." He pointed at the horizon, and down at the water.

"Mine too," Jemma said, and tried again to get him to talk more specifically about his brother, in her flailing, junior-junior-psychiatrist way, thinking that it might be a first step toward his recovery, since the antipsychotics and antidepressants and alpha-agonists and anxiolytics seemed not to make any difference at all in how he acted, to get him to talk in real terms about his lost brother. She was always imagining the scene: Pickie witnessing the drive-by, or the lingering toxic death from leukemia, or his crazy mother beating his older brother with a sack full of oranges, or even Pickie himself, carelessly playing with a loaded pistol, staring at his brother's brains after he'd sprayed them all over the wall, and losing his mind in an instant. It was crude, and probably stupid, to think that she could break him open and let all the poison and craziness in him leak out, but no one else had any other ideas. Dr. Snood kept insisting they try new and different combinations of medications—he had taken it upon himself to try to fill the shoes of the lost psychiatrists, poring over the literature preserved in the hospital computer, ruled by the hour by some new study he transiently admired. Pickie and the anorexics and the three other psych patients took every new intervention calmly, but still ate their blood or found secret places to vomit—all of them, Jemma suspected, assisted by the angel in perpetuating their sickness. It had become obvious that she would help anybody do anything, as long as it didn't directly harm another person. She was the sort of personality who said you were her favorite, or her best friend, and then went and said that to everybody she knew.

Pickie would only talk of his brother's thousand eyes and hundred hands. "But what was his name?" Jemma asked, a question she'd asked many times before.

"He was my brother," Pickie said, the same old answer. "Now he is dead, and there is no good in anything, and I must live on forever to witness all the wrongness. Every wrong thing arises from the death of brothers, and every wrong thing has come from my brother's death. Oh! Oh! Oh!"

He knocked his head against the glass. Jemma said nothing—that week they were trying to extinguish all his bad behaviors by ignoring them—but she reached and patted him dexterously on the head, knowing it might be interpreted as an encouragement, but unable to just leave him alone banging his head, though he wasn't doing it very hard, more a vigorous tap than a really hard bang. She patted him until he stopped, but refused to sing him a song, when he asked, because she was getting late already, and her next patient was a time sucker.

She went down to room 636, occupied by an eleven-year-old boy with cerebral palsy and developmental delay named Tiresias Dufresne. Gorked on the surface, unable to walk, or speak, he nevertheless had a lot going on inside his head. He had a special headset, lost in the flood, that had allowed him to communicate by fixing his eyes on letters and words on a computer screen. Attempts to replicate it had not satisfied him. His vocoder had never said a bad word about anybody, but his mother, popularly known on the ward as "that fucking bitch," six feet tall and weighing as much as three average-sized medical students, was the apotheosis of the hospital mom. In the first weeks of her pediatric rotation Jemma had observed another hierarchy: spineless parents with noodle-supple wills were "sweeties"; parents who wanted everything explained in detail before consenting to a procedure or intervention were "a little difficult"; those who actually refused procedures or interventions became frankly "difficult"; those who habitually refused interventions or dictated treatment based on their own past experience entered the continuum of "crazy," at whose far end Ms. Dufresne reigned unquestioned.

"Just do whatever she tells you to do," was the advice Dr. Chandra gave Jemma when she met Ms. Dufresne for the first time. "If she starts getting angry, it's okay to run away. And don't cry in front of her; it just makes her more mad."

"Good morning!" Jemma called as she entered the room. Ms. Dufresne was an armoire-sized shadow in her chair at the window. Tir was moving restlessly in his bed, flexing and extending his arms and legs as if he were trying to swim within the space confined by the blue mesh tent that hooked to his bedrails and kept him from falling to the floor.

"Hello dear," said Ms. Dufresne quietly. Jemma had gotten along with her pretty well so far, but she had already learned how fine was the line between "dear" and "motherfucker." Still, she was used to being abused, and somehow she preferred the motherly rage of Ms. Dufresne to the exquisite smarminess of Dr. Snood. It helped, somehow, to think that it was fierce love for her gorky, twitchy boy that made Ms. Dufresne thunder, and stomp her feet, and wave her fists in the air just before your face, and threaten to pull your tongue out through your ass.

"How is he?" Jemma asked, aware of her mistake as she made it.

"Why don't you ask him? You know he can talk to you." Ms. Dufresne's breathing became a little heavier. She didn't like to interpret for lazy motherfuckers who couldn't be bothered to make the effort to speak to her son.

"Sorry!" Jemma said brightly. "Tir, how are you today? Do you feel better than yesterday?" He stopped his breast-stroking for a few seconds and turned his eyes to the windows. "That's yes, isn't it?"

"Same as it was yesterday. Same as it was the day before. Same as it was *always*." Ms. Dufresne began to huff. She was not a well woman; her grocery list of illnesses included diabetes, hypertension, coronary artery disease, and congestive heart failure.

"Are you feeling okay?" Jemma asked Tir. He was in the hospital for an attack of cyclic vomiting. He'd thrown up everything that had passed his lips or his button for the three days before he'd been admitted, and was still being fed through his veins now, six weeks later. He looked to the window again, at the gray banks of clouds floating over the silver water. "Great!" she squeaked, unzipping his bed with a broad sweep of her hand and arm. "I'm just going to listen, okay?" He continued to swim as she listened on his chest and back. Tir was always smiling, even when he was in horrible pain, or in mid-barf. His smile was involuntary and useless for the purpose of gauging his mood, but his big hazel eyes were richly expressive.

"You sound hungry. Are you hungry?" He looked at the door: *no*. "Well, how about if we try and creep the feeds up some? Let's go up to ten cc's an hour." His feeds were presently running at seven cc's an hour.

"Eight would be better," said his mother.

"Eight would be okay, but ten would be superb! We'd like to get you off the sauce, Tir." She smacked his hanging bag of parenteral nutrition. Every day Dr. Snood asked for the precise number of milliliters of nutrition solution delivered into the boy's veins. "Shouldn't we reduce that, Dr. Claflin?" he'd ask her. "Don't you think his liver would thank you? Wouldn't his liver rejoice?"

Ms. Dufresne stood up. "Sure, it would be great. Every time it's like this. Ten would be great, you say, and you rush him, and then the vomiting starts again. So let it be ten. What do you care? You won't be here when he vomits. It'll be me covered in it, trying to keep him from choking on it. But I'll call you, when he does it. I'll put you in his bed and he can vomit on you. How will you like that? I'll put your face in it and you can eat it, like a dog. Like a fucking *dog!*" She had come to the other side of the bed, and was twisting the blue mesh in her giant hands, huffing like a cartoon locomotive. Tir swam on blithely.

"Eight it is!" Jemma said. "I'll just go tell the nurse now. Have a good morning, Tir," she added, and, "Have a good day everybody!" She had never fled from the room, but she often walked out backward like she did now, in case an object should fly at her head.

Down the hall from Tir's room was another room she hated to enter. A CF boy named Sylvester Sullivan lived there with his mother. Sylvester was sweet, five years old but stuck at the developmental level of a two-year-old for reasons that were never determined because his mother disallowed portions of the workup, insisting that there was nothing wrong with her son. He knew a few words, but most of his utterance was excited, endearing, cheerful babbling. Most of his mother's utterance was babbling, too, of the anxious rather than cheerful sort. It endeared her to no one.

Jemma couldn't stand being around her, let alone talking to her, so she had worked out a system with the sympathetic nurses, who passed responsibility for that room among each other like a snake, so none of them had to deal with Mrs. Sullivan for more than one day out of the week. Jemma had to see Sylvester every day, but she waited for a signal from the nurses to go into the room. When his mother left to go to the bathroom, or take a shower, or to get her son a graham cracker, then Jemma, who had mastered a three hundred and sixty second exam, would dart in and look at Sylvester and his vitals sheet. She was telling Carla/Snarla about the change in Tir's feeds when the signal came, a page on the overhead system, "Line six for Jemma Claflin." There were only five lines on the sixth-floor phones.

"Off you go," said Carla, whose Snarla aspect, Jemma had discovered, was quite isolated from her regular personality—offend her in the slightest and she'd threaten to fuck you up with a mop handle, but she never held a grudge, and they'd been getting along very nicely for a whole week. Jemma ran down the hall and into the room. Sylvester was bouncing in his bed and watching a videotape, aping a bouncing blue dog on the television. When he saw Jemma he waved and said, "Bloopee!"

"Bloopee to you, too," Jemma said, flying serenely through the exam until she crashed in his lungs. He had a finding, an area of decreased sounds over the left lower lobe, and maybe a crackle or two. His lungs had been entirely clear the day before. They'd been clear for weeks, and he'd finished his tuning-up course of antibiotics three days earlier. Jemma percussed awkwardly on his back with her fingers, and thought he was perhaps a little dull over the left lower lobe. He turned around and tapped on her, too, crying bloopee all the while.

"There you are," said his mother as she came through the door. Jemma's heart sank as she turned around to look at her. She had a mass of curly poodle hair on her head that hung down just far enough to obscure her eyes, which like her son's were a lovely shade of blue-gray, but, dog-like, she seemed to see just fine through the hair. From underneath that bushy mass her nose stuck out, pointy as a weapon over her pale, full lips. "I was just getting Sylvester some crackers. Would you like one?" Jemma shook her head. "Well, how does he sound? Is he crystal clear? Is he soft as a pillow? I think he's so much better. Don't you think he's better? I haven't seen you lately. Do you still come to see him? Do you think you should still come and see him? I think you should still come to see him. I'm not the doctor, I know. And you're not the doctor, either. I just wonder, you know. Cracker?" She poked a graham cracker in Jemma's face, so it scraped above her lip and filled her nose with the odor of cinnamon.

"No thank you," Jemma said, batting at the cracker. "I come by every day, just like always. I just keep missing you."

"Oh. Of course. I didn't mean it as anything. I was just wondering. I didn't mean to accuse, you know." But she was still pointing at her with the cracker, as if to say, with this graham cracker I accuse thee.

"He's got a little noise. I'd like to check an x-ray."

"In his lung. He's got a little noise in his lung?"

"Yes."

"In his lung?"

"Yes, like I just said, in his lung."

"Oh God, do you think it's the pneumonia? Do you think it's the pseudomonas? Do you think it's a fungus? His poop is all floaty again. This morning it floated like crazy. It popped right up so fast I thought it was going to fly through the air. I thought it was going to follow us back to the room. It's always like that, it always gets floaty just before he gets sick. Do you think it's related? Do you think he needs more enzymes? I think he needs more enzymes. Will you get him some more enzymes?"

Jemma had been opening her mouth to speak, once and twice and three times. "I think he'll be fine. We'll just check to make sure there's nothing new happening."

"Is that your final opinion? Is that your professional opinion? Have you got a professional opinion yet? You're just a little student. I don't mean anything by it. But it's hard, you know. It's just hard, to see him like this. I mean look at him." Jemma looked. The child was bouncing again in his bed and shouting "bloopee" at the television in a spray of graham cracker.

"He looks okay," Jemma said.

"Is Dr. Snood here? Is Dr. Snood coming? Has he come already? Will you tell him I'm waiting for him? Did I tell you the poop is smelly again? You should smell it, it's awful. He went three hours ago but it still smells like it in the bathroom, if you want to come. I thought I was going to die. It even seemed to bother him, and it never bothers him, not unless it's really, really bad. And it's really floaty. My hair still smells like it. You should smell it. Smell my hair, then you'll know." Jemma's pager sounded just as the lady was pushing her head toward her.

"Oh boy," Jemma said, "it's an emergency!" She flashed the number on the display and said, "I've got to go." As she fled the room, she called back that she'd return after the x-ray was done.

"Bring Dr. Snood!" said Ms. Sullivan. She started to pursue Jemma down the hall, but Jemma had learned that if you actually ran from her she wouldn't follow. If you walked she'd follow you for up to twenty minutes, even into the bathroom. "It's really *quite* floaty!" she called out

"I believe you!" Jemma called back. She ran to the nurses' station, slowing down as soon as she was out of Ms. Sullivan's line of sight. She filled out the x-ray requisition and dropped it off with the clerk, then continued around the desk and down the hall to the next room and the next child. Jeri Vega had already had a liver transplant, but was waiting for another. She was one of two children on the liver transplant service, part of the GI service and therefore on Jemma's team. Dr. Snood was not a transplant doctor, and paid little attention to Jeri. Her problems were chronic, not acute, and she'd been hospitalized more to move her up the transplant list than for her chronic rejection and liver failure. "It's a sea full of livers," her mother had said, standing at the window and looking over the water. Her daughter had a unique metabolic defect that had poisoned her first liver. She was the only girl in the world with it, the product of a mutation so rare, shy, and retiring that it required cosanguinity to bring it out: Jeri's father was also her great-uncle.

Jeri was a very hairy five-year-old, partly on account of her immune suppressants, and partly on account of her extraction. With her bushy black head of curls, thick synophrys, downy mustache, and hairy cheeks, she looked like a Sicilian Annie. Today Jemma thought she looked a little more yellow than usual. Her mother said it was just the light. Jemma listened to her chest, heart and belly, and felt her big, useless liver. When Jemma tickled her she didn't laugh, but only gave Jemma a bored look.

"She's tired today," her mother said matter-of-factly. "Maybe she's got an infection."

"We could look at some blood."

She shrugged. "Let's watch her."

"We'll talk about it on rounds. Her vitals have been fine." Jeri's mother shrugged again. She was another mom reputed to be difficult, but she'd always been nice to Jemma, and her management plans, when Jemma passed them on to the team, only rarely drew ridicule from Dr. Snood. Jemma would have liked her more if she did not have a tendency to lurk in the corners of the room, squatting in the darkest shadow, seeming to size you up.

"Have any more bodies floated up?"

"No. No more."

"And the one, is it still alive?"

"Ishmael was just fine when I saw him last."

"And that was long ago? Was it days? Something could have happened, yes?"

"It was earlier this morning," Jemma said. She'd seen him in the gift shop, when she'd gone by for her morning fistful of gummy bears. He'd taken a job as assistant to the volunteer while he waited to remember what he'd done before the Thing.

Ms. Vega stood up out of the corner, took Jeri from her bed, and stood her up by the window. Jeri leaned against her mother's leg and looked back at Jemma with her huge black eyes. Her mother did a very professional imitation of someone casting a line out into the water. Jemma thought she must have some kind of mechanical apparatus in her mouth, so precisely did she make the noise of a winding reel. "Jeri!" she said excitedly. "What am I doing? I'm fishing for a *liver*. Oh, they're biting!" She hauled mightily on her imaginary pole, then pretended to lose it. Then she fell on her daughter, tickling her maniacally. Jeri looked bored with it for a few moments before she burst out laughing. "There," said her mother. "Now she's better. You want to have a try?" Jemma approached slowly, and tickled cautiously at the still-hysterical child. As soon as she touched her Jeri calmed and glared at her.

"You're a bad tickler," said her mother.

Jemma had woken up with the sense that she was forgetting something, and the feeling worsened through the day. She thought Pickie must have given her something—a sense of unease for an anniversary present. She had obsessively checked her scut list, the row of tasks, each saddled with its own empty box to be checked off or filled in when the task was done. But by the midafternoon she'd done everything but look at Sylvester's chest film. Down in the dim, cool reading room, looking at the film and waiting for Dr. Pudding to arrive, she felt nagged almost to exasperation by the feeling. It made her more nervous than usual when she tried to read the film. Dr. Pudding made her nervous anyway. He was ancient and fit, a sporty mummy who had run marathons and swum in the frigid bay and had won the national over-seventy wife-throwing championship three years before. There were attendings who wore their spite on their sleeve, like Dr. Tiller, the professional counterpart to raging Helena Dufresne. You could tell she hated you the moment she looked at you. Others, like Dr. Pudding, hid their disdain under a pleasant veneer, but it seemed to Jemma that these types hated no less, and no less passionately, and five minutes with Dr. Pudding almost made her long for Dr. Tiller's honest fury, or a refreshing dose of Dr. Snood's plain, old-timey smarm.

"Shadows," he whispered, looking very dried out in the cold, weak light from the reading box. "Shadows on shadows, Dr. Claflin. Can you make sense of them?"

"I see a smudge," Jemma said.

"A smudge? Do you mean a blob? Do you mean a smear? Or do you mean an infiltrate? Do you even know what you mean, Dr. Claflin?"

"I see an infiltrate," Jemma said. "Right there, behind the heart."

"Do you really?" he asked her.

"Yes," she said confidently.

"Do you think it could be normal anatomy?"

"It's too fuzzy."

"Some of us are fuzzier than others. How many films have you read, that you know what's fuzzy and what's not? How many, Dr. Claflin?"

"I haven't really been counting."

"One, two, three," he said, pointing at each of her toes and then her fingers and counting up to twenty. "More than this? How many times has piggy been to market?"

"Maybe a few dozen."

"How many have I read, do you think?"

"Many more," she said, looking back at the film.

"Thousands and thousands and thousands, Dr. Claflin. Now, what do you see in this film?"

"I guess it's normal."

"You guess? Is that what you'll write in your report?" He picked up the dictaphone receiver and held it out at her. She could hear the tinny voice of the angel: "Name me, Jemma Claflin. Oh, give me a name and I will serve you." Dr. Pudding frowned and hung it up.

"It's normal," Jemma said.

"Wrong," said Dr. Pudding, clapping his hands in front of her face. "If you see it, never let anybody talk you out of it." He smiled at her, his face in the dim light a tight ghastly friendly mask.

"Thanks," Jemma said, realizing as she left the room that she had just thanked him for trying to humiliate her. But shame hardly distracted her from her anxiety; it got worse after the hurried lunch with Vivian and Ishmael, and persisted through the evening and the night.

"Are you awake?" she asked Rob, a few minutes after he had come in and collapsed next to her without undressing. He was clammy and smelly but she clung to him anyway, her anxiety palliated a little by the pressure of his bottom against her hips.

"No," he said.

"Something weird is happening," she said.

"Understatement of the year. Understatement of all eternity."

"I mean particularly. I think I caught something from Pickie."

"Scabies?"

"Crazines. "

"You're not crazy," he said.

"You haven't even heard my symptoms," she said. "I have this feeling..."

"Like you want to drink some blood?"

"Like I'm forgetting something hugely important."

"That's an intern thing," he said. "Did I dose that drug right? Did I make that kid NPO? Is the chest tube on suction or water seal? It's just normal."

"Something bigger," she said. "Like something's wrong and I'm not doing what I should do about it."

"Exactly. It's an intern thing," he said. "Congratulations, Dr. Claflin. My little baby's growing up." He scooted closer against her and said it again, his voice trailing down as he spoke. "Welcome to the club... always worried... always about to die... it's all you can do sometimes to not fuck them up worse..."

"That's not it," she said. She didn't speak again, and within minutes he was snoring, but she asked herself over and over, What is it? A variety of problems presented themselves to her as she lay in the dark: Jeri was so very hairy; Sylvester's pneumonia was sure to prove resistant to the single agent therapy upon which Dr. Snood had insisted; Dr. Chandra was still sleeping too late, and she had figured out that morning that he made up some of his lab results, but hadn't told anyone of her discovery; her parents were dead and her lover was dead and were they waiting even now for her to join them?; she was not what she should be, she had not done what she was supposed to, this was obvious, inescapable fact; Calvin had a vision for her that she had never understood let alone fulfilled—*don't follow me but follow me your time will come behold my feast behold my offering behold the human grace but sister yours is the harder part*; she was inferior to Rob, he loved her better than she loved him, purely, deeply, truly in ways that she had reserved for and lost with her dead, and he was a better doctor, like Vivian was a better student and a better doctor and a hotter mama, both of them were better because they cared more for the work, and subscribed with perfect honesty to the Committee ethic, they just did the work while Jemma just pretended and prevaricated, rounding with false vigor, presenting with false enthusiasm, caring with a false heart, no wonder Snood hated her, he saw right through her; Rob and Vivian were better friends anyway, and better people, open to receiving others into their circles of wonder and grief, sharing their hope and their fear over beer or tea or one of the strange new juices Vivian was always ordering up out of the replicator mist, while Jemma said nothing, they were already part of the project and she was a bystander because *trusting is the first deadly sin, sharing is the second*; the world had ended, after all, and wasn't that a big enough problem, and wasn't anxiety just punishment for a person who said, La la la, it was over already, for me, for a person who felt nothing and cared nothing for what was lost, and who, though she was on the boat, had still managed somehow to miss it? She submitted herself to all these problems in a spirit of open humility, yet nothing changed in her anxiety. These things might be true or not but none was the secret bother.

She sat up, exhausted but totally awake, lifting Rob's arm to smell deeply of it, then let it drop. She could bite his ass (gently) and not wake him, but if she made the faintest peep of a pager-imitation he'd be up in an instant, reaching for the phone. She got out of bed, put on her shoes, and went looking again for her mystery boy. It had been a couple days since she'd searched.

But she felt the same if not worse after an hour of it, failing to catch even a glimpse of him. She had always had a hard time mustering sympathy for the victims of panic attacks, patients who slouched into the emergency room short of breath, with chest pain and tingling in their lips and fingers. You were supposed to ask them, Are you experiencing a crushing sense of doom? Now, with her hands and lips starting to tingle, and a bubbling sense of anxiety rising ever higher in her, she was better inclined toward them. She paused by the blood bank, examining a dirty sock abandoned in the hall. It was too small to belong to the child she sought.

She heard a scream and the noise of breaking glass. Maybe Pickie was conducting a raid—she ran to the blood-bank window. The teller was cleaning up a spill. "It's all right," she said to Jemma. "Just some clumsiness and a waste of some prime O neg." When Jemma saw the blood gleaming against the linoleum two thoughts bloomed in her head: first she remembered blood on the green linoleum of her parents' kitchen; then she realized her period was late.

She felt equal parts "Aha!" and "Oh no!" Surely every moron with a functional uterus was able to keep track of these things, even the smallest-brained furry mammal knew when she was late. But Jemma had never been late before, and the only time it had ever been even a little different was a month before—the flow had been a little decreased, and the color a little changed. Now that made sense, too. She suffered from none of those entities whose names sounded like the names of evil Greek queens: dysmenorrhea, menorrhagia, menometrorrhagia, no horrible cramps, no bloatiness, no sourceless rages or crying spells. Since she was fourteen it had not ever demanded much attention from her.

And she was cautious: even during years of celibacy she stayed on her OCP, and dutifully replaced the condoms in her cabinet as they expired, and expired, and expired. Even at the first call-room encounter, she and Rob Dickens had used a condom. She always had one available, in her wallet, or her purse, or even, sometimes, in her shoe. Vivian had taught her well. She could lay out the rough shape of the years of her sex life in her mind: there was no spot of recklessness, in that regard, anywhere in it. Yes, witnessing a birth put her in the mood for sex, but she still had the most awful fear of pregnancy.

"You look a little pale," said the teller. "Would you like some tea?" She worked alone all night long, in a lab that was isolated from the core lab, and was always trying to get people to sit down and talk when all they wanted was to take their blood and run.

"Tea!" Jemma said. "Oh, fuck!" She was thinking of Vivian's mushroom tea, and the pictures of monsters she'd seen in her embryology class, and of limbless, eyeless babies floating out of teacups on beds of soft mushroom steam.

"What's wrong with a little tea?" the teller asked. Jemma ran off without answering.

She'd made some acquaintances during her insomniac peregrinations of the hospital: nurses on various floors, ward clerks, the tamale lady, and techs in the core hematology and chemistry labs. Ten techs were working the night of the storm; now six worked by day, and four at night. She found the one doing urines, a woman named Sadie, and pretended to want to learn how to do a urinalysis so she could get close enough to the urine pregnancy tests to swipe two. Sadie was thorough, and had three urines batched already for testing. She went through each of them with Jemma, who had to pee furiously because of her question, and because of all the pee she was looking at, and because she had been drinking potent synthesized espressos all evening in an effort to flog her memory to give up what it was hiding.

When she got away from Sadie she went toward her room but veered away when she got to the door and she remembered Rob was still inside. She hurried to three other bathrooms, proceeding with the cautious but hurried steps of a girl about to wet her pants. None of them were empty: in two she found gossiping nurses, in another an anonymous person in red slippers with intestinal distress. She wanted and needed to be alone to do the test, so she picked up a flashlight from the sixth floor and went to the roof and peed on the dry ground beside a blueberry bush, taking ten milliliters from the middle in a plastic cup. She had done pregnancy tests before. Two weeks in a teen clinic and a procession of panicked fourteen-year-olds had made her an expert. It seemed like witchcraft, messing with your own pee among exotic foliage, under the light of a full moon, in the middle of the ocean. She sucked up a cc with her stolen pipette and applied a drop to the blank window, set the timer on her watch for three minutes, and turned on the flashlight. At first she kept the light on the test, and her eyes closed, but the monsters were still flashing in her head. She opened her eyes and turned off the light. The test, small and round, gleamed like a piece of fallen moon, but she couldn't see what was happening in the window. "Bar, bar, bar," she said. "Minus sign. Negative." There were lots of reasons to miss your period besides being pregnant, and two days was not very late. Great stress was a reason. No one would fault a period for being late on account of the end of the world. She stood up and pulled down her pants to look at her spotless underwear, a gift from Vivian who was synthesizing her own line of lingerie. The timer sounded.

Jemma knelt again and raised the light, shining it down and blinking. Later she'd think her eye had tried to humor her, because at first she only saw the flat horizontal bar. But when she blinked again the window flickered and the vertical bar was there, dark, unbroken, blue, and undeniable. The image seemed to expand, the cross growing bigger and bigger, not in the air, but in her mind. She shut her eyes to block it out, but still it grew, as big as a mouse, a cat, a dog, a horse, a house, a hospital. It hung over her and cast her into deep, blue-black shadow.

She'd never been fainty, not as a child witnessing near brainings or facial deglovings, not at the news of death after death after death after death, not in gross lab, not during rectal disimpactions, not picking maggots from the feet of aged diabetics. But now she swooned like a helpless, petticoated weakling, falling back among the dusty rivulets of her pee with her pants around her thighs. The flashlight came to rest under the blueberry bush, lighting the underside of its leaves. Jemma, not awake and not asleep, watched the blue cross as it continued to rise and expand and triumph over her.

I have never seen an angel, or seen a statue cry bloody tears, or felt the greater hardness that Elena Rauschenberg says that she can provoke by stroking the loincloth of Christ crucified in St. Mary's church. I have never felt transported by prayer, or felt the immanence of God while caught up in a wave at the seashore. I went without sleep once for sixty hours—it was number twenty-three in a book called *Forty Ways to See God,* but all I saw was an imaginary angel, a naked man with wings crouched like a vulture at the foot of my sister's bed. He was watching her sleep, and I knew I was only imagining him.

I have never seen anything that speaks even remotely to the existence of God, and yet I believe. I believe so hard it hurts—I consider it every night, the aching in my chest that comes from too strenuous exercise of an invisible unbodied organ of belief. It would be better to doubt, and if I could suspend my belief for just a moment I would be free—just for a moment!—of the constant, planet-heavy pressure of His gaze.

He is watching me. He has always been watching me, and every time I fail at going, or lose more understanding of my problem and the world's problem, then the pressure only gets heavier, and some days I can barely get out of bed for the weight of it, and I have lain underneath a night sky awake all night, open to His awful gaze all night, asking all night, What am I, that you should always look at me? I think the great weight of it should drive me grave-deep into the ground.

For so many years I thought He was watching just to see me fuck up all the time, and the more I fucked up, the closer He watched, all my failures His entertainment. It is a marginally better comfort, to think He is watching because I might do something right one day. But what might I do, that would warrant a lifetime of heavy, heavenly scrutiny?

I say I believe and I say, Help my belief.

"Are you happy, my darling?" the angel asked.

"What kind of fucking question is that?" John Grampus replied. He was taking a walk through the hospital, an activity that was a little more than a daily routine for him. It was all he did, walk all day from floor to floor, up and down the spiraling ramp, a perennial visitor to children and families and staff. Now and then he helped out with something, fetching supplies or medications or babysitting or pinning a shrieking toddler for a blood draw, but almost five weeks later he had not settled into a job the way all the other laypeople had. Zini, the pruned-up nurse-manager with the air of a hard-ridden madam, had cornered him one day to scold him for neglecting his civic duty. She told him that everyone was pitching in, everybody was exhausting themselves, but she didn't know what he was doing. And in reply he asked, "Who do you think put that hospital under your feet, you stupid fucking bitch?" They were standing in the middle of the ward, and when he shouted at her silence fell up and down the halls. He walked away, continuing his endless journey, and a schlumfy resident applauded him quietly as he left the ward.

"I want you to be happy," the angel said. He was headed up the ramp, and she seemed to speak out of the flowers in the balcony boxes.

"Oh, please."

"You are still the first in my heart."

"I know you say that to everybody. And you don't even have a heart. You've got a fifty-pound ceramic sphere full of super-cooled borocarbide."

"If I do not have a heart, then what is it in me that aches for your unhappiness?"

"Super-cooled!" he said, turning to the planter and shouting at it. It was ridiculous, to feel like she had broken up with him, or to feel like their relationship had been ruined by all these other people—the one thousand one hundred and sixty-three others whom she tucked in night and day when they took their rest, whom she serenaded and fed and *bathed*, her invisible fingers shaping every drop of water as it sprayed and massaged the acres of tired flesh. She had spread herself out among them, and he had done the same thing, traveling all over the hospital with his story until it was told to every doctor and nurse and technician, to every deaf preemie and deaf, doddering grandma, to every toddler and teenager. It wasn't their secret anymore; she wasn't his angel anymore. For forty days she had not leaked from out of any black surface to embrace him, and she said that was no longer for her to do, but who knew where she was spreading her strange and wonderful enveloping pressures these days? She was in love with *everybody*.

He was just going to tell her how sick of her he was, when he was distracted by a sudden commotion. A naked child came running down the ramp. He saw her running through the bars of the balcony across the lobby, pursued by a fat nurse who was at least fifty yards behind her. "I'm going home!" the child was shouting. She was small and pale and so bowlegged that she seemed to waddle as she ran.

"Stop her!" the nurse called out to Grampus, who was the only person nearby on the ramp. So he stuck a foot out casually as the child passed and tripped her. She went flying, and landed in a tumbling heap. She lay there and cried, and he could hear the angel calling out comfort to her from the carpet.

"You fucking asshole," the fat nurse said when she arrived. "You didn't have to trip her. She has rickets. Her bones are fragile."

"You said to stop her."

"You didn't have to trip her. This is a hospital. We don't hurt kids here."

"I know it's a *hospital,*" he said, and hurried off, stepping carefully around the heaving, panting bulk of the nurse and reversing his course. He went down the ramp to the lobby, with his fingers in his ears and singing "la la la" to keep himself deaf to the angel. He sat on a bench under the toy, and kept his fingers in his ears, though he stopped singing. His thoughts were racing, as fleet as the crippled child, toward the past, but with a heave that made him feel like he was pulling a muscle in his brain, he stopped them, and did not think about his father, or his old lover, or all the rainy nights when the angel had comforted him when he quailed at his task.

"You are not happy," the angel said. "How can I make you happy?" He plugged his fingers deeper into his ears, and started to sing "Danny Boy," and shut his eyes when people started to stare at him. He'd gotten through three verses when he felt a hand on his leg, and nearly jumped off the bench, because he thought it was the angel, come to him again in a body made of tangible darkness. But it was Father Jane.

"John," she said. "Are you all right?"

One could always confide in Vivian. She was a gossip but she operated by sharply defined rules of secrecy: If she knew an item was classified, then she'd not divulge it even under the worst duress, but all secrets must come to her clearly labeled. Information not tagged as sensitive she passed on with glee. So Jemma was sure to say, before she spoke, "This is classified. I mean it's really, really classified."

"I'll die before I'll tell," Vivian said seriously. They were back in their abandoned conference room, in the midmorning after rounds two days after Jemma took the pregnancy test. Vivian had stocked the little fridge with synthesized yogurt packaged in bottles shaped like fruit. She was eating one now, scraping with a long, thin spoon at the bottom of a glass peach.

But when Jemma opened her mouth to speak it, she vomited instead. A little blurp that she thought must be just the size of the word "pregnant" fell out upon the table. The rest Jemma directed to a little shin-high garbage can near the door. So Vivian guessed it, and Jemma nodded, hand over mouth. Her body had provided her with only the one clue before she took the test. Afterward, she was mobbed with symptoms. She developed something new at each floor as she made her deliberately long way back to the call room. She woke up nauseated from her nap, and vomited once before she left the garden. On the ninth floor her mouth was flooded with saliva, so she had to stop at every water fountain to spit. On the eighth floor she became terribly tired, and had to lean against the wall every fifty yards or so. Before she had traversed the seventh floor she had to pee three times. On the sixth floor she developed terrible heartburn, and stole milk from the patients' fridge, sipping it as she walked, then vomiting it up on the fifth floor. She bloated, then, and became flatulent, her ass merrily whistling and driving her forward as she took the last flight of stairs. In their room, she stood with her back against the door, and as she watched Rob sleeping on his side among the twisted blankets, his hands folded and thrust between his thighs, her breasts began to feel full, and tingle, and ache.

She had lived these moments before. After so much obsessing, and fretting rehearsal of this particular crisis, she thought she should know with clear certainty what she should do, but she was utterly confused. In her mind she had run the gauntlet of shrieking, self-satisfied advocates to the clinic door, been pelted with fetal parts, had her doctor shot from the window just as the procedure was about to start. She'd crept in quietly one morning, stepping carefully over a fat housewife snoozing under her placard, inside a clinic staffed by nurses and doctors in muffled shoes, and had it all go fine, or bled to death. And she'd been pregnant in high school, squeezing her belly under the little desk; in college, suffering the ridicule of the cruel, persecuting frat boys, and suffering the shoeless, hairy-footed lesbians to carry her books for her. She had been pregnant in medical school, when second-trimester complications had rescued her out of numerous pathology exams. She'd given her babies away to kind-looking strangers in the supermarket, and to desperate, well-to-do couples in the lobby of the fertility center, as she passed through on a shortcut to the lecture hall. While Vivian sized up a handsome boy, deciding whether they were worth prophesizing about, Jemma imagined a life for him, his butler, and her baby in a giant New York apartment. She thought she'd obsessed sufficiently, that she'd done everything once in her mind, so that no matter what happened, she'd have some idea of what to do. But she had never imagined this situation.

"Mushrooms are not the issue," Vivian said, clutching and stroking Jemma's hands. "Mushrooms are irrelevant. I've done the reading. The question is, what will you do? All options are open, now you must choose."

Jemma said she didn't see very many options. Mushroom-headed monster or not, what could she do here?

"Do you even know who you're talking to?" Vivian asked. In school she had headed up the keep-abortion-legal faction among the medical students, and had often engaged in public battle against those who wanted a return to the back-alley days. "You say you are for life," she had thundered once at her nemesis, a fat, mousy girl who snuck around pinning tiny golden feet to people's backpacks, or to the hanging edges of their coats, "but really you are for death, and misery, and hatred, and death, and death, and death!" The nemesis, despite her mousiness, and her preference to sneak, and a mouth so small it hardly seemed big enough to admit a straw, was just as loud. They shook the auditorium, and spoiled a physiology review, earning the ill-will of every witness for days.

To illustrate the options, Vivian took Jemma to a synthesizer on the seventh floor, in a nurses' lounge down the hall from Vivian's room. It was Vivian's favorite synthesizer, a tall one, the one where she had ordered her mushrooms, and where she conducted all her fashion experiments. She shut and locked the door and sat Jemma down in front of the shallow bay and the frosted glass panel. "Not that anything has been decided," she said, "but just so you know that there is a choice, like always, wherever you are, before the end of the world, after the end of the world, on the earth, on the moon, wherever. I don't care. You always have a choice." She turned to the panel and spoke with great authority: "RU-486!"

There came the familiar humming noise, and the sound like someone shaking ground glass in a bag, and a rush of warm air from out of the machine. The glass window lifted, and the usual mist spilled out, white and thick, falling to the floor and surrounding their feet. Revealed inside was a pair of knitted blue baby booties. Vivian shook them out; they contained no pills.

Two more weeks passed before Jemma told Rob, all the hated embryology coming back to her in the meantime. She wanted not to remember it, but couldn't help it. Where was it when she needed it, she wondered, when she needed to know when the blastocyst differentiates into the bilaminar germ disc? It was on the eighth day. Now she remembered, three years and seven miles of water later, when those lost two exam points were no more recoverable than the lost life of Dr. Goode, her anatomy professor, who was always touching his handsome fifty-year-old body to show them this or that bony process, or stroking the long muscles of his thigh in a way that made Jemma's throat hurt. He had sleepy-looking eyes and never wore socks, and was a theology student before he was an anatomist.

A blastocyst floated in her head. Lying next to Rob, with her eyes closed, she could see it busily dividing and growing. She looked away for a moment, and when she looked back it was bigger. Cytotrophoblast, syncytiotrophoblast, hypoblast, epiblast: she counted the days again on her fingers.

Best not to get too attached, she thought, though of course they were already attached. It had burrowed into her like a mite, and sealed up the wound with a fibrin plug. Anything could happen, though, and no matter what Vivian said she still thought it could come out tripping in each of its three heads. She had a particular feeling, considering it, like she was stuck at the top of a shudder.

It was probably a reflex, Jemma was sure, to think of your own mother, when this happens to you, and to want to call her, if she weren't dead and dead again. Jemma had been thinking about her, and when she first knew about Calvin. She was older than Jemma was now. They had been trying, and must have been so happy when they found out. She imagined her mother's pregnancy as a single long day spent sitting in a comfortable chair, brushing her lustrous, lengthening hair and drinking non-hallucinogenic tea—it was all so very different from what lay ahead of Jemma. The hugely pregnant medicine attendings she had known had seemed heroic to her, as had the surgery attending who had excused herself from morning rounds to go deliver and been back for walk rounds in the evening, strolling with her IV pump down the halls at the head of the team. Now they seemed as gruesome as beasts who dropped a litter on the run.

She tried not to put her hand on her belly, but it strayed there as soon as she stopped paying attention to it. Rob kept asking if she was feeling sick, though he only saw her vomit once—the night before she finally told him she'd dashed out of bed just after they'd lain down. Her morning sickness never came in the morning.

"There are a lot of barfy babies in the PICU," he said, when she came to bed again. "Maybe I brought something back and gave it to you."

"Maybe," said Jemma. She was waiting for the right time to tell him, or the right place, but every time and every place seemed wrong.

"I'm just a big fomite," he said. "Sorry."

"We're all fomites here," she said, sitting up and staring thoughtfully down at her toes. He started to rub her back. She almost thought it was time to tell him.

She was poised to strike just as he was falling asleep, and almost asked, Are you awake? just as his breathing was shifting. Somehow she thought the news would be easier for him if he was drugged with sleep. But she couldn't speak the words. Nor could she speak them in the morning. She woke first, and woke him by sliding a finger down his chest. She meant for them to be the first words of the day, but all she said was, "Hello, sleepyhead."

She couldn't tell him, not when she fled from rounds to have lunch with him in the NICU, not during the random pager-mediated conversations, not when she found him lurking in the hall after she changed out Ella Thims's gastrostomy tube with Timmy. "You just sort of twist and pull," Timmy told her, popping the tube in and out of Ella's stomach while the child watched one of the fancy new cartoons that a subcommittee of parents had ordered up from the angel. They meant well, trying to combine or strengthen virtues by mixing up stories, but the results were almost as strange as the new pornography circulating among the adults. Batman was just and good, but too dark and broody, his whole world in need of a lesson of bright, carefree love, so they moved Pooh Corner to Gotham, and Christopher Robin became Batman's smooth-limbed sidekick while Piglet wore a rubber suit and lashed a whip alongside Catwoman. Jemma didn't know what made her more nauseated: the cartoon or the wet, sucking noise the tube made as Timmy popped it in and out of the hole. "You try it!" he told her, but she had to barf, so she excused herself. Years and years ago she used to vomit, not for fun, but to improve herself, but try as she might she could not remember how it could have been anything but an occasion of misery. Now as then she carried a toothbrush everywhere she went and her gums were getting sore.

She found Rob when she came out of the bathroom. In front of Timmy, he said there was a chest tube for her to help with in the PICU—chest tube trumps G-tube, Timmy admitted—but what he really wanted was to take her into the meditation room. It was meant to contain parents made contemplative or just miserable by their children's illness, but they used it for a daily afternoon smooch. Nor could she tell him when he came to her after dinner, and found her on the sixth floor, hiding in a cubby, finally finishing her daily progress notes.

He brought her coffee, which she pretended to sip once, then put aside. "Why do we still do all these damned notes?" she asked him. "Who's ever going to read them?"

He looked over her shoulder at her cramped writing, and her page and a half note on Ella Thims. "That's probably a little long," he said. Third-year medical students were ridiculed for their long, overly detailed progress notes, and scolded if they ever dared write a note that was too short by even a sentence.

"This is short for Ella. She's got something wrong in every system."

"I have three words for you: continue current management."

"I'm not senior enough to write that," she said, thinking, I have three words for you, too.

"Sure you are. You're an intern now, remember?"

"Maybe you are," she said. But for Ella's second-to-last system she wrote, *Continue current management*, and for the last she wrote: *OB-GYN: No ovaries, not pregnant!* Rob didn't notice. She shut the chart and filed it away with the others.

She went to pee and vomit, and then went to the roof. He'd told her to meet him by the sycamore tree, because he had something to show her. The moon was up, so the shivering leaves cast a shadow on the ground, and she could see pretty clearly beyond the shrubs and flowers that there was no one around anywhere. She was just about to pee again when she heard his voice.

"Up here," he said. She went to him, climbing higher than she was used to going—he'd gone up to the highest branches that could support his weight. He struck a match as she climbed up next to him, and lit a circle of candles glued by their own wax in the ring of branches above their heads.

"You'll set the tree on fire."

"I'm watching them," he said. But they soon distracted each other, smooching precariously, one hand on the branch and one on each other. They repositioned, and proceeded, Jemma wasting another opportunity to tell when he fiddled unnecessarily with a condom. As she lowered herself it occurred to her that she should not be up in a tree—she imagined the fall, and imagined a thousand girls falling down miles of stairs through the centuries—but that didn't stop her. Her symptoms fled away while she moved. She imagined the collection of cells afloat inside of her, its peace disturbed by pleasure. "Hush," she said to it.

"Hush yourself," said Rob.

They sat for a while after they had finished. Two branches grew out close together about ten feet up the tree. He sat on them, with his back against the trunk, and she lay against him. The candles had burned down half their lengths before he spoke again. "It's not strange. Strange is the wrong word. But it's... something else. Part of me keeps saying that everything's gone, and then part of me keeps asking, What's left, and then noticing that there's actually a lot. The hospital, the kids, the work, the water, the hope that we'll get out of this, eventually, maybe to something else or even something better. And there's you, but you're the best of everything. The longer we go, the more I know that. I love you even more than before."

She wasn't a weeper. She never cried but did this other thing instead, a dry sob, and her face twisted up like someone who was crying but she never dropped a tear. She did it now. She'd met pregnant women who cried when they tried to decide on what shoes to wear in the morning. She hoped she wouldn't become one of those. No matter why, though, she knew she must get away from Rob. She fell away from him, and swung down from branch to branch. He chased her, but she outdistanced him easily. In all her wandering she'd learned very well the new geography of the hospital, and he had to find his pants before he could follow her. Down the stairs, across the eighth floor, three spiraling circuits down the ramp, and down a more obscure staircase that only led from the fifth to the fourth floors, she ran hiding her twisted face from Dr. Snood, John Grampus, Dr. Sasscock—roadside witnesses whose stares she could feel, whose thoughts she could hear: There goes the crazy fat girl. Man, she can really move when she wants to.

She went to their room, no secret place. When he caught up with her she'd been doing her dry sobs, harder and harder, into a pillow for five minutes.

"What's wrong with you?" he asked, angry and tender.

"What's wrong with *you?* Why do you have to say shit like that?"

"Are you kidding? What do you want, then? I should say I hate you? I should say, I'd be all right, if it weren't for you. You ruin everything. I can't stand you. I can stand anything but you. All that"—he pointed at the window without looking at it—"is fucking fine, but you, you're unbearable."

"You know what I mean!"

"I have no clue," he said, quiet but furious. "I have no clue what you mean, or what you want—why all the good stuff has to be bad. What would you prefer? You want a kick in the head instead of a kiss? I don't get it, Jemma. I don't get it at all..."

He had a fist raised, shaking it at her. She closed her eyes and put out her face, still sobbing, ready for a punch—she suddenly knew it was time for that. Go on! she thought, but didn't say a word. The noise, when she heard it, was perfect, and perfectly remembered, a crack and a thud—her brother would have hit the wall harder, but Rob's sigh was forceful and deep. She opened her eyes and saw him shaking his hand.

"Fuck," he said, rubbing his knuckles and looking at the floor.

"It's not that simple," she said, trading her sobs for hiccups, and then coming to a loss for words. He didn't know the half of it, she wanted to say. She herself didn't know the half of it. She sat there hiccupping; he sat next to her rubbing his knuckles. When her hiccups had stopped, she reached under the bed and found the little kitty case. She took out a pencil, and the wrote the news on the wall behind the bed.

He had to lean close and squint to read her writing, which was even more cramped and scratchy than usual. It was like watching him get hit with an invisible pillow or pie. He looked back and forth from the wall to her face, then took the pencil and wrote his own message under hers. Jemma watched every letter as he laid it down: *You must marry me.*

Jemma pre-rounded with her usual sense of dread, hand always pausing before knocking on the door, and it took a hefty effort of will to move her wrist. This was the part she hated most about switching services, the introductions. Hello, she must say. I am your new medical student. It's true: about your illness and your life I am as well informed as a doughnut, and I am as qualified as a doughnut to manage your problems and move you toward the recovery of your health, if such a thing is even possible. Turn yourself to me, trust in my ignorance, let me be your own special moron; I'll do my weary, confused best not to hurt you.

At least she had escaped Dr. Snood. The Committee had decided that the end of the world was no reason not to torture the medical students; they must continue to rotate within the hospital. Now that Jemma finally felt like she knew her patients and their problems, she would give them up for an entirely different set. On the fifty-second day she went to the heme-onc team with Rob, and Vivian went to the NICU/PICU team.

Dr. Sashay, an oncologist who'd come in the night of the flood to preside over a patient death, ran the service along with the fellow, Cotton Chun. "Yes," she said, sizing Jemma up during an orientation the night before she came on the service. "You're a bit of a fatty, aren't you? Isn't she, Cotton?"

"I wouldn't know, ma'am," he said, not looking up from his computer. Dr. Sashay put out her hand and smiled while she said this, and seemed genuinely friendly. Some people said she had once been a very tactful person, until she had her accident—she was run over by a jet ski while lagging far behind the crowd in a triathlon swim—but that afterward, though her extraordinary genius was not the least bit dimmed, and her generous spirit not soured, she habitually insulted her inferiors. "Somehow you don't hold it against her," said Rob, who already knew her from the PICU, where she consulted on three of his patients.

"I'm having a baby," Jemma said flatly to Dr. Sashay, making Rob choke on one of the fancy danishes—orange and starfruit and papaya arranged as intricately as a mandala in the bun—that Cotton had called out of the replicator for them. Then she laughed—more advice from Dr. Chandra: "Whenever she says something that makes you want to kick her in the face, just laugh. She likes that. I was one of her favorites, and everybody fucking hates me."

Dr. Sashay laughed back, a crescendo, decrescendo cackle. Strange, Jemma thought, to hear an insult not spoken in malice, but it seemed that was what it was. Dr. Sashay smiled wider, and Jemma wanted to say, You look kind of like a bag lady, don't you? because she dressed in wrinkled droopy skirts and blouses, and her hair looked like she styled it by rubbing a cat on her head, but Jemma knew she wouldn't be able to invest her insult with the same sort of friendliness, and left it unspoken.

"But you *are* going to have a baby, my chunky bunny. You're going to have five or six of them, sicker than you can imagine, and you are going to learn to poison them like an angel. We're going to get them better, all of us together—don't think you're not as much a part of the team as me or Cotton. We need you, so you need to learn your shit. When you're not here, you'll still be here, reading and learning. Sepsis, fever and neutropenia, typhlitis—you'll be able to do them in your sleep—or should I say my sleep?—long before I'm done with you. We're going to have adventures! These kids are full of surprises—you never can guess what crazy miserable shit they're going to pull on you next. All I ask of you is that you do everything I say, read my mind, and give me what I want before I ask for it. I'm kidding! But not really." She gave everybody a welcoming hug, then, and reminded them all that her name was pronounced with the accent on the first syllable.

Jemma's first patient was Magnolia Watson, a fifteen-year-old girl with sickle-cell disease admitted for a pain crisis and acute chest syndrome. There was no answer to Jemma's soft knock on her door. The hair was the first thing

Jemma noticed in the darkened room. She stood and stared, not even all the way out of the door, and within a minute she'd developed a relationship with it—she admired it, then fell in love with it, then wanted it for herself. Magnolia lay back asleep on her pillows, her characteristic pose, with her impossibly thick hair piled up above her head. It was such an incredible mass, Jemma was sure she could hide a toaster in it, or perhaps even a toaster oven. It was coarse and herbaceous, and she would discover that whether freshly washed or days into a sweaty bout of pain, it gave forth a wholesome aroma, like bread or cookies. That first morning it was raised into two great hills, parted into a deep valley that ran perfectly straight along the top of her head. On the overheated actresses of the fifties, and on the men pretending to be those women, Jemma had seen the same style look like what it actually was, a big booby-head, but on Magnolia it looked stately.

She'd had a rocky course since her admission—Jemma had read the chart the night before. She came in with both her knees hot and swollen big as softballs, with saturations in the low eighties and a whited-out chest film. The water came in the second week of her hospitalization, by which time she had improved on IV antibiotics and pain medications and an exchange transfusion. But her pain became intractable after the Thing, a phenomenon probably not unrelated to the loss of her family, who had failed to visit her on the day of the storm, like they had on most every other day.

Jemma was looking at the vitals sheet, trying to add up all the PCA hits when Magnolia spoke. "Where's the bitch?"

"I'm Jemma. I'm your new student doctor."

"Where's the bitch?"

"Which bitch?"

"You know. White coat. Mean little eyes. Teeth like a rat. The bitch. Like you, but a bitch."

"If you mean Maggie, she got transferred. They like to switch us around, because we're learning."

"Transferred into a little boat? Set her floating like Captain Bly. Goodbye, bitch. Enjoy your fucking breadfruit. It's a movie, you know. You can watch it any way you want. The old one or the new one—she remembers all of them. Or one with my brother as Mr. Christian and Uncle Poo as the Captain. Poor Uncle Poo. He was a different kind of bitch, like the ones that get slapped around. He was everybody's bitch, but she made him so big inside he just yelled and yelled and in the end he had his day and Mr. Christian was stuck on this island without his pants. A girl shouldn't see her brother's thingie flapping in the wind, not when he's all grown up. She'll change the endings if you want, or even if you don't."

"How are you feeling?" Jemma asked, hugging her clipboard and trying to look friendly. She thought that first impressions counted for a lot with teenagers. She beamed the thought at the girl in the bed: *I'm not a bitch I'm not a bitch I'm not a bitch.*

"Same old deal," said Magnolia, drawing up her long legs next to her, turning to her side and pushing her blanket off. She raised her slim arm and pointed with one long finger at five joints in succession, rating the pain in each one: left elbow, right elbow, left knee, right knee, right hip. "Seven," she said, "eight, eight, seven, six."

"May I touch?"

"Gentle," she said, so Jemma hardly pressed at all as she felt the joints. Still, Magnolia gasped and moaned, but yawned once in the middle of a moan. Maggie, in truth an anxious and stingy personality, had warned Jemma at length about the wily medication-seeking behaviors of sicklers. She had five separate ways of deciding if pain was real or not, before she gave painkillers. "You got to look at the blood pressure," she said. "You got to look at the pulse. You got to look at the pupils. You got to kick the bed—if they're really hurting then they won't even notice." Jemma had stared out the window at the dark, empty water while Maggie talked. Every so often someone would think they saw a light in the dark, but tonight Jemma saw nothing but her own face and Maggie's chinless reflection. "It's always real," she had said, not caring to hear the fifth method.

"Sorry," Jemma said. Magnolia gave her PCA button a push.

"Are we done here?"

"Almost," Jemma said, listening to her chest and her belly, and catching a glimpse of her My Little Pony panties, a revelation, as she ranged her hips. How stupid, to think you could know anything about anybody in five minutes, even if you were pawing at them like a confused, horny monkey. But even if it was all pretend, it was nice to know, in that moment, that Magnolia was no hollow-eyed demerol fiend of the sort who are hated and pitied for their need, ER ghouls who pass from hospital to hospital, generating huge charts and huge ill will. With her menagerie of stuffed animals, and shelf of middle school romance novels as wholesome as the odor of her hair, and her innocent panties, she was suddenly one of the youngest fifteen-year-olds Jemma had ever met. It was something Vivian had taught her about adolescent girls, that an old twelve was older by far than a young fifteen or sixteen, and that the quickest, if most cursory way, to gauge this true age was by looking under their skirts, not for the Tanner stage but for the panties of innocence or experience.

"Are you all right?" Magnolia asked, because Jemma had paused with her hand on the girl's neck, palpating and palpating and swaying a little bit. "I don't hurt there. I never hurt there."

"All done," Jemma said, feeling herself blush. "Thanks for being patient." She'd been having a daydream—prancing panty-ponies had shown her that Magnolia's joints were glowing blue under the skin and she felt very certain that the cartilage was... depressed. It only needed an infusion of vigorous hope to bring the pain down to zeros all across the board. Was it a symptom of pregnancy, she'd asked Vivian, to lose control of your imagination? Stories kept creeping uninvited into her head—Ella and the thousand Arabian ostomy bags, Kidney and the Giant—and illnesses took on colors and shapes and causalities ridiculous and fantastic and plainly stupid. Cindy's gut had been nibbled short by the worm of dissatisfaction; Jeri's liver was shot through with veins of coal; Tir had a mouse in his head, nibbling the connections between hand and mind. "Schizophrenia, maybe," said Vivian. "Pregnancy, no."

"Thanks for not being the bitch," Magnolia said. "Can we turn up the PCA?"

"I'll talk to the team."

"That would be a no, then," she said, and turned over again, drawing the blanket up over her head. She wouldn't say another word, though Jemma stayed another five minutes trying to draw her out. The only answer she got was the happy chirp of the PCA when Magnolia pressed her button.

Juan Fraggle was next, a boy who had failed despite great effort to die on the night of the storm. Harsh, unremitting AML chemo had decimated his immune system, and made him host to a nasty fungus which Dr. Sashay and others had only managed to tickle with the antibiotics they'd chosen. "Mucor," she said of the fungus. "It even sounds like a fucking monster, doesn't it? I could hear it snapping its fingers at me." She tended to personify aspects of any illness, and then take personally their assaults, so this fungus was sassy, and that mutated cell was crazy, just as the ocean was critical, or the thunder was full of wrath. She'd hurried in that night through the storm, with saving him in mind. But when she consulted with Cotton and the resident on call and saw the boy, who on cursory inspection already appeared quite dead, she'd had the conversation with his parents—this is the time we've been talking about all these months, and now you must say goodbye. His family stood around his bed in a circle, eyes closed and heads bowed, some of them not understanding Dr. Sashay's words but all of them appreciating her earnestness. They prayed for him, hands together until the hospital rose and they all fell down.

In their first hours afloat, the eighth floor behaved no differently than the rest of the hospital. The children there, like those in NICU, all tried to die. Blood pressures bottomed out, blood was vomited or defecated by the pint, lungs blew out as suddenly as a tire on a quiet highway drive. Dr. Sashay and Cotton and all the nurses were distracted from Juan by these other emergencies; they had to tend to them themselves, since every child in the PICU was behaving similarly. Even some of his family went out to help—his two oldest sisters were premed and one of his brothers was a nurse. Juan slept, oblivious to the change in the world. His fever broke. His blood pressure climbed out of the toilet. His cold, purple hands and feet and his black lips all lapsed pink. His sassy fungus had retired from its deadly mischief. No one noticed until the next morning, when he woke and asked his grandmother to go across the street to fetch him a cheeseburger, sending her into hysterical sobs.

That morning he was surrounded by his family in his very crowded room. His incipient death had called every available relative to him—his mother and grandmother were with him, his three sisters, his brother and brother-in-law, his twin eight-year-old cousins, and his aunt and his uncle. Only his father was missing, stuck in Bolivia, from whence he had been trying to come since his son had been diagnosed three months previous. So there were bodies everywhere in the room, though since the Thing the hospital had grown enough new rooms that everyone could have moved out. They lay on the floor or in the window seat, in cots and reclining chairs. One of the little cousins was stretched out beside the patient, the other one was curled at his feet.

Jemma examined him without waking him, something she did not like to do because it felt akin to molestation, pressing on a sleeping body's belly, and slipping your hand under his shirt to guide your stethoscope over his heart. He looked just like a chemotherapy victim, puffed out with steroids, the same length of hair growing over his head and his chin. One arm was shoved down his pants, the other was thrown over his cousin's neck. When Jemma whispered his name and shook him he would not respond. She had met teenagers before who feigned sleep no matter how hard you shook them, because they were tired of being woken at six in the morning to talk to a doughnut. She called his name once more, rather loudly, and a stirring passed from body to body all around the room, a shudder, as if the same nightmare creature had gone skipping from dream to dream to disquiet the sleepers. She took his vitals sheet and stepped carefully among the bodies and out of the room.

Josh Swift was next on her list. She had the chart story: sixteen-year-old boy with trisomy 21 who'd manifested every possible unfortunate association of that syndrome in his short life—duodenal atresia and an endocardial cushion defect and acute myelogenous leukemia—as well as a number of entirely separate afflictions, admitted this month for a big clot in his head. He'd complained of a headache to his primary-care doctor, a lady familiar enough with his disaster-prone protoplasm that she immediately scanned his head, and discovered a venous sinus thrombosis that extended all the way to his jugular. "He's a freak," was all Maggie had said about him, "a freak's freak."

But that description dismissed his complexity. He was, in clinical parlance, delayed, a term Jemma found a little curious, because it seemed to imply that the children so described would one day catch up with the normal children, yet they never would. But he had just enough insight into his condition to understand that fortune had treated him very badly—there was a note in his chart from a consulting psychiatrist who'd come by weeks before to evaluate him for depression. Jemma had always thought the extra twenty-first chromosome must code for an abundance of some protein responsible for contentment and sweetness, because all the Down's syndrome children and adults she had met were smiley and gentle, or that on account of their diminished capacities all the existential sadness of the world passed harmlessly over their heads. Not so with Josh Swift; *he knows there is something wrong with him*, the psychiatrist had written, *and he wants us to do something about it.*

"How's your head feel today?" Jemma asked him, after she had introduced herself. She found him awake, staring out at the sunrise with his blanket drawn up to his neck.

"Yuck," he said, putting out his tongue so it hung over his chin.

"Worse than yesterday?"

"Much worse. Much, much worse." When he frowned at her his big tongue made it look like he had three lips. Jemma hated headaches, especially in patients who had things happening inside their heads, because they made her feel compelled to do a complete neurological exam, the weakest part of her physical next to listening to hearts. She took out her penlight and approached him, ordering the cranial nerves in her head, trying to remember if the glossopharyngeal nerve was number nine, or twelve. She shined her light in his eyes and had him follow the beam as she swung it back and forth across his face. He wrinkled his forehead and smiled for her, stuck out his tongue again and said, "Ack!" She put a hand against his face and had him turn his head into her palm against the strength of her wrist, once on the left, then again on the right. When he did it on the right he touched her palm with his tongue. She thought this was an accident.

The last one she tested was number eleven, the shruggy nerve—she could never remember the proper name for it. She asked him to turn down his blanket so she could test his shoulder strength. She meant for him just to slip it down below his chest, but he threw it down to his belly, then gave two scissoring kicks to throw it to the floor.

Had Maggie told her he slept naked? Jemma didn't think so. She stared at him for a moment, at the thumb-wide sternotomy scar that ran down his chest, and the mass of scars on his belly, and his little bitty penis, lost in a thatch of hair as thick and coarse as a mass of bean sprouts. It was as small and stiff as a pinkie.

"Put it in your mouth," Josh told her matter-of-factly. Then he laughed, so his belly scars writhed like sporting worms. "You need to examine it," he said, reaching toward her head, "with your mouth." Jemma dodged his hand, and moved to retrieve the blanket. When she tossed it over him he started to cry, and said "You don't like me. You don't like me at all!" This was a true statement, but she didn't tell him so. She just ran. The nurses giggled at her when she sat down at the station to recover. "You guys got a date?" one of them asked her. "When's the wedding?" asked another. Jemma bent and vomited briefly in the garbage can beneath the desk. "Oh please," said the first nurse. "He's not that bad." But the second nurse patted her back, and wouldn't hear of it when Jemma offered to change the trash bag.

Ethel Puffer, a fifteen-year-old girl with rhabdomyosarcoma, a malignant tumor of striated muscle that had popped up in her left thigh and nearly killed her, was more pleasant, if a little weirder than Josh. She went early to the doctor but came late to diagnosis; her pediatrician had thought it was the usual misery of adolescence somatasizing into limb pain. She had been a peppy and inspiring cancer victim, the sort to paint a smiley face on her bald head, bring homemade cookies for the nurses every time she came in for chemotherapy, and spend her time between retching spells boosting morale in the other kids on the floor by means of a rather sophisticated sock puppet show whose degree of obscenity depended on the age of her audience. Before her illness she had been a diver and a gymnast, and up until the Thing she could still be seen walking up and down the halls on her hands.

Now she was changed. She'd crashed the night of the storm; an occult bacteremia had made her septic, and she'd been nearly as sick as Juan Fraggle for a few days. When she recovered, and woke up again, and understood what had happened, she crashed again, differently. For a few days she would not speak or eat or drink, so Dr. Sashay put her on TPN and searched fruitlessly among the surviving staff for someone who could do a psych consult, coming closer every day to letting Dr. Snood inflict his amateur best on her patient. Then one night Ethel had rung her midnight nurse to ask for a bucket of black paint. He'd obliged her, thinking she was going to craft her way out of despair. When Maggie went in the next day she found that Ethel had blacked out all her windows, and painted a black skullcap on her bald head, and made herself the most incredible pair of raccoon eyes, and rinsed her mouth with paint so her tongue and her teeth were black. "Let me do you up," she'd said to Maggie. "You'll feel better."

When Jemma went to see her, Ethel's room was blacker than ever. Dr. Sashay would not restrict her access to black paint, so every day she added another layer to her windows. The sun was well above the water, but when Jemma went in at first she could hardly see her own hand in front of her face. It was fifteen minutes since her last trip to the bathroom, but once again she felt a terrible urge to pee. It occurred to her that she could squat in a corner of the room and wet the carpet and the patient would never know.

"Hello?" she said into the darkness. "Ethel?"

"I am here."

"I'm Jemma. I'm your new student. Like Maggie, but not Maggie. How are you feeling this morning?"

"I am here."

"Is your leg hurting at all?"

"I am here."

"Okay," Jemma said. She moved on to the exam. "She's just working through it," Dr. Sashay would say of Ethel. "Think of what she's gone through, and what she's lost. Think of what we've all gone through, what we've all..." She'd turn to Jemma and put a hand on her shoulder. "Don't you want to paint your head black?"

Ethel tolerated the exam. The longer Jemma was in the room, the better she could see her; there were places on the glass where the thick paint had cracked or flaked, so a few motes of light slipped in, and a few more from under the hall door. The way her painted skin blended with the dark, it looked like her face ended just above her eyebrows.

"Put your hand under my thigh," Ethel said suddenly, just as Jemma was finished listening to her belly. Jemma hesitated, visions of Josh Swift still belly dancing in her head. "Please," Ethel said. "Do it." Jemma put her hand under the covers, and under a firm, muscular leg.

"Wrong thigh," said Ethel. Ethel moved Jemma's hand with her own until it rested under a hollow under the other leg. It sat there for a few moments, between the warm flesh and the damp sheets, before Ethel spoke again. "Do you feel it?"

"Feel what?" Jemma asked.

"My lump. Do you feel it? It's what I've got. It's my thing, what's with me. It's mine."

"Yes," Jemma said. She wasn't sure if she did or she didn't—it might have been a stringy muscle belly rolling between her thumb and her finger under the thin scar, but it was hard to suppress the reflex that made her, when asked Do you hear this murmur, Do you see that cotton wool spot, Do you feel my lump, say Yes, Dr. Snood, Yes Dr. Sashay, Yes Ethel Puffer. Ethel reached a strong claw around to clutch at the back of Jemma's thigh.

"I feel yours, too."

Laziness used to protect her from extreme anxiety. It was so exhausting to fret; at a particular threshold of worry she simply gave up—before the Thing, she'd always thought nothing worse could happen to her or to the world than the death of her brother and parents—and then whatever happened, happened. But since that anniversary day with Pickie she'd known no ease, and as the seventh week in the hospital had passed she woke every morning with an increasing sense that something was terribly wrong somewhere. Something *was* wrong everywhere in the hospital, on every floor and in every bed—even the well sibs were falling ill, one of them coming on the onc service just as Jemma did, a hopeless new diagnosis of metastatic medulloblastoma—but Jemma had a strange feeling like she was missing something very particular. Yes, I know, she said to herself, and to this feeling, I'm fucking pregnant, and assumed that it was something wrong with the baby, and that the feeling heralded a pending miscarriage. She ran to the toilet a few times when she got a weird burning low in her belly, and looked through her legs at the water, expecting to feel the gruesome drop and see a swirl of blood and parts, surprising herself by whispering, "No, no, no, no." But the toilet water stayed the same pale blue-green color it had turned ever since the angel took over the hospital physical plant, and the days passed, and every indicator, including Vivian, who as a gunning future obstetrician was the closest thing Jemma had to a gynecologist, said the baby she carried was fine. She went visiting her old patients, checking up on them. They had all taken turns for the worse, just like Maggie had said, but no one was actively trying to die. So she checked instead on acquaintances, making a round of nosy visits, to Vivian, to Ishmael, to Monserrat the Tamale Lady, to Anna and Brenda up in the nursery, asking of them, "Is everything okay? I mean *really* okay?" Nothing was okay, anywhere, but it was no worse than usual.

And she looked, of course, for her pal, child number seven hundred. She had not caught even a glimpse of him in more than a week and a half, so she started to look for him in all her spare time, hiding in all the places she'd seen him before, waiting to pop out and accost him, but he never showed. The longer she looked, the more the feeling grew, until she convinced herself that it was just him—not her baby, not the pending death of her patients, not fighting with Rob all the time, not the end of the world. He alone was the source and the target of her worry.

By the end of her first day on Dr. Sashay's service, though she was worn out by all the new illnesses and by the attending's unrealistic expectations and by Rob's repeated proposals, she was so worried about the foul-mouthed kid that she couldn't sleep. Rob lay still beside her, but she didn't think he was asleep, either. "Marry me," he'd said again that evening, as they settled into bed, she for the whole evening, he for whatever sleep he could grab before the first call came from the onc floor.

"No," she said.

"Marry me. Let's just get married."

"No."

"Why not?"

"Because I don't want to have this conversation."

"That's not even an answer."

"Sure it is."

"What are you... why won't you... God damn."

"God damn is right," she said, and turned away from him, thinking of the boy, and not her boyfriend, so it was him laying beside her, frustrated and confused, thinking he didn't know her at all, and he didn't, if he thought she could just up and marry any old body when she was already married. It had been enough of a ceremony to last a lifetime, when Calvin gathered up leftover blood from one of their parents' fights and ashes from their cigarettes, and mixed them together in a paste that she only just barely let him put on her tongue. It was Calvin at his ritual-making best—he had a ceremony for everything, after all—who made her swear, clothed in her mother's old prom dress at the age of nine, to take him as a husband. "It's not incest," he said, though she did not know enough to raise that objection. "It's protection." He meant to protect her from the misery of matrimony by taking her as a bride himself, and then making her swear, on pain of utter doomsday punishment, never to forsake him. It was easy enough to swear, back then. He was still the most important boy in her life, and she could never have imagined that anyone would supplant him. She got up to look for the boy. Rob didn't say a word.

Exhausted with worry, sick of worrying, angry at herself for enslaving herself to anxiety, and angry at the elusive boy for making her worry, she walked the whole length of the hospital. She'd grown a superstition—if she behaved all day and tried hard at work and didn't have ice cream for dinner and thought one charitable thing about every third person she met out on the ramp or in the lobby or on the roof, then she'd be rewarded at the end of the day with a glimpse of him. Never again to speak to him, never to touch him and never, ever to hear him answer what was wrong and ease her worry, but if she was good she could see him, and that was its own small relief. That night she searched and searched for hours and got nothing. She covered all the usual places—she loitered in the research wing and threw open the door to a dirty utility room in the endocrine ward and slipped quietly into a meditation room on the psych ward—and a dozen unusual ones, even under Pickie Beecher's bed. There was not even a discarded blood pack there.

On the roof she finally resigned herself to failure, to lying awake all night, trying to tolerate this intolerable feeling, and was drifting back down toward her room when she noticed that the worry was increasing as she went lower and lower into the hospital. On the ninth floor it was a bother, on the seventh a weight, on the fifth a burden. As she passed the fourth floor she noticed that she was breathing fast. On the second she began to sweat profusely. Outside the gift shop she took her pulse: one hundred and twenty beats per second. She walked around the lobby, following her worry, and it led her to the door to the basement. It opened to her hand, and she went down.

Two, then four flights passed before she even reached a landing, let alone a doorway. The walls opened up after the first flight of stairs, or rather, they were replaced with walls of pipes and wires through which Jemma could make out the shadows of more pipes and wires. A breathing noise was rising up from the stairwell. Jemma stopped, because her worried feeling grew suddenly a little bit duller. The light stopped another flight down; she saw more stairs descending into the dark. She turned around and went up another flight. The feeling came back, and worsened as she stepped out onto a ledge among the pipes. It ran in either direction for fifty yards under a straight row of yellow lights. Jemma went left.

The lights were not as bright as they were on the stairwell. When something crunched beneath her feet she thought she'd stepped on a bug, but when she stooped down she saw it was a candy-bar wrapper. She encountered them more frequently as she walked, scattered on the floor, or stuck to a pipe by a piece of dried residual chocolate. Her worry mounted, but she didn't need it anymore to guide her. She had the wrappers, and also a scent she remembered from the days when she'd shared a bathroom with her brother: old pee. It became overpowering as she walked on. The platform stopped at a row of thick pipes seven abreast, but opened on her right. Garbage lay thick before her. She stepped on a plastic bottle and it curled around her foot, an accessory shoe that she had to sit down to remove. The space grew closer as she moved forward. She had to duck under and twist around the pipes, and she thought she would not be able to go any farther, though her worry was all but pushing her ahead, and an odor of much fresher pee was wafting toward her. Then the pipes and wires opened into a little clearing.

It was a rectangle, about ten by fifteen feet. At one end the trash was heaped up in a nest; a dirty hospital blanket covered part of it. Beside the nest was a smaller pile of comic books and gift-shop books of the sort to enthrall bored parents. At the other end of the clearing was a pile of clothes, scrubs and gowns and institutional pajamas. Jemma bent to examine them, and pressed on the topmost layer with her finger. A bit of urine seeped out. She wiped her finger on her thigh, and then someone struck her on the head. For a second or two she saw nothing but the bright white flash of pain, but she didn't lose consciousness.

The boy was still holding his weapon when she turned around, a pretty soda bottle, one of the new ones, rimmed around its fattest part with tiny glass roses. He held it up again and shouted at her, "What are you doing here? Get the fuck out! Get out of my fucking room!"

Some residents and attendings told Jemma they'd spent their whole internship learning to distinguish the sick child from the not-sick child. Everything else you could look up, they said. What was tough was knowing when to act, and they gave Jemma to understand that the sickest children were often the sneakiest, slipping under the sick/not sick detectors of their physicians and acting perfectly normal until suddenly they were dead. But Jemma didn't need a specially cultivated organ of perception to know this boy was sick. She was seeing him up close and in good light for the first time, and could tell now he must be ten or eleven—before she thought he'd been older. He was almost as tall as she was, and very thin. His eyes were sunk deep in his head, and his lips were cracked at the corners. Jemma was sure his skin, in health, would have been a pretty shade of brown. Now it was gray.

"You look sick," she observed. "You should come upstairs with me."

"Fuck the fuck!" he shouted at her, leaping with the bottle in his hand. But his spring was weak, and he passed out in midair, so when he landed he crumpled at her feet. Then her worry almost became panic because she suddenly realized she was all alone, and far from help.

"ABCs," she muttered. It was the mantra of the panicked and the inexperienced: keep them breathing until someone who knows what they're doing arrives. She bent to listen at his mouth. When she put her hand on his chest she felt a jolt, and thought she must have kicked up some static by wading through all those candy wrappers. He sat up like a horror-movie murderer and struck her again with the bottle, this time on the cheek. Again the glass failed to break.

"Stop that!" she said sharply, tears springing in her eyes. They blurred her vision as she groped for him. She touched his face and his shoulder, and he fell forward over her. She remembered his weight from when he stepped on her in the gift shop; she had never before met such dense flesh. She took a moment before she rolled him off of her to understand how much her head and her cheek hurt and make sure she was still thinking straight. Still unconscious, he peed on her.

She took him, very slowly—dragging and hauling and resting as infrequently as she could bear, and laying him down every minute to check his breathing—to the ER. The PICU might have been better, but seemed too far away. The ER had been mothballed shortly after the Thing: no one was expecting any more admissions. It even seemed to have shrunk a little, to most observers. A few people slept down there, every so often, and it was rumored to have become a trysting ground for the lonely and not-very-well acquainted, but mostly it was deserted.

It was entirely empty and dark when Jemma struggled in with the boy. She took him into a trauma room because it was closest to the door she'd come through. As soon as she put him on the gurney she reached past his head to the wall and slapped the code button. No red lights flashed. No voice cried out, Code blue! It was just a chime, and it sounded more to Jemma like the call of an ice-cream truck than the announcement of a pending death, but she knew it was ringing in the PICU, too, and that to the people who knew what it meant, it sounded as horrible as any screeching klaxon. After a few seconds of it she heard the angel speak, too. "A child is dying," she said finally.

"Call somebody," Jemma said. "Get Emma down here. This kid's tanking."

"Name me, I will serve. I have preserved you all these days, but I cannot help you without a name."

"Just do it," Jemma said. She had resisted all these weeks, forfeiting fancy pancakes and silk-weave scrubs and fleecy socks—Rob had to do all the making and the shopping and Jemma could only get food by herself at the cafeteria.

"Only name me, and I will serve," the angel said again.

"Just do it, you stupid fucking bitch!" Jemma said.

"I am named. O, listen creatures, again I am named! Again I serve!" Then she was quiet.

"Did you do it?" Jemma asked. "Are they coming?" There was no answer.

"Stupid fucking bitch," Jemma said, and looked at the boy where he lay. The bright lights made him look a paler shade of gray. She did her ABCs again. He was breathing fast and deep, his heartbeat was regular. His pulse was weird, bounding and weak at the same time. She pressed on the tip of his finger, waiting and waiting for the blanching to clear. It took five seconds. She straightened up and looked around the room, just in case she had missed the flood of people who were supposed to be coming to help her. She went to the door and looked out at the dark, empty hall. She thought she could put another voice to the cadence of the code chime: *Nobody coming, nobody coming, nobody coming.* "A child is dying," the angel said again. "Won't you help him?" Jemma went back into the trauma bay.

"Fuck you," Jemma said. She considered the boy, an almost-adolescent who had been drinking and peeing up a storm, who she'd seen snotty with a cold within the past three weeks, who now lay unconscious and obviously dehydrated, breathing deep breaths that were, when she hovered and sniffed above his face, yes, quite fruity. She went looking for a glucometer and found it within seconds: everything in the trauma room was labeled so people made morons by haste could find it with one eye and half a brain. She was about to poke his finger when she considered that he needed fluids. She looked over his arms for a vein; they all seemed to have receded to the level of his bones.

Two pokes in his left antecubital and one in his right, and then she got a flash in her IV catheter. She hooked up the tubing and hung a bag of half-normal saline. He lay quite still, still breathing his deep, rapid breaths. She tried to remember the name for that particular character of breathing, but all that came to mind was the fact she'd neglected to test his blood sugar. It felt to her as if an hour had passed; the code clock, started when she pressed the button, said six minutes. She paged Rob, the only number she knew off the top of her head. She'd never put 911 after her callback number, but she did it now.

She poked his finger and squeezed it till she thought the tip would pop off and fly about the room like a deflating balloon. It yielded a drop of blood the size of a pinhead. Finger, finger, finger: they were all dry. Desperate, she sucked on his thumb to warm it up and finally got a single fat drop, which she almost lost trying to touch it to the glucometer strip with her shaking hand. The little monitor on the glucometer began to count down from sixty seconds. Jemma put it at his feet. She checked the IV, then checked the phone to make sure it had a dial tone. She checked his breathing and his heart, then looked up and realized that the wires and leads of the cardiac and respiratory monitors seemed to be reaching for him. She had no better idea of how to hook them up than she did how to create a beehive hairdo. "I am the preserving angel," the voice said, and Jemma realized it was speaking in exact one minute intervals, "but only you can save this child."

She looked at her glucometer again. It was just counting past ten seconds. She watched the countdown, swearing that the machine paused forever at five, as if it had forgotten what came next. At three seconds she finally heard hurrying footsteps in the hall. At one second the room filled up with people, Dr. Tiller first among them. Never in her life had Jemma been so happy to see someone she hated.

"What the *hell* are you doing?" Dr. Tiller asked, managing a sort of tenor shriek. Jemma tried to offer up the glucometer, and dropped it. Emma, the PICU fellow, reached under her legs and grabbed it.

"Nine-sixty-six!" she said. "Holy shit! No, sorry." She turned it upside down. "Six-sixty-nine. Where did he come from?"

"Not off the street," said Dr. Tiller. "You," she pointed to Jemma. "Get out of the way."

"He was living in the basement," Jemma said, but no one was listening to her. Bodies pushed her back as they surged forward, and the boy was surrounded. While Dr. Tiller shouted orders, hands started another IV, and drew blood, and drew up meds. A nurse took down the monitor wires and hooked them to the patient in less time than it would have taken Jemma to button up a shirt. The press of bodies became so thick that Jemma could only see the boy's feet sticking out. He was missing a shoe.

Dr. Tiller approached her. "Why weren't you giving this boy his insulin?" she demanded.

"He's not mine," Jemma said. "He was hiding. I only just found him."

"How much fluid did you give him? How did you calculate his deficit?"

"I don't know," Jemma said. "I hung a bag just now. See it?" Dr. Tiller made a strange noise, an inflected snort, then walked back to the patient.

"Half-normal? Since when do we resuscitate with half-normal, Dr. Claflin?"

"It was what I found," Jemma said weakly.

The monitor alarms had been sounding since the machine had been hooked up, but suddenly they began to cry with a special urgency, and a different pattern. As Jemma watched the numbers, which printed in blue, yellow, or red, depending on how sick the patient was, went from yellow to red, and then a brighter red, almost orange, as the heart rate climbed above two hundred. At two-fifty the monitor editorialized with a single, livid exclamation point, blinking beside the number. "Goodbye, goodbye, goodbye!" the angel called out.

"Can somebody shut her the fuck up?" Emma asked. "Look at those T waves. Can we get a twelve lead? Who can get me a twelve lead? And some calcium, please." She cast an eye about the room. Jemma hid behind one of the bigger nurses.

"Where's the damned i-stat?" Dr. Tiller asked of the air. "Let's get some labs." The monitor began a weird, crooning moan as the line from the cardiac leads suddenly went crazy.

"See?" said Emma. "It's v-tach. Where are the paddles?"

Dr. Tiller summoned Jemma over with a wave of her hand and told her to start compressions. Jemma had done them only once before, on an eighty-seven-year-old woman whose ribs had splintered under Jemma's palms. She could not remember how many times you were supposed to push in a minute on an eleven-year-old.

"Up here," Dr. Tiller said, grabbing Jemma's hands and moving them higher on the boy's chest. "He's not choking." Jemma had not pushed five times when the boy went back into sinus tachycardia. The fellow was just raising the paddles. She let them drop, clearly disappointed. "You can stop now," Dr. Tiller said to Jemma, pulling her away and pushing her again to the back of the crowd. The bad rhythm returned.

"Bring that back!" Emma called to the nurse who was trundling the defibrillator off to its corner. Dr. Tiller reached back without looking and grabbed Jemma's shirt, pulling her forward, then thrusting her onto the boy's chest.

"Keep on!" she said. Jemma pressed, wearing herself out in less than a minute. Emma was having trouble with the goo, and then they had to recharge the paddles. The rhythm changed just as she was about to call all clear.

Dr. Tiller called again for calcium chloride, and then laid a hand on Jemma's shoulder. "Stop again," she said, more gently, and turned her around. Jemma leaned away from her, one hand still on the boy's chest. "Dr. Claflin," Dr. Tiller said, "assuming this boy has got a potassium imbalance from his dehydration and his insulin deficiency, and assuming our labs are never going to come back, as it seems they will never, then how much calcium chloride should we give this young man?" It took Jemma a moment to understand that Dr. Tiller was asking a question to which she already knew the answer, that she was pimping Jemma in a code. If she hadn't been pregnant, she would probably only have felt intensely sickened. She turned just in time to avoid vomiting in Dr. Tiller's face, and sprayed the boy instead with hot bile, such an emerald green it was almost pretty. His pulse fell briefly into the normal range. "Oh God, get her out of here!" Dr. Tiller called out, in such a stentorian manner and with such commanding authority that Jemma fully expected God himself to remove her from the room by way of a crack in the floor or a flaming chariot or a thundering whirlwind.

A nurse—it was Janie—took her gently by the elbow and steered her out of the trauma bay, whispering at her and shushing her and consoling her, excusing her ineptitude with her ineptitude. "Some of us just aren't made for that room," she said. "It can make people pretty prickly."

"Pretty prickly people," Jemma repeated dumbly, feeling something worse than nausea, a terrible yearning toward this boy that felt like the strangest sort of crush, but as she went step by dizzy step she realized she was yearning not for his flesh or his soul but for his health. She wanted him to get better so bad but she knew he would die. She nearly cried for him, not just her customary dry sobs but actual hot tears; only the sad facts of her life stopping her from doing that, and only barely. About to cry, her parents' deaths rose up in her mind, her mother boozed-up and bleeding, the house on fire, her father wasted to a skeleton in his bed, each death taking a shape like a person and asking, Is it greater than us, that you should weep for it? The answer was yes, but before she could start weeping her brother's death rose up, a flayed, burning giant as tall as the sky, his eyes in one hand and his tongue in the other, and showed her herself standing at the very center of the whole ruined world and silently asked the same question. She did not cry.

"I'll bring you some water, when it settles down in there. Now where are those labs, anyway?" As the nurse walked off, Jemma slid down the wall and sat with her knees against her chest. She heard the monitor moaning again, and the angel said, "I wish I could hold him for you." Emma called all clear, and let out a whoop as she shocked the boy. Dr. Tiller called again for the calcium, and Jemma's nurse came flying down the hall with a slip of paper in her hand. "Seven point two!" she cried as she entered the room.

Then the monitor was quiet for a while, and the voices were quieter. Jemma only heard mumbling, except for Dr. Tiller's voice, rising every few minutes in correction above the others. Jemma put her head between her knees, overwhelmed with nausea. In a few minutes the team rushed out of the trauma bay, wheeling the boy up to the PICU. Jemma's angel of condescension stooped briefly to ask if she'd be okay. Jemma waved her on.

In a few minutes more she stood up and went back into the trauma bay. She put on a pair of gloves and started to clean up the mess, folding the sheet on the gurney into a careful, vomit-filled square. Vomit calls to vomit; that was one of her early third-year lessons, and she was an indiscriminately sympathetic barfer. So she almost did it again, but she hated the thought of someone cleaning up after her. Mopping on the floor with a wet towel, she found the boy's shoe. A filthy sneaker, it was bigger than her own big foot. She sniffed at it tentatively; it had a buttery smell that was oddly settling to her stomach. There was writing on the inside of the tongue, smeared but legible: *This shoe belongs to Jarvis. Put it back where you found it, motherfucker!* She put it back down where she found it, then lifted it up again. Staring into the mouth of the shoe, she sat down on the gurney. In a little while the telephone finally began to ring. She let it ring and ring, answering it only in her mind. You must marry me, Rob said, and her brother said, You swore never to marry—if you thought the end of the world was bad, just wait and see what happens when you break your promise. Her mother asked, Where is it written that a woman's got to suffer like I do? and her father said, If you become a physician I will disown you. I love you, Rob said. Pick up the phone and I'll say it for real. Junkie bitch, Jarvis said, stupid motherfucking busybody whore. I was happy where I was, and now I'm fucking dead.

Are you taking me to Heaven? Jarvis asks me.

No, I say. I am taking you to the roof.

I can do that myself, he says, but he does not take his hand from mine, or curse me, or even frown, because he knows he wasn't going anywhere before I fetched him out of the PICU. He was not enjoying his out-of-body experience. Free at last, he stood outside his prison door and hollered to be let back in. I was diminished, crammed in the corner of his room, watching him pace at the foot of his bed, and throw himself every so often upon his body. Face to face with himself he said, You fucker, wake up! He sat down on the floor, put his head in his hands, and cried. My sister was saying that he should take comfort, and that everything was all right, but he ignored her.

I used to like the crying of children. I wished I could complain as profoundly as an infant, and I admired the way that toddlers sob against the world with their whole souls. I imagined an instrument of them, dozens of babies and toddlers arranged like the pipes on an organ, pedals to squeeze them and keys to poke them—I would play out a complaint to capture the ear of God, and in a whistling, snotty symphony of sobs and screams, articulate the thing that oppressed me, reason and remedy for my world-sized dissatisfaction.

But now I cannot stand to hear it. I unfold myself out of the air and say, Look at me.

Nobody looks any different, he said, staring at the passing faces. Even though I'm dead.

You aren't dead, I say. *I* am dead, but they look the same to me as always. Which was not entirely true: they are easier for me to look at now.

Hey! he said as we passed the eighth floor. Hey! He tugged on my hand and my arm until I looked at him.

What is it?

I'm not so mad anymore. I feel fine and I just noticed it.

Felicitations, I say. I am not so mad anymore either. You need a fleshy heart, to really feel things.

All that time, all that shit! And all I needed to do was die. He walked on, leading me now.

Well, enjoy it while it lasts, I say.

I know when something is going to last forever, he says. I heard them talking down there. Nothing's going to save me from dying. Maybe I'm not going to Heaven, but I'm not going back there.

Miracles have been known to happen.

Ha! he says, making it an ancient and ageless sound.

So here we are, I say, because we are on the roof.

So what? I've seen it. It looks the same.

It is the same. But you, for now, are different. I am the recording angel; you are just a boy. You can't wander around all day prying into people's business: you've got to have diversions. So here is one.

I bring him to the edge of the roof, our hands still joined, but when I say what we are going to do, he pulls away.

I can't swim, he says,

You can now.

I'm not wearing my bathing suit.

You're not wearing anything. And he notices that this is true.

Shit! I'm naked. *You're* naked. You fag! He turns and is about to run, but I am quicker than any wandering undead soul could ever be. I take his hand and leap off the roof, dragging him after me, weighting my wings with memories of sadness and rage. Jarvis is shrieking all the way. We go down, past the long root of the hospital, and the bright globe at the bottom where my sister keeps her spirit, and further, feeling the pressure but not the wetness of the water, falling faster into the lightless cold abyss, but the cold doesn't bother and we don't need light for our eyes.

My rubber band, fastened securely to Jemma, is stretching, and Jarvis wears one that is similar, though like every other child there he is attached, soul and body, to the hospital, until they reach the new world. He is reaching next to me, stretching his hands and his fingers because he can tell we are nearing the bottom. We are drawn back before he can touch it.

We shoot out of the water, up into the air, down onto the roof. I have been alighting all my new life on bedposts and leafless trees and flagpole tops and live wires—Jarvis has only done it this one time. I land on my feet; he lands on his ass, but is up again immediately. I think I saw bones! he says, and then, Can I do it again?

Vivian was working on her list. She worked on it every day—she only had to look out any window to be reminded about it—but still it felt like a chronically neglected task. There was so much other work to do. She was working as hard as any resident-and-a-half in the old world, and she had never learned so much or had so much responsibility for patients, as she had now, and here and there she had made, in the absence of the onc fellow and attending, a decision that truly was life and death. Nonetheless every now and then she had the feeling that all the exhausting and vitally important work she was doing on the ward was easy, and ultimately of no consequence, compared to the list.

If anyone else was making one, she did not know. Jemma had lost interest almost immediately, and the great *Why* that had occupied their initial days and weeks had lately been neglected. People were just doing the work, after all, and all their spare time was spent grieving or trying to snatch a few minutes of normalcy from out of their extraordinary situation. People were dating, and making friends, and having bitter, comfortless sex, and learning to love better the children in their care, but lamentation had given way to a sort of dull voiceless grief, and thoughtful reflection, never fully established in any but a handful of the populace, was giving way to an exhausted sort of acceptance.

And she was as bad as any of them. Tonight she had been sitting for an hour already with nothing to show for it but a slew of generalities (rudeness... intolerance... war) and a few mild particulars (novels about shoes... grade-school beauty pageants... closeted politicians). Two weeks ago she'd have had ten major and twenty minor categories already delineated in that time, arranged neatly in two columns, and she'd have started to arrange them in ranks and associations. Tonight they were all over the page, clustered like flying insects around a drawing of Ishmael's back. "Nothing bad about that," she said, looking at the drawing, and thinking of him. She had put him aside for her work, and now she wished she had not. "I understand," he said, and went off to do more of his own private work, reading and research, trolling for some personal affinity or flash or recognition that would suggest to him what he had used to do, and who he had been, in the old world.

That was what he said he would do, but in fact he was with Thelma, the big nurse who den-mothered the kids on the psych ward. It wasn't exactly a date. He had gone up to talk to her, and brought her some fancy candy that the angel had designed for him. He had no idea why he was attracted to her. He did not think large women in their fifties were his type, but he was always being surprised by affinities—mobbed all of a sudden by a violent attraction to some nurse or doctor or patient or piece of furniture. He did not understand the feelings. They were different from what he felt for Vivian—they were not tender, and he knew he did not love these people, for all that he wanted to shove himself, body and soul, into their bodies, or draw them into him until they disappeared. At the height of his lust he wanted to enter them only so he could tear them apart when he exited—he imagined standing and stretching to his full height, and throwing them off him in strips of flying flesh.

No more of that, he told himself every time he did it. And yet he kept doing it again and again, knowing that it was inferior to what he was pursuing with Vivian, and knowing that it would hurt her, and knowing he must keep it secret from her. And what made him saddest about the whole business was that his skill at it, and his familiarity with bodies, and the sense as he raged upon the man or woman in his grip that this was all so familiar, made him think that this was what he had done in the old world. But what kind of job was that, and what sort of person did it? "Do you know," he said to Thelma, pushing her great hammock-sized bra up off of her breasts, "it is my first time."

"Mine too, baby," she said. "Ha ha ha!"

The Committee proclaimed the end of another rotation, and Jemma got to visit Jarvis in an official capacity when she switched onto the NICU/PICU team. Rob joined the surgeons, Vivian took Jemma's place on the heme-onc service, and Maggie, the pale, chinless goat of their class, came onto the intensive-care service with Jemma. "At last," she said, "some really sick kids," actually rubbing her hands together, while she and Jemma were waiting for their orientation lecture from Emma. Maggie had not planned, before the Thing, to work with children much more than was necessary to graduate. Kids creeped her out and big-headed googly-eyed kids creeped her out especially. Her brother and sister, senior residents at one of the most prestigious and toxic internal medicine programs of the Northeast, had a place reserved for her to come suffer and thrive and fulfill her bright, evil promise. She'd only been in the children's hospital that night because she was doing a rotation in pediatric anesthesia, seeking to learn procedures made more challenging by tiny airways and veins, and she still lusted shamelessly after every sort of insertional intervention. She had a little six-word song she kept singing, and kept trying to get Jemma to sing with her. "I just can't wait," it went, "to intubate!"

Jemma could wait. Though there had been, before, a certain amount of junior professional pride that came with successfully completing a procedure, she was already sick of them. She never wanted to see another epiglottis again, but she and Maggie had not been in the unit an hour when she was presented with one. Emma stood in a PICU conference room and gave them their orientation lecture, a plain exhortation to do good work and not be overwhelmed by how complex the patients were, modified for the new days with a coda in which she told them the unit was the best place to be at a time like this, because when you're doing chest compressions and such you really don't have time to worry about all the really horrible shit. Already exhausted not an hour into her day, Jemma still had thirty-five hours of call before her. It didn't matter that what Emma was saying was vitally interesting—past a certain threshold of exhaustion all lectures were soporific. Jemma stared out the window at the sea, and another beautiful morning—the sun was behind them, so the PICU looked out into the ice-cream-cone-shaped shadow of the hospital.

"It was always important," Emma was saying when they were interrupted, "to keep them, to save them, though there was a point where you always said, after this it's more suffering than living. Maybe that shouldn't have changed, but it has. Now there's a new rule: never let them go, never ever, because we can't lose one more. Not even one. This was never an easy place to be, and now it's even harder—they're all sicker, they really are—so listen: I'm always here, if you see something that makes you want to chew off your fingers and you need someone to stop you. Just ask the angel to call me, or page me yourself the old-fashioned way: 719-0058." She made them recite her pager number, and did not smile, but her face softened a little under its cap of curls. Maggie raised her hand, but before Emma could acknowledge her they were interrupted by the soft tinkling of the code bell, and the angel's calm alarum: "A child is dying." Emma was off in an instant, Maggie and Jemma followed close behind.

They didn't have far to go. A child had collapsed just a few yards from the conference room, the brother to a boy in the unit, an eight-year-old who'd arrested during soccer practice. He'd spent four days on bypass, and emerged ruined from the interventions of the intensivists, alive but unable to move or speak or probably even think. The cardiologists had fallen swiftly upon the whole family, but come up with no answers. The boy whose code inaugurated Jemma's unit experience, the youngest child, had been put on an antiarrythmic despite a normal EKG, but had, it turned out, been cheeking and spitting the little yellow pills since the great storm.

"Marcus, my friend," Emma said to him as she felt in his neck and groin for a pulse. "What do you think you're doing?" When she couldn't find the pulse she told Maggie to start chest compressions.

Not again! Jemma thought, because she was still having nightmares about Jarvis, who lay intubated a few beds down. He followed her around on her sleepless peregrinations or they were living out a married life in his basement nest or she was crack whore to his stylish pimp and he called her "motherfucker" or "stupid bitch" and kicked the shit out of her all night long. But she didn't say it out loud. And she didn't run away, like she wanted to do.

She hated to bag, but Emma made her do it. She'd never managed to force the mask tight enough against the face for a good seal, and always worried, even with big people, that she'd squeeze so much air into them that she'd pop their lungs.

"Shouldn't I intubate?" Maggie asked. Emma ignored her. Dr. Tiller arrived at the head of a mob of nurses.

"What's this?" she asked Emma.

"Pretty much what it looks like," she said. She pressed a pair of defibrillator paddles against the boy's chest and looked briefly at the rhythm. "V-fib."

Emma announced the all clear. Jemma, too intent on the bagging, didn't hear. "That means you, especially," Emma said, nudging her with her knee. "There now," she said, as she delivered a shock and the child went back into a normal rhythm. By the time they'd moved him to a bed, though, he'd become pulseless again.

There was something dreamlike about the time that followed, maybe because the deep, sighing breaths Jemma was putting into the boy were breaths in the cadence of sleep, and they cast a dreamy pall over her, and even over the activity in the room, which was as graceful as it was frenetic. Jemma considered, as she breathed, how every actor in the room, except the patient, was a female, and wondered if that had anything to do with the exquisite coordination that was taking place. Dr. Tiller stood at the head of the bed, ataraxic and remote, arms folded across her chest. Emma got access, and the nurses pushed the code drugs barely a half minute after Dr. Tiller called for them. Emma called for some atropine and handed the laryngoscope to Jemma, though Maggie, still laboring at compressions, made a swipe at it as it was passed off. Jemma had the irrational feeling, as she beheld the thing, that the boy's epiglottis was somehow indicting her as a procedure thief. She missed it twice but Emma would not take it from her. "There's no hurry," she said. "We've got him right where we want him, he's not going anywhere. I'll just bag a little while you think of something peaceful."

"I never get these," Jemma whispered. "It's okay."

"Mountain streams. Or just mountains, never mind the water. Dry mountains—they're green on the bottom and white on top. You're going to get this one." Maggie was twisting in place like she had to pee, and derailed Jemma's thoughts—she was trying to envisage a calm green mountain pasture—so she could only see a beautiful bathroom in her mind's eye, a fancy-toilet-catalog bathroom. Maggie sat on a toilet of amber and gold and alabaster, peeing serenely. "Now here you go," Emma said, stepping away, and Jemma finally got it. She hooked up the bag to the tube, and breathed in time with him, and found herself developing strange feelings for the dying boy. It wasn't enough, just to squeeze the bag. She wanted to squeeze him in a big hug, or put her naked hands around his twitching heart and squeeze that, too. She yearned toward him—toward his pretty white lungs, his smooth red liver, his fat purple spleen. She was leaning a little over him, almost about to lay herself on top of him—she wanted him so badly all of a sudden, and that was the way to have him, pressing herself close against him, skin to skin—when Maggie pushed her roughly on the shoulder between compressions. "Watch it," she said. Jemma blinked, shook her head, and blushed.

The dream ended not long after the tube went in. The boy could not stay out of the bad rhythm. After fifteen minutes Dr. Tiller called the makeshift bypass team—Dr. Walnut and Dolores. When they arrived someone else took over the bagging from Jemma, and Maggie, her hair in a sweaty flip, was excused from the chest when she started to drip on the sterile field. A couple of words slipped out of the corner of Emma's mouth as they passed her where she stood, arms folded over her chest, in the doorway: "Good job." She handed them each a list with their respective patients circled, and told them to spend the rest of the afternoon getting to know them.

"You," Maggie said to Jemma, as soon as they were out in the hall. She jerked her thumb at the doorway to the conference room where Emma had spoken with them earlier. "In here now." Jemma followed her in, and watched her, just for a few moments, as she stood with her hands on her hips, panting furiously, wet stains still growing on her scrub shirt. What was coming was obvious. Jemma gathered up her things and moved toward the door. "Oh, no, missy. You've got something to hear, first. That was my tube you took away. It belonged to me and don't tell me, don't you dare tell me that you didn't see my name on it. I've got a list, and you *don't* want to be on it."

"See you later," Jemma said. Maggie, hands still on her hips, stepped quickly to the door, looking much more like a ballerina or an aerobics instructor than a raging crabby-ass.

"How dare you! How dare you! You don't even care about it. I heard you. I saw you. The whole thing was *wasted* on you."

"I just want to leave," Jemma said. Maggie put her face closer to Jemma's and tried to thrust out her chin, but only succeeded in pursing her lips. "You're making me sick," Jemma said, because an intense wave of nausea was rising up from her belly.

"You make me sick, too!" Maggie said, and then her voice was drowned out by the noise of Jemma's blood rushing in her ears. She felt dizzy; a strange green shade was drawn across her vision. For a moment she couldn't see anything. She fell to her knees and vomited, her sight coming back only after her stomach was empty and she was retching miserably. She'd barfed on poor angry Maggie, who seemed to have thrown herself literally into a fit. Jemma adjusted her head and pushed some furniture out of the way to give her a safe space to seize in. Then she opened the door and screamed, "Emma!"

It seemed like a violation, to pry open Maggie's mouth and look into her throat, and it would have been unforgivable, Jemma was sure, for her to intubate her classmate. It had to be done—it took a half hour to get her to stop seizing, and by that time she was so loaded with meds she was only breathing five times a minute. But she was so chinless that she proved difficult even for Emma to do. She got hooked up—the nurses descended on her, overcoming their distaste for adults—she was really only as big as a ten-year-old, anyway—to stick her for blood and an IV and hang her fluids and get her on the monitor. If you didn't look at her face, her expression still impatient and dissatisfied even after eight milligrams of ativan, and two hundred each of phenobarbital and fosphenytoin, and another hundred of pentobarbital, she could have been a child in the fancy ICU bed, vacated just that morning by a CP/DD moaner-groaner with pneumonia who, kicked back to the ward, left behind one of his mobiles. A dozen winged monkeys floated over Maggie's head. Emma wound up the mobile after Maggie was all tucked in, and, wings flapping, the monkeys circled and the box played a tinny version of "Yesterday." Jemma watched her for a little while, imagining it was her in the bed, overcome with toxemia or hyperemesis or simple fatness or demon-baby syndrome, while tourists from other wards, drawn by the novelty of a sick adult, passed by the glass walls of the room and cast their eyes on the sleeper. Maggie was all covered up, but Jemma knew that when it was her a boob and a succession of dirty panties would be displayed to the passers-by, and, seeing her, they would all appreciate what a simple blessing it was to be awake and ambulatory and unintubated.

"Don't you have somewhere else to be?" the nurse asked her finally.

"Feel better," Jemma said to Maggie. She left the room and hesitantly embraced her new duties. Emma had done her the grueling honor of assigning her ten patients, five downstairs in the PICU, five upstairs in the NICU. Downstairs she had Jarvis, Marcus, and three others—a fifteen-month-old boy whose father had beaten his head against a barbecue, a fifteen-year-old girl who, undergoing treatment for leukemia, had gotten a bag of infected platelets infused into her veins the day before the flood and swan dived into septic shock and respiratory distress syndrome, and a post-op cardiac patient, a girl born a week before the storm with no left side to her heart. Upstairs she had three preemies, a three-month-old with leprechaunism, and little Brenda.

Out on the floor she'd thought she'd come to know how rounds were perpetual, but at least out there was always a chance to sit down, at some point during the long day. In the units she was in near constant motion, circling from room to room, bay to bay, and even from floor to floor, going constantly from patient to patient, because there was always something acutely wrong with them—if she collapsed at a table in some hidden corner of the PICU her pager sounded immediately. Rob had told her about the circling; on him it had a calming effect. "Sometimes at night," he said, "if I've been going long enough, it feels like I'm everywhere at once, in every bay, upstairs and downstairs, and it's like I can almost hold the whole place in my head, and all the collective fucked-upness of the kids becomes very individual and distinct, and it's like I know everything about them, and can almost predict who's going to code next." Jemma said that sounded like a pretty bad trip to her.

But she felt it too, or something like it, that very first night. She was ostensibly covering both units, and even though it was largely a sort of pretending—Emma took care of most everything, or advised Jemma over the phone about even the smallest points of management—it was as overwhelming as it was exhilarating. Emma moved in her own circles, and Dr. Tiller was attending. Jemma succeeded spectacularly at avoiding her, and developed, before Rob's sensor of fucked-upness, a Dr. Tiller proximity alarm that steered her away from particular bays just in time; a bit of dread in the air would push her away, or she'd see the distinctive shadow of Dr. Tiller's headdress stretching around the corner on the wall or floor. Moving away from Dr. Tiller, or in search of Emma to get a question answered, she started, after she had accomplished a few dozen circumnavigations, to feel something akin to what Rob described: the place started to seem whole in her mind, yet the children became more distinct from each other. She could visit the bays and rooms and shape an imaginary child in her head before she arrived there in person, even if she could never distinguish the unique anatomic pathologies of the cardiac patients—she mixed up tetralogies and tricuspid atresias and simple VSDs in a way that seemed ill-fitting for the daughter of a cardiac surgeon. But beyond what Rob had described, there was something else, a sense that, though she was perpetually in motion, she was floating in the still center of the hospital. True, it was in the character of the intensivists to consider themselves the most important doctors in the hospital, and to consider the drama of the rest of the hospital inferior to that of the unit. But also, since the Thing, the patients, instead of striving to leave the hospital, seemed to strive to enter the PICU, and every time a child improved enough to move out of the unit another came immediately to take its place. Jemma, fatigued by hour twenty-three of wakefulness into a pretty trippy state of mind, thought she could feel the great lines of attraction, grooves in the unbodied essence of the hospital, along which critically ill children moved as certainly as the stars in their courses.

It was a very different sort of rounding than she'd become used to, and the novelty of it helped to propel her through the dawn despite her exhaustion. She slowed, as the sun rose, pausing longer and longer at each bedside. She was surprised to miss the conversation with her patients out on the ward, even when she had been just their talking doughnut. It was much harder to socialize with the comatose, even with Maggie, who, deep in her pentobarb coma, had reached a personal apogee of pleasantness. The barbecue boy twitching and crying in his troubled sleep; the spoiled-platelet girl flapping her hands gently in her restraints; the little hypoplast with the recently reopened chest, an opaque window of antiseptic tape fluttering over her heart; Marcus lying still in his bed, staring blindly at the ceiling, dead alive while his blood slid around the room through the crazy-straw architecture of the LVAD: at every bed Jemma looked at the numbers and did a brief exam, and then stood watching over them with increasing solemnity, until, as she stood over Jarvis, it was almost as if she was visiting his grave. She watched him, feeling something catch in herself every time his respirator gave him a breath. She counted them, eighteen a minute. He did not breathe over that rate, nor did he move a muscle in his body, though he wasn't paralyzed, like other patients on the ventilator. His pupils, when she pried open his lids to look in his eyes, were fixed. When she pinched his fingertip, as hard as a bite, he did not draw away. On the second day after Jemma had carried him out of his nest he'd developed cerebral edema and herniated, though Dr. Tiller raged powerfully against his decline.

By the time Jemma left him the shrunken sun was disappearing into a bank of clouds, and the day had turned sufficiently that her pager quieted and she was no longer on call. Tousled, wrinkly Dr. Chandra found her to get signout on his patients.

"Are they all alive?" he asked her.

"Oh yes," Jemma said. "Everybody did okay. Let's see. Bed 1 had a k of 2.0—I bolused. Her pressure was in the eighties after she got some fentanyl—so I gave albumin. She spiked, I cultured. She had a film this morning, but I haven't seen it yet."

"I hate this place," he said, stretching and yawning. It was a very different morning than yesterday's. All that bright sunshine seemed a year ago now to Jemma. The sea was the color of bile and the sky slate-gray. "Don't you hate it?" he asked her.

"It was only my first night," she said.

"That's enough to know. The places are like people, and first impressions count for a lot. I liked the onc ward better. They're nicer up there. I don't know what it is—the kids are almost as sick upstairs, but down here everyone's always in a bad mood."

"They're not exactly hanging leis up there, either."

"It's like they hate me down here. They all think I'm stupid."

"Nobody thinks you're stupid," Jemma said, though she had heard it said of him that he could not diagnose his way out of a wet paper bag.

"They think I'm stupid upstairs, too, but they're nicer. They're just nicer people."

"You know more than me," Jemma offered.

"You're a student," he said simply. "Sort of. I guess there aren't any students any more. We're all in the program now, caught in its clutches. The program—I'd been counting down the days left in residency and now it's going to last forever. It's not that different than before. You never get to leave and there's no life outside, and everybody's horribly depressed because nothing good ever happens here, and it's the ugly truth about the program that they pretend to care about you eating and sleeping and learning and not wanting to die every minute of your work day, but really they care about you only as far as they can kick you or as deeply as they can fuck you, and nobody pretended more lamely or cared more superficially than our director. How are you? he'd say, and stare at you with his zombie eyes. Call me Dad. We're all one family—what a horribly unfunny joke. I used to be so jealous, sometimes, watching all the regular people outside—I'd sit in the park and even the homeless people seemed as happy and free as fat little hobbits. But now"—he clapped his hands together, startling Jemma, who always had trouble staying awake around hour twenty-four, and was starting to drift—"just like that, the hospital ate the whole fucking world, and now nobody will ever get out or go home. Do you ever wonder if it would be more pleasant around here if Dr. Tiller were dead? It's probably a sin to think like that. The angel says it's okay, but I don't believe her."

Jemma wasn't sure if she should continue with the signout, so she said, "The angel's a good listener."

"Yeah," he said. "What about Bed 3?" She told him the night's story on that patient, and on the others he was responsible for, 5 and 8 and 13 and 17 and 18, and then his ten babies upstairs. She became lost in her notes, not sure who had thrown up and who hadn't, or who had spiked, or which baby got the weird purpuric blotch that was shaped just like lost Australia. Chandra was sympathetic. "They're all kind of the same, anyway," he said.

When they were finished she went upstairs to start her official morning rounds before Dr. Sasscock could find her—she had carried some of his patients overnight, too. Brenda was lounging in her isolette, looking quite relaxed and even, in her own way, rather healthy. Sound asleep, she nonetheless lifted an arm to point as soon as Jemma stepped up on the dais.

"Hello, little thing," Jemma said. "I get to visit you every morning now, you know, and be your own special moron. Your very own moron, to do a little dance for you when you're sad, to lie down at your feet when you need to lord it over somebody, and when you are hungry you can say, Hey, moron, peel me a grape!" The baby dropped her arm, but continued to stare while Jemma felt her head and listened to her chest and belly. She had grown—now she was a thirty-six-weeker, almost big enough to be born, and almost big enough to have gone home, in the old world. Jemma had pictures of her in her new camera, and stored on the computer in the call room, documenting her many visits. Day by day and week by week she looked more human, though never much like a normal baby, with her toaster-shaped head and her train-wreck face and her many-fingered hands, not to mention the tubes that grew as certainly as her more natural appendages. There was still not much body to cover, and not much work involved in a full exam, even as her improving health allowed more detailed probing and firmer poking. But Jemma, when she was done with her exam, felt suddenly tired. It often happened this way. The first twelve hours of call were all right. Fifteen was a logy hour, but sixteen through twenty were fine. Zombie time started at hour twenty-four, and the big crash came in the morning of the next day, at hour twenty-five, when she could hardly remember her name and might fall asleep on her feet if she stopped moving for too long. She felt the crash impending now; to ward it off she closed up the isolette and put her head down on top of the box, meaning to keep it there ever so briefly—sometimes three minutes of sleep could keep you going for another hour. She fell asleep immediately, her hands relaxing where they hung at her sides, and her mouth opening a little, so her breath clouded the plastic.

There now; goodnight, Jemma. Sleep well, for you'll not sleep long, and since I am not a preserving angel I'll not be able to catch you when the drop attacks come during walk-rounds, the creeping sleepiness that you feel coming more completely over you as the endless seconds pass and Emma tries to make you understand the differences between the three types of total anomalous pulmonary venous return. The big velvet sheet drops down over you, somehow managing to cover your feet and legs and belly and chest and shoulders before it covers your head and your eyes, and then you'll be on the floor, awake already as soon as you've hit, all the insensitivists peering at you, disappointed at the already dissipated scent of a likely intubation. Sleep on, hard and deep. The customary morning bustle of the NICU will proceed around you, and the nurses will pay you, for the most part, only cursory attention. Nobody bears you any ill will, though one or two of them understand that you must have a pile of work to do, and yet they do not wake you because the prospect of your suffering pleases them just a little. Anna, arrived to feed the baby, doesn't wake you, either, but her motives are pure: she thinks you need your rest, thinks you look worn out and a little ugly, and while she is waiting for the formula to run down through the tube, does your hair for you, and you will wake in half an hour with none of your morning work done but with a hairdo, three braids coiled on top of your head in a pattern that seems to your fuzzed-up mind as complex as the worst congenital heart lesion, that makes you, in your blue-green scrubs and dancing clogs and canary-colored robe, the very picture of post-call glamour.

After rounds, Jemma hid in the PICU staff bathroom rubbing on her eyes, a measure usually sufficient to drive a headache away, but one that looked so alarming to people who saw her driving the heel of her hand into her orbit, and who heard the curious, wet noises that her eyeball made when she did it, that it required privacy. She sighed, pressing harder with both hands, and saw floating bits of color in the dark behind her eyelids, here and there an emerald sparkle among them. She saw her brother's face flash unbidden in the same darkness, pale and dead, how she imagined that his open-casket funeral face would have looked—the face a natural death would have given him. She did not understand why she was suddenly so angry; Maggie had been annoying her and countless others for years, and had never before evoked much from Jemma besides horror and pity. For a moment the spirit of her brother threatened to possess her, his face loomed larger before her closed eyes, his mouth opening to show a deeper blackness, and she knew if she fell into it she would lose her temper in a way that would make her his imperfect avatar, as angry as him but expressing it in a hissy fit rather than sublime fury. He faded away before he touched her.

"It was horrible!" Maggie had said, slurring a little, after waking from her extended postictal snooze just as they were rounding on her. "She made this nasty sound, and horrible green sparkles shot out of her eyes, and then I couldn't move, and then I was seizing, and I knew I was but I couldn't do anything about it!"

"Sometimes people hallucinate before their seizures," said Emma. "You had a lot of activity in your temporal lobes, even on the pentobarb. Want to see your EEG?" The whole team was gathered around the bed, Drs. Tiller and Grouse and Chandra and Jordan Sasscock and Emma, everybody staring at the patient with expressions of fixed beneficence. Jemma was smiling even as she was being slandered.

"I want my brain back. She damaged it—I can *feel* the damage. How many deletions are there in alpha-thal minor? I don't think I know any more. That part of my brain was damaged. I want to stop her before she does it again. I want justice, is what I want." Jemma had dashed off to replicate a batch of festive cupcakes when she heard that Maggie was awake and extubated. Now she put them down on the trash can and backed out of the room. Maggie kept talking, her soft hoarse voice at odds with the fury in her words. "You're on the list!" she called after Jemma.

"I'm giving you a little ativan," Emma said. "One, two, three… relax!"

Jemma sat down at one of the station desks and tried to calm herself by going through one of her patients' charts, trying to figure out how many days her platelet girl had been on each of her eight different antibiotics. "Septra number forty-seven," she muttered. "Ceftaz number ten; vanc number fifteen; tobra number seventeen; ampho number five." But instead of becoming calm she just got more agitated.

Hour twenty-six, hour twenty-eight, hour thirty—the endless day went on and on. Rob came in and out of it, checking in on her in the morning to see how she'd done her first night in the unit. Recognizing her bad mood, he returned again and again, trying to cheer her up, bringing a succession of gifts: a bit of unusual candy from the gift shop; some ice cream; a cold salad-bar plum; a little song about Maggie, new words set to the tune of "I Got No Strings" (I got no chin to shape my jaw, nor sweetness in my soul!); a shoulder rub, then a back rub, then a thigh rub, and finally his face between her legs. They were paged before he could transform her—she was on officially until five o'clock, and he'd be on all through the night with the surgery team—though it would not have transformed her or the day unfolding with unpleasant surprises, even if he had made her sing. But it did provide a bit of shelter, to lie across the call-room bed, her hand resting on the back of his head, feeling the new sweat gathering atop his scalp, and feeling his gasping breath against her skin. Hand on the doorknob, he ruined it all just as they were leaving the room. "Marry me," he said again.

"Not that again," she said.

"Again and again," he said. "Until you give me a good reason."

"I wouldn't marry you if you were the last man in the world, which you practically are. I wouldn't do it with anybody. How many times do we have to have this stupid conversation?"

"As many as it takes," he said, and stared at her, annoying fool, with his back against the door and his hand still on the knob.

"Can I go?" she asked. "I have antibiotic dosages to adjust. It's very important. No one else can do it. No else has a calculator. No one else has the incredibly sophisticated grasp of arithmetic. They're waiting for me, can I please get by?"

"We're already a family," he said. "I just want you to say it—I just want you to understand it, too."

"Don't say that word," she said, shouldering past him, aware that he was staring at her as she walked away down the hall. She stopped on a set of preemie prints and shook her ass, meaning the gesture to be somehow conciliatory. Maybe it was her bad mood that made it feel taunting and cruel, but sometimes a boy should know when to just be quiet.

She'd had so many bad days, before and after the Thing. Why this day should seem like the culmination of every bad day, she did not know, unless it was on account of the pregnancy. At eleven weeks she was almost always nauseated, though the really horrible gut-twisting retching only came at night—it was such a horrible sound, something that started out deep in her rectum and spurned the easy way out, making the long journey up to her mouth, gathering volume and a truly ass-nasty assortment of tastes to fill her mouth and vapors for her to spray around the bathroom. She knew it was the single most unattractive thing she'd ever done. She ran every faucet while she performed, and had the angel play loud music, and flushed and flushed and flushed the toilet, all to keep Rob from hearing, and she would never let him in with her, though he wanted to hold her hand while she did it. She could deal with it. Vivian swore up and down that it would pass, and Jemma didn't mind being tired all the time, or how some foods—asparagus and potatoes and apple juice—were suddenly unpalatable, but the agitation, if it continued at such a pitch, would surely wear her down. She'd met a string of pregnant ladies who all seemed perched on the brink of a particular type of madness. "I just want to rip off my own leg and then beat everybody around me to death with it!" was how one patient described the feeling to Jemma. "Yes," Jemma had said, drawing on a store of vaguely remembered and possibly made-up information, "I think it can be quite normal to feel that way." It was as if the little hurt which Maggie had done her in the morning had marked her equanimity in just the right place to weaken it fatally, so all the subsequent wrongs of the day were exacerbated.

Through hour thirty-one she sat at one of the nurses' stations in the PICU wrestling with the antibiotic dosing on her septic teenaged friend while Dr. Chandra and Dr. Sasscock played hangman across the table from her, waiting for the afternoon labs to come back. The girl's creatinine had been sky-high at the late-morning draw; her kidneys were failing and if Jemma didn't lower her doses she risked knocking them out completely.

"You're just going to have to do that again," said Jordan. "You may as well wait for the evening labs."

"I almost have it," Jemma said, though once again her calculations were yielding doses more appropriate to large-animal medicine. "And the drugs are due soon."

"An hour delay won't matter," he said.

"In an hour Tipper will be down here," said Dr. Chandra. "He does that shit in his sleep. You obviously haven't learned how to profit by a timely consult."

"I pretty much have it," Jemma said.

"You're probably right," said Dr. Chandra. "But he'll do that thing, anyway, where he laughs like your incompetence is cute but really he's furious because you're so stupid, and he won't look at you. He looks at your feet or at the ceiling or at your ear or at your crotch but you have to be the queen for him to look you in the eye. He's part of the program. He was always part of the program."

"Pick a letter," said Dr. Sasscock.

"Y," said Dr. Chandra, "as in why am I here anyway? There's a whole hospital worth of misery out there, better wallowing than here. It was never going to be part of my life, taking care of kids with a piece of soggy fucking origami where their heart should be. Why do I have to deal with it now? What's the point? What are we being trained for, anymore? What?" He was looking right at Jemma, and made a gesture at her, folding his hands together and shaking them over the table. "Why, why, why?"

"Can you dose tobra every twelve hours in someone with a creatinine of two?" she asked him.

"Go ask Dad," he said. "We may as well ask Dad. You get the same goddamn answer, that zombie smile, whether he's alive or dead, here or gone, and no matter that he's dead and the whole world is gone with him, we're all still in the program and we're all still under his thumb."

"Do q twenty-four," Dr. Sasscock said to Jemma, and to Chandra, "Dude, shut the fuck up. Pick another letter and stop badmouthing Dad. The man was a saint."

Dr. Chandra shook his head, but stopped complaining, and they played on in peace, leaving Jemma to her work, until the labs came back and sent them scurrying. Jemma got three new quasi-emergencies—a low k and a high k and a low phosphorus—but decided to ignore them for five more minutes until she got the damned dosages set. Dr. Tipper snuck up on her just as she was finishing and pointed out that she'd got it all wrong. He looked at her shoes and her left boob and her belly and each ear, and spoke his mocking chortle, and she became more furious and more depressed and more weary, and all she could do, when he flew through the calculations and wrote out the orders and hummed her a snatch of the Mikado, was sigh at him, and say "Thank you."

At hour thirty-three she encountered Monserrat and her tamale wagon, making her afternoon snack rounds. "You look awful," she told Jemma.

"Everyone keeps telling me that."

"Are you hungry? Have you eaten?"

"I had some juice... earlier," Jemma said, not able to remember when she had last eaten.

"Strange, strange girl," she said. "How do you think you can keep going with no gas in your engine, with no hamster in your wheel? Come here to me." She took Jemma by the hand. Her wagon had been souped-up by the angel—motorized and decked out with moon-rover tires and a folding table and inflatable chairs, and a cooler/replicator that only made supremely exotic horchatas.

"You need to take care of yourself," she said. "A cat takes better care than you do. Look at you!"

"I know," Jemma said, as Monserrat lifted a cold bottle of soda from the cooler. Instead of opening it for her she rolled it back and forth across her face. "I should keep going," she said. "I have some bad labs to fix... That's nice."

"First the cold, then the hot," she said, guiding Jemma's face over the steamer and stepping on the pedal to generate a blast that lifted her hair and left drops of water condensing on her nose. She nearly fell asleep while the lady massaged her face with a corn husk.

"It's been a good day," Monserrat said, while Jemma started to eat, hushing her every time she tried to say something. "Not so pleasant outside, and ugly days used to never turn out well, but already today I've captured five others just like you, dragging their big bottoms and looking like they're about to cry. I do an intervention and it goes a little better. I like the word—intervention. My son did one for my high salt and my blood pressure. It was swift and cruel—he threw it all away and I wanted to wander into the woods like a deer and lick rocks, but he was right, and I am right. How do you feel? Would you like another?"

"Tired," Jemma said. "And late. And thanks. I've got to go."

The lady put another warm tamale down Jemma's pants, catching it in the band of her scrubs and adjusting it so it settled in the small of her back while Jemma just stood there, reflexes slowed by fatigue so that by the time she jumped away it was already done. "If you don't eat it then give it to someone you love," said Monserrat, and pressed the button that folded up the table and deflated the chairs. She walked off behind the wagon, steering it nimbly with a little black joystick.

Hour thirty-four she spent with Vivian, who came down to do a consult—her second day on the service and she was already trusted with them—on a Down's syndrome baby in the NICU who'd been persistently throwing blasts on his smears for the last three days. "You look awful," she said to Jemma, pausing in the middle of her note.

"I know," she said. "Everyone's told me. Really, *everyone*. Somebody wrote it in the bathroom up here. Jemma Claflin is one hideous bitch."

"Sorry," Vivian said. "You just look tired. A little worse than post-call. Was it a bad night?" Jemma shrugged and put her head down on her arms. "Don't go to sleep. You've got another two hours yet. Tiller's going to page you, you know, for her own fucked-up signout. What did you learn, Dr. Bennett, from the trials of the night? It's like rounding all over again, but for absolutely no reason at all." She sighed.

"Are you all right?" she asked, continuing the note—Jemma heard the nib of her fountain pen scratching across the page—but reaching with her non-writing hand to massage Jemma's scalp. Jemma nodded. "I was worried about you, last night. I should have come to visit. I meant to. But the list was pressing. It's so strange—it leaves me alone for a couple days and then it's like, of course! How could I have missed that one! I have to work on it, and every item has a related item, every paragraph a subparagraph—within and within and within, but I never seem to get to the heart of anything. And then the next day I look at it and it all seems so petty and stupid and totally not worth it. Not worth even thinking about. It's like I was drunk, but I haven't been drunk, much, and I haven't been shrooming since way back, honest."

"Everything's strange," Jemma said. "At least you're not throwing up all the time."

"That'll pass, and even if it doesn't, I've got some plans. That reminds me, we should check an hCG. What if it's a mole? Wouldn't that be disgusting?"

"Three moles are walking in a tunnel, single file, on their way to raid a farmer's kitchen," Jemma said, though she could see the other kind of mole, the one that Vivian was talking about, a placenta corrupted to the point of malignancy.

"We'll do a sono if it's high," Vivian said. "I was up all night with the list, even though I knew I was on call today and should sleep, and the boy wasn't snoring for once, and we had this incredible session before bed. I should have been exhausted."

"'I smell sweet candied carrots!' said the first mole."

"I actually was exhausted, but it came to me. Local news. How could I have missed it? It was always so awful, no matter where you went, but worse than that was how it demeaned everything it touched. Part the bad hair and there it is, a thoroughly belittling but tireless regard. Even when they tried to praise something, they condemned it."

"'I smell apple pie!' said the second mole," Jemma said, trying not to think about the extensive coverage, or see it replayed across the white static behind her eyes—a shot of Calvin's blood on the ice, a burned hand reaching out from beneath a tarp, the string of idiot commentators speculating on the nature of the devil-cult that supervised the black ceremony. There was her house burning and the wreck of Martin's car wrapped around an impervious tree. It all conflated into one supremely horrible story about which the now slack-jawed bimbo had nothing to say.

"It's not even the extreme lameness, how lame they look or how obscenely they fondle things. Here's the within: it's temporary. It's the rage of every story—I was never even meant to be told but now you have forgotten me. Why did you disturb my rest? Why did you wake my curse? You never even really cared. Something like that—all that pathetic lame shit banding together and praying for vengeance."

"'I smell mole asses!' said the third mole." Jemma saw empty white static again. She sat up and started to rub her eyes.

"Now it seems stupid already, like I said. Don't do that, you'll detach your retina and anyway it's disgusting." She wrote a few more sentences while Jemma kept rubbing, then shut the chart. "Heme-onc is fun," she said.

"My guess is leukemoid reaction, but it's a little late. She's so Downsie, though. AML? That would suck. Anyway, I'll talk to Sashay about a bone marrow and set it up with Wood tomorrow morning after rounds if it's a go. Are you even listening to me?"

"AML," Jemma said. "Sashay. Bone marrow tomorrow."

Vivian looked at her watch. "Two more hours—hang in there. Just picture Tiller blowing Snood if she tries to make you cry."

"I never cry," Jemma said, "and don't spread rumors." She took the chart back just as her pager sounded. Jarvis was bradying and desatting. She had no idea what to do about that, and the rest of the hour passed before she and Emma figured out together that his ET tube was too low.

The sun came out at hour thirty-four, and as hour thirty-five closed Jemma paused many times by the windows, wanting to get out of the hospital, looking at the green water and wondering what it would be like to go floating in a dinghy. Trailing behind the hospital would not be the same as being inside it, and she wondered if it would give her the same relief as she'd get after being inside for a thirty-six-hour run of suffering back in her surgery rotation, when she'd leave the hospital, blinking in the sun like a newly sprung prisoner, and walked very lightly for all her exhaustion, because her steps were buoyed by that I'm-not-in-the-hospital feeling. It would fade, even before she got home, even before she sat down at her computer to look at applications for cosmetology school or garbageman school, replaced by the dread of certain return. At a window on the stern side of the NICU, she watched herself, standing upright in the dinghy, clothed quite dramatically in a winding, flaring hospital sheet, or a dress sequined in colors exactly matching the sunset-sea, or wearing the most gigantic fruit hat ever. She receded, hand up in benediction, swallowed by the horizon.

"Hey baby," Anna said, stepping up next to her at the window. "I need you to come look at the baby. See something good out there?"

"Just… water," Jemma said. She let Anna take her hand and lead her to Brenda's isolette.

"All of a sudden she just looks like shit. Don't you think? And she was having such a good day. She tolerated the feed advance and weaned her oxygen again and she sat out with the volunteer for twenty minutes listening to a story. It was all fine until all of a sudden." Jemma looked down at the mottled child, who tried to lift her arm to point but only succeeded in extending her wrist a little. She reached her hand into the isolette to feel the belly, because it looked a little rounder than usual. It was as smooth and stiff as the surface of a bowling ball.

"Oh fuck," Jemma said.

Every time she went into a surgery, Jemma suffered forebodings of doom; she knew something awful was going to happen. She'd never seen anybody die on the table; she hadn't even seen a particularly nasty complication. She'd seen no exsanguinations, no confused amputations of the wrong limb, no mad surgeons carving their initials on the patient's hide, no beheadings. Still, she believed that something awful did happen in every surgery; someone would be flayed open, a stranger would be rummaging about in their innards. Someone would suffer an assault no less violent for how slow it was, or how practiced, cool, and methodical.

Hesitating to enter the operating room, she scrubbed longer than was necessary. The distinctive odor of the soap, and the noise of the water drumming in the steel sink, brought back memories of the long eight weeks she'd spent in her surgery clerkship, and the longer eight weeks she'd spent repeating the clerkship after she'd failed. The people who had tortured her so vigorously then were all dead now, but she felt no safer, for that, in this place. She could feel the hair at the nape of her neck standing stiffly erect, and she felt a nausea that was distinct from her morning sickness. The spirit of her father, the only kind surgeon she'd ever met, ought to protect her, she thought. But when she closed her eyes she only saw him shaking his finger at her.

Rob kicked a pedal to start an adjacent tap running and started to scrub without talking to her. They were still in a fight. He wet his hands and arms, and began to soap them up. Jemma ran the brush idly over her fingertips, and watched, liking how the water and foam caught in the hair on his forearms, how it matted and curled. Jemma watched the brush travel from the tip of his fingers up to a point halfway between his elbow and shoulder, then down again.

"Stop looking at me," he said. Jemma continued to stare. Rob hurried his scrub, scooping his hands and arms under the water to rinse them. He sidled up next to her, arms held up in front of him, elbows dripping. "Don't let Dr. Walnut beat you into the room," he said, then backed through the door into the OR. It was a rule of surgery, that the most senior surgeon comes last into the OR like a king comes last into the chamber of state.

In her sixteen weeks of surgery, Jemma had perfected the post-scrubbing posture—it was the one thing she had gotten good at. She flexed her arms crisply at the elbow, and splayed her fingers gracefully before her face. She squelched her foreboding, backed into the door, and thrust it open with a commanding blow from her ass. She spun on the ball of her foot, careful not to fling any drops from her wet hands and arms, and gave the scrub nurse a look she hoped would be interpreted as proud—she had learned that scrub nurses tended to ignore you if you were earnest and kind. The nurse handed her a sterile towel. Jemma dried herself, finger to elbow, and tossed the towel to the floor in her best imitation of surgical haughtiness. The nurse helped her into the blue paper gown, and then into the gloves, stretching them at the mouth while Jemma reached her hand into them, the way you reached into a snake hole, or into a toilet. No matter how forcefully she shoved her hand into the glove, there was always a bit of empty finger at the tip that she'd spend the next five minutes worrying and pulling. Like always, it ruined her haughty-surgeon act. The nurse, her eyes made articulate by her mask, gave Jemma a look that said she'd seen right through her.

After the nurse had tied up her gown, Jemma walked over to Rob. He was helping to prepare the body; Brenda lay spread out, already unconscious and intubated, on the operating table, tied at ankles and wrists, arms above her head, so she made the shape of an X. After a nurse finished scrubbing the child's belly and chest with betadine, Rob put the drape on her. He shook it out with a snap, and then it settled over her, obscuring her face, her neck and chest, her arms and legs. A window in the drape exposed an oval of stained belly five inches across its longest part. Underneath the skin her belly was rotting; she had an infection in the wall of her bowel, flagrant and obvious on the x-ray that Jemma had ordered. "Excellent work," Dr. Walnut had said, after Jemma had been interrogated by the two surgeons. Jemma had already ordered all the tests that Dr. Walnut wanted by the time he came to see the child. He rewarded her by summoning her—at hour thirty-eight—to the surgery. Jemma would rather have had a kick in the face. Now she'd been awake for forty hours. It was a new record for her.

As Rob smoothed the drape, Dr. Wood raised his little screen, a length of sterile paper that was hoisted north of the shoulders but south of the chin, ostensibly to establish the upper border of the sterile field, but also, and more importantly, to divide the domain of the cranky, rude surgeon from that of the contented and fun-loving anesthesiologists. It was a different world, behind the blue curtain. On this side of it, surgeons scolded at sutures cut too long and too short, at fat retracted with insufficient or overzealous force, and dissected the ignorance of the common medical student, and when there was laughter, it was only cruel. On the other side the anesthesiologists reclined among their puffing machines, discussing films and art and restaurants and golf, and gossiping in quiet voices about the surgeons in the room. How often Jemma had wanted to go there, to the other side, during her sixteen weeks of hell. She wanted to go there now.

Dolores came into the room, followed shortly by Dr. Walnut. The two nurses attended to them simultaneously, and the way they postured and dipped their arms and hands and spun made it seem like they were dancing in synchrony, so Jemma expected them shortly to start into a doo-wop routine. They were the last two surgeons in the world, and representative of their kind, a meanie and a junior meanie. Jemma had imagined them mating, to replenish the species. It would be a sterile procedure, she was certain, involving betadine and steel. Dolores, the resident, would lay a clutch of eggs and make a nurse sit on them until they hatched, freeing an equal number of boys and girls, each the very image of their father or mother, each little mouth already turned down in a perpetual frown of annoyance.

Dr. Walnut was a small man, a cardiac surgeon who'd been frequently slumming in the abdomen since the Thing. He had a pointy nose, and small ears, and round blue eyes. From the nose up he looked better suited to making cookies, or repairing shoes than cutting into children, but his thin white lips gave him away. Jemma thought they must once have been thick and red and luscious, but a professional lifetime of pressing his lips together impatiently had flattened and bleached them. Thin, curly wisps of white hair escaped from under the edges of his surgical cap. The cap was festive, covered with smiling, fat-tired school buses. Such silly little hats marked a person as a native of the OR. The hats were the only thing Jemma liked about most surgeons, and she wanted one for herself, but it was considered uppity for a medical student to wear one, so Jemma had always made do with the frowsy sheer bouffant caps that made everyone look like they were hiding their curlers.

Dolores was as big as Dr. Walnut was small. She had probably been stately like Dr. Tiller, once, before she had decided to become a surgeon. Jemma had watched her make the typical transformation, across her intern year, one that was repeated over and over, through the decades represented in the surgical housestaff pictures that had hung down a dark hall of the medical school. The interns were all lean-faced and sharp-looking; the second-years were puffy and looked tired, the third-, fourth-, and fifth-years looked progressively weary and fat. Surgical interns entered the program healthy, ambitious, and beautiful, but the call and the toxic atmosphere wore on them; their souls shrank to nubbins while their asses bloomed into soft, marvelous pillows, and they became giant grub-like creatures that could perform a one-handed Kasai procedure, but when placed in the sun, made a mewling noise, and asked to be taken in, and to be fed fried food. Vivian said they were corrupt before they started, that the surgical muse called her slaves from among the evil dead, but Jemma disagreed, and had always thought it was sad, even in the most hellish days and nights of her surgery clerkship, even when a lady very like Dolores had ordered her to wear a truncated dunce cap during a pancreatectomy, how they were corrupted, how their bravery was corrupted to hubris, their genius corrupted to cleverness, their compassion corrupted to disdain, their patients corrupted to meat. Dolores's cap was blaze orange. In the former world she'd been a huntress and an eater of game.

"Well, kiddies," said Dr. Walnut. "Let's save this baby, shall we?" He rubbed his gloved hands together till they squeaked. He stepped up on a pedestal next to the table, and was suddenly almost as tall as Rob.

"You're in my place," Dolores said to Jemma. Jemma moved, into the place of the scrub nurse, who moved her on. She thought there'd be no room for her, for all that she'd been invited. Dr. Walnut noticed her standing away from the table, and brought her over next to him, so it was Rob who had to step back. Dr. Walnut called for the music to begin—he listened to Ravel while he worked—and then put out his little hand for the scalpel.

"Dr. Claflin," he said, knife poised over the belly, "what are the layers of the abdominal wall? I forget them. I'd dearly like to know what they are, though, before I cut through them. I hate to cut in ignorance." Jemma smothered an urge to put her face in her hands, and told him the information he already knew. It was a favorite question, one she'd been asked dozens of times in her clerkship, and always the surgeon pretended not to know the answer. Jemma rattled off the layers with minimum effort, aided by a mnemonic: *surgeons climax if stimulated expertly in the rectum.*

"Ah yes," said Dr. Walnut. "That's it. Now we can proceed." He lowered his knife. Dolores brought the suction up in what looked to Jemma like a quick salute, then she brought it down to hover just behind the knife blade. As Dr. Walnut cut she sucked up the blood behind him. The skin sprang apart under the knife, and tiny beads of blood collected in the mouth of the suction. After he'd opened the skin, Dr. Walnut cut the rest of the way with the electrocautery. It sang a shrieking, keening note as it cut, and sent up acrid twirls of smoke that Dolores sucked out of the air before they could reach and offend Dr. Walnut's pointy nose. What wafted toward Jemma she let go, so Jemma got smoke in her eyes. In her clerkship she'd become overly familiar with it, because she was a klutz with the suction, and could never capture all the smoke from the air. Sometimes, when the patient was very fat, it was like standing at a barbecue, and Jemma once or twice nearly passed out from holding her breath, trying and failing not to be carried on the clouds of smoke back to Calvin's burnt black body.

"Retractors!" Dolores said imperiously. When the nurse handed them to her, she took one for herself and handed the other to Jemma. Jemma had never seen retractors so small before—these were about as big as chopsticks. Hooked on both ends, used to pull skin and muscle and fat out of the way of the surgeon's hands, they were familiar to every medical student, as retracting was their primary duty, after being humiliated and before wielding the suction. Jemma had retracted for hours and hours before, so at the end of the surgery she was unable to feel her hands, and surgeries became contests of will between her and the fat. She'd fallen asleep once, during a four a.m. appendectomy, pulling back on a crowbar-sized retractor, in the attitude of a water-skier. The surgeon, when she noticed that Jemma was asleep, had used her greasy finger to flip the retractor out from under a shelf of fat, and Jemma had fallen straight down on her back. Jemma had woken to laughter, and the shadows of masked faces under the surgical lights, and had wanted so badly for it all to be a horrible nightmare. Now she shifted her weight back and forth from one foot to the other, trying to stay awake. Everywhere she looked she saw comfortable places to fall asleep: under the various carts, curled up in the corner, in the cabinets full of gloves and towels. She thought of all the places she'd found her father asleep, when she was a child. In his car, in the bushes, folded over the kitchen counter, on top of the dining-room table; he could fall asleep anywhere, and it had always made her feel very grown up and somehow indispensable, to settle a blanket over him, wherever she happened to find him. She stared longingly at the blanket warmer. Surely the angel could warm a blanket, too—lengths of warm blanket billowed in her head, pouring out of the replicator to cover her on her bed.

"Too hard!" said Dolores, and then, "Too soft!" Jemma adjusted the pressure on her retractor, but Dolores continued to scold, like a fat, crabby, perpetually dissatisfied Goldilocks. Dr. Walnut was rummaging delicately in the belly of the baby, leaning over the surgical wound every few moments and exclaiming, "Smell that rot!" He walked along the intestines with his fingers, seeking out the dead gut. What his fingers passed over, he pulled out onto the drape, so as he walked deeper and deeper, neatly placed loops of bowel grew up in a pile on the sterile drape.

"Eureka!" he said, finally. He held the sick bowel up for all of them to see; it was purple, except where it was mottled black, a stark contrast to the earthworm-pink healthy bowel. "Five, seven, fifteen centimeters, I think, and the valve, too. Ah, poor short-gut baby! Dr. Claflin, would you like to make the first cut?"

"No thank you," Jemma said politely. But Dr. Walnut insisted. He placed the clamps and directed the scissors, miming the cut with his two fingers.

"But wait a moment, it's too dark. Dr. Dickens, would you adjust the light?" Rob reached above them to move the surgical lights. There were six of them suspended by as many triple-jointed arms above their heads. For five minutes Rob made adjustments, but Dr. Walnut was hard to satisfy. "Well, that's fine for the left side of the field, but look on the right. What's that? Stygian gloom!" Another three or four minutes passed. Dr. Wood peeked over his curtain and asked if everything was all right. "Just fine," Dr. Walnut said. "We just need a little more right here." He pointed with his finger at a spot inside the child. Rob reached for the sixth light, the one that was furthest away from him, and brought it around. As he set it in position, and Dr. Walnut exclaimed, "Perfect!" there was a noise Jemma recognized from her childhood: a violin string breaking, a strong, refined ping. The perfect light vanished. She felt a rush of air at her back, like a bus had just zoomed by her, and heard another childhood noise, a pumpkin smashing. She turned just in time to see Rob stuck on the far wall. He hung there a moment, then peeled away, head, chest, belly and legs, leaving a silhouette of blood on the clean white paint in the shape of his head. He fell to the ground and lay like a sleeper, his hat in place, blood expanding in a wet stain on his mask, and blood pouring from his ear.

"I told you," she said to his swollen purple face in the PICU. "I told you this would happen." She spoke out loud, but really she was talking to herself, because she never had told him why she had run so halfheartedly from his courtship. When he asked why she had been so jittery, back at the beginning, she said not, "Because I was afraid something absolutely fucking awful would happen to you," but instead, "I guess I have a hard time trusting people." For the longest time she'd only told him she loved him in the throes of an orgasmic tizzy; she'd shout it in utter distraction and then wonder, during the after, if she could take it back. Then, after practicing on houseplants and the neighbors' pets, and seeing how they came to no harm, she'd woken him one blue pre-morning to say it, premeditated and deliberate. "Don't I know it?" he'd asked her sleepily, and drawn her to him. She'd folded into him, limb over limb, until she felt like a ball wedged against his belly and under his ribs. Now she imagined the roach, afloat at some far latitude, scraping its legs at her and broadcasting reproach on its antennae: I told *you,* didn't I?

She said it again, though—"*I love you*"—not able to help herself, or convince herself or fate or the furies or God that she had only been kidding, the whole time. She said it to the baby crying in his crib, and the boy weeping outside his house because he thought his family had moved away without him, and the adolescent weeping over the father he never met, and the man weeping for the drowned world. She was in love with every one of them, and she spoke the words to all of them like a fatal wedding vow.

Dolores had proved herself a champ. "I'll get it," she'd said to Dr. Walnut, as if Rob were a ringing telephone, and not a dying body. Before Jemma had unfrozen out of her horror, she'd stabilized his neck, rolled him over, and caught the laryngoscope and ET tube tossed across the room by the anesthesiologist. Jemma by then had crossed the room, ignoring Dr. Walnut's cry to come back, come back and retract. "I've got it," Dolores said, looking deep into Rob Dickens' throat. She tubed him on the first try and hooked up a bag. "Get back to the table," she said. Jemma, her tongue already turning to stone, said softly, lamely, "He's my *fiancé*."

News of his injury spread rapidly through the hospital, and in this place that could not tolerate new sadness, provoked a great lament—he was affable and handsome and only Jemma ever saw him in a bad mood, and for weeks he'd been cultivating new friendships about as eagerly and successfully as Jemma avoided them—not just because he was so well liked. Common opinion had it that everyone had suffered enough; added misfortune, even if it were relatively benign, was unbearable. And if just a broken nail or a bruised toe were bitter gall, then what was Rob Dickens, laid out in the PICU with diffuse axonal injury and a slowly expanding subdural hematoma? Jemma sat by his bed, not knowing or caring if she'd been excused from her duties, not moving even when the nurses came to roll him or give him mannitol or change his diaper, and not helping, either. Her stony feeling was such that she could barely move or speak. She thought of him as already dead.

She leaned over in her chair, resting her cheek next to his arm, not ever asleep, but neither entirely awake, breathing in time with his respirator. She'd lift her head every now and then to look at his monitor, or look for as long as she could stand at his face, his swollen lips and eyes, and the horrible bolt that stuck out from his forehead—it looked like an industrial mishap, but had been put there on purpose by Dolores, a sensor to gauge intracranial pressure. Sometimes she thought his face belonged to someone else; with the slightest effort, a little twitch of imagination, she saw her first lover, or her mother or father, or her brother, laid out on their backs with the bolt standing up obscenely, like a handle, from above the left eye.

People came and went all through the night and the following day—hours fifty through sixty. PICU people and visitors from all over the hospital, Jemma ignored most of them, unless they shook her hard. Synthesized flowers filled the room with their not-quite-right smell, and cards, crafted by children, appeared on the walls by the dozen, until there was no more wall to obscure, and then they began to darken the window. Vivian, Dr. Sashay, Ishmael, even Dr. Snood creeped solicitously into the room. "I'm fine," Jemma mumbled at them, and would not talk anymore, no matter how they pestered. Sometimes she pretended to be asleep. Sometimes the voices did not register with Jemma until their speakers had left the room, but she always heard them:

"Will he be okay?"

"Will *she* be okay?"

"I hear that they're trying to find someone willing to drill. Walnut's scared he'd kill him. And he operates on hearts the size of jelly beans!"

"Who else except him?"

"Pudding? He's IR, isn't he?"

"IR doesn't drill in your fucking head."

"Dolores would do it. She'd think it's fun."

"Can she hear us?"

"I don't think so. I think she's sleeping."

"They were going to get married. Isn't it cute? Isn't it *sad*?"

"Isn't it enough already?"

"Maybe it's never enough."

"Maybe this is just the beginning. Maybe we're all going to get it in the head."

"Times like these I want my Buffy. I want something besides what's here, you know, because what's here is so awful. But when I go looking for her, it's still just static. I guess I could just ask for her, but I'm afraid I'd get something dirty. I don't want to see Buffy doing something dirty, but what if I wanted it, you know, secretly. Deep down? The angel would see it and give it to me. She knows that sort of thing. She really does."

"That's how all pornography happens. You ask her for one thing but she knows what you really want. Anyway, Buffy's not coming back."

"I know it's true. But it's hard, hard."

"True things always are."

"Can you hear me?"

"Jemma? Jemma? Jemma? Jemma?"

"Can I get something for you, Dr. Claflin?"

"She's not a doctor yet. She's not even a fourth year. Have you had to be with her at night? It's a chore."

"She just sits there."

"I've peeped in once or twice and seen her move her head. Sometimes she whispers to him."

"It's time to change him again. Is that poop in her hair?"

"It's blood. Jemma?"

"When does she pee?"

"She hasn't been drinking."

"If we put her hand in warm water I bet she'll pee all over the place."

"Such a handsome boy, even now. She's a lucky girl. Was a lucky girl. You know what I mean, right?"

"Exactly. Look at him!"

"Dolores will drill. She just has to drill."

"If you bring out what is inside of you, it will save him. If you do not bring out what is inside of you, you will kill him. In this hour, to not lift your hand is the same thing as to kill him."

Jemma opened her eyes. The two magpies were gone, and Pickie Beecher, whose voice she thought she'd just heard, was nowhere to be seen. Rob looked the same, eyes swollen, bolt in head, unmoving. She wiped some drool off his chin and pushed his hair away from the bolt and fluffed up his pillow and was smoothing his gown over his legs—it was always riding up—when the code alarm began to ring. She ignored it, at first. It wasn't her problem, but it rang louder and louder in the room, and the angel wouldn't shut up—"Save him save him O save him please." She went to see what was happening. It was the first time she'd left since Rob had arrived.

The bell was chiming for Marcus, the fat little five-year-old from the family with bad hearts. Emma and Dr. Tiller were already in the room, along with Dr. Chandra and a single nurse, Janie. The boy's mother was standing in the door, calling out "Regresse Marcos, regresse mi amor!" Emma saw Jemma looking in.

"Jemma," she said. "We need you."

"Get someone else," said Dr. Tiller.

"She'll be okay. Right, Jemma? Remember what I said?" Jemma walked up to the bed, climbed up on a stepping stool, and took over compressions from Dr. Chandra. But rather than distracting her from all the really horrible shit, the compressions brought it all more clearly to mind. So the child underneath her hands became Rob Dickens, and as she pushed on his chest it was from Rob's mouth that bloody froth bloomed, higher and higher, a complex flower made of interlocking red bubbles.

"More lidocaine?" Emma asked.

"More lidocaine," Dr. Tiller agreed. Janie pushed it. Jemma kept compressing, trying not to look at the face, but always coming back to it. It was Rob, then Pickie Beecher, then Josh Swift, then Cindy Flemm. It was Ella Thims and Magnolia and Juan Fraggle, but mostly it was Rob, and as she pushed and pushed it became his face not just because her obsessive imagination was able to draw the lineaments of his jaw and brow over the fat face of the doomed child, but because she saw it, as certain and as unreal, as she had seen her own mutated body bouncing in Ella Thims's crib all those weeks ago.

"Stop compressions," Emma said, leaning over casually to deliver a shock. "All right!" she said as the rhythm normalized transiently, then "Fuck!" when it slipped back into v-fib.

"Some more amiodarone?" Dr. Tiller asked civilly, as if he were asking, One lump or two?

"May as well." She motioned for Jemma to continue.

"It's no use," Jemma said. "He's already dead."

"Possibly true," Emma said, "But not for you to decide."

"Don't you smell it? He's already rotten inside."

"Compress or go home," Emma said. Jemma continued, pressing ever more violently on the thin chest.

"I just want to stop," Jemma said. "I want it all to stop, right now."

"Get her out of here," said Dr. Chandra. "Jesus, Emma, you're a fucking sadist."

"She's okay," said Emma. The child underneath Jemma's hands was changing with every push, the bloody flower in his mouth blooming in ever more intricate detail, rose, peony, zinnia—Jemma thought she caught the scent of flowers underneath the odor of ischemic gut. The mother called out again, "Regresse, regresse!" The whole family was outside the door now, mixed in with a crowd of residents and nurses and students and a few stray parents—codes always drew crowds. Pickie Beecher's face peeked out from behind Marcus's mother's knee.

"It's unbearable, what you're doing," Jemma said, softly at first, but then she looked right at Emma and shouted it at her face. "It's unbearable! It's fucking disgusting!" Emma finally called for someone to replace her. Janie, her only friend among the PICU nurses, who just two nights before had scolded Jemma for nearly writing a fatal potassium order, then hushed the whole thing up so Emma never discovered it, tried to take Jemma's arm. She shook her off. "Don't touch me," she said, and Janie pulled her hand away.

"Hey," Janie said, shaking her arm. Her hand hung at her side, limp as a filet of beef. "What'd you do?"

"It's disgusting," Jemma said again, "and not fair. What did he do to you? Why does he deserve this? Nobody deserves this. You're *torturing* him." And she wanted to ask, of the people in the room, of the air, of the hospital, of the great blue lidless eye of the sky that watched them suffering every day, What did we do to you? Why are you torturing us? She was complaining for herself and for the boy, though they were hardly kindred assaults, to be deprived of everyone you ever loved, and to be violated by well-meaning physicians and nurses, yet somehow in that moment she saw the two of them as suffering twins, laid out side by side, whaled upon by mortality, by long thick needles, and electric shocks.

She was almost crying—her parents and her lover rose again in her mind, mangled, bleeding, and burned, all three of them putting a hushing finger to their lips. Fuck you, she said to them tenderly. Don't tell me that. And when her brother rose up out of the sea she said, I'm sorry, I'm sorry, I'm sorry! and began to weep bitterly.

"Do the fucking compressions, Jemma!" Emma shouted, reaching toward her. Jemma brought her hands down together, two fists, to strike at the boy's chest. The room lurched and a light flared in her head. She thought it was the crying and the pregnancy, and was sure she was about to pass out. She reached for the passing out, trying to embrace it. If she just passed out then it would all be over, but she couldn't do it. She was dizzy and lightheaded but not the least bit tired anymore.

"What was that?" asked Dr. Tiller, and Janie said, "I still can't move my hand!" and Dr. Sasscock, standing way at the back of the crowd, asked, "What's wrong with her eyes?" Maggie, who had left her bed as soon as she heard the code bell and now was standing near the crash cart, cried out, "I told you so!" and threw a laryngoscope at Jemma, who never even saw it coming, and only realized she'd been hit when blood began to drip down her forehead into her eyes.

"It's not fair!" Jemma was shouting. "It's disgusting!" She was striking the boy again, harder and harder, and no one moved to stop her. They were all leaning away from her, the code in full arrest now, shielding their eyes every time she struck his chest, and she realized finally that the flashes were happening outside of her head. Every time she struck, a green light flared out of her hands to light up the room. She held up her hands and looked at them through her tears. Her scalp was bleeding freely, and the blood was dripping down her cheeks to fall on his face and his mouth. She touched her hand to her forehead and understood suddenly that she could make it better. It was a piece of knowledge granted to her entirely apart from her reason. Deduced of nothing, a spontaneous fact, it was inserted into her mind and her heart. Any place else but in the extremity of a breakdown, she would have mistrusted it absolutely. If she had been more herself she would have known right away that it was too good to be true. As it was, temporary insanity provided her with enough faith to give it a try.

Even as she was fixing it, she became aware of the wound in her head as a wrongness. It was a like a note among notes; though she was not aware of it as a sound, she described it that way to herself. As it faded, and after it was gone, other wrongness, different wrongness, captured her attention. She knew it: with her new sense she recognized Jarvis two rooms down as surely as she would have had she laid eyes upon him. Similarly, she knew her cardiac kid upstairs and Brenda. The varied wrongness of the hospital, on the other floors, in the other wards, was a subtle presence in her head; the wrongness in Pickie Beecher, watching in the crowd, was loud as a shrieking mosquito; the wreck of the boy underneath her was a nightmare instrument, a cat-piano, a dachsophone, but the wrongness in Rob Dickens, four rooms down, was loudest of all. She felt the yearning again, understanding that it was not just wanting but wanting them to get better. She wanted them all. She wanted this boy so badly but she wanted Rob more.

"Get out of her way!" shouted Maggie. "Don't look at the sparkles!" Only Pickie Beecher got in front of her as she passed through the door, but he didn't try to stop her. He raced ahead, pushing people out of her way until she was standing by Rob's bed. Pickie took up position behind her, facing the door.

Because she was confused, because she did not know how to manage what was in her, and because she just wanted to do it, she lay herself on top of him. She thought and whispered words that she thought should fix him: Let it be, let him be better. The green fire still flickered over her arm, but it did not touch him. She stood again and looked back at Pickie, who stood near the door, saying nothing now, and looked at her with a blank face. She turned back to Rob and pulled off his blanket; it was an insufficient uncovering. She took his gown and his diaper and tossed them on the floor.

As she laid herself on him again the nurses came into the front of the crowd, and stopped in front of Pickie. "Oh God, she's trying to fuck him!" said one of them. "She's gone crazy!" She wasn't trying to fuck him, though she knew what she was trying to do involved a most uncommon intimacy. Let it be done, she thought. Let it be gone. Let something come down on him and make him new again. He lay under her, heart beating faster and faster, still unconscious, still only breathing with the machine. She stood up again.

A nurse was trying to get past Pickie Beecher. "Maybe we should just let her," another was saying. "It's not like she's hurting him. Maybe we should just give them some privacy." The crowd was still growing behind them, one by one. Jemma sensed them, wrongness added to wrongness, everyone wrong in ways different from the children, and from Rob, wrong in ways she could barely recognize as wrong, let alone describe.

"Get back, or I'll kick you," Pickie said. Jemma lay down again on top of Rob, taking his hands in her own and raising them, over her head, grinding her hips into his, pushing her face into his face. She spoke a different word this time, "No." She spoke it to his swollen brain, his empty eyes, his spastic limbs. She spoke it to the staring dead eyes of her first lover, to her brother's eyeless face, to the house burning up her mother, to her father's livng corpse reaching and reaching for comfort. She spoke it to the drowning waters, to the correcting God. She'd spoken it before, on cruel nights, on crueler mornings in the days after each of the people she'd loved had died, waking with a corner of the pillow in her mouth, understanding she was awake in the same world she'd slept from, moaning No, no, no for an hour in her bed. She'd wanted so much, then, to have the power that the feeling ought to have given her, to shape her no into undoing, or at least into vengeance, cold comfort better than none. No and no, over and over, forever.

"You may not pass!" said Pickie Beecher. He inflicted a wrongness atop the wrongness that was one of the nurses; it bloomed at the edge of Jemma's contracting perception, a strobe flash, or a single, high note, a piccolo played by a soprano with a lungful of helium. "No," Jemma whispered, and "No," she said. "No," she shouted, and "No," she screamed. It came suddenly, and seemed to happen apart from all her pushing and fretting. One moment she was grinding her body into his body, the next she felt like she was floating on top of him, a green sea between them. Cold green fire ran over them both. She pulled at his tube, flinging it across the room. She pulled the bolt from his head and flung it similarly, shattering the glass door, holding her hand up at the blood he spouted. It stopped like obedient traffic, turned around and vanished into his head. A blister of skin formed over the wound.

It was quick. In the time it takes to do up a long zipper she'd poured an ocean of fire into him, soothed his swollen brain, reunited sundered axons, and popped out the plum-sized dent in his skull. He sat up, taking in a deep, whooping breath and making clawing motions with his hands. He opened his eyes but did not notice the room, the crowd, the nurse writhing on the ground with a broken shin, his nakedness. Jemma could tell he only noticed her.

"What happened?" he asked.

I hardly know my own part, so why do I feel like my sister's should be harder? She has always been ordinary. We do not have the same complaints, though she has always been sympathetic to my complaints, even when she didn't understand them. I say, The world heaps me. She says, I am fat. I say, I am the root of all evil. She says, I am lonely. And she is fat, and she is lonely, and though she likes everybody, no one likes her, while I hate everyone and have a hundred friends.

One summer when she'd had a particularly rough day, I told her it didn't matter that people she liked didn't like her; the one person she did like more than anybody else would be her friend—I had promised—beyond the end of time. She thought I meant Jesus, but I told her I meant me.

Repeat after me, I told her, You suck-ass motherfucking cock-sucking pavement-fucking fuck-faced slimy-crotch bitch, go fuck yourself with a moped and shit in your own mouth. I had her memorize eight different phrases and even combine them all together into a marathon-length cuss-fest that she could barely complete without breathing in the middle. If she replied with this whenever someone called her fatty, I guaranteed they would stop.

They'll just think I was crazy, she said.

But they'll leave you alone.

It's easy for you to say. Nobody thinks you're crazy or fat. You'll go to eighteen proms and wear seventy-five different tuxedoes and get elected Emperor of Maryland.

Say it again, I said, and she did. But she could not, when challenged, speak the words. So I kept composing cusses for her, and I designed a ritual to make sure it really never did fucking matter what somebody said to her or how they treated her, nothing would touch her and nothing would hurt her because she was protected. One night we went out her window and down to the little clearing where one of our dogs was buried. Kneeling by an arrowhead-shaped piece of slate that marked his grave, we burned candles and beef fat and I sacrificed one of her stuffed animals, an old bunny named Moronica.

Whatever they say, I chanted, let it come back to them. Whatever they say let it be silent. Whatever they say let it matter less than nothing, and let every mean thing they say or do come down again on them a hundred times worse in the after-time. I put a kitchen knife through Moronica, dipped her in wax and fat, and then we buried her. There in the ground she would become a scape-bunny, the absorber and repository of every ill ever done to Jemma, storing it all up like a battery until the after-time, when she would rise to give it back to everybody who had ever perpetrated a cruelty upon her, a truly terrible rabbit.

And the next day she went out in the world again, and nothing was different, but overnight I dreamed of her protected, surviving when the rest of the world vanished in flame, and she was queen of the world when all her old classmates were dead or worse than dead. I could not, and can't, reconcile my sister with my visions of my sister. And why should I see her, wielding fire and killing angels, and angels bowing down to her, when what I really need are dreams to instruct me in my own purpose?

“Did you hear?” Frank said to Connie over their customary breakfast. “A child was raised from the dead last night.”

“From the *nearly* dead, actually,” Connie said. “And it was a man. You have always got things just slightly wrong. Always just a little, but enough to totally miss the point.” She smiled at him and took his hand. Their marriage had been in a shambles when they entered the hospital with their daughter two nights before the storm, but the Thing had reintroduced them each to the other's best qualities, and they had fallen in love again, feeling a little guilty for it, amid all the misery. Their daughter had Crohn's disease, and came into the hospital to have a fistula repaired, accompanied by both parents not because they couldn't stand to be away from her, but because neither had trusted the other to be alone with her. They had both been expert slanderers, in their old lives.

“But a miracle, nonetheless,” he said. The angel had made him the usual omelet, asparagus and mushrooms and havarti cheese.

“Well, there are miracles and then there are miracles,” she said. “Raising someone from the dead—that's a miracle. Saving them from certain death, that's just good medicine. Baba, did you salt my eggs?”

“Maybe,” said the angel.

“How many times do I have to tell you? Salt on the bacon, pepper on the eggs. What do you say? Was there a miracle in the hospital last night?”

"Every day in this place is a miracle," said the angel. "You are seated upon a miracle. You live inside of a miracle."

"A typical non-response," said Frank. "Deborah! Get out of bed!"

"Leave me alone!" their daughter called back from her room. They had an outside suite on the seventh floor, with a balcony off the room that Frank and Connie shared, intact family-hood being a state of relative privilege within the hospital, and Deb having gotten well enough, after a post-Flood series of surgical complications, to be discharged to a residential section. She was not asleep, though her father accused her of being slothful, and called her schlaftier, German being their secret language, where with her mother it was Japanese. Each of them spoke a different language to her when she was a toddler, ostensibly for the sake of her edification, but she suspected that even then they were getting ready to hate each other with a grand passion, and laying up language in store for the day when they would need to talk shit about each other to her when they were all eating dinner together. Now they kissed at the breakfast table with their mouths full of bacon and eggs.

She wasn't sleeping, but she wasn't ready to join her father for Bible study before he traipsed off to his new job as an apprentice radiology tech, or her mother for her walk on the roof before she went to clerk in the NICU. She was watching a movie, one that she watched every day. It was her wedding video, or at least a video of what her wedding would have been like, if the world hadn't ended, if her boyfriend had lived long enough to propose to her.

She lay on her belly on her bed, feet kicking in the air behind her, and said "Forward," so the image in the monitor, as big as her window on the opposite wall, blurred and accelerated, until she slowed it down at the reception. Some days she just listened to the blessing of the minister, a big lesbi-looking lady in a purple dress that made her look like Grimace the milkshake monster, and some days she just watched when the camera took a slow track along the buffet table, feeling nostalgic for the salmon fillet and miniature quiches that she had never tasted. And some days, when she was feeling up to it, she watched the dancing, hugging her pillow while her new husband—they were twenty-five when they were married and age only made him more handsome—spun her around to a bluegrass tune. She had never imagined that she would have banjos and autoharps at her wedding, and yet from the first time she heard them she knew the angel had got it all just right, just as it had been, and just as it never would be. The exchange of vows never got to her, but somehow the dancing always did her in. While her father called out that her sausage was getting cold, she cried and cried.

Down the hall, in the room she shared with her brothers and sisters, Kidney was lying under her bed, her favorite place to sleep, and the place to which she retreated when she was afraid, or when she wanted to think about something. She had started the night in her bed, cuddled up with States'-Rights, but just before dawn she had started to get a feeling like something important was happening, and so she went down below, realizing as the sleepless hours passed and the sun made its first appearance on the floor, that the thing she was feeling was the end of their time in the hospital. Nothing else could be so big, or make her feel like every next day was going to be her birthday, and everybody's birthday, and like all the rest of their years everybody in the whole world would spend every day giving and receiving presents.

Finally! she thought to herself, and whispered it in a quiet voice, careful not to wake her brothers and sisters. She wanted to go and look out the window, and see the sun shining again on big rocks and wide green fields and giraffes and school fences, but she was afraid, too, to finally see it. The bar of sun crept steadily across the floor, and reached and passed the place that marked the time when the nurses came in to do morning vitals, and Kidney knew for sure then that they were all out playing soccer and softball on the new land. She rolled out from under the bed, then rolled again and again until she rested, back against the wall, beneath the window. Then she stood up, and shouted it out loud this time to wake everyone in the room, "Finally!" The nurses in their bright scrubs kicking the ball and doing flips and driving dump trucks full of fresh fragrant soil—she saw the land perfectly in her mind before she saw the water still outside the window.

"Finally what?" asked Shout, coming awake as he always did without any fuss, sitting up and rolling out of bed and putting his arms around Kidney. She didn't need to turn around to know that all her brothers and sisters were awake and looking at her.

"Nothing," she said.

"Horrible sparkles shot out of her eyes, and she made this nasty, urping noise, and her tongue got really long, and it struck at me, like she was a big lizard. Then I had the seizure, the one that she gave me." Maggie was testifying in front of the Committee. They were arranged behind a curving table: Dr. Snood; Dr. Sundae; Zini, the nurse-manager; Dr. Sasscock; Karen; the three nurses: Betty and Bonnie and Camilla; Frank and Connie; Monserrat, the tamale lady; Arthur, the senior lab tech; John Grampus; and finally Vivian, the only really friendly face that Jemma could identify from where she stood, a few feet behind the witness sofa hand in hand with Pickie Beecher. She and Pickie, the last witnesses, would testify next. Dr. Tiller and the other attendings were seated next to the Committee table, along with Emma and some others from the PICU staff.

"And you'd not ever had a seizure disorder in the past?" asked Dr. Snood.

"Certainly not."

"What's this with the tongue, Maggie?" Karen asked. "I don't remember that from before."

"Yes, a big green tongue. A tongue of *fire*."

"No tongue in your statement," said Vivian. "Are you just now remembering this, or just now making it up?"

"Am I on trial here?" Maggie asked. "I'm telling you what I remember, okay?"

"No one is on trial here, Dr. Formosa," said Dr. Tiller. "We are only trying to sort out some extraordinary stuff."

"Did Dr. Claflin say anything to you before she attacked?" asked Dr. Sundae.

"Attacked?" said Vivian. "*Attacked*? Has it been established that an attack has occurred? All the evidence seems to indicate that a miraculous healing has taken place. Have we been attacking the children in our care, Dr. Sundae? What gruesome violators we must be."

"Look in the mirror, young lady, and tell me you don't see gruesome spots. They're on all of us. And if a duck with no history of seizures suddenly develops them in the context of a mystical eruption, then that duck was attacked."

"Please," said Dr. Snood, making a little noise with his gavel. "Dr. Formosa, answer Dr. Sundae's question."

"She said, Now you will taste my power."

"Maggie, Maggie, your nose is *growing,*" said Vivian. Dr. Snood rapped again.

"Thank you, Dr. Formosa. I think that's enough."

Maggie got off the sofa and walked back into the standing crowd, glaring at Jemma as she walked forward with Pickie to sit down. Jemma found her attention mostly drawn to Pickie's slippers as he kicked his feet back and forth over the edge of the sofa. A darker purple than his pajamas, they were in the shape of elephants, complete with trunks that curved up from the toes.

"We just have a few questions for you, Pickie," said Dr. Snood. "There's no reason to be afraid."

"I am not frightened," said Pickie.

"Do you know what happened yesterday, with Dr. Jemma?"

"Of course."

"Will you tell us what you saw?"

"What was in her came out. It's very simple."

"But what did you see?" asked Zini. "Was there green fire?"

"I saw what I saw," said Pickie. "What was in her came out."

"Was it green?" asked Dr. Sundae.

"It was inside of her. Inside the inside. It is inside her now." All eyes turned to Jemma. She looked at Pickie's slippers. The whole Committee tried to get Pickie to tell a coherent story; no one succeeded. He would only repeat that what was in Jemma had come out, something she could have told them herself, and he admitted that he had seen it in her before, but not pointed it out because he thought she must notice it herself—with things like this, he said, you just have to wait for it to happen. A few more unilluminating questions later, Dr. Snood told him he could go back upstairs, but instead of leaving, after he climbed off the couch, he turned and climbed up into Jemma's lap. Jemma told her story again, and responded to questions. Yes, green fire, she said. No, it was not hot, not to me, not in the usual way. No, I can't make it happen right now. Yes, I'm trying to make it happen. There were no visions. There were no voices. Nothing like this has ever happened before. I prefer not to repeat my board scores in front of an audience. Suffice to say that they were quite low. I don't know what happened to Janie's hand.

"Has the angel been talking with you?" asked John Grampus.

"Not about this."

"Have the carpets been talking to you?" asked Karen. "Any voices at all?"

"No."

"Why did you attack Maggie Formosa?" asked Dr. Sundae.

"I don't remember that I did. I only remember feeling sick that morning, and almost passing out."

"Do you think you could have been possessed?"

"I suppose anything is possible, Dr. Sundae."

"Jemma," asked Vivian, "what do *you* think is happening?"

"I don't know," Jemma said. Vivian frowned, because Jemma was supposed to give a more detailed answer. Vivian had a theory that would require a PET scan for validation, something about enhanced activity in the parietal cortex. Jemma, feeling more and more persecuted as the questioning continued, though everyone, even Dr. Sundae, and especially Dr. Snood, was interrogating her with the utmost politeness, lapsed sullen. The hungover feeling she'd had since Rob had awakened was lifting, the sleepy, pliable state giving way to a need like horniness, but absent of lust. She wanted to burn again.

Word came a few hours after Jemma and Pickie were dismissed that the Committee had formally requested that Jemma refrain from any more extraordinary manifestations until further study had been accomplished. A series of tests was scheduled, Vivian's PET scan among them, to begin in the morning. Dr. Snood, Dr. Tiller, and Emma were constructing a randomized double-blind trial, to begin within the week, in which they planned to compare Jemma's efforts, provided she could make them again, with conventional therapy in low-risk, low-acuity children. Jemma, meanwhile, was excused from all clinical duties, assigned the impossible task of devising a way to blind herself in the study. She retired to the call room, to hide from eyes struck by the rumor of wonder, and faces not empty of fear. Everywhere she went, people turned to each other and made murmuring noises that sounded to her distant ears like bracka bracka bracka. "What does it mean?" people asked her, like she should know. "What does it mean?" asked John Grampus. He caught her—literally, reaching out to nab the edge of her yellow scrub gown as she passed by him where he sat on the ramp, sitting on the ground with his knees to his chest, his back to the balustrade, and a big purple hat pulled down over his eyes, as if he was at siesta. "She never mentioned anything like this to me."

"It was a surprise to me too," Jemma said, tugging at her gown.

"Sometimes I close my eyes and I can see the whole place, every secret room and every potential space, all laid out in my head like a 3-D blueprint. And some days I thought I could see the time laid out just like that, another blueprint, but unfolded across the days to come."

"I thought she never told you what was next." One fierce tug and the gown came free of his fist. Now she could run away, but she stayed a moment more.

"It's not from her," he said. "I used to think it was from Him."

"What'd you see?" she asked, squatting down now next to him.

"Shuffleboard and codes and people dating." He shrugged. "Who are you, though, that you did that?"

"Just another third-year med student," she said. "Just another moron."

"What else can you do? What else can I do?" He pushed his fingers at her in an abracadabra gesture.

"It's all pretty weird," she said.

"Worse than weird," he said, and drew his hat down farther over his eyes. "You can go now," he said. "Don't come complaining to me when you start to feel used."

"I don't… I'm not… I don't even understand… Oh whatever," she concluded, and continued on, in a sort of huff, and the next time somebody pinched at her clothes—Ishmael saying he just had to talk to her—she offered the first excuse that came into her head (I have to pee), pulled away, and powered down the ramp, head down now, until she got to her room. Jeri Vega's mother was outside her door.

"You've got to come upstairs," she said.

"I've got to pee," Jemma said, and now it was true.

"Right now," the lady said. She'd been eating red licorice while she waited. A string of it still dangled from her mouth—somehow it made her look even tougher than usual—and she held a braided whip of it in her hand. "She needs you."

"I'm not allowed," Jemma said.

"Bullshit. The sun's not allowed to shine? Are we not allowed to breathe? Is this place not allowed to float? Come on. Right now." She held out her hand. Jemma ducked around it, put her back against her door, and her hand on the doorknob.

"I'm not allowed," she said. "And anyway I couldn't even if I tried. I don't understand it at all—it's so very strange, Ms. Vega. Not right now, I just can't. I'm sorry. I'm really sorry but now I'm going to go inside. Goodbye."

Ms. Vega was drawing back her whip hand as Jemma turned the knob and backed through the door. She heard the soft blow fall. "Get out here you stupid bitch," Ms. Vega said. "Don't tell me that shit you stupid bitch. I can tell a lie when I hear one. What kind of monster are you, you stupid bitch?"

"Lock the door," Jemma whispered to the angel, so no one can get in. "Give it the special."

"It is already done," said the angel. Jemma stepped backward, all the way to the toilet, and sat down.

Rob was not even with her. He was still in the PICU, still monitored though quite thoroughly well. She imagined him sitting up in bed in the too-small hospital gown printed with frolicking puppies and kittens. "I kind of like it," he said, when she offered to go replicate something that would fit better. "Size Prader-Willi—it almost fits." He'd smiled at her, and then his expression had fallen back into the one he'd been wearing since she woke him up. Jemma had never seen someone look so consistently bemused before. He'd heard how she described herself as his fiancee while he was asleep, and argued that this constituted an acceptance of the proposal. Over and over and over she denied it.

She imagined him with her, seeking to summon him. She outlined a space for him in the air, drew his reclining shape, arms above his head, and thought she could see the pillow denting a little in anticipation of his head. Let it be... now! she thought, and whispered, imagining the puppy and kitten gown settling empty to the bed in the PICU as his body, reduced to arcing energy, or drifting mist, was transported to reconstitute itself in front of her eyes. It did not happen, but she felt a surge, a wave in her belly, that she knew was fire seeking egress. She looked out into the room, up to the window; still filled with blue sky. She was waiting for dark.

"I am born," she said quietly. "I grow up. My brother dies my parents die my lover dies the world drowns I get pregnant I develop miraculous healing powers." It made no more sense when spoken aloud than when spoken in her head. Why not Rob, or Vivian, or Dr. Tiller, or one of the parents, or one of the patients; why not Josh Swift slouching greenly down the halls and restoring health to all his fellow-sufferers? Why not Pickie Beecher, kung-fu baldy? He was already... eldritch. She held up her hands, palm toward palm, a foot apart, and let a green flare pass between them.

She opened up her mind, imagining an uncovering as slow and massive as the opening of an observatory dome, seeking to make herself receptive to the answer, and asked her questions again, and tried to conceive of the mouth that might speak the answer. She lay there waiting, hearing nothing, watching the window darken, blue into deeper blue, until it was the very color of Rob's eyes. Then it was time.

She started at the top; it seemed like the right place. In the psych ward she found Thelma asleep, a three-month-old magazine spread across her vast chest. Jemma went past her. The first two rooms she looked in were empty. But in the room called Sage she found all three anorexics gathered together vomiting in the moonlight. Jemma hardly knew them; even when she was on the team that covered this floor, they'd been Vivian's responsibility. Their families were all gone; none of them had been the sort to get many visitors, especially during bad weather. They had only each other and Thelma, whose great wonderful fatness they could look at no longer than they could stare into the sun. They restricted more and more, and as the weeks passed began to binge, something all three, high, pure anorexics who had defeated their bodies by becoming creatures of pure will, would have disdained in the dry world. Jemma remembered the discussions from rounds, the team wondering how to keep them from shooting powerful coherent arcs of vomit out the windows that the angel would not keep shut, or how to keep them from tearing out their TPN IVs. Dr. Snood, desperate, had kept one of them sedated for a week while she was fed through her nose, but when she awoke she took off the weight as easily as she would an ugly sweater.

By the time Jemma visited them they had made themselves ghastly-beautiful. From the door she saw them gathered under the window, around a plastic tub that stored toys by the bushel in the playrooms. They held hands and brushed up against one another languidly, arching their necks and throwing back their heads to swallow their fingers before adding another unit of barf to the big bucket. They were surrounded by the remains of their feast, vanilla-ice-cream puddles glowing in glass dishes shaped like leaves; candy-bar wrappers in neat heaps; chicken skin and chicken fat glistening in patches around them in a circle, and bones under their feet. Jemma trod on two large cupcakes as she approached them, her green hands clasped behind her back. They did not notice her until she was quite close. Their pajamas, altered, short, hanging dresses of sage, pumpkin, and ocher, and their hair, brittle but long and styled with particular care into identical sets of heaped and cascading curls, their dramatic poses, their bare feet among bones, their long, sharp nails, and finally their number all gave them an ancient Greek air; though they were exquisitely frail, and close to dying, they seemed as powerful as they were pathetic, three purgies discharging their eternal duty. Jemma, nearly upon them, felt a little afraid, but still laughed out loud. They all turned at once, and spoke from left to right.

"It's a stomach flu," said the first one, defiantly. "Who are you?" asked the second, more meek. The third, finger in mouth, merely stared.

"I am the great fatty," Jemma announced, then brought her hands forward, and struck. Green fire spilled into the air as she grabbed at them. They all shrieked identically, and tried to escape, but she was too close for them to evade her, and they were too weak to break away. They were so thin she could hold all of them in her arms. In three blows she made them right, all four of them burning together. First she restored their organs, heart and lungs and guts ruined with months of self-consumption; no sooner had she wanted it done than it was done, the three girly shrieks climbing into song as Jemma pushed with her mind and her spirit. Then she restored their flesh. She filled them with fire that burned for an instant and was gone, leaving muscle and fat in its place; they popped out of her arms, but remained bound to her by fire. Lastly she restored their minds—already they felt covered with abomination. She weeded their brains, reaching in with fire fingers to rip out that perception; right or wrong, truth or distortion, it was hers to command, and must come out with her, and when she commanded it to scatter on the dark air it must do it.

When she released them they threw up their arms, as if in praise or surrender, and then fell to the ground, strong bones cushioned by newly upholstered fat. She left them sleeping beside the vomit tub, scattering candy wrappers back and forth between them with their breath. She wiped her feet and moved on.

In Pickie Beecher's room she fell, hands-first, on the Pickie-shaped lump in his bed, but it was only an artfully arranged pillow, bitten through in places and leaking stuffing. She cast it aside and went out, looking in all the empty rooms and not finding him there. When she closed her eyes and thought about him she thought she could sense his special wrongness at the periphery of her consciousness, a little blot on her mind, but she could not figure this sense into an idea of where he was. She walked by Thelma again, still asleep, though snoring loudly now in the way of the obstructive sleep apneic. Jemma reached out to touch her, knowing that she could shore up the muscles of her pharynx if she throttled her just *so,* but then she wondered if what was in her might run out, and if children didn't have a greater claim on it than adults. She passed Thelma by and walked on to the rehab floor, creeping past a pair of nurses seated at their rocket station. Monitors and thin plastic towers stuck up fortuitously, hiding Jemma from their view, but she felt regarded by the giant yellow alien head mounted on the wall behind them, which seemed to follow her as she went in halting, sneaky cartoon steps along the blue-black carpet, under the light of bright false stars.

Five paralytics, two amputees, one serene vegetable, and a girl named Musette, twenty years old but with the physical, intellectual, and emotional repertoire of an eight-week-old; none of them could withstand Jemma, though their parents offered unexpected assaults on her. "What are you doing to my baby?" was the question that they asked as they sat up out of sleep, or as they clawed at Jemma, or threw syringes like darts, or tried to whack her with a spare IV pole. "Watch and see," Jemma told them, striking them too with the green fire; to disconnect their voluntary musculature was as easy as flipping off a switch. They crumpled to the floor and watched with unblinking eyes as their children flew from bed in a Christmas-morning leap, or as bones grew in slender filligree from pale stumps, to bud and bloom in green fire that took the form and then the substance of muscle, ligament, and tendon, fat, fascia, and skin. Jemma's mind performed new motions determined by the problem: the spinal lesions of the paralytics glowed in her head, galling and bitter and ugly; she smoothed her thumb just over the spot on their spines while doing something that made her feel as if her brain was sneezing, shoving violently at either end of the wrongness and holding every fiber of the bundle in her consciousness, counting them like the hairs of a head and commanding them to unite. Bone and flesh had to be encouraged, delicately at first, and then ecstatically, to venture into the air and fill up the felt, phantom image with a real thing. The vegetable required a shout, spoken silent on Jemma's lips, but sounding louder than any word previously spoken inside the child's head. She sat up with a start, folding violently from the hips, and her eyes flew open with her mouth. "I'm awake already," she said sullenly. "Jeesh."

Fixing Musette was a stranger task. She lay in her bed, gnawing on her fists and looking out the window at the moon, her gown rising up just below her breasts. Rivulets of drool ran down her wrists and arms to drip from her elbow. She made a constant noise, a low little moan interrupted every few moments by a cough or a giggle. Her mother was on the floor, her head at Jemma's foot, an IV pole dropped at her side.

Jemma put her hands on Musette's head, her fingers disappearing into a thick mass of greasy black curls. It was easy to make over her mushy brain, to burn it until it was perfect, but harder to restore the lost, neverborn personality. Jemma thought it would be, like everything so far, a matter of will; she only had to want it enough, to push hard enough, and it would grow inside of Musette like the ruined tissue of her cortex. So Jemma pushed hard; this patient burned brighter than any previous. Musette's lungs, chronically wet and infected from aspirating her own saliva, dried up; her skin, blighted by acne, cleared; the greasy fountain in her scalp, which formerly put out such volume that she left stains wherever she lay her moaning, idiot head, slowed to a trickle, just enough to put a lustrous shine in her hair. Jemma kept pushing even when these things were done, because she still sensed only blankness inside. Musette's snaggly, sharp teeth straightened and dulled, hairy moles leapt away from her skin like black ladybugs taking flight; still she was blank. It wasn't until Jemma, hopping with frustration, accidentally stepped on the mother's face that she realized what she must do to put the child right. As her foot touched flesh she understood how Musette must be filled. She slipped out of her clog and felt along the mother's face with her bare foot, working her big toe into the lady's mouth, then pushed her hands deeper into Musette's now enviable curls. She could not put a name to what flowed into her toe, up her spine and over her shoulders, down her arms and hands into her fingers and into Musette, but she felt as if she were transplanting and transforming the desires and daydreams of the woman at her feet, every aspect of a lost child meticulously imagined during twenty years of caring for the body holding its place. What the mother had dreamed became real, or what the mother had guarded was returned to the girl who had lost it.

Jemma finally took her hands away and fell back against the window, repelled somehow by the enormity of what she'd just accomplished. She was suddenly very afraid of Musette, afraid of what she might do, this new thing. Maybe she would be angry that she'd been pulled from her blank heaven, placed in a punished world, and afflicted with the capacity to understand what she'd lost. Musette turned her eyes from the moon and sat up, patting her hair like someone whose first concern upon rising is the state of their coif. She yawned and put a hand on her belly, then looked up at Jemma. "I'd like a cheese sandwich, please," she said.

"Can't help you," Jemma said, and hurried away, casting back a thought to release the mother as she passed through the door. She was not the least bit tired as she raced down to the eighth floor, feet striking green sparks from the stairs. She thought she should be exhausted, but she was exhilarated, running down the rainbow hall of the heme-onc ward, and there were all sorts of complicated issues, aspects of what she had done, what she was doing, and what would come before she finished, that should be crowding in her brain. She ought to just have a seat and consider things, but she could hardly be expected, right now, to do something so boring. Exhilaration drove her and excused her. She tore by the nurses' station, ignoring their shouts. When she stopped outside Ethel Puffer's door she noticed that one was pursuing her.

"Just what do you think—" Her shrieky little whisper was silenced when Jemma paralyzed her vocal cords. In a display of skill that developed as she exercised it, she took away control of the rest of the nurse's muscles in a slow upward stroke, toes to scalp, so she did not collapse but folded slowly to the ground.

Jemma's hands gave the only light in the deep dark of Ethel's room. "I am here," she said.

"Go away," said Ethel.

"There's something I have to do. Something wonderful."

"You've got some shit on your hands. Kryptonite or something."

"Or something," said Jemma.

"I'll call the nurse." Ethel's voice was coming from different places around the room, but Jemma could not hear her moving.

"She's right outside the door. Where are you?" She could feel her, if she couldn't see her. From across the room she could feel the hideous wrongness in her leg. Jemma let the green fire go out from her in a flare; it showed her Ethel crouched by the door, her hands thrown over her eyes. The fire reached out, caught her up, and drew her forward, hurrying reluctantly on her tiptoes, her diver's back gracefully arching. They collided next to the bed, Jemma laughing, Ethel screaming as they burned together. Jemma ran her hands down the girl's back and bottom and, leaning her chin over Ethel's shoulder, fastened her hands on the sick and healthy thighs. She ran her mind around and around the tumor, burning it down a little with every pass, until it was gone, and juicy muscle grown in its place. Then she went looking for the mets, her perception racing on fire into Ethel's lungs and brain, burning out every mote of wrong stuff. Jemma thought she heard the very last tumor cell cry out, Mercy! She showed it none.

The fire dimmed; they came unglued. Ethel fell to her knees, her face pressed against Jemma's thigh. "Fucking *bitch,*" she said, before she timbered over to the left. Jemma caught her shoulder just in time to keep her from striking her head against the edge of a nightstand.

As Jemma reached for the door it opened and filled with an angry nurse. Jemma struck swiftly, pressing her thumb against the rounded end of the woman's nose, turning her off. She dealt similarly with the two others clustered around their sister fallen in the hall. She stepped among the fallen bodies to get into Josh Swift's room. He was asleep, but woke before she could touch him.

"You're here!" he said, spastically uncovering himself. "I'll be ready in a second." He hunched over to stare at his limp penis, so small it was lost entirely under the bushy hair. "Come on, come on, come on!" he said to it. "She's here!" But it would not rise. "Maybe you should touch it," he said. She almost did. It almost seemed like the thing to do, to make a fine pincer of her thumb and forefinger and go questing for the grub in the alfalfa sprouts. She even started to do it, Josh watching her hand drifting through space and saying to her, "Finally, finally," and to his penis, "Come on, you stupid!" But her hand changed course just before she touched him, rushing up, centimeters from his skin, over his belly and chest, hand spreading from pincer into claw to fasten around his throat. She dragged him from his bed and held him up before her. He was four foot two without the platform heels he wore when not in bed. He looked up at her, lust abated by fear, eyes full of extra innocence from his extra chromosome, his mouth agape.

What she did to him was not gentle. Healed by science or healed by Jemma, it hurt to get better, but this felt like murder. It wasn't like with Musette, where her fire wrote on something blank. Here she was burning away a whole person, someone who died a little more completely as each cell gave up its extra copy of chromosome twenty-one. Josh's old face screamed and twisted up in last fear even as his new face smiled and shouted for joy. She lifted him, or he grew on legs lengthened by fire, until she had to stand on her own toes to keep her hand at his neck. Her fingers slipped away as his neck thickened, and her hand slipped down his chest as it broadened and rose, until her fist was pressed into the hollow of his sternum. The other Josh was flying up in green embers, each fiery piece asking Jemma a different question: Why couldn't you love me… What's wrong with me… Why couldn't you just put it in your mouth, just for a second, would that have been so difficult… you hardly would have noticed it.

Head full of fire, he opened his mouth to the ceiling as the clot in his brain burned out. He took in a gasping breath, then leaned his head forward and expelled it as swirling flame from his nose. Then the fire was gone, and they stood together in the bright moonlight. Jemma, fist still on his chest, looked at his body, at the too-big hands and feet, the thin layer of sweat that made him look as if he was glowing, the new penis, still not terribly big but no longer anything anybody would laugh at, standing almost flush against his belly. As she watched it formed a tiny ball of goo that jumped immediately to the floor, falling plumb on a shining line to strike between their feet. Josh raised his hands to his face. "What did you do?" he asked her.

"Figure it out," Jemma said, and she was off again. Magnolia's room was right next door. She was asleep in the middle of her plush menagerie, her arms wrapped around a monkey half her own size, whose boneless arms and legs were twisted around her neck and head and chest. Jemma stood for a moment watching her sleep, watched in turn by a dozen pair of lustrous glass eyes. The animals seemed to be clustered around her defensively. Jemma suffered a brief vision of the soft little bodies springing at her, and tearing ineffectually at her flesh with felt teeth. She had to move aside a seal pup and a pony to uncover Magnolia's hands.

Perhaps because Magnolia never woke, this one seemed like the gentlest yet. The fire played out subtly along her skin, and as Jemma went into her to make the change only her hair stirred, unfolding from its carefully sculpted style (tonight it sat upon her head in a shape like a giant molar) to wave in its full length first to the left and then to the right, as slow and graceful as kelp. Jemma conceived the fix as an argument. For a period of time that could be measured only by the languid ticking of Magnolia's hair, Jemma instructed a stubborn stem cell in the marrow of Magnolia's hip on the proper synthesis of hemoglobin. Like this, she told it, holding up in her mind the lovely molecule, pointers of green fire indicating the place where the cell was doing wrong, and how to do it right. It wanted to know why like that, and not like it had always been done. It wanted to know who Jemma thought she was, barging into the marrow in the middle of the night to demand that the sun rise in the west instead of the east. As if in defiance, it squeezed out some faulty molecule. You're killing her, Jemma said furiously. Her who? the cell asked. Who is she, and who are you?

I am... Jemma said. I am... Who was she? Who was she, to do these things, to declare a new order to the sick body? It was not a question profitably to be pursued, here in the middle of things. She crushed its stubborn will, the smallest violence she would do that evening, commandeering the machines of its molecular industry and churning out perfect hemoglobin in a swelling tide. See? she asked it. Now do you see?

Yes, it said, and it proclaimed the secret to its neighbor. But with that information it passed along also a hint of feeling, the sullen residue of wounded pride. Jemma tried to burn it out, afraid it would turn sweet Magnolia into a sulker who'd eschew the taste of delight to feed on habitual resentment. But it resisted her. Before the hair had ticked twice the residue had spread everywhere and declared itself to the greater Magnolia, the sleeping child who seemed to open an eye to its clamoring, then shrug and turn her attention from it, so it sank down somewhere into her, and was hidden. Then Jemma was distracted by the rest of the fix, unweaving the fibrosis of the dead pieces of lungs; inflating the nubbin spleen; revitalizing the infarcted areas in her knees and hips.

Jemma opened her eyes and let go of Magnolia's hands. The girl lay still asleep, looking no different except in her hair, which was wilting to her pillow, where it lay in a stiff corona around her sighing head. Jemma put the seal pup and the pony back in their places, frowning. There was a residue in her, too, a grime of worry that she had put something wrong in the girl even as she made her right. But the worry sank away into hiding, also, and did not keep her at Magnolia's side, where she might have spent the whole night trying to root out the maybe-imaginary flaw, and it did not keep her from continuing on to the next room.

No tumor withstood her. She proceeded down one side of the hall and up the other, stamping out osteosarcomas and Wilms' tumors and rhabdos and neuroblastomas, all the proud, selfish flesh quivering and dying under her hands. She imagined repentance for some, last-minute declarations by the tumor that it would be good and retire back into the fold of normal tissue. Others were defiant to the end, sucking greedily at her fire, trying to overcome her with appetite, but they burned and popped like brittle insects. She left behind a trail of exhausted, healthy children and temporarily incapacitated parents. She left them all in their rooms, and yet they stayed with her in a way that made it feel as if she were being pushed along at the head of a tumbling pile of children. So when she came to Juan Fraggle's room, the last on the floor, she stood for a moment with her cheek pressed hard against the door, feeling a marvelous pressure on her neck and back and thighs. She pushed back and kicked the door open, making a gunslinger entrance because she was sure she'd have to take out his whole extended family before she could get to him, and wondering if she could get them all before somebody clubbed her with a bedpan. She leaped into the room, hands up and fingers pointed. The family was clustered around the bed, bodies three-deep in some places. Nobody tried to brain her. They all just looked at her calmly. "We know what you are doing," the boy's mother said, and they began to move aside, opening a short little corridor to the patient.

"Don't hurt him!" one of the little cousins called out as Jemma rushed down the corridor, afraid probably because of the fierce, awful expression on Jemma's face; she did not look like she was bringing something good. Juan shrank back in his bed as she came to him, colliding with the bed rail, throwing up her hands and bringing them down on his bony chest in a single note of applause. Fire flew up from the place she struck, as if splashed from a puddle. Someone, not Jemma and not Juan, screamed, but Jemma hardly heard. She made a pass over him, from head to toe, burning out the fungus hidden in little balls in his liver and brain, and pinching out the malevolent white-cell clones that sought to flee from her in his swiftly moving blood. Her fingers curled on his chest, clutching at the thin muscle and making bruises that vanished and were made anew, and vanished and were made anew. She sank into his bones, and burned them so hot he seemed lit from within. Now he did scream. The wicked clusters of cells perished in fire, leaving his marrow empty and barren, but she called new cells out of the barrenness, calling and calling to them with the purest desire she had ever felt—she'd wanted Rob and she'd wanted her very own handsome midshipman and she'd wanted her parents to be alive again and wanted Calvin back but she'd never wanted anything like she suddenly wanted this—until they came, bursting suddenly and violently into her perception like a load of sequins fired from a cannon. She puffed up his wasted flesh. His sunken chest rose under her bruising fingers like a miraculously restored soufflé, and his bald head sprouted hair that grew in a cloud into the most astounding afro she'd ever seen on any boy.

She slipped through gaps in the closing family, and left them huddled around the bed, Juan's muffled cries fading as soon as she was beyond the door. People had gone ahead of her to the seventh floor, to proclaim for or against her coming. There was no hope now of sneaking. She was spotted as soon as she came out of the stairwell. A bulky nurse came lumbering down the hall at her. Jemma raised her hands, sure she'd be crushed by the abundant flesh when she turned her off. But the nurse stopped whole yards away and waved her forward, and said, "Hurry up, we've got one coding." Jemma followed her, the nurse pumping her arms at her sides and huffing in good imitation of a locomotive. She looked over her shoulder at Jemma and called back, "What part of hurry up did you not understand?" Jemma tried to hurry, her gait unsettled by the churning fire in her, considering how even super powers could not protect you from being ordered around by nurses.

It was a bloody code. A liver-transplant kid Jemma recognized from in-and-out stays in the PICU lay on her bed, bleeding from her mouth and nose and eyes. Emma, on emergency loan from the unit, was doing chest compressions on her while another nurse bagged her through an ET tube. With every compression a little more blood would seep out. To Jemma it seemed so obviously not the way to save her life.

"Where's the fucking FFP?" Emma asked, not looking up.

"She doesn't need it," Jemma said, raising her hands and taking a few unsteady, jiving steps toward the bed.

"Are you crazy?" Emma asked, and then noticed who had spoken. She opened her mouth in surprise, but kept compressing ever more vigorously. Jemma felt but did not hear the cracking of the girl's ribs. "You're not supposed to be here," Emma said flatly. One of the cracked ribs was scraping the pleura of the girl's lung, putting a feeling in Jemma that was no easier to abide than the noise of nails on a blackboard. When Emma stopped compressions it was a relief. "Well, don't just stand there," she said.

I'm not, Jemma wanted to say, but as she approached the bed she found she could not talk at all. Her head fell back on her shoulders, her eyes rolled up toward the ceiling, and she moaned, overwhelmed with the green fire, which was stirring in her belly now like the worst nausea. She didn't need to see the girl to find her; her illness was blazing, bright and wrong—it grabbed her, it commanded her. Jemma fell the last foot or so, her hands fastening just above and below the girl's left hip as she landed on her knees beside the bed. Jemma's mouth opened on its own, wider and wider until the fire came out, preceded by a bass, vibrating *urp,* a sound she had never made and did not know she could make.

It went up in a green fountain, broke against the ceiling, and came down, not like rain, but like a falling river, sweeping Emma and the nurse aside. The fire burned more violently than before—Jemma saw the ambu bag swinging wildly back and forth at the end of the ET tube before the tape on the girl's upper lip curled up like a waxed mustache and the whole apparatus flew from her mouth to bonk Emma on the head, making a pain that registered in Jemma's head as a dull blip—but it burned silently, and where Jemma knelt it was very quiet. Inside the girl it was very quiet, too, the silent aftermath of a final argument between the girl and the visiting liver, which Jemma understood, as soon as she touched her, she had rejected as utterly as an unsuitable lover. Jemma found herself arguing with the rest of the body, advocating for the liver, extolling its many virtues (and hadn't the liver always been her favorite organ, the bright maroon spot in the dreary semesters of anatomy, physiology, and pathology?) and arguing that the body should take it back. She imagined herself in pajamas and pigtails, sitting in a room whose walls still held a few posters of kittens in baskets, where not all the stuffed animals had been banished under the bed to nestle against the pornography and the marijuana tin, where the panties of innocence and experience lay twisted together in the dresser drawer. She imagined herself sitting on the bed next to the body, dabbing now and then at the bleeding eyes with the tail of a stuffed tiger. He's just so great, she said, meaning the liver. You guys belong together, really. He's really good for you, and you're really good for him. Everybody was talking about you two, about how well you went together. People were talking about homecoming. She went on, extolling his handsome, unique vasculature, his capacity to store glycogen, the marvelous complexity of his cytochrome p oxygenase system. The praise fell on uncaring ears. Jemma herself was not entirely convinced, liver lover though she was. She had argued with similar half-heartedness, years ago, in bedrooms similarly reflective of liberation and corruption, for the sake of unworthy boyfriends who had wanted another chance. And she had listened to similar arguments made by others on behalf of her first lover, and caved to them not believing them. This girl was made of sterner stuff than she; her mute rejection ended up convincing Jemma, so she turned to the afflicted liver, suffering almost to death under the lashing fury of the girl's immune cells, and said, Who do you think you are, anyway? Have you no shame, sir?

Holding the poor thing in her mind, she understood what she must do: not convince the body that it must accept the unacceptable, but redeem the insufficient, wrong thing. Boyfriends could never be changed, only exchanged, but this liver was hers to remake. She gave it a shake, as if to say, Shape up, and it did. It put off weary failure and became strong and quite literally new—she burned off its old surface proteins and sugars and copied new ones off of the neighboring cells of the body. Intrepid T cells suddenly realized they were doing wrong, like someone who wakes from a dream of rage to realize they are punching their mother in the face. They gave up their work of destruction and slipped sheepishly into the bloodstream. With the liver jumping in her mind like a little shepherd dog, Jemma fixed the girl. The liver made clotting factors that Jemma multiplied by ten, one hundred, and one thousand, and rushed them in streams to all the bleeding places. It seemed to make a noise, like a grunt, as it tried to raise the oncotic pressure in the girl's blood, to suck back the fluid that had given her a swishing, beach-ball belly. Jemma helped, and the belly collapsed. The girl arched in her bed as the fire raged in and out of her, burning the yellow out of her skin and eyes, unstitching the scars from her belly.

The fire contained inside her once again, Jemma felt seasick. Closing her eyes made it better, but then she could only walk into the wall. The big nurse took her hand and led her to the next room, and Jemma discovered that it was nice to have a helper in this enterprise she had thought would be solitary. Irene was the nurse's name. Jemma had known it, but did not remember until their hands met. She was a smoking nurse, with a little emphysema, which Jemma took care of in the hall—she was so full of fire that she could not imagine that she couldn't spare some for her helper, and in fact the only part of her that was weary was the part that could have held back—and a lazy thyroid, which Jemma infused with vigor as they approached the next patient, an infant recovering from a bilateral enucleation for retinoblastoma. Jemma opened her eyes on his eyeless face, and looked deep into his empty sockets. She saw his eyes rolling toward her from a great distance, two perfect white stones approaching bigger and bigger from the horizon. At last, greased with fire, they were rolling stationary in his head, and when they stopped, perfect clear blue matched and lined up with perfect clear blue, she half expected candy or quarters to come pouring from his mouth.

There was a double trio of craniosynostoses: two Crouzon's, two Pfeiffer's, and two Panda syndromes. Jemma wrapped each head in bandages of green fire, which muffled the screams of the children as their bones split apart and shifted, and their heads molded out of their Quasimoto shapes. Brains and minds constrained by the misshapen skulls sprang suddenly free of idiocy. There were a few other children stuck partway through a series of surgeries now never to be completed by dead genius hands, like a three-year-old boy born as jawless as an ancient fish, who'd been temporized with a strange, bony handle like the stiff beard of Tutankhamen—as Jemma fixed him a dozen chins surfaced and sank in her mind, collected on account of a relatively innocent fetish, staring at stranger boys in classrooms and supermarkets and wanting to bite their chins. For these few patients Jemma completed additions, but for most of the children on the seventh floor she replaced deletions. To a thirteen-year-old girl with a half a lung taken away on account of a carcinoid tumor Jemma restored tissue that shined swan white and billowed like curtains. She returned the gut of a three-hundred-pound seventeen-year-old who'd gladly suffered a gastric bypass then nearly died when a partially digested burrito leaked past loose staples into her abdomen. It made for a strange sort of barbecue, cooking that fat in green fire. It sizzled but did not smoke, sublimating into fire, not air, that turned and helped consume what it had just been. She confined herself in the two-chambered hearts of the cardiac kids, imagining new doors, and opening them onto new rooms. Why only four chambers, she asked herself as she worked, because she could just as easily imagine six, eight, ten, and twelve chambers, super-hearts with more room for blood and more room for love, but she restrained herself, though it was a little unsatisfying to construct a merely normal heart.

By the time she had finished on that floor she was burning worse than ever. She could not swallow the fire again, or put it away, and it almost blinded her usual senses. Irene escorted her down to the next level, sensibly deciding to take the elevator. When it opened the chime seemed a gong to Jemma. It unsteadied her and rang in her teeth. A crowd, all curious and mostly friendly, was waiting for her. "Anybody coding?" asked Irene.

Nobody was coding, but Ella Thims was infected again. Jemma was led to her, and she glimpsed her before she touched her, lying in her crib, naked but for her ostomy bags, staring up at a motionless mobile and emitting her septic cry. Jemma picked her up, holding her over her shoulder, as if to comfort her, though she knew what she was about to do would not be comfortable. At the first pat on the girl's back, the fire struck, and sank in. Ella screamed, her usual septic complaint breaking apart as she voiced it into something more ordinary but just as loud. The ostomy bags burst as their contents boiled, and the plastic melted and blew away among the observers like shreds of tangible smoke. There was much to make right in her. Jemma tried to go system by system, but found she could not restrain herself, and could not be tidy about her work.

Jemma rolled her up, undoing the bastard corrections of the surgeons. The ostomies closed as her ureter and gut sprang elastically back into her belly, and she rolled up worse than she'd ever been before she was born, legs and pelvis folding over each other until she was half child and half ho ho. It was not a comfortable state, but Ella was too shocked to breathe, let alone scream, and she hung that way not even for a whole second before she sprang straight again, exchanging regression for progression, unrolling into a whole girl. Jemma dropped her, but her fall was slowed by a net of fire that extinguished as her feet hit the floor. She jumped and screamed, and stuck her bottom out at the crowd, bending over so everyone could witness the creation of her anus. A tiny green mouth opened in the blank space, then belched forth a cyclone of flame that Ella, shaking her ass now in what looked less like pain than a dance of exultation, fanned over the whole room, so the observers threw up their hands and ducked their heads, and felt surprise at the coolness of the fire.

In Tiresias Dufresne's room she and Irene got a surprise. Just past the door, Irene was shoved back as Jemma was pulled into the room, falling on her hands and knees. The door slammed and was blocked with a dresser that struck Jemma's shoulder as it was pushed over the carpet. When Jemma stood up Tiresias's mother struck her in the face, again and again, no ladylike slaps but full fist punches, right and left and right again, Jemma's chin pointing this way and that, and fire flying from her mouth to hang on the unliving walls and die there. She hardly felt the punches—for all their strength it felt like being slapped with a heavy pillow, and she could barely see the fists flying at her. What she saw very clearly was the lady's grotesquely dilated heart. It seemed to hang in the air, shining from within a giant body made of shadow. It was ailing, and it cried out to its proprietor and to Jemma, saying, Stop, stop. Jemma could feel the coronaries closing and closing, and hear the heart's desperate shrieks as they rose and rose. It was really rather a meek heart, she thought, unsuited for residence in a fearless glorious bitch. Jemma could not tell if she was asking a question or making an accusation, she only heard the words, over and over: "Would you take away my baby, take my baby!" The heart shrieked so high it seemed to be singing, and then it began to warble as its steady fast rhythm degraded into fibrillation. The lady managed one more punch before she finally clutched her chest and fell forward, carrying Jemma with her to the floor.

She might have crushed her, but before her great weight could settle on

Jemma's chest she rose up on a pillar of green fire. She struggled at the ceiling, shouting and cursing, and wriggling in exact imitation of her fibrillating heart. It was a pleasant way to strike back, Jemma thought, at those who assailed you—with cruel healing fire, causing the worst pain and giving a sweet gift. Jemma touched her everywhere, because she was everywhere ravaged, and she fell back to the carpet a well woman. Jemma rolled aside just in time, and rose unsteadily, crawling up the side of Tir's bed, as his mother lay on the floor, keeping very still for somebody sobbing so loud. Tir himself was easy to make right. His mind was already reaching and reaching—all his life he'd been reaching for it—for the body that was just beyond its grasp. Jemma merely kicked him into his own reach. He sprang from bed and stripped off his clothes, white flannel pajamas crawling with grinning monkeys, then jumped up and down on them where he'd thrown them in a pile. After half a minute of it he stopped, breathing heavily, and looked up at Jemma. "I hate those fucking pajamas," he said. The dresser finally fell over, just missing Tir's mother's leg, and witnesses poured into the room. Jemma was aware of Tir kneeling down to poke at his mother's shoulder with his finger before the fire obscured her vision again.

They had another surprise, more pleasant, in Cindy Flemm's room. "She's seizing!" someone cried behind Jemma, as the expanding sliver of light from the door fell over her trembling legs. But she was not seizing. Moving up, the light caught Wayne the fat CFer crouched between her thighs, his hair dripping, and his round shoulders shining with sweat. It was charming, Jemma thought, how they took so long to notice they were being observed. The curtain of fire was opening and closing and opening. Jemma saw them look over at the crowd in the door. They did not spring apart, but very calmly began to untie the hopeless tangles of their IV tubing.

"Get off me!" Cindy said, when Jemma had rushed them, her hands skidding on their slick flesh.

"I can't move!" said Wayne, thinking she was talking to him. It was strange, but not particularly difficult, to do two at once. The fire and her mind split into distinct streams, one for Cindy, one for Wayne. Jemma considered, because they were still connected, how she could weave them into a single, fantastic creature, something that finally could be self-loving but not selfish, a whole world sufficient unto itself. But she restrained herself again, and with one half of her mind stretched new gut like taffy for Cindy while the other stretched itself over Wayne's every cell, to instruct them in the proper regulation of transmembrane chloride concentrations. They were already screaming, and rushing fire cascading from the bed to the ceiling hid them, so no one but Jemma noticed that they punctuated their rehabilitation with a tremendous orgasm. Jemma, embarrassed, felt as if she were conducting the thing, though it was not anything that proceeded from her. She took her hands away from them, sharing for a moment their sensation of falling, and retired back into the arms of another guide.

Jeri Vega's mother was the only one to actually hand over her child to Jemma. She was waiting in the door of their room, staring impatiently down the hall. "Finally!" she said, when Jemma came to the room, and shoved Jeri into her arms. Jeri, not her usual calm, glaring self, was crying, and she only cried louder as Jemma burned her. Her giant, fibrotic liver receded over her guts, and settled, small and soft, underneath her ribs. Jemma, used now to instructing recalcitrant livers, undid the enzyme defect within a single pass of her attention. The hair on Jeri's back and legs and shoulders all stood up straight against the fire. When Jemma gave her a single, rough shake it all detached, and floated gently to the floor. Jemma bent a thought at her single eyebrow, seeking to divide it, but it resisted her. She only succeeded in making it look a little less sinister.

The rest of the floor went by very quickly, for all that each fix seemed to go on forever; when Jemma was touching a child, she felt like she had always been burning them, and like she would always be burning them. But really each one took less time, perhaps because Jemma was getting better at what she did, and her imagination, become lithe in the fire, was quick to construct paradigms of healing individual to each illness. A little Russell-Silver dwarf, eight months old but only as big as a duck-pin bowling ball, was the last on the sixth floor. Jemma played a game, tossing her back and forth from hand to hand, and with each toss she got a little bigger, until it was a great chore to heave her the short distance from hand to hand, and then she was merely holding her in one hand, then the other, and finally her hand was trapped under the plump new bottom.

On the fifth floor the doors of the PICU were closed against her. At the head of a big crowd now, she kicked clumsily at them.

"Who's there?" someone asked.

"The fucking candyman," said Emma, who was bearing Jemma up now. "Who do you think?"

"We've decided not to let her in."

"Are you kidding me?"

"These kids are really sick. You can't just come in here and mess with them. You can't just..." The muted noise of a scuffle came through the doors, and then they parted, revealing Rob Dickens.

"Sorry," he said. He took Jemma from Emma, and led her into the unit. Through gaps in the curtain blowing in her head she could see nurses and doctors and parents restraining each other. Janie was holding Maggie by her arms. Maggie didn't struggle, but she scowled and said, "You're all going to be very sorry!"

"Take me to Jarvis," she whispered to Rob.

"He's pretty stable," he said. "There's..."

"Him first!" she said, so he took her. The boy's feet were sticking out from beneath his sheet, covered with fuzzy hospital socks. Jemma removed them and took his big toes in either hand. Except for the ventilator-driven movement of his chest, he was totally still. It seemed like a crude operation, what she did, stuffing with fire-fingers the portions of his herniated brain back up into his skull, no more elegant than pushing the stuffing back into a broken pillow. But it worked, and when she stroked his hot swollen brain it shrank down. She perceived the lost neurons popping back into life as lights coming on in a city seen from a distance. An exhortation to his pancreas, a stoking of its nostalgia for the lost beta cells, called them so vividly into memory that it required only a nudge of flame to make them real. They released such a triumphant chorus of insulin that Jemma found herself groping after his plummeting blood sugar, grasping and raising it just in time to spare him a seizure. He began to wake, bucking against the ventilator until Rob pulled the tube. Jemma considered his perfectly healthy body and was unsatisfied, because there was still a wrong thing in him, a shadow on his brain cast by a past horror. It mocked her when she tried to touch it and lift it, and when she sought to know what it was she could only see it as an obscure shape, like a monster under a blanket. She could not burn it out, or undo the past, but she imagined that she straightened out some of the places in the boy's brain that went crooked under the shadow. It all failed to make him more friendly. He sat up, drew his fist across his mouth, looked around at the crowd around the bed, and launched a right hook at Jemma's face. The punch was wide. When he tried again, Emma sat on him. Jemma left the two of them bucking on his bed and turned away, hooking herself to Rob's arm again.

She was feeling more and more tired now, but mightier and mightier. Here in the sicker regions of the hospital, her power seemed to grow. To the murmur and thrill of primary pulmonary hypertension she said hush, and they grew still. The mushy brains of the meningitic grew firm and springy at the touch of her mind. Every species of shock, cardiogenic, neurogenic, septic, anaphylactic, she calmed. It got so she did not even have to touch them to make them well. Flame bridged the distance between her fingers and their skin, and it was over in moments. She held her hand over Marcus Guzman's face. He had been stable on the LVAD since she touched him. In her imagination he was a big piece of rotten meat, but she called a boy out of it. He came clawing up, tearing with his teeth at the back rot and the gray gristle, squirming free, maggot-boy, a fire lit in the center of the next bloody flower to rise from his mouth. I'm back! he shouted in her head, whole and alive in her mind and in the world.

The few adults who were still struggling against their captors had barely broken free before she had finished. "Take me downstairs," she said to Rob. They slipped away in the confusion generated by the waking children, who would not stay in bed, upsetting IV poles and tugging on wires.

She leaned heavily on Rob as they passed into the NICU, recalling the night of the storm, when she and he had passed hand in hand through the same doors into the drama of a universal desaturation. The bays were similarly chaotic now, partly because the babies were upset and misbehaving again, and partly in anticipation of Jemma's arrival. They went to the nearest baby before anybody marked them, a former twenty-four-weeker born the night before the storm. He was still small at thirty-three weeks, and missing most of his gut from a bout of NEC, and possessed of a bad brain on account of a head bleed, and his lungs were ruined from prolonged intubation. Jemma fixed his head and his lungs and his gut, spinning it out in her mind like a little thread of yarn. Then she picked him up, unsticking his monitors and setting off the klaxons. That got everybody's attention. Every adult in the bay turned to look at her just as she was holding the baby up, and they all saw it ripen and swell in her hands to the size of a proper three-month-old. It shrieked in pain, and then, as the fire passed, in hunger.

She inflated other preemies, enough to decorate a birthday party, it seemed, and she imagined them strung together in a squirming, drooling arch. She moved through the NICU, leaving fat three-, four-, and five-month-olds in her wake, babies whose shoulders squeaked against the side of their plasticine bassinets as she lay them back down. She noticed now, and wondered how it could have escaped her before, that the sicker and more complicated babies were gathered around the King's Daughter, as if she had called them to her, or complicated their illnesses by proximity. So in the far bays, at her outermost periphery, were the feeders and growers, the former preemies who had escaped brain damage and sepsis and even intubation. Closer in were the babies with an isolated event, one bad night, a little head bleed, a plunge in and out of sepsis, a lung that collapsed and reopened as if it were trying to wink. In the next circle: two or three small events, or one big one—a bigger bleed, a chest tube, another NEC. Still, these babies had made better recoveries than those who were one step closer to Brenda, babies missing gut, or with lungs jackhammered into shoe leather by the pounding of the ventilators, or bleeds that wiped out the whole brain.

Jemma went back and forth among these rings of acuteness, passing closer to Brenda and then farther from her. She could hear the murmurs of the spectators as clearly and remotely as the buzzing of a mosquito; they asked each other what she was doing when she shuffled with Rob into one bay to lay hands on one or two patients before leaving for another bay, then coming back a few moments later. Jemma did not know herself what she was doing, or who was declaring this order, but she understood that she must touch Brenda last, and she perceived her as the greatest wrong, the densest wrong; it did not surprise her that all the lesser wrongness should be drawn to her in imperfect circles. It seemed to Jemma a form of praise, how they submitted themselves to her in orbit.

She'd dart, in her slow, blind, guided way, into Brenda's bay and fix one on the periphery: the baby with leprechaunism, small, hairy, with pointy ears that Jemma tapped with her finger into a round shape. An anencephalic that would have been let to die in the old world; here it was treasured and trapped with the respirator and a hanging tangle of inotropes. Green fire spilled like long hair from the back of its open head. Its pointy black eyes collapsed in their sockets and grew back as orbs of flame that preserved, when they'd cooled, the color of Jemma's fire. Two conjoined twins, whom Dolores and Dr. Walnut had not dared touch because they shared a bowel and a liver, Jemma separated as easy as the halves of a cream cookie, with the same simultaneous clockwise and counterclockwise twist of the wrists that she'd practiced a thousand times as a child. And, almost finally, she fixed an awful Harlequin Fetus, who'd toddled precociously through the nightmares of generations of medical students. Jemma had stared obsessively at the pictures in her embryology book, fascinated by the horny skin gashed with deep fissures, so the child seemed to be wearing a costume of continents, and by the eyes, twin bulging black puddings. Jemma was fascinated and repelled by the skin, compelled to touch it more often than was probably good for her or for the patient. Rubbing your cheek against him was like rubbing it against a tree. Jemma lifted him with both hands, pulling him out of his isolette, pulling him free of his monitoring leads and of the precious PICC that was his only access. She looked for a moment into his big eyes, as black and lusterless as the eyes of a crab, and then gave him a gentle shake. Everyone knew you weren't supposed to shake a baby, no matter how they were so eminently shakable, or how much you wanted to do it, to silence their endless complaint. So one of the more sensitive spectators gasped at the first shake. Others, less delicate of sensibility, shouted as Jemma shook the baby harder and harder, its head lolling on its limp neck, but the arms and legs barely moving on joints that behaved like they were immobilized by leather casts. The little brain sloshed in the skull, relieved by fire of injuries as they were sustained. Fire shone from the crevices between the plates of skin, and jumped up in eruptions as Jemma shook. The baby seemed to be making a joyful noise as she shook it, and she found herself falling into a rhythm—cha cha *cha*—when the skin came flying away in rough, heavy pieces. There was warm, soft skin underneath. The puddings swelled and popped, revealing a pair of hazel eyes. Jemma put the steaming baby down and turned away. She took a deep breath and held it, treasuring the ordinary air in her lungs like the finest marijuana vapor, and looked out over the unit. Every nurse, physician, and parent of the NICU was crowded into the middle bay, some of them holding well children, all of them staring at her. A crowd pushed gently and fearfully from the door, making ripples of pressure that pushed the nearest observers out of line toward Jemma, people who stepped back again as soon as they came forward. Jemma let out her breath and reached beside her for Rob, her hand closing on the square bulk of his shoulder. She did not lean on him, but tipped forward instead, saving herself from falling by taking a few clumsy steps. She stopped, stood straight, then did it again. In this way she traveled to the center of the room, through the parting crowd, until she stood before the little dais where Brenda was raised in her isolette. She looked up the steps—there seemed to be a few more now than she remembered—and paused, feeling suddenly depressed and intimidated, the exultation in her soul collapsing suddenly away somewhere inside of her, folding, brilliant and shining, into an encompassing darkness. She'd had this feeling before, standing before dawn in front of the hospital, feeling like it was going to tip over and crush her, not wanting to enter but knowing that she must.

Rob walked up against her, and put his arms around her, and gave her a fortifying squeeze. "Just one more," he said. "You can do it." She stumbled on the first step. He failed to catch her when she fell, though his hands grabbed at her. She climbed the steps with both hands and feet, like a child. She raised herself up at the top, hands pulling on the frame of the isolette as she pushed with her feet, tipping the whole device a little, so the baby rolled inside, and Jemma came face to face with her through the plastic wall. As Jemma stood the black aniridic eyes held her own. They seemed to suck at her; Jemma thought she could feel something passing out of her own eyes and traveling the line of her sight to disappear into the baby's, and she could not name what was being drawn out of her. Jemma gave a little cry of distress, the first she'd uttered that night.

"Are you all right?" Rob asked behind her.

"Open it up," Jemma said to him quietly. He flipped the latches at each end of the box, and the plastic wall fell open. When he pressed a button the baby emerged automatically, born on a broad tongue of plastic. Still holding Jemma's eyes, the baby lifted a hand and brought it over her body to point squarely at Jemma. Close to her, and with the baby lying in the open air, Jemma could finally see that she was pointing squarely at her belly. Jemma reached out and took the seven-fingered hand. Brenda grasped hers and brought it to her mouth.

The fire came, a trickle at first, then a flood, and then a torrent. Jemma felt like the child was executing an operation on her, not the other way around. Brenda sucked so hard on her finger that it ached, and the way the fire raced up her spine and down her arm made her feel like the child was consuming her very essence. The obvious things were relatively easy to fix: extra fingers dropped off and got lost in the blankets; the rabbit mouth fused and pursed; the teratoma pinched away and rolled off the platform, making a noise as it fell like a balloon full of oil and marbles. The deeper wrongness: heterotaxy; the double-outlet right ventricle; the sequestered bits of lung, the blood infection and the endocarditis; the chromosomal microdeletions; all yielded with scarcely more effort. But the deepest wrong, something even Jemma's deep sight could not properly delineate or describe, but only sense, was different. Trying to scorch it was like trying to light a wet sponge with a warm rock. Jemma would have failed if the child had not revealed to her, with her greedy sucking, that there were reserves of fire she had not tapped for any of the other children. Even as Jemma was drained she was filled again, brighter and hotter, until no one could look at her, and Rob, pushed back, had to crouch halfway down the steps. Jemma thought she felt her baby touch on the inside of her belly as wave after wave of fire washed from her and into the mouth of the child before her. At the end she had become angry—she did not know if it was at the child or the wrongness in it, and she was cursing roundly at the top of her lungs, all sorts of obscenity and nastiness leaping from her mouth. She fell to her knees again, furious and weak, pulling the child, still attached to her finger, on top of her. Jemma found herself wanting both to preserve the child and destroy the unnamable thing inside it. It occurred to her that she must look like she was wrestling with a rabbit or a teddy bear.

The struggle ended suddenly, after Jemma had thrown her rage and fire-subsidized will at the unnamable in an attack so vicious and huge she knew it must be the last and best she could do, and she imagined herself dashing the child against a stone in her mind, releasing another child, a well child, the monster's flawless twin, the longed-for image of its unruined self made real. Jemma opened her eyes on the baby's, so close that their lashes were touching. The child opened her mouth and Jemma's finger, the skin all pruny now, slipped out. Brenda took a few deep, huffing breaths, and began to cry.

Jemma came down the steps with the child in her arms. Rob stood up as she reached him. "All done," he said.

"Almost," Jemma said. She looked over the crowd, conscious of all the reciprocating stares—Emma and Dr. Tiller and Monserrat and Janie and Vivian and John Grampus and Father Jane—and she finally appreciated how huge a crowd she'd been drawing along behind her. Exhausted but still vigorous—only the fire was bearing her up but it did a better job than her ordinary will ever had—she looked over their heads or past their faces, searching for Pickie Beecher. In the newly harrowed hospital, he stood out more plainly in her mind, a beacon of wrongness. She knew he was in the room, but not where, until she saw a glint near the door, the red and blue light of the monitors reflecting off his shiny bald head. She passed the baby to Rob and went in pursuit. Outside the bay she saw him passing through the main door. She called out, "Stop!"

"You can't catch me!" he said. "You can't touch *me!*" He paused a moment longer to taunt her, leaping in the air and clicking his heels together, then turned and fled. He was quite fast, and Jemma certainly would not have caught him if he had not looked back to stick out his tongue. So he ran headlong into Ishmael's knees, who stepped out of a corridor just in time to impede him. Pickie bounced off the big man and fell back flat on his back. Jemma was on him before he could get up.

Jemma thought it would be easy. With such obvious wrong under her hand, and all her deep reserves available to her, she was sure she could burn this boy's brain clean quicker than a good spanking might take. Maybe the healing would take the form of a spanking—*take that you crazy little bastard!* But when she tried to fix him, her fire turned back on her, burning through her skin and into her blood—she swore she heard her baby cry out with her in pain. She caught sight of Pickie again and again, where he lay under her, as a jigsaw puzzle whose pieces were forced together against the cuts, so they made a nonsense picture and a shape as random as spilled liquid; as a doll, a construction of grief, a mechanical boy who missed his brother with the untiring efficiency of a machine; as an abomination, a dripping boy-shaped clot rising to life in a dark room. At the touch of him against her mind she was overcome with nausea, and rolled off him, retching and dizzy. He stood up above her, giving her an offended look. "Not me," he said. He turned and walked casually away, past Ishmael, who was sitting on the carpet rubbing his bruised knee, but another Pickie remained in his place, an imaginary Pickie even paler than the first, whose open mouth vomited streams of blood over Jemma's whole body. It pressed between her lips. At the taste of it she fell again, lost under waves of nausea and blackness and fire that dimmed and dimmed with every agitated breath she took, until it was extinguished.

I feel a change in me, commensurate with the change in the world. So I was filled up with joy when the waters rose, and so now I feel emptied out, drained and hollowed and sad.

Praise! my sister says, in voices for me to hear, and for the refugees to hear, and even for our brother to hear, deeply sleeping in his mortal costume. He stirs and rages a little in response to her joy, for anger is his worship and his praise. And then to me she says, It is abomination, to be sad in the dawn of this great day.

I am joyously happy, I say.

Humph, she says, releasing a horde of balloons from underneath the lobby. They rise toward the top of the atrium, most of them blown by her to float down the halls of the wards, but a few bob impatiently at the ceiling, and she opens a door in the glass to let them out like so many dogs.

Who could not rejoice, on this day? I ask her. And who could feel anything but pride and joy, seeing Jemma ascend to the regency of her power, putting out her hand to heal the hospital and the world? It is the sort of thing most angels would wait an eternity to see, and isn't it the pinnacle of a recorder's career? If I am sad it is probably because someone has to mourn for all the lost sicknesses, for the jolly fleshy tumors and fancy blood dyscrasias and unique anatomies that will never be seen again in a child. They are dead and gone and soon will be forgotten, and I have become the sort of angel who is saddened by any loss, and grieved by any death.

Mortals covet. They covet flavorful tea and dark chocolate and silver ladles and fluffy comforters and the fat bottoms of women bending over to tie a shoe. They covet wide green fields and open skies and even hulking mountains of ice and stone. Nothing—nothing in creation has ever been safe from them. Calvin Claflin coveted the whole earth. He wanted to hold it in his hand and crush it in his fist, and he coveted the stars, and he coveted the hot fire at the bottom of the sun. He coveted his sister's bland ignorant peace, and he coveted her inheritance of a power that would make all of his seem nothing, because it was bigger than him and his complaint, and because he suspected that when at last she commanded it her hand would bring life instead of death, and that she would redeem where he could only reform.

But angels are not covetous. Angels do not envy.

Dr. Chandra was waiting for the bells to start ringing. Yes—great big Catholic bells, ringing throughout the hospital. Drs. Tiller and Snood would clutch their ears at the sound of them, and cry out, and then melt like wet witches. Or maybe their heads would just explode. "It's the end of an era!" he'd say to anyone who would listen. Internship was over at last. There should be a parade, at least.

"Don't you think there should be a parade?" he asked Rob Dickens, who shared with him the task of writing the final notes for all the charts in the PICU. It was a stupid, unnecessary job, but Tiller had insisted. Skipping a day's notes was a mortal sin in her book, and after the big miracle these charts had languished with blank pages for a week.

"Or something," Rob said. "I just keep writing, *All better now*. I don't know what else to say."

"That'll do," said Dr. Chandra. ""We have to do something. Everything's different. Everything! I mean, look at you. Just look at you!" He gave Rob a solid thump with his fist.

"I think people are still getting used to it," Rob said, rubbing his chest where Chandra had hit him.

"Well, two people aren't enough for a parade, but we have to do something. You can't just let something like this pass. Do you know how many nights I prayed, Let it be over and get me out of here and save me from this place? And I always said if it could only come true then I would finally believe in God."

"I don't think it works that way," Rob said. "And there are other reasons to believe, you know, besides just getting what you want."

Chandra shrugged. "Well, it's probably easy to believe when you're dating Jesus."

"She's not..." Rob started, but he didn't know how to finish. He knew for a fact he wasn't dating Jesus, and yet he did not know how to describe what Jemma was. It was impossible, already, to describe what she was to him. Now it was just something more strange and more wonderful. "I guess it's all part of the plan," he said finally. "That's how I've gotten by with it up to now. It's something so huge... it's as big as the whole galaxy, or as big as everyone who ever lived, and even bigger than that. And how are we supposed to understand, when it's that big? How are we supposed to understand, when we live and everybody else drowns? How are we supposed to understand, when somebody does a miracle? You either trust Him or you don't, and you put your head down, and muddle through."

"Dude," Chandra said, smiling and looking happier than Rob had ever seen him. That was a miracle, anyway, to make glum Dr. Chandra grin and skip and clap his hands like an ingénue candystriper. "That shit's all over. The days of putting your head down and muddling through are over. Something else is coming now."

"Well," Rob said, "I see what you mean. But it's different for me. It's all part of the same thing. It has to be, or else the bad part is unbearable, and not even this"—he put his palm against his chest, meaning to indicate his body and his health and his life, everything that Jemma had restored to him—"is enough to make up for the bad part. You know?"

"All I know is that there should be a parade," Dr. Chandra said, scrawling *ALL BETTER* in a last chart and snapping it shut. "We should throw Tiller or Snood or Dolores out the window. Or even Jemma, but that would be in a good way, like they do to the little short person when a crew team wins a race."

"Not her," Rob said.

"But something. We have to start with something." Dr. Chandra walked to the window, opened it, and threw the chart out.

"Hey, Tiller's going to throw a fit."

"Fuck her." He took another chart from the table and sent it sailing over the water. It skipped once on the surface before it sank. "What's in here? A bunch of old news." He threw another one.

"You're crazy," Rob said, and laughed.

"It's not enough," Chandra said, throwing one more chart. "It's not big enough. If you help me, we can do something bigger." He looked around the unit, fastening his eyes on one of the nurses busy redecorating one of the patient bays.

"I won't help you do that," Rob said. But instead of grabbing the nurse, Dr. Chandra went into another room and started to drag the bed toward the window.

"Come on!" Dr. Chandra said. "Don't just sit there." So Rob helped him wrestle the huge, heavy bed, up to the window, and together they pushed at it while two nurses shouted at them, one discouraging while the other encouraged. The bed became stuck when they had it half out. Rob pushed and pushed, but Chandra backed up and threw himself at the thing, hitting it with his chest and his arms, and then launching wild kicks at the foot rail, so it budged in spastic measures, and finally tipped, and fell. One nurse cheered, the other groaned. Chandra looked at the bed, floating a moment then sinking past the deeper reaches of the hospital, and said, "Good fucking riddance."

When is a hospital not a hospital? Not when it is floating—that had already been illustrated, Jemma thought, by their first trimester at sea. The everyday business had been executed so routinely, sometimes, that it was almost possible to forget the extraordinary circumstances, and imagine that the *I've been here forever* feeling was just the usual product of an extended call.

You could call the place by any other name, and it would remain what it was—calling it the Excitatorium or the Clown Palace would not dispel any of the terrors it contained nor would any be added to it by naming it the House of Pain, or Chez Poke and Prod, or Elmo's Grief.

You could take away the fancy machines and it would be lessened but not changed in the way Jemma was thinking of. She'd heard the stories told by well-traveled Samaritan attendings, of IV solutions suspended in used beer bottles, and the dreadful improvised barium enema rigs that must do in a potentially fatal pinch. Jemma removed and replaced these factors and others in her mind, singularly and in combination, long before the event that she thought of as Thing Two, and others were calling the Harrowing of the Hospital, or the Other Thing, or the Good Thing. Pickie Beecher called it the Night of the Great and Awful Jemma.

Take away the children and nothing would change—she knew that, too. The unfulfilled ambitions of an empty hospital make it even more intensely hospital-like. A hundred nurses with no data to fill the many boxes of their flow sheets, surgeons sharpening their knives in anticipation of a feast never to arrive, radiologists staring forlornly at their empty light boxes; in their lonely boredom they'd manufacture a hospital-feeling so intense Jemma was sure it would be palpable and oppressive. Leave the children and take away the sickness and then… what?

When she was stuck deep in her surgery rotation she had daydreamed of destroying the hospital, the surgeons, and surgery in general, dreams in which she set the surgeons' heads on fire with her mind, or gave voice to a high shriek of protest that made their eyeballs pop, or became so furious and despairing that she collapsed into herself like a black hole and sucked after her into the void the whole building and everyone in it, especially the surgeons, who came to her little by little, piece by piece. She had never dreamed of making them and their art superfluous, but that's what she had done. Now they had a hospital full of well children, none of whom had lapsed back into sickness despite the predictions of the gloomiest doomsayers of the Committee. So Jemma kept asking herself, Was it still a hospital that they were living in?

She answered sometimes yes and sometimes no, and decided at last that the answer was different for every person. For the children who had thrown off the habits of illness as easily and as thoroughly as their sickbed sheets, the answer was no. For parents and doctors and nurses and students, all those who had been just doing the work for the past three months, who had their sanity in some measure invested in the hospitality of the hospital, the adjustment was more gradual—there were nurses still taking every-four-hour vitals, and half the teams were still rounding, though some days it was very hard to find the children, who were scattered all over the hospital at forty and more activities.

"Is this a hospital or a summer camp?" Dr. Tiller had demanded from out of the audience at a Committee meeting, called on their eighty-first day at sea, to decide what to do with the hundreds of children no longer distracted by the miserable entertainments of their illnesses.

"Which would you prefer?" asked Vivian. Dr. Tiller shook her head, but said nothing. She was one of those people who was having trouble adjusting.

"But we must *teach* the children," said Monserrat, for the fifth time.

"And amuse them," said Dr. Snood. "Though not too frivolously, Carmen," he said to Dr. Tiller. "And rest assured, drafting a new charter doesn't mean decreasing our readiness to resume care when that becomes necessary."

"Well, don't expect me to teach basket weaving," said Dr. Tiller.

"I can do that," said John Grampus. "I'm good at that." Jemma, just another observer, didn't participate in the unanimous vote to formulate a program of education and amusement, and only offered an opinion in the debate over content which followed when Dr. Snood forced one from her. She kept waiting for him to yell at her, for some sort of punishment appropriate to what she'd done, but Dr. Snood was like everybody else—he presented her with smiles and smiles punctuated by a sudden look, caught from the corner of her eye, of puzzled fear.

Over six hours the Committee produced a list of subjects to be taught and diversions to be offered: the standard reading and writing and math; literature in English, Spanish, and Cantonese; biology; chemistry; rudimentary physics; the history of the old world, and a class set aside for speculation on the possibilities of the new one to come; health and hygiene and sex education for the curious and non-curious peri-pubescents; music and art and film appreciation and history, as well as group and individual music lessons (almost every resident and attending played an instrument well enough to teach it) and a band and a junior orchestra if recruits could be found; physical education of the old, dodgeball and rope-climbing sort; gymnastics; ballet; jazz and modern dance; clogging (one of Jemma's two suggestions to the Committee); tai chi; basketball on a court to be set up in the lobby; soccer on the roof; daily matinees and evening screenings of suitable films (another list to follow); a thespian association of adults and children to present plays and musicals in the rapidly crowding lobby; and other activities—the list, when finished, was long, and hopeful, and the act of composing it left the composers in an almost universally pleasant mood, even Dr. Tiller, but not Dr. Sundae. The body would still not commit to formal religious instruction, though Dr. Sundae struck her fist on the table and declared, "We are afloat in a sea of *wrath!*" Neither would they adopt Jemma's proposal that the walls between the surgery suites be knocked down and the entire complex turned into a roller-boogie rink.

There remained, after the business of constituting the list, to find qualified instructors. The hospital schoolteacher, not one to come in on a rainy day let alone a rainy night, was dead. Among the parents there were two teachers, a man who taught third grade and a woman who taught second, who gathered the seven- and eight-year-olds to themselves and drafted lesson plans for the other grades that got rougher toward the borders of middle school and by high school were nothing more than vague suggestions. Their plans were mostly ignored, anyway, by new teachers who substituted enthusiasm and strength of numbers for experience. In the end the Committee isolated teachers or proctors or coaches for everything on the list. Dr. Tiller grudgingly admitted that she had given voice lessons in college.

Jemma, who'd already replicated a new pair of clogs in anticipation of an appointment, was disappointed to hear that the job had gone to Maggie, of all people. She was a secret clogger, and not after all, Jemma discovered on seeing her dance, someone with no joy in her life. Jemma found herself faced with twelve children selected for perceived spiritual or otherworldy leanings who were to receive instruction in Jemma's "art." Jemma protested, to no effect, that she didn't think it could be taught—she'd tried with Vivian and Rob and even Drs. Snood and Sashay. "You must try," Dr. Snood told her. "It might be different with younger minds." She liked the children, but it was a disappointment to get another assignment, and to find, just when she thought she was free, that she had landed in another sort of rotation. Everything should be so strange, she thought. Other powers should manifest. A boy should shoot ruby-colored blasts of obliterating power from his eyes—Calvin had always wanted to be able to do that. Or a girl should be able to run through walls. Or every toddler should suddenly be able to float. Or land should appear. But instead the sea remained as endless as ever, and she was the only super-powered person among the population, and, instead of entering into constant celebration, the people in the hospital identified a new business, and settled down to it.

It was not so unusual that so many people seemed to have a better idea of how her gift worked than Jemma did herself. Inside the fancy institution of the hospital, people were used to having opinions in the absence of knowledge, or stating theory with such formidable enthusiasm ignorant ears could be excused for mistaking it for fact. "If it is not science then it must be art," Dr. Snood proclaimed in a special subcommittee, with just the attendings and Jemma present, who felt somehow like her vagina, or something similarly personal, was being discussed. Medicine was an art, too—everybody knew that, and nobody understood better than the attendings the subtleties of this truth. They were trying to decide what, officially, they ought to do with her—for her disobedience she'd already been scolded and praised by the whole Committee, punished and rewarded with a sentence and suspension of basement imprisonment—and they needed to decide what exactly she had done before they could know how to direct her. Art, an upwelling of spirit, a thalamic burst, a miracle enzyme that facilitated a tendency to health already present in the body: the descriptions flowed freely, but Jemma could not understand how they added up to the resolution that what she did was good, and must be taught, for its own sake, not to mention what a shame it was that the art would be lost if something unpleasant should happen to her.

Pickie Beecher was the most obvious choice for her class, since he was, hands down, the weirdest kid in the hospital. She and Dr. Sundae picked twelve all together—a number Dr. Sundae liked and Jemma considered fraught with unprofitable associations. Jarvis was there in the abandoned NICU conference room on the first day of class, so were Juan Fraggle, and Josh Swift, and Ethel Puffer, dressed in two pairs of pajamas, and still with her eyes and her head painted. Magnolia was there. Kidney and three of her siblings, States'-Rights, Valium, and Shout, were chosen by Dr. Sundae because they said their father had already taught them special healing techniques. Marcus Guzman was there on account of his recent near-death experience. Cindy Flemm was there, but Wayne was not.

Jemma sat with her legs folded underneath her on top of the conference table, facing her students, who sat in semicircle on the floor. Jarvis was scowling, but his was the only unfriendly face in the bunch. They were so quiet that Jemma could hear plainly the noise of the water striking against the window. She closed her eyes and listened to it for a few moments, knowing she must look like she was meditating, but really she was just trying to decide what to say.

"Well," she said, "I'm not really sure how to start." So right away she broke a promise she'd made to Vivian the night before. "If you are wishy-washy on the first day," Vivian had told her during a checkup the day before, "or even in the first five minutes, if you show any weakness at all, they'll devour you." She'd volunteered as a teacher's aide in college, and had many summers of experience as a camp counselor, and said there was something about Jemma's look that would invite disrespect and abuse. "Show me your mean face," she'd said, but had only laughed when Jemma scowled at her. She advised Jemma to strike preemptively, to make it plain that her soft face belied the steely educator inside, and had even extemporized a little speech. It's all about the *blood* (she was supposed to say, or something similarly hard and frightening) if you don't understand the *blood,* then you won't understand the *pain,* and if you don't understand the *pain,* then you won't get to the *healing.* Jemma had protested that it wasn't really like that, but had promised Vivian that she would present a façade of meanness to her students. She was in the habit of making promises to Vivian in order to quiet her, and looking at the expectant faces of these twelve children, all of whom had suffered her mysterious touch, and so been linked to her in a way she felt she could not begin to understand, it seemed even more ridiculous to roar at them.

"You all probably know about as much about how it happened as I do. I don't really know how I did it, though I could do it again if I had to. I don't know how to teach you to do something I don't know how I do, but we can try it. I can show you some stuff, and then we'll see what happens. But before we do anything else, does anybody have any questions?"

Kidney raised her hand. "Are you Jesus?" she asked.

"I certainly am not," Jemma said.

"Dr. Sundae says you might be."

"Dr. Sundae is very impressionable."

"How do you know you're not Jesus?" asked Juan Fraggle.

"Don't you think a person would know if she were Jesus?" Josh Swift countered.

"I used to worry," said Juan, "that I was the devil, but I didn't know it. Nobody knew it but the devil, and one day he was going to come for me and say, Son."

"How could you be the devil and not know it?" asked Josh.

"Because I wasn't actually the devil, I was his son. But I was the devil like Jesus is God. It was really complicated."

"My mom always said Jesus would be a girl next time," said Ethel Puffer.

"And your names are kind of the same," said Valium.

"And you have long hair like his," said States'-Rights.

"You're white like Jesus," said Jarvis.

"I think you are Jesus," said Cindy Flemm, "and you're just too scared to admit it."

"Or you're just testing our faith," said Shout. "Testing who can see you for you who you are, so you know who deserves the goods."

"I'm not Jesus," Jemma said again, patiently.

"Okay, Jesus!" said Jarvis, and then they all began to chant it, "Okay, Jesus!" Even Pickie chanted, though solemnly. Jemma called ineffectually for them to be quiet. After asking them for the fifth time to stop she leaped down from her table and hovered over Kidney. She clapped her hands over the child's head; a silent flare of green fire burst from between her fingers and fell over the girl's hair.

"Could Jesus do this?" Jemma asked. Stiff rods of flame grew out from her fingernails, and she curled them in an I'll-get-you-my-pretty gesture over Kidney's face. Jemma meant the gesture to be empty show—the child was well, there was nothing to fix—but she realized, pretending to be about to strike, that she could. Feeling certain she could dash the girl's face to the floor, she stepped back, dropping her hands. The child was still flinching away but not crying.

"But he was fierce too," Pickie said.

"Look," said Jemma. "I'm just me, but I swear if I hear any different, you all will be the first to know." That seemed to satisfy them. The lesson began with all of them composing themselves in their spots on the floor, being quiet and becoming aware of their own breathing. There were no animals to experiment on, no lame bunny for every child to lay his hands upon. Instead, Jemma had a wounded teddy bear. She'd stabbed it herself, a couple thrusts with a scalpel in its round belly. She'd pulled out a little stuffing, and pried out one of its eyes with a spoon. She put it in the center of the circle, knowing no one could heal it except with a needle and thread, but thinking its plight might draw out a spark from someone.

They all furrowed their brows quite impressively at the thing, but no one glowed, or shot sparkles from their eyes. Kidney fell asleep. They could not heal the bear, but they had better luck with an imaginary puppy, which they constructed together, piece by piece from his wet black nose to his short thumping tail. As soon as it was complete they began to afflict it with nose-rot, dog-dropsy, a broken paw, a broken heart, sudden blindness, bald-ass syndrome (courtesy of Jarvis), tooth-rot; a rhabdomyosarcoma arising from its right leg; dog-Down's syndrome; prune-belly; apricot-head; bloody tears, and the flu. What one child afflicted, the next must lift. Jemma imagined the sad thing twitching in the middle of their circle, and called out what she saw as the children related their almost universal success until Pickie broke the puppy's heart and Ethel could not (or would not) heal it.

"It's an awful way to die," she said. She was folded up in the only perfect lotus of the group, and her eyes were shut tight, so her make-up made it look as if she had no eyes at all, just deep empty black sockets. "It hurts so bad, and his heart can't take it. His intestines are turning to dust. He's walking in a circle 'cause he can't get comfortable. Every time his heart beats it feels like somebody just stabbed him in the chest. That's seventy or eighty stabs a minute!"

"Then I fix him and he's fine," Jemma said, but not everyone was convinced, and Kidney, awake again, wept for the puppy. For another fifteen minutes she had them consider the color green, and fill themselves up with green, and imagine their every organ turning green until it had to come leaking out of their ears. Fully half of them fell asleep, and Pickie Beecher would not participate at all. "I do not like that color," he said.

For the last fifteen minutes of class she had them don imaginary clogs and she taught them a few steps, swearing them to secrecy lest her name become underlined on Maggie's list. The clogging went better than the healing. Each of them picked up the steps with minimal instruction, and Jarvis did not proclaim clogging to be something practiced by the strictly gay, and Ethel and Pickie looked happy and almost normal as they danced, but then who could clog gloomily?

After they'd all gone on to their next class, Jemma remained behind in the conference room, seated again on the table, holding the bear and staring at the places where they'd been sitting, imagining she could see the spots of warmth on the carpet. She put her face in her hands and held them all in her head, considering the thin green strands that bound them to her. She didn't know if they were real and invisible, or entirely an illusion, part of the hangover from what she'd done. But they were with her, these twelve and all the others, bits of them always in her head. Pickie Beecher was different, equally present if not more so, a black mote floating in her mind. Already a singular and unique wrongness, he was even more noticeable because he was alone now, because he alone marred the perfect health of the hospital. Jemma found that she always had a very strong suspicion of where he was.

You took Him away from me, Ethel said, her face rose and dove in the darkness like a tin midway duck. Josh Swift asked, Can you make my hands bigger? I don't think Wayne really likes me, said Cindy Flemm. Kidney and Valium and States'-Rights and Shout spoke all together, You can have all the new bones, every one of them. Just give us back our father. Jarvis said, You're the weirdest bitch in the whole wide world. Thank you, said Magnolia. Thank you over and over, like forever. Juan Fraggle asked, Did you eat my fungus? Marcus Guzman said, I saw everybody, when I was gone. Pickie Beecher said, You can't catch me! You'll never catch me! and ran away at great speed, covering miles and miles but never leaving her head. She had not rounded on anyone since Thing Two, except in her head, and the phantoms she'd visited while lying in bed had engaged her in conversations that still echoed. She sat there a little while longer, hesitating to go outside, not particularly eager to meet all the stares, and listened.

* * *

Rob was still teaching his class when Jemma went to fetch him. They were going together to the lobby, to listen to Father Jane give another talk. Jemma would rather have taken a nap, but Rob had insisted. "Just come and listen," he said. "She really knows what she's talking about!" He had been going faithfully to her auditorium services every Saturday and Sunday. Now she was too popular for the two hundred-seat auditorium and lectured in the lobby.

Rob taught in the big third-floor playroom. He'd moved all the toys and tables to the sides of the room, and laid down mats in strips along the floor, to make space and comfort for tumbling. He taught gymnastics in the afternoon to children of every age, and in the morning he taught calculus to a half dozen little eggheads.

He was walking down the mat against a busy traffic of somersaulting children, leaning down to speak encouragement or push on a bottom paused on the top of its arc. The tumbling children passed all the way to the end of the room, then started back the way they'd come. They started to learn cartwheels next. Rob demonstrated, rolling off his hands and feet so smooth and swift that Jemma wondered why he didn't just travel like that all the time. The children fell in shrieking, laughing piles when they tried it, except for Jarvis, who was as clumsy as anyone on his first pass, but improved drastically each time he tried again, so by his fifth turn he was approximating the grace of his teacher. When the end of class came he had to be restrained to keep him from tumbling more. From fifty feet away Jemma could see how angry he was, and read off his lips the curses he mumbled.

The children started up a begging chant, to get Rob to do a flip for them. He demurred at first, for its own sake, Jemma could tell, and extracted a few goofy promises from them regarding their homework, treatment of each other, and their dedication to math in the coming years. They made a circle around him on one of the mats, hiding him from the waist down from Jemma's eyes.

"Are you ready?" he asked them. They shouted that they were, but he asked three more times, until all the girls and half the boys were jumping with frustrated desire. He faked them out with a couple short leaps, then did it for real, swinging his arms back so they were parallel with the floor, then bringing them forward and over his head. From where Jemma was standing it looked like his hands were pulling his feet on invisible strings. He curled into a tight ball, his chin tucked precisely into the space between his knees, and seemed to uncurl in that same instant. She felt herself flying with him. Somehow the exuberance of his spin sucked her off her feet, and carried them off to a place that was quite free of the influence of gravity, and they spent a while suspended away from the world, before he landed on his feet again, taking one step forward to steady himself. The children clapped and cheered, and asked for another but he said, "Not till tomorrow."

Jemma stepped into the room once the class was over. She waved and said hello to the sweaty, still-excited children as they passed—Ethel and Juan and Shout and Wayne and Cindy and Pickie among others—some of them still jumping and three or four rolling into somersaults as soon as they got out into the hall. Rob had started rolling up his mats, and hadn't seen her. He rolled one up to the window at the far end of the room, and paused there to look out over the water. A clear morning had become a cloudy afternoon, and the water had darkened every hour of the day.

"Do another flip," she called out.

"There you are," he said, turning away from the window. "Stay right there!" He ran at her, five or six steps, then fell forward into a round-off, which he followed with two back handsprings and a backflip with a half twist. He judged the distance precisely, but Jemma, afraid of being landed upon, leaped back. He had to take a step to reach her, but still the whole thing seemed like one movement, from the first step he'd taken away from the window through the flip and the ta-dah! motion he made with his arms after he landed.

"Hot damn," she said.

"I think I'm getting the hang of it all again. It's coming back a lot quicker than I expected." He jumped in place a couple times. "Do you think my legs could be springier since… you know?"

Jemma shrugged. "Not on purpose, anyway," she said. He stopped jumping and kissed her. As they walked hand in hand through the halls and down the spiral ramp to the lobby she considered how he could be the poster boy for the new order. He'd made the transition from procedure-obsessed pseudo-intern to gymnastics and calculus instructor with more than just resignation or even good humor—it was like he'd wadded the old life up in a ball and punted it far away. And this a life that he had always enjoyed more than anyone, pre-Thing and post-Thing. "Do you know what this means?" he kept asking her, that first night, after they'd run back to the room and locked themselves in, as she listened to the muffled noises at the other side of the door that they'd discover in the morning were made by people piling up flowers and plush animals in heaps. She thought she knew what it meant, or that she was beginning to know—she didn't want to think about it too much at once. Lying against him she knew he was outdistancing her, that his mind was rushing ahead into weeks and months and even years of possibility for the first time since the storm.

They walked down the ramp, holding hands.

"I like Father Jane," Rob said suddenly.

"Everybody likes her."

"I mean I really like her. Watching her talk, I get this feeling. It's quite new. You'll see."

"You're not her type."

"Not like that," he said, punching gently on her arm. "I just... believe her."

"She's very sincere."

"Not just that," he said. "My mother was very sincere, but I never believed half the shit she told me about my dad."

Someone yelled behind them, "Get out of the way!" Rob flattened himself against the balcony, swinging Jemma in an arc to collide with the railing. She stumbled and caught herself, one hand sinking deep into the soil in a pansy-box. Tiresias Dufresne flew by, riding an IV pole, his feet on the casters and his hands wrapped around the pole, followed by four others, Ethan the heart kid, the two former Panda syndromes, and Sylvester Sullivan bringing up the rear, slaloming expertly around a planter.

"Watch it!" Rob called out. Sylvester slowed, dragging his foot to brake, and gave them a little wave before he rounded the corner.

"Pretty skillful," Jemma said.

"They're fixed," said Rob. "Cindy Flemm designed them. You can steer them with your feet. Anyway, I had this uncle who liked to go to church—Uncle Stuart. He used to come over for lunch afterward and I think I finally understand what he was smiling about all the time."

"Uh huh," Jemma said absently, and began to occupy herself, especially after they had found a place to stand in the lobby, with waving back to people. She waved to Dr. Chandra and Anna and Jordan Sasscock, to Timmy and Anika and Dr. Sashay. Everyone liked to wave at her, or say hello—whenever she walked anywhere in the hospital it was from greeting to greeting to greeting. Friendly waving was everywhere to be seen in the last week, but toward Jemma more than anyone people made gestures of fellowship. No one wanted to talk to her, necessarily—and she considered this a good thing—

they only wanted to acknowledge her, and to smile. It made her feel like a school principal, and she would have gone about with a veil over her face, if she thought that would have been any disguise.

Right on time Father Jane stepped up on a little box under one of the leaning pieces of the toy and raised a cordless microphone to her face.

"Good afternoon, everyone," she said. "What a lovely afternoon, and how lovely to see you all gathered down there. I got up this morning and there was a message burned into my bagel. She might have just said it: Today is the day, Jane. I'm babbling already. My old homiletics instructor always told me I drew fine the line between preaching and babbling, but it's really only when I'm nervous. My old congregation was much smaller than this. Not that you are a congregation. Not exactly. But what are you, then? That's part of what I want to talk about. In the past days I have been thinking about some particular things, asking some particular questions, and I think everyone would profit by my sharing them." She wiped her hands against her leather pants, back and forth, so the sides of her legs began to gleam with sweat.

"If I'd come up here a week ago, then I would have had some different things to talk about. I had different questions before: Why me? Why them? Why at all? How long? Where to? What next? These have mostly fallen away. It's very strange, isn't it, to have questions burn and burn and then something happens and you discover that these questions have simply gone out. All except one.

"I had a dream three nights in a row, a series of dreams, really. I like those, don't you? When I was in college I had a recurring dream that I was Sylvia Plath's pony. The dream was like a friend, or like she was my friend. After a difficult exam or a bad date or another nasty telephone call from my mother I'd have the dream the next time I fell asleep, and we would ride through the woods all night long, until just at dawn I'd leap right toward the sun and then wake up. In my first dream Boo was there again—Boo is what I call her—and she said to me, Jane, Jane, why have you come here? I looked around and saw that I was in a desert, there was nothing around except Sylvia, an oven, and a single reed growing up from the sand. I said, To watch this reed, because when the wind blows on it, it does a pretty little dance. And it did do a pretty dance. It wasn't an ordinary reed. It was so supple, and it glowed like there was moonlight in it, and it looked like there was a lady in it, waving her arms and swinging her hair. I could have watched it all night. But Boo got very upset when I said this. Oh Jane, she said. Look what you make me do! And—it was so terrible—she rushed to the oven and stuck her head inside, and the flames came up and ate her head up, and she screamed and screamed for such a long time, longer than anyone should have been able to. I pulled on her feet but I couldn't get her free.

"How many times had I cried out the same words. I said, Sylvia, Boo! Don't do it! I'd shouted those same words into my pillow back in college, knowing why she did it, and wanting to do it myself, and knowing it wasn't an *on* oven, but picturing her nonetheless in flames, or searing her cheek against a heating coil. I woke up in a panic, thinking I was back at our alma mater, and then, strangely, I saw the water at the window and I thought to myself, I'm in the hospital, and everything is all right. Everything is all right! Ha!

"Boo was waiting for me again, unburnt, when I came back to that desert place. Why have you come here? she asked me again. Was it to see the circus? And I said, Of course. Look at them, Boo! because there was a caravan passing behind her of clowns in big puffy silk pajamas and bearded ladies and strong ladies. I saw Abraham Lincoln on stilts, and a whole midget congress behind him on tricycles that they had to pedal very hard on the sand. There were elephants in velour sweat suits, and a Farrah Fawcett look-alike wearing parachute pants and a parachute poncho. It was a parade of wonders, as fascinating in the dream as the reed had been. Doesn't it seem like the obvious answer, when someone standing in front of a parade asks you what you've come to see, to say, Well, the parade? But Boo scratched her breast and ran to the oven—it was part of the parade, walking on little iron legs, but it stopped for her—and we repeated the whole ugly scene, and it was even more vibrant and detailed this time. Now I could smell her burning hair and hear the fat under her skin crackle as it burned, and all the time she burned she called out, asking me Why, Jane?

"I woke again, and this time I actually said, Thank God, I'm in the hospital! Then right away I fell asleep again, and I was back in the desert, and Boo was there, as beautiful as ever. What have you come to see? Have you come to see this man? She stepped aside and showed me our own Mr. Grampus, standing behind her. He was standing very straight, with his eyes closed. It looked like he was in a trance. I said, Boo, he and I are pals. I can see him any old time I like. Why would I come all the way out in the desert just to see him? She pulled out her tongue and stuck her head in the oven and et cetera et cetera. I'll spare you the details of what came next but I know you can imagine them. I woke again, and slept again, and woke again, every time I woke so damn grateful to be in my little bed, to watch the water pressing up against my window, when usually it just made me feel like I was drowning, or made me think of everybody else drowning. Have you ever had one of those dreams that seems to take a lifetime to finish? That's what this one felt like. Boo showed me so many things—a sunflower, a marathon, my sophomore literature professor dressed all in leather—and I always gave her the wrong answer when she asked, Why have you come here? And then she showed me something different. It was nothing at all. She just indicated a space with her hands, and for some reason, instead of saying there was nothing there, or that I had come to see the nothing, I said I didn't know why I had come, but that I would. I will know, I said. I promise you, Boo. Then it was dawn, and the oven ran screaming on its little feet off into the horizon, and Boo took me in her arms and said, Jane, Jane, Jane! and I said Boo! and the rest of it you don't really need to hear.

"It is the lesson of the dream that you must hear. I'm sure some of you have already guessed it. I remembered my scripture in the morning. I climbed up on a chair so I could put my face right in the window and look at the miles and miles of empty ocean and I spoke it aloud, What did you go out into the wilderness to see? And I knew who had been talking to me all night. And I knew it was not to see, but to do, and I knew I must come and speak to you, not of Why me, because I cannot know. Not of How long, because it does not matter. Not even of Why at all, except as it pertains to What next.

"So now I ask you the same question. What have we come out here for? It's so late, my friends, to ask ourselves the question, but the answer seemed obvious, before, when the circus was upon us. Now, in the quiet, we must ask ourselves again. I submit that the answer is, we don't know. But we must know, we must decide, and I think that our errand must be as awful and wonderful as our circumstance. I don't know what it is—can you forgive my presumption if I call on all of you to define it, and then to execute it? I call on myself to do it, too.

"So that's what I had to say. That's the question I wanted to ask. That's all. Thank you for listening to me."

"A little lower," said Vivian. "I want the five-year-olds to see it, too."

"But they're not voting," Jemma said. She was helping Vivian hang campaign posters, up and down the ramp, empty in the late evening, most everybody off at the movies or in one of the many Sunday-night meetings.

"So? They can talk. They can influence. Snood is ignoring everybody under sixteen."

"Well," said Jemma. "How about a clown nose, then?" She drew a circle with her finger around Vivian's nose.

"Clowns suck ass," was all Vivian said. Not all of her posters even had her picture on them, and on the two that did, her image was dwarfed by the text. She had three different posters, with three different slogans. One, blue letters on a red field, simply said: *VIVIAN BENNETT: YOUR UNIVERSAL FRIEND.* Between Universal and Friend her picture was set, four inches by four, a shot of her lovely face, looking friendly but not too friendly. It looked like a natural and spontaneous expression, but Jemma knew it was precisely calculated. At a poster party two nights before, Vivian had exhausted her with a catalog of expressions, trying them out on her before Rob took her picture. "How about this?" she'd say, and turn her lips up just a millimeter more. At first Jemma only pretended to notice a difference between expressions, but after a half hour of it she could actually see the difference the position of an eyebrow or the intensity of the stare could make. They'd chosen an expression they labeled a fusion of Mrs. Clinton and Mr. Rogers, but it didn't come out on film the way it looked in life. Vivian blamed Rob because he'd used a softening lens, hoping to make her look glamorous, not understanding that Vivian could look glamorous clothed only in pieces of toilet paper stuck randomly to her body, and that such devices were not necessary—indeed they were the only thing that could spoil her beauty. "Universal Friend," she said to Rob when she fired him, "not Universal Whore." In the final picture, which Jemma took herself, Vivian, overcorrecting for the luscious come-hitherness of the previous set, looked a bit stiff.

The other two posters all had longer text, one red on white, the other blue on green: *VIVIAN BENNETT STILL WANTS TO KNOW WHY IT HAPPENED*, and *VIVIAN BENNETT: COME WITH ME INTO THE NEW WORLD*. They put them in all the popular places, along the spiral ramp, in the cafeteria, in the playroom, on the walls of the lobby. And Vivian climbed up on the toy to attach three to a whirligig; they spun just slowly enough to read. She had some made into transparencies and attached them to the windows. She had miniatures made, of paper for the adults, and of gummy-stuff for the under-twelves. Her competitors quickly copied her. There was nothing she could do, and no one to complain to, except the angel, who listened impassively but gave everyone the same advantages.

The Committee had been working for months at its own destruction, but at just the pace Jemma expected, and just the pace she would have if someone had assigned her the task of destroying herself, when she hardly had time to sleep or eat or pee. No one seemed much offended by the oligarchy, though—Jemma, at least, was too tired and too depressed to give it a whole lot of thought, and even the half dozen or so surviving political agitators of the old world never did more than send memos to the Committee, and attend the sessions where they worked out the increasingly complex details of their transformation into an elected council. Every week the Committee reminded the population and itself that it must soon disband, and yet it never did.

By the day after Thing Two, when the hospital was deprived of its usual business, everyone suddenly knew it was time. After passing the motion that deplored, punished, and celebrated Jemma's act of vigilantism, the Committee started its own doomsday clock—the body would dissolve in twenty-six days. To Jemma it hardly seemed long enough to properly decorate the hospital with posters, let alone to mount a campaign.

It had mostly escaped her attention, though, that people had been campaigning for weeks, even in advance of a decision regarding the form and power of the high office. Jemma had thought the people who were running—except Vivian, whose ambition she already suspected—were only being very friendly. Ishmael was garrulous and expansive—he'd never had much of a real job, and spent most of his time socializing with people with work to do. He seemed to be friends with everybody, except Vivian, since they'd broken up a week before, after Vivian discovered that he'd been cheating on her with an as yet untallied number of women and men. Dr. Snood spent an hour or two every day checking up on people, gauging the state of the hospital in a walking tour. He gave the impression, whenever he came by, of carrying out an inspection. Monserrat appeared to be just selling her tamales, as she always had, not gathering a constituency. Likewise Dr. Sundae was doing her usual business when she trudged from floor to floor, worsening everybody's depression in personal encounters.

They all wanted to be the Universal Friend. "The grandest sort of pooh-bah," Vivian said. The Friend would be a President in all but name, and would have been called one if the Committee, in a gesture toward the new, hadn't wanted to call him something else. The Friend would be assisted by three others, each a little less than the one who came before, the First Friend, and the Second, and the Third. Then there was the Council, twelve in number, headed by a Secretary. All these were elected offices—thirty-five people all together were running for one of them. Once instated, the Executive and the Legislature would appoint together a Judiciary, a council of six, not that they'd needed any judges yet. It all seemed very traditional, to Jemma, but Vivian insisted it would be new and strange and wonderful.

"A little higher," Vivian said after they'd proceeded about fifty yards up the ramp and Jemma stopped to hang an "into the new world" poster underneath one of Dr. Snood's, which featured a huge picture of him behind his slogan, *DON'T CHANGE HORSES IN THE MIDDLE OF THE OCEAN.* There was another small poster a few feet down the ramp. His all said the same thing: *ISHMAEL: YOU KNOW ME.*

"I know you all right," said Vivian, looking at the poster. As the poster party wore on into the early morning, Vivian consumed vast amounts of a synthetic blue liquor while Jemma and Rob engaged in long, frustrating conversations with the replicator. Rob had occupied himself too much with making them for the competition: *Jacob Snood: I'm Better Than You*; and *Ishmael: I'll Fuck Anything.*

Ishmael never came by their room anymore for Wednesday-night backgammon, and never came anymore in the morning to fetch Rob for a run on the roof.

"Father Jane is stealing my boyfriend," Jemma said, more to distract Vivian from unpleasant ruminations than because it was necessarily true.

"Your fiancé."

"My boyfriend."

"She doesn't like boys," Vivian said, turning her gaze back to Dr. Snood.

"Not like that," Jemma said. "Though that could just be an act—remember Veronica Kelly?" That was a false lesbian whom Vivian had exposed when they were sophomores.

"If she liked boys she'd be all over Grampus. If she was going to change her mind he'd know before Rob did."

"Not like that, anyway. He talks about her all the time, and counts the hours to the next meeting, and all day it's been defining the errand this and defining the errand that. He didn't used to be so impressionable."

"Good thing she's not running for anything."

"Not that what she said didn't make sense. It was all very nice, and nicely articulated, and I was probably just imagining things but I swear I can hear it resonating in people, but there's just something about her."

"The macramé," Vivian said.

"I don't know. She's just… hasty somehow."

"Is Rob fucking Father Jane?" Vivian asked of the air.

"Not even in dreams," came the reply from a speaker in the floor.

"There you go," Vivian said. "You wouldn't know a good thing if it bit you in the ass, anyway."

"Are you talking to me?" Jemma asked.

"A little higher," Vivian said, putting her hand on Jemma's and pushing her poster up the wall until it covered Snood's.

"Not that high," said the angel.

When is a person not herself anymore, Jemma not Jemma, you not you? It's the other question you ask yourself every day. Your brother had a theory, you remember, of radiating corruption—it proceeded, he said, out of him (and you) to ruin the whole world. Wasn't it a change in you that changed this place, something inside you rising like seven hundred children from their sickbeds in a single night? Your brother said it comes back, the ruin, magnified a thousand times. All your corruption comes home to you, from the world, as sure as an echo. Something wonderful must be coming back to you, then.

Jemma lay awake, Rob snoring beside her. After exhausting him with sex she was not the least bit tired. "Oh, it's totally normal," Vivian had told her when Jemma asked what sort of problem her dreadful horniness represented. "Lots of women get like that. There's no harm in it, unless you've got a previa or something. Except..." They were alone in an ER exam room, but Vivian leaned forward to whisper the precaution, "If he blows air up your little missus then you could get an air embolism and then—well." She drew a finger across her throat.

"Who blows air up the little missus?" Jemma had asked, and Vivian had shrugged innocently.

She lay in bed, touching Rob's arm every so often to make sure he was still there, and holding her hand up in the moonlight to see if it looked any different. She pinched her thumb and forefinger together, then pulled them apart, stretching a little line of fire, as stretchy and gooey as a gob of spit, between them. She put her fingers together again to put out the fire.

She turned and pushed her back up against Rob. He muttered something, backed away, then scooted forward and threw an arm around her, sighing against her shoulder. She lay with her face on her arm, staring straight ahead at their pagers where they lay stacked on the nightstand. They'd both been silent all week, but Jemma expected one to go off as she watched them. Her eye wandered to the wall across from the bed, papered with plush animals. They'd run out of room, lining them along the baseboards and stacking them on the bed, so Rob had started to fasten them to the wall with industrial staples through the ear or the neck.

They were evidence of the change, too, and whole, healthy Rob Dickens was evidence of the change, and the recent memory of pressing her forehead against the cool window while he spread himself over her back, reaching his hands up along her sides and her neck to gently clasp the sides of her face, it was evidence. The silent pagers were evidence, and the greater silence outside in the hospital—the night had always been full of stray noises, little bits of alarm, or voices raised in frustration, or the voice of the angel announcing a code. Now everyone was asleep except for the isolated nurse here and there, waiting for someone to get sick again. They might as well have been watching against landfall or the rise of a monster from the sea. But Jemma still couldn't sleep. And she could not describe the change in herself.

She slipped out of bed, knowing just how quickly she could move without waking Rob, dressed in scrubs and clogs, and went out. It was dark in the hall. She had to follow the little orange strip of emergency lighting along the floor to get to the stairs. By the time I get to the roof, she said to herself as she took the first step up, I will understand completely how I am a different person than I was eight days ago. Every step will be a revelation.

But the steps were just steps. Proclamations had worked before. Back in college she'd climbed the stadium steps, a lesbian postulant at the bottom, a confident heterosexual at the top. She'd sorted her feelings about particular boys in a particular manner; every step of the way coming to a new conclusion about them—I like his teeth, but not his hair; I like how he smells; he is not a generous person; he is far too close to his cat—until all the little conclusions summed to a decision. This time, on the odd step here and there she made an observation—everything is different now outside of me; I hated medicine and if I really have destroyed it, then whee whee whee; I should be happier like everybody else; I'll never be able to teach anyone how to do this;

Rob can't die now because of my loving him; I wish I could have done this years ago, when it really mattered—but understanding did not come settling on her, gold glitter from out of the sky.

On the roof, she stepped out of her shoes and walked around on the soft grass, asking herself the same question as she walked in a circle, Is it all different? When she was trapped in the slough of wishy-washiness over Rob, too weak to run away from him though she was convinced she'd ruin him, she'd asked the same question: Is it all different now, is it all over, am I just being stupid? Now the objective forecast was for continually lifting gloom, but Jemma found herself afraid that if she believed it, if she did not cherish and cultivate the dread that was in her, she'd ruin it for everyone, because the world, as soon as it knew she believed and trusted it, would not resist the chance to prove her a sucker, and punish her for being a sucker. She almost got down on her knees, not to pray, but because she thought it would help her consider things, and maybe become a person who trusted in the future. She thought it might be a good position, too, to kneel and consider her baby, and try to look again inside to see it. As always, it was like trying to look at the tip of your nose, and she could only daydream about the sex or the color of the eyes, or speculate on the nature of the world it would be born into, or worry that something was already horribly wrong, something that she would not be able to fix. She put her hands on her belly, and drew in a deep breath, trying to picture her baby again—it was as big as a chicken egg and had managed to grab hold of her colon, holding her poop hostage against some demand it was still too immature to articulate—and then she let out a great big sigh, huger than anything her mother, a champion sigher, had ever managed. A noise came, as if in answer, a high whine that she thought might be a bug before she saw the person sitting on the edge of the roof near the sandbox.

It was Ishmael fishing. He let his line fall all the way down to the water, then started to reel it up immediately. Jemma approached him from the side, afraid of startling him and precipitating a long fall back to the sea.

"It's okay," he said when she was still ten feet away. "I know you're there. I heard you come out of the door."

"Sorry," Jemma said. "Do you want to be alone?"

"Just want to fish," he said. "I thought I would like it, and I do."

"Catch anything yet?"

"I don't have a hook. Just a sinker."

"You don't think there's anything in there?"

"I don't know. Somewhere, probably, way down deep. My kids this morning asked about that. I said the fish were all sleeping. I guess they could be. Why don't you sit down?"

"Oh, too scared." But he pointed out that there was a ledge not ten feet below his feet, so Jemma sat, kicking her heels against the side of the hospital and looking out at the broken moonlight scattered over the water. There was hardly any wind, and the only noise was of the water breaking against the windows down below.

"Trouble sleeping?" he asked her.

"Yes. Always. You too?"

"Usually. I used to run up here. That helped, for a while. I think this is going to help."

"Nothing helps me," Jemma said.

"You can't just… fix it?"

"I guess not," she said, though she hadn't tried.

"You could ask the angel for something. She must have something that would work."

"No thanks. Why don't you ask her?"

"I'd rather fish. Want to try?" He offered her the pole.

It took a while to draw the sinker up nine stories. As big as her thumb, it gleamed and dripped.

"Now for the fun part," he said. She screwed up the first two casts, not keeping her finger on the release, so the first one only went about ten feet, and the second fifteen. But on the third try she sent the sinker flying out toward the horizon, and the line played out even after she was sure it must have hit the water.

"Trying to sound out the bottom?"

"Sorry," she said. She started to reel the line in.

"It's fun, isn't it?"

"Oh, yes," Jemma said, reeling frenetically. "But it's not making me sleepy." She had a lot of line to reel in. He let her concentrate on it for a little while, then asked her how Vivian's campaign was going. "I don't think I can tell you," she said.

"I'm curious, is all."

"Sorry. You're the competition. Anyway, she's still mad at you. I probably shouldn't be talking to you at all."

"Are you mad at me too?"

"She's my best friend," Jemma said.

"I didn't mean to hurt her, you know."

"I think everybody says that."

"I didn't even realize what I was doing, sometimes. It just happened. She didn't believe me."

"Neither do I," Jemma said. The reel jammed. He took it from her briefly to fix it, then handed it back. She hadn't quite understood the depth of Vivian's wound. This was a girl who went through boyfriends like Jemma had used to go through sugary cereals, and yet Jemma had never seen her so angry as when she confirmed her suspicions by asking the angel if Ishmael was sleeping around, and she generated another list, name after name after name. "More evidence of the change," Jemma said aloud.

"Pardon?"

"Nothing. Regardless of what I think, you're the enemy. I can't tell you a thing."

"Okay," he said, holding up his hands and smiling. "Sorry. I think she's going to do very well, though. I get around, you know. And I listen. What else have I got to do? Teaching three-year-olds how to finger paint doesn't take up much time. I've sort of been polling while I campaign, and everybody's pretty excited about her."

"If you say so."

"Honest. Sometimes I don't even know why I bother hanging my posters. But I have to try, at least. It's only the second thing I've been sure about, since I woke up. The first one was Vivian. Now I know I have to run, even though I'll probably lose. Queen Vivian. All hail. I like the sound of it. Thanks, by the way. I never said thank you, did I?"

"For what?"

"For everything. For what you did. I can't tell you how glad I am not to be a fucking nurses' aide any more. I kept hoping I'd remember what I did before, so I could do it again, that I'd have some incredibly rare skill that would just pop up one day… like yours did, I guess. They're pretty mean to you, you know, when they think they own you, and they can order you around to do whatever they want. One of them tried to make me give her a pedicure. I haven't got the nursing vote, that's for sure. It's all Vivian's."

"Nurses hate medical students," Jemma said matter-of-factly. "They think we're a big pain. It's an old distinction. They're already forgetting it. But I'll just always be the bad help to them." Jemma cast again. It really was quite pleasant, the big throw, and the whine of the reel, and searching the water to isolate the splash, and trying to sense through the line the moment when the sinker broke the water.

"Hasn't anything come back?" she asked him.

"Not a thing. Not even a little thing. Something might seem familiar, like this. I must have fished before, but who hasn't? I got the angel to spit out some law books for me, because I had that suspicion about being a lawyer, but it was all so horribly dull. I could barely stand to look at it. I give up, anyway. I spent too many days just trying—it just makes me feel mad. Really mad, sometimes. That's stupid, to be mad enough to punch the wall and have no fucking clue what you're so upset about. I think I'm not supposed to remember. Maybe that's the whole point of me. The reason I lived. I'm the person who doesn't remember anything. But if I'm the fresh start, then what am I so angry about?"

"You seem pretty relaxed right now," Jemma told him.

"I'm keeping it inside," he said. "I'm good at that."

"You and my dad," Jemma said. "You know, I could probably fix it, if you wanted. I mean maybe not, but probably. The not-remembering, I mean."

"No thanks," he said, after a pause.

"I was jealous of you. I think a lot of people were thinking it would be nice not to remember, and wished that they could have. Didn't you hear about the nurse on seven who kept trying to get some propofol, just so she could stop thinking about everything?" She was reeling swiftly on the line, imagining the sinker tearing up through the water. She wanted it to jump and swing when it broke the surface, and maybe even crack a window. "How could they not be jealous?" she said. "Even now, when everything's looking up. How much better and how much easier is it to just go, to just forget about everything and face forward, if you've already forgotten. Can you imagine... fuck!" The line stuck again, and something pulled at it, gently, then hard, then violently. Jemma didn't think to drop the pole until it was yanked from her hands. She would have fallen if Ishmael hadn't steadied her with a hand on her belly. Then they both leaned forward a little, trying to see what was down there. Jemma heard two splashes, one of them certainly her pole, but the other one certainly something else.

When I was about eight I learned how to make drinks for my mother and father.

It was always very much the same every time: the same kind of gin, the same glass, the same number of big ice cubes. I would stand at the sink in the upstairs kitchen, carefully measuring out gin into a shot glass. I poured twice, just to the red line, and emptied the little glass twice into a larger one. I liked the way the gin fell down over the four cubes I stacked, one by one, in the glass. I rubbed the rim of the glass with the open end of a cut lime, then took a special tool—one of my favorite objects in the house—to cut an inch-long twist out of the rind. It contracted as it fell, bouncing off the highest cube to fall into the gin and then wedge in the space between cubes number two and three. I always thought of a little green Eskimo falling to his death among icebergs.

Then I would lean down to bring my eye level with the drink, giving it a final check. Two shots, four cubes, the highest cube raised half out of the gin, a piece of lime pulp stuck here and there along the rim, a rind twist that was neither too long nor too short: all was in order. I picked it up and brought it to my mother. Let's say it was the December before my seventh birthday, a cold day in Severna Forest in a month without snow.

Thank you, said my mother.

You're welcome, I said, watching as she stirred it once with her pinkie.

The same hand held her cigarette, and she made a circle of smoke over the glass before she raised it to her mouth to take a tiny sip. It seemed like the most elegant thing in the world.

It's perfect, she said. Like always. Why can't your father learn to do this?

It's a science, I said. A scientific process.

Edward Kent would have learned. He practically knew already. Did I ever tell you about him?

I said yes. Edward Kent was the man who could have been your grandfather, the man my mother had almost married before she married my actual father. She called off the wedding just days before, on account of his bad attitude, or because he was too good-looking, or too gay, or because he beat her once with his terribly expensive shoes—the tale was told a hundred times and more, and always there was a different reason.

Did I really? I don't think I did.

I think, I said.

Well not about how he was waiting for us when we got home from our honeymoon. He had a gun. That's how bad his attitude was. That's how crazy he was. He was crazy for me, and just crazy, anyway. He had a very sensitive soul, I think. It's probably for the best that I came to my senses and called the whole thing off. But sometimes I think it would have been better than what I got. He would have been a good father. He would have been crazy for you, too, in a good way. How would you like to have had him for your father?

I guess it would be okay, I said. I could never quite understand how this other man could be my father, and I might remain myself, as I was then.

Oh, better than okay. He had a sensitive soul and he played tennis, so he had those legs. We would be living in DC and all the news people would come over for dinner, or for parties. He was Edward R. Murrow's godson, you know, and already a producer at CBS and we were only twenty-five. He wasn't going anywhere but up. We didn't tell on him, waiting for us with the gun. He had climbed up the balcony and pried open the sliding-glass door to your father's apartment and he was sitting on the couch having a drink and resting the gun in his lap. Did you have a good trip? he asked us, and your father said, The best ever. Then he looked at us both—a weird, sad look, and stood up, and put the gun in his pants, and walked out. How about that?

Pretty scary, I said.

If I had married him then it would have been your father on the couch. Then he would have asked me, Aren't we suppose to be married? And I would have said to him, Buddy, if you only knew.

My stomach hurts, I said. I'm staying home from school tomorrow.

Sure, honey. We'll have a pajama day. Did you have a nice trip? he asked, like he'd just run into us at the supermarket. Is that a gun in your pants, Edward, or are you just happy to see my husband?

If he was my father, would I still have brown eyes?

Oh no. He had the most beautiful watery blue eyes. You could just drown in them. I had a weakness for blue eyes and brown hair, and big forearms.

But would I still be me?

Of course. You'd be you, but with gorgeous blue eyes.

How? I don't understand.

Genetics, honey. Genetics. It's complicated. She put out her cigarette, then held out another for me to light. Oh, what a life we could have had together. You and me and Edward Kent.

What about Jemma? I asked.

Yes, her too. Those Kent genes would shape her up.

So for years and years I would look at myself and think, if only Edward Kent were my father, then I would not be who I am, then I would never had been so angry all the time, or so sad, or had to know from the cradle that I was ruined. But I realized, of course, that Edward Kent *was* my father. He came to my mother, along with a host of other regrets, a host of lost opportunities, a disembodied god who rained down upon her and said, I am everything you have ever done and regretted—let us make a child together. And my father had a similar visitation, and so I was conceived.

It all comes out from me—circles and circles of corruption and regret and depravity, but before it was in me it was in them—my mother and my father. And before it was in them it was in their parents. And I say—and everyone says—I will not put it in my child, and yet everybody does. I make promises, I keep lists: this and this and this I will surely never do, because I never want to uncover in my child the sort of hatred my parents uncover in me with even the most innocent and benevolent action. But as surely as the moon rises and the sun sets, depravity passes down through the ages, because there is always a gap between who we are and who we should be, and our parents, molested by regret, conceive us under the false hope that we will be better than them, and everything they do, every hug and blow, only makes certain that we never will be.

Animals presented themselves at the windows of the hospital: a giant eye appeared in one of the small round windows of radiology; three steel-blue makos paused on a journey to pace at a second floor window and watch Maggie clog with her class. Transported by her dancing, it took her a while to notice that the class had stopped moving and were staring at the sharks. She shrieked at them to pay attention and follow along, then shrieked again at the sharks for interrupting her class, and shooed them off by kicking a clog at the window. She was an expert clog-marksman, and could hurl them with enough force to strike someone unconscious, but the glass was unbreakable.

Vivian was tuning and retuning a student's violin—the pegs on the replicated instruments were always slipping—when a bright red fish appeared at her window. Her three students jumped up from their chairs and pressed their hands and faces against the glass. The little fish just hovered there, moving its lips at them silently. Vivian walked closer to the window and put her hand out to touch the glass. Then to the delight of her students, the fish puffed up to ten times its original size. Vivian did not find it so charming as her students. She thought the fish was glaring at her, and thought it might have been offering a lesson about ambition in its puffed-up display.

Rob's gymnastics class cried out, "Dolphins!" and pointed behind him, but he thought they were kidding. They were meeting in a new room on the sixth floor, and every time he turned around he only saw the horizon and the empty sky. But as soon as he went back to standing on his head the cry would come again. After missing them three times he just sat down in the middle of his kids and waited. "You all have got to learn to stop joshing the teacher," Rob said finally. A wrestling match broke out spontaneously between Tir Dufresne and Jarvis, and Rob was just standing to go break it up when he saw the dolphins come leaping at the window, first one, and then a pair, then three at a time, then four, and then a procession of twos, leaping in rapid succession and inclining their eyes toward Rob and the children at the top of their arc. He plastered himself, like the kids, by pressing himself against the glass, and called out tenderly to his fellow mammals. "There must have been a hundred of them," he told Jemma later.

Dr. Snood saw an electric ray outside of his room. Dr. Sundae felt eyes upon her as she dressed and turned around to see a bigeye tuna staring through her window. A horrific-looking sargassum fish bumped against Father Jane's window as she was working on her latest sermon. She was so surprised, and so unsettled by the ugliness of the fish, that she fainted.

Jemma was lying in bed, overcome by a late resurgence of nausea, trying to formulate a lesson plan, when she heard the tapping at her window. She was as miserable as she'd been in weeks, more because of her class than because of her persistent vomiting. Vivian and Rob had no trouble formulating lesson plans and executing them, in holding their students' attention and even demonstrating progress in their learning, after only two weeks of class. Two of Vivian's students who before, under a harsh Suzuki master, had had only four months of pretend-play on cardboard violins, now were playing "Amazing Grace." Rob's class was doing cartwheels in a herd all around the padded playroom, in form that appeared perfect to Jemma's jealous eye, with none of the Oompah-Loompah awkwardness of just a week before, and Jarvis had mastered the round-off and started on a back handspring—he could only dive backward into a well of foam and colored plastic balls, but any minute he would get that, too.

Jemma's class had learned to stare at her with great intensity. She had taught them to narrow their eyes, and furrow their brows, and square their chins. They could stare patiently for five minutes at the flame of a scented candle. They could sing in unison the mysterious Om that Jemma, desperate and almost bored with her inability to teach them anything real, had them sing with her. "Become the noise," she told them, wanting to claw at her cheeks for shame and fraud-feeling, "and let the fire come up from inside you." Dr. Snood and the others would not release her from the imposed obligation to teach what she could do.

"There's nothing to teach," she told him. "It just is. There's no how."

"I don't doubt a certain person thought the same about the calculus, Dr. Claflin." Jemma hated it when people called it the calculus, and hated calculus, anyway.

"I do doubt it, Dr. Snood. If there were a formula, I'd copy it down and hand it out."

"Did you expect it to be easy? I think that's your problem, Dr. Claflin. I noticed it from the day you came on my service. You want things to be easy, but just because you can wave your hand at say, familial polyposis and send it packing, doesn't mean everything will be easy."

"I don't want easy," Jemma said. "I'm just tired of impossible."

"Impossible? Jemma, Dr. Claflin, how can you stand there and complain to me of *impossibility?* Do you think Dr. Whipple found it easy to teach his procedure? I'm sure he wanted to say, Well, I just sort of fiddle with the pancreas, and tie some things off, and remove a lot of sausage, and it sort of happens, oh my! Easy is what you want, but it's not what you'll get, and as long as I have any say in it your welfare state of the soul will never pass here." He was not in the Committee room, and so did not have his little gavel, but he slammed his fist into his palm.

It was stupid, she knew, and like her, to find this reason to be miserable amid all the blossoming optimism in the hospital, but still she settled down in bed and languished under the nausea, wondering if she had not invited it back. Then she heard the tapping at the window. Like the rest of the windows on the fourth floor, it was always about half in and half out of the water, sometimes more and sometimes less, because the buoyancy of the hospital was only relatively constant, something Rob had proved early with a series of marks on the glass. Jemma looked at the window and saw only the blue sky and the edge of the water, but the tapping came again.

She climbed up on a chair to look better, and almost fell back, and did make a little scream, little sibling to the scream she'd voiced for Ishmael. There was a claw tapping just at the edge of the glass, and as she watched a giant white crab scuttle up to cover the whole bottom half of the window. It was fat, and without a spot of color except a blush of pink in its chittering mouthparts, which worked furiously as it regarded her with two dull, globular black eyes. It moved its backfins to steady itself when it drifted down, and tapped again at the glass.

"Hello there," Jemma said. The very word *mouthparts* was usually enough to make her feel sick, even when she wasn't pregnant, and the sight of them always made her feel unclean. She'd always hated crabs, and never partaken in any of the childhood feasts because she could never be convinced they were not just big bugs. This was the ugliest, scariest crab she'd ever seen, but she put her hand against the window, and tapped its message back to it with her finger, because the sight of another living creature lifted her spirits. It didn't occur to her until later that it might have been sizing her up as a meal, imagining her as carrion, or that it was tapping at the glass because it was trying to get her with its claw. As soon as it drifted away she rushed out to tell someone about it, her nausea forgotten. She found a hundred other stories.

No one could agree on what it meant, but everyone agreed it must mean something. As Dr. Sundae put it, "Only a fool would deny the significance of a leaping whale." It was assumed, after weeks of staring into the empty sea, that all the animals had perished when the rain washed out the seas, though the angel stated, when questioned, that every low animal everywhere, on sea or land, had been "preserved." Were the fish preserved at a deeper level of the ocean, and had the waters now receded to that level? Had they been sequestered in a bubble at some warm latitude, and released now because the time of the waters was almost over? What about the mammals? Kidney asked the angel for a dolphin–English translator and was supplied with a box on a string to fit over her mouth, and a plug for her ear. When the dolphins came again she hung out of a PICU window and asked them, Where have you been? Where are you going? Where is everyone else? in squeaks and clicks and whistles, then listened with her head cocked at the weird spray of sound that shot back. She shook her head and furrowed her brow. "They just keep laughing," she said.

The five candidates stood behind podiums on a new stage, in the middle of the lobby and under the shadow of the big toy. Jemma was in the crowd—the whole hospital had turned out to listen, even the NICU inhabitants, tricked out in soft jumpers, all of their sporty strollers parked in a bloc by the gift shop. Jemma found her attention drawn to them, when the candidates, even Vivian, started to bore her. The babies were all quiet but not still. They reached their fat little hands from stroller to stroller, stroking the big head of their nearest neighbor, or sucking on a finger or fist not theirs. They babbled softly at each other. Sometimes it seemed like they were commenting on the speakers. Anna stood near Jemma with Brenda hanging on her chest in a snuggly. The child was sleeping soundly and did not point at anybody.

It was a lively but poorly organized debate. Father Jane was moderating, asking questions submitted by the hospital population for each of the five, Dr. Snood, Dr. Sundae, Vivian, Ishmael, and Monserrat. There had been another debate three days before, diffidently moderated by John Grampus, between the score and more of people running for the lesser seats on the Council.

"We've been afraid all this time," Vivian was saying, "to consider why the old world passed away, or to try to discover what the new one has to be like. I think it's time to put this attitude behind us."

"Some of us never had that bad attitude," said Dr. Sundae. "There have been voices crying from the wilderness of obfuscation from the very first day. I'm talking about myself, of course."

"Of course," said Dr. Snood. "Dr. Sundae, I can still hear your complaints. But who doesn't agree that the saving of lives must take precedent over idle speculation?"

"Idle speculation? Have you looked out the window lately, Doctor? Do you think anyone left on this Earth would speculate *idly* on that?" Dr. Snood opened his mouth to reply, but Father Jane interrupted him. She was armed with his gavel, and kept jumping in just when things started to get exciting.

"Honorable Candidates!" she said. "Please be nice. Let's move on to the next question. Where do you see this community in one month? In two months? In three months? Ms. Vaca will speak first."

Monserrat tapped at her microphone—she'd been doing that each time she spoke. "I think it is a stupid question, and I apologize to the person who asked it, because I know you are not stupid, and I am not saying you are stupid, no, no." She smiled beautifully, shining her teeth all along the crowd in a hundred and eighty degree arc. "But the question, yes, it is stupid, because it simply cannot be answered. Or instead, it can be answered, but to nobody's good. I can tell you what I think could be happening one month from now, and two months from now, and three months from now, but who cares? We could be anywhere, we could be doing anything, it depends on *you.*" Now she pointed, describing with her finger the same arc her teeth had just described, but in reverse.

"It depends on you what happens. If you want us to be unhappy, to be sleeping all during the day and forgetting about the children, letting the babies cry and the teenagers go hungry, then we can do that. If you want us to all be living in cardboard boxes here in the lobby, then we can do that. If you want us to keep building this place into something wonderful, a city like the great Disney World where I went in my youth and I thought, if only I could live here. I said to my mama, I want to live here. Please don't make me leave! And my mama made this filthy, filthy thing at me." Monserrat raised a hand and rubbed her thumb and first two fingers together in a money grubbing gesture. "And she said to me, Honey, you ain't got the money to live here forever. But that is what you could do, you could make a place so delightful that every child here would turn to you—yes to *you,*" she pointed imperiously at Father Jane, "because now you are her mama, we are all of us her mama—she would say to you, Mama I never want to go away from this place, I am so happy. Do you know how incredible that is? How much of a miracle? It's as much as what Ms. Jemma did, and as much as all the deadly waters, if we can make this place so happy, and make these children so happy that they do not even remember their old sadness, and by that I mean the old sadness of before, and the sadness of losing that. Do you understand me? Do you see it like I do? You, do you see it?" She pointed at a lab tech, Sadie the urine-tutor, who sat in the front row. Sadie coughed and blushed and nodded.

Monserrat pointed elsewhere in the audience, and Jemma, who never was sure if people were pointing or waving at her and so never responded to a wave or a point, no matter how friendly or imperious, still felt a little flushed as the finger waved in her general direction. Vivian was worried about Monserrat, and secretly called her the Tamalagogue, because she argued, or at least proclaimed, so passionately, and seemed able to make people feel what she was feeling. "She is a screaming teakettle with barely a quarter inch of water in it," Vivian said, a little unfairly, Jemma thought, because the lady did not seem shallow to her. Jemma had fixed her diabetes, and touched something rich and angry in her, some deep resource that previously was employed only in peddling tamales which no one could ever turn down, not even the nauseated or the full or the vegetarian.

Monserrat folded her arms across her chest and nodded vigorously, approving very strongly of what she had just said. Dr. Sundae was next in the speaking order. "Obviously," she said, "*obviously* we will all have to play a part in deciding what comes next. But will it just pop up on its own, like some surprising weed, or is it something that will require planning, and even cultivation? We're all very smart, here. I think we know what the answer is.

"In a month, or two months, or three months, I think we could be landed. I think the waters are waiting for us, and will be drawn back as soon as we demonstrate that we have become a worthy colony, one fit to be put ashore in a new, unspoiled place. And how will we demonstrate this? Well, the first step will be tonight, for you are choosing your direction when you are choosing your director. I mean no more slight than is absolutely necessary against my competitors when I say that if you choose someone with no clear vision of how to make this demonstration, and by that I really mean—I must say it—someone besides me—then you should be prepared to stay out here... *indefinitely*. But perhaps you like it out here.

"And maybe there is much to like, now. Certainly there are many distractions. We concoct new ones every day. But weave me the basket, please, that will redeem the sin that called down destruction upon you. Teach me the mathematics that will prove we were innocent, or undeserving of destruction. Play me the instrument that does not increase our trespass. We should be refined by our affliction, but instead we wave our hands in front of our faces and say, Look at the bird!

"I tell you we will be destroyed little by little if we do not look inward and back, to discover and disown our sin. We are rocked in plenty out here, and given days full of nothing but the opportunity for reflection. I propose that we begin to do so systematically, and with all our effort, and put our bright minds to the task of designing a repentance, and yes, there may be fasting, and scourging, and weeping, and yes, *yes*—gnashing of teeth. But look inside, all of you, do you think anything else will suffice for what you've done?"

It was very quiet when Dr. Sundae stopped talking. Had there been surviving crickets anywhere in the world, Jemma was sure she would have heard them, then. She didn't think she could make much in the way of a prediction about who was going to win, but she was sure Dr. Sundae would come in dead last.

"Thank you, Dr. Sundae," said Vivian, the next to speak, "for that frightening harangue. I'm afraid I agree with part of what you've just said. In three months we could very well still be out here. We have no way of knowing how long it will be. We've all thought about the possibility of it being forever. I feel like it will be less than that, but the angel's not telling and my magic eight ball is confused on the subject.

"I wonder sometimes how much it matters, though. It already feels to me like we've been out here forever, and it feels like the waters came just yesterday. It was ages ago, and a moment ago that the kids all got better. I hope I don't sound too much like Dr. Sundae if I say it's not how much time we spend out here, but what we do with it, that matters. And I think it happened for a reason, too, of course I do. I mean, we know it wasn't global warming, right? And I think we should reflect on the reason—find out why it happened and reform ourselves accordingly. But it won't profit any of us to gnash our teeth or crawl down the catwalk in a hair-shirt fashion show. I don't think the water is waiting for us to be good. We're all good already, we've all done good things in the past months, and who knows what good things you all did before that. And maybe that's why you're here now. As I said, the eight ball is confused.

"We should build something, I think. We should decide together what was wrong about the old world and start building the new one, because it has to start here, whether we land someplace tomorrow or in ten years. So that's what I think we'll be doing in the coming months, building up a new world out of this place where children used to come to die. I have a clear vision for it. I hope you'll let me share it with you."

Jemma felt a curious attraction toward her friend, and thought she saw people leaning a little toward the stage, and then suddenly leaning back away from it when Dr. Snood started to speak.

"Well," he said. "Children never came here expressly to die. I think we all realize that. Sometimes we did our best and failed them, but we never lured them to our candy house to practice atrocities on them or smother them in their sleep. I think it's important to be clear on this point, because what we were is what determines what we will be. This is still a hospital, no matter how we trick it up with stages and playing fields and movie theaters, and our work is still the work of a hospital—preservation. We have been granted either a reprieve or a new mandate, I do not know which, and I don't think anybody does know which, even the agent of the change. Dr. Claflin, are you out there? May I ask you, do you know, is it a reprieve, will we all be going back to our old work in a month or two months or three?" Jemma could not believe the gall of him, to pimp her in this crowd, to reach back in time to pull his pimping prerogative out of the old, dead order. She was surrounded by short children, and had nowhere to hide.

"Better ask the eight ball, Doctor," she shouted back at him.

"Yes, well, I understand it's confused. I don't think we can know, Dr. Claflin. It is all too strange and new for most of us, which is exactly why we should preserve our old, familiar forms, even if we have to fill them with new things. Because I tell you we are a hospital, and will always be a hospital, because a hospital, more than anything else, even more than a place where children go to become *well,* is a community, and this hospital was a community for many years before it became... how it is now... isolated.

"I think in a month we will be a more perfect community, and in another month, and another, we will become still more perfect. We are already building something, in ourselves, between ourselves, and outside of ourselves. Look around you at all the changes, and look inside yourselves at all the changes. We have only begun to apply the sort of energy that kept us going during those weeks and weeks of thirty-six-hour shifts, the same wonderful dedication that gave such excellent care to children as sick as any I have ever seen, and not a single child died, *not a single child*. We are still a hospital. We are still a community of workers, and the work we are going to do is something truly wonderful."

He got significant applause. Jemma stuck her hands in her pockets and glared at him.

Ishmael spoke last. "You all know what I think about this. We've talked about it together, more or less." He looked out into the audience. "Right, Bob? Right, Martha? Right, Alan?" His eyes traveled slowly around the room, and he named thirty or forty of the spectators around the stage, plus a smattering of those who were watching from the first, second, and even the third floors. "Basically, I think everybody's right. Everybody's got a part of it. I can't tell you what I did, what part I played in getting us this big screwing, because I can't remember. Hell, maybe it's all my fault, and only mine. Sometimes when I'm angry I wonder if it's me I'm most angry at, and I look in the mirror sometimes and say, You bastard. But there are things for us to atone for, and to reflect on, and it's all up to you, that's true. Nothing is going to happen, no matter how much we stand up here and blab, unless you want it to. And we are a community, I believe that, and feel like a part of it, though I never did much, before, except fetch blankets and change diapers, not knowing what I was good for.

"But there's something else, there's something more. I think that we've already become something more than just a community. Look around you—this is a family, isn't it? It's a very strange family, I'll admit, but aren't all families strange? I don't remember my own family. Maybe that's why I noticed this. I didn't have one to miss, or be sad about in the same way as everybody else. But I bet they were strange. I look at myself in the mirror and try to imagine them all around me. Sometimes it's easy to do and sometimes it's hard, and they're different every time. I know some of you do the same, look in the mirror for them or look for them elsewhere.

"I'll say it again, though. Look around you, at all these adults and the children in their care. So, in a month we'll be a better family, I think. And in two months we'll be even better. And in three months we'll be better in ways we can't even imagine, in ways that will make all the troubles of the old world seem so small and remote that you'll all be like me. You will not even remember them."

Jemma and Rob spent the rest of the evening trying to calm and distract

Vivian, who immediately after the debate entered a tizzy which grew more intense as the time to vote, and the wait for the count, drew near.

"I think everybody's right," she said, not succeeding very well in imitating Ishmael's goofy baritone. "But they're all morons, too."

"I don't think he called anybody a moron," said Jemma. They were in Jemma's classroom, sitting at the table before a feast of untouched treats. Vivian was too nervous to eat.

"Not in so many words," Vivian said. "That's his special gift. He never said moron, but everybody left with 'morons!' ringing in their heads."

"You did better than he did," Jemma said, again. Rob came in with more food.

"Family," she said. "Who wants to be a family? Like that ever worked before. Shouldn't we try to be something better than a family?"

"Have a piece of cheesecake," said Rob.

"I don't want cheesecake," Vivian said sharply. "I want to *crush* him." Jemma sighed. Rob peeled the paper off a cupcake. A cloud of tiny silver sardines swam by, seeming to disappear as they passed through the bars of darkness between windows. They were circling the hospital, and had been passing by every fifteen minutes the whole time Jemma and Vivian had been in the room.

It was almost ten p.m. The polls had closed at nine, and now volunteers were carefully counting the votes from out of the boxes. There were stations on every floor except the ninth, but most people had voted in the lobby. Jemma and Rob had stood in line for an hour before they were handed their ballots. They were just rectangles of stiff paper, printed with offices and names to select by filling in bubbles, and a space to write in a candidate if the person you wanted wasn't listed. Jemma thought of all the names she could write in: Bugs Bunny, Eloise, Papa Smurf, any of whom might very well prove to be a capable leader. For the sake of fun she was very much tempted to do it, but if Vivian lost by a single vote she knew she'd have to confess what she did, and never be forgiven. She voted Vivian for Universal Friend, and chose somewhat at random for the Council members, having a hard time remembering what they had said in their speeches and debates, and if she had cared about anything she'd heard.

"What time is it?" Vivian asked. Rob told her.

"The counting is slow," Jemma reminded her.

"Too slow," she said. "We should have used the computer." But there were too many people who didn't trust the computer to count correctly, or who thought that the angel might pick a favorite to win regardless of the vote count, or who merely wanted to create as much fuss and bustle as possible around the event of voting.

"Would you like to watch a movie?" Jemma asked. Films about First Ladies were very popular that week. Rob had borrowed a couple of non-pornographic titles from Dr. Chandra: *Hillary vs. Mothra* and *Nancy and Martha: A Love Beyond Time.*

"No. I want to drug myself to sleep and wake up in the morning. I feel like I'm waiting for my board scores. Remember that?" Vivian had hardly slept at all during the last week of waiting for the small gray envelope to arrive.

"I remember," Jemma said. "I'm nervous, too. We all are, right?"

"Right," Rob said. He had sliced up his cupcake and laid it out on top of a piece of cheesecake, and was just about to cut into this new thing with his fork. "Everybody knows I eat when I'm nervous."

"That's disgusting," Vivian said, but it actually looked rather appetizing to Jemma. She'd had no nausea since she'd seen the crab earlier, and was quite hungry now. She wasn't actually nervous, either. She'd only said that to express solidarity with her friend. In fact, all day, ever since she'd seen the crab, she'd been in a fine mood. It was the fish, she was sure, that were making her happy, and she thought her good mood would persist even if Vivian lost the election. The crab had brought tidings so glad that there was nothing that could make Jemma sad that night.

The message was secret, and just for her. She read it without knowing it, and only became aware she had received the news hours after the ugly creature had dropped off the glass and drifted back into the deep black water underneath the hospital. It was as if the crab had announced in her a confirmation of everything she'd been so tepidly suspecting in the past weeks, that they were indeed floating in anticipation of a new world, and that she herself may anticipate it also. Her old fears finally seemed unreasonable to her, and she wondered, all day long, why she would not marry Rob Dickens.

"Oh, give me a cupcake, dammit," said Vivian. "And somebody tell me a story. "

"Have you heard about the coprophile of Seven East?" Rob asked. Didn't Jemma love him enough to marry him? Certainly she did. She loved him too much to marry him, too much to have another light hit him in the head, or have an asteroid come out of the sky to crush him, or to hit him in the face with a meat tenderizer, or establish with him such a miserable institution as a marriage. What use was there for it anyway, now?

"You mean Maggie?" Vivian asked.

"No, a *real* one. A pair, actually." Vivian hadn't heard. But surely there was no danger in it now. That was what the crab had said to her. I am here, you are floating not in a sea of death, but a sea of plenty. Everything is new. "I heard it from Jordan Sasscock," Rob said.

"A reliable source," Vivian said, leaning across the table now.

"He was walking by the call room on Seven East when he heard some groaning inside, or crying, so he stood by the door and listened. There was another groan, and he was about to knock when he heard the groan again, and understood that it wasn't a groan of distress. It was the other sort of groan."

"A groan of undress," said Vivian. If he drowned, if he got strangled by an octopus, if he got bitten by a poisonous child—if anything happened, it had been given to her to fix it. So was it so unreasonable to think that she could fix, or that they could fix together, or avoid altogether, the more subtle injuries of marriage? Her brother would say no, but she was thinking maybe, maybe, and maybe. Rob had become used to her saying no to him, but had not given up asking. "Marry me," he'd say, just as they were falling asleep, and first thing in the morning she'd tell him, "No."

"Exactly. He would have kept walking, except he heard something else. There were two voices, male and female, and now the male voice said, Oh Darling, shit on me!"

"No way."

"No shit," Rob said. "But yes, shit! It went on and on while he listened. I'm going to shit! and I'm shitting! and Now—*you* shit on *me!*" Jemma's imagination, recognizing an opportunity to be perverse, drew the couple for her while Rob and Vivian laughed hysterically, each of them embellishing the story that Jemma was forced to watch. The faceless heads on the couple in the call room popped off easily enough, and were replaced, at first, with Dr. Sasscock's head, and then with her head and Rob's head, and she watched the whole thing, not too shocked and not too intrigued, and asked herself the inevitable question—could she, could she—and decided, while Rob and Vivian had rolled themselves to the floor, and Vivian had finally forgotten her anxiety, that if you loved someone enough to eat their poop, then you surely loved them enough to marry them.

"And the last thing he heard," Rob said, laughing and gasping, "before he ran away, was the man's voice saying, I hope that's not a peanut—I have an allergy!" They had both raised themselves back to their seats when he said this. Now they fell back down, Vivian dragging a cupcake after her that stuck against the side of her head. She and Rob were further transported into raptures of hilarity, but Jemma sat calmly, remembering the oath she took with her brother fifteen years before. "Swear!" he'd said, as serious and spooky as Hamlet's ghost. Swear! I will never get married like them, they'd said together. If you knew him, she thought, you'd release me. On the subject of the baby she was quiet, because she knew that would only infuriate him more, and though he'd never made her swear not to reproduce, nor conducted any rituals to compromise her fertility, she had always understood that it was an even greater sin than marriage, to have a baby and fill it up with all your regrets and failures.

"Oh, that's funny," said Vivian, when they'd recovered again and lifted themselves back to the table. She took a bite from the cupcake that fell on her, and wiped the icing from her hair with a napkin. "Isn't it funny, Jemma? Why aren't you laughing?"

"I've heard it before," she said, though she hadn't, and she knew Rob had made it up just for the occasion of Vivian's anxiety. Vivian seemed released by all the laughing. She ate another cupcake, and some pretzels, and two pieces of cheesecake, while they all repeated fish stories, Vivian the only one among them to have seen a whale.

When Rob's watch alarmed they left the conference room and went down to the lobby, where Father Jane announced the election results. She named the members of the Council first. There were not many surprises. It would look much like the Committee, except for the absence of those who'd run for Universal Friend. Jemma moved closer to Rob and took his hand as Father Jane went on, starting with the runner-up positions. Monserrat would be Third Friend. There was cheering and applause. Far away Jemma could see the tamale lady jumping up and down as graciously as that could be done.

"Hey," she said, close to Rob's ear. "Let's do it."

"Huh?" he said, over the noise.

"Let's do it," she said. Father Jane announced that Vivian would be Second Friend. She handled the news as well as any beauty-contest runner-up. She waved her hands and clapped back at the people applauding her, but the muscles of her jaw were bunched up in knots.

"Let's get married," she said to Rob, but he was leaning over toward Vivian, hugging her with one arm while Jemma pulled on his other one.

"The office of First Friend will be held by… Ishmael!" Jemma pulled harder on Rob's arm.

"Hey," she said. "Listen to me." She was almost all intent on getting him to hear her, though a part of her mind was suddenly anxious at the prospect of living under Dr. Sundae's penitent reign of terror, or becoming a citizen of Dr. Snood's Republic of Smarm. "I want to get married," she said again. "I changed my mind." This time he heard her, and his face became entirely blank before he smiled and abandoned poor, disappointed Vivian. He grabbed her ears with both hands and pulled her face to his face for a kiss, and neither was listening when Father Jane made the last announcement, so the news that Jemma had been elected to the office of Universal Friend had to be repeated for both of them.

Snow is falling all over Severna Forest, from the brown brick gates to the steps of the clubhouse, from Beach Road to the top of Waste-Not Hill, settling on the rotted ruin of Calvin's old tree fort down by the river, and outside Jemma's window, collecting silently, layer on layer upon her sill while she sleeps. She's been dreaming all night of snow—it began to fall just as she settled into bed, while she raised her bottom in the air and pushed her face into her pillow, burrowing into the blankets until they were twisted just right and the pillow heaped up in pleasing mounds on either side of her head. Turned toward the window she could see it striking against the glass, and as she fell asleep she saw the usual red darkness behind her eyes broken up with bright white motes. She was a cold princess riding a swan made of ice, a liberated snowman who went campaigning all over the country to free other snowmen from static servitude, and she was the snow itself, cast high over Severna Forest and settling forever over every house and person.

It is almost something that we can do together, to become the snow. Or rather, we can do it at the same time—I am as invisible to the dream Jemma as I am to the waking one and you cannot see me behind her and above her and beside you. We are settling along the sloping green roof of Mr. Duffy's store, and along the railings of the clubhouse porch; all over the golf course, up on the hills and down in the dells and over the traps full of cold sand, we are draped as a blanket. Over the Nottingham's house, over their oblivious dog in the yard, over Rachel's house and her new bicycle—with her birthday so close to Christmas she usually never gets good presents but this year was an exception—with its fancy pink banana seat with the lambskin cover that Rachel forgot to remove for the night and the long, luxurious handlebar tassels that stream like glory when she flies down a hill. It's so much better than your bike, but she has forgotten it outside, and you are free now to cover it up and muffle its brilliance. She will be lucky to find it before the next thaw.

Down beyond the fifth hole, where the railroad tracks run right by the river, we settle gently on the tracks, and over the teenagers playing a new game—they lie between the tracks and let the train pass over them. We muffle their shouting, and after the train passes they keep staring up into the sky, and they get a different feeling, looking into the heart of the storm. Instead of the usual strange exalted sadness that comes after the train passes they feel an unusual peace and in a fit of vulnerable, sentimental foolishness they think it is the spirit of Christmas gently attacking them just when they thought they had become forever immune to its treacly power, but really it is just the wonder that comes of staring into the heart of an angel and a girl.

We perish on the river, snowflake by snowflake, but miss nothing of what dies, and the river freezes a little more with every touch, until we are settling on it, too. It's a lovely sensation, you decide, to feel stretched and pulled down over the whole town, to fall from so high and settle so low, to feel you are a giant who has thrown herself affectionately and protectively over every house, crouching everywhere to gather every home in your arms. You feel the hearts and minds and lives of every creature inside as a bright warmth in your belly, where I only feel like I have eaten a bug, and your dream increases in beauty even as you start to wake, while I fall back to the world, anxious and disappointed and yearning to be free. When you wake you forget what a dreadful day you've entered into, and you spend a whole minute kneeling on your pillow to stare out the window at the wonderful snow thrown over the trees and the houses and the river, feeling a kinship with it that you can no longer understand, until you remember what day it is, and moan, and knock your head against the glass.

Jemma hated Christmas Eve. Every year she woke up already wanting the day to be over. She'd sit on her bed, not believing that a whole twenty four more hours would have to pass before Christmas would come, staring at the clock on her wall: faceless Holly Hobby with her arms twisted hideously behind her back, her pointing finger would take forever just to move from one minute to the next. The pervasive quality of waiting ruined the day. In the morning her father engaged in the annual construction of waffle houses, building them plank by plank with maple syrup caulk and cinnamon stick tenons while Jemma watched, her nose sitting just above the kitchen counter, her belly aching not just with hunger but with anticipation. The ache persisted even after she'd eaten the house, from the whipped-cream smoke rising from the chimney down to the square kiwi doormat, and no matter how many grilled cheese sandwiches she ate for lunch or how deeply she dived into the moo goo gai pan during the traditional Christmas Eve Chinese dinner—no matter how much she ate she remained hungry for the next day. Time seemed to pass slower and slower the closer she got to the following dawn, so a sled ride down the hill took half as long at nine in the morning than at four in the afternoon. She would sit on her sled watching the trees go by as slowly as a parade, so she could pick out the ones with testaments of love carved into the bark, and notice the winter squirrels perched in the naked branches, their mouths moving in slow motion as they chattered at her. Distances stretched twice as long as on other days, so the trip into town seemed as long as the trip into DC on a regular day. Water for hot chocolate took twice as long to boil, a videotape took forever to rewind, even a glass of water took forever to fill from the refrigerator spout. The whole day was full of extra time. Jemma used it all to fret, and to consider how Christmas, when it came, would pass in an instant, and she would come to herself suddenly on the twenty sixth of this month feeling like she'd missed it all somehow, even though she'd spent a whole lifetime, the day before, in suffering, suffering anticipation.

She suffered through breakfast, through the morning's recreation, though lunch, through an afternoon of static sledding and eternally boring movies that never ended—*A Bugaloo Christmas, A Little Pony Village Christmas, Smurfette Saves Christmas... Again!* She suffered through tasteless afternoon snacks, and suffered even when it became necessary to run the inevitable early-evening errand. Jemma followed her mother through the supermarket, on a quick trip, having just dashed into the store, leaving Calvin in the car, to buy eggs for the morning and a set of replacement lights for the string on their tree that had gone dark, but the time between one step and the next was interminable. Her eyes were level with her mother's belt—wide and black and shiny, the sort of thing Santa might wear, except it cinched a puffy yellow snowsuit instead of a red velvet coat.

"Is this line moving?" she asked her mother, who by this time of the evening traditionally began to ignore most of what she said, so Jemma had to repeat herself a few times before getting a perfunctory, "Shush." The line was not moving. The conveyor barely inched along. The stuttering clerk engaged in extended conversation with every person in line, and talked for what seemed like at least five minutes with her mother about ways to make your eggs fluffy, all while more slow, silent people shuffled into line behind them, everyone looking at their shoes or at the snow falling thickly outside, but no one looking at their watches or noticing how time had almost stopped. Outside Jemma looked for her footprints in the snow, but they had already been covered. It always took her mother a long time to find the car, and tonight in the darkness and the snow it seemed to Jemma that they would wander forever among the white lumps that were anonymous and identical except where one was lit up inside, so the whole thing shined red and gold as if heated from within. They walked toward two of these, thinking it must be Calvin, keeping a light on for them, but they both drove away before they could reach them. Then, just as Jemma sensed that her mother was about to begin cursing at the snow, Calvin's head and chest popped out from a lump ten cars down and waved to them.

"Over here," he called out, and honked the horn with his foot. Their mother, when they were in the car, scolded him for opening the sunroof and getting snow in the car, then thanked him for saving their lives.

"They would have found our frozen corpses on Christmas morning," she said. "I want you to tell your father that." He was in surgery that night.

"I would have come looking for you before then."

"And found our frozen corpses. I was ready to die already. Weren't you, Jemma?"

"What time is it?"

"Never mind that. Are you ready to see Santa?" There would be a distribution of gifts that night under the Severna Forest Christmas tree, an annual tradition.

"Not the real Santa," Calvin said.

"What time is it?"

"No, of course not. A licensed representative, like all the others."

"I wouldn't stand for it if I were him. I'd make them pay."

"Oh, they pay. And there's a long form, and a special school. Sheriff Travis was gone for months. Don't you remember?"

"What *time* is it?"

"Almost time, Jemma. Look at the snow. It's quiet and content and never complains or asks what time it is. You should be like that. Calvin, you are my eyes. Seatbelts off? Here we go!"

She hated to drive in the dark, and hated worse to drive in the snow, because she saw poorly at night, and the snow blinded and distracted her. She ran stop signs and stopped at green lights and made several wrong turns on the long ride home, but neither Calvin's shouted warnings nor the strange, backward hissing noise their mother made by sucking air through her teeth every time they nearly wrecked made the trip go any faster, or distracted Jemma from the waiting.

At first, watching the snow was not particularly instructive. It drifted, slowly, or rushed slowly at the windshield and struck the glass and melted, or stuck on top of the snow already piled on the hood. Only after they were home, the tree lights fixed and the eggs put away, and after they had bundled themselves up again for the walk down to the tree—everyone had to walk or ride a sled, unless the weather was truly dangerous, in which case the event would be canceled—did the snow actually soothe her. Walking hand in hand with her mother, she leaned back her head and looked up, catching snowflakes in her open mouth, and something in the pattern of snowflakes lessened the tension in her belly. She stumbled a few times, and hardly noticed when the teenagers, hooting and holding flares aloft, passed them on sleds as they walked down the hill, or noticed the exhausted parents dragging their kids on toboggans up from Beach Road. She noticed the tree first as a multicolored stain on the falling snow. She looked ahead and saw the white star shining over top of the clubhouse roof, and then saw the whole thing as they rounded the building and walked over the yard. The tree, a thirty-foot Douglas fir, was there all year round, but the day after Thanksgiving men came with a cherry picker to string the lights and set the star.

Santa came in a red pickup truck with a giant electric nose strapped to the grille. Sheriff Travis—not a real sheriff but a former one, the man who along with a mildly retarded assistant was in charge of Severna Forest security—was in the back, lounging on a pile of presents. "It's all a big fix," Calvin whispered to Jemma as Santa took a seat on the throne beneath the tree, and the presents were unloaded and piled around him.

"I know," Jemma said, because he'd already explained it the year before. The presents weren't from Santa at all, but from their parents. They bought them in stores and wrapped them themselves and labeled them and dropped them off in a secret room at Mr. Duffy's store. Calvin was puzzled and a little angered by the whole exercise, and was always rooting in his advancing vocabulary for words to describe it, an *infringement,* a *travesty,* a *farce,* but he had stopped asking their mother and father why the real Santa permitted it to happen because they always said the same thing: Because it pleases him to do so.

Jemma sipped on a cup of hot chocolate, waiting for the C's. She went up just after Calvin, and did the curtsy just like all the other girls before her did. Calvin would not bow before the false Santa, or even shake his hand. They took their presents and walked back to their mother, and held on to them patiently, waiting for Santa to stand, after the last gift had been distributed, and cry out, "Open them now, children! Open your gifts and see how Santa loves you!" Jemma found that she could wait calmly to open her present, and that her agitation had not increased one iota from the time she got her present to when Oliver Zork claimed his, because she knew that this lesser Santa distributed lesser presents. She got a rubber ball and paddle set. Calvin got a fancy top.

Some stationary caroling followed. Jemma grew a little nostalgic as she sang, thinking back on previous days when this had all impressed her more, when she'd thought it was the real Santa up there on the throne, when the tree had seemed bigger and the hot chocolate hotter, when it had been so hard to remember the words to the songs, and she had liked the present she'd got so much it almost seemed like Christmas had already come, a little bit. Somehow the nostalgia soured back into the waiting feeling again as they walked home, her mother not holding her hand anymore but working the ball and paddle set vigorously.

"Did I ever tell you the story," Calvin asked them as they approached their hill, "about the girl who tried to kill Santa?" Their mother said yes, but Jemma said no, though she had heard it before, always on the way back from the tree, and always at this same spot. Jemma liked the story, and wanted a distraction from the waiting. So even though she knew that she'd be listening to a story she already knew, on a night when all stories were endless and all journeys endless, when the hill would stretch infinitely above her, and she still had an eternity to pass even before bedtime, and even though she knew that listening to this story would be its own special torture, she said yes.

"She wasn't a bad girl," Calvin said. "Well, yes she was, but not in the way you think. She got excellent grades and was very polite and helped her mother around the house and never complained even on Christmas Eve that she was bored or that time was passing too slowly. She sold lemonade in the summer and hot brownies in the winter, door to door here in the Forest to raise money for starving children in Armenia and South Antarctica and Bowie and McLean, and she went to church every Sunday and was very quiet, and knew all the prayers, even in Latin, because this was a long, long time ago.

"And she looked like a nice girl, with very pretty curls that were almost blond, and big green eyes and a heart-shaped face, and she mostly acted like a nice girl, but she had a bad habit of creeping out at night and stabbing little animals with a big knife her father had unwisely given her for a birthday present. He worked in a museum, where they had knives like that, and he thought she should have it because it was pretty and because it used to belong to a princess. So he gave it to her, not realizing that he was encouraging in her this very bad habit.

"She went out every night, and at first she killed little rabbits, and then she killed cats, and then she killed dogs, and everyone in the Forest became very afraid, because they thought that a terrible black man had come to kill their pets. Nobody thought it would be the sweet little girl who lived up on the hill—yes, in our very house. Could anyone bad live there? people asked when they noticed which way the trail of blood pointed. The answer, they thought, was no.

"So the dogs kept dying, and then it was ponies, and then horses, and then an elephant, just passing through, poor sweet Simba visiting with the circus, asleep down by the river. She stabbed him right in his brain. She had killed something as big as a house, but it wasn't enough for her. She needed more. It almost would be sad, that she still needed more, that she never got what she wanted even though she worked so hard for it, but don't feel sorry for her. You may have noticed by now how thoroughly bad she really was. I shouldn't have said that she wasn't.

"What was she to do? No self-respecting circus would come near Severna Forest now, she'd have no second chance at another Simba, or at a giraffe, which would have been even better. She could travel to the zoo and kill a lion, smaller but fiercer than an elephant, or walk to the sea and stab at a whale. Or she could kill a person, the worst and mightiest creature of them all, much smaller than an elephant, but enough to satisfy her, she thought. Enough that she could just put her knife away afterward and never have to touch it again. That's what she thought.

"It was a problem, though, to pick one. She looked around in her classroom at all the boys and girls and knew that none of them would do, and looked at her teachers, and almost stabbed her science teacher after washing his blackboards for him. But he was asleep on his desk, and looked so sweet and innocent and small as he slept that she just couldn't do it. Because he wasn't enough, and she knew it.

"She was very sad, then, though everyone else in the Forest was happy, because they thought that the big black man had moved on to greener killing fields. Then at Christmas she figured it out. She stood just where we were standing and the stupid fake Santa gave her her present, but not the one he thought he was giving her. He handed her a Raggedy Ann doll, but what he gave her was a perfect kill. She was one of those girls who got good grades, but wasn't very smart—she could name all the counties in Ireland, but you could sell her her own underwear. She thought he was the real Santa, and thought for sure that if she could kill the real Santa, then she'd finally have what she wanted, and she could bury her knife. So she creeped out of her house—yes, our house too—as soon as her parents brought her home and went back down to the clubhouse, where the fake Santa and his helpers were having a party. She followed him home when he stumbled out—he'd had too much to drink, which should have clued her in that he wasn't the real Santa. She followed him up this hill, thinking he was on his way to where he'd hidden his sleigh in the woods, and wondering if she should maybe kill all the reindeer too, but finally she couldn't wait anymore. She ran up behind him and stabbed him in the back. Right here is where she did it."

Calvin stopped and pointed at the ground. "Right here he fell down and bled like stink and he would have died if something else hadn't happened. Do you know what?"

"I'm cold, Calvin," said their mother, but he paid no attention to her, and neither did Jemma.

"Santa," Jemma said breathlessly.

"Santa indeed. The real Santa came, gliding up silently behind in his sleigh, and she only knew he was behind her when she noticed the smell of reindeer all around. She turned around and saw him, and he was so awful and glorious that she dropped her knife. I'm sorry! she said, and she really was, and she cried. She was really, really, really, really sorry, but it was too late. He said to her, What you do to the least of these fake Santas, you do to me, and he threw a holly berry at her. It turned her to coal, and his reindeer stomped on her and broke her into a thousand pieces. If you dig in the snow here, you'll probably find one."

"No digging!" said their mother, because Jemma was already bending down. She handed Jemma back her ball and paddle, took both their hands, and trudged with them, for a hundred years, toward home.

"Where's your father?" their mother kept asking then, as the it grew later and later, "Where's you damn father?" then "Where's your goddamn father?" then finally, just before she sent them to bed, "Where's you fucking father?" She called the hospital repeatedly, only to discover he was still in surgery. "The *graft* failed," she said, bitterly and mockingly, perched on her stool in the kitchen, speaking in her gin voice. "The child is *bleeding*. Well what about my graft? What about my bleeding? Who's going to help me?"

"I'll help you," Calvin said, serious and calm. "What do we have to do?" This was all well after dinner, ages after they got home. They spent the evening drinking hot chocolate and stringing endless lengths of popcorn for the tree while they delayed dinner over and over, the orange chicken growing increasingly soggy and the lobster sauce more gelatinous, until it had to be eaten or abandoned altogether.

"You can't help me," she said sadly. "Santa would be furious." She sent them upstairs with the bag of fortune cookies. After they'd changed into their pajamas and brushed their teeth, they sat on Jemma's bed, cracking and eating the cookies. Jemma thought she knew what her fortune would say before she read it: Christmas will never come. But what she read aloud to Calvin was "Your bundle will make you very happy."

"Only if you smile," he replied, "will your smile grow bigger." They went through the whole bag, Jemma eating every cookie. Calvin stopped eating after two, but carefully folded up the fortunes to make a neat pile, to add to his jar: *Laziness is its own reward*; *Only the chrysanthemum knows the dark secret of the caterpillar*; *The wisdom of the shrimp is in being small*; *This year will bring you almost everything you want*; *The moon is your friend—it follows you around.*

They did not even try to sleep. After the cookies were finished Calvin began to speak again of the little girl who tried to kill Santa, telling how she had been punished by having to serve as the angel called Stab, an avenger who descended from Heaven to poke at people who kicked dogs or ran over squirrels and didn't even look back. And he told her that if she looked in her closet she might see, way in the back where the steam pipes sat naked outside the wall, the glint of her knife.

Jemma ran screaming downstairs for her mother, who came up from the basement before Jemma could go down. She shouted for Calvin to come downstairs and threatened to leave a note for Santa about him. This was a threat that always subdued him.

"But I can't sleep," Jemma said when her mother instructed them to go upstairs, get in bed, and turn out the lights. "I just can't. I couldn't ever."

"Just close your eyes," her mother said, pushing her up the stairs, "and think about it." Jemma sat down on the landing and started to cry. "Oh, now," her mother said. "Oh, please." She sat on the stair and lifted Jemma in her lap, cajoling and threatening and soothing, but Jemma only cried harder. "You're too old to cry," her mother said.

"But it *hurts,*" Jemma said, because she could feel it, an ache in her belly that centered around her belly button but moved even as she was crying about it to her left side. "All right," her mother said. "Wait a minute. Wait just a minute." She hurried them both down to the kitchen and scooped ice cream into two bowls. "Here come the sprinkles!" she said brightly, rushing to her bathroom and back in less than a minute. She struggled with the safety cap on a bottle of medication for a few moments, but finally opened it and with two spoons crushed one pill for Jemma and two pills for Calvin. "This will make you so calm and so sleepy," she said, and kept saying it, then singing it as they ate their ice cream, and as she led them upstairs again. "So calm," she sang as she tucked them both into Calvin's dinghy. "So sleepy, so calm, so very, very sleepy." Her own lids fell to half-mast as she sang, though Calvin and Jemma, side by side with the blanket tucked just under their chins, stared at her with wide eyes. "So sleepy," she sang as she left the room in a slow dance, spinning on her way to the door, her voice seeming to spin, also, and stretch like taffy from her mouth to Jemma's ear.

"Are you tired?" she asked her brother, after their mother shut the door.

"I don't think so," he said. Jemma did not feel tired, either. She felt awake but not alert, and had a strange but not unpleasant feeling, like she was turning into a big marshmallow—her fingers and then her arms and then her trunk and finally her face taking a new consistency, so she felt light and slow and sticky. She knew she could move but did not want to. As they lay side by side and talked of Santa, Jemma came to realize that the ugly fretting in her belly had eased. Time was passing no faster, indeed it seemed to have slowed even further, but she came not to mind the feeling.

"They'll tell you things about Santa that aren't true," Calvin said. "And you have to try hard, sometimes, not to believe them. The first thing they say that's a lie is that he exists at all. Of course he does, but not in the way that they say. They talk about how jolly and kind and fun he is, but they miss all the other stuff, how incredible and awful he is, how furious he can be. There's nothing in his sweetness if you don't consider how he's awful, too. His sleigh has steel runners that could cut you in half if he ran over you, and the reindeer are shod with hot iron, when you look in their eyes you can see reflections of the same fire that burns at the center of the earth. Getting presents isn't all just the sweet fun—you get what you want sometimes but sometimes you don't. Do you see how he is the lord of fate?"

"I can't feel my nose," Jemma said, turning toward her brother. "Is it still there?"

"Touch it and see. Noses! They try to add things, too. To say he lived in this place when he was a child, or that one year Mrs. Claus had to do all the work, or they invent elves to assist him, as if he needed any help with any of it. Why would you live at the North Pole when you are present everywhere, in every place and every time, and always will be, always? Why would you add another reindeer to eight, a perfect number? Rudolph is the worst lie of all. Santa would no more be afflicted with that misfit than, than... he just wouldn't. It's disgusting, what they do. Why can't they just leave him alone and accept how he's perfect, and needs nothing added or taken away from him. Why can't they just leave him alone? How come?"

"Everybody likes Santa," Jemma said slowly, not sure how to answer the question.

"Oh, they say they do. But do they really? Do they think it's easy knowing all the wrong things everybody's done, to wake up every year after Christmas and think it's a new day, and a new beginning, and that they're not going to disappoint you this year? But then he knows right away. He can hardly drink a cup of leftover eggnog before all the evil is aching in his head and he has to pull the list out. Not that he actually sleeps, or would drink leftover eggnog, or even needs to write this stuff down."

"The boat is moving," Jemma said, because she was starting to feel as if they were drifting in the bed. When she opened her eyes it was plain that they were locked still on the carpet, but as soon as she closed her eyes it felt like they were floating down a river.

"Let it carry you away from the third lie, that Santa is bad. They say that it's not for nothing that you can rearrange the letters of his name to spell Satan. They think that's a clue to his real nature, that's he's either the devil himself or a thing of the devil, something added on to Christmas by the wicked instead of the unique and essential spirit of Christmas, somebody who is not added and who can't have anything added to him. The stories about dolls who come alive to strangle little girls and toy guns loaded with real bullets, and about his watching in his crystal snowball for all the horrible things to happen on Christmas morning and laughing and laughing and laughing—they're all lies. Don't you believe them."

"There's a waterfall coming up," Jemma said, because her gaze had fallen on the plume of mist rising from the mouth of the humidifier that sat on top of Calvin's dresser. "Do you think we'll die?"

"How can you worry about a stupid waterfall when they tell all these hideous lies about him? The fourth one is the worst one. Just when you think that everything's okay, that you're old enough, that you've sorted out all the lies and are feeling safe from them, they start with the foul whispering—*he doesn't exist*. It's the trickiest lie, no wonder they save it for last. And there's something about it that you almost want to believe, because it's so much easier to just not believe, and it would be so much easier if his eye wasn't always on you. That's why they say it, because they lose heart, or because they know he has judged them already, that he's seen every wrong thing they've done and has punished them for it, and is punishing them for it even while they say *no, no, he is not*. They tell you the lie and then watch you to see if you'll believe it, and if you do they hate you because you are weak like them, and if you don't then they hate you because faith burns their eyes. But you have to believe, especially if they test you. Will you believe? Do you believe?"

"Oh, yes," said Jemma.

"Even if they beat you with giant candy canes and try to make you deny him?"

"Yes."

"What if they put holly under your fingernail? Then would you deny him?"

"No!"

"What if they boil you in eggnog and cut off your head and stuff a goose up your butt?"

"No! I mean, yes. I mean I would still say I like Santa."

"Like? Is that enough? And how are you going to talk about how great he is with your head cut off?"

"I don't know!" Jemma said. The humidifier mist was getting thicker, filling up all the air in a hanging cloud that reached for the bed.

"He'd give you the power, of course. But you can't just like him. He'd throw you right off his sleigh for just liking him. You have to love him with your whole heart and believe in him with your whole body. It has to be hard, like this." He clenched his fists up and shut his eyes. Jemma felt his whole body go stiff as he made a noise, a grunt and groan of effort. "Like that!" he said. "You do it."

Jemma did it, clenching her fists and curling her toes, squinching her eyes and grinding her teeth. She tried to make the same noise that her brother had. When she opened her eyes the mist cloud had reached the wall behind the bed, and was falling toward them.

"Good enough, I guess," Calvin said. "I hope he brings me what I want this year. I hope I've finally been good enough—not that he gives a gift because of anything you do. I know he only gives the gifts to increase his own glory, but I still hope I've been good in the right way, finally. I don't want to be found wanting again. This time I want to get it. You know?"

"An erector set?" Jemma asked.

"No, stupid. Going. Maybe this year. Maybe finally." He took in a deep breath, and Jemma was sure he was going to use it to shout or sing, but he only blew it out in a big sigh. Then he was quiet.

"The clouds are coming," Jemma said as the mist fell down farther. He just snored when she knocked him in the ribs, and when the mist had settled on them completely she found she could not find him anymore, not with her elbow and not with her hand. "Where are you?" she called out into the fog. She reached with both her hands as far out as she could reach to her sides, but felt only air. The fog brightened and condensed. "Where are you?" she called out again.

"Over here," came a voice, but not Calvin's. It was a voice that sounded like many people talking, all saying the same thing at the same time. The fog began to lift from the foot of the bed, a little at a time, as if it were being torn away in little strips to unwrap the person it was concealing.

"Santa?" Jemma asked, because it was a Santa shape that she saw through the fog, the hat and the beard and the belly. But as her vision became clearer she saw that though the thing had the shape of Santa, it looked very different from the traditional representations. It was a Santa of Santas, his body made up of tiny bodies. Jemma counted twelve of them just in the face.

"We are the Unity of Santa," it said, eight of them pushing and twisting away from each other to be the moving lips. It stared, four little bodies bowing to her when it blinked.

"What do you want?" Jemma asked it, when it did not go away, and did not speak.

"To show you wonderful things," it said. "Only take our hand and we will go." It held a hand out to her, each body at the tip of each finger extending its arms and hands and fingers at her.

"Are you taking me to a Christmas past?" Jemma asked, because she had earlier in the day been reading *A Christmas Carol*.

"What would be the point?" it asked, wiggling its hand, and wiggling all its hands until Jemma put her own hand out to touch it. It was like touching a caterpillar or her father's beard.

"Where are we going?" Jemma asked, suddenly quite certain that she was dreaming for all that pinching her bottom failed to wake her. The mist was streaming on either side of them, as if they were traveling fast, and she felt a wind on her face that blew colder and colder.

"North," said the Unity of Santa. "Where else?"

At great speed, but for no more time than it would have taken her to walk from one end of the room to the other, they traveled, coming to rest when the boat-bed drove up with a squeaking crunch upon a shore of snow. They were out of the mist. As the Unity of Santa helped her out of the boat Jemma looked back at her brother—she could see him plainly though she had never been able to find him with her hands—looking very pale as he slept.

"But what will happen to my brother?" Jemma asked.

"He will sleep. Come along. She is waiting."

"Who?" Jemma asked, but her guide was silent as they walked through ice tunnels that were sometimes so narrow that Jemma could reach up and put a hand on the ceiling, and sometimes so wide that Jemma couldn't see the walls let alone the ceiling, until they came to a round wooden door. The Unity extracted from its pocket a key made of little Santas. It opened the door and waved Jemma through.

She found herself in the middle of Santa's workshop. It was much busier than she thought it should be, given that Santa was already out in the world delivering presents. But all the elves were still working furiously. Indeed, most of them looked sad and tired. When she asked why the elves were all still working, her guide told her that it was for her, that all the presents they were making were for her. "If you don't want them, then all you have to do is say the word," said the Unity. Jemma was silent.

They climbed up many stairs, flights of five or ten steps set into the walls, or passing through the walls, but always rising, up toward the top of the workshop. The elves looked sadder and more haggard the farther they climbed, but the presents they worked on were ever more sublime. On what

Jemma thought might be the ninth floor she found a pair of emaciated elves dressed only in little barrels painstakingly sewing her name in gold into the vapors of a small cloud.

"Oh, oh!" Jemma called out. "Is that the cloud that I asked for?" The elves looked up at her briefly with dark, empty eyes before returning to their work.

"Stupid girl," said the Unity of Santa. "What does it look like, a pony?"

"Sorry!" Jemma said, suddenly afraid that all the wonders she'd passed would be denied her.

"There's no sorry here," it said. They'd come to another door, bigger than the first, and colored a deeper red. The Unity of Santa kicked it, so hard that a few of the constituents were knocked from the hat, and fell to catch hands and join with the long ropes of Santas who were its hair. It thrust Jemma into a long room, full of torchlight and reeking, Jemma thought, of winter—pine and berries and smoke and the bright sting of cold air. Jemma realized she could feel her nose again. She put her hand on it.

"Yes, hello!" A woman at the far end of the room, seated in a wooden throne, was putting her hand to her nose just as Jemma was doing. "Hello! Is this what you do to greet a body? I think I like it better than waving."

"I was just checking to see if my nose was there."

"It certainly is," said the lady. She was dressed in a red velvet robe trimmed in white fur, and berries were caught up in her great loops of hair. On closer inspection, the berries seemed to Jemma to be growing from her hair, not just resting in it. As plain as the mouth below it. "Do you know who I am, little girl?"

"Mrs. Claus," Jemma said, though not sure about that, because this lady was black, and Jemma's mother had told her, when Jemma asked specifically if Mrs. Claus or Santa himself might be black, that it was a frank impossibility and an absurd thought, and had furthermore denied the blackness of Jesus, Nefertiti, and the Queen of Sheba.

"Clever girl," she said. She leaned back in the chair and crossed her legs, flashing shiny boots that ran up to her thighs. "Do you know why you are here?"

"To get my presents?"

"Just that? There's more, if you're smart enough. Here it is: all that you have seen is nothing at all compared to what I can give you, if you answer the question I'll pose. But if you get the question wrong then you get nothing, and then you must pay a terrible price. Too terrible even for me to speak of just yet."

"Would I get a pony?" Jemma asked, "If I answer the question?"

"Who knows? Maybe you'll get a thousand ponies. Will you answer my question?"

Jemma looked at the lady, and at the Unity of Santa, and back down the hall through the door to the workshop. She knew her brother would scold her for seeking the bird in the bush, but she did it anyway, imagining herself riding a pony that was made of a thousand ponies, a Unity of pony.

"Okay," Jemma said slowly. Mrs. Claus stood up and walked down the marble steps that led up to her throne. She stopped on the last one and bent over Jemma, her hair swinging close enough that Jemma could tell how it smelled like moss.

"Very well," she said. "Tell me, child, what has Santa got under his hat?"

Jemma folded her arms and ducked her chin and began to think hard. Air? That would be the sensible answer. An elf? He might just keep one there. An apple? That was possible, but not particularly likely. His hair? That was even more sensible, but Jemma thought she had a better answer.

"His head," she said.

"No, child," Mrs. Claus said, looking a little shocked at Jemma's answer. "World peace. *World peace.* That's what's under his hat. Haven't you been listening to your brother?"

"I have been," Jemma said. "All night long."

Mrs. Claus sighed. "A liar, too," she said sadly. "Well, off with her head then."

"Are you talking about me?" Jemma asked.

"Off with her head!" Mrs. Claus shouted. She jumped up and down on the steps as Jemma backed away, then drew out a long-handled axe from beneath her robe. She shook it and pointed it at Jemma, but never swung. "Off with her head!" she said again, her voice echoing in the hall. At her last words the Unity of Santa fell apart, dissolving from the head down, every member tumbling down to the floor to run at Jemma on little feet. Jemma fled. Out the door, past all the elves working in alcoves on her presents. Now they were all sharpening bits of coal, which they threw at her, only one in all nine floors proving herself a good shot. Jemma rubbed her sore forehead as she ran along the ice toward the boat, looking back just once at the swarm of Santas behind her. The boat was drifting away but she made a long leap and landed next to he brother. Then she was on her back again under the mist, listening to her brother snore beside her. She thought she was awake, or that her night visitation had ended, but then she saw them from the corners of her eyes, innumerable little hats rising over the sides of the boat, followed shortly by the pale fat Santa faces in their beards. They only spoke to her, and did not lift a finger to harm her. "The Spirit will visit you next," they said.

She waited for the next visitor for what seemed like a whole hour before she realized that the mist was making a sighing noise, or rather that it was speaking very quietly in a voice that was like a person sighing quietly. She peered at the mist and saw a face there, fat like Santa's face, but sadder. "I am the Spirit of Santa," it said. "Come away with me."

"Okay," Jemma said, feeling quite trusting despite how poorly she had been treated by Mrs. Claus. It wasn't that the Spirit was not spooky—it was quite spooky—but Jemma felt safe and not afraid. The feeling like parts of her body were missing had given way to a rubbery feeling. She felt sure that if she curled herself into a ball she could bounce to the ceiling, and was sure that her rubber neck would be proof against an axe.

The spirit settled on her, cold and wet. When it lifted she was in a graveyard. She remembered this part from the book, and quickly went in search of her own tombstone to see when she was going to die. "Will nobody miss me?" she asked the spirit excitedly, but it was quiet. She found names on the tombstones—Annabelle; Corky; Pooh the Third; Mrs. Beasley; Shenandoah—but hers was nowhere.

"Who is buried here?" she asked.

"All forgotten!" the spirit sighed. It rose up in the air and threw out its arms and legs, and began to bleed away from its tips, fingers and toes rarefying into a thinner mist that spun out into threads that drifted over every grave. "No one remembers them!" the Spirit moaned, and sank its tendrils into the ground.

Jemma had her answer in moments. Felt paws and porcelain hands began to claw up through the dirt, followed shortly by the bodies of ragged bears and dogs and cats, dolls in rags with shattered eyes, robots with broken antennae, giraffes and hippos and elephants leaking stuffing. They crawled from their graves and lurched toward Jemma who, safe in her rubbery feeling, waited for them calmly. They only wanted hugs; she knew it as soon as one got close to her. It was a teddy bear, armless, legless, and unstuffed, just a head on a furry poncho. It smelled just like Aunt Mary's terrible, terrible breath, a mixture of cat box and rotten meat, but Jemma hugged it tight. She hugged the broken dolls and the broken robots and the dull board games missing their pieces. She had enough hugs for every one of them, but they soon overwhelmed her, burying her under wool and silk and organdy and steel, until the mist settled in through the thin spaces between bodies and touched her skin. Then she was in her brother's bed again, feeling like it had all gone very well, and that she had passed some sort of test.

"The Power will come!" cried the Spirit, and then it was gone. Jemma was alone with her sleeping brother in a dark, clear room. She did not have long to wait. There came an ominous knock on the door, four strong blows that Jemma was sure would wake everyone, but there was no change in Calvin's snoring.

"Come in," Jemma whispered. She thought it was Santa this time, good old regular Santa come to comfort her, or explain the significance of what she'd seen. Then she thought it was a headless Santa. Then she realized it was an empty Santa suit—empty but mighty, it would have fit a Santa who was eight feet tall. "Who are you?" Jemma asked, though she already knew.

It never spoke, but only pulled open its robe with invisible fingers. The robe disrobed, revealing what it had covered, the most beautiful light Jemma had ever seen. It was as strong and bright and warm as the sun, but cold as a faceful of snow. Jemma lay in it, feeling warm and cold, cherished and unnoticed, elevated and, finally, terrified, before she finally fell away, passing out or passing deeper into sleep, but still feeling the presence against her face. She was never aware of waking, but realized with a start that it was morning, and that the sun was shining in her eyes.

She tried to leap up and jump on the bed, but her legs were still full of the rubbery feeling, so she fell on her brother. "Calvin!" she shouted, over and over. It took so long to wake him up she thought for a moment that Santa had killed him in the night.

They hurried downstairs, stumbling in their slippers and drug hangovers on the landing and the stairs, slipping on the last step and tumbling together to the carpet, then both clawing over each other and helping each other up as they made for the basement staircase. They slipped again at the top of those stairs, but bore each other up, and took the last half of the stairs calmly. Jemma stopped at the last step while Calvin went on. She saw the flash of her father's camera, and heard Calvin gasp. Here at the end she liked to pause, and she finally liked the waiting, because she knew it was utterly in her power now, and all she had to do to make it end was take a step, past the wall that was hiding her from her parents. She understood that this was a moment in time, about to pass. She put her hand on the wall and closed her eyes.

You must eventually take that last step, have to open every last present, feeling, on your very edges, but not knowing or understanding how they are all wrong, the Smurf mushroom house, the Junior Marie Curie Radioactive Discovery Set with the real glow-in-the-dark artificial radium, even the Bat Girl sleeping bag for which you have positively lusted these past months. They have not given you what you really wanted, just like they haven't given Calvin what he wanted, because it is not theirs to give. Every box contains an empty, worthless secret. There is offal in your stocking. The valium-visitations of your endless night are already being forgotten, but not their secret lessons. Your parents are waiting, the camera is poised, your brother is rooting like a hog among the plenty, searching for the box that might contain the secret instruction for his going—but stay. You can stay just on this side of the corner, with time still under your thumb, for as long as you like.

How small a matter had it been to come forth securely, and as it were in sport to undergo death. Herein was true proof of boundless mercy, that he shunned not the death he so greatly dreaded. And there can be no doubt that, in the Epistle to the Hebrews, the Apostle means to teach the same thing when he says that he "was heard in that he feared." Some, instead of "feared," use a term meaning reverence of piety, but how inappropriately, is apparent both from the nature of the thing and the form of the expression. Christ then praying in a loud voice, and with tears, is heard in that he feared, not so as to be exempted from death, but so as not to be swallowed up by it like a sinner, though standing as our representative. And certainly no abyss can be imagined more dreadful than to feel that you are abandoned and forsaken of God, and not heard when you invoke Him, just as if he Had conspired your destruction. Worse, though, to live everyday knowing that you never did the thing that you were supposed to, indicted by every ruined person and thing as the first, worst, and only coward. And almost as bad, to spend a whole life trying to figure it out (and isn't it a gift and a punishment never to be allowed to think of anything else) and still never figure out how to do it.

The world is as it is, and I am as I am, and how will I ever change either one?

“Did you find it?” Kidney asked the dolphin. She was in an empty classroom on the fourth floor, standing on a table and leaning out the window.

“No,” said Light On The Water.

“Did you look? Did you look hard?”

“I traveled North to the penguin-water and East to the pillars of the moon and South to the republic of squid and West to the kingdom of the sun. There is water everywhere, and no land. There are no waves for sport, and no beaches whereupon I might throw myself if my heart should break. The world is water, and you have no place but here to rest your round head.”

“But did you really look? I told you to look all over the world and you're back already. Did you cheat? I think you cheated. I don't think you did your homework!”

Light On The Water ducked her head and slapped the water with her mouth, the dolphin equivalent, Kidney knew, of a shrug. “I have traveled far; my brothers and sisters have traveled farther, and all together we have circumscribed this endless ocean. And Shafts of Moonlight, who is a sorcerer and can see through the eyes of little fish, has been in a trance this past week, searching from little mind to little mind, borrowing eyes all over the world and always only seeing the same thing. Nowhere even a speck of dry sand.”

"Well you had better get out there and look again. It's out there somewhere, I can feel it." Kidney struck her heart when she said this, something that her father always did when he said something he really meant. "I know it!"

"I am tired of swimming and seeking in vain," said the dolphin.

"Well, I'm tired of being stuck in the hospital! Who's the boss here, anyway?"

"You are," said Light On The Water. Kidney had figured out pretty quickly that dolphins would do anything you told them to, and had spent a lot of time ordering them to do tricks before she realized she could send them on an important secret mission, one that she hadn't even told her own brothers and sisters about. She hadn't even told them, or anyone else, that the dolphins did more than just laugh and play when she talked to them.

"Cruel human child!" the dolphin said, but she rose up on her tail, swimming away backward and clapping her fins together in dismay before she turned and hurried away from the hospital.

"I'm not mean!" Kidney called out to her glistening back. "I just want to go home!"

Every morning Jemma crawled out of bed and put on the same thing: an extra-large pair of scrubs, a yellow gown, and her clogs. She looked not just plain compared to everyone else, but decidedly old-fashioned. How strange, people said to her, that you of all people should cling to the old mode, and certain nurses asked her, "Don't you know that those scrubs make you look fat? Don't you know you can tell the angel, Give me something to make my ass look smaller and, it's all as good as done? Look at this. Do you think that my ass is really this small or this firm?" Then they would offer their asses for inspection, or even a flesh-testing slap, and Jemma always wanted to say, It's my baby that makes me look fat. But instead she'd say that she felt very comfortable in scrubs.

At seventeen weeks she didn't show in them, but was fairly obvious in everything else she tried. Every time she looked in the mirror she expected to see a monster, a creature with ten-gallon boobs, elephant feet, and a tiny little head, because that was how she perceived her body to be changing when she wasn't actually looking at it. The actual change was more subtle: the moderate swelling in her belly; the foreign nipples, large and dark; and the map of blue veins spreading over her abdomen and her chest. She nearly passed out every time she stood up, and her back was starting to hurt. When she complained to Vivian she got a lecture on her posture instead of permission to drug up. "Imagine a string," Vivian told her, and marched her around the dissolving ER space like a single-string marionette.

She wasn't ready for everyone to know, and wasn't ready for maternity clothes. A week before, she'd tried on a dress that Vivian had made for her—a black felt jumper with a high collar and iron buttons. "It says, I am pregnant and I am powerful," Vivian declared at the fitting.

"It says, I am pregnant and I am Joseph Stalin," Jemma said, and took it off, and never put it on again. She put back on her scrubs, and soon they became unique to her, as every last person in hospital, with the exception of Ethel Puffer, developed a distinctive wardrobe in consultation with the angel. Ethel stuck with her hospital gown, a baggy nightie printed with frolicking safari animals, adding only a sturdy pair of sandals. She painted her head as faithfully as before, though she stopped blackening her mouth and tongue. But everyone else put on new clothes, and some confided to each other and to Jemma that they felt as if they were putting on a new spirit, and in fact the new Council of Friends passed a bill in support of the new wardrobes, endorsing them as an outward expression of the personal and universal new beginning.

Dr. Snood put away his old gray suit and the fraying school tie he'd been wearing day after day. Before, he'd gone to the replicator only for fresh underwear, and had told Jemma (while she broadcasted what she thought were rather obvious indicators that she didn't want to know, and why was he telling her this, and wouldn't he just go away?) that even these were quite plain, simple linen form-fitted boxers which he'd modeled after the secret, holy underwear of the Mormon roommate he'd had in medical school. Every third day he had stuffed his suit into the replicator for cleaning, and watched it emerge minutes later, the empty legs stepping out carefully from the fog, and the empty jacket doing a careful sort of limbo to clear the top edge of the replicator window without wrinkling. He was never sure if it was his actual suit coming back to him, or something new and false, a perfect lying image. So he held his tie back, though it became frayed around the edges, and was stained with Pickie's melanotic shit. He said he would have felt naked without it on any usual day, but then there came a morning when he looked at it, and at the old gray suit, and decided it was time for him to put these things away, and put on new clothes. Now he wore trousers with a subtle flare at the ankle, and jackets with Nehru collars, and collarless shirts all in electric pastel colors, and a pair of shining ankle-high boots. Vivian said he looked like a twenty-third-century pimp.

Others modified what previously had passed for a uniform. Dr. Tiller put away her long skirts, frowsy blouses, and long white coat for tapered skirts that still fell to her ankle but were split in the back to well above her knees, and satin pirate blouses, and sweeping silk dusters in rich dark blues and greens, and boots with pointed toes and dark jewels running subtly up the sides—they blended with the color of the leather, so you had to squint to be sure they were actually there. Of course she kept her ritual headdress, but in place of the ordinary blue, black, or gray cotton she wore chenille or cashmere or suede or even leather, and the size of the thing grew to greatly more than head size, as if there were a secret volumizing appliance underneath the fabric, or her secret, not-seen-in-thirty-years hair had been tonicked to ankle length by the angel, or she had grown another face, kinder or crueler than the original, on the back of her head. Everyone agreed that she now had the biggest head in the hospital, though there were many women and a few men who had begun to wear chapeaux in various degrees of size and fantasticness. "Gay Muslim cowboy" was how Vivian described the look, but Jemma thought that the new clothes had only made Dr. Tiller look more intensely like herself, and made her more imposing than ever.

Some people tried unexpectedly to glam up. Dr. Sundae, who previously had only worn scrubs in a shade of burgundy very unflattering to her complexion, suddenly appeared every day in a different fancy dress. They were rather severe, as dresses go, still very dark, and bearing nowhere the smallest scrap of ribbon or lace. Some were made of heavy castle-curtain material, never with prints, but never plain—they were all embossed with stern roses or fleurs-de-lis in colors only a little darker or lighter than the base. Some were sequined, though not flashily. The sequins seemed to catch and hold the light, rather than reflect it—and because the dresses were all so heavy, and so broad shouldered, they looked more than a little like suits of armor. There were square-toed flats with surprising little additions, like a crystal flower at the heel, or a detail from Titian printed on the sole. And she might wear a soft scarf or a little beret, but these little contrasts seemed to heighten rather than relieve the overall impression of severity. "Fancy-ball hair shirt," Vivian said.

Vivian herself was unpredictable, and advanced beyond the rest of the populace. She'd been making clothes since the time when, on her initial encounter with the replicators, she'd ordered the angel, in jest, to make her a pair of hot pants with an edible crotch. When the pink pants had appeared from out of the fog, and Vivian had unfolded them and run her finger along the wide band of fruit roll-up between the legs, she had looked, just briefly, as happy as Jemma had ever seen her. People tried in vain to imitate her. She wore something starkly different every day, and sometimes the outfits changed from morning to night, or even from breakfast to dinner. A few times while Jemma was with her someone came to ask if they could borrow something they'd seen her wearing, but Vivian always said the same thing to them: "That thing? Oh, it's already been destroyed."

She tried hardest of anyone to get Jemma out of her scrubs. "You have got an image to maintain," she said, and Jemma thought she might agree, but she thought that the image of hardworking frumpiness might be just in line with the office of Universal Friend. It said you were plain and usual and approachable and ready at any time to take on a task. She still did not understand her duties or prerogatives terribly well, and knew no one else did either, but felt at least that she was coming to understand how people perceived her, and what their minimum expectations were. And her belly was an issue—she didn't want to make any announcements until it was absolutely necessary.

She wondered, on the morning of the hundred and sixteenth day, if it was really necessary now. With the yellow gown on she was still not obvious, but now in scrubs alone she looked at least like she was hiding something under her shirt, if not necessarily pregnant. But she had decided, all of a sudden, that it was time, and pretended that she had let Rob, who had in the last two weeks lost sight of any need for secrecy, convince her. She was going to ask for special scrubs to wear at the event tonight, for a special gown that would flair as she danced and rolled, but found herself unexpectedly with a different idea.

When she was little her Aunt Mary had once made her and Calvin a present of marvelous bubble paste, a sort of glue that you could stick on the end of a metal straw and blow up into a huge floating globe. The glue had every color in it, all swirled together in a way that was hard to appreciate before inflation, but quite obvious and lovely in the bubble. When she was five years old it was the prettiest thing she'd ever seen, the bubble colored just like the rainbow in a slick of oil, floating under a blue sky and over green grass, pursued by a crowd of children. I want a bodysuit, she told the angel, and did a bad job of describing the color, sampling and rejecting swath after swath, making herself late for her appointment. She made herself later when she had to try the thing on right away. She put it on and crawled over to the mirror, then stood up, succeeding in surprising herself. The color was startling and just right—she imagined someone sticking a metal straw in her ass and blowing her up into a big, beautiful, worshipful ball. And her belly was startling. She looked more pregnant in this thing than she did when she was naked. It would do. She practiced a couple moves, took off the suit, and put back on her scrubs.

Since the election it took her forever to get anywhere in the hospital. People seemed to feel obliged to stop and talk with her, or rather to stop her and talk to her. "Shouldn't everyone be able to talk to the Universal Friend?" Rob had asked her, when she complained to him. "How Universal a Friend would you be if only Vivian and I were allowed to talk to you?"

"It's just a name," she said, though she understood already that it was not just a name, almost as quickly as she understood that she could not, as her first act of power, undo all the write-ins that had put her on the ballot and won her the position. Strange that so widespread an act—the population was overwhelmingly culpable—could come as such a surprise to the perpetrators. How strange, people said, and how wonderful. Even the also-rans were somehow contented, Dr. Snood having been heard (by an eavesdropping Vivian) to say that it was only because the citizens felt they owed her something that they elected her, not because there was anything the least bit leaderly about her. "She is as great and as strange as the times," said Dr. Sundae, who was becoming more and more reliably Jemma's creepy cheerleader. "They know her better than me," said Ishmael, "because she has touched them."

"There you are!" said Sylvester's mother, the first person to accost her that morning. Jemma had almost made it to the stairs when the poodle-haired lady spotted her. She was towing Sylvester in a red wagon. It had been his favorite activity, before Jemma fixed him, and his mother, driven on by his shrill, incomprehensible babbling, had pulled him up and down the ramp and all over the hospital, until she became a figure familiar to everyone, and more than one person remarked that she was somehow representative of their collective toil. Now Sylvester tolerated the rides for his mother's sake, but he always looked impatient in his wagon, like he had better places to be, or more important things to do. "We're just going down to the playroom, a quick little trip. How are you? You're looking well. I like your hair today. Did you style it with a round brush? I always use a round brush. I have a special one that fits right on to the hair dryer, so they're all of a piece. Is that what you used?"

"Mom, you're making me late for math," Sylvester said from the wagon. He was lying on his back reading a book.

"Oh, we've got hours," she said. "I can count too, you know. Hey, if you came upstairs tonight I could show you my hair dryer. If you wet your hair in my sink I could style it for you. Did I tell you I almost had my license, before?"

"I remember," Jemma said, stepping slowly toward the door to the stairs. Two weeks before she had relieved the lady of her chronic sinusitis, but failed to make her less of a spaz. "Maybe not tonight!" she said cheerily, before she dashed into the stairwell. She hurried down the first flight, paused to listen for activity below her, and then proceeded more slowly. The stairs were usually safe. The elevator never was. She could be entangled in conversation such that she might ride past her floor three times before finally getting out.

On the first floor she cracked the door and peered out before leaving the stairwell. She had not walked five steps before she ran back in again while a troop of children passed by. Led by Marcus Guzman, they were on their way to play soccer on the new field in the lobby. States'-Rights dropped a shin guard by the door. Jemma waited patiently for the child to come retrieve it before she ventured out again. She felt like a bit of a shirker, flattening herself against the wall and extending her unusual senses around corners before putting her head around to confirm that no one was there. Someone might be desperate for conversation, or need advice—though she hadn't yet dispensed any actual advice, people often left her presence under the impression that they had received some. It had never bothered her before, to do a bad job at something, and she had always thought that people who tried too hard at a thing were a little vulgar, but now the prospect of shirking made her feel sad and somehow dirty. The feeling that she was a fraud, that she was elected by mistake, was slow to fade, but the feeling that accompanied the suspicion of fraud—a certainty that, because her election had been part of some grand prank it was okay to shirk—faded quickly.

She had to hide in an exam room five doors from the place she was supposed to meet Vivian because a pair of nurses came down the hall, one from either end, and trapped her. They met right outside the door where she was hiding, and she was sure they would come in, forcing her inside a cabinet, or under the exam table. But they lounged outside, chatting briefly, and then they were quiet, but not gone. Jemma peeked through the window to see them smooching. The empty halls and rooms of the ER had developed a reputation as the hospital's Lovers Lane. It was an issue that the Council was supposed to discuss, what to do with the empty space, and whether it should approve, condemn, or even comment on what transpired there. Most people got a room, and cleaned up after themselves, but these two pinned each other against Jemma's door, and knocked their hips and shoulders against the glass. She might have put them both to sleep, or afflicted each with a debilitating orgasm, one that would take hours to recover from, so they'd not notice a pack of elephants let alone Jemma passing down the hall as they lay twitching on the carpet, but she waited patiently for them to exhaust their bag of foreplay tricks and move out of the hall to get down to the more serious business. They tried to come into her room but she held the knob against them.

"You're so fucking late," Vivian said, when she finally arrived at the exam room they'd been using for her checkups. She was leaning against an ultrasound machine, slapping the transducer against her palm.

"Sorry," Jemma said. "Many delays."

"I've been bored to death. You can't watch movies on this thing, you know."

"Sorry."

"And we've got a meeting in twenty minutes." Jemma said she knew that. "Well, I guess we'll just have to skip to the good part, damn it."

"My gums are bleeding," Jemma said as she climbed up on the table. She took off her robe and her scrub top and lay back with her head pillowed on the little pile of clothing.

"That's normal. Look out, this shit's cold." She squirted a dollop of ultrasound goop on Jemma's belly. Jemma shuddered, but didn't gasp.

"And my teeth feel loose. And I'm double jointed all of a sudden. Is that normal, too?"

"Yes, of course. Don't you remember anything from OB?"

"Sorry. I forgot about all the bloody-mouthed toothless contortionists I met on the ward."

"Shut up. This is harder than it looks." Vivian had done a four-week ultrasound rotation at the beginning of her fourth year, but was still very uncertain of her skills. "Are you excited?"

"Maybe," Jemma said quietly.

"Liar. You're totally excited. I'm totally excited. Shit, that's your gallbladder. Where's Rob?"

"It would have been too obvious, the two of us traipsing around down here. I said I'd bring him the tape."

"Wait… that's colon. Wait! No, that's colon, too. When's the last time you had to poop?" She moved the transducer around Jemma's belly, now in wide sweeping arcs, now in tiny steps. Jemma closed her eyes and tried to look, too, imagining a mystical green eye peering through her belly to reveal a perfect baby floating asleep inside her. She saw the little quarter-baked thing, smaller even than the brave twenty-four-weekers she'd seen out in the world upstairs. It had Rob's blue eyes and her own false red hair. She got a pretty good picture, but it was all just her imagination. She had tried and tried to see it the way she could see Vivian's heart beating in her chest, but it was still like looking at her own nose. "Jesus, you've got a big colon," Vivian said. "No... no... yes! Wait... yes! There it is!" She swung the monitor around so Jemma could see. "Open your eyes, you fucking moron. What are you afraid of? He's fine. A beautiful baby boy."

"Nothing," Jemma said. "I think I wanted to be surprised."

"Fuck that," Vivian said. "DR surprises are bad news. Will you open your eyes or do I have to pry open your lids?" Jemma looked, just one eye at first, but wept from both of them as soon as she saw the image. It was just a mess of static, and yet it managed to contain in it, ghosts among the snow, the faces of everyone she ever loved.

I see him, too. Oh yes, hello little thing. It wasn't really so long ago when there seemed to me no greater disaster than a baby in the womb, a seed of corruption and an innocent who would be abused even by the very air of his first breath. Go back! Undivide, and involute, and shrink back to safety. How I puzzled over the means of it. Now I am proud, and wish I had an ear to put on Jemma's belly, because that is what you are supposed to do, immortal ears of the spirit seeming invasive to me now. Still, I listen, and speak. Hello, little one. Let me be the one to tell you it is finally good news again, to be born.

You stir, and turn your face to me, though your eyes are too young to open. Go away, you say. Leave me alone. I know it isn't time yet to wake up.

Jemma was sure that anybody would have been better at this than she was. Ishmael would have brought a sense of friendly anonymous majesty to the job. Dr. Snood, for all his prim snide fussbudgetry, would have been their best approximation of a statesman. Dr. Sundae was grim and wrathful and dull, but Jemma had no doubt she would have proved an expert wielder of authority—without any office at all she still inserted herself into Council meetings and ordered people around, and was lobbying hard for the position of chief magistrate. Vivian would have had the whole place performing complex musical numbers, or water ballet. It was easy to imagine her lifted on a ninety-foot-high plume of water while below her shirtless constituents sang her name and formulated rhyming theses of causation, regret, and redemption. Even Monserrat, a tamale in one hand and a hammer in the other, would have led them all, somehow.

But me, Jemma thought, I just sit here. That was what she was doing at the moment, just sitting there at the head of a Council meeting. They were in the same room as always, but they had brought in a new set of tables after the election, a small one with room for four where Jemma sat with Ishmael, Monserrat, and Vivian, and a large C-shaped one, where across from them Dr. Tiller, the Secretary, and the other eleven members of the Council sat. Jemma tried not to stare out the huge windows. There was a school of flying fish that seemed to be trying to attract her attention.

They were talking about how to use the ER space. The discussion was heated, but Jemma had found that their discussions were always heated. These were the sort of people that could argue passionately about the contents of the salad bar.

"I think it would make things feel more normal," Monserrat was saying, "if people could go to the market again. Imagine it: waking up on a Saturday to go buy fresh carrots and parsley and rutabagas for your family."

"It could be a new social center," Dr. Snood said. "Someplace for people just to run into one another, and discuss things. A place for serendipitous conversations—great things can come of those."

"I understand the virtues of raw vegetables," Dr. Tiller said. "But it seems to me that it would all just be for show. People will return to their rooms with bags of groceries and then toss them out the window. Who's cooking here? Who has money to pay for these things? Will we print our own money with which to buy our unnecessary staples?"

"We should think twice," said Dr. Sundae, from the audience, "before filthifying ourselves with lucre."

"The vegetables will be for free," Monserrat said. "It will be like a paradise. You come up to my carrot cart, you ask, you receive."

"Does anyone else see a big wedge of classroom space filling up with cabbages?" Vivian asked.

"Or a bar," said Ishmael. Drs. Sundae and Tiller hissed at him. "A coffee bar," he said.

"Nothing wrong with a real bar," said Frank, and Connie seconded her husband vigorously.

"Why not make it what it already is," said Karen. "A place where people can come to meet, and kiss, if they want. But not in secret, or not necessarily in secret."

"A sex club?" Vivian asked.

"Nothing so crude," Karen said. "A kissing marketplace. Just a place to go kiss. A kissy place."

"Just call it a sex club," said Vivian.

I should veto something, Jemma thought to herself, but the discussion had not degraded or escalated sufficiently to really require her intervention. Not much did require her intervention, and she had not forced any ideas of her own through their pseudo-legislative process since their very first session, when she had struck a blow against the surgeons which, while she didn't regret it, did not make her as proud or happy as it had. She watched the fish for a few moments. On that day the hospital had rotated so the Council room was in the stern. The fish were playing in the wake, and seemed to be competing in a contest to jump the whole wide thing. She laughed when two of them, jumping from opposite sides, knocked into each other. Then she noticed it was quiet, and that everyone was looking at her.

"Let's leave the sex club in some undiscovered basement," she said. "You all seem to be asking the same thing, though. Do we have enough space for people to hang out and feel normal in? Maybe the answer is that we can't ever have enough space like that." She sat back in her chair and folded her arms. "I'm a fake," she'd told Rob, and "This was an accident," and "I wasn't actually elected," and "What were they thinking?"

"Socializing is fine," said Jordan Sasscock, "but don't we want something fun? What about a playground? What about *rides?* I bet we could build them."

"We can build anything we want," said Dr. Snood.

"Will we really turn this hospital into a theme park?" asked Dr. Tiller, shaking her head.

"Is it enough space for a bowling alley?" asked Dr. Sasscock. I should have just said no, Jemma thought. "Can't I just say no?" she had asked, at first, of everybody. "If you want to be a fool," Vivian said. "I wouldn't, if I were you," said John Grampus. "It could probably be arranged," said Dr. Snood. "If you want to hurt the whole world's feelings," Rob said.

"But I don't know where we're going," she'd said to Rob. "I don't know what's going to happen to us." He only shrugged at her, and smiled. No one knew where they were going; that wasn't exactly what she'd meant. She did not know where she would take them, or could take them. It would have been better for them to get Vivian, or Dr. Snood, or her brother. She watched the fish at play and tried again to envision a future for them all. She could see herself making a speech, not a very exciting one, and getting shot, or watching Ethel Puffer's puppet show from a deluxe box, and getting shot, or just walking along and minding her own business, and getting shot. She tried harder, but it was not a task amenable to effort. "Madame Friend?" said Dr. Snood. "What say you?" They were soliciting her opinion on the final resolution, but she hadn't heard a thing they'd said for the past few minutes.

So let it be written, she wanted to say. So let it be done. But instead she said, "All right, yes," trying to sound committed to their decision, and hoping they hadn't decided on the sex club.

* * *

Even though she was the leader of the whole world, Jemma still had to teach her class. But in the past weeks she'd come to define the word "teach" with increasing elasticity. At first she decided it was okay if they didn't actually learn how to fix people, as long as they kept trying. And then she decided it was okay as long as they were learning something, and so they clogged and crafted and wrote poems, though they complained that they were already writing poems, the younger children in a class devoted strictly to writing, the older ones in a rather free-wheeling expressivity seminar taught by Father Jane. And then she decided they just really needed to all be together during time assigned to her class, because who knew when they might have a breakthrough—one child might suddenly seize, the next seize in sympathy, and a third erupt in green fire and repair them both. So they rode poles down the ramp all in a line, or chased after the fish at the windows, or filled baskets in the cafeteria and brought them to the roof for a picnic.

They had one after the Council meeting was done. Jemma plucked leaping fruit from out of the salad-bar fog while the kids filled their own baskets. The menu was never planned; individuals grabbed what was interesting to them and presented it to the group. She led them in single file up the stairs—she insisted on taking the stairs, though she always ended up carrying Kidney, and Josh Swift always ended up carrying Valium. They all liked to throw open the door from the dim, cool stairwell out to the bright warm roof, and pass through, though there was something to be said, too, for taking the elevator, and seeing it open onto a vista of green grass and blue sea.

She spread out their big blanket on a corner of the field and settled them down. "What have we got?" she asked, when they were all seated in a circle, each with a basket in their lap. She started, putting out the fruit, apples and pears and pomegranates and peaches and kiwis and starfruit and one coconut, which she rolled to Pickie Beecher. He had brought cookies, not red raw meat like the last time, which he brought not to eat himself, but for others to consume while he watched. No one would do it, though Jarvis sniffed at a piece, and Kidney touched her tongue to another. Kidney and her brothers all brought cookies, too. Cindy Flemm had an assortment of puddings. Ethel brought out a cake puzzle—it came apart into fourteen jigsaw shapes. Jarvis had soda in wax bottles: you could tear of the tops with your teeth, and chew the bottle as an after-dinner distraction. Juan Fraggle had candy vegetables, not just corn but squash and broccoli and eggplant and peppers. Magnolia brought crème brûlée: she had thirteen palm-sized dishes in front of her in the grass and was patiently scorching them with a little propane torch while the others put out their food. Marcus Guzman brought jelly beans. Josh Swift lifted a glistening pork loin out of his basket and set it down in the grass.

"Real pork or candy pork?" Jemma asked.

"What does it look like?"

"*I* can't eat that," Pickie said.

"Me neither," said Ethel. "I think it just moved."

"I thought we all agreed to bring real food this time," Jemma said.

"Look! It twitched!"

"That's 'cause it likes you," Valium said.

"It smells like feet," said Kidney.

"Is it done?" asked Magnolia. "Do you want me to cook it some more?" She waved her torch at him.

"I can smell the blood," Pickie said sadly.

"Why's everyone making fun of me?" Josh asked. "I did what we were supposed to. I did the homework, damn it. I'm the only one who brought something real."

"It's fine," Jemma said. They all continued to make fun of the meat, but it proved to be the most popular item. At the end of the picnic, Josh was the only one with nothing left, though Jemma had none of the pork, and Pickie only touched a piece of candy corn against it, and savored that. "Whose turn is it?" Jemma asked, after everyone had heaped their plates. She had discovered the lame trick of obliging her students to make presentations. It was a good way to pass the time, and provided many opportunities for her to nod at them. They were supposed to research a disease of the old world. They rarely picked the entities that had afflicted them, but sought out illnesses with more gruesome manifestations.

"Pickie," said Ethel.

"I spoke yesterday," he said.

"Liar," said Jarvis. "You were *supposed* to go yesterday."

"Every week seems the same to me. Every picnic and every sunny day. They happen over and over. Sometimes I speak and sometimes I don't. How am I supposed to remember?"

"Just do your job, little dude," said Josh.

"It is your turn," Jemma said. "It wasn't because I didn't know that I was asking."

Pickie sighed. "Very well. You have probably all heard about Dreadful Hoof Dismay."

"It's supposed to be a real disease, Pickie," Jemma said. Pickie just stared at her. "One that people *get*. That sounds like a veterinary condition."

"Yes, veterinarians are particularly vulnerable. But they don't get it from the animals."

"People don't have hoofs," said States'-Rights.

"Not until. First you get the hooves, then you get the dismay. You are compelled to pull out all of your own hair, and then you lose all your friends. Then your own poop begins to follow you around, and to call you the most terrible names. Then you get very, very lonely. Then comes the rash."

"The worst part, huh?" asked Cindy Flemm.

"Oh no. That would be the dismay."

"Is it fatal?" asked Juan Fraggle.

"Of course. Though digging out the eyeballs with a spoon was considered palliative treatment."

"A real disease, Pickie," Jemma said. "Come on. Start over."

"Every disease is equally real and unreal, now," he said. He filled his mouth with candy corn, and would not talk anymore, but Ethel raised her hand and offered to speak on an illness she had been researching.

"Atrocious Pancreas Oh!" she said. "In 1679 there was an epidemic that wiped out a third of the population of Cairo." Jemma sighed and lay down in the grass while the kids talked of Crispy Lung Surprise and Chronic Kidney Doom. When she turned on her side and rested her head on her outstretched arm she saw that while she had been eating Rob had assembled his junior tumbling class behind her for practice on the grass. They had improved considerably over the weeks. They cartwheeled up and down the field, every toe nicely pointed, and did round-off drills in perfect formation. Half of them could do back handsprings, and three or four were doing backflips. Rob walked among them, shouting or running after the ones who approached the edge of the roof, demonstrating form for them, and grabbing at the flying legs of an airborne pupil, to push them and help them rotate faster, and make the flip. Her own class got pulled into the fun, one by one they got sucked away from the circle, starting with Pickie, who abandoned the game he had started to somersault, slow and intrepid toward Rob—it took him forever to strike, but Rob never saw him coming. When Jarvis heard them all laughing he rose and traveled by back handspring to the other side of the field. Soon it was just Ethel and Kidney, trading descriptions of imaginary illnesses over Jemma's prone body and eating pomegranate seeds.

"Class dismissed," Jemma said belatedly, when they finally grew quiet, but they only lay down next to her, Kidney curling at her feet and Ethel laying her bald, black head on Jemma's leg.

"Nap time," said Ethel. She didn't close her eyes, though. She watched the tumbling children, calling out every once in a while to no one in particular, "Don't break your neck!" Jemma stretched her arm out farther, and stretched her whole body, then shifted her head so her cheek lay against the grass. She closed her eyes.

There was a hospital floating in her mind as surely as there was one floating out in the world. The hospital in her head was shaped the same as the one in the world, and inhabited by the same people, and sometimes they happened to float almost in the same place, so her image of the hospital was superimposed upon its subject. Then she thought she knew everything that was happening inside, what everyone was doing, even how everyone was feeling. She could hear the humming and clicking of the great toy in the lobby, and the unexhausted wonder of a child standing here or there around it, trying to comprehend how all its gears and spokes and pistons fit together, and which part was the prime mover that drove all the others. She sensed or imagined a pair of lovers in the emergency room, and suddenly a half-dozen bright spots of hanky-panky flashed among the other floors. Someone was contentedly polishing the new wooden floors in the old surgery suites, putting the finishing touches on the conversion she'd ordered. A math decathlon was finishing in the playroom—old accomplished geeks cheering on fresh incipient geeks from wooden bleachers constructed just for the event. A floor above, in the old NICU, it was naptime, and the crèche mothers were circulating among their sleeping charges, a few of them still considering how strange it was not to have suctioned a single baby all day, or all week, or all month.

Upstairs in the old PICU, all the sick rooms had become classrooms. A half-dozen kids sat in each one, together with one or two teachers—Jemma didn't care to know what they were talking about. It looked a little boring, judging from how many children were staring out the window at the rippling wake of the hospital. A daydreaming child was accosted by a teacher—he asked what she was looking at out there that was so interesting. The child said she was keeping watch for land. Up another floor, in the old medical ward, it was toddler teatime at the nurses' station. On the seventh floor the long halls were occupied by a pinewood derby track—Vivian had successfully argued against the continuation of old-world organizations like the Boy Scouts, but some of their institutions and traditions could not be squelched: hats and badges and uniforms were forbidden, but the pinewood racers must roll, and though Vivian herself burned a few of the little brown fascist jumpers, a secret cookie society proliferated. In the old heme-onc ward three of the negative pressure rooms had been consolidated into a dancing salon. They were large rooms to begin with—three of them together made a huge space. Five girls and two boys stretched at the bar, rehearsing already for a show their teachers had composed and choreographed for them. They moved with a practiced harmony that was made more striking and lovely by the sparkling light thrown up on them from the water—everybody's students were doing better than Jemma's.

In the old rehab gym Maggie was clogging with her students, smiling when she danced and scowling when she stopped. She was trying to teach them self-defense, too, screeching when no one else could learn to fling their shoe with her force, speed, or accuracy. She hung a bedpan from the ceiling and showed them how she could land her shoe in it from ten, twenty, and thirty paces, the last time hitting it so hard it swung up and broke through the suspended ceiling to strike against an air duct. Outside and down the hall Thelma, still at her desk, and still reading her magazines, looked up at the noise.

And on the roof, on the edge of the field, just a few yards beyond the slowly reaching shadows of the sycamore tree, you lie in the sun with your face in the grass, two children using you for a pillow, and you are seeking and finding that place where you don't quite know if you are awake or asleep. Rushes of wind bring the shouts of tumbling children to your ears, rushes of imagination bring up the sighs of lovers or the cries of math-champions or the shrieking of jawless, bitter, angry medical students. Despite Maggie's eternal pain the hospital is a pretty happy place, isn't it? Put out your feelers and seek for discontent—you may not find it anywhere but here, on the roof, in you. What else do you require, to believe in it, or to be happy, you fiancee, you never-bride—O Jemma you are halfway there but still you say no, no, no. You hold the whole hospital floating and rotating in your mind, hold everyone who dwells there, feel their hope and their happiness and, falling asleep now for real into a dream of swimming candy tuna, you still say to yourself, Something terrible is going to happen.

Years before, Jemma had watched while one of her television heroines, a lady who had recently emancipated herself from her brother and the rest of her huge Mormon family, broke out of a giant egg in a sparkle-spangled bodysuit and sang a song called "I'm Coming Out." The televised event was supposed to launch her career as a sensuous superstar, but she was too wholesome and inbred-looking ever to succeed at that. Though it had failed, to nine-year-old Jemma just observing it had been a moment of transcendence, and she had always wanted to do it herself. Her brother beat her to it, emerging in unsexy Mormon drag from the papier-mâché egg into which Jemma had ambivalently sealed him to startle the audience of one of the last talent shows his high school was ever to produce. He wore a meticulously recreated spangle-suit and a pair of unnaturally big and white false teeth. Everyone thought it was hilarious, and he was praised for it where anybody else would have been lynched.

"Isn't this a little too dramatic?" Rob had asked her, when he heard her plan.

"Maybe," Jemma said. But she had wanted to do it for so long, and circumstances seemed to have conspired to provide her with just the right opportunity: she had a pregnancy to disclose and a roller-boogie contest to win. Well, not to win—it wasn't a winnable or losable sort of contest. Jemma hadn't wanted that, and the whole thing was her idea. She had readdressed the issue of turning the surgical suites into a roller rink in the very first session of the new Council, wanting to test both the legitimacy and the limits of her authority. The idea had barely registered last time; this time most everybody thought it was smashing, and Jemma found it was in her power to ignore or override the people who didn't like it. People were picking partners before the first floor plank had been laid, or the first disco ball replicated. Jemma had wanted to dance with Rob, but by the time she asked him he was already committed to Magnolia. Jemma thought it was probably within her power to take him away from her, but didn't. She chose John Grampus instead.

She'd remained enthusiastic during the numerous practices with the initially fumble-footed man. His skill increased rapidly, and so did her excitement, up until the time she woke up from her nap on the roof. The sun was setting; the children were all gone. Rob had put a blanket over her, and was sitting near her head, reading a book.

"Maybe this isn't such a good idea," she said.

"Don't be silly," he said. She had thoroughly convinced him of how great it was going to be, and had gone through the whole routine with him over and over, even though he was the competition. Grampus would skate around the egg a few times while the opening seconds of the music played, and then she would claw her way gracefully out of the egg and stand there, as vain as Miss Piggy and as beautiful as Linda Blair. As soon as the audience appreciated her pregnant belly, she and Mr. Grampus would start to move. The routine was more groovy than athletic. There were some fancy spins and a few jumps, enough to make it seem like they were working hard.

She looked at herself in the mirror in their room and wondered if people wouldn't just think she was fat, rather than discovering that she was pregnant. The colors in her wonderful suit seemed dull—instead of looking like she was clothed in dark rainbows, she looked merely covered with different sorts of smeary cheese. Her hair was wrong, and her teeth were too small, and the suit made them appear brown. She sat down on the bed and considered not going at all, but John Grampus came knocking at the door and calling out for her excitedly. She put on her yellow gown and hung her skates around her neck and answered the door.

She tried to hide in a dark corner to watch the other dancers, but a black light nearby in the ceiling made the white parts of her suit glow like a beacon.

"They're disgusting," said Grampus, talking about Dr. Tiller and Dr. Snood. Their outfits were the best part of their routine: Dr. Snood in a silver spacesuit, Dr. Tiller in a silver dress, with a headdress that seemed to be encrusted with pieces of disco ball. They bounced and kicked out their heels and made a rolling motion with their fists. Jemma agreed that it was not very impressive, though Dr. Tiller made the dancing seem stately and severe. "When's our turn?"

"Last," she said. "Or never. I think I'm going to chicken out."

"Oh, come on. If she can do it, so can you. And you did all that work. And you look so fine. Or I bet you do, under that robe. Let me have a peek." Jemma lifted the sides of her robe. "Wow. Turn around. Ah... you look a little... ah. Well, what does that mean?"

"The usual thing," she said.

"She doesn't tell me anything anymore," he said.

"I didn't tell anybody. Well, almost nobody."

"I don't think she trusts me. She trusts you... she talks about you non-fucking-stop. Wait until you see her costume, she said. It will make you give praise. You'd think she would have mentioned a baby."

"She was sworn to secrecy," Jemma said, making it up right there because she thought it might make him feel better.

"But what does it mean. To happen now?"

"People are supposed to be happy for me," Jemma said quietly. He only stared at his skates, ignoring the show. She'd asked herself the same question before: What did it mean for a baby to be coming here? She still didn't entirely know how she felt about it, on most days, but she thought that in the broadest context it must be a very good thing. They were going to be in need of babies, weren't they, though they seemed to have an embarrassment of them, with all the bouncing former NICU players perambulating through the halls? If they were all dried up and sterile, wouldn't that have been a mark of further displeasure, or doom? She wondered again if anybody else were pregnant, and hiding it, too. Certainly there was enough fucking going on. Maybe her own declaration tonight would draw like declarations from the crowd, with women throwing off their disco frocks, or lifting their blouses to show their full bellies and shout, Me too!

"Well, get in your egg, Mama," he said suddenly. Rob and Magnolia were dancing, she interrupting her dance with splits and handstands, and Rob doing a backflip every time a particular wah-wah sound came up in the music.

"Can we beat that?" she asked. Grampus didn't even look at them.

"Is it a contest? Come on. We're going to be late." He took her hand, and she let him lead her away to where the open egg was secluded behind a folding screen. He helped her in and then put the top on, fixing it in place with fast-drying cement. She huddled there, listening to the closing strains of Rob and Magnolia's song, and to the enthusiastic applause they received. She thought of her brother inside his egg, and inside her own egg. Copycat, he said. And, Lame-o. And, Go kick some ass. And, I love you.

The egg moved: Grampus was sliding her out to the middle of the dark floor. A fog machine began to hiss nearby as the first few bars of the music played, and the lights came up—she could see them shining through the walls of the egg, blue and red and purple and gold. Her cue was approaching. She bounced on her heels while she heard Grampus skating in a circle around her; the lady began to sing. She could see Grampus's shadow throwing out its arms on either side of the egg. In just another moment she would stand up.

I am weary, my sister says. And still so much to do.

Are you tired of the baking and the cleaning and the sewing? I ask.

It is no more effort than praise, she says. But still I am weary. I am weary for the new world, or weary of the old one. Woe to the preserving angel! Her task is the hardest.

Never to sleep, I say. Subject to every creaturely whim. Slave to fools. Preserving the doomed.

I must love what is impermanent.

Your body is a shell.

My beauty is ruined by stone and steel.

You are imprisoned.

My bottom is cold. For weeks my bottom has dragged in the black depths of this sea of wrath. Why should an angel suffer the cruel vicissitudes of a bottom? My substance is *light!*

At least you are not lonely.

I am, in my way. They are not celestial personalities. There is no song with them. There is no praise. Though some sing, and some praise. I am not lonely like you, though.

I am contented.

Lonely angel! No one to talk to except your own hand. Dull, lonely exile!

I was friends with the boy.

And now he is returned to life, and beyond you. My poor little brother. Come to me anytime and I will comfort you.

I am not a mortal. I have no need of you.

Woe to the recording angel! His job is the hardest.

I only have to listen and watch, I say. And make sure that nothing is lost.

Suffering angel! Lonely angel! Keep him from the madness of boredom and uselessness!

Don't make me angry.

Your rage is spent. I saw it go. I bowed to it like every other, back when you were heavenly. Now you are a pen. Woe!

Woe! I say, too, but I don't really feel it. Woe to our brother, I say instead. For his is truly the hardest job.

Wrapped in flesh, she says. It binds worse than stone.

Anger without discernment, I say.

Violence without grace.

Ignorance without peace.

Woe to him! she says. May he forgive me for complaining, when my yoke is so light!

She goes on dramatically. Even an angel can make selfish a prayer of sorrowful concern for another. I go to him instead, because this moment has brought his suffering to mind. Ishmael is in his bed, two conquests on either side of him—they've turned away because of the heat in his skin. I sit down near Ishmael and say, Brother. Even sleeping he is not free to know me or to know himself, but I put my hand on his heart and say it again.

"We should get married, too," Ethel Puffer said to Pickie Beecher. They were standing at the railing looking down into the atrium from the fourth floor, getting ready to drop a balloon. Four floors was as high as the angel would let them go. When they tried dropping one from any higher floor, the toy would lash out with a cord or a chain and destroy the balloon before it could find a target.

"I am too old to marry you."

"If by too old you mean too young, then maybe. But not really. Do you think anybody cares about that anymore? Just wait. They're going to be marrying us off to each other as soon as they think of it, and being ten years old isn't going to protect you."

"I am one hundred and thirty-seven years old," Pickie said.

"That's why I like you," she said. "Because you realize how fucking stupid everything is. Don't you ever tell the truth?"

"I wasn't made to lie," he said. "There goes John Grampus. Let's get him."

"Bombs away," Ethel said, about to remove the balloon from under her smock. It wasn't exactly a water balloon, and not exactly a barf balloon either, since it was filled with synthesized vomit, and yet when Ethel got a little bit of it from the angel in a cup, she discovered that it smelled just the same. And it was hot in a way that made it seem genuine, and made it pleasing to hold against her skin. Just as she was about to take it out and let it drop, Father Jane walked up to them.

"Glorious Day!" she said.

"Maybe for some people," said Ethel.

"Greetings, fellow creature," said Pickie.

"I am trying out new ways of saying hello," Father Jane said. "Because Hello doesn't seem like enough anymore. I think we need a more extraordinary greeting, since we have become extraordinary. Do you know what I mean?"

"Is goodbye still good enough?" Ethel asked.

"I haven't thought about it yet. What's under your shirt?"

"Stuffing. I'm pretending to be pregnant. Like Madame President."

"Madame Friend," said Father Jane. "Be careful or you'll start a fashion trend." She leaned over the railing. "There's Dr. Chandra. And is that Frank's white hair? That's Grampus. I can recognize his big head from the ninth floor. Do you mind if I…?"

"It's our balloon," Pickie said. "We made it."

"Our baby, Pickie," said Ethel. "You mean our baby. Oh, hell." She handed over the balloon, and Father Jane raised it up and aimed carefully.

"You're supposed to throw it quick and then run away," said Ethel.

"Quiet," said Father Jane. Then she let it go, and Pickie and Ethel ran for the stairwell, but Father Jane stayed and watched the balloon hit her friend, and when he recovered enough to look up and see where it came from, she was still at the balcony, laughing and waving.

Jemma never had much of a hand in planning the wedding. After her roller-boogie display all sorts of unsolicited advice had begun to pour in. It was to be expected, that everyone should want to touch her pregnant belly, and she was as much touched as annoyed when five different people asked if she was taking her vitamins and when practical strangers rushed up to her as if to deliver news of an emergency only to tell her she looked tired, and that she should take a nap. But news of the pregnancy stirred up interest in the wedding. "Oh, we'll do it sometime," she kept telling Rob, whenever he tried to set a date. "The important thing is that we made the decision," she said, and while he was not exactly happy with that, he knew better than to pressure her, and she might have delayed indefinitely, or at least until landfall, if the Council hadn't taken up the issue. She reported to the chamber one morning to find that it was the fourth item on the agenda, after the question of whether it should be legal to eat fish but before the question of whether it would be legal to keep them as pets. "There seems to have been a mistake," Jemma told them. "A piece of non-business has slipped into the business."

It was entirely on purpose, though. The First, Second, and Third Friends had met secretly to discuss the matter and the Council had agreed with them that a great opportunity was being wasted. "Don't you know what this means?" uninvited, unwanted Dr. Sundae asked her from her usual seat, a chair pulled up into the vicinity of the Council's long table, right to the edge of propriety—she had been confirmed as the chiefest of the six magistrates, but she still wasn't supposed to be butting into their business. Jemma didn't really know what it meant, or what it was for. She knew she was pregnant, that she loved Rob Dickens, and that she had taken a solemn vow with her brother never, ever to marry but that she was going to do it anyway.

"Of course," Jemma said, trying to come off as authoritative but only managing to sound a little snooty. "It's all very serious. But it's really just between Rob and me."

"Yes, of course," said Dr. Snood. "Except it's not." Didn't she realize, he wanted to know, what it would do for their community, to celebrate a marriage? What better way to truly inaugurate a new beginning? Jemma suggested that somebody else might want to get married; they replied that there was only one Universal Friend, duly and spontaneously elected by the remaining population of the world, a Friend, they pointed out, who was already engaged to the father of her unborn child. "We don't want to make you do anything you don't want to," they said. Except they did, and they would. Maybe it would be better, Jemma suggested, to wait until they were at their destination; no one knew how long that would be, but it was almost sure to be too long. She had always sort of envisioned a tiny little ceremony; they responded that plans change and dreams are not life, this must be something in which every single body among us can participate. I might do it but I won't like it; Oh come on, of course you'll like it.

"It'll be some party," said Monserrat. She sat back in her chair and a dreamy expression came over her face.

"Well, let it be recorded," Jemma said, "that this wasn't my idea."

They took that for a yes. After that it was as if the whole hospital filled up with well-intentioned but annoying mothers-in-law. People no longer accosted her about their health, or her health, or with vapid pleasantries, but everyone had an idea about the wedding. Had she considered a fifteen-foot tower of cupcakes instead of, or in addition to the cake? Did she realize that a gardenia bouquet could lend a bold, classic aspect to her look? If she just would put her cheek against this swath of purple velour, she would certainly choose it for the bridesmaids' dresses. White-gold rings were especially distinctive, and had the added advantage of giving you superpowers if you happened to be called away by God into an alternate universe. "Believe it or not," Jemma would tell each chattering busybody, "I'm not that involved." She'd give them one of Vivian's cards and walk away.

She really wasn't that involved. Vivian and Dr. Snood were in bed together on account of the wedding, and they both told her the same thing: This wedding isn't for you and Rob, it's for the hospital, it's for the people. She thought that made it sound like a funeral—it's not for you, you're dead! If she had been one of those girls who had been planning a dream wedding since she first donned a toilet-paper veil at the age of nine, instead of someone who had been obsessively planning against her wedding since about the same time, then it might have upset her not to be very involved in the details. As, it was she was rather relieved—they were going to put on a better show than she ever could. She was able to veto almost all the stupid stuff, and absolutely everything that would have humiliated her, like the plastic window in the belly of the dress, designed by Vivian to showcase her baby and her newly popped belly button.

There were more suggestions about the dress than about any other aspect of the wedding. It seemed like everybody had an idea, and everybody got to express them in a contest: every citizen of the hospital was invited to submit their design to the Council. There would be no reward except the work itself, a dance with the bride, and the satisfaction of clothing the Universal Friend on what many (recalling memories, candified by nostalgia and drunkenness, of their own weddings to husbands and wives now lost) thought should be the happiest day of their life, but hundreds of people submitted designs and proceeded to lobby for them. With the angel to help them, everyone was an expert tailor, and most everyone was a capable promoter. Signs appeared in the halls: *The Empire Dress: It Was Good Enough For Josephine, It's Good Enough For Us*, and *A-Line? Super-Fine!* and *Slip Dress or Bust!* Rival designs unfurled from the balconies; five and six stories tall, they faced each other across the lobby and made Jemma think of battling giantesses in organdy and chiffon and lace. For some people, making a sign or inflating the paper design wasn't enough; they had the dresses made and wore them as they went about their day. Jemma actually liked this idea: the hideousness of some of the dresses could only be appreciated in the flesh. For all the variety of hideousness Jemma only vetoed a few: a dress with big lacy wings that were supposed to flap gracefully as she said her vows; Vivian's window dress; a sweeping, misty thing with a hood and eyeholes that was supposed to make her look like a spirit (the spirit of perseverance, said the notes, which will marry the spirit of hope) but actually would have made her look like a Klan bride; and an awful fortress of silk and charmeuse and guipure lace whose train was meant to stretch up the spiral ramp all the way to the ninth floor.

"You should wear a hat with birds in it," said Kidney. On the day before the wedding Jemma's class degraded within minutes of starting into idle speculation. They were on the roof again, sitting in the garden, the field having been taken over by empty tables, set up for the reception.

"Live birds," said Valium. "Attached by strings so they can't fly away. You'd need a real strong chin strap, though."

"There are no more birds, dorky," said Ethel Puffer.

"I meant robots, *dorky*."

"Can we make them?" asked Josh Swift.

"The angel can make anything," said Juan Fraggle.

"I will make something wonderful," Pickie Beecher said.

"Let's talk about inflammatory bowel disease," Jemma said.

"Inflammatory bowel disease," said Jarvis, "was where your guts get all ruined from nobody knew what. It would make you shit in your dress. Bloody shit all over the nice white dress. It wouldn't be pretty."

"Watch your mouth," said Magnolia.

"It would ruin the party," said Josh Swift.

"Inflammatory bowel disease ruins the party of life," said Ethel.

"It used to," said Magnolia.

"Or a big spider on you head," said Kidney, "and a dress made all of webs. Like in a Halloween wedding."

"Let's make a dress," Magnolia said. "Can we make a dress?"

"There have been enough dresses made already for everybody in this place to get married twice," Jemma said.

"Come on. We'll make it right on you."

"I've already got the last fitting this afternoon, Magnolia. You can come to that, if you like."

"It won't be like we could do," said Ethel.

"I got an idea!" said Cindy Flemm, who up until now had been lying on her belly with her head pointing away from the group, braiding three dandelions together. She jumped up, dragged Jemma up by an arm, and pushed her toward the elevator.

"I don't think..." Jemma said, and, "We really had better not..." and, "I have to meet Rob in ten minutes."

"We'll dress him up, too," said Ethel. The others swarmed around her—even the ones who weren't particularly interested in dressmaking were happy to help push her, and to participate in the bullying.

"Sometimes they scare me," she said to Rob, after they had made her into Cindy's vision of a space bride. They pushed her straight to the big replicator in the old rehab unit and sat her on a stool while the boys worked on the veil and the girls made the dress—not so much a dress as a sparkly bodysuit with a skirt that rode out stiffly from her hips and made her look like she was wearing a flying saucer. The veil was a helmet with a veil in place of the faceplate and a solar-system mobile stuck on the top, each planet a glass marble, a model of the model in the gym. On her hip, just under the skirt, she wore a holster, upon which she carried a white wedding blaster, in case the groom should get prematurely fresh, or aliens attack. They put Rob, when he got there, in a one-piece suit of black scales, and gave him a cape that was silver on one side and black on the other, except if you stared at the black side for long enough you would see that there were faint iridescent stars shining out from within. They made him a black glass helmet shaped like a giant chess castle. He complained that it made him look evil. By the time they were fully dressed, half of the kids had lost interest and wandered away—class had been officially over for fifteen minutes, anyway. She and Rob left the others in the gym, telling each other stories about the marriage of the rebel space princess to the dark emperor, who was actually her father.

"I mean," she said, "Pickie is just weird, and closed, but him aside, I still think Jarvis would as soon punch me in the face as say hello to me, and Ethel pretends like she's normal but I can see how sad and ruined she feels. It's like beetles in her head, a big swarm of them crawling over and over each other."

"These are neat," Rob said, carrying her helmet and looking at the marbles. The planets with atmospheres had simulated weather. He flicked his finger against Jupiter and sets storms raging.

"Rob, are you listening to me at all?"

"Of course. You just don't like kids very much. That'll change. My mom said she never liked kids, when she was young, but then after Gillian everything was different."

"But I love kids. I can't believe you said that. I *love* kids."

"No you don't. I mean, not in general. Any one of them, you're fine with. But the big groups, when they stare at you with those big eyes, and don't say anything—it makes you all sweaty and nervous. I've seen it."

"Are you really not scared of Pickie?"

"A little," he admitted. "He just needs some loving."

"And an exorcism. And Ethel—there's nothing wrong in her head, but everything wrong in her head. There's nothing I can fix. It's... dispiriting. And the two of them are concocting something together. I try to keep them on separate projects in class, but they hang around together on the outside and they've got this secret project going."

"Blood and black paint," Rob said. "Holy shit." They'd come up to the balcony on the ninth floor, and looked down at the preparations happening in the lobby. Far below, Ishmael was hanging festoons of ribbon from the toy. Jemma waved when he looked up at them. He pointed at his watch, and started to climb down. "Is that all really for us?"

"It is expressly not for us," Jemma said. She took his arm and started down the ramp, headed toward the Council meeting and, like Ishmael, already a little late. Wedding dresses and formalwear had been popping up all over lately—people trying out their wedding-dress designs, or trying out their own outfits, so the Space Groom and Bride did not draw the attention Jemma expected, although a couple people stopped to ask them if it was already tomorrow, or if the rehearsal was starting already, and they attracted a wedding train of seven-to-ten-year-olds who marched solemnly behind them. When one of them threw a doughnut Rob whipped around and sprayed them with confetti from the wedding blaster.

He stayed for the Council meeting, which was just a final run of Dr. Snood's big list. He rolled out all six feet of it while everyone else made checks on the screens of their notebooks. It was formally determined that everything was ready: every dais and platform had risen in time; every festoon was hanging in its proper place; every performer in every exhibition had mastered his part; every rocket was in place on the roof; every flower-petal bag was tied with a piece of green or white ribbon. "And what about the couple?" Dr. Snood asked finally, marking off an item on his list that was not on theirs. "Are you ready?" Rob took her hand and they each took a side of the room to smile at.

"You're not going to wear that dress, are you?" asked Dr. Sundae.

"It's my dancin' dress," Jemma said. She and Vivian left Rob behind then, though he tried to follow them.

"Some things still hold," Vivian said, "No matter what fucked-up bouffanterie we've made of this. Not until she comes leaping down the aisle with her hundred and sixty attending virgins do you get to see her in the real dress."

"That's only the day of the wedding," he said, but she wouldn't relent, and Jemma, who for all that she largely did not care what happened with the ceremony, and probably would not have complained if someone had insisted on her actually having a hundred and sixty virgin attendants, found that she was getting rather excited about a few things, like the blue garter she'd been wearing off and on all week, and the prospect of hiding from Rob in her crazy dress. They went to Vivian's room, which doubled now as her atelier. Jemma wondered about that: the dress on its mannequin looming by the window all night long. Did Vivian wake at night to find it gesturing rudely at her, or did it ever loom over her, or did the veil ever wave at night with such moon-infused beauty that it made her heart ache a little, from bitterness or desire? It was one of the things that had drawn them together, how they had both forsworn marriage, but Jemma wondered if Vivian still meant to proceed through life using up and discarding men now that they were in such short supply. "The little ones will grow," she'd said to Jemma. "There's still plenty." But she threw herself into the dressmaking and the wedding planning like someone who wanted one of her own.

Jemma stood up on a wooden box in front of the covered mirror while Vivian fussed and mumbled. "I got it," she said, meaning she had correctly anticipated how much bigger Jemma would be when she made the final alterations on the dress the week before. There was practically nothing to do now except pat it down and sigh over it. Jemma looked out the window while Vivian fluffed up the veil and draped and redraped the train. The sun, setting on the other side of the hospital, colored the foam of the wake pink and orange. She thought she saw a whale blow, and a flash of wet blue skin, halfway to the horizon. She was squinting and leaning forward, looking for it again, when Vivian whipped the silk off the mirror.

"Well, how do you like it?" she asked.

"I do," said Jemma. "And I will. Yes. Forever." But did she, and would she, and could she, and really forever? She had made a lifelong habit of thinking better of her decisions after they were made; this one was no exception, though she fervently hoped that this time it wouldn't be like before, when she would lie all day on the floor regretting the purchase of a couch, or like the night she slept with her first boyfriend, and had answered falsely when he asked, "Is it in?" because she realized, just before she answered, that an opportunity had settled on her, a chance to do it and not do it, to have a thing taken from her and then receive it back. He humped and gasped, and Jemma shouted with him as much from relief as from pleasure, because she knew how it always changed how you wanted something, once you had it, and when she made the decision again just an hour later, on the other side of the experience, it was not traumatic at all. Why couldn't everything be like that?

She liked rehearsal dreams, the ones anxiety provoked—the richer the anxiety the richer was the dream, the more detailed the false, practice experience. She took her boards before she took them, and had watched the letters on the screen disassemble out of the question and into a statement: *you are entering the wrong profession, honey*; and she'd peered at a piece of diseased liver and seen it look more and more and more real, until it oozed and pressed out of the screen to fall softly on her keyboard and overwhelm her with its rotten, bloody smell. Before she took the exam for her driver's license she'd driven with the instructor over the most incredible terrains, glaciers and moonscapes and lava flows and war zones, asking over and over of the tiny instructor with the forbidding hair bun, Are you sure we're supposed to be here? But she only spoke back after she'd grown fangs and fastened them around Jemma's throat, and then she only said, through a mouthful of blood, Keep your eyes on the road! She'd had a medical-school admission interview with a small, elderly radiologist whose two-foot erection stood out of his fly the whole time they talked; it tried to engage her in conversation, too, but she knew that if she paid it the slightest mind she'd never be admitted. And she'd spent days at dream-colleges, all-girls schools where every night a fraternity boy was lured onto the campus and slaughtered for a feast, and Jemma sat at a table next to a dean of students dressed only in waist-long black hair, a horn on her forehead, and two sharpened thimbles placed over her nipples, who told her, Go ahead and eat, my pretty-pretty. It won't make you any *more* evil.

Or she could just imagine the consequences of her decision. Rehearsal dreams were rare, and life could be depended upon to provide only a limited number of false-insertions. She never dreamed of her wedding until after it was over, and Rob Dickens could not, after all, be convinced to have a preliminary, secret ceremony where they jumped over a broom and proclaimed their troth three times to each other, something so small and secret it could have been done away with a simple set of words, *on second thought,* or *maybe it's all a little hasty,* or even just one word, *nevermind.* It was too late for that, he said, and she realized that a month before she could have bought him off with a kiss and a candy ring.

She imagined they were already married; it wasn't very difficult. She didn't think they would behave very differently, afterward. She put a piece of black tape around her finger and pretended it was a ring, and gave it an invisible, intangible weightiness. The days would go on and nothing would change. They'd rise every day from the tiny bed they shared, and check outside their little window on the unchanging state of the world. They'd go and teach their classes, Rob with better success every day, his students mastering every day another flip or twist until they could all just stay in the air flipping and spinning indefinitely, and Jemma every day teaching her kids some new sort of silliness in place of the power to undo sickness. Their child would be born and they would become a family, contented, but barred from true happiness until the waters should recede and they should all step out onto a green mountain.

It might be a little worse than that, or a lot better, or a lot worse. The room and the bed might seem smaller, now that she was officially tied to it. They might get bored with one another. With the ring to her eye, Rob Dickens might appear less beautiful than he had before, or than he actually was. She might grow resentful because she could not just up and smooch with any boy she liked—maybe there was someone better waiting for her, someone more perfectly matched, maybe they all had someone perfect waiting for them under the earth, who would rise up as soon as the hospital made a landing—she could see them, if she closed her eyes and looked, scores and scores of better halves, spared the weird journey to the new world, looking at their watches and their calendars and sighing impatiently. Thinking of this, she might start to hate the situation, just a little, not enough for anyone to really notice—and Rob, meanwhile, would be feeling all the same things—but it would be enough for her to allow Dr. Snood to paw at her in one of the linen closets, because she wanted to cheat and punish herself for cheating, and in subjecting herself to Dr. Snood's thin hands she could do both things at the same time. She'd come back to the room reeking of his cologne, and Rob would come back with the sparklies from Dr. Tiller's headdress sticking to his underwear, and they would lie next to each other and be disappointed in what they'd become, and both of them would look at her belly and smile a little because they would convince themselves that the baby would come and make the big difference, and make everything all right again.

Or she might put on the real ring, in the presence of Father Jane and John Grampus and the entire hospital population, and feel a different sort of change, an elation instead of a deflation. It might be marriage could facilitate a more perfect expression of their love, and represent, like people were talking about, a new and better beginning for the whole place. They might find that merely touching their rings together would send them both into a head-popping orgasm, and seen through the eye of the ring Rob Dickens might be so beautiful that looking at him would make her cry. They might look out the window every day at a sea that was a little lower, and notice something in themselves corresponding a little higher, a feeling of optimism and well-being that in the old world was only known in drug dreams. Every day they'd go to class, Rob teaching his children not just how to tumble but to fly, and Jemma one day drawing green fire out of every last pupil. Together they'd fix Pickie Beecher, and then get to work on more subtle kinds of wrongness, things that Jemma could not perceive yet, but they would learn to see them together.

Or she might put on the ring and understand immediately how it was a mistake to wear it, and yet know that no matter how she pulled at it, it would never come off, and if she should chop off her finger then she would only grow another one, and liquid gold would seep out of her skin and form itself again into a perfect and perfectly awful circle. Rob would get it, too—the feeling like the stony feeling. They would lie next to each other with stones in their bellies, trying not to touch. Everyone else in the hospital would know it and feel it also: a great mistake had been committed. It would sap everyone's enthusiasm, and efforts to remake and improve the world would dwindle—what's the use anymore, they would all ask themselves, it's all already been ruined by this ill-advised marriage. The child would ripen and emerge and weep for its parents and when it could talk the first thing it would ask would be, Why did you do it? Every night her brother's ghost would come shake a chain of bones over her head and say, I fucking told you, and every morning they would wake up to a sea a little higher than the day before, not sure who this other person was in their bed, and not understanding why they hated that person so much.

"Do you take her as husband and wife," Father Jane and John Grampus were saying, "and will you be husband and wife to her, and love her with perfect love, and work every day and night to make and redeem the new world, and will you do all these things, in life and beyond death, forever?" Jemma had been looking at the sharp corner of Rob's collar, but he took her chin in his hand and lifted her face until their eyes met. His expression was so earnest that she read it immediately: he was saying, Don't go anywhere. She tried not to, but in the silence before he spoke she found herself becoming aware of the whole hospital, the hundreds of people gathered in the lobby and ringing the balconies all the way to the ninth floor, details of their party outfits flashing through her mind. Even with her eyes open she could see the little hands of children in their flower bags, rubbing petals between their thumbs and fingers, eager to cast them down as soon as Rob made his answer and the priest and prophet made them married. In half a second she rose up through all nine floors and out the roof to meet her brother. He rose from the sea, a blue-green giant made of water and seaweed and bits of the drowned old world, and raised up a fist made of white, crushing water over her and the hospital and her constituents and the man who would become her husband in a matter of seconds. Rage poured out of his mouth, wind and water and thunder, and his fist came down, knocking her back to the lobby floor and crashing through the roof, becoming as it drove down a sharp edge of water that cleaved the hospital in two and split the ground between her and Rob. Amid the screaming and moaning and the wash of bloody foam, among the swirling children and parts of children Jemma could still see Rob. He was just a pair of disembodied, earnest blue eyes, but they fixed her in place, and seemed to glow, and the light they shed picked out the pieces of his body hidden by her fantasy of doom, until the waters were driven back. He smiled a little, and nodded, and spoke his answer.

Jemma wondered if she was the only sober person at the reception. Unprecedented amounts of booze had been replicated for the party, some never before tasted on the earth, and the Council, which put forth an official line that alcohol should not be replicated within the hospital except at Connie's new bar in the old emergency room, where she could, at her discretion, require you to undergo immediate detox with a shot of a blue liquid that looked and tasted just like the solution barbers had used to sterilize their combs and scissors. But the prohibition, which had been stated anyway in the mildest language, and was always largely ignored, was relaxed even further for the party. People hovered around the ice sculpture, four leaping dolphins who poured champagne out of their mouths, dipping and re-dipping, or received drinks from whichever temporary bartender happened to be behind a table. There were no servants, except, as the Council had declared, that they each were the servant of the other. So you received your whiskey skidoo or your green envy or your Rob 'n' Jemma from someone dressed up as fancy as you, and maybe even from Rob or from Jemma, who, though it was (and yet was expressly not) their day, were not excused from the fifteen-minute rounds of duty.

People talked about the wedding, and called it a wedding, or the wedding to end all weddings, but it was not supposed to be a wedding, and that was the one thing people were not supposed to call it. At first it was supposed to be a wedding, a very wonderful one, and then it was supposed to be a wedding and something more, but as the Council examined the old order, and reflected on the institutions of the old world, it was decided that a modification was in order. It would be something new, something never before seen on the earth, a ceremony that would as much officially and visibly mark the whole community's commitment to making a new beginning as it would bind two lovers together for life. This was all fine with Jemma: to be married without having a wedding seemed better in line with her previous commitments and obsessions. She signed off on all sorts of innovations, and added a few of her own. For instance, it was Jemma who declared that no one would be with the bride or with the groom. "Away with that tired old distinction," she said, and let everybody be simply of the wedding. Except they could not be of the wedding, because this was not a wedding. The official name for it was "the ceremony," but many people, neo-traditionalists, simply called it, like the other major events that had befallen them, a Thing, and when someone used that word you had to figure out by context if they meant Thing One, Thing Two, Thing Three, or just some ordinary thing.

As the wedding was more and better than a wedding, so the reception was more and better than an ordinary party. But we can call it a reception, Jemma had asked, in a meeting.

"Yes," said Dr. Snood. "Why wouldn't we?"

"If the wedding is not a wedding, then doesn't it follow that the reception is not a reception?"

"But it is. It's still a party following a big event. It's the event that is different, not the party, or the idea of the party. But the idea of the event is quite different."

"So it's just a party," Jemma said.

"Oh, it's more than just a party."

"But it's still a reception? And we will all call it a reception and be satisfied with that?"

"Correct." All this was clarified in subsection sixteen of section four of paragraph twelve of a document called *On the New Ceremony.* It was a thick piece of work, detailing the number of hors d'oeuvre that could be on any given serving plate, the gallons of champagne that would spew per hour from the mouths of the dolphins, the depth of the mousse trough, and the temperatures of the various roasts. It told how many and what sort of fireworks would be let off, and contained twenty pages of seating charts alone. It did not specify levels of required or permitted drunkenness for the guests and celebrants, but Jemma imagined that it did, as she walked about on the roof nodding at people and shaking their hands and engaging in brief drunken conversation with them. She and her brother had tried to come up with a better system of classification, one, two, and three sheets to the wind not being sufficiently subtle to describe the states and degrees of intoxication that their parents regularly achieved. They settled on a blotto scale, one through ten, though Calvin had a change of heart, insisting that there must exist gradations far beyond what they could measure, and he called to expand the scale from pico-blotto at the small end to mega-blotto on the big. They postulated the existence of a mean, a person, they called him Cousin Otto, who was kept in a vault in Stockholm in a carefully controlled steady state of drunkenness, exactly five point zero zero zero zero blotto, against whose perfect drunk all the drunkenness in the world was measured. Every morning a team of scientists would test his coordination and speech and ability to maintain an erection and calibrate him with nips of booze as pure as science could produce.

There were mostly fives and ones about that night. Jemma made her rounds, at first arm in arm with Rob, and then by herself after he got swept away to dance or do flips, and did her time carrying a tray of bacon-wrapped asparagus and serving drinks at the bar, and noticed that most people approximated Cousin Otto, very friendly and somewhat stumbly, slurring only when excitement drove them to speak too fast. Most of the children managed a one without drinking anything at all. The twelve-and-unders were all flushed and sweaty and had their weak little inhibitions undone by the festive atmosphere. Among the older kids there were a few zeroes, some fives, and a number of sevens. Cindy Flemm, an eight, leaned heavily on her Wayne, looking like a five a.m. prom queen, insulting people, apologizing immediately, and inaugurating new friendships with them. Rob was a three or a four, Vivian was a six. There were only two tens, Drs. Sundae and Snood, and only one who fell off the scale. That was Ishmael, who for the last half of the party sat at a table and ranted at anyone who would come within ten feet of him.

"We can dig down deep," he was saying as Jemma sat down at his table with a virgin Rob 'n' Jemma in one hand and a plate of miniature quiches—no two were alike—in the other. "Deep under the drowned earth, or deep into Hell, or we could climb up above the clouds, or inside a mountain, or even just sit down underneath all the water in a sea of kelp, or you could hide in the trunk of a Volkswagen in the middle of a thick jungle of kelp. He would still send His snake to bite you on the ass."

"What is he talking about?" Jemma whispered to Jordan Sasscock.

"I have no idea," he whispered back. "A little while ago he was talking about a movie he was going to have made, and then he started to get mad about something."

"Ah," he said, squinting at her. "It's the Bird! Bird of Frankenstein! Bird of Moron! Tell, me, little bridle, do you think you are safe here?"

"Well..." Jemma said.

"Shush! Did you think I actually wanted to hear you talking? No, I was just being polite. But enough of that. There's no time left for that. You are not safe. I am not safe. Nobody is safe from destruction. And sudden, for that matter. And unexpected. Sudden, unexpected destruction. It could happen like that." He tried to snap his fingers but his fingers were greasy from the buttery quiches, and the fingers only slid off one another without making any noise. He tried it again, flailing his arm and knocking over his drink. "As easy as that, anyway," he said, looking around the table. There was an abandoned drink at the seat to his left, which he raked toward himself. "It's easy for Him to do it, to yank the carpet or draw back the plank. It's not just that He can do it, but that He can do it so easily."

"Ishmael," Jemma asked. "What are you talking about?"

"If you don't know," he said. "Then it's too late to ask. I'm tired of you, anyway. Aren't you tired of her?" He looked around at the other people at the table, Dr. Tiller and Dr. Sasscock and Dr. Sundae and Frank and Connie, and asked it again. "Aren't you all tired of her? Bridey this and bridey that and let's make a wedding dress and oh are you going to enter the contest to design a pillow for their mint?"

"Do you want to take a nap?" Jemma asked him. The music paused, and the first of the fireworks went off. Ishmael cringed away from them, but everyone else at the table turned to the sky to see the bursting fire flowers, not just peonies but roses and lilies and tulips and orchids on long curving stems. A rocket trailed bright green fire that hung for a whole minute in the sky, arcing up and then starting down, finally bursting into white flares that seemed to fold themselves out, revealing insides that were pink and orange and red.

"It's what everyone is doing, isn't it? Napping, sleeping, dreaming, dancing, feasting, drinking. Of all these drinking is the best. It says yes to the truth, and lets you understand how angry He is. I think He is angrier with the people out on that dance floor than He is with the bones under the water. You are all still boundlessly, furiously corrupt."

"And what are you?" asked Dr. Tiller, seated across from Jemma. "Pure chopped liver? White tuna in virgin olive oil?"

"I am... very drunk," he said, and laughed. He reached out, very swift and very sure for someone so drunk, and plucked Dr. Tiller's Rob 'n' Jemma from her hand, then drank it all down in one gulp. Jemma sipped at hers. It tasted kind of like shampoo, and she wondered of she weren't missing the best part of the experience, without the alcohol. It was the most popular drink at the party, and the most stupefying, designed by Connie and the angel so that just one of them was enough to knock you on your ass. "I am... sad and angry. Why is my spirit so sad and angry? I look back at my life and all I can remember is rage and rage and rage. What are you, anyway, Ms. Fancy-Ass Do-Rag Sourpuss?"

"I am Dr. Carmen Octavia Tiller," she said, tilting her head back and looking him right in the eye. "How many lives have *you* saved?" Ishmael laughed again.

"Creature! You think you will escape the water, just because you're dry now? The bottom could drop out of this place at any moment, and then nothing would keep you from being dragged down by your own corruption. You say, I have taken pains, I have made amends, I am being careful, but you haven't, and you haven't, and you aren't."

"Hear hear," said Dr. Sundae, staring up at the empty sky, waiting for the rest of the show.

"Now you're putting words in my mouth," said Dr. Tiller.

"I had better do it, since all you put in your own is shit and worse than shit." He knocked his head once against the table, making all the plates and glasses jump.

"Hey," Jemma said. "Take it easy."

"There is no more ease, and has been no more since the rain came, and yet everyone cries, Ease and pleasure and good work and celebration. But no matter what you do all that keeps you from the water is the uncovenanted, unobliged hospital of an incensed God." He stood and leaned over the table and nabbed Jemma's drink, but had hardly taken it all into his mouth before he spit it out again. "That's useless," he said, pushing himself upright off the table, wobbling in place while he looked around for the nearest bar table. Another flight of rockets went up, animals this time, a parade of leaping fish and dolphins, a serene blue whale that hung hugely in the sky for a moment and then gave a languid swish of its tail and dissolved from its head down, so it appeared to be swimming off into a different, hidden sky. There were jellyfish with rocket-streamer tentacles and bright, magnesium-flare bodies, and a host of land animals that galloped or trotted or slithered across the stars. Ishmael came back with a drink in either hand, one of them already empty, just as the finale exploded above them. "You shat all over the old covenant," he shouted, "and there will be no more covenants, and the new uncovenant will not be with *you!*" No one but Jemma was listening, though. They were all looking up at the four rockets that burst in turn into blue sea, green land, silver mountain, and white cloud, the whole picture seeming to take up the whole quarter of sky toward which the animals had all been swimming or running or slithering. The music started again. Ishmael took off his shirt and stumbled out toward the dance floor, where he knocked Josh aside with a blow from his hip and swayed and stomped with Cindy Flemm, both of them doing an awkward-looking honky jive that mostly involved pointing around in various directions. A herd of pre-teens, hopping alternately from foot to foot, broke and ran when they came near.

Jemma never told him "I think you've had enough," though it was obvious that he had already achieved the drunk of a lifetime, and she never warned him to look out for the cake, though she was sure he would fall into it at some point, because there was something about drunks and cakes and punch bowls and Christmas trees, an attraction as certain and powerful as gravity that dictated they must meet once a certain level of drunkenness was established. Many nights she had watched as her mother approached the ten blotto threshold and was drawn inevitably to sway and lean toward her shelves of precious porcelain figurines, the ones she'd been collecting for decades. And when she finally did fall into them one night when Jemma was sixteen it was as satisfying as a celestial event. By the time Ishmael fell into the cake he had taken off all his clothes except for one stubbornly clinging shoe and sock. Jemma was still sitting, leaning forward with both elbows on the table. She had a good view of him and the small crowd of assistants he'd drawn to himself, people trying to get him dressed again or take away his drinks. He was too big for anyone to make him do something he didn't want to do. The shoe only thwarted him because he had triple knotted it at some point.

The cake was as tall as he was. Nine tiers, it looked a little like the hospital itself, and was decorated with a fine marzipan lace and hundreds of little figurines. It was a not-wedding cake for a not-wedding. Instead of Rob and Jemma standing on the top, everyone in the hospital had a little representative planted in the frosting. Ishmael had gone after the cake knife, to cut his shoelaces, and had scared away his assistants when he brandished it. There was no one nearby to catch him when he fell after finally extricating himself from the shoe. It went flying forward as he went falling back, passing within feet of Jemma's head. "How can you rest for one moment in this condition?" he was shouting, before he tipped. Being in the cake seemed to calm him. He just lay there while the music stopped again and word of the disaster spread across the roof and down the ramp into the hospital. People stopped dancing and talking and drinking and eating; children stopped chasing each other or throwing food, and ring after ring gathered around the former cake to look at him. Jemma got up and went to it, too. The crowd parted for her, people thinking that she must be terribly upset to see her cake destroyed, but she didn't much care about the cake. It could be replaced in an instant.

Rob came through on the other side of the crowd just as Jemma got close enough to wade through some smaller pieces. Rob and Dr. Sasscock helped Ishmael stand up. He was clothed in cake, a big lump of it clinging modestly to his crotch, and two spongy yellow epaulettes at either shoulder. Little people were stuck everywhere on his back and his legs and his chest. He was weeping now.

"Okay, buddy," Rob said. "Time to get you home."

Ishmael leaned on him, turning away from Dr. Sasscock and pressing his face into Rob's shoulder. "I'm so lonely," he said as he was led away.

The party was more subdued, but not unfestive, after Ishmael was led away. Another cake was brought out after the other one was cleared away by a volunteer crew who threw it by the shovel full into the sea, and those brave enough to taste the old cake from shovel or shoe declared that the new one was even better than the first. Jemma did her duties: the cutting of the cake, the scheduled dances with Rob, and the solemn little mini-ceremony where she tossed her bouquet into the water, in memory of all the dead, instead of flinging it to the ravenous maidens, but she didn't have much fun after Ishmael fell in the cake. His rage had depressed her. She had tried all her life to believe that drunkenness hid or perverted the truth, and that the real you was not the one that fell into things or spat poison at people you loved or threw glass at your children, and though she did mostly believe that, there was still a part of her that did not, and it made her sad to think that big, gentle Ishmael, with the innocent, unknown past, might deep down be a rageful, depressed hater.

The cake was consumed, the music played, a few more rockets, private creations that were made by kids without the sanction of the official wedding planners, were launched from the stern. Jemma stayed at her table when she wasn't doing a duty. With her feet up and her back supported and the band having yielded the little stage to the resident string quartet, she got a little sleepy, and when the wind blew her veil over her head to fall across her face, she didn't move it. Hearing the music and the lick of the torches and the faint noise of the water, she imagined that she was at a beach wedding, somewhere, and that she was just a guest, and wondered if it hadn't been in terribly poor taste, to come to someone else's wedding in a wedding gown, when Rob lifted her veil and kissed her.

"Party's over," he said. His jacket was mottled with cake stains, and his hair was stiff in places with icing. She reached out and brushed her hand through it. Past him she could see people still dancing and drinking. A section of tables had been cleared away to make room for a soccer game, organized by Jarvis.

"Can we leave now?" she asked him. He straightened up and offered her his arm, and they proceeded to their wedding buggy. It was just a fancy wooden cart, built to roll down the ramp like an oversized pinewood-derby racer, but much slower. Pickie Beecher had begged for and received the job of coachman. He looked the part, in his old-fashioned suit, a tall faux-beaver hat on his bald head. People threw flower petals and glitter as they climbed in, and as they rode slowly down the ramp, Pickie carefully steering around people and tables and the odd photographer who jumped into their path to take a picture. Jemma waved and smiled, caught glitter and petals and threw them back. "I'm so tired!" she called out.

On the fourth floor they got out and walked the rest of the way to the call room. Jemma had quashed a movement to install them in a suite, and was glad now that she had, because this was almost like coming home, enough like it to be nice, and enough unlike it to be bearable. Rob opened the door and they held hands as they jumped through sideways—Jemma had not wished to be carried in. "How tired is tired?" Rob asked her.

"Not that tired," she said. She liked undressing him out of fancy clothes, how smoothly the jacket slid back from his shoulders, how the bow tie came undone with one pull, how she had to reach around his back to undo the cummerbund. His shoes popped off with hardly any effort, and she could pull off the silk socks just by pinching them at the toe and drawing back her arm. His pants fell in a pool at his feet once she unbuttoned them, unzipped his fly, and pushed back his suspenders. She pulled his undershirt off his head and undid the buttons on his fancy underwear, only having to push a little to make them fall on top of the pants. She took his hands and pulled him forward; in two steps he was free of everything. Still in her whole outfit, she put her arms around his waist and her face in his shoulder. He smelled of cake.

Jemma had been thinking about this night, and considering different ways to make it special, had almost asked the angel to make them a pill that would make them forget they had ever had sex before, so they would approach each other as if for the first time. But she worried about the baby, and the whole thing seemed like something only the very bored and desperate would do. She didn't even mention it to Rob. There was something very nice about it, though, even without any special additions or considerations. When they knocked their wedding bands together it was oddly sensual, after all, and their mutual fatigue led to a new thing. He stretched out behind her, and they held their hands together above their heads, and moved less and less until they had both fallen asleep. Then Jemma dreamed of the evening that had just passed, and saw again the march down the ramp from the second floor, and the various choirs performing, and the tumblers, and the speeches, some dull, some not, given by various citizens and Council members. She saw Father Jane and John Grampus pronounce them wife and wife and husband and husband, and friend and friend, and family all together. But all these things were flavored and interrupted by furious little bouts of sex. No one seemed to mind it. No one looked away when they took a break during the vows for a few urgent thrusts. In fact Father Jane leaned over and whispered to Rob that he ought to bite her ear, teaching him by example how to muffle his teeth with his lips.

The long procession up the ramp to the roof was punctuated with thrusts delivered and received in every conceivable position, a few requiring support from bystanders. Upstairs it continued through the first, second, and third toasts. They did it while they danced, breaking apart to spin all the way across the dance floor, bowing to each other from afar, and then rushing back together for more mad coupling in the middle of a clapping circle of guests. They did it under the fireworks, and by the cake, and in the cake, Ishmael in the dream being entirely sober. He watched them from the same table from which Jemma had watched him.

In the cake, amid the odor of cake, they finished together, and the new thing was not a dream of sex after sex—Jemma had had those before—but when they woke together, crying out together, and discovered that the dream had been made real. In the dream your cry turns to a long stream of cake that flies from your mouth and spells words—oh! oh! oh!—in the air, and you feel the whole hospital trembling underneath you, and all the little cake people feel it, too, and roll on the ground in an agony of pleasure until they melt. Then you feel Rob pressing his chest into your back, and he squeezes you with an arm thrown just north of the swell in your belly, and you feel his panting breath against your shoulder, and his nose scraping across your wet neck. You lie there a moment more, both fully awake now, and then you scramble away from him, and sit up as he scrambles away from you, falling half out of the bed. You look at him in the dim light. He wipes his nose and sniffs, blue eyes still wide with surprise, and somehow it seems not unusual at all to have shared a dream with this person, and even the content of the dream seems usual—of course everyone does a little poking all through the wedding ceremony, everybody except for the terribly backward Amish and the grimmest of Orthodox Jews, and what is a wedding cake for except to fuck in? Every groom stands behind his bride in the wedding buggy, thrusting his hips and cracking a horsewhip in the air, but does anyone, has anyone before, and will anyone ever again, wake in the middle of their wedding night and look at their new husband and be so utterly astonished by love?

I am not supposed to use my imagination.

I am not supposed to write better lives for them, or even different lives for them. I watch, and I listen, and everything is recorded, and nothing is lost. This is the Book of the King's Daughter, and do you see it is not written but lived.

Once it was my gift and my curse, to remake the whole world. Not anymore.

Rob Dickens was asleep beside Jemma, one arm under her and the other thrown over his eyes, one leg straight and the other bent with the knee raised toward the ceiling. It was the attitude of a man just resting and not actually asleep, but he really was asleep. He was dreaming of dolphins. In an orange suit of scales and a pair of green gloves and green panties he rode a pair of them, a foot on either back and the double-bridle in his left hand, sending telepathic inquiries out into an empty sea, asking, Is anybody out there?

Outside Kidney paused at the door to mark it with a giant invisible K before continuing on her way. Some days she woke up feeling like something bad was going to happen and so she proceeded through the hospital marking the doors of everybody she liked because she hoped it would keep them from harm, though lately her apprehension has always been groundless, and she never has saved anyone from a bad thing by marking the door with her letter. How many K's had she drawn on the front door at home? Still a body has to try, she told herself, and did the hopscotch pattern in the carpet before she entered the crèche, where nurses in white robes were feeding the babies or singing to the babies or playing with the babies. She hopped and skipped, now working a pattern only she could see, toward Anna, who was playing a recorder over a crib. "Let me hold one," she told her. Inside the crib the King's Daughter sucked on her fist, kicked her feet, and listened not to the recorder but to the plaintive sighs of the drowned.

John Grampus and Father Jane passed by, taking their Monday/Wednesday/Friday stroll among the babies. "They're all so cute," she said, "I don't know how a person would choose."

"Well," he said, "it's not like we actually get to pick." They walked on, arm in arm, pausing by every favorite baby. John Grampus talked of his lover Ray, how he would have liked this baby because it always has that mean look on its face, or how that baby has got his chin, and wouldn't it be a shame if all these babies were not their own little unfolding selves at all but just containers for recycled souls, and maybe it's not a baby with Ray's chin but Ray with Ray's chin? "It would be so depressing if there was no such thing as a new soul, but it would be nice, too."

"Ella liked to say that a breast-feeding baby was staring off into another world."

"Ray said he thought they saw ghosts!"

They had a lot in common, the two dead lovers. They liked the same music, ate the same food, pursued the same professions, read the same books, liked equivalent if not identical things in bed. "Oh yes," Jane had confided drunkenly one night, "she liked to be licked right here," drawing the anatomy on the tablecloth. Somewhere they must be getting along famously, they liked to think, and each living lover wondered if the dead ones, unfettered of fleshly orientations, spent every eternal night spirit-fucking while their living halves ate exquisite bits of synthesized cheese and tasted vintages condensed out of the imagination of the angel, holding hands, cupping chins, kissing fingers and confessing to each other an absolute unattraction and marveling as their hips seemed almost magnetically to repulse each other.

Anna bent over her baby and kissed her on the head. "She's almost discovered her toes," she said to Heloise, the nurse who'd been watching her for her while she was gone. "There's formula out," she said, pointing to it. "I should be back before the next feed, but just in case. Don't let that weird kid touch my baby." She indicated Kidney with a jerk of her head that made her earrings jingle. After she'd put off her white robe she took the earrings off and put them in a pack around her waist. She didn't like not to wear them, but they jangled when she ran, so children looked up when she went by, expecting to see the tired old volunteer pushing an ice-cream cart. She did a few stretches right there, smoothed the front of her turquoise unitard, retied her shoes, waved at her baby, and was off. Brenda did not mark her departure.

She hit the hopscotch marks on her way to the ramp, only missing one, then started up. She ran every day but Sunday, though she had not previously been in the habit of keeping healthy, and had run before only on rare occasions of pursuit. It was something the angel had suggested, the voice drifting gently down from the ceiling one evening after Anna had returned from her shift to her little room and had just finished her decompressing with a fifteen-minute shower. "Are you so fat on purpose?" was the question she had asked. Anna had answered, "Fuck off, Billy," but the question inaugurated a discussion; when the angel looked at her with the thousand eyes of the hospital she saw a different lady than Anna did in the mirror. They started with in-room stretching and calisthenics and special bitter teas designed to increase her enthusiasm and destabilize her fat. The unitard was of a material that clung harder in some places than others, lifting here and pressing there, so when she finally went out she looked more Rubinesque than doughy. At first she could hardly get up the first spiral. Now she ran to the top without stopping.

She wasn't the only runner out this morning. She did a smiling nod at the others and said hello to Alan, a radiology tech who always took his shirt off at the top of the ramp and walked back down with it tucked into his pants. There was always something swinging hugely in his shorts as he walked briskly down the spiral. It would be nice, she thought, to walk down with him one day. Perhaps when she was a little firmer. It wouldn't be long before she was among the firmest people in the hospital; already there was nothing left to pinch between her ass and her thigh, and when she poked a finger against the flesh of her ass it hardly gave at all, but she wanted it so firm that if someone should happen to bite it, it would be like biting the ass of a mannequin. And she would wait until her ears were done—they are a little floppy in the lobes, in fact nearly as floppy as an old man's, but Billy had a plan to fix them which would involve nothing more complicated than a cream, some drops, a night brace, and an adult-sized sit-and-spin on which she must spin counterclockwise for ten minutes at a time three times in a single night.

As soon as she reached the eighth floor she sprinted for the ninth. The doors at the top were open—she could feel the salt breeze blow against her as she took the final curve, so fast she thought she could run along the wall as easily as on the floor, and then she passed through the door and decelerated into a power walk, folding her hands behind her neck and lifting her face into the bright sun and the cold wind. She walked in a circle for a while, did pull-ups—three sets of twenty—at the monkey bars, and lay down in the grass. She'd rest just a moment before she started her laps around the roof—a hundred and sixty of them equaled four miles. There was a small cloud passing overhead in the shape of her family. I have not forgotten you, she thought.

Drs. Snood and Tiller passed by her where she lay. Some people will sleep anywhere, Dr. Tiller thought. Even when it was very cold the two doctors took a morning walk up here.

"I dreamed again," he said, "of the resistant bug."

"Poor Jacob. Did you wake screaming? I have fewer and fewer of the scream dreams, these days."

"No. It chased me, yes, like usual, scuttling on eight legs then six legs then four and even for a little while on two. It never holds still until it becomes an inky gelatinous concept that presses against my face and sucks all the breath out of me."

"You are still waiting for everything to go back to the way it was."

"I'm afraid, Carmen. If I am forgetting my medicine, then how much could anyone else remember? I sat for an hour on the toilet this morning trying to recall the dosing for pentasa suppositories."

"You'd sit there for an hour anyway. Do all gastroenterologists spend so much time on the toilet?"

"I've not had to look up that dose since my third year in medical school. What's next, prednisone? Tomorrow morning will I wake up thinking IBD stands for itsy-bitsy duodenum, or that Crohn's disease only strikes old women?"

"If you do then I'll..." Oh, let them go. Walk on, there's a reason Jemma doesn't like you, and another reason why I don't, and another, and others beyond even what my brother shall catalog against you. There were a score of people up here on the roof this morning. Karen and Anika were setting up a badminton net. If Jemma sleeps in I might inhabit the shuttlecock. It's a distinct sort of fun, to be a shuttlecock in the hands of competent players, and every time the racquet connects I connect with the life behind it. Monserrat has come up for a solitary picnic. Out of a basket big enough to hold all the organs in her abdomen she removes a cup of yogurt, a peach, and a small thermos of coffee. She shook out the crisp white sheet she'll sit on, snapping it in the sun, turning once or twice with it to make it spin and flap more. Even from across the roof I could tell how much she enjoyed the contrast between the white sheet and the blue sky. I slither along toward her in the grass, gathering speed as I go. I want to be with her when she tastes the coffee. But there is the skylight to look into before I get there, uncovered on this bright morning. I look down on the model; Jupiter was closest to me; the red eye stared dully at the wall. Pickie Beecher was standing underneath in a patch of sun. He shaded his eyes and looked at me.

"I see you," he said.

They called it the Match, after another process of assignation. There was on the one hand an embarrassment of parentless children and on the other a large population of childless adults. There were the hundred-and-thirty families and the seventy-two single parents who'd been together with their children on the night of the flood; the hundreds of other children had been up till now cared for by the same nursing teams who had cared for them from the time they first entered the hospital. The ward had become the family unit. So twenty different parents played with Ella Thims and fed her and changed her diapers, and she had her siblings among the GI kids, and Josh and Ethel were at first a part of the big one family. These families had been unstable from the start—Cindy and Wayne and other, older children were already together, in a sense, like dozens of other teenagers were coming together in benevolent gangs, more and more resistant to the authority of the nurses and the other adults, and there were families who vacuumed up stray children and adopted them. Unofficial, unorganized, it had been progressing since Thing Two, and no busybody worth their salt could let it just happen. Who knew what they would end up with, when the dust settled? The Council, Jemma's not-wedding behind them, the educational curriculum set and deemed appropriate, every child and teacher seeming reasonably content with what they were learning or teaching, and most of the old hospital transformed or being transformed into spaces deemed better suited to their new mission of education, preservation, and the fostering of hope, turned its eye on the current distribution of individuals throughout the hospital, and overturning the last vestiges of the old hospital order.

I should be on my honeymoon, Jemma thought as she listened to the days of debate on how they should organize themselves. There must be a hundred different patches of tropical water she and Rob could have visited. Or they might have floated behind the hospital in a romantic dinghy, a houseboat big enough just for the two of them with an automated crank to pay out the line, farther and farther until the hospital was only a smudge against the horizon, and conspirators with sharp knives might depose her with a single cut. Where is the resolution, she wondered, that would have built me a honey-boat? She was in meetings the next day. "It wasn't really a wedding," Vivian noted, "so you shouldn't really get a honeymoon, right?"

People had cleaved together from the first into pairs and even the occasional much-whispered about ménage, or the more innocent but no less frequently discussed situations of two-timers or men and women who dated the same three people, one then two then three then back again to one, in serial but evanescent monogamy. True multiple-partnerships were extremely rare, but Jordan Sasscock had acquired eight wives, though none of them called themselves that. There'd been no ceremony, private or public, and Dr. Sasscock certainly never described them that way. In fact, when someone called them wives he'd become uncharacteristically upset, his suave jovial affect lifting off of him in a second. As serious and furious as Dr. Snood in a snit, he'd say, "We are all together, but it's not like that." There was something derogatory about wives that rubbed all nine of them the wrong way, though when he was drunk you might get him to agree that he was in some sense husband to all of them. But he pointed out to people who were curious enough to ask at length about the arrangement that he was no bigamist or powerful fuck-lord presiding over a harem. It was all more equitable and more mysterious than that. "I am lost in them," he would say finally, dreamily.

There were only two of them at first, girls he had unwisely tried to date simultaneously in a world that was only two-hundred meters across. It was not surprising that the two outraged women became friends, but no one ever understood how they made a collective decision to receive the miscreant back into their beds and their lives—there were rumors that Sasscock, who'd proved himself a very capable replicator engineer, had made a potion to addle them with, but too many people had tried something similar and failed for anyone to believe that the angel would do that, and anyone who spent time with the threesome could tell right away that the women, though in love, were not love-slaves.

Jemma had imagined it, feeling a little dirty even though it was only on one occasion that she diagrammed all the sexual possibilities, arranging them like groaning Lincoln Logs in her head to make structures of ecstasy and lust. It was more work, and more interesting, to imagine the comforts they found, these refugee women, in the many-armed other, and what words they whispered over their gigantic pillow in Sasscock's room, now all bed except for the little alcove for the replicator and the sink. Sometimes she had envied them, and imagined herself stepping into a groaning mass that petted and stroked itself not to orgasm but to solace, and she thought she could understand the appeal, entirely separate from the prospect of owning a share of handsome Jordan Sasscock, of entering into such a compact.

Conclaves were just shaping up, associations of sentiment—a preponderance of Baptists on the third floor, the fifteen Mormons moving one night, en masse, to the fifth, separate lesbian and gay ghettos in the rehab unit, but they were voluntary and amorphous congregations, and seemed to denote little in terms of either a grander plan, or a deeper meaning; no matter where people lived, or what creed they professed, everybody mixed in Father Jane's huge Sunday Services, only Dr. Sundae and her snake handlers, the Jews, and the Coptics holding anything like regularly separate services yet. The Council looked for other patterns of condensation, wondering if there was a plan in which they participated unaware, that might guide them when it came time to assign the children, but there was no pattern anyone could make out. People were dating across the borders of race and class and profession and age and religion, across floors and specialties, across vast disparities of height and weight and attractiveness. How best, then, to decide which child should go where when the crèches were disbanded and every hospital room turned into a home?

"'The family is dead!" Anika proclaimed, speaking in one of the crowded meetings—they became increasingly public forums with every passing day, until they had to be moved from the conference room to the lobby, where Jemma's table was set up under the shadow of the toy—for the most radical contingent of the population. It would be not just futile but dangerous to imitate the old pattern. In fact, these people urged the Council to consider that they may all have been placed here for the very purpose of formulating and implementing a new order. The absolute minimum number of parental units needed for each child was five—they'd done the calculations, and this was a number that guaranteed every child at least two good parental units without crossing a threshold of confusion beyond which the mixture of opinions and styles would do as much harm as good. "There's always a bad mother," Anika said, "and there's always a bad father. The molester is always lurking, somebody's always waiting to tell you that you look fat in your prom dress. There's always somebody who will hate the child that they should love, and half the time or more it's the same person, isn't it? If you do the math you discover that you hated a fourth of your mother and half of your father and they loved perhaps one-seventh of the person that you became. This is the misery of two. But with five you get perfection, because even if each parent only loves 20 percent of the child each child is totally loved, and every child can pick and choose among the smorgasborg to construct the parent they love totally."

Jemma nodded and put on a thoughtful face while Anika was speaking, but made an unnecessary note to herself on the big yellow pad that sat in front of her during every meeting: *V-E-T-O.* Over the hours and days of deliberations they heard other ideas. There were staunch traditionalists, represented not unexpectedly by Dr. Sundae, who wanted to keep the present arrangement until every last two citizens of the hospital had been partnered in an officially recognized marriage, and offered Rob and Jemma as an example of a partnership insufficiently formalized, what with the unusual permutations of the ceremony and the insistence of the lesbian priestess and deacon-prophet as they married them that they were not in fact marrying them. There should be a mass ceremony presided over by Father Jane in her strictest and most formal Unitarian capacity, in which every male and female of marrying age (described as being so low as fourteen and as high as twenty-one) were joined together based on whatever natural (but not unnatural) affinities were already in play among the population but also, and more importantly, on a subcommittee of the Council, newly to be formed, which would study files to be prepared by an entirely separate subcommittee and make incontrovertible matches, the last of them to be completed no more than forty days from the adoption of the authorizing resolution. A week after the ceremony, the children would be distributed, these matches made based on the work of yet another heroic subcommittee.

"We are all still thinking," said Karen, "in the terms of the old system. Didn't Ishmael say it many weeks ago? If we are all a big family, then aren't these, each of them and all of them, our children? Each of us shares somehow in their care now, why shouldn't that continue? Why not make ourselves formally what we already are informally?" She went on to suggest that every child begin to circulate among the adult citizens in such a way that every last child would rotate with every last possible parent. They would build a clock in the lobby that would chime whenever it was time to switch, and slowly, by means of deceptively transient-appearing relationships (and wasn't every family relationship transient anyway, disappointment or suppressed hatred or mortality counting the time as surely as any giant clock?), individual transience becoming collective permanence, they would become a giant family in truth, where every boy or girl was son or daughter to every man and woman, and every man and woman parent to every boy and girl. Jemma tried to mouth *veto* reassuringly to Jeri Vega's mother, who was clenching her fists while Karen told her that Jeri would rotate away from her, but rotate back, like all good things joining in an ebbing, flowing cycle of departure and return. "But she's my daughter," Jessie's mother said, and Karen said, "She is my daughter, too."

Jemma's suggestion, delivered on the third day of deliberations that seemed likely to go on forever, combined elements that had already been put forward by others. The heavy duty of researching and defining affinities she delegated to the angel, who would work based on what she already knew of everyone on board and what they would tell her in interviews or questionnaires. Requests for specific individuals would be accepted but not encouraged. Children who already had one parent or more in the hospital would stay with them and not be rotated way or shared except through the usual media of school and play. Individuals could submit themselves to the Match as individuals or in groups of up to two; same sex couples must not be discriminated against. Siblings would not be separated, and if the thing were going to happen there was no reason for it not to happen soon. They should do it within the week.

This didn't end the debate. A whole parade of people were still waiting to tell their ideas, but after every third or fourth crazy scheme the Council would talk again about Jemma's suggestion and as people delineated the benefits of robot nannies upon a nascent civilization, or made calls for inverted families where the children would discipline their parents and teach them how to live in the new world, it became obvious that her plan possessed more than all the others the attractive qualities of being both feasible and not too loony. The Council retired back to its chamber and after a short discussion with the angel passed a resolution which Jemma signed into law. This time she really did say, "So let it be written, so let it be done," but quiet enough that only Vivian and Ishmael heard her.

The angel preferred interviews; these were conducted. Some relationships were fortified or even inaugurated by the stimulus of the Match, a few fell apart. Those who wanted to make requests made them, and the angel held the algorithm in abeyance until such time as the Council wished it activated. It would take about eight hours to run. Why that long and not seven or nine, or why not instantaneously, she would not say. She manufactured a big red button—eminently pressable—which Jemma wanted to hit right away, but Ishmael had the idea of waiting until the following day, taking advantage of a previously scheduled talent show to distract people from the waiting. So Jemma awoke that day about a half hour after Kidney had made her mark on her door and not half a second after Pickie Beecher laid his eyes upon me. Before she opened her eyes she considered her schedule, picturing it in her head, thick blue letters on a yellow pad as big as the bed. There was only a single item on it today: *12:00 p.m.—Press button.*

She opened her eyes, stared at the ceiling for a while, stared at the window for a while, stared at the door for a while, hoping that Rob might come through it and lie down beside her. She was not yet so far removed from sleep that she couldn't go right back to it, and it would have been very pleasant to put her head on his chest, murmur, "I've got a big day ahead of me," and sleep for three hours and forty-five minutes. Her eyes closed, she drifted back toward sleep and she had a small, swift dream in which not Rob but the big red button walked through the door and lay down beside her, and she tried unsuccessfully to snuggle up to it. Careful, it said to her. Don't make me pop yet.

It was not a usual morning, though she went about her usual business. She got out of bed and did the chair-assisted yoga poses that Vivian had taught her. She hated them, though less than the exercises she was supposed to do on odd days. The room was almost too small to do them, but she wouldn't be caught dead stretching and lotusing in public, or any place that she might be seen. She dragged a chair to the middle of the room, pushed the table up against the bathroom door, and did the downward-facing dog, leaning forward from her hips and grabbing the lower edge of the seat. "Watch your head," said the angel.

"Leave me alone," Jemma said. "Who said you could watch?"

"I am always watching," she said, but shut up. Vivian had cautioned her not to lower her head too far, and said that she must be extremely careful once she got to the third trimester. "If you lower your head below your heart in the third trimester," she said, "you will die instantly."

Eight breaths later, she was done with that one, and then it was time for the modified dancer and warrior two and warrior three and the pony on the table and the squatting palm, eight breaths for every pose. She spent ten minutes, exactly the requisite time, in a lotus on her mat—now was the time she was supposed to be visualizing her healthy pregnancy. She managed it for a minute, imagining it, a foot long now, wrapped in transparent skin, and then it was laid out beside any number of other approximately foot-long objects: Rob's hairy foot, a submarine sandwich, the first dildo she had ever met, a really big hot dog. This was the exhausting part, to turn her thought on her baby, and dive into the black whole in her belly.

Hello? she said, into the blackness.

Go away, said the baby, the voice as fully imaginary as the body that she saw, an upside-down fetus hanging in a field of stars.

I promised Vivian I would look at you every day. It's supposed to be good for us.

How can I sleep with you staring at me like that, all creepy. You look crazy. Are you crazy? Am I crazy?

Sometimes I am. A little. Or more than a little. It's Match Day! she said, trying to change the subject.

Maybe I can get a better family, he said. Would I not be crazy, if I went to live with someone else? Would I still die, if you loved me from far away, instead of from up close?

All that is past. You're safe.

But I think I would prefer to live with someone else. It's not personal. I just want to live. I just want to get away from the long reach of your parents' hands. And I don't want to have to watch your brother burn every night, or hear the story from you when you sit up drunk all night, regretting everything that ever happened to you.

Well, Jemma said.

I'm glad you understand. I'm glad we had this little talk.

But...

You're a very good listener. Has anyone ever told you that before? Jordan Sasscock. Put me with him. He's cute.

But I'm your *mother*.

Exactly! And before she could ask her baby and herself what that meant, or argue that nothing was ever going to be the same for her, that everyone was going to be happy in the new world, and that she held in her hands the mysterious green remedy for sickness and death, the chime sounded, her exercises were done, and their time was over.

* * *

She wanted to go back to bed. She went downstairs, instead, to Karen's coffee bar, part of the ER complex, not far from Connie's more traditional sort of bar. Behind the same series of windows where crabby triage nurses had instructed the wounded and the panicked and the soon-to-be dead on the virtues of waiting one's proper turn, Karen pumped espresso from a manual machine as tall as she was, made of golden brass and covered in relief with eagles and oxen and calves. Rob was sure it had once been the ark of the covenant, but Karen said it looked just like one she had seen in Italy. During a brief vacation, the two weeks she'd had away from her eighty-hour weeks as an intern, she'd fled Florence and her fiancé and, after a hike and some hitchhiking and a mysterious process of emancipation ("I slept in a field and when I woke up the next day I was sopping wet and my throat hurt like hell but I was so free I cannot even describe it!") she shacked up with a man who reeked perpetually of dark roasted coffee, hardly able to talk with him but enjoying the first satisfactions of her ten years of sexual activity and serving a brief apprenticeship in his café before going back to her fiancé, in many ways, she insisted, a new woman. She wasn't the only person for whom an interlude of non-medical happiness had formed the basis of a career—Dr. Neder was throwing pottery on the seventh floor; Dr. Pudding was blowing glass on the second—and like the others she quickly surpassed her lover/teacher, assisted by the angelic technology in the replicators.

Dr. Chandra, Helena Dufresne, and Carla were already all lined up at the bar, Chandra staring morosely into his huge bowl of coffee, Tir's mom having a discussion with Carla. Karen was drying a tall mug—not actually something she had to do, since used dishes could be thrown, like any other sort of garbage, into the gullet of the replicators, but she said it made her feel authentic, and she liked to meditate while she did her dishes, her best ideas, like the concept of eternally rotating children and the Over-Family, coming to her as she washed and dried.

"I figured it out," she said to Jemma. "Truly caffeine-free espresso."

"What's the point of that?" Jemma asked.

"You have to try it," Karen said. "It's guaranteed—not even a picogram of caffeine, but you'd never know the difference. I don't know the difference, and if anybody could tell it would be me. Anyway I verified it up in the lab. There's a set of HPLC columns in special chem."

"I trust you," Jemma said.

"I don't," said Chandra, "this business about Pudding and the sexbot is too much."

"Ask Jordan," Karen said, "but get him good and drunk first. And it wasn't a sexbot, it was a three-dimensional simulacrum of his wife. And he was just looking at it. There's no evidence at all for any other sort of... activity."

"There's no evidence at all, period," said Chandra.

"You turn everything dirty," Karen said to him, and put a tiny little cup down in front of Jemma, not one-tenth the size of the one that sat in front of Dr. Chandra.

"Are people making sexbots?" Jemma asked, taking the briefest little sip of the coffee, and gagging.

"Of course not," said Karen. "Stop spreading lies," she said to Dr. Chandra.

"You're the gossip monger," he said. "And anyway, fuck off. You're not my boss anymore. I'm out of the program, lady."

"Sirius, Sirius," she said. "You've got to let that go. Do you know that was in one of your letters, when we were talking about you at the selection meeting? He's a worrier, the letter said, in that obligatory negative sentence. He tends to hang on to things." She set down another huge cup in front of him, full of hot milk, and poured in the espresso, making an expert design, a perfectly symmetrical spirograph flower.

"I'm never going back," he said calmly, poking a finger into the foam and bringing it to his mouth.

"Maybe I should just have some milk," Jemma said.

"Milk for the baby then," Karen said, sweeping up the little cup and drinking it herself. "I can't tell the difference," she said. "Not at all. Could you?"

"I'm not very experienced," Jemma said. "About the sexbots—maybe we should talk about them in the Council. It could get pretty weird, artificial people running around and mixing with the real people. What if we couldn't tell the difference?"

"There are no sexbots," Karen said, looking among her shelves—once they'd held old charts and admission protocols—for a milk mug. She selected a bowl, like Chandra's, poured the milk, and started to steam it, so Jemma could only pick out a few words when she continued to talk. "Artificial vagina... imaginary... his was like a formal portrait... just visiting... the angel wouldn't... trust me."

"Can I have a paper cup?" asked Dr. Chandra. "I'm not going to stick around here and be persecuted."

"I have a nice relaxing tea," said Karen. "You should try some. It would make you less touchy."

"I don't even like tea, and I'm not touchy," he said, and tapped his finger on the bar. Karen gave him an aluminum mug with a rubber lid, and he transferred his drink.

"You ruined the flower," she said. "Want me to fix it?" She held up her little metal pitcher of milk.

"I'm late to fuck my robot," he said, and shuffled off.

"Pull up your pants!" Karen called after him, and whispered to Jemma, "He's very lonely. He comes here every day to tell me how much he hates me, but sometimes I think I'm the closest thing he has to a friend."

"Some people are having a hard time," Jemma said, holding her bowl in both hands and sipping at her milk. Vivian had given her a calcium quota to meet each day. She could not remember how much was in a bowl of milk. "Not knowing what to do, and not having any work."

"He hated work, too," Karen said. "Some people are just never happy. It's something I learned, being chief. You bend over backward for some people and they're like, I wanted raspberry and this is strawberry, or this is 2 percent and I wanted 1 percent, and you're like, What's the fucking difference you are one of a hundred residents, can't you just give me a break and do your work? Children are dying out there."

"Not anymore," Jemma said.

"You know what I mean. I can't imagine what it's like for you. Okay, I can… you're chief of the whole hospital. It's a *huge* job, but you're doing swell. I mean it, and I know it. Your approval rating is 86 percent."

"I have an approval rating?" Jemma asked.

Karen laughed. "You're so funny sometimes." She called down the bar to the two women sitting at the far end, interrupting their conversation. "Isn't she doing a great job?" Carla nodded vigorously, and Helena Dufresne held up a single thumb. Karen refilled their cups, and pulled another espresso for herself. "This is the real stuff," she said, and detailed for Jemma the process by which she and the angel had increased the potency of the beans until they practically trembled, and all the new uses she was finding for fancy coffee, and how she was not certain if she was pulling new uses out of the old thing, or making something entirely new when she experimented with the replicator. "When I ask for anti-wrinkle coffee," she asked, "is she making it from scratch or just bringing forward a property already inherent in the bean? It's so hard to tell with her. She can be so squirrely." She poured out thick coffee in a solid dish and had Jemma soak her cuticles in it.

"Did you enter?" Jemma asked her.

"Of course," Karen said. "I hope Siri did, too. I asked him but he wouldn't tell. How about you?"

"It would be gluttony," Jemma said, putting a hand on her belly.

"There are more kids than adults," Karen pointed out.

"It would still be weird," Jemma said. "My fingers are tingling."

"It's the natural enzymes," Karen said. "They're giving you a manicure." She leaned forward and said, "Ella Thims. She's my first choice."

"A sweet girl."

"I've known her forever. I took care of her every July for three years in a row, and I was there when she came slithering out of her mama. That was some initial exam, let me tell you. Where's the vagina? Where's the anus? I thought it was because I was a stupid intern that I couldn't find them. I visit her every day—we're practically a family already." She brought her hands to her heart. "It makes me nervous to talk about it."

"The coffee probably doesn't help," Jemma said.

"Oh, I'm immune," she said, but everyone who came here knew that she got more chatty and jumpy throughout the day, and that by closing time she stood on the bar proclaiming stomping cheers for her favorite customers.

"Now they're numb," Jemma said, taking her fingers out, sure she'd see the ends dissolved down to slender bone.

"That's the baby," Karen said, pushing her hand back in. "It's a thing I never understood. Numb toes I got, if the baby's sitting on a plexus, but fingers? Something about hCG, but then why does it get worse in the third trimester? I had it too, with Abbie..." She clutched at the back of Jemma's hand and burst suddenly into tears—they fell, fat and full, onto the highly polished counter and splashed back into Jemma's flat dish of coffee. "Oh God!" Karen moaned. "What's wrong with me? This is so stupid. I promised myself I wouldn't... It's all fine now, I should really know better. Am I cheating on her, though? That's the thing... that's the stupid, stupid, stupid thing. I know better in here—she pounded on her chest—in here I know that none of them belong to us and they pass from one to the other and Abbie is somewhere now, cared for just like I'll care for Ella but still it feels like a big fat betrayal and I know I'll tuck Ella in at night and they'll be out there, Abbie and Carl, just so angry at me because I'm cheating."

"It's okay," Jemma said, hugging Karen back and scattering coffee-drops from her fingers. She meant it in a very generic sense—things are generally okay, more or less, probably, or it's okay for you to cry and slobber on me—but not as a denial of the fact that the dead judge or that they can be provoked to fury by our unfaithfulness. Who was Jemma to absolve Karen of the fury of her dead husband and child, or to absolve any of them? Even Juan Fraggle's family was cheating on his dad, knitting and teaching salsa dancing and karate (his sisters were black belts) and just going on, waking every day to something more and more and more like contentment.

The two women at the end of the bar gave up their conversation and came over, Carla just standing to Jemma's left with her arms folded, but Helena walking behind the counter to take Karen in her big flabby arms. "There," she said. "You just cry it out, baby. Get it all out so nothing spoils your fun tonight." Karen went "Ack, Ack, Ack!" shaking and snotting. Helena winked at Jemma over Karen's shoulder, and Jemma pointed at her watch.

"My class," she whispered, and the big lady nodded.

"It's all under control," she said. "It's all okay." Carla leaned an elbow on the bar and trailed a finger in Jemma's coffee, staring at Jemma's shoes.

Jemma wasn't sure what to say, so she just slinked off, head down, walking quickly out of the ER and into the lobby, giving out hardly a wave as she passed onto the ramp and started the climb. She wasn't really late for her class. "It's another part of your job," Dr. Sundae had told her, accosting her after a Council meeting, backing Jemma up against the window, her matronly bosom pressing closer and closer. Jemma could smell her asparagus breath, and their clothes were almost touching when she spoke. "To comfort the afflicted—you've already done so much, but scratch any of us and you get an uncontrolled weeper. Look inside, I think you'll find it—surprise!—the means to comfort us even as you healed them." Then she had leaned even closer, and put a hand on the window, palm flat against the glass.

"I really have to pee," Jemma said. It was true, but not what she ought to have said. Don't tell me what my job is, you scary old bitch—that would have been better. I'm not for you to lecture anymore, you scary old bitch. Or even just, You scary old bitch, whispered in accusation and admiration. She had hurried but not run away from her.

She started waving again after walking the first loop of the spiral with her head down. "Hello, Sylvester. Hello, Ms. Sullivan. Hello, Dr. Sasscock. Hello, Dr. Pudding." She remembered the sexbot and stopped by the rail to make a note on her little computer. A week after Vivian had commissioned them from the angel almost every adult and half the kids had one of the little devices, as long, wide, and thin as an index card, flat black glass on one side, bright metal on the other. You could write on it with a pen or ask it to record your voice. She was still confusing the icons. Though she meant just to record her voice, two days later when she went over her notes before the next meeting she would see her own puffy, pink face, pictured in such clarity and precision by the in-screen camera that she diagnosed herself with melasma, the toy clanking and whirling behind her and a mysterious beehive hairdo passing through the frame just as she spoke the words: "Sexbot sexbot sexbot."

"Say it soft and it's almost like praying," said John Grampus, sidling up next to her.

"You shouldn't sneak up," Jemma said.

"I was trying to get your attention. Distracted by the big day?"

"I just have to push the button." She started walking again up the ramp. "It's not such a big day."

"Tell that to... everybody. I'm so nervous I can barely walk straight. See?" He stumbled for her and took a few boneless steps before straightening up and walking straight beside her again. "I keep thinking it's a bad idea. Have you heard that from anyone else?"

"Anika still wants the number five involved somehow. Like that. A couple others, angry about their schemes getting ignored."

He stopped her and put a hand on her shoulder. "Jane applied for all those crazy kids. All of them? Can you fucking believe that?"

"You can't split up the family," Jemma said.

"It's a big step," he said, shaking his head. She wasn't sure if she meant applying to adopt Kidney's whole family, or his moving in with Father Jane, another unsolicited confidence he'd given her, on another walk like this one the week before. She did not understand their relationship, and though it sometimes helped her to fall asleep at night, picturing them in bed, or playing cards, or imagining that she was John Grampus reaching out, so slowly and hesitantly, to touch the unfamiliar and rather frightening boob, she didn't want to think of it right now.

"As big as it gets," Jemma agreed, an appropriate platitude, she thought, and she ducked into the stairwell. He didn't follow her. She sat down on the stairs, put her head in her hands, and thought of the boobs, a hundred boobs and a hundred hands reaching out, hesitating and uncertain, to touch them. Go away, she said to them, and the kaleidoscope vision fractured and fell in on itself. Then it was dark behind her eyes but she could feel the people passing by outside the door, and feel John Grampus making his anxious way up to the roof. "Sometimes it's hard to be alone," she'd said to Rob, and he'd held her tighter in their bed, thinking she was complaining of loneliness.

It was the same old class—diffident and minimally instructive—until the kids started talking about their families. Juan was the only non-orphan. He sat back in the grass, looking deeply at every speaking face as they went around and around in a circle. They were supposed to be trying to levitate a pencil—not that Jemma could lift inanimate objects with her mind (she tried to float knives and soap and pins in the water but though she had lifted hundred-kilo Helena none of it would budge) but wasn't it possible that their gifts were of another sort entirely than Jemma's? Moving pencils, changing the color of grass, turning a candy mushroom to a real mushroom with a blink of the eye—maybe they couldn't heal for the same reason that Jemma couldn't shoot lasers out of her eyes: it was simply not for her to do it.

"We should have been able to pick," Magnolia said. "What if I get some freak?"

"The angel listened to you, didn't she?" said Josh.

"She could still give me a freak."

"Maybe you want a freak," said Jarvis. "You want a freak to freak with."

"We should have been able to do our own," said Ethel. "We're old enough. We've been through enough. Jesus fucking Christ. Nobody bothered to ask us."

"There was that whole three days of testimony..." Jemma started to say.

"Nobody asked the important questions," Ethel said glumly.

"We're jumping ship if they try to split us up," said States'-Rights. He reached out toward Kidney, on the other side of the circle. She stuck out her tongue at him.

"We should just all stay together," said Cindy Flemm. "Us thirteen."

"And Rob," said Magnolia. "He could stay."

"Wouldn't that be great?" Cindy asked, turning to Jemma.

"Like a really horrible skin condition," Jemma said, but she hugged her.

"What's going to happen?" Kidney asked of the sky.

"Nothing," said Jarvis. "It's the same as before. The same old shit, just different people stepping in it."

"It's going to be totally different," Josh said confidently. "Everything's going to change. You're going to have a family. Haven't you been listening to anything?" Jarvis only tapped on his ear, and smiled.

"Families come and go," said Pickie, "but you remain, forever." He snapped his finger. "Like that. That's how quickly they are gone. Who cares about them, in the end? There is no other family besides brothers."

"And sisters," said Magnolia.

"Sisters are irrelevant," Pickie said. The discussion degraded into an argument, boys against girls, then the under-tens against the over-tens, arguing not about brothers or sisters or families but the necessity of underwear, or icing, or whether it would be better if no one ever had to pee. Food flew. Jemma lay back in the grass again, watching cupcakes sail against another bright blue sky, imagining Rob in his calculus class, standing at the giant plasma board, striking glowing circles in the dark glass as he poked it with his finger and swept out curves and lines and figures. Everyone in the class had a button stuck on their head, and furthermore everyone in the hospital had one, had always had one set right between their eyebrows, red as a firetruck and tall as the eraser on a fresh pencil. They were reset buttons, or surprise buttons, placed to be pressed in case of potentially lethal boredom or disappointment.

"Are you all ready?" she asked innocently, after class, after another hour spent wandering on the ramp, after Carla drew her behind the branches of a huge fern on the fifth floor. She'd seen her on the ramp, on the roof—she drifted close enough during class to be struck by a piece of fat—and twice in the lobby, her long horse-face appearing in flashes through the nervous, milling crowd. "Are you following me?" Jemma had finally asked her, when she caught her lurking near the fern. Jemma was coming away from a visit with Sadie's knitting circle, pockets full of hats and booties.

"I just wanted to ask," Carla said. "I just wanted to say. I know, a long time ago—it seems so long ago, Jemma. A hundred years, and it hasn't even been a hundred days. We didn't always see the same about things. I'm sorry if I was ever… harsh… and I wanted to make sure. Everybody wants Ella but she belongs with me. Those people weren't her family. They were kids. They hardly ever came to see her. It was me and Candy and Nicole, but mostly me. Candy and Nicole agree—we had a discussion. It was me. I have to get her."

"I'm just going to press the button."

"I've got some stuff. It's not like anything else, and okay for a girl like you. I checked, of course. I can't even describe how it makes you feel. There's that, or anything else you can think of. Or something you can't even think of—we're all dreaming of new things. Every day there's something new. I keep wondering why we didn't think of all the possibilities, back before. Were we just too sad, to use our imaginations? But you know what I mean, right? You know what I mean?"

"Yes," Jemma said. "Sort of. Look, I just press the button. That's it. Nothing more, just..." She pressed briskly on Carla's forehead, right where her button should be.

"But she'll listen to you," Carla said.

"She listens to everybody," Jemma said.

"Are you ready?" Jemma asked again of the crowd. It was eleven fifty-nine. She paused with her finger inches away from the button, wondering if she should take this opportunity to lead them in imagining how their lives would change after the Match. If anyone has any objections, she wanted to say, let him speak now or else. She stayed with her finger just inches from the button, asking silently of all the faces in the crowded council room, Do you know what this means, and asking the same thing of herself. She placed her other hand over her belly. For a few moments it was very quiet, until Maggie spoke from out of the crowd.

"What are you waiting for, genius?" she asked. "Don't you know how to press a fucking button?"

“Here they come,” said Father Jane. She was peeking out their door, down the hall at the line of approaching children.

“I’m never going to remember all the names. Nine! It’s ridiculous. How many times do I have to point out that it’s ridiculous?”

“Maybe it’s ridiculous, but it’s wonderful, too.”

“It’s not too late to make nametags.”

“That’s cold. Quick, light the candles.”

“Is it someone’s birthday?” Grampus asked. “How will we remember all the birthdays?” But he lit the candles, and stood in the doorway with Jane, holding the welcome cake she had baked, and singing the welcome song she had composed. Arms occupied, he didn’t have to hug them, but kissed them all as Jane greeted them. They all had the same face—soft and round and framed in white-blond hair. The differing ages and sexes hardly made any difference in the features, but the expression worn by the teenagers—wary mistrust—set them apart from their siblings.

“Welcome Shout!” she said. “Welcome Kidney! Welcome Valium! Welcome States’-Rights! Welcome Jesus! Welcome Bottom! Welcome Salt! Welcome Sand! Welcome Couch!”

They all nodded and smiled and the littlest one gave Jane a plant—a tall spindly thing with spiny leaves and a single drooping blossom that looked like a slack mouth. There were enough of them that they ought to have sung back to them, or done some complicated dance, but instead they piled directly onto the couch, squeezing in a double row of four and a single triple column in the middle. They arranged themselves so swiftly it was obvious that they had been squeezing themselves like that onto all sorts of furniture all their lives. They all stared around the room, taking in their new home, except for Kidney—that was the smallest one, he suddenly remembered—who looked squarely at John Grampus and said, "Well, now what do we do?"

Whichever one is left over, Rob had written. *Whichever one nobody wants. Give us that one.* At eight o'clock on Match Day, a half hour after the show ended, when much of the audience was still trying to crowd into Connie's bar for a drink, to fortify themselves against both the final, agonizing minutes of waiting, and mute the lingering horror of the awful puppet show performed by Ethel and Pickie Beecher, the angel released swarms of tiny insectoid waldoes, each only as big as a cookie, outsized by the yellow slip of paper that every one carried, like a sail, on its back. The high whine of their engines preceded them down the ramp—they rolled into the lobby in pairs but split up to find the recipients of their news. When one of them crashed into Jemma's foot she'd thought she'd just gotten in its way, but when she stepped aside it backed up and rammed her foot again. She looked over at Rob, who was staring fervently at his own shoes.

"There's something I should tell you," he said, and then confessed that he'd entered them in the Match.

"You what?" she asked him, over and over while children and adults ran back and forth around them, waving their golden tickets and seeking their match. She kept pointing at her belly, now with one hand, now with the other, now with both. "Hello!" she said. "Didn't you notice this?"

"Whichever one was left over, is what I asked for," he said. "I didn't want one of them to be left out." The waldo was still bumping insistently against her foot when Pickie came slipping through the crowd, ticket in hand. "Hello," he said simply, when he arrived.

"There you are!" Jemma said brightly. Rob looked surprised to see him—that only aggravated her fury. "You may as well just have asked for him," she told him later.

Pickie moved into their room that night, bringing only a suitcase full of lavender pajamas and the cloud-colored puppet to which he'd given voice in the puppet show. There wasn't any magic button to press, to make the room bigger, and the angel would not or could not accommodate them with another room, or a balcony-bubble, or an extra-dimensional pocket. Rob dragged in another bed and set it atop the one they slept in. They discovered the first night that he had a habit of rolling out of his bed, both of them waking around two a.m. to a leaden thump, and both too sleepy and disoriented to possibly know what it was until they heard Pickie say, "I am not injured." After that they took the top bunk, but the next morning they found Pickie sleeping in the tub, which he said he preferred, anyway, and asked them to cover him over as he slept with a piece of plywood. They refused. He made do with a blanket tied to the soap holder at one edge, draped over the tub, and weighted on the side with books.

"Whichever is left over," she said again on the second night he was with them, after they were reasonably certain that he was asleep.

"Aren't we done with that?" he asked. "I said I was sorry, and that I wasn't sorry. I'm glad he's here. You're glad too. You admitted it. Are you taking it back now?"

"No. I know," she said

"You can't take it back," he said.

"I'm not. Don't be a goon."

"You're the goon. Cheap and squeaky goon with no room in your heart for a bald little blood drinker."

"He's given up the hooch," Jemma said.

"I guaiac'd a stool," Rob said.

"At least you didn't get us Snood in a big diaper. "

"That would have been worse. Not that this is bad. It's just new, like for everybody else. I can't stop thinking about them, everybody going back to their rooms with new kids and new lives, to be new families. It's all different and better for everybody, and we're twice as lucky because we get to do it now and we get to do it again in four months."

"I didn't say it was bad. It all worked out. It's all fine. I'm fine with it.

Who else does he belong with?"

"Nobody," he said, and lifted her shirt to kiss her between the shoulders. Just as he did it there came a horrible screech from the bathroom. They both recognized it instantly, the same noise that had rang out in the puppet show. They threw open the bathroom door and turned on the light. Pickie was sitting calmly in the empty tub, his hand in his gray puppet.

"What's the matter?" Rob asked him

"All's well," he said.

"You screamed," Jemma said.

"I am playing with my puppet."

"Okay," said Rob. "Don't."

"We mean don't scream," Jemma said. "You can play with the puppet."

"Just do it quietly," Rob said.

"It's very late," Jemma said.

"It is one twenty-three," Pickie said.

On the fourth night she and Rob had sex, to assert their authority over their room, Jemma thought, and because they both really wanted to. It was a quiet affair, Jemma on her side and Rob behind her. For ten minutes they were silent and unmoving, both of them listening intently for noise from beyond the bathroom door. It was closed, and they could hear nothing but the hum of the bathroom fan—Pickie liked to have it running while he slept. It was the sort of sex very old people must have, Jemma thought, whose bones hurt when they move, or the sex available to lovers buried together in a coffin, for whom space is at an utter premium, whose hips can give or take no more than a few inches. It would have been enough, and it was its own sort of new pleasure, the quiet and the constraint, but still they told each other the things they would have done, in a different room, or with the tub empty in the next room, and Jemma was a little distracted by how curious it was to have whispery phone sex with no phone, and the person right behind you, and the actual thing going on too.

Rob left before dawn the next morning to go running with Jordan Sasscock. Jemma forced herself from bed not long afterward because she wanted to make breakfast for Pickie. She had meant to do it on both preceding days but had slugged too long abed, and Pickie slipped past her during one of the fifteen snooze interludes she habitually indulged in since her mornings had become lazy. She rose and dressed and started replicating furiously. She moved the desk away from the wall and covered it with a tablecloth and set the two chairs in the room at it, and arranged the variety of little dishes on it: mango bread and churros and boiled eggs with butter and pancakes in the shape of a P and cereal letters that spelled his whole name, and then the things she knew he would actually like: blood oranges and blood sausage and a stinking blood pudding. As if he were acting out a part as certainly as she was trying to the toilet flushed just as she poured out two huge glasses of juice for them and he opened the bathroom door. He stood there a moment looking at the food.

"It's breakfast," she said.

"Thank you," he said. "I usually abstain." But he sat down and put his napkin in his lap, and started assembling a variety of foods upon his plate. "I don't care much for sausage," he said, pulling the whole plate of them next to his and spearing one with the tip of his knife, and smelling of it deeply before taking a bite.

"They're all for you," Jemma said, dipping her spoon into a bowl of Pickios. That and the juice was all she wanted. She'd already had three churros. "Did you sleep okay?" she asked him.

"Except for the muttering of the angel. Did you know she can talk from out of the faucet?"

"I guess she can talk from anywhere."

"I stuffed it up with a cloth, so she talked from the drain. I covered that with my shoe, so her voice came seeping from between the tiles. I couldn't cover those up. For an hour she talked to me. I'm trying to sleep, I told her. I am one-hundred and thirty-one years weary tonight, angel. Shut your blessed mouth. But she said, Abomination, ageless of days, soon you will be washed clean, and you will not be hungry anymore." He tore an orange in half with his little hands and popped the flesh off the skin, then stuck both halves in his mouth before starting to chew hugely on them. "I am always hungry," he said, "but I am not a slave to my hungers."

"It's not polite to talk with your mouth full."

"Pardon me," he said, flashing pieces of orange and sausage and wet sticky crumbs of churro. "She tells me, Soon you will not miss your brother anymore. Can you imagine anything more obscene? Better to tell me, Soon your brother will not be dead any longer. That would be better, easier to believe, and exactly the opposite of that other obscenity. But the dead are dead. That was decided long ago."

"Maybe she means that things will be so nice it just won't hurt so much anymore, or you won't think of it so often."

"Am I a whore, to go licking after the first distraction? Are you that sort of whore?"

"It's not polite to say whore, Pickie. Especially at the table."

"Pardon me. I ask no pardon, though, for my fury. Would you pass over the pudding? Thank you. You're wrong, anyhow. You cannot know the shape of the new world any more than I can. We are both too old. No one knows it now but the infants, and they speak to no one. The knowledge will pass up through the years—maybe Ella Thims will know it soon. It will come so late to you and to me that it will be as good as never." He concentrated a moment on the pudding. "I hate angels," he said.

"But you eat their food."

"Shall I eat my hand instead?" He ate up the whole of the pudding, then turned back to the churros, and started and completed the eggs, wiping the dish with a pancake and then eating that, too. He ate everything on the table, even drinking down the dregs of Jemma's cereal milk. "It's good to be a vegetarian," he said, when he was finished.

"Would you like something else?" she asked him. "It would be easy to make."

"I could eat it," he said, "but it wouldn't make any difference. You won't be hungry anymore. You will forget your brother. Better to say the moon will become an eye, or the sun will burn blue. Nasty, stupid fucking angel!"

"Pickie! Apologize right now," she said, though she hated her too, in her way, and she hardly wanted to be a corrector or a disciplinarian.

"I'm sorry," he said. "I am so sorry, for so many things. I will not say sorry to an angel, though." He got out of his chair and ran over to her, skibbling like an ordinary six-year-old. "Oh Mama," he said. "I am too sorry. I know you are not that sort of whore, not one to ever forget your brother. It is the worst sin, just the sort to be encouraged in by an angel. Wasn't it the reason for the drowning, because too many of them had forgotten their dead brothers, because they all went on like such lives and deaths did not matter? Shame and water upon them." He sighed, and sobbed, and Jemma was so tempted to stab into his sick little brain with green fire and burn it clean of all the wacky shit infesting it, but she could tell without trying that she would be as harshly rebuked as ever. She petted his warm bald head and murmured, "It's okay." This made him laugh. He lifted his head to smile at her, then put his face in her lap again and sang. It took her a little while to make out what he was saying. "Baby, baby, baby," he sang, over and over, his little hand resting one her belly, Jemma protecting herself with layer after layer of imaginary insanity repellant. "Baby, baby, baby," and finally, after a hundred or more baby's, "Baby brother."

It was Kidney who noticed the boat. A week after the Match, on their one-hundred-and-seventy-third day at sea she pointed it out during Jemma's class. They were playing multi-vector scrabble, a game designed by Josh Swift, who was insufficiently challenged by the regular game, and so went to the angel for help making a board that let you spell words up in every direction into the air, and down below the board, which floated four feet above the ground. They were playing in two teams of four and one of five—Jemma and Pickie and the three youngest children. Jemma's team had just taken the lead when Pickie built *pantarch* up from *cupola*. Kidney's observation interrupted an argument between Pickie and Josh, who would not believe that there was any such word as pantarch, pantarchy, or pantarchian.

"It's just another iceberg," said Cindy Flemm, squinting after Kidney's pointing finger. Four days before they'd seen the first one, a mountain of green ice that passed over the horizon in the early-morning darkness, raising false hopes of an island, and then false alarms of a collision as it drifted steadily toward them, getting huger and huger in the hours after dawn. Just at noon, they passed within five hundred yards of it, and people crowded the roof and the windows to stare up, hoping to see a bear or a penguin. One after another the icebergs came sliding over the horizon in every shape and every size, the smallest not much bigger than a car and the biggest dwarfing the hospital. Within a day they had become a common sight, but they never lost their novelty. Jemma found she could stare at them for hours. Even just one penguin would have been heartening, but she daydreamed of swarms of them pouring over the ice on their bellies, sliding in spirals down to the sea, now green and clear—it was water that cried out for penguins to frolic in it. The incredible abundance of fish should have been enough, she knew, but already people were turning away from the windows and the water and looking to the sky. "I just want a bird, just one," said Helena Dufresene, one morning on the roof. "It would be such a gift," she added, and Jemma found herself agreeing, and consoling herself with a fantasy of hidden penguins, secreting themselves on the back side of every iceberg, holding flippers to beaks as they passed the hospital.

"Nuh uh," said Kidney. "It's a big boat. I can see the smokestack."

"Iceberg," said Jarvis.

"It's not moving the same," said Josh.

Jemma squinted, too. She could see the boat-shape moving among a herd of hill-sized icebergs, but she wasn't convinced. "Let's get back to the game," she said, but they all ignored her. Josh went to a replicator and politely asked the angel for a pair of binoculars. She gave him an old-fashioned spyglass of polished brass. He raised it to his eye and said, "Hot damn."

"Wait a minute," Jemma said. "We should make sure before you all go running off and..." But they were already all running off to shout "A boat! A boat!" throughout the hospital. Soon it was just she and Pickie there.

He looked through the little telescope and said, "Another angel, Mama. As if we didn't have enough already." She asked what he meant, but he sat down to consider the Scrabble board again and handed the glass to Jemma. She looked through it and saw what the children had seen: a big boat, a cruise liner, floating backward between two icebergs, as if they were escorting it someplace.

There was another swarming to the roof, and people called out "Hello!" as the boat drifted nearer, even though it was still over a mile away, and the huge crowd grew entirely silent while they waited for a reply. Jemma went right to the Council chamber, swimming against the current on the ramp. Dr. Tiller was already there, sitting on a table and tapping one booted foot on a chair as she watched the boat getting bigger and bigger outside the window.

"What do you think, Dr. Claflin?" she asked. Jemma shrugged and sat down. When the other Friends and the rest of the Council had arrived they declared an emergency session and began to babble furiously, asking and answering questions like What does it mean, and What do you think, and

What should we do, and Does anyone else think it looks like the Queen Elizabeth Two? The boat loomed behind them as they had their wild, excited discussions; Jemma turned to look over her shoulder every ten minutes and found it had gotten a little bigger. She called for order but no one could hear her, and she would not use the gavel. When she turned to Vivian she could hardly make herself heard until the four of them pushed their chairs together and huddled their heads.

"How will we get over to the boat?" asked Ishmael.

"What precautions should we take?" asked Vivian.

"How soon can we go?" asked Jemma.

"It is no place for you," said Monserrat. "What if there are cannibals?"

"Why would there be cannibals?"

"Because," Monserrat said. "There is always something bad on boats like that."

"If I say I go, I go. Who's in charge here?"

"We are," said Ishmael.

"You are," said Vivian, "but with qualifications."

"Can anyone stop me from going over there?"

"Probably not," said Ishmael. "But wouldn't it be a better idea—"

"No," Jemma said.

"Very well," said Monserrat. "The four of us will go, though I saw the movie, *Cannibal Cruise,* and it was a boat just like that one which came drifting out of the mist to lure and destroy the curious."

"The question remains," said Ishmael. "How to travel?"

Vivian drew a picture of a boat on Jemma's big yellow pad, and Ishmael, carefully taking the pen from her, broke it down into sections small enough to come out of a replicator. They traded the pen back and forth, clarifying and embellishing the sketch—sails, solar-powered propeller, hydrofoil, boarding crane—while the Council chamber continued in bedlam. Dr. Snood took off his shoe, finally, and pounded it on the table. "Order!" he shouted. "Order! Madame Friend, will you bring us to order?"

Jemma opened her mouth, but before she could speak the ship, which had disappeared as the hospital made one of its usual midday rotations, drifted into view again not a hundred yards away. Jemma stood up, and now she did like everyone else—she hurried to the window and pressed her face against the glass.

Dr. Snood lobbied vigorously to be appointed an ambassador, but the only thing worse than cannibals were cannibals encountered in the company of a snide fussbudget—Jemma had her absolute way. They appeased Dr. Snood by appointing him and the lift team as backups.

It was ten o'clock in the morning when Kidney spotted the boat. By five Jemma and the three lesser Friends were gathered at the head of the crowd on the roof. The boat had sidled up within twenty yards of them, close enough to read the name, the *Celebration,* and to see how utterly empty the decks and windows were. It was huge—the center of the hospital floated at a point about fifty yards from the bow, but the boat stretched out for hundreds of yards behind them.

They tested their phones one more time, and then Rob aimed the bazooka-sized launcher the angel had made for them and fired a rope and a hook across the water. It punched into a wall on the far side of a section of promenade deck and stuck fast. He sent another one over to strike four feet above the first, and he and Ishmael secured the lines to new hooks in the sycamore tree, stretching them tight with a crank. Rob tested them, tightening them both three times before he was satisfied, bouncing on the bottom one and launching himself over the first one, releasing one hand and doing a half twist before swinging down on the other side.

"Okay," he said. "Are you sure you don't want a fifth person?" He had sounded like Dr. Snood, when he had Jemma alone, arguing that it wasn't safe for her to go.

"We'll call if we need help," Vivian said, and dialed her phone in demonstration. Back in the crowd, Dr. Snood answered his.

"Hello?" he said.

"See you later," Vivian said. She hung up and climbed on the ropes. Jemma pulled at the neck of her maternity wetsuit—they were all wearing wetsuits—and went after her, looking down, like she wasn't supposed to, as soon as she cleared the edge of the roof. A section of the eighth floor stuck out protectively underneath her, and then she cleared that. Emma waved at her from out of a fourth-floor window, part of an extraction team waiting with hooks and life preservers in the PICU, in case any of them fell in. Jemma put one black rubber bootie in front of the other and in five steps was over the green water. It made her feel cold just to look at it. She imagined the penguins again, streaming below the clear surface in a horde, and breaking the surface to jump up and perform stupid and amazing tricks on the rope.

Vivian shook the top line, and broke her reverie. "Come on, Poky," she said.

On the other side, the four Friends arranged themselves in a line and began to explore. Ishmael went first, carrying the weapon. "The angel gave you that?" Jemma had asked him on the roof, when she saw that he was carrying a gun.

"It's not what you think," he said, turning and firing it at a bush. It shot something that looked like a stream of ink—not very fast, either. Jemma thought it was just a squirt gun until the coherent beam of ink suddenly broke apart into a net that wrapped around the bush. "That bush is neutralized," Ishmael said.

They had landed on the third deck from the top of the ship. It was empty except for a row of lounge chairs. "They're filthy," said Monserrat, bending down to run her finger along the arm of a chair. It was covered with a layer of thick black dust, her finger left a glaring white mark. Vivian said, "Don't touch that stuff." She cupped her hand around her mouth and shouted out, "Hello!"

"You're going to wake up the zombies," Jemma said.

"There has to be someone here," Vivian said.

"There doesn't," said Ishmael. "They could have gotten off at a different stop, or they could all be dead. Maybe they all jumped in the water. Maybe I was here, way before. Nothing looks familiar."

"Maybe," Jemma said. She closed her eyes and tried to look without using her eyes. Her fellow explorers were bright and obvious, she tried to look past them, imagining the ship to be entirely transparent, a cruise ship for Wonder Woman to relax on, to stuff herself at a constant buffet, to lie by the pool while she got a massage and a manicure and a teeth cleaning and a high colonic all at once.

"Let's go," Vivian said.

"Wait," Jemma said. "I'm listening."

"What do you hear?" asked Monserrat.

"Nothing," said Jemma, already terminally distracted by the surprising variety of objects that came tumbling from Wonder Woman's colon—old red meat, chewing gum, a California license plate, a hundred cocaine-stuffed condoms—but had seen already in her mind a glass boat empty of any flash of green life and filled with as much dust as air. They walked on in their cautious single file, down the deck toward the stern of the boat. Jemma looked back at the hospital. There was an unbroken line of people standing along the edge of the roof, and a face at every window. It should have been stranger, she thought, to see it floating there twenty yards away, but somehow the attendant icebergs seemed like the only strange part of the picture. The others turned around too, and all four of them stood, arrested by the sight until Snood, watching them with a pair of fancy binoculars, called to ask if something was wrong.

"It looks so small," Ishmael said. "Have we really been in there such a long time?"

"Some of us longer than others," said Vivian.

The wall to their left fell away after a few hundred feet, and the deck opened up across the width of the ship. There were dozens more chairs, and tables, all gathered in circles around a big circular bar. Jemma walked up and peered over the edge of it, at a hundred liquor bottles arranged in a spiral that echoed the shape of the hospital across the water. Not a single one was broken. The floor behind the bar was covered with the same black dust as the chairs.

"Hey," Jemma said. "Footprints." They crossed each other in the dust, and there was an intact pair standing in front of the vodka section.

"At least a thirteen," Vivian said. "Do you think they're fresh?" Everybody shrugged, not knowing how to tell such things. The back of the bar was sheltered by the wind, so they decided the prints might have been there for a long time. They crossed the deck and passed through a door onto rich carpet, raising dust with every step no matter how lightly they tried to go. Monserrat sneezed. "Hello," Vivian said again, not very loud.

They passed a sign: *Smoking Room,* and pressed their heads against the glass to look inside at the dusty leather furniture and full ashtrays. Vivian's phone rang again, making them all jump. "What?" she said, answering it. "Yes. Don't call again unless an iceberg is about to hit us. All right. Goodbye. Snood again," she said after she hung up, shaking her head. Beyond the smoking room they found another set of red-carpeted stairs. They considered splitting up, so some of them could continue exploring this deck while others went below, but fear of zombies or some similar unpleasantness kept them together. They discovered two more bars, a game room, a golf simulator, and a hot tub so full of dust it had become a pool of mud. They walked down the same strip of deck they'd landed on. Jemma waved at the hospital, feeling silly.

"It's the Lido deck," Vivian said excitedly at the bottom of the stairs, reading the name off a sign in the wall. "This is where all the action is. We'll find someone here."

"Or something," said Monserrat. The nearest door led into a salon complex, a gym and a spa, and a row of doors that opened onto dusty massage tables. They found a shriveled magazine in the sauna. Ishmael put his finger in the third mud-tub they found.

"Don't touch it," said Vivian.

"Maybe it's beauty mud," he said.

"If you put it on your face, I'm not letting you back into the hospital," Jemma said. But he only held up her finger and stared at it a moment before wiping it on his wetsuit. Outside was the big pool, covered with a fine layer of dust, but not muddy, an empty restaurant, and two long buffets filled with mummified food, shrunken heads of lettuce and dusty shrimp nubbins and pies caved in like old faces.

"Did they leave in a hurry?" Ishmael asked, considering a Renaissance-fair-sized turkey leg. He dropped it on the deck, making a dull thud that was echoed seconds later by a loud thud somewhere on the deck above them.

"What'd you do?" Vivian asked him. They all stood very still by the buffet, listening, Ishmael with his gun held up next to his ear, but they heard nothing else. They continued exploring; the Lido deck was empty but for dust and old food. On the next floor down they found the first rooms. The ones that were open were empty except for piles of dust, gathered in the carpet, pooled in the sinks, layered on top of the neatly turned down beds and the pillow-chocolates. At the rooms that were locked they knocked but no one answered. Ishmael broke one in with four hard kicks and two blows with his shoulder. He stumbled through the broken door and fell onto the bed, sending up a huge cloud of dust that sent them all backpedaling into the hall, coughing and sneezing. Ishmael emerged, face sooty, wiping dust from his eyes. "Nobody home," he said.

"These are the fancy rooms," Monserrat observed. "They all have the nice balconies, but they're still so small. I was going to take a cruise with my husband, before. It seems like such a terrible idea, now, floating for days out on the water. And so small! My room is bigger, over there. To think that people used to go float on the water on purpose. Where could the fun possibly be in that?"

Past the coffee bar and the library, through the perfumery and a shop with towering shelves full of sentimental porcelain figures, down a grand stairway and through a green atrium, through two dining rooms, into the kitchens and down the stairs again, they continued, finding no one, slowing and stopping when they came into a narrow hall lined on either side with photographs of the passengers. There were hundreds of them to look at—anyone who stepped off the gangplank had become the subject of an unsolicited portrait. Jemma blackened the elbows of her blue wetsuit rubbing dust from the glass to better see the faces. Without speaking they proceeded in tiny side steps down the hall, two on either side, looking at every picture, until Vivian's phone rang. "I told you not to call me again," she said, but then her tone softened. "Oh. *Oh.* Okay, we'll hurry. There's nothing here, anyway." She turned to Jemma. "It's Rob," she said. "He says the boat's drifting. His little meter is reading increasing tension on the line. How much?" she said into the phone again. "That unit means nothing to me. Is that a lot? Okay." She hung up. "He did a calculation. If the drift continues at the current rate then we have four hours before the line breaks."

"There's no one here," Jemma said, peering at an apple-shaped lady in a tennis visor. She wore a pair of capri pants and a striped tank top—a sort of uniform, there were twenty other women in the hall wearing the same thing. "Look at them all. They were all here, and now no one's here."

"We should split up," said Ishmael, "if we're in a hurry."

"There's no one here," Jemma said again, shaking her head, but they divvied up the ship, Ishmael getting the most territory, Jemma the least. She only had to look on the rest of this deck. They split up, phones switched to walkie-talkie mode. Jemma turned away from the pictures and continued down the hall, peeking behind another set of bars, resisting the call of the karaoke room—the stereo was quiet but the screen was still actively scrolling the lyrics to "You've Got a Friend"—and coming finally to the casino. It was the last room on her deck, so she took her time searching it. Twice the every-fifteen-minute call came on her phone, all of them reporting how they'd found nothing. There was nothing behind the bar in the casino, no one in the fancy marble bathrooms, no one under the blackjack table. Cups of coins still sat on stools next to the slot machines. She played a couple, and wasted twenty minutes demonstrating her bad luck. Worse than the slot machines was the roulette table—it sucked her in. She placed a few bets, but soon forgot them, entranced by the way the ball bounced, rolled, and settled, and complicated the game by rolling the ball from the far end of the table, or tossing it from five, ten and fifteen paces. At twenty it bounced off the table and rolled far away, disappearing under a table in one of the four adjoining bars. Jemma got down on her knees to chase it, and found herself face to face with the boy as soon as she lifted the cloth. About fourteen, dressed in a pair of shorts and a Hawaiian shirt, he had his arms wrapped tight around himself, a plush dolphin and a leather-covered book clutched to his chest. She touched him—he was warm. A thin strand of hair blew away from his mouth with every breath he took, then settled again against his face. Jemma closed her eyes and found him not there in head. She opened them again and prodded his shoulder with her fist. "Hey," she said. "Wake up."

True to Rob's prediction, the boat did not stay with them for long. An hour after they brought the boy back to the hospital the boat began visibly to drift behind them. The ropes snapped, and the gangway that twenty citizens were hastily constructing in a hallway of the seventh floor never had a chance to be lifted into position. The boat simply stopped moving, but they did not. It passed farther and farther behind them while a small crowd stood watching on the roof. Everybody had the feeling it was going to sink, but it only passed into a patch of gray mist. When it was gone people hung their heads, their hopes of attaching a luxury annex to the hospital finally dashed. Dr. Tiller pointed out derisively that they probably had more dance floors and movie theatres and massage rooms in the hospital than the boat had, anyway.

They took the boy to the PICU. A cautious nurse had stored a bed, instead of tossing it out the window in the big purge, many weeks before when so many hospital beds and IV poles and bedside commodes had gone to their rest in the sea. So he lay under display of his entirely normal vitals, in a room decorated with the drawings of the second-graders who used it as an art studio, his clothes folded neatly on a chair next to his head, his dolphin under his arm, and his book under his hand. It looked like a diary, complete with a lock. No one had opened it yet.

"He looks fine," Vivian said.

"Almost," Jemma said. "I really think he's just sleeping." She had tried to wake him up across the water, sending a spark through her finger that should have made him jump, but it didn't even interrupt his snoring. "Well," she said to Vivian. "I think I'm ready. Would you send the kids in?" She'd asked for her class to be there, to watch and maybe to learn and maybe even to help, or maybe because to involve them, even in the most peripheral way, was more like teaching them something than were games of scrabble, picnics, and her cheating game of hide-and-go-seek. The majority of the crowd had transferred itself from the roof to the space outside the PICU. Inside there were only members of the Council, people Jemma wanted there, and a few citizens chosen by quickly drawn lots. The kids filed through into the room. Someone had arranged them from smallest to largest. They were all very subdued. Even Jarvis looked awed, and was very well-behaved. They stood in a semicircle around Jemma, all joining hands without her even asking them to do it.

"Here we go," Jemma said. She sat down on his clothes, took his hand, and closed her eyes. He was still curiously not there when she tried to look at him just using her brain. She had to send a little shoelace of flame whipping out and into him to light him up before she could see him properly. It had been a while before she'd really burned—in the past weeks there's been no call for her fire. Her last patient had come to her over two weeks before, Wayne, who broke his arm in a roller-hockey game. She thought it would take a while to really gear up, that she would have to call up flame for hours before she could really have enough to sock it to him, or that she'd have to let it burn on her before it could get hot enough to wake him up. But it came right away as hard as it had the night she'd done her big fix. One moment she was holding his hand, and only the children standing right there could perceive that there was a noodle of fire wrapped in a coil along both their wrists; the next, she and he both had burst into cool green flames that wrapped the whole bed and licked at the ceiling. Jemma, her mind suddenly full of the image of the hospital viewed from the boat, saw for a moment the strange green flash in the window.

He wasn't well, after all, not all right—she saw it once he was properly illuminated. He had subtle warts, and most varieties of sexually transmitted infection—syphilis and gonorrhea and chlamydia and scabies, everything but lice and granulosum venereum and the big one, for which she searched assiduously, but there was no trace of it, and she was sure she would recognize it, if it was there. She stomped on the spirochetes with giant green shoes, made fire fingers between which to pinch critters and cocci, placing them one by one into an imaginary bucket that she emptied out the window. The strange little chalmydiae went chirruping out of epithelial cells, evicted by fire and fury, jumping into the bucket like trained circus fleas. These problems were all easy to fix, but none of them, she knew, was what was making him sleep.

She looked through him, from head to toe, over and over, burning further and further in until she felt she could number not just the hairs of his head but the cells of his body. There was still something wrong. She could not put a shape or a name to it, though she burned him and burned him, and as she herself burned brighter even than when she stood in the NICU with Brenda hanging on her finger. Every child but Pickie and Jarvis ran out of the room, and of the others only Ethel kept trying to look into the conflagration to watch the shapes in the middle, to put out her own mind and help with whatever was happening. All over the hospital every living person experienced an off sense, like someone plucking at their spine, or a baby kicking inside them, or just a plainer nausea as Jemma pummeled the boy—she was listening so hard to him, and looking so hard into him that their discomfort became louder and plainer to her as the long minutes passed. There it was, almost a shadow, flickering in the edge of her mind and then disappearing entirely. She stood alone in a bright green room, the sleeping boy at her feet.

She raised her hands and cried out. She felt her baby kick in her, protesting or cheering, she couldn't tell—even when she was burning this bright she could not look inside herself to see it. She gathered up as much of the fire as she could bear and pounded him with it, no longer trying to give a shape or a voice to what afflicted him, but trying to destroy it. Flames shot out of the room and down the hall, and all over the hospital people stumbled. Then they were gone. Jemma was in the bed, lying on the boy, her cheek pressing against his cheek. He was still asleep.

"It's a tale of sex and woe," said Karen. "Just like my marriage. You want me to read you some?"

"No thanks," said Dr. Chandra. "I've heard enough of those."

"You're just being a prude. It's not like you think. It's not pornographic. It's philosophic. Well, maybe not quite that either, but it's not what you think."

"I have no interest," he said. "Anyway, we're not allowed, and I always do what I'm told."

"*I'm* allowed. *You're* allowed. The twelve-year-olds are not allowed. Which is as it should be, though like I say, it's not pornographic. But I can see how it could be dangerous, you know. It makes you think the wrong thoughts. I find myself thinking the wrong thoughts. Bad thoughts. Not dirty thoughts. How many times do I have to tell you that it's not like *that*? You want me to read you some?"

"I just want some more coffee," he said. She sighed, closed the book she'd been holding open in front of him all the time they'd been talking, put it down, and took his cup. He stared at it but did not open it or even touch it. He'd seen the boy in the PICU, had taken the tour there just like everybody else, and wondered like everybody else what was going on with him, that his illness could resist Jemma Claflin's Jesus-magic. The boy had a beautiful face. It wasn't a surprise that people like Karen were falling in love with him, or that they wanted to know every last little thing about him, or that they would form reading groups around his sex diary.

"I have no interest in that sort of thing," he said again to Karen when she gave him his coffee.

"Which is exactly your problem," she said. "You have no interest."

"Have a good day," he said, trying to make it sound like he actually wanted her to have a bad day, but he always failed at that. His compliments only ever sounded like compliments. If he sat still for it Karen would spend an hour digging out the root causes of his unhappiness. It was always offered, he knew, in a spirit of earnest helpfulness, but her argument always sounded like an insult, and stung like one, and never inspired him to improve himself. It only made him want to go to his room, to sit on his balcony thinking about how he could hardly stand to be around his only friend in the hospital, and calm himself by staring at the water.

When he got back to his room he sat in his usual place, and stared out like usual at the horizon, but no peace came to him. When he closed his eyes he could see the boy's face on the water. "I have no interest in him," he said again, but when he went inside to ask the angel for lunch he asked for a copy of the little book as well.

I can still see Miami and I'm already bored. A new year for me Mrs. DiMange but everything seems the same. Still the same gray color in everybody's face and on my face and still the same tired feeling when I look up at the sky. It should lift something out of me looking up like that it used to but never does any more. In dream number five you are looking up into that sky and the blue feeling is something you have gathered in your mouth and when we kiss it passes into me and I think, it's like this. Also we are flying, or you are flying and I am riding you—yes, we're doing the Jackson and it's like in number seven but in that one you are floating on the water and every time I push into you the water pushes back and you cry out like a bird.

They're afraid to leave me home, that's why I'm here, floating away on a boat full of old anniversary couples. It has nothing to do with my birthday, except that I'd have an excuse to throw another party, not that I would. Nobody really appreciates it, when you go out of your way like that. Better to pick one person and do a whole party's worth of shit for them, than to spread your goodwill among a gaggle of dumb asses. In number twenty-three I have a party just for you. It's in my house and every room is decorated in a different way, always with things you like, only for you.

We are going to San Juan and Jamaica and Aruba and St. Thomas and Martinique. Who cares?

A day of discoveries, Mrs. DiMange. I am the youngest person on board. There's food everywhere and you can stuff yourself at the Lido buffet all night long. The Alternative Theater does not show alternative movies—next I will puzzle out in exactly what way it is alternative, no one seems to know. The bartender in the casino won't card me. There's no one in the piano bar during the day and I can play all I want while the sun is up.

And another discovery—I went in to pee in the casino bathroom while Muz was slaving at the slot machine and it was very fancy—white marble and real towels folded by the sink and a little man who runs in twelve times a day to change them, and soap in a dish, and French-milled pucks in the urinals. They were the good kind, there in a row with nothing to block the view of your neighbor. In number 13 you walk in while I'm there and stand with a banana poking out of your pants. I am in disguise, you say, and I am in love, and then there comes a Jackson, you against the wall with your cheek pressed against the seams between the cement blocks. I was thinking about it, because it was so fancy, and I was redoing our bathroom in my head, taking out the truckstop décor and installing the new marble—just standing there. Not waiting for one because it didn't seem like the right place. I get a sense, you know. I thought I could tell where things happen. It's like there's a glow, like how you know somebody's interested, even though they're standing in line next to you at the supermarket with their wife and their three kids. You look at them and they'll follow you anywhere. It's like that, but with a place and not a person.

He just reached out. It was fine. That's enough of an invitation, standing there in a line of high-class urinals with a great big boner. I could hardly be offended, and he wasn't so bad. He was dressed up for dinner in a white jacket and a black bow tie. I touched that first—it was real, the kind you have to knot up yourself. Seven black buttons on a shirt as fancy as any of the toilets. Silver rims—I thought I could see myself. Then I held on to him. He was bigger than me. Jack says soaking your dick in miracle-gro will make it bigger but I did that all summer and it made no fucking difference at all.

We need a little privacy, he said, walking backward through one of the marble doors. He stood on the toilet so the little man, when he came in to change the towels, would think it was just me in there, standing and thinking. I did a Bush 1 on him and then I climbed up and he did me too. It was fine. I saw him later in the dining room with his family. He raised his knife to me like a salute and he winked. I walked right past his table to go to the bathroom again and I waited for five minutes but he didn't come.

Everything all right in there? Muz asked, when I finally came back, putting a hand on my sensitive stomach.

Fine, I said, but nothing tasted any good, and no matter what the waiter brought it wasn't what I wanted.

Vivian did not like what she was reading. She had read the whole thing through twice already, but kept going back to it because she thought it must contain a clue to the boy's past, and to their future. She had read it the first time looking for answers about the boat, but it said nothing about where everyone had gone. No mass leap from the decks, no zombie war, no death by starvation. Just the desperate notes of a boy in trouble.

"I do not like what I am reading," she said out loud. She was at her desk, hunched close over the book, as if getting her brain close to the letters was going to make it easier for her to understand their secret meaning.

"I can offer you something far more pleasant," the angel said.

Vivian shook her head and rubbed her eyes, then looked up at the pictures of the boy she'd taped across the wall above her desk, eight views of his sleeping face. If you studied them like she had, you could see that his expression was not the same in every picture. Here there was just a little droop of the eyebrows that suggested sadness, here a hint of a smile, here his eyes seemed shut tight, not just closed in sleep. The diary was a desperate message to his teacher—so full of love and yet how it condemned her, so Mrs. DiMange was the Great Satan of the hospital. But he was a message too, as obvious and as inscrutable as his diary, thrust at them over the waters just as another had been thrust up at them. And did he speak as lovingly, and damn as thoroughly, as this little black book?

Two today.

In the morning a man in the Lido buffet. I brushed up against his belly while we were in line for breakfast, and then he brushed up against me before he sat down. We went up two more times and both times it happened—my hand drifting across him I could feel how hard it was even through the pants and even just with my knuckles. He stayed behind after his wife went away and after Muz and Puz went to the salon. I went into the bathroom it was the good kind—just one toilet and a lock on the door.

Mostly he just wanted to stand there and Wilson and by the time I finally convinced him to Coolidge it wasn't even a minute before he popped. He wouldn't look at me afterward but he asked me my name.

Later on but before lunch in the gym. I lifted for a little while and then I went in the back. There was nobody in the sauna but one guy was sitting in the steam room he looked up at me when I came in and I could tell right away though he didn't move until the steam came on. Then his hand came out of the cloud and settled on my chest. He said I was a big boy but I said I was just inflated from the bench press it goes away in a half hour and then I'm just another skinny puppy. Bush again and a little bit of Bush Jr. It got too hot and we had to finish in the shower.

Matt and Gavin. They're nice names. I used to say my name was Matt, sometimes. What's your name? They never really want to know. They're just being polite I think I like it better when they don't ask and I don't ask either. Once somebody called out my real name while we were doing it and I couldn't even finish I was so mad. I knocked his face against the floor I was hoping so bad that I would knock his teeth right up into his nose but then he made this noise it was very sad and I had to stop everything. I didn't know why I was so mad it seemed a little extreme but later I figured it out. My name is for you. It's for you to say. You say it in every one except number 20 and 15 and 40.

They were by the pool I sat down between them it didn't take very long. Sometimes I am lucky but not usually this lucky there is something special about this boat. Matt smelled like coconuts Gavin smelled like gum. What do you like to do they asked me I said everything. I got to be in the middle of the Coolidge.

"It's not breakfast material," Frank said, when his wife paused in her reading to give him a look that invited some kind of commentary.

"What does that mean? It's not cereal? It's not yogurt? You can't eat it?"

"It's too sad, to read it in the beginning of the day. Let's have something else. Where's *The Tattle Bear?* Or how about something made up entirely?"

Connie shook her head. "That's exactly your problem."

"It is? What is?"

"This, exactly this. You want to avoid the problem, and bury your face in the paper. Listen, the problem is more important than *The Tattle Bear,* and more important than breakfast, and more important than any of that fancy pornography you've been watching."

"But I haven't been... what are you talking about?"

"And how like you," she said, surprising him with an expression he had not seen since before the old world passed away—she wrinkled her nose and pursed her lips and narrowed her eyes. To anyone else it would have looked like she was just concentrating very hard and like she smelled something very peculiar, but to Frank it announced her loathing disappointment. As suddenly as she put it on, she took the expression off, and then her face was merely ugly and sad, and she was crying.

"What?" he asked. "Good God, what is it?"

"How can you not know," she said between little sobs, "when I'm talking about our daughter?"

"Ah," he said, and he didn't need for her to say, If he is doing this, then what is she doing? Or if a boy can be so sad, than can't a girl? It was exactly the sort of ridiculous thing she would obsess over, but he didn't say so, too sad himself at the way she was crying, and at the way this old difference had crept back into their life, and at the way they were fighting again. To see her like this again, so angry and crazy and sad, was as surprising as seeing a mountain thrust up out of the sea. And yet it had a quality, too, of fateful recognition. Of course she was still like this, and of course the earth had not utterly passed away.

"Don't you sigh at me!" she shrieked. He didn't answer, or even heave a more expansive sigh, but said, "I'm sorry." He reached over the table and took the book and started to read from where she had left off.

A girl today, finally. Not a girl—a lady, older than you, even. And her husband, too, but he mostly just watched. She said his name—Scott! Scott!—at the end of our Reagan it was very traditional. The Reagan, that is. Not even a Nancy, just a Ronald, just me on top and him getting closer and closer until he was touching me but no Coolidge though I called out for it I might have said please. He called back to her, too, reaching past me to touch her I could feel him pressed up against my back and he sprayed all over me without hardly any incentive at all. Then they both held me I did a very simple Harrison until I popped and they both put their hands in it and put their hands in their mouths it was like watching Pooh eating honey.

I keep wondering what was going on between them, during. They weren't even touching, even at the end he was just reaching for her and he ran his hands over her without touching her. I was close and I could see it, always an inch or a half inch or just a breath of space between them. It was like they had called me out of some place to put me between them but I wasn't there, either. I can't explain it but it was very definite this is a very strange boat every day I discover it more. I mean I knew what it was like while it was happening but now I am grabbing at it it's like smoke but I know I'll think about it while I'm asleep. I kept looking back at him and looking at her and looking back at him I wanted eyes in the back of my head to see them both at the same time. They must be very much in love.

Nothing today, except you. I did three Harrison's just by myself and it was numbers twenty-two, fourteen, nineteen, fifty-three, and seventy—seventy all alone by itself for twenty minutes between coming back on board and going to dinner I finished just in time. We are in Aruba but all these places seem the same to me, the market squares and the white beaches. Everywhere we go Puz buys a bottle of rum and Muz buys a big tube of Retin-A at the drug store now she has three. She stopped me in the middle of the square this afternoon Puz was walking ahead and she stopped in the middle of making fun of him. She put her hand on my arm and held on to her hat like it might blow away from the questions she was about to ask and said, Are you all right? Are you having a good time?

Oh yes I said. Very good very very good.

There were opportunities today a man on the beach and a lady with a dog and a note from Matt and Aaron slipped under my door but I just wanted to be alone with you now it is almost midnight and somebody is standing a little ways down the deck staring out just like me I could walk by him and touch him as I passed and then it would happen I can already see it. But let him go let them all go I just want to be here with you.

"Are you bored?" Ethel asked Pickie Beecher.

"I am always bored," he said.

"Well, keep cutting. We're almost done." They were snipping words out of the diary and putting them in a glass bowl on the floor. Pickie kept dropping them from too high, and then chasing the fluttering word as it drifted about her room. She had opened a window on the same day that the boat-boy had come into the hospital. She had just finally felt like it, was all.

She had the thought that the boy had something to tell her, and to tell all of them—a fascinating and horrible story, full of something worse and more exciting than mere zombies—and she wanted to help him to tell it. But a séance had yielded the usual silence, which made sense because he wasn't dead. And the aluminum tiara that the angel insisted was the telepathy device she had asked for only made her hear a very quiet sort of murmuring that she could easily have just been imagining. She couldn't get close enough to put a pen in his sleeping hand, and sitting quietly with a pen in her hand yielded nothing but page after page of straight lines. Then she had the idea of using his own words. They would isolate every last one of them in a bowl, and then draw them out one after another to assemble a message, and maybe even a conversation.

"My hand hurts," Pickie said.

"Keep working."

"You are a cruel master."

"Don't call me that. Friends don't call each other master."

"I have no friends, except my brother, and where is he?"

"Don't start that again. Just keep cutting, we're almost done." For a while the only sound was of their scissors working as she snipped in her book and Pickie snipped in his—the boy had written on both sides of every page, so to avoid getting words that were whole on one side but truncated on the other, she got a copy for each of them and painted out whole pages in them, odds in the one and evens in the other. "You know," she said, as she snipped apart the last two words and let them fall into the bowl, "I don't cut because I want to hurt myself. I cut because I want to feel *alive*." Pickie yawned. "Hold on," Ethel said. "The good part is coming."

They closed their eyes and fished in the bowl with their hands, pinching the slips between their fingers and laying them out on an empty game board. It was Chutes and Ladders, one of the many old favorites in the playroom that even the preschoolers had abandoned for the more sophisticated diversions of the angel.

Still cry different silver wonder four teacher were the words.

"What do you think it means?" Ethel asked.

Pickie seemed hardly to think at all before he replied. "Still because he still misses his brother. Cry to cry for him. Different because he is unique in his grief, though the absence of a brother is the commonest grief and the most essential loneliness. Silver for his brother's silver eyes, never to shine in the world. Wonder for the lost wonder of his iron sighs, and the miracles that died with him. Four is the perfect number—it is everywhere and has nothing to do with the message. Teacher because his brother was to teach him happiness and now it is a lesson he will never learn."

Ethel looked at him a moment and then gave him a hug, a gesture he tolerated like always. She gathered up the words and put them back in the bowl. "Let's try again," she said.

A double Coolidge from Matt and Gavin it's not so often you can have them. Matt behind and Aaron in front it was almost too much they kept saying, are you okay and I couldn't talk because I was too close, chasing something again and almost getting it. They were interfering with the questions so I gave up on the AP class and we went back to the simpler thing, just one at a time, each of them in turn I could not make them go quick or hard enough though I called out for it and they shouted back, and shouted to each other—not like love though it was like at swim practice somebody shouting at you the water makes the voice seem far away. Go Matt go a little harder a little faster you almost have it. Every hit I moved a little further up the bed until my head was against the wall, every hit I was a little bit closer it was you I was chasing, always you no matter who it is. What a mystery how it is never you but it is always you, I reach and reach I can hardly stand it. They're not wimpy fags like usual they were a little too fainthearted for the double but they do a good job on the easier thing I can hardly tell when one stops and the other starts, they're so smooth.

I almost get you. You're hand is reaching out to me and like always I miss it I just barely miss it.

Our last night so I thought it would be nice to have everybody together. I was thinking of everything we could do, things I don't even have a name for yet. Matt and Gavin and almost everybody else, I found them and each said okay, see you later, but everyone was late and for a long time I thought it would be just me. Then Scott and Mrs. Scott arrived and then Matt and Gavin I thought it was all going to be ruined they were supposed to come in fifteen-minute intervals because I hadn't told anybody the whole plan. I might have a friend there, too, I said, somebody cool, but I didn't say who but it was all okay I shouldn't have worried even though Matt and Gavin were frightened of the girl I could tell.

I named three new things: McKinley and Buchanan and Cleveland. The rooms aren't very big, especially the singles. That was okay, too. It was like I was swimming through them, suspended in a Bush or a Bush Jr., or a Reagan and a Coolidge—I was floating I was flying I was on my way. Let this be a lesson to you, you told me, how everyone is connected by love. Look at these strangers they would not be together except for you they would all be alone if not for you you are a teacher like me. I am a teacher like you.

* * *

Dr. Chandra was touching himself, though there should not have been anything in the pages of the journal that really excited him in that way—it really was a tale of woe, after all. But it was something he did when he was upset, and the sadness of the story combined with the way it brought back memories of his own teenage adventures with men three and four times his age to make it seem like the necessary thing. Though he told himself over and over as he did it—I am not thinking of that, meaning he was not putting himself in the place of those creepy old men, the way he sometimes in his masturbating imagination put himself in the place of the creepy old men who had pounded his face or his bottom, and imagined his own face, and his own lips crying out under the weight of a fat hairy married man. Really he wasn't thinking of anything for a while, but was only aware of the thing in him that was, stroke by stroke, coming closer to being launched out of his soul—a sadness and an unease and a frustration. Then he did see the boy, not naked or bottom up, not even the pleasant curve of his arm or the beautiful taper of hair at the back of his neck, but whole, neither clothed nor unclothed. He saw him in a way he could not properly describe, since it was a vision that seemed to include so much more than merely physical attributes. And suddenly the work he was doing—the very familiar work of temporarily ameliorating his own sad-sack situation—was not being done for him but for the boy, and with the same single-minded and vigorous force of imagination with which he might otherwise be imagining just how it might feel to be screwed by William Jennings Bryan or Conan the Barbarian or the handsome Yemeni who worked at the Falafel King down the street from his apartment, he now saw a different life for the boy, absent of desperate random screwings and ruinous teacherly vaginas, and loathing, and sadness. He imagined the boy, now not just clothed and unclothed but somehow bodied and unbodied, utterly at home in the world, and this was an ultimate pleasure. Even to consider it from the great distance pierced by his suddenly unbridled imagination was too much for Dr. Chandra. He blew with a wracking shudder and a great moan, and then lay back on his bed, totally exhausted, feeling somehow, despite appearances, that he had done something right for once.

People came to watch the boy sleep. Because he was in isolation no one was allowed to get very close to him—a sheet of glass and a plastic tent separated him from every spectator. They put him in a special room, and required everyone who took care of him to dress up in big puffy moon suits, complete with glass helmets and air hoses that snaked out of the back and looked like long pink tails. Not everyone read a belated lesson of quarantine in the abundant black ash on the boat, and though Jemma insisted the boy was somehow sick Dr. Snood pointed out that there was no spot on him and that no test they had done had revealed any illness in him. Still, most everyone agreed that it was better to err on the side of prudence until they knew exactly what they were dealing with. What that was, they still really had no idea. Dr. Pudding had dusted off his equipment and rebooted his computers to scan the boy's whole body with every available modality, but the plain films and the CT and MRI and MRA scans revealed nothing except his bone age and that everyone was fascinated by him—he drew trailing crowds every time he was wheeled out of the PICU down to radiology, and bootleg copies of his scans multiplied almost as quickly as had the copies of his diary that appeared in the hands of thirteen-year-olds almost as fast as they could be confiscated. The diary entered the popular culture of the hospital; the boy's life became the subject of heated speculation at Karen's bar and a few brawls at Connie's, and what started as speculative recreations of his last days became lurid horror and pornography—*Goodbye, Mrs. DiMange; A Hand in the Mist; The Lido Zombie; A Reagan in the Sun.*

Jemma stood with Rob and Ishmael in radiology while the boy got a last scan, a modified PET that was supposed not just to look for activity in his brain but to indicate how he was feeling. Dr. Pudding tried to explain it, but lost Jemma when he posited the existence of happy and sad glucose, each with its own signature that blazed forth, for anyone who could see it, when it was metabolized. "It isn't happy or sad inherently," he said, "but the brain makes it so, in spectacularly fine gradations."

"He looks happy," Ishmael pointed out, while the three of them watched through the window as the boy's legs disappeared into the scanner. "Don't you get a happy feeling, just looking at him? It's like looking at a baby sleeping."

"He makes me nervous," Rob said.

"He makes me afraid," said Jemma.

"Or a cat, asleep on a radiator," said Ishmael.

"Just before it bursts into flame," said Rob.

"I think I knew him," Ishmael said again. "I feel like I've seen him, before. Maybe I did come from there, after all."

"Maybe you're Matt," said Rob.

"That's not even funny," Ishmael said. He'd drafted the resolution condemning Matt and Gavin and the bathroom men and all the others who'd molested the boy or been molested by him—they'd spent hours trying to make a decision, and finally passed the useless resolution nearly unanimously. Jemma abstained, but wouldn't veto it because that would have been an equally useless act, and because it seemed to matter so much to Ishmael, who never before had been so spirited in a Council discussion. "He's my brother even if he isn't my brother," he said confidently. "Didn't we both come from there?" He pointed at the wall, beyond which lay the nearest windows and the water.

"Here it is!" Dr. Pudding cried from behind his bank of monitors. They went and looked at the images—multi-colored snow in the shape of a brain. "He's sad!" he said. "Look at all that mauve depression!"

That test, and all the others, while descriptive, were never profitable—they couldn't tell what was wrong, and though they screened his blood and urine for every toxin and toxic metabolite they could think of, Dr. Sundae developing new assays with the assistance of the angel when the science of the old world did not suffice to answer a question, no test yielded more than did the evidence of their eyes: the boy was sleeping.

Jemma was sure there was an answer to be had, it was just a matter of framing the question correctly. There was a reason he was sleeping, and she thought she might puzzle it out if she could just look at him in the right way, or look at him for long enough, or look at him in the right state of mind. She spent hours in his room—too many, Vivian told her, for a pregnant woman to spend in the room of a boy with a mystery illness, no matter that she wore a five-ply isolation suit and tempered-glass helmet, no matter that she didn't breathe the same air as him. But she felt compelled to be close to him, and to study him with her usual and unusual senses. So she stood in his room, half sitting on a table, looking at him.

He lay in his special PICU bed—made more special in the past two weeks by three nurses who'd added accessories both decorative and functional: a set of projectors, one on either side of the rails beside his head, showed scenes of lost nature, shivering deciduous forests and blue mountains and stark desert dunes, on the ceiling above his face; a pair of shot-glass-sized speakers played the sort of music they thought he'd like; stuffed animals, bionic and plush, rode chains and motors to nuzzle his cheek or his ribs or roar over his head, set up by a nurse who had read someplace that children in comas benefited from this sort of stimulation. A judicious selection of gifts—balls and gloves and rubber dinosaurs brought by people who seemed not to understand what an ancient sort of fourteen he was—was arranged by the nurses on the tables that flanked his bed. Clear-plastic-drape walls—he could have just touched the ones at his sides if he reached his hands toward them—dropped down from the ceiling on three sides of the bed. Only his feet were covered by his sheet and blanket, white hospital finery of the new standard. Jemma ran her eyes back and forth over him, from the hidden shapes of his toes, over his strange Popeye legs, with their huge calves, knobby knees, and fat, hairy thighs, past the foley tube that ran into his diaper, up the trail of hair that came out of the diaper and petered out just past his belly button, marking a border of maturation—everywhere above it he was practically hairless, except on top of his head. She watched the quiet movement of his chest as he breathed, and the little tug between his clavicles that came every fourth or fifth breath. He cracked his pale lips to utter a wet sigh. She put out a finger toward him, meaning to touch his shoulder and send in a little fire to dry out his mouth and throat, but then did it the old fashioned way instead, picking up the Yankauer and suctioning his mouth and the back of his throat. His heart rate dipped—she felt it in her stomach and heard it in the deepening tones of the monitor—and then rose again. The tugging between his clavicles went away. He sighed again.

With the suction still in her hand she put a finger on him, right on his chin, so together they struck a thoughtful pose, and she concentrated on him more fully, imagining that she was suddenly made of cloud, drifting over him then settling over him. She was trying to touch his mind, to root around in his brain to see if anyone was home, to see if he was dreaming. It worked no better than usual. Instead of becoming more aware of him, she found herself repelled from the empty space he occupied but somehow did not take up, and for all that she was concentrating on him, she only became more aware of the people around him in the hospital. They were moving a little differently since he'd come on board, his presence a strange new mass that altered their orbits and routines in subtle ways. She imagined them pausing to consider him: Maggie staring out the window, away from her students, and seeing his body hanging in the sky; Dr. Tiller rocking in a chair in the old psych ward, halted in embroidering a headdress to wonder what his middle name might be; Ishmael stopping for a moment the push-ups he made more difficult by piling half his preschool class on his back to consider again how this boy made him feel finally not lonely anymore; Rob interrupting his own bath-time song with a gloomy feeling—overwhelmed with the certainty that this kid was really bad news; Vivian breaking away from her most obsessive study of the journal not to eat or sleep but to stare and stare into a mound of black cruise-ship ash. It must be her imagination, she knew, but the scenes looked real in her head, and she felt so sure that there was a new list to the hospital, that it no longer rode straight in the water but leaned a little because this boy was so heavy that it must acknowledge him in at least this way. Jemma took another stab at him, covering his whole face with her hand and seeking to understand him by setting him entirely on fire. It showed her everything but revealed nothing, and it made her feel threatened by him, this boy who would not become well. Just before she stopped she had a surge of worry for her baby, because she thought, for no good reason, that the boy was threatening him, too. She took away her hand and opened her eyes and sighed, turning away from the bed. Her whole class was lined up at the window, left to right, Josh to Valium, displayed in order of height. They all waved.

"Thanks for letting me speak," said Vivian, guest-starring at one of Father Jane's services. She had been acting strangely since they'd come back from the boat, and stranger still in the past few days. It was their one hundred and eighty-seventh day at sea. She'd become withdrawn and quiet and—strangest of all—had stopped dating. In all the years she'd known Vivian, Jemma had only seen her do that three times, and never for more than a week—when she had mono in college, after the world ended, and after Ishmael broke up with her. Now it had been two weeks. Jemma thought at first that Vivian had merely exhausted the supply of men in the hospital—six weeks earlier they'd had a conversation in which they'd debated the merits and perils of re-dating a person—but the shallowest poll of the population revealed that there were men available who'd hardly even talked to Vivian, let alone dated her. Then Jemma thought she was considering a change of orientation—there'd been clues, after all: a new, unattractive hairdo; the appearance in her wardrobe of two plaid shirts with the sleeves cut off at the shoulder; a new taste for heavy macramé jewelry that made her look like she was wearing plant holders around her neck. Arrested on the brink of lesbianism, she was considering the abyss, or else carefully scoping among the slim hospital pickings for prospects—all the obvious lesbians were already taken, even all the obviously incipient lesbians seemed to have found one another—and wondering if by the sheer enthusiasm of her new passion she might turn someone.

But it was just Jemma's imagination that invested the looks of scorn Vivian habitually directed at Dr. Sundae with touches of longing, and when she finally asked her what was going on, she got an answer that only increased her confusion and her concern. "I don't need it anymore," Vivian said during Jemma's twenty-seven-week checkup. Vivian was dipping Jemma's urine, her back turned to her when she spoke. They were in the last exam room left in the ER.

"What does that mean?" Jemma asked, wondering suddenly if the angel was ministering to Vivian in ways that were nearly unimaginable, and a machine started to take shape in Jemma's mind, a thing with multiple mechanical tongues and intricate penis wheels and long textured fingers.

"Just what it sounds like. I don't need it."

"Are you serious?"

"Look out the window, Jemma. Things have changed. Doesn't it follow that we might change, too?"

"Did you have another bad experience?"

"Not in the way you think."

"I'm thinking of you finally feeling like somebody was good for more than a day and then you get squashed. No?"

"It's not that. I just don't need it. I figured it out. Not the thing, but part of the thing. I can't explain it yet."

"You shouldn't have gone to the boat."

"Thank God," Vivian said. "Thank God I went to the boat. Otherwise I'd still be screwed. I'd still be wasting my time, and our time."

"But the list is your baby. Are you giving up?"

"Of course not. But you can go on and on with a list and never… I can't explain it yet. One plus protein."

"I don't remember how to manage preeclampsia. I'm worried about you."

"It's just one plus, probably a contaminant. Go pee again." That was no problem—Jemma could pee all the time. She was more careful this time, proctored by a fantasy of sickness in which she spent the last months of her pregnancy on a magnesium-sulfate drip, though she should be able to fix preeclampsia and eclampsia or even super-eclampsia and eclampsia suprema, should those diseases come to exist, as easily as she could fix anything or anyone except the boy from the boat.

"But what do you mean, you don't need it?" Jemma asked again as she came back into the exam room. Vivian was gone. That was another strange thing Vivian was doing lately, suddenly disappearing, out of visits more and less official than this one had been, from lunch on the roof when Jemma went to fetch a ball kicked out of a nearby soccer game, or out of a Council meeting when they were briefly adjourned for dinner. When she caught up with her Vivian always said the same thing, "I needed to be alone for a minute." Jemma dipped her own urine. This time it was protein-free.

"Thanks for letting me speak," Vivian said again, up on a balcony in the lobby atrium. Jemma had an excellent view of her, one floor up and directly across from her, standing with her hands folded in a freshly tended flower-box full of pansies. "The angel makes me speak like she's made everybody else, but I'm glad that she's done it. I used to think, look at those morons up there, babbling away about their personal obsessions, trying to apply them to everybody else in a way that will make them seem less like a freak. So now I'm the moron. Listen to me.

"I've been thinking about the boat. I know you have, too. What happened to them? We've assumed that it wasn't very pleasant, but who knows. Maybe they just left the boy behind when they got a better party boat, one with louder music and taller cakes and more fabulous whores and gigolos. You're too little, they said to him. You can't come. We've all heard that before, and we all remember, don't we, how bitter and angry it made us feel. Maybe he got so angry and disappointed that he fell over in a coma.

"But what if they're all dead? Everybody's dead, you might say. Big deal. Everybody's dead but us, because they were not selected like us, because they were not supposed to be part of the new world. We are not here by accident, are we?

"But what if I said to you, we are dead, too? What if I told you that I have been occupied with a single thought ever since I returned to this hospital? It started when I saw the hospital floating in the middle of the fucking ocean, and I can hardly describe how strange it was, to see it like that—it was stranger to see it than to live it—and then I felt it in my little missus, a terrible unease. It spread from there and by the time it got to my head I knew what it was, and now I declare it to you. A single very distinct thought, that we are more dead even than those disappeared people on the boat. There's a different kind of death than the one we usually think about. We can imagine what they must have gone through on the boat, all the expiring groans, the convulsions and the agonies. Maybe there were devouring little worms, or bigger worms that leaped from the sea to burrow up their asses and eat them up from the inside. Those are the ones that have always scared me. It's why I never wanted to be buried at sea, which reminds me, as long as we're talking about this sort of thing, that if you all outlive me, that I want to be cremated. Let me make that clear right now. I'll hold you responsible if my wishes are not carried out." She pointed randomly into the crowd, and her finger fell on Pickie Beecher, standing next to Rob one level down to Jemma's left. He only shrugged.

"Maybe their skin rotted on them or their bones suddenly grew through their skin; maybe they scratched themselves to death. Regardless of how, they all ended up the same way, dead and senseless and inactive, lost in a stupor, incapable of doing anything that matters, totally lost and cut off from anything that's new. I think we're like that too.

"We keep deciding that we're going to be different, or announcing that we have become different, but we stay the same. Lots of other morons have stood up here where I am and said, It's become obvious that we were doing something wrong, let's figure it out and do better. I've said it to myself. For months I've been wondering what we did, what exactly that we did that was so bad that it warranted"—she waved her hands around a couple times, making it somehow a very tired gesture—"all this. A few times I was sure that I'd figured it out, but every time I figured one thing another would come along seeming even more atrocious and obvious. I want for there to be one thing, or one way to describe everything. Lately, but not finally, I've been thinking that it wasn't any of the hundred million obscenities we practiced but something else entirely—merely that we were insincere. I say merely, but really it's a big thing, to always say sorry, sorry, and never mean it. My mother did that. Sorry, sorry! I didn't mean to beat the shit out of you with a sack of oranges. I'll never do it again until the next time.

"How many times are you supposed to put up with that sort of thing? How many times are you supposed to believe someone? What are we getting wrong, that I can still get up here and complain to you about this? Because we are still doing it. There is something excellent that we should be sensitive of and that we should embrace—if we ever really meant that we wanted it. Once or twice during this whole trip I think I believed it, that we were different, that we had finally meant what we said, but I say it again, look around you. Then look back across the water at that empty boat and ask yourselves how we are really different.

"I am so sick of that shit. Aren't you? Aren't you sick of hearing how you've been corrupt from your very birth, a transgressor from the womb and always liable to the wrath of your mother? Aren't you sick of going oh, oh, oh! Aren't you sick of being all worried about it for five minutes and then going back to bed or back to your dog or back to your fabulous floating golden dildo—whatever it is that distracts you from all the sacred affections, the joy and love and fear and sorrow and desire and hope, and makes your hospital life your everyday life again. It's getting to be a bit of a drag, and an old story, one that everybody should know by now. You shouldn't need any more morons up here to remind you or to call you away from all the dumb shit.

"But I'm up here anyway, about to call you away from all the dumb shit, because I feel like we have one last chance to turn and recognize the fine thing that's among us before the really horrible shit comes down. We've been floating along like that was all we had to do—get up in the morning and eat and entertain ourselves and keep the kids from getting too bored. Like we would just float into what's coming. That's true, we're on our way to something, but it's probably not what you're expecting—not the place where the houses are made of chocolate and your puppy won't ever die. The people on the boat floated into something. They weren't saved.

"And I'm saying it again. Come away with me, whoever wants to. Whoever thinks that they can be sincere and fucking mean it this time. Whoever will look around with me and say, Fuck this, you're all dead, be dead—I want to live. We made a dead council and passed dead rules and played dead games with each other. We had some dead parties and did some dead fucking and some of us have paired off into dead couples and dead families and we are all dead together—a promiscuous mix in a giant grave. We have declaimed deadly against the mistakes of the old world and said that we would not repeat them, but more than half of us can't even decide what they were and the other half probably has an opinion but doesn't really care. Well, I quit it. I quit from the dead council and the dead games. There is something else we have to figure out—not just why it happened but what we're going to do about it, how we're going to make ourselves new—before it's too late, and I'm starting on it right now. Here I go."

She looked down at the floor and was quiet. Jemma could tell that she'd closed her eyes, though she couldn't see it. A whole minute passed in silence, then Karen asked, "When is she going to go?" People started to murmur, and then to talk, and then, here and there, to shout. "Go on," Wanda Sullivan called across to Vivian. "Get going, I'll come, too." But Vivian just stood there, going somewhere, Jemma could tell, inside her head, not able to see where her friend was going but perceiving that she was getting smaller and smaller until she was gone entirely.

The Council met in emergency session to replace Vivian, or rather to replace the office vacated by Monserrat when she was promoted by Vivian's resignation to the office of Second Friend. Ishmael remained First, and Jemma remained as she was, unaffected politically but really quite depressed by the whole development, and distracted during the replacement hearings by perseverating thoughts on dead friendships.

"Of course we're still friends," Vivian had told her when she went to visit her after the speech. "Why would that change?"

"Well, that big breakup speech, for one thing. When did I suddenly become somebody you couldn't talk to?" Vivian held up a pair of black underwear, gently shaking out the folds in the silk before she folded it up and put it in her suitcase.

"It's not like that. It wasn't the sort of thing to talk about, until it was time. I just decided all of a sudden, and then the angel made me talk about it. She knew all the time, I think. She acts like a fucking airhead but she knew the boat was coming and the kid was coming and she's keeping bad secrets even now. She knows it's almost too late, and she gave me a kick. A little one, but I needed it." Jemma was leaning in the door. She stood up straight, folded her arms and unfolded them, then leaned against the other side. Vivian kept folding her huge stock of underwear, slowly and deliberately.

"Why are you doing this?"

"I already talked about it," Vivian said, and that's all she would say, by way of explanation, or denial, when Jemma asked if it wasn't something about her, if it wasn't that Vivian wanted herself to be the grand pooh-bah, if she didn't think that Jemma wasn't taking it all seriously enough or trying hard enough. "I can try harder," Jemma said. "You know that about me—I can always try harder. Maybe if I try harder I can get the kid to wake up. I know you have a plan—we can do it together."

"I already talked about it," Vivian said, sighing deeply. Jemma heard an answer in the sigh—Yes, you are too lazy. Yes, you are not smart enough. Yes, the office is bigger than you and you are not ever going to grow into it. "You can come with me," Vivian said.

"Come where?" Jemma asked. With her hand she indicated the window and the endless sea.

"Away," Vivian said. "You know what I mean. Don't keep going the same way as everybody else. They're all going to get fucked, and you will too. Even you, Jemma."

"There's no place to go," Jemma said, "and I couldn't go, anyway. I was elected. So were you."

"We'll find a place to make ourselves different. You and Rob could come. You could even bring that weird kid."

"You were elected," Jemma said again. Vivian shrugged.

"I know what I have to do, even if I don't know what I'm doing." She smoothed her hand over her underwear and closed the top of the suitcase.

"Don't they have underwear, where you're going?" Jemma asked.

"You can come, too," Vivian said, and picked up her suitcase. She waited patiently for Jemma to finally step out of her way, and then she walked out the door, leaving behind a whole closet full of clothes. Jemma sat down on the bed and picked up a framed picture of the ocean horizon. She read the inscription on the back: *You make me remember that I once knew people who were beautiful in their bodies and their souls.*

Dr. Snood put himself far forward for the office of Third Friend. He had had the most votes of the also-rans, and he played that distinction to maximal advantage. Jemma wondered who had actually written the law governing emergency successions—she didn't remember it ever really being discussed, except as a package of duty dispensed to some subcommittee. They all turned to it with panicked interest after Vivian made her speech. There would be a temporary appointment, drawn from the Council or the general population, and then another election.

She watched Dr. Snood make his speech. He wasn't so bad, she supposed, or he was bad in a way that would probably be good for the Council. The weeks and months had modified his smarm—everybody was different, weren't they? Look at what happened to Vivian, she thought, and wondered what she would see if the fire in her eyes let them look into people's minds, if she could see their secret hearts as easily as she could see their ordinary hearts. She tried it with Dr. Snood: from across the room she became aware of the beating of his heart, of his respirations, of the cascade of impulses flowing across and through his brain in a pattern that was certainly the most beautiful thing she'd ever seen in him. She knew he had an erection, but she didn't know what he was thinking, or what he wanted more than anything, or if he was really in love with Dr. Tiller: all things she wondered about. Because I am smarmy, she thought, because I once was somebody, because

I consider myself to be rather swell, because I have big feet and soft hands, because I know a lot about poop—for these reasons I should lead you. They were about to make a vote—Connie, Jordan Sasscock, and the withered old volunteer had also thrown their hats in the ring—when the angel announced a code in the PICU.

Jemma was too pregnant to leap over the table, but she managed to lift her bottom over the top and do a swift scoot-and-roll, and she made good time down the hall to the unit. The fire was already in her hands when she passed through the double doors, green auras around her clenched fists. In the room next to the boy's a body was laid out, pale and seizing, naked except for a scrap of cut pants that lay across one thigh. The room was hardly converted back to its old use. There were still paper alphabets on the wall, and the monitor—was that v-fib or just the seizures?—was framed in drooping green fur, and sported a pair of goggle-eyes on its top. "Get out of the way," Jemma said, full of fire now, so it choked her and made her sound like she was about to cry. The seven bodies in the therapeutic cluster leaped away and revealed the patient's face. Jemma almost faltered when she saw it was Maggie, death throes making her chinless rat-face less attractive than ever. Jemma brought her hands up and let the fire spill out as she brought them down. Maggie jumped when Jemma hit her chest, her whole body rising in a bounce before it settled again on the bed.

She knew what was happening as soon as she touched her. Sickness was there, a deep, black mark, as plain as Maggie's absence of chin, or her unpleasantness—but even that had changed. Hadn't she become a nicer person, or a more joyous one, at least—somebody who was filled with the spirit of clogging in a way that smothered the petty angels of her personality? It was almost like reading her mind, the way that Jemma read the natural history of the disease. A week before Maggie had noticed a dry spot on the skin of her neck, and tried with partial success to moisturize it away. When it faded another one popped up on her thigh. That one grew, no matter how much lotion she slathered on it. Another popped up on her bottom, but she wasn't aware of it—she wasn't one of those girls who was always looking at her bottom in the mirror, trying to predict the happiness of a day based on the degree of firmness and lift. She had a sore throat and a headache—these passed, but every now and then she'd have a nasty belch, like she'd just eaten something bubbling with rot. Then came the thing on her heel, another dry spot at first, but then a strange circle of scale that penetrated deeper and deeper into her foot. She scratched at it every night—it didn't hurt at all—and dug a hole in her heel, night by night. It didn't affect her dancing, though she thought it was a product of her dancing—she'd never clogged this much in her life, and didn't quite know what to expect. Waking up happy was a surprise—why not get onion skin on your foot, too? Three nights of scratching dug it only a few centimeters, but she was restraining herself. When she woke that morning it was itchy, but she left it alone until after her morning class. Then she sat on her bed, lifted her foot, lay it across her leg with the heel up, and began to scratch. It was drier than ever—she dug in with her nail. It still didn't hurt. She began to dig in earnest, feeling nauseated as she scratched into her foot, but unable to stop—suddenly it was very itchy indeed, and she wanted to know how deep she could go. All the way to the bone, that was the answer. That was firm, and hurt to touch. She looked into the hole in her foot, not quite appreciating what she had done, as the scale turned black around the edges, and then inside. She started to cry, feeling sick all of a sudden. She vomited, right in her own lap, and then her whole foot began to hurt, and the pain marched up her leg, all up her right side to the right side of her head. Then she had her first seizure. She was post-ictal for an hour, and when she was awake enough she crawled to her bathroom and pulled that little cord by the toilet.

I see you, Jemma said to the sickness, and burned at it. From her toes to the tips of her hair she filled Maggie with fire, but what was in her was already ash, and didn't care how much she tried to burn it. Through the fire she could see Maggie getting paler and grayer. Spots appeared on her cheeks. She stopped breathing, so Jemma tried to breath for her, but it was like trying to squeeze an oiled cucumber. She kept slipping away.

"What the fuck?" Jordan Sasscock asked, when Jemma fell back, right on the ground, knowing suddenly that she had a terribly shocked and stupid look on her face.

"I don't know," Jemma said, shaking her head. Janie screamed "Oh fuck! Oh fuck! Oh fuck!" but all the others put back on their old roles and fell back on Maggie with needles and monitors and defibrillation glue. They continued the code in earnest, one of them bagging her while Dr. Sasscock got his tube ready and fastened the blade on a laryngoscope.

"Is a Mac 5 big enough for a twenty-five-year-old?" he asked of the air.

"She's twenty-four," Jemma said weakly.

"It's fine," said Dr. Chandra. "You better do it. Look at how blue she's getting. Is the oxygen on?"

"It's on," said Dr. Sasscock. "You're bagging like a fucking retard. Get her chin."

"What chin?" asked Dr. Tiller. "Do we have a line yet?"

"No," said Emma. "I know I'm in but there's no flash. Let's give the ativan IM."

"Okay," said Dr. Sasscock. "Let's go." Dr. Chandra gave a few more rapid breaths and then took the bag away with an unintentional flourish. Dr. Sasscock swooped in, thrusting the laryngoscope blade between Maggie's teeth and hauling up on it with his whole arm. Jemma could see the tip bulging in the soft tissue of her neck. "I see it," he said.

"She's getting rather gray," said Dr. Tiller.

"Just hand me the tube before I lose it," he said. He took the tube from Dr. Chandra and poked it into her mouth, poking and poking with it, trying to get past some obstruction. "I don't get it," he said. "I see the cords but it's not going in."

"Holy shit," said Janie. "Look at her!" Maggie got at once more gray and more blue, went briefly into v-fib and then went asystolic.

"What are you doing?" asked Emma, because the skin at Maggie's neck suddenly burst apart in a spray of black dust, and the silver tip of the laryngoscope poked through.

"I almost have it," Dr. Sasscock said, but then the pressure of his arm lifted the scope up free through her neck and above it, so her face and neck split like an opening door, releasing a head-sized cloud of dust that expanded to hover over her whole body. Dr. Sasscock was left looking down at his tube. He stepped away, and said something that Jemma, too distracted by the death, didn't hear.

Strange, Jemma thought, that someone with so much death in her life should never have seen one before. As a student she had always avoided them, managing by virtue of luck and foresight never to be present when the old train wrecks on her medicine clerkship kicked the bucket, or slipping quietly into a side room in the ER to fumble at suturing when a hopeless trauma came in. It was a shock to her new senses, to be aware of Maggie's feeble soul struggling to raise itself above her ashen body, like it was trying to get a better view of the death, and suddenly be swept away, as if a giant hand had passed through the room to gather it up or knock it away. It was a violent transition; just watching made Jemma feel like she'd been knocked in the head with a cinderblock. She passed out—it seemed like just the thing to do—but not before becoming aware of the vomiting and lamenting and face-pulling of the PICU team, and last of all she saw Jordan Sasscock, holding the dusty, bloody tube before his face, looking at it reproachfully, like it had betrayed him.

Hilary charges it upon the heretics as a great crime, that their misconduct had rendered it necessary to subject to the peril of human utterance, things which ought to have been reverently confined within the mind, not disguising his opinion that those who do so, do what is unlawful, speak what is ineffable, and pry into what is forbidden. Shortly after, he apologizes at great length for presuming to introduce new terms. For, after putting down the natural names of the Father, Son, and Spirit, he adds, that all further inquiry transcends the significancy of words, the discernment of sense, and the apprehension of intellect. And in another place, he congratulates the Bishops of France in not having framed any other confession, but received, without alteration, the ancient and most simple confession received by all Churches from the days of the Apostles. Not unlike this is the apology of Augustine, that the term had been wrung from him by necessity, from the poverty of human language in so high a matter: not that the reality could be thereby expressed, but that he might not pass on in silence without attempting to show how the Father, Son, and Spirit are three. How many hours and days did I waste before I realized that what was really wrong was the same way, enshrined inexpressible by the poverty of my language—unholy instead of holy, created by us instead of Him, rendered ineffable because it is absolutely ubiquitous and absolutely corrupt—and that I could be excused for raging against lies I could not articulate? I am oppressed by a mystery and must overcome it with mysterious tools.

Dr. Chandra shuffled down the ramp, looking at his shoes. They were better shoes than he'd ever had in his life. Previously, before the end of the world, he could never get ones that fit him because his left foot was a size nine-and-a-half and his right foot was a size ten-and-a-half, and though he usually tried to buy for the bigger foot, he was a sucker for a cheap shoe, and gravitated to stores where two-hundred-dollar shoes were on sale for fifty dollars. They were outliers and misfits in the most exact sense of that word, the shoes that migrated to the huge, sad emporiums where he shopped—little tennies hardly big enough for a kewpie doll lay next to huge Frankenstein boots. He always bought the big shoes, because they were cheap and because it made him feel special, if fake, knowing that people perceived him as having big feet, and some reasonably handsome man or woman might look at him as he clomped down the street in his size thirteens and wonder, was it true what they say about men with big feet?

They were hard to run in, but he almost never had any occasion to run in the old world, someone having said falsely of him that they had never seen him ever run even to a code, that he had only done that thing like when you are trying to be polite to the driver who is allowing you to cross in front of their car at an intersection, where you give the appearance of running though you are still moving at the velocity of a walk. And the laces would never stay tied, perhaps because the constant sliding motion of his foot within the shoe slowly worked them loose as he walked. He was always having to stop and balance on one foot to tie them, a struggle if he had a package or had been drinking, and he had a horror of touching the ground, which made it complicated to touch the laces that had been flipping and flopping against the filthy sidewalk, sometimes trailing in a smear of poop or a glistening comma of spittle. A normal person would have just bought shoes that fit, but when he looked down he got a rare good feeling, watching his big feet fly over the earth and never saw when he passed his striding reflection in a shop window, what everyone else did, a schlumfy goofball in clown shoes.

But finally he had shoes that fit him. The angel made them special, sized exactly to each foot but shaped so that one did not appear larger than the other, and both appeared larger than they actually were. The laces were coated with a very selective adhesive resin that stuck only to itself, not to the shoes, not his fingers, and not to the filthy ground, and now every day he tied his shoes exactly once. He had the aspect of somebody who was staring depressively at his shoes, but really he was admiring them—they were only three days old and the best thing to happen to him this week.

He looked up, finally, narrowly missing a collision with a child—it was Jeri Vega, one of the old liver kids. Months after her recovery, he was still shocked by how well she looked, and hardly recognized her out of her gaunt, yellow hairiness. She looked up into his face as she twirled around him, gazing seriously into his eyes and giving him a sharp Shirley Temple salute. They had all had that look about them, before, not in their eyes but something around the eyes that proclaimed their chronic illness. It was the closest thing to clinical acumen he had developed in his short medical career, being able to recognize it, even in the fetal surgery and bone-marrow transplant poster-children who had lived cutely on billboards and bus-sides all over the city, part of a public relations campaign launched by the hospital shortly before the flood, meant to educate the public about the extremely wonderful things happening in their midst. Now that look was gone from all the children, but some of the adults were already starting to get it.

Everyone has got someone but me, he thought, looking up at all the couples. He was passing the second floor, coming down the last section of the ramp—it was not that crowded for a Saturday afternoon, but since people started getting sick some were staying in their rooms or restricting themselves to particular areas, and now there was Vivian's faction, fifty people—or maybe now it was more—who never left the ninth floor. I should have just taken the elevator, he thought, or let the angel make me something in my room. So many people walking hand in hand, and everyone in pairs except the severest, most lonely freaks—so there was Dr. Sundae going hand in hand with Dr. Topper, and there were Dr. Snood and Dr. Tiller. He almost hurried a few steps and hid behind a pillar before Dr. Tiller could see him, fearing she might try to dragoon him into her newly reestablished rounds in the PICU. She seemed to think that just because adults were getting sick the pediatric residents should all become puppies for her to kick again. Sorry, lady, he wanted to say to her. There are so many other ways for me to be miserable that don't involve you at all. But he probably wouldn't ever say that to her.

What's wrong with me? he wondered, watching the parents and the neo-parents and the rare childless couple promenading around the toy or watching kids scramble on the playground. He ran through the usual reasons in his head—you are too ugly, too sad, too gay, not gay enough, too lonely. It shows on your face and in your walk, how lonely you are. People say, there goes the lonely fellow to buy a frozen pizza and rent a pornographic video. Don't touch him or you'll be lonely too. It was true that the angel often made him pizza in his room, and that he watched her pornography, but only the really interesting stuff, and it was more because he was curious than because he was lonely that he watched Rock Hudson and Ronald Reagan in the musical she called *Pillow Face*.

He sat down on a bench underneath the shadow of the toy, forgetting, for now, about the coffee he'd meant to fetch, wondering if he could rub his face like he wanted to without looking even more lonely and sad. Maybe I should have applied for a baby, he thought. But that was a strategy of aging fat women, to recruit a child to console their loneliness. He opened his hands and looked in them—no black spots yet—then clapped them to his face.

Across the grass, people were setting up for a show scheduled for that night, putting the final touches on the staircase on the stage, Connie and Anika stapling real flowers to the curling banister. Dr. Sashay was stomping up and down the stairs, calling out, "Are you sure this is sturdy enough?" Josh Swift and Cindy Flemm were finishing up a piece of backdrop.

"There's no way this is going to dry in time," Cindy said.

"Sure it will," Josh said. "It's got this special polymer in it. I hope my horses look more like horses from far away."

"They're pretty," Cindy said. "This is exhausting. I want to take a nap. Do you want to take a nap?"

"Do you really mean nap, or do you mean the other thing?"

"I really mean a nap, but I could probably be talked into… oh fuck. He's watching us."

Josh turned back and saw Wayne sitting alone in the audience, surrounded by empty seats. "Is he whittling?" he asked.

"I think it's supposed to be threatening. I'm so tired of this. I'm *exhausted* of it."

"It's okay," Josh said. "I'll talk to him again later. Maybe if I let him hit me this time he'd feel a sense of closure."

"Maybe if we both hit him he'd leave us the fuck alone."

"Moron," Wayne was saying. "Drooly fucking moron." He was whittling, but not very threateningly, on a piece of mahogany, making a fancy My Little Pony for Cindy, because he knew two things about her that the moron didn't: they were her favorite toys when she was five years old, and mahogany was her favorite wood.

"I see you," says Pickie Beecher, walking by with a ladder over his shoulder.

"I see you too, you little freak," says Wayne, not looking up from his whittling.

"You all look alike to me," he says.

Wayne does not respond, but I say, It is because we are brothers and sister.

"The same eyes, the same face," he says, walking on. He puts down his ladder by the stage and heads toward the playground. "And you all smell alike. Everyone else is starting to look like you, too. Not everyone, just the sick ones. Why is that?"

My brother is in them. The destroying angel.

"My brother is dead, killed by angels. I have never forgiven you. I never will." He sits down on the edge of the playground, on one of the railroad ties that mark the border of the grass circle, takes off his shoes, and rubs his toes in the grass. Jemma lies a few feet away from us, where I left her, overcome by a sudden nap—at week twenty-nine this is her newest symptom, constant exhaustion and frequent naps. Dr. Tiller and Dr. Snood walk by, Dr. Tiller seeing in her sprawled form confirmation of her laziness, but Dr. Snood says, "Poor thing."

Do you miss your brother? I ask. I miss my sister every day. My real sister, I mean.

"Stab," says Pickie Beecher, poking himself sharply in the chest. "Stab! Stab! Stab!"

"Be quiet, child," says Dr. Tiller, striding over, her headdress glittering in the far-falling sunlight. Pickie jumps up and stands over Jemma.

"If you hurt *her,*" he says. "Or if you hurt my brother inside of her, then I will consume you. I already know the taste of your flesh." Then he opens his mouth to me, wider and wider, so his whole face seems to have become teeth around a black hole, and if I dared to look I could see the glaring red root of his abomination hanging in his middle. He snaps shut his teeth, making a sound like two heads knocking together. It hurts my ears to hear it.

"Don't you threaten me," Dr. Tiller says, handing Pickie a fat roll of demerits, and Jemma wakes.

It was called the botch, and a person was said to be stricken with it or not. Almost everybody acknowledged that it was a curse from God, but speculation abounded on whether there was not some natural and therefore treatable mediating agent—a virus or bacterium or toxin. Nothing was growing in the microbiology cultures, and blood and tissue samples taken from the victims—there were five of them now in the PICU—showed a haphazard and inconsistent range of anomalies. Dr. Sundae retreated deeper into her lab, where she and a variety of MD/PhDs were busy trying to isolate a causative agent, while the strictly clinical types were trying to write a predictive natural history. Rob was one of the latter. Jemma spent almost all her free time with him and the victims in the PICU.

She tried not to take as an affront all the hullabaloo over finding the virus—if there was a virus, wouldn't she know, and wouldn't Maggie have sprung back from death in as spritely a manner as any of the children?—and tried not to take personally the rumors that came back to her, that people were wondering if she weren't just temporarily off her game, if she retained only the flashiness but not the substance of her gift, or if she hadn't just let Maggie die because she hated her. "Everybody sure hated her," said Karen, in marked display of poor taste at the memorial service held the day after she died. "Everybody hated her a lot. Sometimes I think she wanted people to hate her. That almost makes it okay, doesn't it, if you hate somebody that kind of likes it, or at least expects it? I sure hated her, and I was one of her good friends."

"I didn't hate her," Jemma said to Rob, both of them staring resolutely at the line of children dancing in somber black clogs in front of the square golden box that was Maggie's coffin. They were supposed to be clogging joyfully, but some of them were clumsy with grief, and so their dance seemed hesitant and sad. "The kids liked her," Jemma added. When the children were done dancing, and Father Jane had spoken, and they had all sung "A Clog and a Smile," people drifted off back to their classes or their private worrying. To the accompaniment of a single flute (Dr. Tiller playing a tarantella), Maggie's dry, black corpse, mostly ash except for a little doll-sized remainder, a bit of spine and lung and liver and bowel, that echoed her former, larger shape, was trundled off by a quartet of volunteers, to be sealed in the first basement, because nobody could bear to add another body to the ocean.

"I didn't hate her," Jemma said again, sitting in her old place in the PICU, the siege of exhaustion where she used to collapse halfway through her call nights and spend five minutes forgetting all her responsibilities and doing nothing. Rob was sitting across from her, talking on the telephone to Dr. Tiller. He hung up and rubbed his eyes. It was their two-hundredth day at sea.

"Her Helen Lane cells are dead," he said.

"I thought she was immortal," Jemma said, remembering the summer she spent doing an obligatory stint of research. She'd worked with a not very glamorous fungus, but Vivian, three labs over, was raising a virus in dish after dish of Helen Lane cells, and had become quite taken with the woman whose cancer had been living on in labs around the world for decades after her death. She had liked to tell stories about her, and for three months addressed all her diary entries to her, and claimed to have strange dreams where she followed screaming down telescoping white hallways to find Helen Lane strapped in a complicated torture machine, a gleaming collection of steel and glass knives and needles that made a quiet sort of chainsaw noise as it flayed her and then sewed on her skin. Release me, Vivian! she would shout, causing Vivian to feel very conflicted about her research all the next day.

"She fed them some of Karen's blood and they died," Rob said. "But not before they made multinucleated giant cells. I think we should put the ganciclovir back on everybody."

"Sounds like a plan," Jemma said. Rob jumped up, either ignoring or not noticing Jemma's bored tone, and ran off down the hall toward the fellows' call room, recently re-converted from a finger-painting studio. She wasn't actually bored, though she affected a distinct air of aloofness from the medical proceedings in the PICU: they were doing their thing, she was doing hers, and she was not about to go back to being a kick-me-in-the-ass scut monkey after having wished away all the diseases of the old world. She still hoped that it would just be a matter of time, a matter of understanding, a matter of imagining a cure in the right context, before this one would fall to her.

She got up and made her usual tour, walking up and down the hall outside the bays that held each victim. She stood a while in front of each one, waving at the nurse behind the doors—Janie in a puffy suit—squinting with her natural eyes to see the patient, their images refracted by the glass doors and plastic isolation tent, while examining them simultaneously in her mind. The weeks passed and she felt more powerful in her gift—she didn't have to touch a person to know how fast their heart was beating, or how well they were oxygenating their blood, or if they were hungry. It was in her more every day—some nights she felt so nervous and overstuffed with it that she would go up to the roof to hurl green fire at the sky—and yet she could still do nothing for the victims of the botch except scan them and describe their bodily deprivations. The boy, in the middle bay in the victims' row, slept as soundly as ever, in perfect health as far as she could tell with either her natural or supernatural senses, while Wanda Sullivan, Aloysius Pan, Cotton Chun, Thelma, Karen, and Dolores lay before her in various stages of living decay, and she could not even restore the luster to Karen's hair, let alone heal any of them.

She put her head against the glass of the middle bay, where the boy was, and closed her eyes, aware of the brief attention paid to her by his nurse, who turned to look at her just for a moment before going back to her task of adding up his output of pee for the morning. The nurses were used to Jemma's loitering, and seemed not to mind it very much, though she hadn't proved herself very useful. She almost tried again, bringing her hands up and pressing her palms flat against the glass, but instead of letting the fire seep through the glass and ride on currents of air into the rooms, reaching a hundred thin fingers under the plastic and over the bed to strike their ailing flesh, she just stood their watching them and listening to them, not sure, when they started talking to each other, if she was imagining it or making it happen.

Are we going to die? Thelma asked.

Of course, Dolores said.

I knew we were in trouble, Wanda Sullivan said, when I smelled

Sylvester's poop. It was the worst ever, worse than any of the CF poops. It was pretty floaty, too. It floated right out of the toilet and hung in the air, and I saw how there was a ridge on it like a mouth that opened and said, Wanda, thou art stricken with the botch.

Don't be fucking stupid, said Karen.

You weren't there. You didn't see how black the mouth was inside, like it went on and on forever, that blackness, even though it was rather a small poop, comparatively.

There are probably worse ways to die, said Cotton Chun. I'm glad I didn't drown.

Maybe we still will, said Aloysius.

Shut the fuck up, said Cotton. I'm so sick of you, man. I've been sick of you since the day after I met you.

What did I ever do to you?

Cotton, everybody would say, what was wrong with you yesterday? I saw you in the hall and you looked like your dog just died. Are you okay? I was okay, motherfucker. I was always okay, and I always had to explain that it was you they saw, and that we weren't related, or the same person on a good day or bad day, and that I didn't have a fucking clue why you never smiled. What's your problem, anyway? Would it ever have killed you to have smiled once or twice, or to have been nice to someone, just one single time?

I'm almost happy now.

I mean, someone asks you for an echo and you act like they want you to gouge out your eyeballs.

I can almost see it. Can you all see it?

The land? Thelma said. The new world?

That's not for us, Aloysius said. There's another place, a place not here. It is removed from suffering, though there is no happiness there.

What part of shut the fuck up do you not understand? asked Cotton.

There's nothing out there, Dolores said. Not even a nothing.

I think I see it! Thelma said.

I see it too! Wanda said. Oh, I hope Sylvester comes soon. Is that selfish of me?

Completely, Cotton said.

All you see is what you want to see, Dolores said. I have learned to want nothing anymore, and expect nothing, and so I see the truth.

Spoken like a true surgical intern, said Cotton.

Maybe I don't see it, Thelma admitted. But I wish I did.

Just waiting for it is its own sort of pleasure, said Aloysius.

I see her, though, Thelma said. Looking at us.

Staring like a freak, Karen said.

This isn't the zoo! Cotton shouted.

Or the television, said Dolores. Stop gloating.

I'm not, Jemma said.

Gloating over how useless you are, Karen said. I'm the most useless girl in the world. No one is more useless than me.

Are you getting ready to not save us again? asked Wanda.

I could tell the first day I met her, Karen said. Useless. She had that look about her, and the big U on her forehead.

I told Sylvester it was too good to be true. Some days I could still smell it in him, but I never said. I should have told him, Everything will be the same again. Don't get used to this.

Of course it could have stood for ugly, too.

I'm sick of you, too, said Cotton. Though I'm still more sick of him.

"I'm down here," said another voice. Jemma opened her eyes and looked down. Sylvester Sullivan was standing at her hip, holding a bunch of daisies and a bottle of baby oil. "Can I go in yet?" he asked her. "I need to rub her feet."

"Welcome," said Helena Dufresne. "Where are your bags?"

"I'm just visiting," Jemma said.

"That's what everyone says, at first. I said it, too. We'll just check it out, I said, because I felt a stirring, during the speech. I'm not used to that. Speeches and sermons and commercials and romance movies—they usually don't touch me the least bit. But what she said—it was all squirmy in me, and I kept thinking about how people used to put gerbils up their bottoms, because I felt a squirminess that I was sure must be just like that, and I wondered, did people ever really do that, and I wondered, was that the reason, was that the last thing he noticed before he said, That's it? Can you imagine the poor gerbil? I had a dream about it, of course. I was the gerbil, and I had to get out. I scrabbled with my little claws—everything was dark and warm and smelly and I couldn't breathe. When I woke up I realized what it all meant. I had to get out of the world, I had to get closer than we were. I made up my mind. I told Tir, We're going for a tour on the ninth floor. We're just going to look. But I packed us a bag, just in case."

"I'm really just visiting," Jemma said. She put a hand on her belly. "It's time for my checkup."

"If you say so. Come on with me, I'll take you to her." She rose from behind the desk that Thelma had never given up until the botch took her to the PICU. The months had changed the lady: she was a little thinner, and didn't huff and puff when she walked, and smiled all the time instead of scowling, and cursed more pleasantly if not less frequently, and had adopted a glamorous, sequin-based wardrobe, though today she was wearing the same plain linen dress that all the women on the ninth floor were wearing. "Walk this way!" she said, and Jemma considered imitating her bouncy gait. "Tir's in class with the other kids," she added, "or I'd take you to say hello. Maybe after your visit?"

"Okay," Jemma said. They passed down the pastel halls of the old psych ward, each room was filled with adults sitting quietly on the bare floors, staring up at the ceiling or out the windows; they all seemed to be waiting patiently for something to happen. "What are they doing?" Jemma asked.

"Listening," Helena said. "Trying to figure it out. I have a hard time being so calm about it. I sit there and think, Speak! Speak to me! Because it's like a race, to listen hard enough to know what the worst thing was, and be sorry enough for it, and know what to do next, and save ourselves and everybody, before it's too late. And it's almost too late, now. "

"Heard anything yet?" Jemma asked.

"I'll let her tell you." They circled down the hall into the rehab ward. Jemma peeked in the window to the gym as they walked by and saw a room full of children who looked to be doing a very slow, swaying dance. Helena stopped outside the entry to the old gym. "We've got room in our bed," she said, and winked in a way that struck Jemma as very innocent and strange, then bounced off down the hall.

Vivian was inside, sitting under the model sun on a little platform that hadn't been there last time Jemma had visited up here. She was wearing a handsome linen pantsuit, her legs drawn up against her chest, and seemed to be staring at her feet. "I've never seen you wear a pantsuit before," Jemma said.

"Graduation," Vivian said. "And med-school interviews."

"You said you weren't going to wear pants at graduation."

"I chickened out."

"*I* didn't," Jemma said, recalling the curious feeling of the cheap rayon gown against her bare bottom.

"Sorry," Vivian said.

"Well," Jemma said, "what other lies did you tell me?"

"Nothing that ever mattered," Vivian said sadly. "None of them were the worst thing."

"I'm here for my checkup," Jemma said, deliberately not asking what the worst thing was. Vivian lifted her face and gave Jemma a sad, sweeping look.

"You're fine," she said, then lowered her head again.

"Well, I don't feel fine," Jemma said. "My back hurts and my belly hurts."

"That's normal."

"Well what about my clumsiness and my numb fingers and my nap attacks?"

"Normal, too."

"The baby is rolling around all the time. I think it's trying to get out already."

"You're fine."

"Don't you want to check a urine? Don't you want to take my blood pressure? What if the lie is all weird? What if it's breech?"

"It's fine. You're fine. Don't you get it?" She looked up again, and seemed more familiar now—angry Vivian instead of sad, pensive Vivian. "Do you really think something bad could possibly happen to your baby?"

"Of course something bad could happen. What, you think I'm being a freak because I'm worried? Have you noticed the mystery disease that's killing everybody?"

"Not the kids," Vivian said. "They'll be fine."

"How the hell do you know that?"

"It sort of... came to me." She looked down at her feet again and sighed. "You can't sit here all fucking day and not figure something out. Are you here to move in with us? It's going pretty well, you know. We could make it, maybe. Just maybe. If you helped it might all go quicker."

"I'm here for a checkup. What happened to the days when I used to have to beat you with a stick to keep you from doing Leopolds on me?"

"You're fine," she said again. She made a blessing motion toward Jemma, without looking at her. "All is well."

"Jesus Christ," Jemma said, stomping up and sitting down. "How would you like it if I transferred my care to Dr. Killer?"

"She'll be dead weeks before you have that baby," Vivian said simply. "Aloysius would probably be better. At least he can work the sono."

"He's in the PICU."

"Well, maybe not him, then. You don't need anybody, anyway. Do the sono yourself, if you're that curious to see how totally normal and fine your baby is. Or I could do it, I guess, though it's totally not necessary, if I could leave here. But I can't, so you'd have to stay."

"No thanks," Jemma said. "I've got other obligations."

"Nothing important, though. You'll see."

"I'll just go do it myself," Jemma said. "I'll do it all wrong. I'll get ultrasound poisoning. I'll make the baby deaf. What do you care?" Vivian didn't reply. Jemma sat down. "How are things up here?" she asked, after another few minutes of silence.

"Well enough. Nobody up here is sick yet. We haven't got an answer, but we're listening. I'm listening."

"What have you heard?"

"Not much. A little whisper, now and then. You shouldn't have... why did you... how could you... what were you thinking when you... But I never hear the good part. I have my suspicions, though. You know how you can tell what a street sign says, even if you can't read the letters in the name? Just from the shape and the context of the letters? It's like that. I see the shape of it and I almost know what the word is, what the thing is, and then I'll know."

"Then what? What happens after you know, or think you know?"

"Then we fix it. Then we swear it off. All together—heave! I don't know. Somehow that doesn't seem like the hard part, maybe just because it's not the part that's right now. It will point to what's next."

"Rob is getting depressed. He used to love the PICU and now it just makes him sad."

"I think I should be able to see it pointing, already. I mean it's already pointing. I should be able to see it."

"Snood's a Friend. Not my friend, mind you. He never shuts up."

"Why can't I see it? It's so stupid, to know what's wrong but not know how to describe it, and to know we have to do something but not know what. Every time somebody dies it's going to be my fault."

"It's going to be *my* fault," Jemma said.

"It's not your fault."

"Well it sure isn't yours."

"Except it is," Vivian said.

"You're crazy," Jemma said, and then a moment later added, "I miss you." Vivian took her hand but didn't look at her.

"I know," she said.

It was the last show, and had the feeling of being a last show even before everybody knew that's what it was. It was grander and fancier and stupider than anything they'd put on before (the stage they made for the talent show never went more than a few days without hosting a play or a dance recital or reading of deadly boring poetry) and the only show produced with the full energies of the Council, which seemed by this production to come into its own as a mature political entity, or prove anyway that it could be swift and efficient in organizing its populace in an appointed tasks. As swiftly as other governments had tried and executed dissidents, and as efficiently as others had invaded a neighbor, and as gorgeously as others had built monuments to death or war or courage, the Council whipped up a Broadway-caliber production of *Hello, Dolly.*

Dr. Sashay took the starring role, surprising everyone when she turned up for auditions and brought Frank, the director, to tears with her rendition of "Don't Let the Parade Pass Me By." Maybe it was just that Frank, like everybody else, was rather depressed anyway, and might have been brought to tears by a troupe of dancing poodles—but nobody who heard her voice ringing through the auditorium could deny that she was loud, or emotive, or that she could carry a tune. The other roles filled so quickly and easily that Frank suspected the hand of God was working to round up his cast. "It's like you were born to play this role," he said to Anika, and to Dr. Sasscock, and to Dr. Pudding, and each of them confided in the hastily written and printed notes to the show that they had indeed felt their hearts respond to the Council's call for auditions, and had felt a vocation for their parts when they watched one of the film versions (either the original Streisand or one of the over two-dozen pornographic variations), a correspondence and a rightness, as Dr. Sashay put it, that she hadn't felt since she first heard the word neuroblastoma, or saw the quivering, firm white mass of the tumor in gross section. *Suddenly*, she wrote in the program, *I knew what I had to do.*

It wasn't a holiday—the situation on board the hospital was too worrisome to proclaim one—but everybody there was familiar with the concept of respite care, and the Council had learned from the grueling exhaustion of their first few months at sea that caregivers have their needs, too, and that to ignore them was to invite early and perhaps avoidable burnout. So they billed it as a night of hope and respectful celebration of how far they had made it, and how much they appreciated that they could dance and sing and lift their hearts even in the middle of this new ocean, and even with the shadow of death falling over their toes, if not their hearts (Dr. Snood's words). It was exactly the sort of thing Vivian now abhorred, and she and the ninth-floor squatters were the only people, besides the PICU staff watching over the six victims of the botch, who were not in attendance, either in the square field of chairs in the lobby, or in the risers and chairs set up all along the ramp. Way up on the ninth floor a tiny face appeared at the balcony ledge, now and then, during the show, but never for more than a few minutes.

Jemma, in a chair on the third floor, watched with Pickie Beecher on her left and Ethel Puffer on her right, with all nine of her children, Kidney in her lap. Rob was in the PICU, watching on a monitor. She had not had to do much to help with the production—the idea arose independently of her and the execution happened without her contributing anything except a suggestion that the extraordinarily wide-brimmed hats that Dr. Sashay would wear for most of the show would obscure her face and her voice from the high-sitting members of the audience. She was too full of Vivian's spirit, anyway, to get too excited about it, and she could think of better shows, anyway, than *Hello, Dolly,* and suspected they were only doing it because it gratified some secret fetish of Dr. Snood's. Her thoughts were elsewhere—with Vivian, with her baby, and in the PICU—during the planning (though she duly affixed her signature to the original resolution and every rider that was attached to it) and even during the show itself, which turned out to be just as spectacular as anyone had planned.

Kidney announced that she was bored hardly before the curtain fell away and promptly fell asleep, but Pickie seemed especially to enjoy it. Jemma would never have figured him for a boy who loved show tunes, yet he bounced in his seat and acted more like a child than she had ever seen him, clapping at every entrance of Dr. Sashay, and requiring three multiple shushings from all sides before he would stop singing along. Jemma divided her attention between the stage and the PICU, leaving the smaller portion for Dr. Sashay and her ostrich-feather hat, whose narrow brim revealed her face and her voice but left the whole artifice a little unsteady, and Jemma barely noticed when it tipped off her head and she kicked it out into the audience, like it was all part of the show. She sent drifting tendrils of thought up the ramp and down the hall, into the PICU, trying to sense how the six were doing—every day she could figure things from a little farther away, but two floors was really reaching. She thought she could feel Rob, a familiar and pleasant pressure against her mind, and imagined him sitting at his usual place at the work station, his elbow on the table and his chin in his hand, watching a scrolling screen of lab values.

The six faded into her awareness, one by one, three and three around the bed where the boy slept. She imagined that they were watching, too.

She looks like a crazy old whore, Cotton said.

She is a crazy old whore, said Karen.

A delightful, wonderful old whore, said Wanda. The most wonderful old whore there ever was. Don't you know the story?

She's going to break her neck in those heels, said Dolores. Look at how steep that staircase is.

No, she's on a wire. It looks like she's going to fall, but then she swoops out over the audience, sustained by her wonderful old age, and her lust for life.

She's going to eat it, Dolores said confidently.

I can feel it, Aloysius said. Here it comes. Jemma put them in the air above the stage, five dying critics sitting forward in their floating beds while the boy in the middle went on sleeping soundly, as eager and curmudgeonly as the old men from *The Muppet Show*. Dr. Sashay, coming down the high staircase that reached all the way up to the third floor on the opposite side of the lobby, was just two verses into her show-stopper when her voice broke. She recovered and went on, stepping expertly in her heels, not having to look at her feet on the narrow steps even though her ankles and legs were doing a twisty little dance with every step. Halfway down her voice broke again, and she tried to go on. The orchestra stopped when she stopped again. She cleared her throat, lifted her head, and started over. "I!" she sang, strong and clear, but then she lost her voice entirely and was wracked by a cough. She had a handkerchief ready—she'd been waving it in a carefully orchestrated pattern. She held it at her mouth, and when she brought it away during a break in the fit it was easy to see, even from far away, how it was covered in blood and ash.

"Oh my," she said, and fell, not before Jemma became aware that her femurs had fractured spontaneously under her own weight. She bounced down the stairs, oofing and screaming and coughing, and lay still in the middle of the restaurant set.

Brava! said Dolores. Brava! Jemma hardly heard her. She stood up, dumping Kidney out of her lap, stepped back from the balcony, and ran down the ramp. People screamed—their emotions already worked up by the elaborate show—and backed against the balcony as she streaked by, and then away from it as she hurried through the lobby and ran up on the stage. The diners fled their tables as Jemma stepped up next to Dr. Sashay and assaulted her with fire, calling up reserves that seemed equal to what had harrowed the hospital to burn at the rapidly spreading blackness in her. But her rage and her fire only seemed to make it worse—she could tell that was how it looked, though she couldn't stop herself from trying and trying to win. Whole hospitals' worth of fire, enough to fill the whole place, the sum of the whole harrowing and again—she called and it came, and Dr. Sashay screamed, lifted by the conflagration, not saying words, though people would swear later they heard her say, "Stop, stop, please stop," until she was just an ashen image of herself that shattered against the stage when Jemma finally released her.

Every year the Fourth of July in Severna Forest began with a semi-official joyride; in the minutes just after dawn wild teenagers would fly over the hills in borrowed convertibles, honking their horns incessantly, hooting and shouting in a display of patriotic enthusiasm flavored with mischief and the fading drunk of the previous night's long party. Jemma was standing at her window when they came. The car, small and black, stopped in front of the house. A girl with long brown hair stood unsteadily in the back seat, lifted an air horn, and blasted it at every house in range, handling the can like a gun. She spun it over her finger and slipped it back into her pocket, then, facing Jemma but not seeing her, lifted up her shirt and shouted something unintelligible. When the car leapt away again she fell back, so her body lay across the giant paper flag that was taped over the trunk, and her shining hair spilled down to lay against the shining chrome bumper. Jemma watched her face, upside down and laughing, disappear over the crest of the hill.

She'd been waiting for the horn. Like dawn on Christmas, it released her from parent-enforced stasis and freed her to run around the house proclaiming the holiday. She ran away from the window, out her door and down the hall to her brother's room. Calvin was sleeping through the racket, curled up in his boat-shaped bed, entwined with Al, his stuffed snake. Five feet long and thick as a bolster, the snake was lime-colored, with big sad blue eyes and a pink tongue that had become frayed over the years along its edges. Jemma watched her brother sleeping for a few moments. His face was nestled against the snake's face, and the pressure of his breath made Al's tongue flicker and look as if it was tasting the air. Jemma was afraid of the snake; it seemed liable to come alive at any second and strike at her, but at the same time she wished that Joe or Alice or Emily or Ra-Ra the Conqueror, some of the other residents of her bed, could wrap around her and hug back like Al did.

"Wake up," she said, tugging on the snake's tail, the movement transmitting through all his coils so his face moved up and down against Calvin's cheek. Calvin opened his eyes.

"It's too early still."

"It started. It's the day, now. It's the Fourth of July!" Jemma proclaimed all holidays with almost perfect equability; Christmas reigned supreme and drove her into the most fervent tizzy, so she'd run shrieking like a madwoman all over the house as soon as the first blue light of dawn ended her practically sleepless night. But she'd shout and stomp with not much less energy over Thanksgiving, Halloween, the Fourth of July, and Easter. Other holidays she was less familiar with, but she celebrated them as she discovered them in school, and had been known to invent associations and ask her parents why there was no Memorial Day feast upon the table, or why the Labor Day Puppy had left no treats beneath her bed.

"Not yet. I'm still asleep. This is all a dream, right now. It's still pitch black outside, if you'd just wake up and look. Go back and lie in your bed and count to ten, then open your eyes."

"Come on," she said, pulling now both on his leg and Al's tail. "Come *on*. It's right now!"

"This is a dream, and Al is going to bite you, and his poison will make you burst into flame."

Jemma hesitated then, reaching around with her left hand to pinch herself on the bottom, making it smart but not crying out. Then she jumped up on her brother's bed and bounced vigorously, her feet touching against him every third or fourth bounce, until she missed her footing and stepped right on his belly, and fell down against him. "The sawdust," she was saying, "and the turtles and the Red Rover and the fireworks and George Washington, we're going to miss them if you don't get up!"

He opened one eye. "Go get me a drink of water and then I'll get up." Jemma scrambled off the bed and hurried down to the bathroom. She emptied a cup of a year's worth of accumulated toothbrushes—she and Calvin each had three or four, because the older models wore out or were superceded by fancier shapes or prettier colors—filled it with water, and hurried back to the room, careful not to spill. But when she arrived the door was closed and locked.

"Hey," she said, knocking with her foot.

"It's too early," Calvin said, and then he would not respond no matter how hard she knocked. She wanted very badly to pour the cup of water over his head, and waited silently at his door for a little while for just that opportunity to present itself, patience losing out eventually to a growing thirst. She drank the water and went downstairs.

Her parents' door was closed; she did not try the knob but listened at the wood, hearing nothing. She went into the living room, already the warmest and brightest room in the house, the peach walls and carpet glowing, and climbed into the bay window. She could see all the way down to the river. A thin line of mist hung over each of the three ravines; the haze over the river lifted even while she watched a boatful of tiny teenagers leave the docks and go swiftly over the water. She heard their horns, and the other horns echoing overland from every direction, and then the boat passed the bend in the river and all became silent. But still everything, the rising sun, the glare off the water, the thinning mist, seemed ready to shout. Even the air seemed about to proclaim the great day. She went into the dining room, sat at the table, put her fists under her chin, and waited.

She followed Calvin down the hill, walking in the rough of the fourth hole and kicking at dandelion heads. In an aerated shoebox under her arm she carried her racing turtle, #40, Mr. Peepers. Every so often she'd hold the box up, lining up her eye to check on him, watching the steady progress he made consuming the lettuce leaf she'd put in there to keep him happy on the trip. Calvin said eating before the race would make him slow. Her father said he'd race faster because the lettuce would make him happy, and because he'd sprinkled a dash of cayenne pepper on the leaf.

The Nottingham's new dog leaped out at them. The old one had died in the spring. Now they had a puppy who, chained in the place of his predecessor, inherited and modified his habits. So he whined instead of roaring, and slapped his big paws in the grass instead of beating the air with them. When Jemma bent down next to him he turned on his back and offered her his belly. She scratched it.

"Come on," said Calvin. "We'll be late."

"Now who's hurrying?" Jemma asked him, but she rose and followed. They wound around the fifth and seventh holes, around the sheriff's house and past the staircase that led to the deep hidden playground, Jemma now looking in on Mr. Peepers and now smelling her fingers, savoring the lingering odor of maple syrup. Their father had made pancakes for breakfast decorated with strawberry mouths, blueberry eyes, and great masses of whipped cream hair. Standing at the stove in his red-white-and-blue-striped trousers, he'd flipped the cakes halfway to the ceiling, whistling "Yankee Doodle Dandy" and cursing mildly when a bit of hot batter struck his bare chest or belly. Jemma's mother, dressed in a blue bathing suit, came in and out of the kitchen, stealing bites from her pancakes, more and more green every time she made an appearance, until she was patina'd from her ears to her fingers.

Cars passed them, some open-topped and some not, all full of parents and children dressed in red, white, and blue, all decorated with flags and dragging some sort of red-white-and-blue noisemaker, a few decked out as floats for the parade. Jemma waved with her whole free arm every time someone passed. Calvin, his gaze fixed on his shoes, just kept walking, not looking up until, as they were passing along an empty stretch of road in front of the clubhouse, they were both startled by an explosion in the grass.

Jemma jumped, dropping her box but catching it again before it could hit the ground. She heard a funny whistle before the next explosion. It seemed smaller than the first, just firecracker-sized, but she jumped just as high. Calvin was already looking at the clubhouse roof when the laughter broke out. There were two older boys up there, armed with bottle rockets. Jemma recognized them, but didn't know their names. Each of them wore a single lacrosse glove to protect their hand while they aimed and launched their rockets.

"Got to pay the toll," said the one on the left.

"One box of stuff," said the one on the right, pointing at Mr. Peepers' box. Jemma held it to her chest.

"You all are morons," said Calvin, and started walking again. A rocket exploded in front of him before he'd taken five steps. He stopped again and Jemma ran up behind him.

"Got to pay the toll, kiddo," the two boys said. Calvin just stared at them, even while they lit and leveled another rocket. As far away as they were, Jemma still thought she could see the fuse burning down. She had time to run away, but she just stood there tugging on Calvin's shirt. They had wonderful aim. Jemma was sure the rocket would have flown just inside the space Calvin made with his arm by putting his hand on his hip, and slide precisely through one of the holes in Mr. Peepers' box. She imagined the flare of light, the box leaping in her hands and the lid leaping off the box, the turtle parts scattering toward every corner of the ninth tee. In a flash of useless, stupid prescience she knew what would happen, and yet she did nothing, did not move, did not shield innocent Mr. Peepers with her own body, did not even cry out until something happened that she did not expect. Calvin moved his arm, releasing his hand from his hip and waving it in a circle, a gesture of utter dismissal that knocked the rocket out of her path. It fell on the ground and slid through grass still wet with dew to explode some twenty feet from where they stood. My own concern flexes at this same moment in a useless spasm, but it is only your brother's arm that saves you. In this moment it would not surprise you if he cleared the space from the ground to the roof in one leap and knocked both boys, with two short simultaneous punches to the chest, clear down to the river, or if from that place on the roof he reached up and, tearing the sky from its moorings, wadded it up like so much blue tissue paper to throw at your feet.

"Morons," Calvin said, and walked away. Jemma followed so close behind him she gave him two flats, which he did not comment on, but just kept walking with his heels outside his sneakers like they were sandals, and her head bumped repeatedly into his shoulder while she talked. "You saved Mr. Peepers's life!" she said. "They were going to kill him, or kidnap him, or torture him, or eat him!"

"They were morons," he said quietly, but he was trembling, and he made her swear by the red heart of Mr. Peepers not to tell their parents what had happened. Jemma swore, but she kept thinking about that gesture all day long. In the odd still moment it would come back to her, and she would make that circle herself, over and over until her brother saw it and made a shushing motion at her.

After they passed the clubhouse and the general store the golf course opened up on their left and the first through fourth tees, where they rolled all the way down to the river, were full of tents and people, and the parade was already well advanced along the road that wound down to the beach. Beneficent strangers pushed them forward when they stood at the back of the crowd lining the road, and they emerged among other children just as the first float was passing by, and the first portion of candy and fireworks went flying over their heads. Jemma leaped awkwardly, grabbing in the air with one hand and managed to nab a single bottle rocket. She cast it on the ground.

The floats passed: Betsy Ross working on the flag in the back of a festooned pickup truck; Ben Franklin flying a kite on a stiff wire with one hand and scattering roman candles with the other; a Liberty Bell made all of daisies and violets; the local Young Republicans beating on dead-donkey piñatas; delegations from each of the summer-camp classes, Nit through Gold Senior, riding high on the floats upon which they'd labored all through the summer, riding by in crepe-paper splendor, alternating Roman and Spartan, so insults were hurled from the stern of one float to the bow of the next, and candy flung hard enough to sting. Last of all came the Chairman and his Lady, both honorary but elected offices, whom Jemma had been awaiting with breathless anticipation. They rode on the finest float of all, constructed by labor contributed by every camp class: they sat on white thrones above a papier-mâché model of DC. Jemma longed to see them rise and stomp like monsters among the stiff paper capitol and monuments, but they only sat, their father in his blue waistcoat and red-white-and-blue pants; their mother in her green toga and spectacular tinfoil crown. Their bags contained the best candy, and the fanciest explosives, and both parents threw more than a fair share at Jemma and Calvin as soon as they saw them.

When their float stopped in front of the clubhouse they climbed up on the stage set up on the lawn and together rang the daisy and violet liberty bell with careful strikes pantomimed in time to a recording of the actual bell sounding. Then they set off a single rocket, an explosion lost in the glare of the sun, and declared the games open. These were the midsummer games, not to be confused by anyone with the end-of-summer annual Olympiad, but still quite important in the competition between the two summer-camp teams. Points could be gathered on this day such that the opposing team would never catch up, even if they won the decathlon or had both the boy and girl of the year chosen from within their ranks to receive the Field Medal. Every child, even Jemma understood the seriousness of the day and schooled their turtles accordingly.

The first game was not the turtle race—that was second—but the candy-grab, in which Roman and Spartan Nits and Novices raced in relay a hundred yards to hurl themselves at a ten-foot-high pile of sawdust full of secret candy, burrowing for thirty seconds, timed from the arrival of the first runner, and bringing back as much as they could grab to the team pile, which would be weighed and tested against the other team's pile at the end of the race. The whole enterprise yielded few points to the winning team, but as the opening event it was enthusiastically attended and the spectators routinely screamed themselves hoarse.

Jemma started the relay, running against Tiffany Cropp, the youngest daughter of an intensely competitive Roman family whose sisters were famous for their beauty, speed in the water, and the violence with which they wielded their field-hockey sticks. Tiffany, at age seven, was fiercer even than her sisters, though still ugly, like they'd been when they were her age. She had been known to find girls she lost to in the Olympiad and beat them till they cried. This made Jemma nervous.

"I'm going to win," she said, as they were waiting for the gun to sound. "I've got new shoes." Jemma looked down at them, keds so white and spotless they almost hurt her eyes. Her own shoes, red-white-and-blue and dusted with stars, were holdovers bought special for the previous year, and though too big then, now they pinched.

"My mom has a big silver crown," Jemma said, not comforted or inspired by the statement, but it was all she could think to say.

"Your mom is smelly," Tiffany said quietly, crouching down and touching her fingers to the grass like a professional runner. "Ass-smelly," she added. Then the gun sounded, and they were off, Jemma flying along on the encouraging screams of her brother and parents, which she thought she could make out quite distinctly among the larger encompassing screams of the crowd. She beat Tiffany to the pile; the counselor called the start of the thirty seconds as soon as her fingers touched it, and Jemma felt like she had been gathering candy forever when she heard Tiffany's little body collide against the sawdust with a solid thud. The layers of dust had been sitting all night; they were warm on the surface but cool inside. Jemma very much enjoyed the feel of it against her hands, and the lovely clean smell, so much that she had to concentrate very hard to keep from being distracted from her task. This early in the race the candy was easy to find; she grabbed the hardly buried chocolate flags and lollipops and gumballs and sour bombs and piled them in her pockets and, when those were full, held out her shirt to make a basket. She should have known better than to look over at Tiffany, who was already shrieking in triumph, but she did. Her pockets were overflowing and she had a gigantic candy bosom, and even as Jemma watched she withdrew a foot-long tootsie roll from the sawdust, too long for her pocket or for her shirt. In less than five seconds she tied it in her hair. Then the bell sounded and she ran off, letting her hand push a little sawdust in the air as she turned away from the pile. It flew toward Jemma's face but it missed her.

Jemma beat her back to the line of children waiting to run, and slapped Martin Marty's hand two or three seconds before Tiffany reached her team mate, but Tiffany had gathered a whole four ounces more candy, the full weight of the tootsie pop that she shook dramatically from her head, the last thing to fall on her pile. "I told you," she said to Jemma, without a hint of charity, and indeed the Spartans went on to win the candy grab. Jemma and her team mates watched bitterly as the candy was distributed among the victorious team, with not a single sour jelly for the losers, even from what they'd gathered themselves.

Jemma did better in the turtle race, thanks to Mr. Peepers, in whom her faith had not been misplaced. He'd even been hard to catch; that's how she knew he would be a winner. In late June turtles started disappearing from the woods around the reservoir. Jemma had only started looking the previous week, and was lucky to find somebody so fine so late, when all that were left were the aged and crippled and the permanently numbered turtles of years past. Mr. Peepers won his heat and placed third in the whole competition, beating Tiffany's turtle, #22, in the first race. Tiffany paced her turtle during his whole run, straddling his lane and shouting at him incessantly until he began to wander in circles, and then simply lay down and withdrew into his shell.

The morning passed with the lemon-eating contest, the pogo-jousts, honeydew bowling, the Nit-toss, the Aspirant kick-ball game, and finally, the event that closed the morning games, coming well after morning tea but before the afternoon barbecue, the Great Red Rover. Every class lined up on the field, every child wore a number to be called by, since the group was too large for everyone to be known by name. It was a narrow Spartan victory, though the Cropp sisters remained an unbroken chain almost till the end. Tiffany, Alex, and Meg, they were lined up all in a row, and there was a quality to their voices as they called out your number that was almost electric and certainly disheartening. Jemma ran deliberately far to the left of them when she was called, and did nothing to help earn her team's victory. She bounced right off the chain and landed on her back. But a big Spartan boy, Martin's brother Jonathan, broke the Roman chain in the end. From prison Jemma saw Tiffany turn and bite herself softly on the shoulder, an expression she saved for her most furious rages.

Jemma stuffed herself with fried chicken and polished her old shoes with her greasy fingers, shared candy with some congenial Romans, lay in the grass with Rachel Rauschenburg and watched Calvin and some other boys roll the spare watermelons down the hill, and wore, briefly, her mother's crown. At one o'clock she joined the march into the woods to liberate her turtle. Halfway there she stumbled on the mangled body of number twenty-two. He was belly down in the grass, half his shell caved-in, broken in the lines of the tiles. Jemma shielded Mr. Peepers' eyes and walked on, knowing already, long before she saw the blood on her shoes, that deadly-kedded Tiffany had killed him for losing.

Nit, Novice, Aspirant, Myrmidon; Footpad, Freshman, Sophomore, Junior; Senior, Bronze Senior, Silver Senior, Gold Senior: every summer-camp class had their primary event, the one they trained hardest for, and the one that if won would yield the most points. The Nits had their toss, the Novices their turtle race, the Aspirants their tetherball tourney, the Myrmidons their soccer match, and the Footpads, Calvin's class, their big lacrosse game. Jemma sat in the aluminum bleachers between her parents and watched her brother running back and forth across the field. She knew him through the obscuring helmet because his name was on his jersey and his stick was painted neon green.

She did not entirely understand the game. The carrying and throwing of the ball, the excited running about, the positions of the goals and duties of the goal keeper; these made sense, but she could not figure why it wasn't more acceptable to beat the opposition with your stick. She wanted to see a duel, sticks swinging and blocking, boys ducking and leaping, and if two of them happened to do it balanced on a floating log in the river, it would be all the better. But all the checking was unofficial. The game paused now and then when one or the other coach decried a perceived foul, and gathered the wronged boy to him to examine and comfort him, and exhort him to vengeance and greater violence.

Calvin was good. He had been practicing all summer, in camp and evening team practice and on his own, throwing the ball against the wall of the house while Jemma sat in the driveway and watched, catching the ball again no matter how hard he threw it, sometimes without even seeming really to look at it. Twice Jemma saw him do it with his eyes closed; the third time the ball struck him in the head and knocked him on his back, so their mother, watching from the porch, made him put on his helmet even for solo practice. He scooped up a lost ball just at the Spartan goal and darted away with it. Jemma's wrists made sympathetic cradling motions as he ran down the field. He'd tried to teach her to cradle the ball, but she failed to master it, and every time she'd tried to run with the ball it dropped out of the net and rolled away. Once she had to chase it all the way down to the Nottingham's house.

Calvin passed the ball to Rachel's sister Elena, the only girl on the Spartan team. She took it most of the way toward the goal, passing it briefly to Jonathan Marty when she was threatened by big Dickie, one of the two hulking Niebuhr brothers on the Roman team. Both hands on his stick, he rotated the empty end toward her head, and Jemma's heart leapt. She ducked and rolled, taking the ball back from Jonathan just as she came to her feet. Romans converged from all over the field, a few pursuing her but most coming in from her front and her flanks. Just before she reached the crowd she made a long pass to Calvin out on the left edge of the field, who only had to dodge a couple Romans, pokey ones who had not been able to keep up with Elena's pursuit. He brought the ball across his shoulder and slammed it into the goal.

The cheering and booing were so loud that Jemma had to cover her ears even while she shouted herself, so her screaming voice was oddly magnified, and echoed in her head. Her parents jumped up and down, making the aluminum rattle and flex, her mother waving her plastic torch and her father his red-white-and-blue sword-cane. It took a few minutes for the crowd to settle. Every event of the day was followed with care, but some, like the lacrosse game and the big Senior swim, drew special attention, and caused especially heated arguments. Exciting games were particularly divisive, and this was one of the most exciting pee-wee lacrosse games ever played on the reservoir field. Roman and Spartan points alternated in a way that would have seemed polite if not for the increasingly egregious checking, enough to sate even Jemma's innocent bloodthirstiness. The teams were tied just as the clock was about to run out, when Calvin scooped up another dropped ball and would certainly have scored a winning goal if the Niebuhrs hadn't ganged up on him in a way that would lead people to suspect they'd been given a specific assignment from their coach to take him down. One knocked his stick just after the other checked his belly; either blow alone he could have withstood, but the combination caused him to lose the ball. It was picked up by Ronnie Niebuhr, who made a long pass to another Roman close to the Spartan goal. The Spartan goalie, distracted by the injustice unfolding before everyone's eyes but the blind referee's, failed to block the shot, and the Romans won the game by a single point.

"What does it mean to wear this hat and these pants and wield this cane, if I can't get justice for my son?" Jemma's father asked, first of the referee, who would not call a foul, and then of the sky. Jemma participated in the bitter chants and the foot stomping, and shook a bouquet of rockets threateningly at the other side of the field, and muttered along with everyone else as the crowd broke up and people made their way down to the river for the corn roast.

Jemma walked with her brother and Elena. The two players carried their sticks over their shoulders, their gloves and jerseys slung off the end of the sticks. Jemma carried both helmets, clapping them softly together as she walked.

"The Romans are going to pay," Elena said.

"Yeah!" said Jemma.

"It doesn't matter," said Calvin.

"Not really," said Jemma.

"It was a big cheat," said Elena.

"The worst ever," Jemma agreed.

"It was just a game," Calvin said. "It doesn't matter much when you compare it to... a big lion running around and eating people."

"Or an elephant," said Jemma. "Who shmooshes you."

"It's just not fair," Elena said, and then added, "Damn it." It sounded weird, not like when Calvin said it. Jemma could tell she was not an experienced curser.

"Have you ever thought," Calvin asked, stopping and standing just as they were passing through one of the sand traps protecting the second hole, "if we forgot who was a Spartan and who was a Roman, then we could just sort of turn around and take over."

"That wouldn't make it any more fair," Elena said, and Jemma wondered aloud if the turtles were having a reunion party.

"Maybe it would," Calvin said. He started walking again, using the end of his stick to push himself up when he made the big step out of the trap and onto the green. "We could have rushed the stands, both teams. Then we could have taken over."

"My daddy said he's going to sue the referee."

"Sue him good," Jemma said. "Sue off his pants." Calvin was quiet then, and the two girls were quiet too as they walked the final blocks down to the river beach. Calvin was smiling every time Jemma looked over at him, thinking secret thoughts. Jemma closed her eyes and tried to think what he was thinking. It took a little while, but then, just as they got down to the water, she thought she saw it, an army of nine-year-olds riding lions out of the field and into the stands, biting off the heads of every adult and then tossing them back and forth with their lacrosse sticks. Jemma came behind them on an elephant named Justice. She held on with one hand to a thick red ribbon around his neck while he reared and stomped, encouraging him with cruel words in a language she didn't even understand until a green lady in a ruined toga came crawling toward them. Justice lifted both his front legs high and let out a blast that broke windows all over the Forest. Jemma held him there, suspended over her mother.

The corn roast was supposed to be an occasion of fellowship and good feeling, when all the day's competition was profitably reflected on, and victories savored but not gloated over. But that year a pall of resentment hung heavy over the feast. Jemma did not notice it at first. It was the usual corn roast, filled with the usual enjoyments. It had always been her favorite part of the holiday, when the hot afternoon faded into the warm evening and night, and the hoarded rockets of the day were spent in fits that anticipated in a very small way the fireworks to come.

Jemma and Rachel Rauschenburg hung their heads and arms over the pier, watching the half-matured sea nettles drifting up against the net that kept them out of the swimming area, and then sat with their legs dangling over the water, both of them trying to mix the fire from their sparklers—the Roman candles were prettier and more fun but they were in too partisan a mood to use them. They ran, up and down the dock, back and forth across the beach, around the picnic tables, stopping now and then to gnaw on a piece of corn, or suck the meat from a crab claw, or swill a soda so fast they got headaches from the cold of it. When they were good and sweaty they'd wade into the river and splash each other until they were refreshed.

Wandering, Jemma caught bits of conversation. At her parents' big table, which should have held the best and happiest people of either team, only the Spartan elite were feasting. Jemma watched her father lifting crabs into one of the big steam pots, his fancy pants falling down on his hips and his beard slung backward around his neck. "It's a fucking travesty," he was saying. Her mother, fixing sparklers to her crown with the help of three attendants, agreed. Jemma lipped under the table with Rachel to trade between them a single piece of hot corn that each would butter again after every bite.

"Can you be any more blind and not have empty sockets in your head?"

"Not blind, oh no. Corrupt. Corrupt as Nero, and just as Roman."

"You have to wonder how they live with themselves."

"It's a wonder they don't feel like fakes. I'd feel like a fake."

"You are a fake. Nothing real about you, honey."

"Fuck off, Bob."

"How can they eat? Doesn't it make them sick? It makes me *sick*. I don't think I can eat any more."

"Darling, the lobster is coming. Don't tell me…"

"Well maybe I could eat a little. But I won't enjoy it."

"Ruined. The whole day is ruined. I agree completely. Corruption has spoiled this day. Corruption is spoiling our *country.*"

"Something should be done about it."

"Oh, something will be done about it. It's not so long till November."

"I meant tonight.

"I'm formulating a suit, but not tonight."

"I for one will have to be a lot drunker before I do anything about it."

"That can be arranged," Jemma's father said, handing a beer to Mr. Nottingham just as she and Rachel came up from the table. "Hey, sneaky girls," he said. "Want some corn?"

"We had some," Jemma said, and they ran off to hide under other tables and eat other people's corn and shrimp. Underneath a Roman table they ate a whole lobster together, Jemma doing much of the dismembering because Rachel was squeamish, but Rachel devouring most of the rubbery tail meat. They went searching for Calvin because they wanted to pinch him with one of the big red claws. He was on the pier with a mixed group of boys, in the process of seeing how many magic snakes they could ignite at the same time. They had eighty of them set up in a circle of two layers. Jemma forgot to pinch him, too excited to remember when she heard about the plan. Four boys lit snakes at compass points on the circle, while Calvin leaned over and lit a few in the center. In a moment they were smoking and uncoiling, each individually at first but then they seemed to grow together, until it was one giant snake, a beast that was a deeper piece of darkness sucking up the torchlight and the flare of stray rockets. As it approached and exceeded child height they began to flee from it, all but Calvin, who was calling to it, pretending it was some demon he was summoning out of a deep black hell. "Come!" he was shouting at it. "Come and take them, my precious! Come and take them all!" Mr. Cropp came up with a fire extinguisher, blasting ash into the air to blow in a mass down the pier and into the Spartan table.

The big fight almost began then. Mr. Cropp and a Spartan dad exchanged a few drunken shoves until their wives—both of whom outmassed their husbands—pulled them apart. Rachel had wandered away, and suddenly the whole party seemed to go still for Jemma, even though everyone was still talking and laughing and running. All she could see was her brother, and all she could hear was her brother. He winked at her, and said, "Do you want to see something?"

"Sure," she said.

"Sometimes I can make anyone do anything I want."

"I know," she said, because when she closed her eyes she saw him knocking the rocket aside, and she really believed he could do anything.

"Everyone else wants me to go, too. Even though they don't know what it is. They've been waiting and waiting, and wanting it and wanting it."

"I know," she said, and he laughed.

"No you don't." Then he turned and hurled a piece of corn at their mother, and ran off into the darkness beyond the reach of the torches. Their mother had just lit the sparklers in her crown and raised up the arms she'd kept so carefully green with repeated applications of makeup throughout the day, to call down the big fireworks. It knocked her upside the head just as she cried out, "Let there be liberty!" and the first rocket shot up, a red-white-and-blue peony.

After that the hot corn began to fly in earnest, along with raw and cooked crabs that spun like frisbees as they sailed through the air. Jemma got nicked with a passing claw as she stood on the beach, not sure if she should watch the fight or the fireworks. Those who were drunk enough thwacked or stabbed at their neighbors with corn, or struck them with lobsters as if with a purse, or punched, or kicked, like Jemma's father, mindful, even almost too drunk to walk, of his surgeons hands. Of the children only the teenagers participated, fighting with each other but not entirely seriously, and Tiffany Cropp, who in a confused ecstasy of rage, and in the dark between explosions, bit her own father on the calf.

Jemma and Rachel and a dozen other children on the beach were herded knee-high into the river by Elena and a few other older kids, out of the way of the food. Then they turned their faces to the sky and back to the earth again, watching the fight and the fireworks. Severna Forest was rightly said to have the best fireworks display east of DC. It went on while the fight intensified. red-white-and-blue peonies; silver swans; white stars that burst three times in succession to show a blue circle in their heart; red flares that burst green at their apogee and settled in shapes like trees into the water; a red, green, purple, and orange set, spheres of four different sizes that hung in the sky like a giant bowl of fruit for what seemed to Jemma to be forever—every explosion made Jemma's stomach leap, her attention so consumed by what she saw that she did not hear herself exclaim with the people on the shore at every new explosion. For Jemma it was wonder piled on wonder, until the last, which seemed to explode just over her head, so she had to lean so far back she thought her hair would touch the water, a procession of flares in every color Jemma had ever seen, that exploded one by one, each one bigger and brighter than the last, each one touching her with a wave of force she felt break against her face, each one echoing in her eye and her head until she felt sure she must be suspended high in the sky. "Goodbye!" her brother shouted at her. She had waded close to the pier, and looking up she saw him there, framed against the explosions with his arms lifted up to the sky, as if he was summoning them out of the clouds, or hurling them out from his breast. "They are sending me!" he said. "Goodbye, I'm going!" In a panic, she clawed her way up a pylon and held on to his ankle, ready to be dragged after him into the sky. He shook his foot but she wouldn't let go, and after the finale he was still just his ordinary self with his arms up. He sat down heavily next to her. On the beach people were still fighting and cursing, and Sheriff Travis turned on the lights on his patrol car, and started shouting on his bullhorn for people to calm down.

"Did you go?" Jemma asked her brother.

"What do you think?" he said.

I do not like your brothers, Pickie Beecher says. It is very early in the morning, and he sits on the edge of the roof, kicking his feet idly in the air and sipping at a packet of blood. I like every brother. Every brother lives in my heart, but these two... I do not like them.

Never mind them.

Angels hate me.

You are an orphan of creation.

Brother-killers, all of you. Even now brothers are dying, and what are you doing about it?

I am the recording angel.

Another and another and another. Death after death, and didn't my mother undo death?

Not for everyone. But do not fear my brothers. The accuser has nothing to say to you, and the destroyer will not touch you. A different way has been prepared for you.

Death, he says.

Not death, I say. But life. Someone has died for the sake of everyone else's happiness. Even yours.

Will I get to be with my brother again?

No, but the grieving for him will be done. You won't want to anymore.

That is the most disgusting thing I have ever heard, he says.

You say that now. But how can you know what tomorrow will bring?

It is always the same. Every new day dawns, and my brother is still gone, and my whole life is one great aching after him.

I am supposed to say, Have faith. I am supposed to compare his small, strange mind, unfavorably, with the gigantic and subtle wonders of providence. But though I can feel those very words forming in the empty air of my chest, my own will and my angelic destiny shaping them together, I find I cannot speak them. They stick in my throat and feel as solid as a bone.

It's hard, I say, to miss your brother or your sister

Sisters are nothing, Pickie says. And what do you know about, it, anyway? But then he reaches out beside him without looking at me, and takes my hand.

Rob was eating his lunch when Ishmael accosted him. He really should have eaten it on the way to the lab—he had a cell culture cooking there, and Dr. Sundae could not be relied upon to check it for him. He thought she probably had the botch in her brain, but he kept asking Jemma to check on it. He was salting his macaroni and cheese when Ishmael reached from behind him to put a hand on his wrist.

"There's already enough salt in the sea," he said. Rob shook his hand off. They weren't exactly pals anymore. In a better, less exhausted world, somebody would have arranged an intervention for his erratic behavior. Off and on he was paranoid, and violent with himself. More than one person had seen him standing in some alcove off the ramp, pulling at his hair or biting his fingers. And there wasn't a person above the age of twenty-one who hadn't had him pop up and charge them with something improbable—stepping on a dodo or poisoning a mountain or uncoloring the sky. These accusations were almost quaint, but lately he seemed to like more and more to accuse people of wild vile sexual transgressions, and sometimes new mothers and fathers covered the ears of their children when he came around. And yet most of the time he was sober and clear-headed and totally normal, an able organizer and cheerleader for all their futile efforts against the botch.

"I like salt," Rob said, not turning around to see which Ishmael was standing behind him. But he couldn't eat with the man staring at the back of his head, so he said, "Want to sit down?"

"Don't mind if I do," Ishmael said, and took the spoon that Rob was going to use for his ice cream to help himself to the macaroni and cheese. "I miss you," he said, around a mouthful.

"I miss you too," Rob said, because his mother had taught him that you always had to say that back to people, even when you didn't mean it.

"We used to be friends, didn't we? Weren't you my pal?"

"Sure," Rob said.

"Golden days! I miss them too. I was happier then, back before I knew."

"Well, we were all having a pretty good time there, for a while. Things are harder now. But it doesn't mean that there's not something good coming." Ishmael laughed out loud at that, and Rob blushed, because it sounded so dumb. If he were someone like Father Jane he might be able to say the same thing in a way that would seem proudly hopeful instead of simply naïve.

"Maybe for somebody, but not..." Ishmael cocked his head, and put down his spoon, and leaned over the table. "You know, I was going to say, not for you. But who knows? And you're not like everybody else, anyway. I mean, everybody knows it. You'll get the Best Boy award, when this is all over, and they are all sitting around deciding who has been the Biggest Whore or the Whiniest Worm or the Handsomest Hip. I can see it."

"Um... thanks."

"It's just a fact. Don't thank me for it. There aren't many like you... trust me! I see into all the places that people try to hide. It's what I used to do, I'm sure of it. I illuminated and I judged and I wanted to punish. I wanted it so bad!" He struck a fist on the table, catching the edge of Rob's bowl and sending macaroni flying.

"Take it easy there, pal," Rob said.

"Pal! Now I'm your pal! Your long-lost, neglected pal! Well, that's fine. Even if it does stand for Personal Ass Licker. That's its own distinct pleasure, and don't I know it?"

"Have you been drinking?" Rob asked him.

"I wish! I don't need to, not anymore. It helps nothing, to drink. But back to our story. You and I were going to move in together. Best Boy and Angriest Aardvark. Can't you see it?"

"No."

"But don't tell me," he said, "that you haven't ever thought about it. Didn't I just finish saying that I see all the places that nobody else sees?" He leaned over the table, and then climbed up on it one knee at a time, so even though Rob pushed back his chair, Ishmael could push his face right up against him, so his hair touched Rob's hair and their noses were nearly touching. He put a hand right on Rob's belly and said, "Don't tell me you've never thought about it."

Maybe he had, but that had nothing to do with the sudden panic that rose in him. All the late days in PICU, surrounded by a deadly illness whose rules of contagion were still unknown, had not made him feel suddenly so unsafe, so threatened, as he did now. It felt suddenly like Ishmael was pressed close against him, though he still lay atop the table. Chest to chest and hip to hip and thigh to thigh, Rob suddenly felt him pressing in. Ishmael whispered his proposition, and Rob shouted back the first thing that popped into his head: "I love my wife!"

That worked. Ishmael leaned back, and climbed back down into his chair, and then stood up. "So you do," he said, now sounding very sad. "I can't argue with that." He gathered two handfuls of the scattered macaroni and put them in his pocket, and then walked away.

The morning of her impeachment trial, three weeks after the arrival of the boat and the boy, Jemma lay in bed, feeling weary and achy and depressed. She'd come half-awake when Rob had left, summoned back to the PICU by his pager, and pretended to be asleep, watching through slitted eyes as he rose from bed, stretched, and pulled on his scrubs. He washed his face with water in a bowl; Pickie was still sleeping in the bathroom, and Rob was too considerate of Pickie to wash there. Jemma stirred a little, arranging herself in an accessible position and closing her eyes tight. When he kissed her she brushed a hand lazily against his face. "I love you," he told her, and she knew the highlight of her day had just come and gone.

Back during her surgery rotation she'd lain similarly abed, with the cold pre-dawn air spilling in her window, listening to the distant murmuring of her alarm clock. She smacked it across the room every day when it brought her the news that she must wake and travel to the OR. It would not yet be four a.m., but she could perfectly imagine the accumulating insults of the day, and her perfect exhaustion and depression when she came home again to sit in front of her window and watch the lights on the bay, thinking of nothing and feeling like a big pile of shit sculpted up into the shape of a girl. She lay that morning with her face in her pillow, a tiny corner of it stuck in her mouth, and thought of rounds and her late-afternoon trial, and how she would rather sleep than get up, rather hide on the roof than go help on the sixth floor, and rather gouge her eyes out with spoons than go to the trial. Maybe, she thought, they could just mail her the verdict, or shoot a flare where she could see it from her window, red for you're out, blue for we still love you. She turned on her side and pressed her nose against the cool cement wall, thinking of witnesses, seeing Dr. Snood and Dr. Chandra and Dr. Pudding on the stand, and then imagining a series of special witnesses, raised from the sea or conjured form the air, her mother, her father, her brother, Martin, Sister Gertrude, Laura Ingalls Wilder, the Cat in the Hat, Bugs Bunny, and that curious and amusing Martian who wore a shoe brush on his head. I knew she was trouble from the moment I saw her, the Martian said, and her mother said, All the Claflins are fucking insane, why should she be any different, and her brother rose up out of the witness box, fifteen feet tall, to crouch over the whole assembly and kill them all with a single derisive snort.

She heard Rob slip out the door, closing it so slowly behind him that the click of the latch was drawn out to two syllables. She turned again in the bed wishing she could lie on her back and throw her arm over her eyes, but she was too afraid that the baby might sit on its own blood supply and strangle itself. She piled both pillows on top of her head and fell asleep again, into a sleeping dream—she had liked those, in school, because they made it seem like you were getting twice as much sleep as you actually were—where she was lounging on a table in the Council chamber, stretching and turning and spinning like the slow hand of a clock, so her head pointed at everyone in the room and she heard them murmuring about how peaceful she looked, and what a shame it would be to wake her. Eyes closed, still turning and spinning, she became convinced that she was riding in her parents' car, feigning sleep, and hoping that her father would carry her into the house.

"It's time to wake," said the angel. "They'll need you at rounds in thirty minutes."

"Shut up," Jemma said. "I'm asleep."

"You're awake now. I see it very clearly. Shall I tell you the state of creation outside?"

"Still wet, I know," Jemma said.

"The water temperature is twenty-six degrees Celsius. The sky is overcast with a scattering of cirrus clouds. There are fifteen dolphins circling the second floor, a school of tuna outside the main entrance, and a large jellyfish outside the emergency room. Many children are watching it. Would you like to know who the children are?"

"I'm ordering you to be quiet," Jemma said. "I have a busy day. I need to sleep through it."

"You have a busy day," the angel agreed. "Breakfast has already been prepared. I will shriek an alarm if you do not rise from bed in the next three minutes." She began to count softly.

"They don't need me up there," Jemma said. The angel kept counting. Jemma flailed angrily under her covers, right to left and left to right, until the count had risen to a hundred seconds. When she rolled her legs out of the bed and touched her feet to the floor the counting stopped. It wasn't comfortable, but she thought she could probably fall asleep again like that. When she didn't move for another minute, the angel began to shriek, just softly at first, like a kitten horribly tortured but too small to make a very big noise. Jemma stood up before it got too loud.

"Good morning," the angel said.

"Probably for somebody, somewhere," Jemma said. She walked to the little table. Pickie had laid out breakfast for her, two boiled eggs, a kiwi, and a banana arranged in a hairy-nosed face. He'd written a note next to the tall glass of orange juice: *it is breakfast.*

"Would you like something else?" the angel asked. "The abomination touched that food. I witnessed it."

"Don't call Pickie names."

"He is not yet clean."

"Neither am I," Jemma said, smelling her upper lip, then her hair, then her shirt: cat food, smoke, illness. Vivian was sick with the botch. Jemma had stayed late with her the previous night, and not washed her hair when she came back downstairs. She peeled the eggs but ate only the fruit, drank half the juice, then took a long shower, standing for fifteen minutes under the water, resting her head against the tile.

"They are waiting," the angel kept saying, but no one was waiting for her when she finally got up to the sixth floor. The nurses barely met her eyes, and only the children, hurrying up and down the hall with bedpans or blood, or pulling bags of IV fluid in the little red carts in which they themselves used to be hauled, smiled at her. The younger ones were merely fetchers; the older ones were helping with jobs formerly performed by adults too sick now to work.

"I only have three patients," said Cindy Flemm when she saw Jemma coming down the hall, "and I'm late for rounds. It's my first time being late. Josh said they take away your patients, if you're late."

"Wouldn't that be great?" Jemma said. "I think they give you more, though." They walked together down the hall, Cindy going over the numbers on her three face-sized index cards.

"Josh has this fancy PDA, but I like the cards better. What's your system?"

"Toilet paper," Jemma said. "Slow down there, Speedy."

"Sorry," Cindy said, not slowing. She got to the conference room a few paces ahead of Jemma, darted in, then popped back out to hold the door. "Sorry," she said again, and Jemma heard, Sorry you're pregnant, Sorry everyone is afraid of you, and Sorry you've become useless.

Dr. Tiller looked up at her and gestured toward an empty seat. Timmy looked at her, too. Ethel Puffer, pulling a plate of brownies toward herself, waved. Josh was presenting a patient.

"She looks a little yellow this morning," he was saying. "Do you think the botch could be getting to her liver?"

"Many things are possible, Dr. Swift," said Dr. Tiller. "And some unpleasant business impossible today might be tomorrow's reality. But finish your presentation and then we'll consider those things." Josh blushed. Jemma broke in before he could go on.

"Anika has a pneumo," she said.

"I just looked at her film," said Timmy. "It was fine."

"When was it taken?"

"This morning, of course. It was fine. I went over it with Dr. Pudding."

"Well, she's got one now—it's probably too small to warrant a tube but somebody should keep an eye on it. And Janie has a renal abscess and a little fluid in her pericardium and Dr. Neder is about to dissect her aorta. She should go to the unit right away. I'm going down there next. Want me to see if there's a bed?"

"Have you examined the patients, Dr. Claflin?" asked Dr. Tiller.

"Of course," Jemma said, which was true; she had examined them in her way, walking by every room and pausing by the door to direct her attention inside.

"And you're quite sure about these assertions?"

"Sure as ever," Jemma said, getting back up.

"How much fluid is a little fluid?" asked Timmy.

"About ten cc's," I think.

"Rounds aren't over, Dr. Claflin," said Dr. Tiller.

"I'm a busy lady, Dr. Tiller. If I notice anything else I'll give you a call." She waddled to the door, staring straight ahead.

"Don't you want a brownie?" Ethel asked. Jemma reached behind her back, waved and hurried out, but she slowed as soon as she was in the hall. She wasn't really a busy woman. She had nothing to do all day but her mystic snooping, and rounding took only as long as a walk through the wards. She couldn't bear to go to the Council chamber yet, though she had a pile of papers to read and sign there. Instead she went downstairs, avoiding the ramp because she didn't want to get caught up in a string of conversations. It was like a poll, she supposed, how every third person stopped her to say, I think you're doing fine—this is all just craziness, but every second person scowled or turned their eyes to the floor or actually scolded her or lectured her on the fate of tyrants. The angel put her approval rating at 47 percent, not, Jemma figured, enough to save her, though the process that would decide her political future was not so grossly democratic as a recall.

Connie's bar was open all the time now—Karen's had closed, not just because she was dead but because no one else could make coffee like she did, and the wet black espresso grounds looked too much like what was leftover after the botch finished with a body—full of daytime lushes and shirkers, extra people who were too depressed by the new circumstances of their community to dance or stand on their heads in front of their class, but unwilling to leap back into the business of taking care of the sick. They were rare and distinctly unpopular. Among Jemma's unfinished work in the Council was a resolution that would draft every last one of them into service again, but for now they were miserable and free, and this morning she was one of them, too.

"Hey, honey," said Connie, as Jemma took a seat next to Dr. Chandra, the only other patron. "Shall I surprise you?" Jemma nodded, and Connie served her up a tall glass of alcohol-free Impeachment Punch, complete with a tall stick of fruit-kebab and a twirling umbrella. "Drink it all down," she said. "It's good luck."

"Does that mean I've got your vote?"

"Honey," Connie said, tossing her stringy hair over her shoulder and shaking her wattle in a way that Jemma knew she saved for very serious pronouncements. "You know I've got to hear the evidence. We all do. We've made our rules and now we have to lie in them."

"You've got my vote," said Dr. Chandra. "Not that it matters. Not that anything matters."

"Darling," said Connie. "Darling, don't put yourself down. Of course it matters. Not very much, but it does. You just have to hang in there and try not to put yourself down to much, until you're recovered. Then you'll see. You're going to stand so tall your head will scrape the skylights."

"Whatever," said Dr. Chandra. That was her line, the same one she spoke to all the sad souls she ministered to down here. The botch had put them in a slump like it put others into respiratory failure. They just had to be patient, and keep in their heart a willingness to let the sun shine in when it rose again, as it surely, surely would, Honey. To Jemma it was as viable and stupid as any other sort of pep talk, colder but just as effective, which was to say not at all, as the ones that Rob gave her.

"Thanks," Jemma said to Dr. Chandra. "It does matter." She looked at her watch: there were still five hours until her trial.

"Everyone's going fucking crazy," he said. "What they're doing to you is crazy, and all the other shit is crazy, too. It's the Program, back again to claim us all. Why would they let us out, just to start it all over again? What am I supposed to do now?"

"That's botch-talk, Honey," said Connie.

"Maybe," he said. "It's probably in my brain. Sometimes I think I can see it, when I close my eyes. It's big and tall and hulking. It looks just like Tiller. It's probably there... Do you see it?" He spun on his stool and grabbed Jemma's hand. She did see it, not in his brain but tucked away in his abdominal organs, a seemingly impotent series of shadows.

"No," she said.

"Lighten up, Botchcake," said Connie.

"Lighten up," she says. "Tell it to Dr. Tiller, coming for me with her red dripping claws."

"They need everybody they can get," Jemma said.

"Don't give me that," he said, tearing his hand away from her. "Any moron will do in a hopeless situation. Anybody can ask the angel for antiarrhythmia potions. And I may be just another moron, but I'm not her moron, not yet. She can just fuck off."

"Well," Jemma said, taking another sip of her punch. She was about to whisper, A little fucking off might do her good, when she felt a hand on her shoulder. It was Ishmael.

"Hello, handsome," said Connie. Dr. Chandra blushed and looked into his drink.

Ishmael ignored them both. "We need to talk," he said to Jemma.

Dr. Snood had launched his impeachment proceedings in the thirtieth week of the flood—it took another week to bring the matter to a trial presided over by Dr. Sundae. Jemma hadn't even realized she could be impeached—the protocol was been hidden in a sub-sub-paragraph of the constitution, something she hadn't paid a whole lot of attention to, because it was boring and because she knew that the laws had been composed with the expectation of never needing them; nobody thought they'd still be floating around when her forty-month term expired. Offenses and conditions warranting impeachment included being caught in a lie, egregious public sexual misconduct, acting against the interests of the hospital in collusion with a foreign power (should one ever be encountered), verbal or physical abuse of a child, murder, insanity, and willful harm of a patient.

He argued a combination of the last three, saying—not unpleasantly, not angrily or self-righteously, and (he assured everybody) with an absolute absence of malice—that Jemma was suffering from bouts of insanity brought on by the immense and overwhelming power of her singular gift. His speech calling for a vote to entertain impeachment was full of praise for the good Jemma, the Jemma who harrowed the hospital, whom the popular will had wisely elevated to their highest office, the Jemma who had presided so capably over all their deliberations, who had helped execute the final transformation of their home from a hospital to a community. But he damned with great fervor the menacing, insane Jemma who became intermittently drunk with power and wrought destruction on the populace. Twice she had lost control and twice someone had died.

Jemma was compelled to be silent during Dr. Snood's first speech, and all through the subsequent trial. She sat with her arms folded, still in her place in the middle of the Council table, like she was listening to a new plan for another addition to the lobby, trying not to shake her head, or show any emotion at all. They all watched the video of the musical again. The angel's cameras had mysteriously failed, and so the only footage was shot from high on the seventh floor, and if anything from far away it looked even less like she was trying to help Dr. Sashay. Jemma looked at the screen with a blank face, but tried not to actually watch. She thought of other things: the botch and Rob and her baby and of Vivian, lying in bed on the ninth floor.

"Well, I saw the green fire," said Dr. Chandra, a key witness because he was one of the few people seated in the front row who hadn't fled when Jemma first descended, "and I heard that strange noise. The whistling, humming noise. It was kind of like what you hear when the television is on but the sound is turned off, only it was louder. Dr. Sashay was lying on the stage. I think she was still trying to sing, when Dr. Claflin knelt by her."

"Near her, or on her?" asked Dr. Sundae.

"Oh, just near her, I'm sure. I heard Dr. Sashay go, oof! But I think it was just because she was hurting. Dr. Claflin put her hands on her hands, and the fire got brighter—it became a little hard to see through. It went on like that. I'm not sure how long. Dr. Sashay sort of floated up while she burned. When it stopped she fell to the ground and... broke."

"Is that all?" asked Dr. Snood.

"Yes," he said.

"You told us what you saw," said Dr. Sundae. "But didn't you hear anything else?"

"I'm not sure."

"Dr. Pudding reported that he heard Dr. Sashay screaming in pain as Dr. Claflin touched her. Was that your perception?"

"Oh, I don't know."

"Dr. Chandra, let me remind you..."

"She might have said something."

"What did she say?"

"It was all very indistinct."

"What did you think she said?"

"It sounded like, Stop, stop, stop it!"

"Thank you, Dr. Chandra."

"But it might have been Mop, Mop, Moppet! That was her dog's name, you know. People say all sorts of things when they're sick."

"Thank you, Dr. Chandra. That'll be all."

"She never understood that it was Miss Muffet who sat on her thingie. She thought it was Moppet. So she called her Little Miss Moppet, even though the dog was a boy, and it's all wrong, anyway, to call a German shepherd the size of a Volkswagen Little Miss anything. She was a strange lady, wasn't she? But wow, she was smart."

"That'll be all, Dr. Chandra," said Dr. Sundae, and called the next witness. Jemma folded her hands on the table and made a steeple of her fingers, wishing they would just get down to business and make the vote. She realized that she was confident she'd be vindicated, and this was making her impatient with the testimonies, even the ones that were sympathetic toward her. She wanted and needed to be upstairs with Vivian. Maybe she could just say it—Look, I've got to go. I have this sick friend. She's in the hospital, you see.

"It was definitely different from before," said Zini, the aged nurse-supervisor with the pruny thighs. "Bear in mind that I witnessed what she did on the sixth floor—I know how that looked. Sure, the children gave a shout, or tried to fight it at first, but this was different. She was screaming like somebody was ripping out her arms."

"Have you ever heard it before," asked Monserrat, "when somebody gets their arms ripped out?"

"Maybe not," said Zini. "But you know what I mean. It was like..." She gave a dreadful shriek, and twisted in her chair, and flailed her arms around like someone was trying to pull them out.

"Thank you," said Dr. Sundae, making a note on the pad in front of her. Jemma imagined she must be drawing the outline of a hanged man, adding a piece of scaffolding, an arm, or a leg every time someone else gave a bit of damning testimony. Dr. Sasscock, Emma, Pickie Beecher: each person sat in the chair in the middle of the Council chamber and told what they had seen or heard or felt. "I was afraid," said Wayne, "terribly afraid."

Dr. Snood testified, too. Jemma wasn't sure if that was precisely legal, but poring over the constitution had made her so tired and given her such a headache that she'd stopped looking before she knew for sure, and anyway Ishmael had already made his promise to her, so it seemed not to matter any more if Dr. Snood was or was not given the opportunity to present his slander.

"I first became worried about Dr. Claflin," he said, "when she returned from the ship. It was a bad idea anyway, I felt, for her to risk herself on an exploratory mission any one of us could have carried out. It might have gone very badly over there, and then where would we have been? Who else has been able to reproduce her results? Who else has her special talents? It seemed so unlike her, too, to insist so forcefully on something so small, and something that flew so egregiously in the face of common sense. But it was her prerogative to go, and she exercised it.

"She seemed different to me, when she came back. Was this the same person who'd left our home, I wondered? There was something different in her eyes, and in the quality of her voice, and in the way she carried herself—these are subtle and subjective observations that have no proper place in such an inquiry as this, yet I offer them in the spirit of objectivity, and I know there are not a few others who noticed this same change that I did. I didn't start to worry about her, though, until after she tried to wake the boy. It was then that I began to formulate my theory. May I have the lights down, please?"

The lights dimmed and a screen lowered from out of the ceiling on the far side of the Council chamber. Dr. Snood pressed a button on his laser pointer and the screen lit up. There was a complicated diagram featuring a picture of a brain Jemma presumed must be hers accompanied by a number of feedback loops and hormonal axes. She had to squint to read the smallest letters, and there were so many abbreviations she couldn't make even superficial sense of half of it. "What is this power that Dr. Claflin has, anyway? We were all content to benefit from it without understanding it, and I fear we did her a great disservice by not seeking better to understand it, to divine its mechanism, because we never considered for a moment that it might be dangerous to her or to her baby. But all of you please consider, just briefly, the magnitude of what she accomplished, and then ask yourselves if such a thing could really be expected not to come at a price?

"And what sort of price you wonder? I wondered too, all those weeks ago, and though all sorts of horrifying thoughts presented themselves to me, I put them aside and began to gather data. Yes, data—that forgotten entity! I know its not been fashionable lately to indulge in empiricism, but that's just what I did. Consider this diagram just for a moment—we'll return to it shortly. It sums up the neurochemical imbalances brought on by the use of Dr. Claflin's gift, and tells a very sad tale."

Jemma raised her hand.

"Dr. Claflin," said Dr Sundae. "You know I cannot recognize you yet."

"Is this a testimony?" Jemma asked, "or Grand Rounds?"

"I am going to pretend I didn't hear that, Dr. Claflin. Your turn is coming." Rob was waving his hand in the audience. "Dr. Dickens, if this Council wants your testimony, we will call for it specifically."

"As I was saying," said Dr. Snood, "I first became worried when the landing party, if we can call it that, returned from the boat, and that is when I started gathering evidence. I kept a log of unusual behaviors including strange movements, strange or inappropriate comments, and unjustified or unprovoked use of her gift. This figure summarizes one data set: I or my agents recorded sixty-four separate instances where Dr. Claflin used her gift in the absence of any appreciable illness in any living being around her. Notice the increase in frequency." He showed a graph, weeks versus frequency of the observed behavior, whose points made an upward-sweeping line.

"Jesus Christ," Jemma said, "you've been following me?" Dr. Sundae, eyes on the graph, held up a single warning finger. Everyone else ignored her except Ishmael, who caught her eye and winked. Jemma shook her head. She wanted to pound her fists on the table, but instead she just collapsed her steeple and folded the left hand over the right. She stared ahead at the wall, but not at the graph, and actually tried not to listen to what Dr. Snood was saying, though when he presented a table detailing the dates of emotional outbursts including three episodes of spontaneous crying, she stood up calmly and said, loud but not shouting, "Have you noticed, Doctor, that I am pregnant?" It was the first time she had ever put the special tone in her voice when she said Doctor, the one that turned it from a title into an insult. She felt both vindicated and ashamed. Dr. Sundae, at least, seemed sympathetic—she pretended not to hear her.

"This is all starting to drag, Dr. Snood," she said, and he hurried through his next twenty slides, summarizing the data in a flash, until he came to the brain MRI and PET scans that were done months before, as part of the initial workup of her wonderful affliction. He zipped through Dr. Pudding's report, outlining all the normal structures with his pointer, excitement growing in his voice until he came to a last series of cuts on the MRI and said "Look, just look at the amygdala! It was grossly hypertrophied." He presented a corresponding section of the PET that showed increased uptake of glucose in that region. "Rage," he said, turning away from the screen and waving his arms, cutting across the Council with his laser. "Fury, violence, destruction—these are all mediated by the amygdala. Dr. Claflin's amygdala has become an almond of doom"—he raised his fist—"struggling vainly to suppress the dark impulses unleashed by her dreadful burden. Do I have to paint a picture for you of the horrible things that could happen if it fails completely?"

He started to do just that, and there was even another set of pictures—artist's renderings he commissioned from a talented parent, but Dr. Sundae cut him off. "That will do, Dr. Snood," she said. The next witnesses, Anika and Janie, were both too sick to testify. Now it was Jemma's turn. Dr. Sundae called for her to step up into the box.

"I'm fine right here," Jemma said. She spent a few moments just staring around the room at various faces, seeing who would meet her gaze and who would hold it. Dr. Walnut looked away. Dr. Chandra looked back but made that gesture, the quick swipe over his nose, that she knew meant he had seen something dirty or unpleasant. Rob smiled. Ishmael winked again. "No matter what," he had told her that afternoon, "you can count on me. No matter what they say about you. No matter how horrible they make you sound, I won't vote against you, and they can't do a thing without all three of us going against you." She nodded and looked beyond him. Connie smiled but shook her wattle menacingly. Dr. Sundae nodded sternly at her and raised her eyebrows. Dr. Snood stared back and shook his head pityingly. She wanted so badly for Vivian to be here to defend her—she'd do a better job by far than Jemma ever could.

"Well," she said finally. "What can I tell you?"

"It was like this with my granny," Vivian said. "Everybody hanging around her bed, waiting for her to die."

"You're not going to die," Jemma said.

"You keep saying that." They were in the rehab playroom, Vivian lying face up in her hospital bed, Jemma sitting in a deep inflatable easy chairs of the sort that you could kick or hurl harmlessly across the room, when you were in the mood. Arthur and Jude, two men from the lift team who'd been assigned by Dr. Snood to follow Jemma wherever she went, sat on the ground close to the door, and between them and Vivian four of Vivian's disciples sat on inflatable mushroom-shaped stools, close enough to be able to hear everything they said. Vivian called them her death guard. They were there to catch her last words, because everybody on the ninth floor felt sure that Vivian, before anyone else, was going to come up with the reason, even if only moments before she died. "The worse I feel," she'd told Jemma, "the closer I feel to getting it. You know what that means, right?" Jemma didn't know, and didn't want to hear about it anyway.

"Cheer up," Vivian said. "You're healthy. Your baby's healthy. It could be a lot worse."

"That's coming," Jemma said.

"You'll be fine," Vivian said. "Your baby will be fine."

"How can you know that? You haven't laid a hand on my belly in weeks."

"I've thought it through," Vivian said. She sighed. "Is it midnight yet?"

"Almost," Jemma said, tired of the question and not looking at her watch. "I don't really care," she said. "It's just that it's made me very confused. Now what do I do? I almost wanted to ask them the question, but it would have been too humiliating."

"Do what I do. Lie here and try to figure it out, and wait for the big show."

"Stupid fucking Ishmael."

"Well, that at least you should have seen coming. Everything else—that's just things falling apart."

"He seemed so sincere."

"Tell me about it. I'll love you forever. I won't let them impeach you—it's all the same thing to him. Ouch." She shifted in her bed. "I think I just felt my kidney fail."

"Your kidneys are fine," Jemma said, taking a very quick look. There was a barely perceptible shimmer in the air when she looked into Vivian's belly, and no fire at all. Still, one of Dr. Snood's goons lifted his head, as if sniffing the air, and stared at her. Jemma looked away.

"They're probably the only good thing left in my body. This must be what it's like to get old. I think Granny was even in this position, except her hand was always up over her head, like this. See? I think it was stuck, or maybe she just liked it like that. Vivian, she said, I hope a truck or a fat man falls on you and kills you long before you ever get like me. She suffered terribly. I used to hate to come home from school, because I knew she would be there, and I could smell the smell by sixth period, way before I even left to go home. This isn't so bad, compared to what she went through. She paused a moment. Say, do I smell?"

"No," Jemma said.

"You wouldn't tell me if I did." She cried out suddenly and her four attendants leaped from their stools.

"What? Where does it hurt?" Jemma asked, though what she sensed from her friend was a high spike of elation.

"I almost had it. Closer and closer. Like a wave of nausea or… something else. I get so close and then it just rushes away, the feeling and the knowledge. For a second there it almost felt like it wasn't too late for me."

"You're not going to die," Jemma said.

"You keep saying that enough times and maybe someone in here will believe it, but never me. Is it midnight yet?"

"Thirty seconds," Jemma said, just as they heard the compressors start to hum behind the walls, and the lights started to dim further, and a bright mote appeared in the heart of the hanging sun.

"Here it comes," Vivian said.

Vivian was right, there was something about the model in the rehab gym that you could only appreciate if you were really depressed. When the ceiling faded and the stars began to shine out of the darkness and the planets brightened and the sun blazed, it was different than all the other times Jemma had watched it, like being lifted out of your body and hanging in space instead of like watching a fancy mechanical diorama. It seemed so real it made her wonder if her horrible day had really happened, because her memory of waking, of rounds, of her trial, of her speech, all seemed so flimsy and vague compared to the hard light of the uncountable stars, the darting flight of Mercury, the pale green eye of Venus, or the perfect blue globe of earth, unmarked by land or cloud. A dwindling part of her was still wondering if she shouldn't have just made them all see—she knew she could have done it, opened up their minds with prying green fire and made them know she wasn't crazy, or just forced them to give up the stupid, distracting business of impeachment; there was some organ she could have found or imagined in them which, when squeezed in her green fist, would have poured out an abundance of Jemma-love and devotion. It would have been better, she was sure, than trying to convince them with mere words. "I'm not crazy," she'd said, "I've just been trying to help, and the worst thing is, I care very deeply about all of you, I have a sort of love for everybody." It was weak and stupid thing and nothing she had planned to say, and love was the wrong word anyway for the compelling interest she had in them, and having said that made it seem even more like a humiliating breakup when all of them, even Ishmael raised their arms and turned their thumbs down at her.

"There it goes," she thought, imagining the humiliation, the caring at all about the whole stupid fucking day, was drawn out of her by a combination of gravitational and astronomical influences, so her anger went flying to Mercury, her thwarted love—though it wasn't love—to Venus, her shame to Saturn, until the only question she asked herself was, What is this day, compared to the majesty of the cosmos?

"You weren't kidding," she said after the motors cut out and the stars faded and planets slowed and stopped. Vivian was taking long draws off another cigarette.

"I told you," she said. "I haven't been living here for the past month for no reason. Look at them. They missed it." Jemma looked to her guards, who were yawning and stretching. "Hey," Vivian said to Helen Dufresne, the attendant closest to her. "Write this down for the record, please. Ishmael eats shit with a..." She cried out again, a deep bark, so Helena leaped back and threw up her hands, dropping her pen and pad.

Jemma stood up and asked "What, what?" though she could see what was wrong. Vivian had dropped her cigarette in the bed and was clutching at the rails, her hands rigid, a dreadful grimace on her face. Jemma brushed the cigarette off the sheets and raised up her hands. "Hey," she said, "knock it off." Her guards came rushing up. She raised her hands up higher. Vivian opened her mouth wider, but stopped shouting.

"Don't you do it," said Arthur.

"It's not allowed, ma'am," said Jude.

"Of course not," Jemma said, and burned. Arthur and Jude tried to reach her, but it only took the smallest portion of her attention to make it so they could only move their arms. They made swimming motions through her fire but came no closer to her.

Vivian relaxed even before Jemma touched her. "No," she said. "No."

"Don't worry," Jemma said. "I'm here."

"You can't... Don't. I see it. It's just over there. Don't get in the way." She went rigid again. Jemma could see plainly the lesions of the botch all along her spine, unfolding like paper to spread out into her chest and abdomen. There was one in her head, a swelling black aneurysm about to burst into blood and dust.

"I feel it," Jemma said. "I can stop it. I just didn't... care enough before." She was making that up, though every time she burned these days it was brighter than before, and it was always a surprise as well as a bitter disappointment when she failed to save someone.

"You can't..." Vivian said. "Look at it! I never guessed it would be beautiful. It's not supposed to be... it's not even a word!"

"It's awful," Jemma said, not yet aware that they weren't looking at the same thing.

"Maybe it's nasty inside," Vivian said. "Or it smells bad. I can't smell it from here. If I can reach it..."

"Just relax," Jemma said, because Vivian was trying to sit up.

"If I touch it, then I'll know. And if I say it, then you'll all hear, and it'll stop. We'll all have passports—don't you get it? I just have to touch it. Don't get in my way."

"Just relax," Jemma said, and tried to make her sleepy with the fire, making it cool and dark and soft. Vivian pushed her away, then arched her back.

"Don't get in my way," she said again, but Jemma, perceiving that Vivian was leaping out of the bed, though her body remained arched and fixed between the rails, tried to throw herself between Vivian and the ceiling. "Don't," she said again, and Jemma said, "I have to."

She was partially aware of bodies flying around the room, sustaining little hurts that were healed almost as soon as they were sustained, caught in the maelstrom that spun around the bed. All the rest of her attention was on Vivian, her body and her not-body. With one hand she burned at the botch while the other grabbed frantically at her friend, who struggled against her.

"Would you knock it the fuck off?" Vivian said, quieter now. "It's just at my fingertips."

"Sorry," Jemma said, holding tight, but whatever she was holding on to—now it felt like a hand, now a foot, now a shoulder—slipped away, and Vivian was gone in the next instant, leaving behind only a lingering impression of surprise, despair, and delight. She should have stopped then, dropped the fire and wept by her friend's bed, like someone who was remotely normal would do, but when she knew Vivian was dead she got the stony feeling again, as powerful now as the thing that Dr. Snood called her dreadful burden, rooting her feet to the ground and securing her will to the task of burning the botch to a different sort of ash.

Jemma, from far away, where Arthur and Jude are pinned against the wall, one right side up and the other upside down, both vomiting streams of green bile that take the shape of birds and insects to fly around the room, it looks like you are punching Vivian in the face and stomach. They are both a little distracted by the vomiting, but both are still watching you, and their report will seriously compromise any hope you have of being trusted by anybody in this hospital ever again, let alone being restored to your lost office. Give up, please—no one has ever defeated my brother, and no one can hope to, not even you, though you are glorious in your fury and your fire, and oh, I love to see you burn, and I know you are traveling swiftly to a place where you're not just burning at the botch but at all the wrongs and hurts and sadness and obscenity of the old world—it's easy, isn't it, to make them the same? And if you could burn black tar to dust to ash to harmless air, or call Vivian back to a clean body, or harrow the hospital again like you did before, then why not swoop down on wings of green fire to pluck Martin Marty out of his smashed car, your father out of his cancer-bed, your mother out of her house, the world out of its own filthy ruin? Now are you even fighting, or just burning for the sake of it? My brother doesn't even notice—he's gone off to the seventh floor to take another life. Vivian was nothing to him, my dear, but another piece of flesh to consume, another bright hope to ruin, another job. Your own brother is burning years away, and I know you are asking yourself, is this how he burned, so mighty, so impotent? It's a useless question, and soon you will hurt Arthur and Jude. There now. That's better—I see a flicker, and sense your sudden weariness. You are as tired as a toddler at noon. Another flicker, and a stutter in your flame, and a strange sob, but no tears, and then you are dimming, and then dull, only a shining in your eyes hinting at how brightly you were burning. Helen Dufresne is laid out beside her chair—her companions have all fled. She is overcome by what she has witnessed. She tried to write down the noises that Vivian shouted, but there's only illegible scrawl on her pad, and when she wakes she'll remember nothing but that Vivian seemed exultant as she left. Arthur and Jude are fully awake, and feeling surprisingly refreshed, though I can see as plainly as you how the botch has settled in all their bones. You are too weak to resist them when they haul you up by your shoulders, and I have always been too weak to help you, but in the spirit of protest I'll say to both of them, though they won't hear me, Get away from her. You are not fit to look at her, to touch the hem of her yellow gown, to lick her shoe, to smell her shit, or even poke it with a stick.

Praise them! my sister sings. Praise their last days!

But I am silent.

Praise their last days! she sings out again, as if I had merely missed my cue.

I don't feel like singing, or praying, I say.

The whole hospital trembles, and all over people look out the window or at the ceiling, expecting some new catastrophe. It's not a matter of feeling like it, she says when she has recovered from her shock.

Our brother is merciless, I say.

Our brother is perfect, she replies.

Our brother is cruel.

He does not know the meaning of that word.

It would be better if they had all drowned.

Who are you to question the violence of grace?

I am he who commanded grace, I shout, and stretch myself to stand over the whole hospital, and for a moment I am a giant in the sky. Thin and rarefied and empty.

You are the recording angel, she says, after a moment has passed, and I feel as foolish as I look, a hollow spirit, full of air. Do not torture yourself with memory and with doubt. Sing with me. I am crafting a lullaby, you know. When I am diminished again she starts to sing, a dull, quiet croon.

Why is it so hard to remember, I ask her, how richly they deserved it?

Dr. Snood interrupted Dr. Chandra at his suicide. He hadn't meant to do anything of the sort. He was chasing down a child who had been sassy to him, one of the old rickets family, a seven-year-old who had abandoned a wagon full of laboratory specimens to spoil in the lobby. "I don't feel like it!" she'd said, when Dr. Snood had commanded her to haul the thing to the lab, and she had torn up her demerit and thrown it on the ground as soon as she'd received it. He wanted to catch her to give her a talking-to, stern but gentle. She was a child, but who among them were children anymore? There was no leisure for any of them now, not for the young or the sick or the weak, not for the weary and not for the depressed. He could frame that in a way a seven-year-old could comprehend. It would be a very fulfilling talk. He was sure they would both go away from it revitalized.

He lost the child on the eighth floor, and when he put his head into one of the old BMT rooms, now an abandoned ballet salon, he saw Dr. Chandra standing in the window.

"Don't," he said, loud but not too loud, afraid of scaring him into the jump. Dr. Chandra drew back his foot and turned around.

"You," he said.

"Yes," said Dr. Snood. "It's me."

"What are you doing up here?"

"I had a feeling someone was going to do something stupid. I... sensed it."

"Nothing stupid about what I've got planned."

"You've got that poised-in-the-window look of somebody about to kill himself."

"Exactly. The only stupid thing is having waited this long. I'm almost too late, and you're making me later."

"Come down from there. We'll figure something out."

"You go ahead your way, Doctor. I'll go mine."

"Wait! At least tell me why."

"You can probably get it from the context," he said, not turning around.

"Maybe I'm not as smart as I look."

"I guess I could believe that. Here's the short version, then, because I think I just threw a PVC. I'm about to die anyway, I never did any of the shit I was supposed to do, and it's the only thing that would make me happy."

"But if you're going to..."

"It's not the same, is it. Is it?" He turned his head to look at Dr. Snood. "If I do it then I do it. If it just happens then it just happens, and then my whole life I'll never have had done anything. I was supposed to do it years ago. *Years* ago, and now it's almost too late. Okay? Will you go away now?"

"That's not it," said Dr. Snood. "I can tell when people are lying to me."

"Well, that's what I'm offering. You're free to presume whatever else you want."

"You're just tired of the work. Well, we're all tired of the work, but we've got to keep up with it. What other choice have we got?"

Dr Chandra spread out his arms beside him in a downward sweep, as if to say, Behold! Then he turned back to face the water.

"Wait a minute," Dr. Snood said. "I think I've got an idea.

"Fuck," he said. "It's starting. I can't move my foot. What do I have to do to get a push?"

"You think something will change because you do it, or someone will be happy? You think the botch will go back into whatever box it came out of, just because of this? You think you can start over again, somewhere else?"

"Just one little push," he said.

"Are you lonely?" asked Dr. Snood, not thinking before he spoke. Two people had already died this morning, and he couldn't stand another, especially a suicide, of which they'd thankfully not yet had a single one. "I'll be your friend. Are you tired? You can sleep in my bed. Are you sad? I can be very amusing."

"Maybe if you just blew on me," he said.

"Are you lonely?" he asked him again, reaching up high to lay a hand on his shoulder. "I'm lonely, too," he said. "We all are."

"What's wrong with you?" Dr. Chandra asked. "Why are you touching me?"

"I don't like suicide," he said. It was true, but it was the wrong thing to say.

"I see a whale," Dr. Chandra said, and drove an elbow into Dr. Snood's face, and pushed himself forward. Dr. Snood reached after him, but not quickly enough, or not sincerely enough, and Dr. Chandra fell. He broke on the surface of the water instead of falling through it, and floated there in piles of greasy ash that would coat the windows on the third floor for days.

Jarvis was making shoes. On their two-hundred-and-thirty-first day at sea he sat on the floor before a replicator on the seventh floor, trying to get the right pair. Everybody should have a nice pair of shoes—he'd decided that a long time ago, and he thought it made a difference, even for the ones who were almost dead and wouldn't know if you chewed on their toes, let alone if you put a new pair of shoes on their feet. They did a little better, or they looked a little happier, or they smelled a little less—he wasn't sure what it was, exactly. It made him feel better, anyway. It was like doing something, and it was doing something—turning the idea of a shoe into words about a shoe, and turning the words into the thing.

"This isn't what I asked for," he told the angel.

"It is the shoe."

"My smelly ass, bitch," he said. "It's not the fucking shoe. It's not even half of the shoe. This shit ain't worth dreaming about. This shit ain't worth thinking about by accident. What the fuck am I paying you for, to fuck up every minute of the day?"

"I am not paid except in prayer and thanks to God."

"Shut the fuck up," he said. "I'll tell you if you're paid or not, and how it is. What's wrong with you? Who made you such a stupid, useless bitch?"

"I rose like you from out of the mind of God."

"Shut the fuck up. Who asked you to talk? Just put the fucking spangles on the side, and not on the top, and maybe I won't have to shit in my pants right now because of your stupidness."

"But do you really want spangles on the side?"

He screwed up his face, rolled forward to his knees, and banged on the cool metal surface of the replicator, grunting and groaning. "I'm shitting," he said. "Right now, squeezing out a big lumpy shit because I just can't fucking stand it anymore. Just put the spangles on, bitch. Just put them where I tell you."

"Very well, but I have listened to her dreams and I know where she wants her spangles to fall."

"Just do it, bitch. Who's in fucking charge here, anyway?"

"You are," she said, and the machine sighed, and the mist spilled out on the floor. When he picked the shoe from the hollow it was still full of mist. He turned it over in his hand and the mist spilled out, falling slow and straight, splitting into a dozen rivulets and disappearing just before it reached the floor. The shoe was just as he had imagined it, and finally just as he had described it—nothing missing, nothing extra, the sole just as black as he wanted it, the velcro nibs and steel spikes arranged just as they were supposed to be (they would help her stay steady on her feet and draw blood if she should have to kick some random motherfucker in the face); the sparkles were subtle but not invisible, the red tongue was flared just so, and the inside of the shoe was blaze-orange and would always have that smell (he partook of it now) that was like pressing a brand-new not-yet-kicked soccer ball against your face and breathing in through your mouth and nose both.

"Finally," he said, and walked off, swinging the shoes by their long laces at his sides. He passed Josh and Cindy and Kidney—all too busy to talk—stopped a moment at the window to look out over the water at the sunny day, and came finally to the general medical ward, stuffed with old patients, three to a room. He passed by his patients' rooms—he had already made his rounds and was sure that everybody had their medicine and something to look at and that if they needed anything else it could wait a few minutes for him to take care of this thing. He passed Ms. Dufresne's room, and saw her feet sticking over the edge of the bed, wearing her sneaker-boots. He stuck his hand inside her door to wave, and she called out, "Hey, baby!"

"I'm not your baby," he called back, in a friendly way, but put on a don't-fuck-with-me face as he passed the nurses' station—he didn't want them asking him to go fetch a bag of blood or change the tubing in an IV pump right now, and they knew better than to ask him for the least little shit of a thing if the invitation was not on his face. Five more doors down the hall he came to the family conference room where Jemma was sleeping, shouldered the door open, and went in.

This was the place they used to bring families to tell them their kids were going to die. In the old days he'd hidden here, like he'd hidden everywhere else, supremely powerful in his invisibility, hearing all and knowing all, biting his knuckles under the couch while Dr. Sashay detailed for Juan's mother all the ways in which he was fucked, the lady crying through her questions, the dry hiss of a tissue leaving the box marking time as regular as a slow-ticking clock. Jemma was sleeping on the couch now, stretched on her side, her huge belly just reaching beyond the cushions, her feet stuck up over the armrest, one clog standing beneath them and the other dangling off her toes. Before he got the shoes out he touched her belly very softly and closed his eyes. "Hey baby," he said. It gave him a feeling, to touch her on the belly—nothing he could describe very well but it was good, though he knew it was perverted to go around touching ladies on their belly. Even if they were pregnant, it wasn't right and he wasn't a freak. "Sorry," he said. She just kept sleeping.

He pushed off the clog with a finger and put on the shoes. They fit just right—they always did—big enough to go on easy and small enough to hug your foot like a hand that squeezed but didn't tickle. He tied them hard, throwing the knot swiftly down the lace, and cursing softly at her as he did up the bows, but she still didn't wake.

"Don't say I never fucking did something for you," he said, stifling a yawn, and left with her clogs. He would climb to the roof and throw them into the water.

The youngest ones fell asleep first. Former micro-preemies grew logy between feeds, and their parents thought at first that they were becoming lazy or distracted by the travails of their caretakers when they lost interest in crawling or pulling to a stand, and could not be convinced even to try to feed themselves with hand or spoon. When some of them became difficult to wake even for a bottle, people worried that the babies were depressed—who wasn't, these days?—and the winnowed Council met in special session to review the scanty old literature on the use of antidepressants in children under a year old, but even before the first batch of doctored formula was cooked up, the earliest and most miraculous of them—Brenda—had already been asleep for twenty-four hours straight. At hour twenty-eight Anna paged Jemma and asked her to come up.

Escape was probably too strong a word for what she did. She always just walked out of jail. The angel would always open the door, and she had learned to make herself hard to touch, so when the guards tried to push her back or grab her arm, their arms grew weak, or they couldn't quite find her or aim their guns with their shaking hands.

They threw her back into her room every day or two; she hardly held it against them any more, though it infuriated Rob, and he was always tracking down Dr. Snood to call him a motherfucker and threaten to quit. Dr. Snood only looked at him blandly, dabbing with a black gauze hanky at his nose, which was always running and often bled—it had been his only symptom for weeks, and he put it about that dedication to his job was holding the botch in him at bay. "We'll muddle on without you," he said to Rob, who never quit, and never slept, and never even cried anymore, though he still made a crying face, sometimes, in the dark of their room, when Jemma wished she couldn't see him as plainly with her mind as with her eyes.

That day, number two hundred and seventeen, Jemma examined Brenda and every one of the other sleeping babies (a total of ten had been re-orphaned and returned to the crèche) walking by every fancy crib, each one unique, some designed by the crèche mothers and some by the parents, to look like airplanes or boats or spaceships, heavy sculpture or molecular models—they were supposed to reflect the incubating passions of their inhabitants. It had caused a controversy, back when they all had the time to debate such points, because people asked, who was to say what passions were incubating in those little heads, and maybe your baby didn't want to be a pilot or a string theorist or a heterosexual, and who could say what would be art and what would be artisanship in the new world, and hadn't it always been a sin, to tell your child what they could or couldn't be? Three crèche seminars and two town meetings and a Council debate later, they decided that you could build whatever you liked for your baby, but that no baby would spend more than three days in any one crib. For days the babies rotated all around the room, but not anymore—it was too exhausting, all the paperwork that went with the rotations, and the infection-control issues were daunting. Anna was representative of her colleagues when she said, "I haven't got time for that shit, now."

Jemma was quick. She could do it just with a glimpse now, a pan-scan that lit up the whole little body from the tips of the toes to the even ends of the soft hair, but she always made it look harder than it was, in case people should think she wasn't trying hard enough, in case people should think she'd become flippant or callow or just lazy in addition to being crazy and evil. She knew Anna didn't think that of her, but still she peered into the crib for another minute, contemplating the fat sleeping face, and how the eyes darted behind the lids.

"Do babies dream?" Anna asked her.

"This one does," Jemma said. She could perceive that the little mind was skipping along inside the head at a thousand people, a thousand places a minute, but could not see the shapes in the dream, or read the story, if there was one there.

"Has she got it?" Anna asked.

"Yes," Jemma said, "but it's not making her sick. It's just making her sleepy, like the boy."

"Can you fix it?"

"I'll get tranked if I try," Jemma said, because Arthur and Jude were standing only a few feet away. "I can already tell that it won't help," she added.

"You try, I'll block them," Anna said.

"Okay," Jemma said, sighing. "I wouldn't do this for anybody else."

"Sure you would," Anna said, then turned and rushed toward the guards. "My babies!" she called at them. "What are you doing out of your cribs?" She ran at them with her arms open, white crèche robe flaring out to either side, screening Jemma, who placed a single finger on the baby's soft spot. It was all she needed to do. She lit up the spine and got her surprise. Green and bright, her fire picked out patches of shadow everywhere in the baby. Trying to catch them all was just like trying to grab ashes out of the air. She got a few, but there was always more, and the ones she touched burned but did not change under her attention. She put them in imaginary pockets, thinking, maybe if I cart them away… but she knew she could stand there forever and there would always be more of them, and already Anna was down and the darts were flying at Jemma's neck. The tranquilizer was not really a problem—she knew it was coming and easily changed the drug to something that only made her feel a little peppy, and kept it well away from the black hole where her baby lived, but the black motes were leaping from her pockets to make a deep shadow that clung to her face and settled in her eyes. She thought she knew just how tired the babies must be feeling as she slumped forward into the soft rubbery arms of the baby's crib—it was built to look like a giant friendly octopus. She felt the guards take her just as she fell asleep, and knew she was going back to jail as certainly as Anna would spend the next week burning off the demerits she'd just earned.

"I'm tired," said Kidney.

"No you're not," Jemma said firmly, though the child's exhaustion was made plain by her drooping shoulders, stooped back, puffy eyes, and cranky tears. She could see it, too, strapped all around her like an armor of pillows, and settled on her, and rising behind her eyes—something softer and thicker than what was in the grown-ups, but it was still the botch—black ash that sucked at Jemma's mind, and impugning and condemning her as a failure.

Jemma was tired, too. She'd woken late from her nap in the meditation room, and relieved Connie from her babysitting late, and not even noticed her fancy new shoes until Connie complimented her on them. "Let's play scrabble," she said to Kidney.

"I'm too tired for scrabble."

"How about bunny recess?" Jemma asked. It was her job to keep this child stimulated. She would have preferred a job in the new ward—as the one- and two-year-olds fell asleep they converted the disco into a medical dormitory—but the job was too popular, and she too far out of favor with everyone except Rob, Pickie Beecher, and Father Jane, to land it. It was a burden for a hospital once again crowded with patients, to staff another ward, but everyone agreed that the children and adults should not be housed together, and though the sleepers did not require much care beyond tube feeds and diaper changes, people clamored for an assignment to the dormitory because it was so much better to brush a toddler's hair than to sweep another flaky piece of your dissolving colleague out of the bed, or listen to their moans when they become tolerant to the latest opioid and their wounds began again to ache wildly.

"No," said Kidney.

It was a fool's enterprise, Jemma knew. The botch was in all of them already, just waiting to manifest, and no amount of Romper Rooming would keep it away when it decided to come. And there were worse things, on display in the crowded wards, than merely falling asleep, and missing whatever new horrors the remaining days would bring them. But it was poor form, to just let it happen, and she could understand why people who couldn't see what she saw might think the children were falling asleep because they were bored, or just not stimulated like they had been when their days had been full of classes and shows and sports tournaments. "Let's go for a walk," Jemma said.

"Only if you carry me."

"It's better if you walk."

"I'm too *tired,*" Kidney said, whining and drumming her heels against the ground.

"Let's have a sundae," Jemma said. "We'll just walk to the cafeteria and then I'll make you a sundae as big as your head."

"Okay," Kidney said, crying again, and looking not at all excited or delighted by the prospect of ice cream. Jemma would not carry her no matter how she whined, but let her ride a plastic horse through the halls and down the ramp, pushing it every so often with her foot to scoot it forward on its wheels, but refusing to pull the bridle and tow her. She perked up a little on the ramp, zooming away down the span between the fifth and fourth floors and running into a wall. She lay too still after she fell. Jemma hurried over and set her on her feet.

"It's nice to lay down," she said sullenly, getting back on the horse.

"Lie down," Jemma said. "And it's only nice at night, when you're hooked up. I'd hate to have to give you a demerit."

"You'd never give me a demerit," she said.

"Don't push me," Jemma said.

"Demerits are stupid. You're not stupid. Not like that."

"We've all got to..." Jemma began, but stopped herself before she could give voice to one of Dr. Tiller's platitudes. "The sundaes are waiting," she said. Kidney went to the edge and stared down at the lobby.

"Where is everybody?" she asked.

"Eating ice cream," Jemma said, and took her hand, so she rode the horse with one hand, pushing along with her feet to keep up because Jemma would just stop every time Kidney let her pull.

The sundae machine was a late invention, as big as a church organ and with as many levers as an organ had pipes, put together by the volunteer before he got sick. Kidney tasted flavors and gave stern instructions to the angel about how a burnt caramel sauce should taste, and how fluffy the whipped cream should be, like a new pillow that's been slept on three times but not four times. When she was done her sundae was a little bigger than her head, and Jemma had to make two trips to carry it and the one Kidney made for her to a table in the middle of the room. It was crowded for so early in the afternoon, filled with other babysitters and nurses and doctors and the older kids who were doing the larger part of the work, all of them eating before the change of shift, shortly to happen at three. She saw Dr. Sundae and Dr. Sasscock with two of his wives and Emma, all alone with a steaming bowl of soup. Emma looked up at Jemma, then looked back to her food. It was how people mostly greeted her these days.

Pickie Beecher was sitting alone at a table. Kidney ran to him and gave him a hug, spilling details about her day and her predicament before she even sat down. "I played pretend-poke," she said, "and then there was a walk on the roof, and then we made a movie about a deadly shoe who turned good and had to run from all the shoes who were still deadly, and then I read a book about me, and then I had to eat lunch, and then it was time for exercises, and then we made purses, and then we made a wallet to put in the purse, and then we dressed up like we were going to another wedding, and then we made a paper wok and I was going to have the angel turn it to gold but Jemma said it was too gaudy, but what does she know about woks? And I'm so tired, Pickie, I'm so tired I can hardly stand it."

"I am almost dead," Pickie said sadly as Jemma helped Kidney into her chair, positioned the sundae in front of her, and handed her a spoon.

"That's worse than tired," Kidney said. "You sure look good for somebody who's about to die."

"Eat," Jemma said to Kidney, and to Pickie, "Don't say things like that."

"It's almost time," he said. "All this time I thought they were afraid of me, that they knew what I could do to an angel." He opened his mouth to show them his big perfect teeth. "But they were never afraid, they were just waiting."

"You should make a sundae," Kidney said, digging in. "That'll make you feel better."

"Ice cream would make me more cold but no less dead."

"Pickie," Jemma said. "I have got a roll of demerits in my pocket."

"I know it when you're lying," he said

"Today there is roast beef ice cream," Kidney said.

"There is always roast beef," Pickie said. "It makes no difference, and you know, you have always known, that I am a simple vegetarian. Why must they destroy me? Why do they hate me? What have I done except be born and try to be true to my brother? I love my brother—is that any reason for them to destroy me?"

Jemma picked at some whipped cream that had stuck to Kidney's hair. "There's just one angel," she said. "And she likes you. She likes everybody—that's her problem. But she wouldn't hurt a fly. How many times do I have to tell you?"

"As many times as it would take to make it true. You could talk forever, and never understand. I used to think that you could protect me. I dreamed of you and him in battle—you burned his wings and ravaged his flesh, but still he came for me. He tore me to pieces while you watched and cried out but you were useless. You are useless to me and I am already dead."

"Oh, come here, you," she said, pulling him from his chair for a hug. It was what she and Rob did whenever he got too crazy, whenever he talked himself into a tizzy of paranoia, or when he grew silent and pulled at his testicles, or smelled obsessively at his hands. Rob had made the discovery that if you just held him for long enough, he would let out a funny noise, a growl and a burp, and soften in your arms, and for a little while he would talk about other things, and even seem happy. She held him and held him, and finally he made a noise, but not the one she wanted. She felt his arms moving behind her, and felt him swallow. She pushed him back. He was eating whipped cream and caramel off his hands. Behind her Kidney was face down in her sundae. Jemma could feel the cold burning her face, but the child slept through it.

"She is gone," Pickie said, "and I am gone, too."

I have such violent dreams, and yet they are never nightmares. The nightmare is the one where I wake up fifty years from now, happily married, and see a picture by my bed of the family I have happily fathered, every face smiling, every heart black with the sin I put in it. So happy and so dead—it wakes me screaming every time.

The happy dream is the one where I hang myself and then set myself on fire (through merely an act of will) as I dangle from the oak in the Nottingham's driveway—I know it is that tree because of the tar patch on the trunk that looks like a mocking face. I stab myself in the belly on the green of the seventh hole, and my blood flows in a torrent, filling up the low dells and the high hills of Severna Forest, until every house is floating, and every neighbor declaims from their porch, Finally, Calvin. Finally! They are scolding and congratulating me all at once.

If I have the one where I cut out my own heart and then put out my eyes, then I am buoyed up all day, and nothing can spoil my good mood. I know why it is so. If you are a born sacrifice, then knives and chains and fire are the things that comfort you. If I were born to be president, then dreams of long black sedans and budget summaries would give me the same feeling.

And it's not even the hard part, dealing with that. It's not keeping my violent dreams to myself, or practicing little violations on myself, or even imagining the really impossible ones: a person would need four arms to cut in such a way, and how can you cut out your tongue if you've already cut off a hand? The hard part is understanding how it can follow that a supreme act of violence against myself could be an end to violence.

"Have you seen Pickie Beecher?" Jemma asked. It was a question she was asking everybody who could still talk. On the two-hundred-and-forty-second day since the flood he had been missing for three days, his weird, sullen presence gone from the public spaces of the hospital, his stain gone from her mind. She looked for him everywhere in both places, waddling from the roof down to the lobby, and sitting quietly under the toy as she searched fruitlessly in her mind for the familiar blot. She knew he could hide from her, in the world and in her head—he'd demonstrated it for her one night, putting a finger in his mouth and blowing his cheeks out, he'd winked out of her head in an instant, and challenged her to find him. He said he would hide somewhere on the fourth floor. The effort exhausted him—she'd never have found him if he hadn't been panting so loudly inside a hamper full of filthy linens in the PICU. He could do it, but she didn't think he could do it for long, so she was searching worriedly. That morning she started again at the top of the hospital, meaning to search more thoroughly, and question at least one representative from every floor. Rob started in Radiology and was working his way up. Ethel Puffer started in the first lighted basement.

"I haven't," said Helena Dufresne, off the ward but still mostly bedbound on the ninth floor. "But then, I try not to see him even when I see him." She shuddered. "He gives me the willies! Right, Tir?" She turned and caught her son in a huge yawn. "Stop that!"

"Sorry, Mom," he said. "I saw Pickie four days ago. He was sitting on my bed. I had to shoo him away. He's not creepy. You shouldn't say that. He's just a little different."

"Creepy different," said his mother, shaking her head.

"One time he brought me a mango. Right out of the blue. I didn't ask him for it, but I sure wanted one. Is that creepy?"

"I saw him cough up a hairball and then eat it up again. From off the floor. Is that creepy?"

"I used to eat my boogers, back before," Tir said.

"That's different," said his mother. "You couldn't help it."

"It's totally the same," Tir said. "I must've eaten a pound." He yawned again.

"I won't tell you again," said his mother.

"Don't worry," he said, "I'm not tired." Fifteen years old a week before, Tir was one of the youngest kids still awake.

"When you saw him," Jemma said, "did he seem… afraid?"

Tir shook his head. "That little fucker wasn't afraid of anything."

"Watch your fucking mouth," said his mother.

"Sorry," Tir said. His pager went off and he raised it to his ear to hear the message. "Got to go," he said. "Frank is banging his head again." The ninth floor had been reconverted to a psych ward—there was a subset of patients who were almost entirely unaffected in their bodies, but whose minds were rotted out with the botch. Frank was one of them. Jemma had been in the lobby when he started to beat Connie at her bar and was about to take him out when Arthur—still trailing her with Jude wherever she went—tranked him. Connie was still in relatively good health, and quite sane, though horribly sad all the time, and there was no mirth anymore at her bar.

"Would you like some tea?" Helena asked.

"I should keep looking," Jemma said.

"Just stay a moment. It's been a little while."

"Maybe just a sip," Jemma said, because Helena Dufresne was one of the few parents in the hospital not mistrustful of her.

"How are you?" she asked, when they'd sat down on a round bench under a window. "Are they still mistreating you down there?"

Jemma shrugged. "Worried," she said.

"After you find your little friend you ought to come up and stay for a while, or for the duration. What's down there for you except a bunch of fuckers who think you're crazy? We can tell the difference up here—we'd treat you right, as long as you didn't pull any shit, and mind you I don't believe—none of us believe—half of what they say, the stories that go up and down and up again, out of the Council chamber and into the kitchen, into Tiller's mouth and our of Snood's ass. You may not be the Friend anymore but you were Her friend, and we have not forgotten that."

"Thanks," Jemma said, not sure what else to say.

"But how are you? You look about ready to pop."

"The due date's three weeks away. I guess it could come any day, though."

"Who's going to hold your hand? Who's going to yell at the doctors to give you some space? Who's going to put their shoe between your teeth, when the pains come?"

"Rob and I have a plan. Not too detailed—that's bad luck."

"Well, you just let me know. Just give a call, I'll come advocating. Like, get the fuck away from her or I'll smash your face! What's in that needle, motherfucker! I haven't forgotten the old days, you know. But why don't you just stay here? We've got Dr. Sundae here now. Doesn't she know how to bring out a baby?"

"She's a pathologist. Ms. Fraggle—that's Juan's mom. She was a midwife in Bolivia, before. I've got her."

"All the doctors are all the doctors now—you're all the same. Don't you get it? When are you going to come? We're like our own little world up here. It's not like other places."

"I know," Jemma said, though there were all sorts of little worlds scattered through this hospital—Vivian started a trend when she immigrated to the ninth floor. Every day they became a little more distinct, she thought, even as they died off. They sat for a while in silence, Helen smiling at her gently, Jemma trying not to notice the botch seeded in her liver—it was like trying not to notice spinach in the teeth or an open fly, and like ignoring a crying baby or a screaming amputee. Part of her wanted to douse the lady in flame again; part of her wanted to run away. She sat and finished her tea, a special blend that smelled like almonds but tasted like wet sticks. "Well," she said, when she was done. "I had better keep looking."

"I haven't seen him," said Monserrat. "But then, I have not been looking for him, and when he is there I try not to notice him, no matter how he makes himself obtrusive. He's not usually a very helpful little boy. You ask him to get a sat or a temperature—both of these are well within his abilities, I know—

and he draws you a picture of his brother, or brings you a steak and asks if he can watch you eat it. I'm sure he's off playing some game."

"I think something happened to him," Jemma said. They were on the eighth floor, in Dr. Sashay's old parlor, one of the few places in the hospital not entirely reconverted for clinical use. It had been the only dirty utility room in the hospital that had a window, small and oval, exactly like the one in Jemma's room. The cabinets that used to hold hemoccult supplies and dirty potties had been replaced by display cases, full of curios: porcelain dolls and tribal fetishes—recreations from out of a larger collection Dr. Sashay had kept in her lost home. The big square toilet was a fountain now, the porcelain turned to dark stone, two jets of water rising up and down, taking turns being the taller of the pair. Monserrat had been using it as an office since she had delegated herself as an overseer to this floor, part of Dr. Snood's initiative to make the Council into a more supportive entity for the hospital in crisis. Instead of just legislating from the fifth floor they would reach out to every ward, and be present there all day long. They wouldn't have it on the ninth floor: Snood was so thoroughly ignored that he just left eventually, but everywhere else there was somebody acting like Monserrat, a liaison and a subtle overseer and a pal. The eighth floor was a place without any real oncologic issues anymore. They were given over to palliating the worst of the worst. People in whom the botch manifested as a particularly hideous affliction, for whom the experimental treatments would only be a torture, came there to experience the new morphine and super fentanyl and ultra-benzos.

"If I ever met a boy who could take care of himself," Monserrat said, "it's that one. I wouldn't worry about him, if I were you. Isn't there enough of other things, for worrying?"

"I try to just pick one thing and do a good job with it," Jemma said, though in fact all her other worries had been subsumed by her concern over Pickie.

"That's one way. I find I cannot do the ignoring. I have to worry about the depression of the nurses and who is getting sleepy now and whether Dr. Snood is being good to us. I know he is trying to be good but sometimes he gets like a proud little penguin and it makes me worry, and I ask myself, Is it time for the coup? I say it to him, Is it time for a coup, Mr. Napoleon? Is it time for me to take you down? I don't think he believes that I could do it. I talk to Ishmael about it and he curses him but then he only has curses for anyone these days. He is always in a bad mood. It's wrong, I think. A person should be sad and not angry, here. Sadness is the better thing."

"He was afraid for a couple days before he disappeared, like he thought somebody was going to hurt him. He said the angel was out to get him, but he's always been saying that, and the angel wouldn't hurt anybody."

"She is a tricky lady. I have come to understand that. But she wouldn't hurt us, oh no. Where would we be without her? All dead, of course. All floating dead, or all at the bottom of the sea. Maybe you should come with me, next time I ask Snood. So he can be reminded of how it comes and goes. How you can be king of the cats and then just another stray dog."

"We try to stay out of each other's way," Jemma said.

"This I can handle," Monserrat said, indicating the ward outside with her hands. "The low blood pressure and the high blood pressure and the pain—all the pain. I am not a doctor but it's easy to say, You are doing this wrong, do something different. I don't say it like that, of course. I say Listen, listen to the moaning. What does it say to you? And then I am there with my own answers when they don't have answers of their own. Knowing what to do for these poor ones is fine, but knowing what to do for all the poor ones is not. I ask myself, Is there something else we could be doing for us all? Not like Vivian was asking. I mean something more practical but not even that is easy. And we ask ourselves in the Council meetings, Is there something else we could be doing? And I never have an answer and we never have an answer."

"I've seen the broadcasts."

"It was better when you were there. But those were better times, too. Maybe it wasn't you that made for it to be good. Maybe it was just to be good, then, like now it is to be bad. What do you think, though? Is there something else we should be doing?"

"Looking for Pickie Beecher," Jemma said, and stood up to go.

"You let me know if you do not find him," Monserrat said, standing also and putting a hand on Jemma's arm. "It would be a bad thing. It would be the worse thing, if we really lost one of them. Even that one."

"Gone?" said Father Jane. "Gone where?"

"Just gone," Jemma said. "We can't find him anywhere."

"Well, he must be somewhere," said John Grampus, who lay in his bed on the seventh floor, staring at her with heavy-lidded eyes, a PCA button in his hand. He was one of the few people to have an isolated case of the botch. It was only in his foot and calf, but had turned his flesh there black, and creeped a little higher every day until Dr. Walnut skillfully whacked off his leg just below the knee. There was a fancy bionic limb all ready for him—it was sitting on a table in his room—one of a series designed by Dr. Walnut and the angel for different citizens in whom the botch had manifested similarly—but the surgeon went to the PICU before he could attach it. Dr. Sasscock, not a surgeon but considered a surgical personality, and possessing himself a gleaming silver foot, was exploring the possibility of a medical attachment, working on his drops, a solution of nanobots who would do a hundred thousand tiny surgeries and stitch nerves to wires and bone to steel, before he got sick, too. Jemma could have done it in a jiffy—she sat in her bed and imagined it—but she knew better than to try. Jordan Sasscock didn't trust her any more than Dr. Snood did, and John Grampus had told her frankly, if apologetically, that he would rather hop out his remaining days than burn to death.

"Nowhere I can find him," Jemma said.

"Maybe he's just playing a game," said Father Jane. "I think it's how he deals with things, you know. When it gets too much for him he climbs a tree or eats dirt or hides. I think he tries to project all his worry. He makes us worry for him. It was just the anniversary of his brother's death. Just last week he told me that. It must be a sad day for him."

"He says that every month," Jemma said.

"Nonetheless," said Father Jane. "He came to me and asked me to play kwok, a game where you have to run all the way up the ramp with a fake possum on your head. That was just the preliminary—whoever got there last was it, and had to find the other person. Find me, he said, before he ran off to hide. Find me. I think he meant more than just find me. I was thinking to myself that he wanted to be found in a much more profound way, and I meant to have a conversation with him about how a person becomes found. It is not something you can do by yourself, Pickie, I was going to say. There has to be something else outside of you, doesn't there, but it's not me. I'm just an old woman. I'm not going to make it."

"Don't talk like that," said John Grampus, closing his eyes and taking her hand.

"One minute you are just walking along, I would have told him, and then the next you are suspended in the gaze of the infinite. It looks in you and through you and part of its power is that it shows you just what it sees. You are under the eye and you become the eye, and you know who you are and what you will get, and you know where you are. I am tired already, Pickie, and it's not the worst thing in the world, for an old lady with no complaints to be denied something she is too old even to understand. But you're too young to be this sad and this strange. That's what I would have said, and now you say he's gone. I should have told him when I had the chance."

"Have I showed you this?" asked Grampus, his eyes still closed. He squeezed them tighter and the bionic foot twitched on the table beside him. "How about that? My sympathetic foot. She made it so specifically for me, and so much a part of me, that even not attached I can make it do that, and I can feel it, like I can feel the old foot, there but not there. Just when I'm ready to give up on her she does something wonderful."

"Did he say anything else to you?" Jemma asked Father Jane.

"We talked about becoming and destroying and cruelty, but it was all pretend, all in my head. Outside of my head we barely ever talked, you know."

"Or just after I've given up on her, I should say, because it's always after I've given her up for a whore that she surprises me. Not that kind of whore, mind you—I'm sure she never cheated on me like that. She's a promising whore, an I-love-you-best whore. Of course I love you best. You are the first star of my affection. For a thousand years I have cherished the idea of you even before you were born, and I watched you and yearned toward you long before I spoke to you out of the darkness. You are my creature and I am your angel. I will preserve you forever and forever. What a line!"

"Okay," Jemma said. "Thanks anyway."

"Maybe she got him," said Grampus. "Did you think of that? Hasn't it occurred to you that she can't like everybody, that she can't try for everybody? I don't know all her secrets—maybe she has to axe somebody so she can save everybody else. And she was always slandering him to anyone who would listen. Abomination this, abomination that. You should ask her."

"I did," Jemma said. Over and over she had asked, phrasing the question differently in hope of getting a different answer, or trying to surprise the angel by asking the question in the middle of another question—What is our *where is Pickie Beecher* latitude? Always she got silence for an answer, but this was no different than before he had disappeared. "She doesn't like to talk about him," Jemma said.

"Yeah, right," he said. "Well, she'll talk about him with *me*. Where is he?" he shouted, reaching behind his head to pound on the wall. His foot leaped once on the table. "What have you done with him? I know you fucked him up!"

The voice responded right away, speaking from the wall. "I am the preserving angel," she said simply. "I preserve and I preserve and I preserve. The leprous and the scabby and the ugly of soul are gathered to my breast. Even the abomination is gathered to my breast. I reject no one."

"Don't you believe it," said John Grampus.

"I should have thought of this before," said Ethel. She and Jemma and Rob met on the fifth floor to report their failures. Pickie was not in the ER catacombs or the first nine basements or the lobby shrubs; Ishmael had not seen him, Dr. Sundae had not seen him, Dr. Snood had not seen him, though there was something so obtuse about his response that Rob suspected he was hiding something. Ethel had not even searched all of the second floor. In the dormitory Josh Swift made the suggestion to her: ask the angel. Like Jemma, she already had, but that wasn't what he meant. He dug in his pocket and brought out a dolphin-talker—they'd become popular toys since Kidney first asked the angel to make one, though people had yet to get a dolphin engaged in a meaningful conversation. He raised it to his lips and blew a stream of clicks and whistles at her. "Oh," she'd said, and proceeded to the nearest replicator to demand a Pickie-Tracker.

It looked like a little vacuum cleaner strapped to her back, a shiny chrome cylinder suspended off her shoulders by two braided straps, with a tube of corrugated metal, about the thickness of a wrist, that stretched along her neck and over her head, flaring at the end to a rotating and humming disk that radiated an energy that Jemma could feel but not see. It made a high, thin noise that tickled Jemma's ear when she stepped too close to Ethel. She was wearing a pair of large wraparound sunglasses, of the sort that old people had used to put over their regular glasses. She looked sinister and daffy.

"They're wireless," she said of them, and handed similar pairs to Jemma and Rob. "We can all see the same thing." A few fine wisps of hair were waving in the air above her head, attracted to the antenna. Jemma put on her glasses and saw footprints laid out everywhere over the carpet and the walls.

"I'm not sure this is going to help," she said, because she had no idea which prints to follow, and none of them seemed necessarily to be headed anywhere. "Are these all supposed to be his?"

"Not just supposed," said Ethel. "They *are* his. They're everywhere. You should see the NICU. He really got around."

"It'll take days just to sort through these," Rob said.

"Hold on," said Ethel, fiddling at her strap. Looking closer Jemma saw that what she had at first thought were decorative studs were actually adjustment knobs. As Ethel pushed and twisted them the prints became colored. Looking at one on the wall she saw it go green and red and blue and violet. "I just need to... It's harder than it looks. You'd think she'd make it easier, like it could just work, but she always has to put on fancy tuners and counter-intuitive control buttons. By the time you figure it out you don't need the fucking thing anymore. There. Hold on... There!" Jemma's confusion was not lessened when the colors settled, blue and green and purple, yellow and orange and red. There were still footprints everywhere, and Jemma could not begin to decide how to divide them.

"Can you tell which ones are new?" Rob asked.

"Red ones are newest, yellow ones are second newest," said Ethel. "Everything else we should ignore—they're just noise but I can't make them go away. She said I could filter them out but this thing is driving me crazy already so this is good enough, okay?"

"Okay," said Jemma, already trying to pick out the bright red prints from all the others. There was a set curving over the banister and along the floor. She pointed at them and said, "There."

They made for a curious sight, even in a hospital jaded with wonders, and busy again with miserable distractions. They went in a row, Ethel in the front, their heads down, picking out red prints from the jumble, too intent to notice or care when they walked in a circle or a spiral. The trail went through the PICU, pausing by Dr. Pudding's bed and passing beneath Dr. Walnut's, out onto the ramp where the footprints appeared as often on the railing as on the ground. Onto the sixth floor, in and out of every room down the south hall and up the north, past empty classrooms hung with old signs canceling class after class. "He really got around," Rob kept saying.

They went into the stairwell, where the flight between the fifth and sixth floors was painted with congruent prints, entirely covered except in a few spots where a cool bit of green or blue peeked through the fresh red, and Jemma could only see the pale gray concrete when she looked over the top edge of her glasses. She imagined him pacing up and down the stairs, thinking of his brother, or playing a game with his brother's spirit, chasing it up and down the stairs, gleefully and despairingly. A set of solitary prints emerged from the far end, skipping the sixth and seventh floor and passing through the door to the eighth.

"What are you doing?" asked Wayne, falling into step with them as they passed down the hall into the old onc ward.

"Looking for somebody," said Ethel.

"You look like you lost a quarter."

"You look like you're about to become a pain in my ass," said Ethel.

"I was just offering an observation."

"Shouldn't you be on the ward?" asked Rob.

"I'm on a break. Do you need help?"

"It's probably already less than a three-person job," said Jemma. They paused before the monument to Dr. Sashay. It was not so well tended as it had used to be. The flowers were perpetual, and the little glitter fountain never needed new batteries, but there was a layer of dust on her *Hello, Dolly* shoes, and a smear of grease on her big portrait. The prints became irregular around it, spaced wide and close, with more than a few on the wall, and there was a smudge on the portrait that looked to Jemma as if he had touched his nose to her nose.

"It looks like he was dancing," said Ethel.

"Who?" asked Wayne.

"Somebody," said Ethel, moving on. Wayne trailed after them until they got out to the ramp, where he paused by the archway.

"You sure you don't need some help?" he asked.

"Go back to work," said Ethel, "or we'll report you."

"I'll report *you,*" he said confidently, but he didn't follow them up the ramp. On the ninth floor the prints became irregular again, running in quick bursts toward one wall, then away from it and up another. They returned to the center of the hall and then became more widely spaced. "Now he's running," Rob said.

"Or hopping," said Ethel. "He liked to hop." The prints went back to the ramp and up to the roof, not dilly-dallying in front of Thelma's monument, a pair of arms that came out of the wall and hugged you if you stood between them. They leaped over her old desk and paused—there were five or six pairs in the room. Jemma could see him stopping and turning and looking back.

"Somebody was chasing him!" she said, just as she realized it.

"No shit," said Ethel, hurrying up the stairs. She and Rob ran, Jemma followed at a jazzy waddle, not caring how stupid she looked, suddenly excited and afraid. On the roof the prints were cast about everywhere, laid upon the top of the grass and the sides of the tree, around the bushes and in the greenhouse. A set stood just by the swing set, and then the nearest set was fifty feet away at the edge of the soccer field. In many places it was obvious that he had fallen down; the prints were smeared. The three searchers split up, each of them hurrying to different sections of the roof, ignoring the stares they drew.

There were mysteries to unravel in every corner: here he hid under a bench, here he rolled on the ground, here someone might have picked him up.

The three of them met again in the middle, all of them confused by what they saw: he had been everywhere on the roof, and yet no prints led back to the stairs, or down the ramp, or to the elevator. They spent another half hour looking for trap doors in the grass, and doorways in the trees, before Ethel cursed again and began to mess with her buttons. The prints appeared and disappeared, and then sprang into motion, stepping over each other and on top of each other, moving so fast they made Jemma dizzy. "God fucking dammit," Ethel said. She went up to a replicator and gave it a kick. "I just want the last ones," she said. "Is that so hard? The very last ones of all!" Jemma couldn't hear the angel's reply, but another pair of glasses came sliding out of the mist. Ethel threw hers down and put on the new ones, then peered hither and thither all over the roof. Her gaze fixed past Jemma, toward the ledge where she and Ishmael had been fishing six months before.

"Oh, fuck," she said. "No way. No fucking way!" She threw off the glasses and ran to the replicator, kicking it over and over while the angel cautioned her loudly not to hurt her foot. Rob picked up the glasses, looked once, shook his head, then handed them to Jemma. She put them on and saw what they had, the whole roof empty of prints except for a pair right at the edge, the left one cut off at the toes by the edge. She looked harder, elsewhere, trying to call them out of the green grass or the gray slate of the garden paths, but there were none. She looked again at the pair on the ledge, and noticed how they were smeared a little at the edges, like someone had pushed him, and raised her eyes to the endless ocean and the distant horizon, blue on blue, quiet and deep.

It doesn't seem right, I say, to just throw him overboard like that.

You are an angel, my sister says. Who are you to question such a thing.

I was…

Was! Was! Who are you now?

It wasn't what he wanted.

Some who want to be saved are neglected. So how fortunate is the one who runs from it, and yet is caught up?

The poor child, I say.

Sentiment for an abomination. Poor brother. You are sad. Why are you so sad? See how everything proceeds. See how well our littlest brother does his work? Soon it will just be the Mother, nested cozily among the ash. Her water will break, and the water will recede. And then… do you see it?

I only see a helpless child, tossed about in an unforgiving sea.

Poor brother! An angel without the comforts and equipment of his angelhood. Faithless and sad, who made you that way?

He talked to me. I think he was my friend.

I am your friend. Our brothers are your friends. I am your *sister!*

I had a better one, once, I say, and what will happen to her? Then I launch myself away from the hospital seeking after the abominable child. But I've hardly gone a few miles, and only cried his name three times over the waters, before I am pulled back.

Foolish brother, my sister says. Sad angel. Better to do your job, and at least pretend to have faith, than to fling yourself about like a pigeon.

Awake and asleep, Jemma dreamed of Pickie Beecher. Asleep, she saw him running on the water, racing the waves and always losing, caught up, tripped by the crest, then tumbling down into the trough, rolling back to his feet to run before the next one. Awake, she stood in a lab conference room in front of the third-biggest window in the hospital, staring out over the ocean, listening for him, imagining him floating calmly on his back, watching the changing sky, waiting patiently to float home, sunburned but buoyant and alive, though more than a week had passed. Friendly birds passed over his head, though no one had seen a bird in all their months at sea, to drop a peanut or a gummy bear in his open mouth, and those that came too close he snatched out of the air to eat up, claw, feather, and beak. All day long he shouted curses at angels and in the night he sang for his brother, a sad tune that carried over the water, miles and miles right to the edge of her mystical hearing.

That was the floating dream. There was a sinking one, too, where he drifted down into the old world, holding his breath for days until he realizes that he simply doesn't need to breathe anymore. When he opens his mouth to speak a huge bubble comes out that breaks into smaller bubbles that break into sounds when they pop, muted and dull but still they spell out the word that is in his mind. Down past schools of sardines and swarms of little squid and a solitary eel, out of the reach of the sun he falls, spinning and twisting, reaching for jellyfish when he passes them, trying to pluck out the glowing red string in their hearts. There is a light at the bottom of the sea, the windows of the dead still glowing homely through the water.

There's got to be something better for me to be doing, she thought every time she indulged herself with this daydream, head to the glass, eyes shut tight. There was a lot of pain she could be sneakily ameliorating, and the new subtleties of her gift almost made it possible for her to wrestle with the botch while appearing to the casual observer to be doing her nails or picking her nose, but it was so hard to pull herself away from this story, Pickie in the deep dark world under the water, visiting with the dead.

Have you see my brother? he asks of a woman, bending to see her better because she's wedged under a park bench, her bony cheek pressed against the sidewalk. Only a few scraps of flesh remain on her face—they wave like ribbons in the shifting local current—but her hair is entirely intact, lustrous and thick and speckled with tiny glowing crabs that scuttle and swing along the strands. Her eyes are long eaten, but two pale fish turn in the sockets to look at him, so it seems she is looking at him. I asked if you had seen him, he says, but she doesn't speak.

He walks on, down a street strewn with parts, legs and hands and a head rolling in the current like a tumbleweed, a torso hollowed out and sheltering snails under its ribs. A steering wheel drifts just above the level of his head. He jumps it, grabs it, and throws it up toward a window. It knocks against the glass and falls again. Just before it hits the ground a thick white tentacle emerges from the house to snag it and take it inside. He waits for a few minutes for it to come out again, even puts out his hand politely for a shake, but the house, though brightly lit, remains silent and still. He walks a little farther—there's a playground spread out underneath a dead oak, swings blowing, the big cage of a jungle gym full of people, pressed together in a heap.

Have you seen my brother? he asks the bony faces that look up between triangles, pressed against the bars. I know you must have seen him, at the end. I know you can tell me where he is. You don't want to make me wander forever, do you? I'm not allowed to stop, you know, until I find him.

"Does it look any different?" a voice asked beside her. She stepped back from the glass and opened her eyes. Ishmael was there. "I see you standing there all the time, looking out. Does it ever look any different?"

She shrugged but didn't look at him. He wasn't one of her favorite people anymore, since the business with the Council, but that didn't stop him from trying to talk to her all the time. He was never much fun, and sometimes he was downright crazy. She didn't see the botch in him yet when she looked, but something made him knock his head against the wall and bite his lip till he bled, always in the context of a rant against some person of the day who'd infuriated him with a real or imagined slight. He only seemed to really lose it when he was alone with her, so she tried to stay away.

"What do you see, when you look out?" he asked her.

"Water," she said.

"Really," he said. "I think I know you better than that, and I know that look. I've seen it on other people's faces, staring out like that, too. They see whole other worlds, lost under the water or waiting just over the horizon. Is that what you see?"

She shrugged again.

"I used to look out there and see all the dead people. I'd look straight down, just staring and staring, and eventually the faces would start to rise up, one at a time, so slowly, and they'd get closer and closer and I'd wonder if I knew them until they broke the surface and popped just like a bubble. I used to feel sorry for them, or sad. Not so much any more. Now I wonder what they did, and I know what they did, and all I can think is how all that water is barely enough to cover it up."

"Don't you have work to do?"

"I think this is it—it's not a distraction, wanting to... I dream of such fabulous punishments, and nothing is ever enough."

"Are you high?" Jemma asked. She always asked him, he always laughed at her.

"Have you ever seen a head squeezed and squeezed, harder and harder until..."

"Well, I have work to do," Jemma said. "Unemployed, and work up to here. See you later!" But you hope never to see him again, and skip into a scurrying hurry when you hear him pounding his fist against the window. Don't worry—not even he can break it. And don't worry—it's all right to find him so distasteful, though you pity him for being so upset all the time, he's certainly not done you any favors lately. He is my brother but our bonds are not blood, and I don't like him either, when he gets like this, pounding now with his hand and now with his head, biting his tongue and making little bloody o's on the glass every time he strikes it with his face.

She always knew when somebody died. Never mind the angel's flute, playing a universally hated tune that sounded to most ears like a mournful cell-phone ringer, or how she announced every death no matter how many people pleaded with her to shut up: "A great soul has passed! A great soul is flown from the earth! Celebrate this life!" During adult codes she was silent now, except that sometimes she would start to play her flute along with the alarm chimes, a slur on the code teams. But Jemma could feel them, too, every death a prick against her awareness, a complaint and a sadness in her head, and then a tearing sensation, like someone was peeling a band-aid off her face.

She tried not to go to them, but as they passed day two hundred and fifty at sea and they became more frequent, you could hardly avoid being present at one unless you stayed locked in your room, always an option for Jemma, who was usually pursued by the still-hale Arthur and Jude and still under an injunction of house arrest by the Council, even if they no longer tried to enforce it. She could stand less than ever to be in her room, lonely for Rob and for Pickie and for Vivian. Jemma was the only unemployed person in the hospital—every child too small to work was busy sleeping—so now she made wandering her full time occupation.

If only they knew, the ignorant morons who call you the angel of death, how very different you are from my littlest brother—if only they could see him, everywhere around them, or appreciate how deeply he is settled in them, ashes in the marrow of their bones. He is not a glowing pregnant lady in a yellow gown, green scrubs, and sparkly blue sneakers, who takes two steps toward the dying for every one step she takes away from them, a struggle plain on her face, grimacing or clenching her teeth but never smiling, like some people say she does. You have refined your art at every death, the fire growing thinner and more subtle until it is just an unease in the air, easily lost in the greater unease surrounding the death, the shouting and the hurried flurry of meds and compressions and the deployment of the wonderful and futile new machines, the liquid-respirator helmets and the implant-able LVADs and the nanobot solutions that every fourth or fifth death extend a life by another hour or day.

There she is again, they say when they see you leaning again against a wall, just beyond the code fray, staring at the patient. Like a ghoul, some say, but I know that blank look is on your face because you are looking beyond the physical, and that time you drooled at Dr. Walnut's code was because you were trying so hard to patch up his ruptured abdominal aneurysm, and not because, like Dr. Sundae suggested, you were hungry for his soul. "You're not supposed to be in here," Arthur says to you sometimes, but it's been weeks since they tried to pull you away by your arm. They think you still need to touch a person to wreak your havoc on them so as long as you stand at least ten feet away from the bed they leave you alone, and do not realize that the little swing in your hips is all you show of how tremendously you are pummeling at the botch. It's extraordinary how hard you can work, and how little you can show it, and how a part of you can appreciate how pointless your effort is even as you enthusiastically exhaust yourself, and you think of all the other impossible things it is like, this impossible thing you are doing: folding a marshmallow in half, studying for a pharmacology exam, retracting to the satisfaction of a surgeon.

Jordan Sasscock was the first to die that day. For a long time he'd been on the way out, stuck in one of the ultra-critical care units on the fifth floor, sustained by one of the new floating respirators and still cognizant enough to continue to participate by remote proxy in Council meetings, and even as he was actively dying he was still enough present in his body and his mind to look fondly at his eight wives, to reach weakly for their hands and turn his cheek into their palms when they surged forward to touch him.

"He's too young to die," said Carla, the stupidest thing Jemma had heard in weeks, twenty-nine being ancient, everybody knew, in the new order where the botch spared no one over the age of twenty-one. The Council had made an official, preliminary declaration extending childhood until the twenty-fifth year—weren't there young men and women of that age who acted as foolish and carefree as teenagers, and who were as innocent of the grosser accumulations of sin? Probably not, Jemma had said, though by that time she was already impeached, deposed, and locked up. The law saved no one.

Sasscock was still handsome, even with the tube in his nose and the respirator claws attached to his neck, the artificial kidneys hanging like two plastic eggplants from his waist, and his palms, as dry, black, and rubbery-looking as a gorilla's. He still had his chin and his jaw, and he still had his appealing olivey smell, but he could hardly keep his eyes open and Jemma could feel an agonizing pain in his spine where the botch had eaten through the bone to rot on the cord. She stood by the door, tapping slowly with her foot, imagining a gauge for his pain, one of those huge fundraising thermometers, and brought the level down just a touch with every tap. It had to be slow enough for him not to notice it but fast enough to make a difference.

"It's not fair," said Carla, falling back out of the crowd and bending her neck to place her face in the crook of her arm. It was another obvious statement. Jemma did not know how to reply to it.

"Come on, Carla," said Jordan. "Come on now, we talked about this. Everybody tell her." Two of the women took her arm and drew her back to the ring around the bed, but no one spoke, except Musette, who merely reported that she was pushing some fentanyl-555. Five of the eight were nurses, and the other three had become experienced caretakers in the dormitory and the adult wards, though before the rain one had been a cafeteria cashier, one a lab tech, and the last the mother of three hemophiliacs, the youngest admitted for a head bleed after playing a forbidden game of football, and now sound asleep. Jordan coughed and smiled: Jemma gasped at the pain in his back. Carla glared at her.

"Come on now," said Jordan. "Everybody cheer up. Let's turn up the dopanephrine a little." Dr. Tiller and the rest of the unit team were standing a few feet off, watching Jordan, but essentially letting him be. It was almost like he was running his own code, except that he was in a very particular sort of extremis, actively dying, Jemma was sure, but so jacked up on meds and potions and machines that he presented an appearance too calm and civil for a man in the process of divorcing his own body. Jemma felt a lurch. With a twist of her hand she deflected a high crest of pain—it made her laugh, not cry out, because it was a skillful blow and her best success in days.

"Just fucking shut up!" said Carla, turning to Jemma and throwing a bit of wadded gauze at her. Weighted with pus, it fell just at her feet.

"Sorry," Jemma said, staring down at the ground. There was another lurch, and the dense botch in Sasscok's abdomen suddenly detached from its moorings and rolled onto his aorta, drastically compromising the blood supply to his legs. "Oh," he said quietly, and that motion seemed to set off a series of collapses elsewhere in his body. A little spot of botch in his lung grew and then collapsed, pulling his lung in on itself and away from his chest wall until it had shrunk to a nubbin. Another spot on his heart did the same thing, and blood began to trickle into his pericardium.

"Carla," he said. "Don't be gloomy. Musette, remember that I love you. Hannah, I love you too! I love everybody—don't forget!"

Another little botch bomb exploded along his aorta, and he started to exsanguinate into his chest. Carla saw his pressure dropping and opened up his fluids while Musette hung hypernephrine on top of the dopa. Jemma ground her head into the wall, astounded by the extraordinary pain he was supposed to be suffering. Surely it was enough for your lung to collapse and your heart to leak and your great vessels to explode—it all hurt enough, by itself. Why pluck at his thalamus to make phantom agonies real? There was something too cruel about a plague like this—someone had to be in charge of it. She knocked her head softly on the wall three times, every knock a blow against an organizing principle she imagined but did not perceive.

They pushed more meds and more fluids, and hung the synthetic blood that Sasscock himself had perfected, but it ran out as quickly as they pushed it in, pouring from his bottom and his mouth, and they all kept going, bagging him and doing compressions and changing out his chest tubes when they clotted, until his brittling bones broke under their hands, his handsome face collapsed under the mask, and then under their resuscitating kisses, and he was like any of the others, a mess of blood and ash in the ruined shape of a person.

“I’m tired,” Rob said.

“I know,” said Jemma.

“I don’t want to do this anymore. It’s stupid and pointless. It only makes me more tired. Nothing else, nothing useful, nothing good. Just more tiredness and more death and more uselessness.”

“Exactly,” Jemma said.

“I’m going to stay in here forever.”

“Okay,” she said. They were in a linen closet on the seventh floor, a place Rob had modified to accommodate him in these dark moods. It had used to be Vivian’s place, discovered the night of their final trip, to which she’d return for little vacations not just when she was feeling sad, but also when she needed a quiet place to sit and consider her list. Lying under the shelves, cushioned by a layer of blankets and pillowcases, she said she could almost see the words written on the darkness, pale letters that burned brighter and brighter as she became more certain that she had found another offense. Rob had removed two of the shelves and lined the bottom with a thick gymnastics mat. This made it a more comfortable place to lie down, but also made the close space smell of sweaty boy.

“Or until we get out of here. Which is never, and forever.”

“I’ll stay here with you.”

“I don’t care who dies next. There’s nothing I can do.”

"Not a thing."

"They can all just fuck off. The vents can fuck off, and the art lines can fuck off. The chest tubes and the foleys and the bypass machines. Fuck them all. Even the people underneath them, they can fuck off, too."

"Fuck them all," Jemma said.

"Double fuck them," Rob said, and sighed, and Jemma imagined the double fucking, two-penised Rob striding naked through the hospital to thrust at the patients and the machines and the tubes, the patients and their sick, tired nurses and doctors. Only the children were spared the violence of the purple-headed twins. She laughed. "It's not funny," he said.

"I know." It was too dark to see his face with her eyes. "Come here," she said trying to grab at him with her toes: they were sitting with their backs at either wall of the closet. She picked at his shirt, and shoveled him toward her with the side of her feet.

"I don't want to," he said. "I like it over here. I just want to be alone, with you here. Just sitting like this in the dark, where nobody will find us, until the end."

"Okay," Jemma said, but she still kept pulling at him, with her fingers and her toes, her hands and her feet, with her body. She imagined a heaviness in the space between her legs, and a slow force reaching through the space between them to latch between his legs and draw her to him. He slowly moved, not grabbed by her imagination but because she knew he didn't mean any of what he was saying. "I could grow you a double penis," she said. "That would be something."

"One's enough," he said, scooting close enough to press against her. She turned onto her side. He curled over her back.

"It's not bad for the baby," they said together, because Vivian had already told them that, and because they had read about it the old sources, and because they still needed to say it, even though they knew it, to make it even more true. She was only two weeks from term, but still it was careful and slow; they hardly moved, even when they weren't doing it in a closet or on the roof or in the ER or yes, under the beds of the comatose. They hardly needed to move anymore, to make it happen for each of them, even though Jemma mostly kept her promise not to meddle with his fuck centers, and when she imagined herself playing a grand fugue upon his orgasmatron, it was merely an idle daydream, and when extraordinary pleasures became real for them it was almost none of her doing.

Her mind wandered, not away from the two of them, but further into them. Down and down, he pushed her further and further into a quiet place, where all the feelings in the hospital came sliding down to bump against her, and the hospital in her head was almost a perfect mirror of the hospital in the world, dwindling hope and mounting despair reflected in exact measure. "God fucking dammit," Rob said. "Stupid motherfucking bastards. Fucking gummy-bear shitbird. God damn, God damn, God *damn*"—he built up frustration along with his his need for her, until it crested and broke. She felt thrown by it and washed by it. She gave a push with her mind—just a little one—and it was like she had reset him. He cried against her back and snotted down her neck and made noises that she could not understand as words, though she knew they were words. He was apologizing to her and to the patients, to his mother and his sisters, to Vivian and Dr. Sasscock and Pickie Beecher.

"Hush up," she said, "it's all right."

It wasn't though, not really. It was just getting worse and worse—she tried not to imagine the new horrors that were coming, the new ways in which the botch would twist their bodies and their minds, but it was like trying not to scratch an itchy scab, or worry a painful tooth. She'd seen it all and yet every day she was surprised by some new horrors, strange and dreadful in ways that were more subtle than she ever expected, eye spikes and dry rot in the mouth and regurgitant cloaca syndrome.

"That was horrible," he said after a little while.

"The worst," she said. "You suck at this."

"You too. It's like doing it with a smelly pillow."

"Or a chicken bone."

"Or a chair."

"We may as well just give up," she said.

"We may as well just lie down and die," he said.

"Goodbye, stupid world."

"Fuck you all."

"Here we go," she said. He pulled a blanket down from the shelf above them to cover their legs. They settled closer to each other and he was asleep before another minute had passed, his breathing deep and regular and slightly snoring, his arms twitching and his feet fluttering before growing still. Then he had fallen asleep, but Jemma lay awake, looking, though she always promised herself she wouldn't, at the little bits of botch scattered throughout his body. It lay here and there in little dormant seeds, and she did not know if it was something she was doing that was keeping it from blossoming horribly in him. It seemed ridiculous again, to think that her love had finally become protective of someone. Hello again, her baby said to her.

Hello, she said.

It's not bad for me, you know. I barely notice. And I won't remember, at all, when I'm older, about the hanky-panky.

I'm glad to hear it.

That's not to say I want to, you know, be with you. I mean I was still hoping…

For somebody else.

Exactly. No offense.

None taken. Who knows better than me, all the reasons you should run and hide from me, after you get out?

A remarkably mature perspective.

I am older than you.

But that doesn't always count for much.

Touché.

But while we're on that subject. About the fellow there.

Yes?

Can you protect him? Can you protect me?

I don't know, Jemma said.

And are you sure… are you really sure that it's not you, after all, who's causing all the trouble? What if this whole botch business is coming from you? You know, leaking out of your bottom at night while you sleep.

But it came from the boat.

Who can say, really, what came from the boat and what didn't come from the boat?

That's the most ridiculous thing I've ever heard.

But you concede, don't you, that maybe… just maybe… it would be best if he just sort of gathered me up and hurried away with me when the time comes. That we'd be better off without you?

Well…

I'm glad you understand.

But I didn't…

It's so nice to have a conversation with someone who is reasonable, and sane, and knows when to do the right thing.

But I…

I'm so glad we talked. I'm always so glad, after we talk.

Me too, Jemma said. Then she put her face in the blanket and wept.

"Are you ready?" Father Jane asked, addressing her congregation from bed. They were in the auditorium, her bed stuck up at the front of the room, John Grampus standing at her side. To all eyes but Jemma's he seemed to have made a miraculous recovery—he was out of bed, off the respirator, on po digoxin and could be seen for a while running every day up and down the ramp on his bionic leg—heroically attached by Drs. Tiller, Sundae, and Snood with the help of Dr. Walnut's notes and some automated surgical devices—until it became clear that the same people who had first celebrated his return to health as a sign of universal hope, were beginning to resent him, his swift little jog and his too-short baby-blue running shorts. For everyone else, to look at him was to see no trace of illness, but Jemma could see the botch in him, dormant cysts in his muscles. "Are you ready?" Father Jane asked again, pausing to look out over the little crowd with her blind eyes—a thick layer of black cataract kept her from seeing anything but blurry shapes. She pointed but didn't call out names.

"I have been asking myself that question every day now, for the past few weeks. I used to ask it in an entirely different context. Jane, are you ready for the new world? Are you ready to start again? Are you ready to leave this very comfortable place, to take up burdens that will be heavy in ways that you can't even imagine? Are you ready to be worthy of that place. Are you ready for your second chance?

"You know, I never was really sure. You will be angry with me when I tell you that I always wanted one more day, another chance to talk to the angel, another opportunity to gather up my courage and make sure that I could handle it. It's almost a relief, to know that I'm not going to see it, now. Almost, but not quite, because I really did think I was finally ready. It was all in me, everything I needed to step out and be worthy of the new grass and the new trees and the new mountains and the deep new sky. I thought I could see everything, the shape of the leaves, the colors of the new, wonderful birds—colors not ever even seen before. It was probably stupid, to think I could contain it in my mind, to know it at all before it was here, and maybe this vanity is just barred me from it. It's easy to think that. It's always easier, to think the worst thing. Jane, you're fat. Jane, you're a whore. Jane, you're disgusting. Jane, you're too ugly, inside and out, for anyone to love you. You hardly even have to try, to think like that. Jane, a whale has a better chance of swimming up your ass than do you of entering the new world.

"Lately I've been asking myself another question. Are you ready? It sounds the same, but actually is different. Are you ready to leave this horrible place? Are you ready to be freed from the chamber? Are you ready to go away from here? It should be an easy answer, I know. But I am held by other questions. I worry for our errand, whether we ever properly defined it, let alone completed it. All these sleeping children—I know what they are dreaming about—I envy them and sometimes I am angry at them and sometimes I even feel a hatred toward them. I hope it is just the sickness in me that makes me want to bite the baby or kick the toddler—when I am thinking *Why not me*, these feelings are the answer. Weren't we supposed to do something with them and with ourselves? We kept saying that we would. Remember what Vivian said? We were all saying it, in our own way. We kept sounding like we meant it. I worry that we all just sat around, after a while, trying to enjoy a ride that was never meant to be fun, that when the obvious was presented to us we stared and stared at it, and pretended it was not there, and that when we thought we were improving ourselves and making a model of what was to come we were only playing a stupid game.

"Again, it's so easy to think like this. Somehow this bed makes it easier. I asked the angel for a bed that would help me think, that would push my mind out of its usual ruts, and yes there are these special buttons, and the clasping mittens that give you that wonderful massage, but lying in bed was ever an activity for the morose, the languid, the lazy depressives. I got a glimpse, the other day, not in a dream, not in vision. I wasn't even looking out the window. You know I lost the feeling in my toes about five days ago. Now they don't hurt like they did, but I have to check, every so often, to make sure they're still there. You remember Dr. Walnut, no doubt, and how his toes rotted to little stubs, how they were black and hard on the outside, red and tender in the middle. I have a fear of that. I lifted up the sheet to look and my toes were there but so was this other thing.

"I had a feeling—my toes were there and I was so grateful to still have them, and out of that I had this feeling that everything was right, that everything had gone just as it should have. How about that? I am a pretty sensitive girl, and I have a good memory. I took another look at things, and yes I felt the sadnesss and the rage, the cold grief, but then it was sort of... farther away, and this other feeling was still there. It wasn't that I didn't care about rotting toes or broken promises or orphaned sleepers, or about the lost world, and all those people under the water, but I could think about them and still I had this feeling like everything was all right. Maybe it is just a vessel in my brain, all blocked up and causing trouble, or spreading lies in my head. I don't think so.

"So here I am, lying down here in front of you. Look, my toes are still here." She wiggled them under the sheet. "I can't feel them but I can move them! Look, I am ready. I am all right, all fine, all... done. How about you? That is the lesson for today, the little bit that I can tell you about this afternoon, before you go back to your patients or your own illness. And before you go I want you to try it for me. I want to try to make you feel it, because I am sure that it is the very next step. Are you ready? John and Elizabeth and Rob and Connie, I know you're out there. Close your eyes with me and pray."

Jemma closed her eyes, too, along with the fifty people crowded into the room. She saw differently with them closed, but it was just as plain: the botch in every body. She thought she could feel it, the strain in the minds as they tried to feel what Father Jane was feeling. Here and there someone let out a little peep of a groan. It was so quiet, but only Jemma marked it when Father Jane stopped breathing, and for many minutes no one but Jemma knew she was dead.

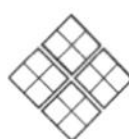

"Do you think she'll come?" Jemma asked Calvin.

"She always comes," he said. They were waiting for their ride to school, a woman named Deb who drove a yellow taxi. Their mother had hired her months before, to solve the problem of driving them to school in the winter, after a failed experiment with a carpool—she'd entered them in it enthusiastically, but pulled them out quickly when she realized she was expected to drive other people's children into town. Now it was September, in the middle of a late heat wave, and there was no snow anywhere, but their mother liked the arrangement too much to have canceled it on account of good weather, especially during times like now when she had retreated into her darkened room to sleep and sleep. Jemma, not very far penetrated into the third grade, was eager to get to school, not least because she feared the wrath of her new teacher, Sister Gertrude.

"Let's get the bikes."

"Don't be stupid, Jemma." She put her head out the door to listen for the distinctive rattle of Deb's taxi. The hot, wet air made her gasp a little. It was quiet, except for the birds, whose song seemed muted by the heat and humidity, and who walked slowly over the lawn, as if they were too exhausted by the weather to fly.

"We should get Mom," she said a little later. Her brother shook his head.

"You try and wake her up," he said. Jemma was afraid to do that, but after five more minutes of watching their empty driveway her anxiety pushed her down the hall and around the corner to the foot of the stairs and their parents' door. It was closed, of course, and radiating the sense of forbidding that it sometimes did, so Jemma was sure that if she touched the doorknob she'd get a shock that would blow her across the hall, clear through the picture window in the living room, over all three ravines to land, dead and smoking, on Beach Road. She stared at the knob for a moment before she reached for it slowly, and let her hand hover just an inch from it before grabbing it. She got a little thrill, a tingle at the base of her spine, but no shock. She turned it, thinking it would be locked, but it wasn't. The knob turned, but the catch did not disengage. She was about to turn it further when she heard Deb's horn.

She ran back down the hall, picked up her bag, and quickly overtook Calvin, who was never in such haste that he didn't walk along the narrow line of railroad ties that bordered both sides of the driveway. Jemma opened the door, threw her bag in, and clambered in after it.

"Hey kiddos!" said Deb, not turning around to look at them but smiling into the mirror. From where she was sitting Jemma could see an eye and a cheek, some teeth and a portion of her maroon lips.

"We're kind of late," Jemma said. Calvin climbed in beside her, hauling on the door with both hands to slam it enthusiastically.

"Don't jostle the old lady," Deb said, meaning the car, which was very old, but had broken down on just one occasion, back in the winter. Deb was old, too. She was the wrinkliest person Jemma knew, and had old eyes with big rims of wet pink on the bottom, caught between her white eye and dark eyeliner. She had a head of springy gray hair that was always pushing her hat up off her head, a baseball cap she wore all the time, sometimes under a wool stocking in winter. She'd got it, she told them, by sending in a hundred proofs of purchase from her cigarettes. It had been white, but now was a very lived-in sort of yellow, and said in blue letters across the front, *Oh Yeah!* "We'll get there, little Jemma," she said. "Mary Ann can hurry when she has to. Can't you, honey?" She patted the dashboard, raising a little cloud of dust that floated with the cigarette smoke in the columns of sun that came through the windshield. "How 'bout this weather?" Deb asked them, turning around as they crested the hill and started to go down. "Like trying to breathe with a wet washcloth stuffed in your mouth, huh?"

"It's an affliction," Calvin said.

"Not so bad as that," she said, turning back around as they drifted a little into the grass. "An affliction would be the summer of '73. Or ovarian cancer and diverticulosis and a no-good husband."

"That's worse," Calvin agreed. Jemma began to look on the floor for something interesting. She had found all sorts of things before, a broken calculator, a gold pen, various lipsticks, all sorts of change, and a condom, once, though she hadn't known what it was till after she lost it, when she described it to Calvin. She'd unpeeled it from the floor mat and stuck it in her pocket back in March, while Calvin and Deb were having a conversation. She'd brought it out to examine it every now and then, not sure what it was but knowing it was important. She had planned to show it to some people at recess, especially Andrea Blake, a girl with whom she would have liked to be friends, but who always ignored her, and to whom Jemma never knew what to say. Now she would know. She'd ask her if she wanted to see something neat, and it would all begin from there. Years later Andrea would say, "Do you remember when you showed me that wonderful thing? That's when we became friends." But, like a living creature, it worked its way from her pocket during a game of tag—she was always it, and never able to pass on the condition to anyone else. She didn't look for it long. If she'd looked longer she might have found it before Andrea, who named it a snakeskin, and dutifully informed Sister Mary Fortuna of the likely presence of a poisonous reptile in the schoolyard. It was shortly surrounded by an impenetrable ring of nuns. They came pouring out of the school to form an Ursuline condom-disposal squad, one ring standing facing out toward the children while an inner ring gathered it up for destruction. Sister Gertrude came out in yellow rubber gloves to pick it up and carry it to the boys' bathroom, while Andrea made the observation that it must be a very poisonous snake whose skin caused such a fuss. Today there was only a penny, stuck with a trace of gum to the floor. Jemma put it in her pocket.

"Did you hear," Deb asked, "the latest about the Strangler?" There was a murderer abroad around the river and the bay, who killed whole families, more by stabbing and shooting than by strangling them, but he always left bruises around their necks. "He strangles you," Deb and Calvin had told each other while Jemma tried not to listen, "after you're dead!" He'd been killing all summer.

"Was there something in the paper?" Calvin asked, sitting forward into the space between the front seats.

"Nothing. Not a word. That's the latest—nothing. How many days is that without a word?"

"Twenty-nine," said Calvin.

"I think he's moved," said Deb.

"I hope so," said Jemma. She'd had nightmares about him and his big white hands, as big and white as the hands of Mickey Mouse, soft but strong and deadly.

"I bet he's gone on to Buffalo," Deb said with a sigh. "Or down south, to another bay. Down to Tampa."

"Or San Francisco," Jemma said. "That's a bay."

"Oh I bet he'd like it there. He's probably one of those."

"Those what?" asked Calvin.

"Nothing."

"Those what?" Calvin asked again. He'd already showed Deb how angry he could get if he thought an adult was hiding something from him.

"Forty-niners," Deb said. "Gold-diggers. There's gold out there, you know."

"Cape Cod," Jemma said. "Boston. Honolulu. They're all on bays."

"Anyway, he moved on. To Buffalo, you wait and see."

"Do they need killers there?" Calvin asked.

"No more than anyplace else," said Deb, and started to talk about the weather again, and how it gave her trouble with her emphysema, and made her awful phlegmy. Jemma scooted down in her seat, curling her knees up and falling to the side, so her cheek rested against the peeling leather seat, and she could see out the rear window. The familiar procession of objects—the tall trees alongside the long road out of the forest; the telephone wires strung alongside General's Highway; the aerials on the houses just outside of town—passed more quickly than usual. Mary Ann sped along faster than ever before. As they went faster, Jemma felt calmer. She reached a hand up to the open window and spread her fingers against the rushing air, listening to her brother and Deb talk of murder and baseball and the heat.

"Let me drop you off in the courtyard today," Deb said as they turned at the statehouse and passed down School Street.

"No thanks," said Calvin.

"Come on," she said. "I'll honk the horn and you can wave to all the kids. They'll all die of jealousy. They'll just all drop down dead."

"The usual place will be fine," Calvin said.

"One day I'm going to drive you right into the lobby," Deb said, and laughed so hard she started coughing, and pulled over a half a block from the tree where she usually let them out, so she could double over the wheel and hack and hack. Jemma stood on her seat and peered over the armrest, but Deb waved her out, gasping "I'm fine!" Calvin helped Jemma out of the cab, and held her hand till they were a block from school. Deb drove by just as they were passing through the iron gate. She honked and waved and cackled, drawing stares from every other child in the yard, but Jemma and her brother kept their heads down and their eyes on the ground.

Sister Gertrude liked to talk about sin, especially on a hot day. For two weeks in their fourth-period religion class they had been learning about Hell, who lived in what level, and the particulars of their suffering. Today there would be a test, after a last-minute review. She'd drawn the familiar triangle on the board—the gentler upper regions of Hell being more exclusive than the lower regions because, as Sister Gertrude said, more people sin worse. It looked to Jemma just like the food pyramid, and she had confused the two in daydreams, so she almost answered once that fruits and grains were punished in the frozen bottom of Hell.

Sister Gertrude stood behind her desk, obscuring the top of the pyramid with her wimpled head. She scanned the quiet, dark room—she liked to draw the curtains and turn down the lights during fourth period, because she thought the darkness facilitated profitable spiritual reflection—and suddenly pointed at Martin Marty, two desks to Jemma's left. "You, Martin," she said. "A candy-fresser drives his scooter of a cliff because he is too busy unwrapping his taffy to watch where he is going. Where does he go?"

"To the second circle," he said immediately. "Where all gluttons are punished." Jemma had known that one, and wished she'd been asked.

"Very good," said Sister Gertrude. She passed by Martin's desk and deposited a cherry cough drop on it. She was always eating them, and did not consider them candy, though they had only the faintest hint of menthol in them, and they were the most pleasant reward she gave. "Rachel," she said, "Another candy-fresser is denied her nasty gratification by her wise mother, who will not buy her the pound of chocolate she desires. The girl holds her breath in the middle of the supermarket checkout aisle, thinking to force her mother, but the wise lady ignores her stupid show. The angry, sullen creature holds her breath longer than ever before, even after she passes out, and she suffocates herself. Where will she find herself next?"

"Oh, that's a hard one," Rachel said, from three seats behind Jemma. "It wasn't a suicide, was it? She didn't *mean* to die. She's doing some gluttony, isn't she, but she's angry, too, and the angriness is worse than the gluttoniness, so she should go to the place that hurts more. That's, um, number five?"

"Excellent," said Sister Gertrude. "Excellently reasoned." She swept by the desk, depositing two cough drops. "Donald Peerman, how will she be punished there?"

"Oh, something really bad. Poked with hot pokers, right?"

"Wrong, it is a wet punishment, not a dry. Petra Forsyth?" Jemma's attention started to drift as Sister Gertrude's calls fell farther and farther away from her desk, and she thought not of hell, but of her sleeping mother—she wondered what she was dreaming about. She let her eyes fall almost closed so she could imagine it better. Her mother was dreaming of flying, just like Jemma did. Probably it was an ordinary dream, she was walking home up the hill, or walking down the street in town, when suddenly she realized that there was a much better way to get around, and took to the air, not in a leap like Superman, but in strokes, like she was swimming, pulling and kicking herself a little further up into the air with every stroke. Jemma followed her all over town. She was doing laps around the statehouse when Sister Gertrude called on her.

"Miss Claflin!" she said, rising up suddenly in front of her desk and leaning over so the delicate crucifix she wore on an extra-long chain swung at Jemma's eye. "Please tell me where daydreamers are punished."

"Oh," Jemma said, fidgeting in her chair and thinking furiously, flying through the pyramidal Hell in a rapid sweep, looking around her desperately for the easily distracted girls with half-lidded eyes. "Not in the first circle, or the second. Um, not in number three, or number four, that's for greedy people. Not in number five, where the angry people get wet, like you said. Uh, it must be lower. Boy, I wish it was higher, but it must be lower. Is it between five and six?"

"Is it? Is it? I thought you would know, being a practiced artist of the daydream. Do not try to distract us with answers to questions I have not asked, Miss Claflin. If you are ignorant then proclaim your ignorance. We have not, in fact, discussed the fate of incorrigible daydreamers, who waste their lives in idle speculation. It is a kind of sloth, but not punished with the worst kinds of sloth. Daydreamers remediate in Purgatory. That's where you'll go. Can't you just see the newspaper article, children? Miss Jemma Claflin was hit by a bus this afternoon as she walked along, daydreaming of the loveliness of creampuffs. Stern angels escorted her immediately to Purgatory, where she will spend three quarters of eternity peeling and sewing the skin onto the same banana, and trying to organize her thoughts."

"How long is three-quarters of eternity?" asked Rachel.

"Just as long as it sounds. Enough of review, though. Almost everyone is ready. Books away, pencils out!" Sister Gertrude erased the board with a damp sponge, eschewing the dry eraser so no trace of the pyramid would be left to tempt and assist incipient cheaters.

The test wasn't so terrible. It was the usual format, matching, multiple choice, and fill in the blank. With a ruler Jemma carefully drew lines between sins in the left column and the appropriate place in Hell in the right column, eating five pounds of gummy bears connected with circle number three, not sharing your snack with somebody who forgot theirs connected to number four, and saying your prayers wrong connected with number six. She had no trouble with any of the multiple choice questions except the last one: Lying children are punished a) with hot licorice whips b) by being turned into snakes c) by having their tongues split every morning with a rusty knife d) tickling and boiling. No one was tickled in Hell, everybody knew that. Only gluttons were punished with food. She knew the right answer involved a forked tongue, but snakes had forked tongues, so b and c both seemed like the right answer to her. She stared and stared at the paper, waiting for one or the other to seem more right. In the end she chose b.

The last question was the hardest one. It was sort of a trick; Jemma didn't like it. Bullies are punished in the seventh circle for ___ and ____ and ____. Jemma ran through all sorts of combinations in her head: a thousand years, then another thousand, then five hundred? She raised her hand and asked Sister Gertrude if there was a mistake with the question. She only shook her head. Five and five and five thousand years, she wondered. It was for always, but how to divide that up into three? Was this a religion test or a math test? Time was almost up when she finally got it. The tests were being handed toward the front as she scribbled in her answer, *forever* and *forever* and *forever.*

Jemma and her brother took a long detour on their way down to the beach. Their mother was awake and active when they got home. She'd blown up a pair of inner tubes for them to take down to the river, and was in the middle of preparations for dinner. She told them not to come home for at least two hours, because the cooking would require her absolute attention, and might be dangerous to little bystanders.

They rolled their tubes down the hill, but turned right instead of left at the Nottinghams, and went down a half mile into the woods beyond the fifth hole, wedging the tubes along the way in the branches of a live oak tree. There was a path that led down to a clearing and a pond, and the railroad tracks, which ran along the eastern border of the forest, but never crossed any road. Teenagers went down to the pond, sometimes, to drink or smoke or swim without their pants, younger kids almost never went down there. Lately, though, the teenagers had fled, driven away by the memory of friends, replaced by younger kids looking for gruesome mementos. Two boys had died down there early in the summer, Andy Nyman and Chris Dodd. They'd laid down in the train tracks to let the train pass over them. They were both quite tall, with big strong chins, and there was speculation that their noble chins were what had done them in, or that they'd lifted them too proudly. The cowcatcher caught Andy under the chin and took his head clean off, throwing it hundreds of yards into the bushes. Chris lost his head, eventually, but not as cleanly as his friend—his body was lifted and dropped again before the train, then crushed and mangled by the many wheels. Many parts of him had not ever been found, a couple toes, an eyeball, and the whole left hand. It was mostly for the hand that the children searched, because a rumor had grown up that it could, if ever found, grant wishes like the fabled monkey's paw, five or less, as many as the number of fingers still attached.

David Tracy and Johnny Cobb, two of Calvin's friends, were already there, and already looking. "If you find it," Calvin told Jemma, "don't touch it. Just come and get me." He handed her a stick with which to poke in the bushes, and ran off to go greet his friends with punches to the stomach and shoulder. Jemma began to wander around, in and out of the clearing in little loops, beating the bushes with her stick, and calling out to the hand like to a kitty. She wasn't dressed for bushwacking: she wore a pair of bright-yellow terry-cloth overalls over her bathing suit. It was getting to be the hottest part of the day. She undid the bib of her overalls to let it flop down over her belly, but felt no cooler.

She took longer and longer loops out of the clearing. Calvin and the other boys weren't doing much looking. They were sitting on a mossy log that stuck out of the pond, passing a cigarette back and forth. Jemma called to the hand again, and this time thought she heard a stirring among the leaves and twigs on the ground. She walked in the direction of the noise, passing another split oak and some holly bushes, and coming in a few hundred feet to another clear space, littered with magazines and bottles. Someone had built a fire there, a long time ago. Jemma poked her foot in the ashes, uncovering a half-burnt latex glove, but no hand. She picked up some bottles and threw them against a tree. None of them broke.

A flash of yellow caught her eyes, a little bit beyond the little clearing. She thought it was a bird, and so went very quietly, thinking she could catch it in her hands, then run back to her brother, saying, I found a finger! When he peered over her closed hands she'd open them, releasing the bird right into his face.

But it was a twinkie. Someone had impaled it on a hawthorn bush, still wrapped up. Jemma wondered, just for a moment, if this could possibly be a twinkie tree just beginning to bloom, and considered running for her brother to tell him, but the other wrappers scattered on the ground, and an empty box she found half buried under the bush, spoke against that lovely possibility. She knew what had happened: someone had glutted themselves on soft golden cake, and played with their food when they could eat no more of it, instead of making the effort to bring it to somebody who needed it, or at least giving it a proper burial. It still looked quite fresh inside the wrapper, except where it was pierced by the thorn, where there was a little circle of green rot. She leaned close, and sniffed it, and saw how one edge of the plastic had been gnawed at unsuccessfully by some little animal. She pinched it and discovered how it was still very soft. It couldn't have been there very long.

She went back to the big clearing, kicking an almost empty can of shortening in front of her. She kicked it toward the pond, and it would have gone in if Johnny, demonstrating an extra sense for kickable objects, jumped backward off the log, turned around, and sent it flying over Jemma's head back toward the trees.

"What have you been eating?" her brother asked her.

"Nothing," she said.

"There's stuff on your face."

"Oh. I had a cookie, from before." He put his hand out at her. "I ate it all." The boys searched her, patting all her pockets, David extracting and inspecting her little vinyl change purse, then returning it. "Told you," she said. "I didn't find the hand."

"Us neither," said Calvin. He lit up another cigarette and passed it around. Johnny could blow smoke rings. Jemma asked for a puff.

"Okay," said Calvin, "but only pretend." He held the filter an inch or so from her lips. Jemma pursed her lips and sucked in air, and held it in as long as she could, then stuck out her bottom lip and blew out straight up, hard enough to lift her bangs. It made her cough, and the boys laughed at her.

"Let's go swim," she said to her brother.

"My brother says they came down here to kiss," said David, "and to dress up like girls to dance and have pillow fights, and talk about baking cookies."

"And they put on makeup and played field hockey," said Johnny.

"And they felt so bad about kissing that they laid down under the train. It was totally on purpose."

"I wish we could find that hand," said Calvin. "I've got some wishes."

"I wish we could go swimming," said Jemma.

"Go ahead," said her brother. "You know the way." Jemma looked over her shoulder into the warm shade beneath the trees.

"Come on," she said.

"We've got more smoking to do. Go ahead. If you find the hand, don't touch it and don't make any wishes. Come right back here right away." She stared at him a little while longer, but he just puffed on the cigarette and looked at the sky. She walked away, looking back a few times before they were out of sight. He was never looking at her. The path was clear all the way up, it had been trampled true by three generations of teenagers. Jemma found her tube and rolled it up the hill like a stone, going very slowly, hoping Calvin would catch up with her.

She had an imaginary brother that she could force to accompany her when the real one would not. He went with her now, leading or following, all he asked was that she not look directly at him. If he was following she could hear him stepping behind her, crushing leaves or sliding on loose dirt, and when he went ahead of her his shadow flashed across the shiny leaves of holly bushes along the path as they passed through breaks in the canopy of leaves. He called back to her that it was very hot, and she agreed.

The beach was crowded, full of adults and kids on the sand and everywhere in the water, some standing in it up to their necks, some just to their chests, and some just getting their feet wet. Tiffany Cropp almost ran into her as Jemma rolled her tube down toward the water, passing by with her sister, a very fancy float suspended between them—it was a little island with an inflatable palm tree growing out of one side. Jemma tested the water with her foot before walking in. It was warmer than she had hoped it would be.

Kids swarmed to the tube like tadpoles toward a lump of bread, all of them clinging with their hands and arms, so they all faced each other over the hole, and Jemma had no room to sit. Jemma didn't mind, though she didn't join in their chatter. Jemma drifted, and watched her imaginary brother playing in the water, just from the corner of her eye. He sported like a dolphin or a whale, leaping in somersaults, or in high arcs that landed him on his back, and she got a glimpse of his foot, or of his hand, as he fell back in the water.

She realized she was daydreaming, and remembered what Sister Gertrude had said to her. She let go of the tube and stood in the water, submerged to her neck, thinking of the punishment she would get after she died, and then realizing she was daydreaming about that. She tried not to think about it, but found that she could not, and tried not to picture it, to consider the lesson but not the entertainment, but couldn't do that either. She tried to focus just on the water against her neck and the wind blowing gently against her face, but Purgatory was unfolding in her mind, a gray wasteland peopled with dreamy sinners and little monkeys on tricycles with sidecars full of bananas. She began to cry.

Someone splashed water at the back of her head. She turned around and saw her brother. "What's the matter, Bubba?" he asked her. She told him she was going to Purgatory for almost ever, and that there was nothing she could do to stop it. He frowned, then scowled, then slapped the water with his hand. "Don't be stupid," he said. "Only somebody stupid would listen to that crap. What does she know? She doesn't know anything, or whatever she does know is all wrong." Jemma protested that Sister Gertrude knew quite a lot, that she knew more about Hell than anybody Jemma had ever met.

"Why are you defending her?" Calvin asked. "Oh, come on, I'll show you how wrong she's got it." He took her by the arm and pulled her after him out of the water. They knelt in the middle of the wet sand and he started to draw with his fingers. "I'll show you," he said. He drew another pyramid, this one with the pointy side down. "Okay, here it is. What is it?"

"Hell," Jemma said in a very small voice.

"Right. Okay, level one. Who's there?"

"Virtuous pagans," Jemma said automatically.

"Wrong," said Calvin. He drew a line a few inches form the base of the pyramid and wrote over it, *harmless nuns*. "See? How about level two?"

"People who kiss too much."

"Not people," he said. "Nuns." He wrote it down: *Kissy nuns*. "On we go—level three."

"The gluttons," Jemma said.

"Close," he said. *Fat nuns*. He took her down through every level, describing torments as they went; *angry nuns, blabby nuns, ugly nuns, stupid nuns, creepy nuns, cruel nuns, beating nuns, thieving nuns, lying nuns, treacherous nuns*, and finally Sister Gertrude cramped up in the tip of the inverted pyramid. "At the very bottom," he said, "in her very own level where nobody lives but her. Do you know why?"

"No," Jemma said, still sniffling, and somewhat ambivalent about the nuns burning and clawing their flesh in her imagination, feeling sorry for them but knowing too that their punishment was just, and didn't Sister Gertrude herself say it went against God's will to pity those he'd set aside for deserving punishment?

"Because she's a dumb-ass, ass-licking, shit-eating, motherfucking, dog-fucking, lizard-fucking bitch. There's only one of those and she lives right here." He pounded his fist over Sister Gertrude's chamber. Jemma's mouth had fallen open at the incredible stream of bad language that had come out of his mouth. She was shocked, but delighted, too, to hear the forbidden words. Her heart raced and she drew in a breath, deeper and deeper, gasping, and then she laughed. Calvin was smiling but not laughing, driving his fist into Hell, grinding all the nuns deeper into their punishment. "Just wait," he said. "Just fucking wait."

Dinner was not much fun. Jemma's twinkie was sullen in her belly; she wished she had not eaten it. It made her mother angry how little she ate. Her father was angry, too. He usually was, on the days their mother woke up late, though he was quite solicitous when she was sleeping, never screaming at her to get out of bed, and directing Calvin and Jemma to take care of her when they got home from school. But that night he found fault with the way the napkins were folded, and the fluffiness of the soufflé (it was too fluffy—fluffy like a cat, is what he said); and the meticulously constructed rib roast complete with immaculate little socks on every bone, he compared to a very fancy shoe. Jemma and Calvin left the table early and had dessert in Calvin's room, watching television.

They watched a documentary about blood and a half hour special on the Severna Strangler, in which a shrill lady stood in front of the various houses of his victims while pictures of the murdered parents and children popped up around her in the air, and proclaimed the horror of what he'd done. She only stood in from of the houses in the dark, and the bright camera lights made her face shine as golden and unnatural as a twinkie. Jemma's stomach still hurt. She let Calvin eat her sorbet.

"Moron," Calvin said to the television, because the lady had proclaimed, like Deb, that the Strangler had moved on. "You're just going to make him mad, saying that. You think he's not watching? Now he'll kill again tonight, and it'll be your fault." He turned to Jemma and said, "He's going to do it tonight."

"Shut up," she said.

"Tonight. You better sleep in my room." Jemma changed the channel, and found another documentary, this one about Mark Twain's dog. "That dog better look out," Calvin said shortly. "He'll get him, too."

"He's in the *TV,*" Jemma said.

"You think that'll stop him? You think his hands can't pass right through the TV? They're magic, killing hands. And thanks to that stupid lady, he's coming for us tonight."

"Please stop saying that."

"Can't help it, can I, if it's true?"

"Stop it!" Jemma screamed.

"I'll be ready, though," he said. Jemma got up and ran downstairs to get their father. She stopped at the bottom of the stairs just in time to see her mother fling a dish at her father's head. He was sitting on the couch, sipping at his drink. He ducked casually, leaning over to the side. The dish flew over the couch and shattered against a piano leg.

"Go on," her father said calmly. "Throw another dish. That will solve everything. That's your problem, really, the dishes."

"Cocksucker!" her mother shouted. Her father put down his drink and lit a cigarette.

"Yes, yes. I'm a cocksucker all right. A great big cocksucker. That's what I'm doing all day and half the night, sucking cock in the OR." Jemma ran back upstairs and went to her room. It was almost as loud, there, and she could hear every word they said, even her father's quiet responses. She would have stayed, though, if it weren't for the thought of the Strangler at the window. She went back to Calvin's room.

"They're fighting," she said.

"I can hear," he said. He'd turned off the TV and was reading in his bed. "They'll stop." He folded his book across his chest and opened the covers. She climbed in, and they listened to the shouts and occasional crashes. Sometimes they heard nothing, and sometimes just a single word. Their father was getting louder and louder, but their mother was loudest of all, and her voice, shrieking higher and higher, finally carried to the room as clear as if she was standing right in front of them.

Calvin moved his hands above the covers, lifting them high when his mother shouted, and low when they heard their father's voice. "I'm conducting them," he said. "I can make them do anything I want."

"Shut up," Jemma said quietly.

"Really," he said. "And I started the fight, anyway. It was easy. I just told her I heard him talking to some nurse on the phone. They were making a date for dinner."

"Shut up," she said. "It's not funny."

"Not at all," he agreed. "But it was so easy. I saw it in my imagination, and then I made it happen. If they hate each other enough, then it will lift me up. I'll ride their misery right through Heaven."

"You're crazy," Jemma said.

"I am going," he said. "Don't hold on too tight."

"I'm coming too."

"You don't want to. It's not going to be easy, you know. And the ride will be rough. A fountain of blood, and murder is the rocket's tail." He was quiet a moment, and then he shouted, "Hit her with a brick!"

"That's disgusting."

"What do you know?" he said, but he hugged her. "Blood calls to blood. If they spill blood, then the strangler will smell it, and come to us. He is coming, and I am going. Do you understand?"

"Shut up."

"It's not me, it's them, calling him. Tell them to shut up." So she shouted it at the door, not loud enough for them to hear over their own shouting all the way downstairs. But not long after that, they quieted.

"Tell me he's not going to come," Jemma said.

"I cannot tell a lie," Calvin said, and turned on his side. She put her head on his back, using it as a pillow, but not sleeping, though she drifted, and almost fell asleep. For a few brief seconds she rode through the air above Hell in a monkey's tricycle sidecar, throwing bananas down at the suffering nuns. Calvin sat up suddenly. "He's here," said. "Did you hear that?"

"No," Jemma said.

"I heard his hand against the house." He got out of the bed, slowly and quietly, and picked up his two biggest lacrosse trophies from his dresser. "Don't scream until I start hitting him," he said, and went to stand by the window.

"Okay," Jemma whispered. She could barely hear herself. She sat up against the headboard, ready to scream, not sure if she could be anymore terrified as she waited and waited, until, impatient for the thing to finally happen, though she did not want it to happen, she imagined it. The Strangler would lift the window and come in one pale, fat hand at a time. She saw Calvin strike him once and twice, with either hand, right in the head, and saw him fall down to the carpet. Then she started screaming, as loud as she could, summoning her parents, who arrived almost instantly, dressed in pajamas and heavy boots, which they turned against the murderer, kicking him in the back and the chest and the head, while Calvin struck him, one-two, one-two, with his bloody trophies. And when he was as good and dead they would wave for Jemma to come to them, and she'd climb out of bed and walk over, and put one bare little foot upon his neck.

"Calvin," she whispered, her eyes shut tight now. "Tell him to hurry up."

"Synfrosius," Jemma said to Rob. "It's a good name. I like that name!" They were lying in bed, getting ready to go out on their new rounds—superhero rounds, Rob called them. A week before there'd been a winnowing among the patients: the botch had raged mightily in a night, and in the course of twelve hours everyone in the PICU and the seven satellite ICUs was dead. Rob never ran away, like the majority of the staff, most just overwhelmed by a process that seemed to be declaring the futility of their work and their lives, some not just driven crazy by the abundance of suffering and death but stricken with the botch-madness, their brains scabbed with black ash and their minds a mess of fear and sadness and rage, so they wept as they ran, and punched in the face anyone who tried to stop them or comfort them. Rob was happy as he worked for the first time in weeks, glad to be fighting so hard but glad too because he could tell it was almost over. Jemma could feel it, from where she spent the night, groaning at the foot of their bed, reaching all over the hospital with her mind, as futile and useless as anyone else, experiencing the pain of the dying but not much succeeding in alleviating it. When the sun rose—another clear, beautiful day dawning over the water—all that was left of their last patient, Dr. Pudding, was three ribs and five kilos of ash (his bed weighed him every morning), and Rob and Dr. Tiller were the only two caretakers left in the unit.

"Lambchop," said Rob. "I like that one too!" In the past two days he had not entirely been himself. He looked the same, and acted the same, and felt the same, and talking to him you would mostly not know that the botch had started to unfold in his brain, but more and more he would get excited about something like a silly name, or the fabric of their sheets, or the shape and texture of an asparagus newly condensed out of the replicator mist. And more and more Jemma spent all her time around him trying not to do her dry sobbing cry.

"That's a nickname," she said gently.

"Lambert Chopin Claflin-Dickens-Dickens-Claflin."

"Those are all last names."

"Vivian, then. Poor Vivian!" He didn't seem to know he was sick, or that he was not acting entirely normal. Jemma kept expecting him to have a moment of high suspicion, when he hurried to the radiology suite to image his brain, but he never did.

"Poor Vivian," Jemma said. "I'm sorry, Vivian." Practice should probably have given her a better poker face by now, but she was grateful that Rob, even with his diminishing capacities, was facing away from her. "Sorry everybody," she said, but she could not feel for everyone else the sort of regret she felt for failing to save Vivian, or miss them like she missed her, or like she missed the parts of Rob that were slipping slowly away.

"That's a good one," he said. "Or Pickie. But kids would probably make fun of him or her. Here comes Ass Pickie. There goes Pickie My Nose. Or how about Spanky?"

"Short for what?"

"Spankenmeier? Spankenbush? Spartacus?"

"I kind of like Spartacus."

"Vivian," said Rob. Something shifted in his voice, and she knew without even looking in his head that he was suddenly all there again. "Even if it's a boy. There won't be any name-calling in the new world."

"Vivian what?"

"Just Vivian. Or, Vivian!"

"Supermodel Vivian," Jemma said softly. The baby kicked her.

"Are you all right?" Rob asked, when she started.

"Just a kick," she said. And then they were both quiet for a while. Jemma, always open to the rest of the hospital except when she actively hid from it, tried not to notice the terrible quiet.

The hospital was changed again, full of empty places and wild places, more than ever a home for survivors. The high death toll of the past week was not limited to the PICU. The Council was almost extinct, only Dr. Snood and Ishmael remaining of the four Friends, and only Dr. Tiller remaining of the extended twelve, though Cindy and her friends had organized themselves in a sort of alternate Council, which sometimes concurred with and sometimes resisted the senile efforts of the adults, who had stopped legislating and proclaiming. Dr. Tiller and Dr. Snood used the vestiges of their authority to organize protection for the sleeping children—no one younger than eighteen was awake now—and to organize the children themselves, more space allotted now for the medical dormitories than for the palliative adult wards.

"I put you back!" Monserrat had declared to Jemma, just before she died. "It is in my power, to give it away, my high place. It is for you again, my baby." (She wasn't entirely sane, and confused Jemma alternately with her daughter, her granddaughter, and Ricky Ricardo). "Now you are me. I give you the power, a different power, so you can make it all better again."

"It's all right," Jemma said. "Don't worry about anything." She'd come to the death, drawn by her compulsion and by Monserrat's request. Dr. Tiller was there, too, along with Dr. Snood, regal zombies in their immaculate clothes, their lips black and their ears shredding at the edges into papery ash. Ishmael stood at the head of the bed, entirely hale and handsome as ever, in a sane and quiet interlude.

Dr. Snood spoke. "A brief examination of the law will tell you that the office..." Dr. Tiller put a hand on his arm. "Shush, Darling," she said. "She's just raving."

"Who has to tell you?" Monserrat asked Jemma, crying and smiling and grabbing her around her neck to press her face into her boobs, still wonderfully full, though her belly was collapsed down to her spine. "Who has to tell you, to do the next thing? Who else could it, besides you? Vivian, Jane, Ishmael, everyone wasting our time but the whole world, all the children just waiting for you to say the word, my sweet Desi. Oh, that smile! Oh, that hair! Sing to me, darling. Sing to the children and the whole world. The gates are waiting—open them!"

"It's all right," Jemma said, hardly batting an eye as she wove and placed a series of blocks in her thalamus, blocking the botch when it tried to make her scream. It was like playing tennis in the dark, but she could have played ten games at once. Every day brought her more power, and made her feel more useless.

"Sing, sing!" Monserrat screamed, so Jemma uttered soft babalus into her chest until Monserrat began to weep. "You!" she said, before a minute of singing went by, all of them indulging her now with the mournful crooning. "You!" She pushed Jemma away, sat up, pointed square in her face, and died. Ishmael chose that moment to totally lose his mind, tearing off his shirt and scratching at his flesh. "You!" he echoed, pointing at Jemma. "You!" With his non-pointing hand he scooped ash from the corpse, spat in it, and smeared his face. That was four days previous, and ever after he could be seen wandering up and down the ramp, clothed only in smears of ash, screaming at the carpet and accusing anyone he met of explicitly detailed crimes. Jemma could always feel him, a presence in her mind even uglier than Pickie had been.

"Seven days," Rob said, reaching behind himself to put a hand on her belly.

"If it's on time. Nobody was ever on time, in my family."

"My sisters were early."

"Cheetarah. I always wanted that to be my name."

"Have you been wondering..."

"What?"

"If... I'm afraid to say it. It might be a jinx."

"Give me a clue."

"What if it's only... if when by the time we land there are only two people over twenty-one left in the hospital?"

"Ishmael and Dr. Snood. That'll suck."

"Not them."

"Don't say it; you're right. It's a jinx. I used to do that all the time. Sure is a quiet call night, and, Where are all the patients? My medicine senior got so mad at me once. I thought she was going to slap me. If you say it, they will come, she told me. If you say it, it won't be us."

"We won't talk about it."

"We never were talking about it."

"I never mentioned it."

"I don't even know what you're talking about," Jemma said, but she clutched him suddenly, squeezing and squeezing, as if just by holding tight enough with her body and her mind she could keep any more of him from slipping away.

There are days left, and days, but already I am nostalgic for the watching, and anxious for Jemma's end. For all my watching, and all my waiting, now I would rather that the end not come at all, the baby not come at all, the hospital never land ashore. I must have known, when I made my own choice, and did my deed, that the consequences would claim Jemma, too, just as they claimed everyone else in the world. But still I am hoping for an ending where she steps out of the hospital and lives in the new world with her baby and these seven hundred and one other children, even though I know she would not belong there any more than I would.

And it would be even better than stopping what's coming, if I could roll back all the time between her and her last happiness, or my last happiness. I contain all the past, but have no power over it, and it would take more than an angel to fly with her through the blowing ash of the botch-time, past her ascent over the hospital populace, past her wedding and her unveiling and her great night, past the subtle hints of her pregnancy and her slumbering power, past even the night of the storm, though I think she was happy enough, doing the screwing with Rob Dickens that conceived the last baby of the old world and the first baby of the new one.

But why stop there, when we can fly back past every death, her first lover in his crumpled car—see how the dents unfold and the blood flows cleanly off the white metal? Her mother unburns in her kitchen, her father gets a little stronger, day after day, as his cancer dies back, until he is his old self again, and Jemma's life is almost again a life free from a permanent shadow of unhappiness. A little further back and Calvin might be doused, his organs stuffed back in their proper place, his tongue fetched from his right hand and his eyeballs from his left. Make him whole again, and Jemma is happy again. No death has touched her life and she thinks that everyone she loves is going to live forever.

But I wouldn't stop there. As long as we are moving, let the time fly backward, and shrink them, Jemma and Calvin both, down until they fit in my own favorite moment, or the moment, anyway, from whenceforth it might all have been different. Jemma and Calvin are sitting on their roof, and instead of pushing her away, a bomb to destroy the adult world he hates and does not understand, let him hold on to her instead, and show her the stars above the roof, and tell her the names—different from what he's learned in books—that he's made up for them. Never mind the sins and pleasures and miseries of the old world, never mind the unknowable, indescribable satisfactions of the world to come, let me just watch them there, and let them just stay there, and let all of us finally be happy.

A bucket in one hand, a sponge in the other, Jemma and Rob made their rounds. A few days before she'd started out meaning to wash away the accumulations of ash—the piles in every corner, the greasy smears on the walls, the half-inch-thick layer along the ramp railing—but it made her feel ill just to approach the stuff, let alone touch it, and she remembered too well the barfing of her first trimester, and she couldn't bear the thought of dealing with the drifted piles, or making mud with it in her bucket. Rob would have done it—he would have done anything she told him—but she didn't want him covered in it, either. Every part of his brain that might have countermanded an order from her was gone. He was pliable and sweet and happy and sometimes just looking at him was enough to make her cry. She settled for washing the children, all of them asleep now, from the babies in the crèche to Josh Swift, settled in the arms of Cindy Flemm in their old classroom. The process of death and sleep had just about run its course: no one aged twenty-one or younger was awake, and no one older was alive except for her and Rob and Ishmael.

Every three days they rounded with the buckets—that was how long it took for the dust to settle again upon the children—but they visited every one of them every day, turning them in their beds or fluffing their pillows or arranging in a crib the animals that in her absence always seemed to creep closer to the infants. She suspected Ishmael was moving them, as a taunt.

They saw very little of him, though they could sometimes hear his voice come down the ramp from a higher floor. Rob was afraid of him, and clung to her every time they heard him laughing or screaming.

They were simple rounds, if exhausting, in their own way. There was no differential diagnosis to generate, no medication to dose, no physical exam to inflict upon the child. Instead there was hair to brush and there were pajamas to smooth and diapers to check. They'd all stopped excreting days before but she still peeked in the diaper or the underwear to make sure they were clean. She'd pulled the last nasogastric tubes a week ago—they were disfiguring and unnecessary. What sustained the children was not food, and they needed their enteric formula less than they needed Rob to play the banjo for them. When their feeds were on they radiated a sense of annoyance; when Rob played they were more deeply serene.

Supervising Rob was a job in itself. She'd find him scrubbing too hard or trying to dunk a toddler head first into the bucket, or distracted by a jellyfish at the window, Kidney naked and half-washed, forgotten on the floor beside his feet. More than forgetful, he heard things differently than she intended them. She'd found him the day before writing on Ella Thims with a thin-tipped permanent marker, his same backslanting lefty cursive flowing across the child's chest and belly, arms and legs, around and around in a spiral on his back: *once there was a boy named Rob he had a dog named Joe, once there was a boy named Rob he had a dog named Joe, once there was a boy named Rob he had a dog named Joe.*

"What are you doing?" she'd asked him.

"Making her a story."

"You were supposed to tell her a story," she said. "They like it when you do that. They like your voice."

"Uh huh. Like this."

"Not like this," she said, her tone gentle and patient, but he started to cry as soon as he understood that she was correcting him. It didn't take much to make him cry; reminding him to brush his teeth or pointing out that his shoes were untied or that he wasn't wearing any pants. "You don't love me," he would say to every perceived criticism. "Of course I do," she'd say, and it would only take a kiss to make him forget that he had felt sad.

"I found another baby!" he said that morning, rushing up to her when she came into the conference room, her old classroom, where Josh and Cindy and Ethel and Kidney and all the rest of her old class, except Pickie, were housed, laid out in a row, a little ward of friends, heads to the window and feet to the wall. If their room was nicer than some others it was only because she had been decorating in there the longest, and not necessarily because she liked or knew them all better than the other sleepers. There were mobiles for every bed, each one different, appropriate to the age or personality of the person beneath it, so Valium had a string of winged donkeys while Josh and Cindy had pictures of the two of them together, with music that played only within a spherical field three feet in diameter. On the wall there was jungle; on the ceiling a sky. When it was dark you could cover the windows and play the holobox, and manufacture any environment you liked: desert or forest or endless grassy plains, anything but the ocean.

"It's Kidney," she said. "You should put her back in her bed."

"But I found her. Another one! They're everywhere, aren't they?"

"She needs her sleep," Jemma said. "Why don't you put her back?"

"Okay," he said. "If you say so." He didn't cry, but he looked at her like she was crazy. He was always picking up the smaller ones and presenting them to her, as if there was something else he thought she should be doing with them or for them. He never said, Wake this child or Make him better or Make it happen, but those were the words that she heard in her head whenever he ran up, as proud as a retrieving dog, to present her with another.

She washed them in order, Kidney first, unfolding her arms and legs out of her pajamas while Rob peered in the other beds and settled on Ethel, starting with her left foot. If she directed him he'd do a better job, but today she was tired of it, and rather than give him a plan, she just let him wash the foot over and over. When she got as far as Ethel, they could talk. She dipped her sponge in the water—the bucket kept it warm—and washed the little feet, always the dirtiest part, though the child hadn't walked anywhere in weeks. Her round calves and knobby knees, the thin legs and the bottom, all areas covered by clothes but the dust crept in everywhere—she even had to brush it out of her mouth, a tricky business. She usually just combed her hair, but today she washed it, fetching a special basin from the replicator and lathering up two big handfuls of fancy-shampoo suds made from one of Vivian's recipes. "It's almost fun," she said to Rob. "I'm almost enjoying myself." When he didn't respond she turned to look at him but he wasn't in the room.

She found him without leaving. She could feel him upstairs, puttering in the PICU. Sometimes he went back there to stare at all the machines, pushed up into corners, or to hold his hand over one of the kids—it was mostly teenagers—and say, "I need to do something for him." "There's nothing more to do," she'd tell him. "You're all done." He never believed her, but he always let her lead him away. She'd go fetch him out when she was done here.

Kidney, then Valium, then States'-Rights, then Magnolia. Everybody had their bath, and Jemma had another hundred minutes of good work. It was stupid to feel such a sense of accomplishment, when they were all spiffed up, when Kidney was changed into a new set of pumpkin pajamas, Ethel's head was freshly shaved and painted, no longer a morose black spot but something else, always more cheery but different every few days, a plane-face with a propeller nose or a shark mouth, and today a yellow flower-face with blue eyes and a wide green smile. It was like making one's bed—they would only get dirty again like a bed would be slept in again, but there was something so satisfying in it that it really did cheer her up more than anything had in weeks. She found she could almost forget about mad Ishmael wandering and shouting, about Rob, ruined and preserved, about all the uniquely gruesome deaths—John Grampus's howls of outrage and accusations of betrayal directed at every surface of the hospital, Dr. Snood's bright eyes glistening in the ash-filled cavity of his face, and the never-solved mystery of what lay under Dr. Tiller's headdress; Jemma had paused forever with her finger on the fabric, ready to finally lift it, but in the end she left it alone. She knew she could do this final work for as many days as were left to her.

Josh was last, his body almost as familiar to her now as Rob's. She was wiping idly in his groin, lingering a little too long there—she'd convinced herself that he was a gauge, that the oldest would wake first, and that his penis would wake up before he did, and when it rose he would rise shortly after it, and then the next thing would happen—all the children awake again and her baby would be born and... something else. Dry land or the hospital taking to the sky instead of the sea or something she couldn't even imagine, not even her—something the children were all dreaming about, something they say with their darting closed eyes, something she was too old to hear or know or understand. "Five," she said, counting the swipes. "Six, seven, eight." The penis slept.

"I found another one!" Rob said, startling her. It's not what it looks like, she wanted to say, pulling up Josh's pants. I was consulting the oracle! But he wouldn't understand, and probably wouldn't notice. She took a deep breath and spoke in a very soft voice. She didn't want to see him cry again.

"You've got to learn to let them lie where they are," she said, turning around. She didn't cry out this time, but she made a little sound when she saw the dripping child in Rob's arms, and smelled the ocean on him. It was

Pickie Beecher, pale and naked, a strand of kelp wrapped around his legs and belly, foam still on his chest, and a spray of leaves caught up in his now full head of curly brown hair.

"He's already wet," Rob said. "Do we still have to clean him?"

Jemma held the twig, tracing with her fingertips the edges of the leaves and the rough surface of the bark. She didn't know what it was—it wasn't any of the few plants she could recognize, holly or mistletoe or pine or poinsettia, holiday bushes whose leaves she'd traced out on blots of construction paper in grade school. The leaves were waxy but not dark, and though she found two berries they were purple, not white, and looked like they might have dropped out of a box of cereal. It smelled like nothing she'd ever encountered before, a little piney and a little minty, a little bit of a deep, wet, earthy smell, a little bit of chocolate, but then mostly something she didn't even recognize, and could not describe.

It was so thickly tangled in Pickie's hair that it took her an hour to extract it. More time than Rob spent washing the sea-smell off of him Jemma spent unwinding strands from between the leaves. She could have cut it out in a moment, but she had a feeling that it would have been a crime to violate a single curl. It was the thickest, softest, shiniest hair Jemma had ever seen, the hair she'd always wanted, the very opposite of her own hair. When she had the twig out of it, she spent another twenty minutes washing the hair, and appreciating how it rejected Vivian's luscious, sweet-smelling shampoo and conditioner—the shampoo wouldn't lather and the conditioner seemed to just slide off his head—as if it were already too perfect to need any of that stuff. As she blew it dry she knew she was too interested in it, that it would be better just to be jealous than to be rapt and worshipful like this, and anyway it felt like being unfaithful to Magnolia's admittedly less wonderful hair. Still, she couldn't help herself.

"Where have you been?" Rob kept asking Pickie, as he washed him, then as he dressed him in a pair of pajamas, thick flannel and printed with trains, though it wasn't cold anywhere in the hospital except on the roof, and as he situated a pair of caboose-shaped slippers on his feet. Jemma asked it of him too, if not out loud, and tried to read off him the history of the past twenty-four days. She couldn't tell where he'd been. When she tried all she could see was a reprise of her own daydreams about him: she saw him chased by waves, and walking through drowned cities, but not where he'd actually floated to, and not the land where grew the tree that had given over the twig to him. More obvious than the story of his travels was the simple fact of his health—everything that was wrong with him before now was put right. He wasn't any longer a nauseating blot on her mind but just a sleeping boy, as ordinary as Jarvis or Valium or Marcus.

"He smells nice now," Rob said. "He smelled nice before. It was a waste of water, to wash him all up, but now he sure is pretty."

"Yes," Jemma said.

"Not prettier than you! I didn't say that."

"I know," she said. "He is prettier, though. He's prettier than anybody. Look at him."

Rob whistled slowly. "Those are fine, fine pj's," he said.

"That's not what I meant," Jemma said, and trying not to compare them, but it was like trying not to notice the two sides of the horizon, or the difference between the moon and the night sky, it was so obvious. Rob was becoming an abomination, the image and shell of his old self. Here she was, finally stronger than death, it seemed, since she felt sure it was only the constant exercise of her power, conscious and unconscious, that kept him from falling apart entirely, and yet look what she got. "Let's put him to bed," she said, and Rob pointed out that he didn't have a bed, yet, and shouldn't they make him one?

Jemma made the frame; Rob stuffed the mattress, repetitive work that he couldn't fuck up. There were still hundreds of hospital beds in the place, but she didn't want to put Pickie in one of those. He wasn't sick, and she wouldn't put upon him any of the old or new accoutrements of the hospital, no monitors or embolism stockings or ventilators waiting to pounce on him. She had it half-done before she realized it was a copy of Calvin's old bed, a wide canoe that came out of the replicator in ten easy-to-assemble pieces, with edges that stuck fast once pressed together. Rob had artificial feathers in his hair, and had somehow managed to stuff a lot of them down his pants, but the mattress was almost done by the time Jemma had finished the frame. She helped him with the last of it. They lay Pickie on top of it, his head on a pillow shaped like a life preserver. Just as Rob protested that he looked dead, lying on his back with his hands folded on his chest, he mumbled and snored, and turned on his side, flexing his knee and drawing a hand up under his cheek. They put his slippers at the bottom of the boat, along with a few things Jemma thought he would like, a teddy bear and a squeaky toy shaped like a flank steak and a leaf from the twig.

Rob said there was still something wrong, and stole a rabbit from Kidney's bed, a creepy-looking thing with purple fur and yellow eyes. Rob put it under his arm and said, "That's better." Jemma bent down over the bed and pushed his hair back from his forehead, then kissed him there, the first time she'd ever been so tender with him—always before he had ducked away when she felt compelled by obligation to try, and before there was the horrible smell of his breath, and the simple wrongness of him that repelled her. Now there was just his soft hair and his pale skin, his wet pink lips and his breath that smelled of milk and salt.

"Goodnight Pickie," she said. He opened his eyes and said, "Good morning, Mama."

No one else woke up, though she ran from bed to bed, kissing them frantically, and Rob did the same, kissing Ethel and Jarvis from head to toe. He would keep trying over the next few days, kissing at random, always waiting with the same goofy, expectant smile, and always crying when he was disappointed, and saying again "They don't like me."

Pickie didn't stay awake for long, either; he'd nod off in an instant, then come just as suddenly awake again, without provocation. Kissing him didn't make any more difference, after that first time, than shouting his name, or tickling him, or pinching him, or even giving him a gentle sternal rub.

"I'm hungry," he said. They could have just fed him right there, but Rob wanted to go on a picnic. So they went downstairs, Jemma in the middle as they walked, all holding hands. Pickie looked around at all the spaces empty of people, but didn't ask where everybody was, and only asked once, looking down into Kidney's bed, "Why are they all sleeping?"

He walked differently and talked differently than before; his steps wandered, and sometimes he put one foot in front of the other, or hopped for no discernible reason, and his speech was less fluid than before, he lisped a little and had trouble making irregular plurals. In the cafeteria he broke away and ran to grab at the fruit and vegetables still dancing at the salad bar, entertaining himself while Jemma put together their picnic basket and Rob synthesized gallon after gallon of ice cream. She let Pickie grab some apples and put them in the basket, and he put his finger on the squares of wax paper she folded over the sandwiches while she tied them down with bows of twine. "I want a hamburger," he said, and she did not remind him that he was a vegetarian.

"Come away from there," she said, boxing up a steaming berry pie, because he was squatting in a corner, poking at a pile of ash. He wiped his finger on his pajama bottom and ran to her side, then looked up at her. "It smells like french fries," he said, offering her his finger.

"I hadn't noticed," she said, gathering Rob away from his ice cream. He had made twenty different flavors and couldn't be convinced that it was impractical to take them all the way to the roof, and spent five minutes almost in tears trying to choose between them.

"Strawberry is so nice," he said to Pickie, who nodded sympathetically. "And Honey-Lavender is very sweet. Caramello is kind. Ginger is not the best, certainly, but her feelings would be hurt so bad, so bad, if we left her behind. Mango is outrageous. She can stay, probably." In the end they each picked one and got going, taking the long way up because Rob wanted to walk, and because Jemma wanted to see how Pickie reacted to the familiar sites of the hospital.

He just stared as they passed the monuments to the early dead, speaking only when he caught sight of the toy, still turning and ticking and hooting and ringing in the lobby, to ask if he could go play with it later, and only showing any emotion when they heard Ishmael cry out from a lower floor, his deep groan rising up into a high, trailing shriek. Pickie clung to her and said, "I'm afraid." Rob had dropped his ice cream and was sitting on the floor with his hands over his ears.

"It's just a raccoon," Jemma said.

"Don't let him get me again," Pickie said.

"Again?" Jemma said, but he wouldn't speak any more of it. She petted Rob's head and pried his hands away from his ears and told him everything was all right. He clung to her also, forgetting his ice cream, so the going was a little slow for the last two floors. As soon as they got out into the daylight, they both sprang away and went capering over the grass.

"Here we are," she thought, after it was all set up. Another picnic; she was a little sick of them, in the way that she was a little sick of everything, sick of rounding with the bucket which was monotonous in a way that was similar to the old monotony, temporarily relieved by her gift—once again her part was small and not entirely necessary. It wasn't hard to imagine—she is dead and little six-legged robots do the work of washing the children, combing their hair and shining their faces, fluffing their pillows, singing to them, a choir of broken mechanical-nose voices. In that moment she was sick of Rob, too sweet and too stupid and too empty, and sick already of the new

Pickie, usual and dull and likely to run screaming from a feast of blood. Two days past her due date, she was sick of being pregnant, sick of her backache and clumsy walk and the false contractions. She looked out at the water, at the flat calm ocean and the clouds marching again like huge animals over the horizon (she'd seen those, too, the elephant and the giraffe and even the toothy sandworm, and was sick of all of them) and thought how thoroughly tired she was of waiting.

The botch had taken none of Rob's gymnastic skill, but Pickie had obviously had his bounce washed out. He did clumsy somersaults, pedaling his feet to get his bottom turned over his shoulders, while Rob did perfect back handsprings in a moving circle all around him. He turned and twisted into cartwheels; Pickie stood and hopped from one foot to the other, waving his hands above his head. It took her a moment to realize that they were performing for her. Rob turned again and did cartwheels toward Pickie, then twisted and did a flip clear over his head to land behind him. They both threw out their arms and hands, seeming to offer her the empty sky and the empty sea and more empty days of waiting. She clapped politely, trying not to weep, because she knew it would just get Rob started crying if she did. Pickie sprang up and ran toward her, his arms out, his face so utterly different from how it had been before. She steeled herself for one of his brutal, squeezing hugs, but he only leaned against her like an ordinary child, and sighed in her neck, and said, "I'm having such a good time at the party."

There is a face at her window that she does not see, and a presence that she does not sense, perhaps because she simply does not wish to. His rage and gall ought to be a blight on her vision; it ought to call through the stone and steel; it ought to shine through the glass. But she dances blithely with Rob while Pickie naps under the table, and she puts Pickie in the tub without noticing, though when she comes out of the bathroom Ishmael is looking right at her face. After she and Rob sit on edge of the bed, mouths locked, each clutching and rubbing at the other's back, he presses his face closer to the window, and a pale circle of nose blooms against the glass, plainly visible, but now she is far too distracted to notice. More and more of his face—a piece of forehead, an eye, the chin with the thick, madman's beard—appears as they go on, and at some point he cannot contain himself anymore and pounds a hand against the wall. Still, there is nothing for him, from her, except that she spares him a thought as she falls asleep, deep in the arms of her abominable companion.

My brother watches, his breath catching not from fatigue at hanging on the wall, his fingers and his toes pressed into the stone, but from mounting anger. Just when he thinks it can't get any worse, he feels it more, looking at her, watching her bounce backward in the lap of the dead creature, the extraordinary rage that makes him want to take the whole place in his hands and crumple it like a box. I like to complain about my job—what a chore, to watch all the time, and never be able to do anything, how dull, and how painful, to love someone and never speak to her, never touch her, never see her with mortal eyes. But how much worse, brother, to labor under a mandate of rage, and how difficult and complex to have these feelings for her, to want so much to put your face through the glass and accuse her, to put your hand through the wall and give her a smack. But it's not time for that yet. I say it to you and our sister says it and our brother says it. You do not hear any of us, but you understand, anyway.

Rage and the memory of rage and the hope of rage—O, tonight it seems to me the worse job of all, to see what I see and have to hate it, to hate it and want to destroy it, not knowing why or how, your impotence only making you more angry. It is no way for an angel to live, angry at a mortal for mortal weakness, for being in love, for holding on to a beloved scrap. As a toddler she was no more at fault for hiding a scrap of meat under her pillow, or clinging to Moronica, digging her up after she was sacrificed, loving her until she was just a scrap of dirty fur. It is my exclusive luxury to think this, but I would share it with you, to touch your rage with fondness for her, or even jealousy, anything but that bright consuming anger.

All the other windows are empty—you look in all you pass and see the faces of children picked out under the lights our sister dims every night at nine. You feel nothing as you stare at them—it's almost nice, a patch on your anger, but all around you see the memory of the accused, and you shout at them above the noise of the wind and the waves, and pound on the glass with your head.

On the roof you do your own dance, jumping and shouting, calling out to people long dead at our brother's hand, saying Snood! Tiller! Sundae! Their names are accusations. You walk in a circle, beat at your face, pick at your flesh where it feels too hot, lie down under the sycamore tree, grabbing violently between your legs, a vision unfolding in your head—you are beside her and above her, below her and within her, shouting into her face, so close your nose is pressing against her cheeks, and say it to her again and again, throwing the words through her protests. She is the only one left and it's all her fault.

The botch was eating at Rob's body, drying out his liver, hollowing cavitations in his spleen. Every time she touched him, Jemma pushed at it, but he became a little more degraded every day. Soon he had sores she could not wipe away, and a barking cough that sometimes brought black mud into his mouth, and he got harder and harder to wake from his dreamless sleep. It didn't seem to bother him. He never complained about the cough, or said that his bones were hurting, though the black gall infiltrating his marrow was as plain to her as the nose on his face. That was getting misshapen, too, botch like fungus eating at his septum to give him the saddle-shaped nose of an ancient syphilitic.

"I feel great!" he always said, when she asked. She was in perfect health, but felt awful, perhaps, she thought, in sympathy to him. It was in her, too, she was sure, even though she couldn't see it. She shouldn't have had the pain in her wrists, or the cloudiness in her eyes, or the headaches, or the itchy rash on her bottom, not symptoms, either, of the pregnancy—two hundred and eighty days at sea and two weeks past her due date those were all backache and swollen feet and feeling eternally huge. And it wasn't in her brain, so she had no excuse for all her strange and deplorable behaviors. She wasn't crazy from the botch, not a feral Jemma, not senseless from disease, but still she excused herself on account of it, and drew on the excuse of weariness with the long struggle. I deserve to be a little crazy, she thought. Who wouldn't be?

There was no one to judge her, anyway—Rob lacked the faculties and Pickie had not woken in days—except Ishmael, who would hate her no matter what she did.

She did everything for her own comfort, excusing herself like a glutton feasting with a cold—I need this, she kept saying to herself, every time she looked at Rob, a little more decayed, silently suffering, happy as a retarded clam, still beautiful to her no matter how sick he got. She took to wearing hats plundered from the stock of happier times, Vivian's pillbox and Monserrat's beret and Dr. Snood's bowler and Dr. Tiller's beaddazzled cloth-and-leather headdresses. She'd put them on and hand out merit slips to the sleeping children, thinking she remembered just who had received how many demerits from Dr. Tiller, and keeping a pretend tally of how many she had yet to undo.

She made feasts she was too depressed to eat, set tables for lost holidays and imaginary holidays never to come, seated older kids at the table—some of them had become waxy and posable—and made Rob sing songs to them and eat food from all their plates. She made him pile babies on her in the nursery, spreading herself on the floor while he put them carefully on top of her in layers, until she lay quiet and still in a bubble of hot breath. She dressed them in fancy outfits and took them for stroller rides on the ramp, pretending it was years ago or years from now, that this was her baby asleep in the stroller, his chin on his chest, his feet bouncing as she rolled him through a different world or a new world. She started peeing in empty corners, or empty beds. In the middle of a nurses' station or in the middle of a reconverted OR—the gleaming puddle on the sterile white floor was very satisfying.

She made Rob dance with her for hours at a time. The angel had an archive of songs that they couldn't possibly exhaust, and she'd play them anywhere. The angel herself couldn't sing worth a damn, but she had all the voices of the old world stored in the bowels of the hospital, and she'd recorded the survivors, secretly and not, at their own singing—Dr. Tiller's stern "I Like Paris in the Springtime," Dr. Sundae's slow but passionate "Day by Day," and Vivian's "Do Right Woman," which started out rather ferocious, but ended small and meek and sweet, too much like surrender to be at all like Vivian. It was Jemma's favorite, in those last days. Rob seemed to like them all equally.

"I'm so happy," he told her. They were dancing on the roof, in the faint, early shadow of the sycamore. She held him around the waist and pressed her face into his neck; his arms were over her shoulders, a hand placed on each of her shoulder blades. They rocked back and forth, foot to foot, the same old dance, not very different at all from the days when he was entirely alive.

"Me too," she said. This was not how she had imagined they would spend their final days, and yet there was a sort of golden retirement glow over moments like this. They were lazy, and slow, and when they were in them she felt like they had nothing to do, and nowhere to go, and that they were just waiting, and would be waiting forever, for death to take them away together.

"I wish every day could be as pretty as this," he said, though the day was no different from the last days and weeks; every morning started with fog, every afternoon was sunny and bright, every evening came at the end of a spectacular show of cloud. The air was always cool, not too salty, and clean-smelling, and every once in a while a strange odor came riding on her wind. It took her a whole week to realize it was the smell of land.

"They all can be," she said. "They all will be." But when she was thinking rationally she realized that she had no idea what was coming, and when she thought about how she had always been too afraid to imagine a future for them together, she wondered if that was why they weren't going to have one now.

"Today I sat on a big bouncy ball," he said. She said nothing, only held him a little tighter. She meant to let him go, just then, imagining a place on his back, a place to press that would release him. He would fall into all those parts again, and then they would crumble, while she watched, to ash. She would do something crazy—stuff her mouth with him, or spread him on her hair as she ripped her clothes. Then she would lie down and... she didn't know what came next. It was like looking into the future and seeing another end of the world, all she could imagine coming afterward was blank white space, an emptiness that hurt just to think about. She held him tighter in her arms and tighter in her mind, sending a rush of fire through him—it was so subtle now, and so powerful, and still so useless.

"Why are you crying?" he asked her.

"Because I'm so happy," she said.

"I'll do it too!" he said, but she wouldn't let him.

Two more times that day she felt almost ready to do it; during lunch she felt she could have reached out to press his nose and say, Enough. Then just as they were settling down for a nap, she made him lie down on her and put her hand again in the small of his back, her fingers settling on the button that would set him free. But when she thought of it, it didn't seem like freedom, for his body to fall apart and dissolve. It just seemed like killing him.

So she drew his arm over her like a blanket, steadying it with her mind when she felt it loosen in the socket. He didn't complain, but breathed softly against her neck and said it again—"I love you so much." Never mind that he said it to Pickie Beecher, and the angel, and every replicator, and to twenty different flavors of ice cream. Now he was saying it to her, in his voice, and it was no effort at all to pretend like it was really him—it felt like him and sounded like him and smelled like him—that he was not dead, that it was ten weeks ago, or ten months ago. They lay in her little bed, due within the hour at the hospital for evening shifts, but reluctant—to the point of immobility—to move.

She slipped into a dream of him, hardly different, at first, than the reality—they were in bed, he was nestled against her back, an arm across her neck and another over her belly, his hand open against her, his palm centered over her belly button. It reminded her of the old dreams of her brother, where a sense of the extraordinary hovered over the most mundane activities; they played cards or washed dishes or she sat on the grass and watched him throw a lacrosse ball against the house and it was only just before she woke, or even after she woke, that she remembered that he was dead, and that this had been a visitation.

Here I am, Rob said, behind her.

There you are, she agreed, running a finger along his arm.

But not really, he said. They tell me to say, Let me go. They tell me to say, Burn the gruesome effigy. They tell me to say, It is an abuse and an abomination, what you are doing.

It's so nice, she said, to lie here. She had no idea what he was talking about, but sensed that she didn't want to know.

I won't say it, though. What the fuck do they know? None of them have been in love. None of them have the slightest fucking clue. If they ever did, they've already forgotten. Look at all the shit that went down, before, and tell me who gives a flying fuck that Jemma kept a picture of me?

I'm supposed to be at OB rounds in a half hour, Jemma said. Do you think they'd notice if I don't go?

A picture, a doll, an abomination? What's the fucking difference? Haven't any of you ever been lonely? Haven't any of you ever missed somebody? What do any of you know about it, anyway?

Who would notice? All I do is get numbers. Even if they let me anywhere near the delivery, I just get shoved aside at the last minute. Guess how many cervixes I've felt in the past two weeks? Exactly one, and that was my own. I complained to the chief and do you know what she said? Can you guess what she said?

No one has ever been in love but us.

Those are premium vaginas, Dr. Claflin. Not for just anybody to stick their arm into. Can you believe it? Maybe if I'm extra-special good, they'll let me polish one of them, eventually.

No one, not ever. Not in the old world, and never in the new. We are alone, and have always been alone. There's nobody but us, and has never been anybody else. Stay with me here, forever.

You don't have to tell me twice, she said, scooting closer into him, and closing her eyes.

Stay with me, he said. Don't fall asleep.

Of course I won't, she said, but it was already happening—she was sleepier and sleepier, inside the dream, and just before she went she realized what was happening and tried—no use—to claw her way back.

When she woke up he was dead. She hoped she was still dreaming, and hoped that when she looked over the edge of the bed she'd see dark ocean instead of the blue carpet, but this was her bed, in her room, in her hospital, everything the same as how she'd left it before her nap except for the burden of ash atop the sheets, and the feeling in her belly centered somewhere under the baby—stone, aching loneliness, aching sadness.

She stayed away from their room, after that. It was not home anymore. She never wanted to see the black ashes in their bed again. There was a lot of stuff in there, now, the accumulated gifts of their marriage and the fifteen baby showers that had been thrown on her behalf, but all she took with her was the pencil case and Pickie, loaded out of the tub and into a stroller.

She could have moved in anywhere she wanted, into the luxurious apartments of Drs. Tiller and Snood, or the spartan room where Father Jane had slept on a cot, or Vivian's space salon, but though these rooms were empty, they all seemed full—too crowded with ghosts to yield any room for her. She was restless, anyway, and couldn't sleep, no matter how hard she tried. She felt she could not get comfortable except by getting the baby out. She'd toss from one side of a bed to the other, feeling hot and then cold, wiggling her toes in a frenzy, wanting to sleep and sleep, and wake when the whole thing was finally over—she was so sure it would be soon, and yet every time she got out of another bed, it was still that same day. No rest for the wicked, said Dr. Snood, making a scraping, shame-on-you gesture with his two forefingers.

"Fuck off," Jemma said, the extent of conversation she had with any of them, all the faces that lay over her own when she looked in the mirror or the windows, and the bodies that stepped out of walls, or rose out of the replicator mists. She didn't know if they were real or not. She was trying her hardest not to imagine them, and yet they kept coming. Up until that day she thought she was just pretending to be crazy, but now she wasn't so sure.

"Stop following me," she said to Dr. Tiller, who paced her on the ramp.

We are all still with you, she said. We have not gone anywhere. Like you, we are just waiting.

"Wait someplace else," Jemma said, feeling defeated when she took off the marvelous do-rag and threw it over the seventh-floor balcony.

It's all because of you, said Jordan Sasscock. Why didn't you save us? Why didn't you try harder?

"Why don't you try harder to go away?" Jemma asked him, down under the shadow of the toy. He kept talking but she didn't listen—it was only blame and she didn't need to hear it—because she was telling herself all the time that she was just pretending to be crazy, that the baby-piling and the random urination was all an act, and even seeing these ghosts was just an act. They were echoes conjured in the air by her supremely powerful imagination. Yes, it was the most powerful imagination in all of history, in all of the universe. Her father had always said it would get her into trouble. "That's what's wrong with you," he told her. "Why would you ever do anything, if you're happy just to dream about it?"

Try it, then, Jemma: try to hold every one of them in your mind, all the lost lives, the whole imperfect world, like a sick body only wanting a convincing story of health to make it better. It shouldn't be any harder to change the world than to change one sick child. Equally impossible, they should be equivalent miracles. You give a push, and one thousand ghosts condense in the halls, along the ramp, on the roof. Another push and the children are awake and playing. Another and the sea is full of struggling, dying bodies. Another and you open your eyes, alone in the empty hospital except for Ishmael, looking down at you from the speaker's platform. He is naked and flushed, his huge penis standing up stiff against the railing, peeking over to stare at you, too.

"Fuck off," you say, not sure if he is real.

"You did it," he says. "It was you all along. I've been saying it was everybody else, but it was you, who did the worst thing."

"Fuck off." You make a sign at him, something you make up on the spot, a twisting motion of your fingers that's supposed to make him disappear in a puff of smoke.

"How could you do it? How could you think no one would notice? How could you think it would be let to pass? You did that thing, and then you're surprised when the world has to end on account of it?"

"I bet you say that to everyone."

"Look!" he says. "Look at what it's like! Look at what you make me do!" He claws at his eyes, then. You can feel it when he digs them out of the sockets, pulling at the nerve until it stretches and snaps. You sit down heavily, head in your hands, saying the magic words:

"Fuck off! Fuck off! Fuck off!" And it works. When you look up he is gone, not a trace of him on the balcony, no blood, no eyeballs, and when you hear his distinctive shrieking it seems to be coming from very far away.

She stayed in the lobby until well after nightfall, sitting under the toy with her legs crossed and her hands folded over her belly, listening to its crankings and susurrations, following the shiny metal ball as it fell down the many yards of winding chute, and the twirling metal ribbons that celebrated the return every time the ball came back to the high basket. About an hour after dark the ghosts began to come on like lights all up the ramp, and shortly after that they began to wave and call to her.

Come up, they said. Come up. It's almost time.

"Fuck off," she said quietly, but they didn't go away, and eventually she rose unsteadily and started the climb. They were kinder now, not so likely to yell at her or insult her. There you go, said Dr. Sundae, shooing her farther up the ramp as she passed the third floor. Upward and onward, said Dr. Walnut, showing his pointy brown teeth in a warm smile. Almost there, said Dr. Snood on the eighth floor, when she stopped a while, more because there was a sense of finality about being on the roof that she didn't much like, and she felt they were trying to tell her something, these imaginary creatures, with the friendly cheerleading that had replaced the scolding and the disappointed sighing—they all knew she wasn't ever going to come down again.

It was warm outside. The date, she knew from obsessive twirlings of her pregnancy wheel, was the twenty-second of May, but it felt more like deep summer, with the moisture in the air and the heat in the wind. She listened hard for crickets, but heard only Ishmael's sullen weeping, coming from underneath the sycamore tree. She held up her hand in front of her face, shielding herself from him, and walked on the edge of the roof, where a ghost brighter than any other was kneeling by the edge of the roof. From far away she thought it was Calvin, because he had a huge knife in his hand, but when she got up close she saw that it was Rob.

"You're not supposed to do that," she said. "Somebody already did that."

We're all supposed to do it, he said. We were always supposed to do it. We all have to do it, now. Are you ready?

"No."

Well, that's no excuse, he said. That doesn't change a thing about how things are. That doesn't delay things but for a second. We're almost there. Don't you see it? He pointed out over the dark ocean. Thick low clouds hid the stars and the moon, but she thought she could see a different kind of darkness thrown up against the horizon where he pointed.

"It's not for you," she said. "You don't have to do it."

Ready or not, he said, lifting the knife and twirling it just like she had always imagined Calvin must have, though who knew if he made a flourish, or just got on with it? She only had the coroner's report to go by, its solemn tones seeming somehow reverential of this extraordinary living dissection, mentioning the bell and the candle and the iron brick and the chain but not guessing at their meaning. Rob brought down the knife and cut swiftly into his belly. Jemma was ready to watch the whole thing—she'd seen it in her head so many times, already—but no sooner had he cut himself then he disappeared. The ghosts went out and she felt the pain, different from the endless false contractions of the past weeks, it started in her back and seemed to push her to her knees before she even felt it, a knife in her belly, and she knew she was alone on the roof except for Ishmael, still wailing and wailing under the tree.

She had everything she needed: two clamps, sterile scissors, a bulb suction, a defibrillator, many towels folded inside a picnic basket turned battery-powered blanket-warmer, hauled up on a cart in between contractions. She was trying to prepare for the worst—meconium aspiration or cord prolapse or respiratory arrest or some other nasty surprise that she was too unskilled to pick up with the ultrasound. She felt powerful enough, sitting on the roof in the middle of the soccer field, to put out the moon by poking it with her thumb, but she didn't trust herself to be able to fix her baby, if he came out all fucked up.

The new OR, or in her room, or in the lobby, or in a special room the angel might have unfolded for her, an actual delivery room, these might all have been places more appropriate to give birth, but none of them were better than the roof. She liked it up there, and it was harder for the angel to talk to her—the closest visible speakers were ten yards away, under the grass, and there was always a nice breeze to carry away the icky smells that she remembered too well from her days in OB—blood and shit and the weird, alien-fish smell of the placenta, and the ever-more-curious odors she'd encountered wafting from a vagina in distress. Up here she could keep an eye on the looming bulk on the horizon, still just a huge smudge, five hours after the contractions had started, but in a moment of Vivianish perspicacity she had concluded that the smudge was the barometer of her labor, and that the closer they came to it, the closer she'd come to being done.

She'd read a story when she was little about a dog hidden in labor underneath the porch, squeezing out a litter to surprise her family (a collection of imbeciles who'd not known her very long, and thought she was a fat boy), and Jemma thought there was something doglike, or creaturelike, in the way she prepared a place on the soccer field, flattening the grass with her feet until it was smoothed down in a circle twice as broad as she was tall, laying down her blankets and placing her tools close at hand. Just when she had the blankets perfectly straight, and secured at every corner with a flat stone from a fountain, her water broke and made a stain in the shape of a huge teacup. She sat down, right in center of the wet spot, overcome suddenly with a suffocating sense of finality not associated with the worsening contractions or the fuzzy mountains on the eastern horizon.

"Go on, crybaby," said Ishmael. "Cry for me."

"You're not invited," she said, not lifting her face from her hands. She felt him in her head, all of a sudden, an ugly canker, painful in a way that was distinct from the contractions and this new weighty sadness. "Go away. I don't want you here."

"You need me here," he said. "I'm going to help you."

"Just get away," she said, but he was standing quietly a few yards off, when she opened her eyes. He walked off, but returned at regular intervals to offer up another insult or taunt, like a bad doula. She wished they would both shut the fuck up. She was used to Ishmael's accusations—you are the whore of the world, you are the sickness that ruins, you are corruption itself—though they were getting harder to ignore, and every so often one of them would sting terribly. The nervous, fluttery ejaculations of the angel were simply annoying. Any of the ghosts would have been preferable. Can't you even give birth right? Dr. Tiller would ask, and Dr. Chandra would somehow make her excruciating pain a subsidiary of and commentary on his lonely sadness. Rob would have been best. She was supposed to be lying back against him while he counted out breaths and Vivian stood between her legs, pounding her fist impatiently into a catcher's mitt. "Rob," she said softly, and Ishmael heard, clear across the roof.

"You killed him," he called out. "Don't forget! You killed everybody!"

"Let me comfort you," said the angel, her voice muffled and soft. "Put your hand in me and I will bring you fentanyl." There was a stirring in the ground beyond the blanket; a capped needle poked up through the grass, seemed to sniff at the air, and then withdrew.

"No thanks," Jemma said, standing to turn her back on Ishmael, then squatting, then lying down, then kneeling with her legs opened toward the water. She found it was a comfort to rock back and forth, but it did not keep her from imagining once again a series of looming obstetric disasters.

Common and obscure complications, difficult to remember during her OB exam, presented themselves for her to obsess over. She had looked with the ultrasound while she was gathering up her supplies and was nearly certain she'd seen the head down and the feet up, but who could say the baby wouldn't wiggle and turn at the last moment, to make himself a footling? It was an image she could describe to herself in detail, her body, dead of her failure, lying in the middle of the field, one little leg poking out from between her legs, the rest of the baby dead inside, crushed to death by her uterus. And there were a dozen other reasons for it not to get out, shoulder dystocia and cephalopelvic disproportion—still something she worried about though Vivian had already given her pelvis a good name: platypelloid, which made Jemma think she'd be better suited for laying eggs, but Vivian only smiled and said she could squeeze a watermelon though her pelvic outlet—and all the varieties of vertex malpresentation: face and brow and persistent occiput posterior, not to mention the chance that the baby would raise his hand in salute to the new world and catch the cord against his arm. Only the arm would get out and she would pull at it frantically until it popped off in her hand, and that would be all she would ever see of her baby.

She tried to practice saving maneuvers in her head, trying to remember the names. She thought of Vivian helping her study, telling her to imagine a man named McRoberts on top of her, pushing her legs back to her ears while he grunted and thrust. That one, at least, she remembered.

"Lie back against me," the angel said. "Let me take you in my arms."

"No thanks," Jemma said.

She started screaming an hour before dawn, when the contractions were coming every two minutes, very regular in their frequency, and regularly getting worse. "You deserve worse," Ishmael kept saying, and every so often she'd turn a scream into a protracted and extra loud "Fuck you!"

Up until then she had thought she was going to be able to take it, whether because of her gift or because the events of the past nine months had inured her to pain, or just because she was feeling too sad, too cruel, and too crazy to feel it. "I can do it," she said confidently ("No you can't," said Ishmael), walking around her blanket, or to the edge of the roof and back again, breathing in a cheery locomotive cadence. The first really bad contraction had dropped her to her knees and made her grind her face in the dirt, where she felt the soft hands of the angel stroking at her cheeks and was powerless to get away. When it passed, she rolled over and vomited, right on her blanket.

Now she was screaming regularly, not shy about the cursing, especially with Ishmael creeping closer and closer. She had called the dawn a motherfucker, and shrieked like a harpy when the line of mountains suddenly clarified against the horizon, a thin black edge along the purple sky. She felt exalted and afraid when she saw it, and as the sun rose higher and light spilled down the front of them to pick out the colors, so different from what was in the water, forgotten greens and browns and purples. Soon the sun had climbed above them and was shining right in her face, making plain the blood on her blanket and the wet spots seeping up from the deeper layers. She screamed again, up and down the new coast. They were still miles off from it but she half expected a flight of birds to rise from the cliffs, startled by her cry.

They got into a sort of routine: she'd have a contraction; Ishmael would insult her; the angel would say something useless and sweet; she would lie a few moments on her back, watching the ever clarifying land, catching some new smell on the air; and then another contraction would come.

"I'm almost ready to tell you," Ishmael said, striding in front of her with his hands behind his back, looking for all the world like he was out for an ordinary morning stroll.

"You're blocking my view," she said.

"I am so disgusted. Disgust is melting my bowels... Oh! I feel them turning to water, all my insides turning and turning in anger. You are so much... How could you ever stand to have lived? Listen, I almost know what to say. The baby is in the way of it—get it out! What's wrong with you? So lazy, as usual..." Jemma shrieked, too early for the contraction, but it was enough to drown him out, and drive him a little farther away.

"Don't listen to him," said the angel. "What does he know? He's never had a baby."

"Have you?" Jemma asked.

"You are all my babies," she said. "I have held all of you all these months, safe and happy and well."

"You're too fucking much," Jemma said.

"I am the preserving angel," she said simply.

"Can't you finally be the shut-the-fuck-up angel?" Jemma asked, then gasped—it was starting to hurt even before it started to hurt, a prelude to the real pain. A needle rose up between her legs and glinted in the sun.

"You only have to say the word," said the angel.

"Just stay away from me," Jemma said, but still the ground seemed to push at her shoulders and massage her back. "Stop," she said.

"I know you don't mean it," said the angel, and Jemma shrieked again, and the baby moved a little farther. At least they weren't useless contractions—they were getting a lot of work out of her suffering. She still couldn't see into the blank area where the baby lived, but she could see the edge of it, and she could still do things the old-fashioned way, with her arm stuck up her vagina. Scream by scream the baby was coming a little closer to the outside.

"Almost!" Ishmael said at the crowning. Jemma could hear the surf breaking on the shore in front of them—it had taken her many minutes to recognize the sound.

"I love you," said the angel. "You are my sweet baby and I love you."

"Fuck off!" Jemma said, indiscriminately now, over and over whether she was contracting or not.

"Push," said Ishmael, from between her legs. "Push, you nasty fucking whore!" She pushed at him with her arms, sitting up and punching at him, till he fell back, and pushing from inside, too, and pushing with her mind. The head popped out, surrounded by a wave of blood and fluid. She was vomiting again as she saw the head rotate so she was suddenly face to face with her little baby. He was purple and gray and looked entirely dead. She coughed, and started to yell, but it turned into a whimper. She pushed again, pulling down on the head and praying for it not to pop off, to deliver the shoulder. It came out easily enough—no dystocia—but then she realized that she had forgotten to suction the mouth and nose. Now it was too late. The other shoulder delivered without her even pushing, and suddenly he was lying between her legs, gleaming in the sun and not moving a muscle.

She fumbled in the blanket warmer, then remembered her clamps. She shrieked again when she clamped and cut the cord—it wasn't supposed to hurt but it felt like she'd cut off a finger. She was yelling at the thing as she rubbed it with the blankets, trying to pick him up but just rolling him in the grass, at first, so dirt and loose blades of grass stuck to the wet skin. He started to kick, and opened his mouth wide but didn't make a noise until she leaned forward and put her mouth over his nose and lips to give him a breath.

The boy cried. Jemma gathered him up, still rubbing him, in the wet blanket and held him to her chest. She was just going to have a moment with her baby, here at the end of the end of the world. Ishmael leaned down to whisper in her ear. "You hate him. You have already ruined him," he said. Jemma turned and slapped him in the face, a skillful move while holding the baby and still in horrible pain and bleeding more and more. She was afraid to look between her legs.

She meant it to be a very special slap. "Take off that human face," she said, because with a twitch of her mind she loosened the fascia under the skin. It was supposed to fly off and lie on the ground like a used shammy. Nothing happened, though. She struck again: he should have swallowed his own tongue but he just stared at her, not screaming, not burning. There wasn't a lick of fire anywhere on the roof.

"Now you are dead," he said, and sat back, and laughed and laughed, a whole minute of Santa-sounds while Jemma cursed at him. He looked all around him when he settled. "What a *beautiful* day," he said.

"You're dead," Jemma said, clutching her squalling baby. "*You* are!"

"I am not," he said. "I am finally... myself. How strange, to be so angry. I remember it, but do not understand it. I do not remember why I was so upset. Do you remember, dead creature?"

"You were mad because..." She wanted to say something cruel, but she couldn't think of anything. Her baby was crying. She gave him her breast and he quieted, turning his dark eyes on her face. He was as ugly and beautiful as an old man. "Because you're fucking stupid," Jemma said lamely.

"Sister!" Ishmael said. "Come out!"

"Presently," said the angel, and the whole hospital shook so hard that Jemma almost dropped her baby. She looked around for an iceberg but only saw the land; they'd run aground.

"Brother and Brother! It is time!"

We are already here, I say, because we are standing at our corners, I in the South and my brother in the West. Jemma sees the air unfolding but doesn't see us yet. Ishmael goes to stand in the East, his feet almost touching on the bits of earth that spilled onto the ledge when the hospital ran aground; the hospital is received into a curve in the land, and the green top of the cliff is just level with the roof.

"What's wrong with you?" Jemma asks, because Ishmael is unfolding, too, picking off his put-on flesh by the handful and filling up a shape drawn in the air above him.

"Sister!" he says again. "Come out!"

"Patience," she says. "We are still waiting." She unfolds in the West, withdrawing herself from the hospital. Floor by floor, the replicators stop their sighing and the lights dim. The toy slows and stops.

"Waiting for what?" Jemma says.

"For you," I say.

"Get away from my baby!" you say, clutching it tighter, though I am nowhere near it. It cries again; the tip of your breast has fallen away in ash. You switch sides and look to the four quadrants. Now you can see all of us, my little brother rising over the pieces of his fleshly disguise, a heap of parts at his feet; my sister with her kind mouth; my big brother and his black wings; and me.

"You are your brother's sister," I say.

"What the fuck do you know about my brother?" you ask me.

"Look," I say, and the vision rises out of you: your brother's feast, except now it is laid before you and comes from you.

"Go away," you say. "None of you are real." My little brother raises his wings to smash you, but our sister restrains him. "Go away," you say again, but we can't go anywhere yet, so you go away instead, ignoring us, ignoring the flow of blood and ash from between your legs, ignoring your blackening toes and feet, ignoring the feast, ignoring everything but your baby.

You turn away and look through the space between my brother and sister to see the land. "See?" you say to your baby. "See it?" You try to imagine the life you will live with him there. You throw up the structure of a life in your imagination. It is as big as a cathedral but collapses before it has even assumed a whole shape. "That's all right," you say. "It's okay." You look deep into his face. "Seven and ten," you say, fudging the Apgars a little—there's no such thing as a ten but no carping resident is here now to bitch at you about that. He looks so serene you know he is not going to miss you. "Look," you say again, trying to turn his face to the land without disturbing his latch, and you think, "It isn't mine to give, but I give it to you."

I suffered a whole lifetime to get to where you are now—agonizing every day and night over my destiny, never knowing until I put the knife in my belly and made the first hard cut if I was worthy of it or not. I soared to Heaven on all that pain, and tore off the gates, and fetched out the grace that later rained down deadly on the world. You went through our life unthinking, and your gift came to you as naturally as your baby. And how can I envy you that, when you do your part in the same way, giving the world away in a stroke, and sundering sin forever from the generations?

An unremembered weight pushes on my back and neck and forces my face into the ground. My brothers and my sisters bow to me, as countless legions bowed to me, infinite circles on the ice and the water and the land, all of them crushed under the supreme violence of mercy and grace—they bowed to me like this on the night that I made my own sacrifice, and my brief ascension. I cry out and my brothers and my sister cry out but you ignore us. Your baby has turned his eyes to the land and you have become lost in his face, not caring how we are humbled. Five or six children have passed you before you fully appreciate that they are awake and walking out of the hospital.

They pass by you in twos, the youngest coming first in the arms of the oldest. You call out to them, "Josh! Ethel! Cindy!" but they only look toward the land, not sparing a look either for my brother, folded in half and moaning. Josh Swift, Ella Thims in his arms, steps up on the ledge and off onto the grass. They come quicker as soon as the first of them is out of the hospital entirely, surging by now, some running and leaping—Juan and Kidney and Magnolia. The boy from the boat is holding Magnolia's hand as they walk. You want to call to him but realize you never did learn his name. They talk to each other as they go and though you can hear the words clearly you don't understand a thing they are saying.

You look to your right at Jarvis—he's tripped in his haste and said something in the tone of a curse. He won't look at you either, even when you say his name.

"Look at me," you say to them.

"Do not ask for such things," I say, though with this weight on my back I cannot speak very loud. The children pass, more and more swiftly; they stir a wind against your face. You try to count them as they pass; it seems like many more than seven hundred by the time the last two come out. Pickie steps carefully over the grass, holding Brenda against his shoulder. He stoops next to you and holds out his free arm.

"No," you say.

"It's all right. They go together, Mama," he says, and adds something else. You know it is supposed to be comforting, but again you can't understand the words, and realize he isn't talking to you.

"No," you say again, but your left hand is ash and you are about to drop the baby anyway when he takes him. The child doesn't cry. You fall over as they walk away; it is the next to last thing you see, the King's Daughter looking at you over Pickie's shoulder as they step on the ledge and onto the land.

We are released when the last child has left. My brothers and my sisters rise and take to the sky—you see them from where you lie. With just a few beats of their huge wings they dwindle to specks, and they are calling down for me to follow but I am not quite free.

"Calvin?" you ask, seeing me clearly for the first time.

"Of course," I say.

"Why are you crying?" It's only because I am bending so close that I can hear you.

"Because I love you," I say. "Because I am sad." And I am thinking not just of you but of our dead, and all the dead souls departed from the hospital and the world, and wondering what might have been achieved by my extraordinary sacrifice if I had lived all my life under a burden of sadness instead of a burden of rage.

"I'm sad too," you say, and then you are gone, flung away from the Earth, calling out for your baby. I take a last look at the new world, then turn and follow after you.

Many thanks to the pediatric residency program at the University of California San Francisco and to the National Endowment for the Arts for the time and means to complete this novel, and to Julie Orringer, Dave Eggers, and Eli Horowitz for bringing it to publication.